Praise for David Farland and *The Golden Queen* books

"They leap from planet to planet via Gates opened with Keys, enduring perils at every turn, until a final showdown decides the fate of the galaxy."
—*Kirkus Reviews*

"When you want to slap a character for her naïve arrogance on one page and comfort her on the next, you know you've found a writer with a gift for characterization. . . . This is an enjoyable story. Recommended."
—*Starlog*

"It's a long, colorful book. There's a pleasure, a richness, or a surprise on every page—sometimes all three. There's immense scope to *The Golden Queen*, and a wonderful sense of presence. Any reader can simply plunge into this novel and be off to alien worlds and wonderful adventures."
—Richard A. Lupoff, KPFA (San Francisco)

Tor Books by David Farland

The Runelords
Brotherhood of the Wolf
Wizardborn
The Lair of Bones

Worlds of the Golden Queen
(comprising *The Golden Queen* and *Beyond the Gate*)

WORLDS OF THE GOLDEN QUEEN

David Farland

TOR®

A Tom Doherty Associates Book
New York

WORLDS OF THE GOLDEN QUEEN

The Golden Queen copyright © 1994 by Dave Wolverton.
Beyond the Gate copyright © 1995 by Dave Wolverton.

This omnibus edition comprises *The Golden Queen* and *Beyond the Gate* by David Farland, which were originally published under the name Dave Wolverton.

Edited by David G. Hartwell

Book design by Jane Adele Regina

A Tor Book
Published by Tom Doherty Associates, LLC
175 Fifth Avenue
New York, NY 10010

www.tor.com

Tor® is a registered trademark of Tom Doherty Associates, LLC.

Library of Congress Cataloging-in-Publication Data

Farland, David.
    Worlds of the golden queen / David Farland.—1st trade pbk. ed.
        p.   cm.
    "A Tom Doherty Associates book."
    ISBN 0-765-31315-4
    EAN 978-0-765-31315-7
    1. Kings and rulers—Succession—Fiction.   2. Cloning—Fiction.   3. Queens—Fiction.
    I. Title.

    PS3556.A71558W67 2005
    813'.54—dc22

                                                                                2004063753

First Trade Paperback Edition: June 2005

Printed in the United States of America

0 9 8 7 6 5 4 3 2 1

Contents

THE GOLDEN QUEEN

For Mary, who makes it all possible

One

Veriasse could taste the scent of vanquishers in the crisp mountain air. Beneath the sweaty odor of the horses, lying deep below the aroma of pine needles and leaf mold, he could barely detect the acrid scent of a dronon vanquisher's stomach acids. This was the third time he had caught that scent in as many days, but this time it was closer than in the past.

He reined in his mare at the crest of the mountain, raised his right hand as a sign for those behind to halt. His big mare whinnied and stamped its feet, eager to forge ahead. Obviously, the horse tasted the strange scent, too.

On the muddy road behind him, the Lady Everynne reined in her stallion, and Veriasse just sat a moment, looking back at her. She had the hood of her blue cloak pulled up, and she hunched wearily in her saddle, too tired to remain alert any longer. The wind was blowing at his back in wild bursts, rushing through trees with the sound of an ocean, gusting first from the east, then from the south. In such weather, one could seldom tell where a scent originated. A vast forest spread below them, and Veriasse could see little of the road they had just traversed—only a thinning of the pines in the valley. Overhead, thunderclouds rolled across the evening sky. In minutes, full dark would fall upon them, with the storm.

Veriasse raised his hands. The olfactory nerves running up his wrists could detect the subtlest smells. He could taste a person's nervousness from across a room, detect the scent of an enemy across a valley. Now, he could smell a man's fear behind him, along with the acrid odor of a vanquisher.

"Calt?" Veriasse called softly. The big warrior was supposed to be trailing them as a rear guard. With Calt's sharp ears, he should have heard the call even at half a mile. But he didn't answer. Veriasse waited for a count of four.

Downhill, far behind them, Calt whistled like a thrush, three short calls. It was a code: "Our enemy is upon us in force! I will engage!"

Everynne gouged her stallion's flanks, and the horse jumped forward. In a heartbeat she was beside Veriasse, looking back down the trail in confusion, as if to wait for Calt.

"Flee!" Veriasse hissed, slapping her stallion's rump.

"Calt!" Everynne cried, trying to slow and turn her horse. Only her ineptitude as a rider kept her from rushing headlong back down the mountain.

"We can do nothing for him! He has chosen his fate!" Veriasse growled. He spurred his own mare, grabbed Everynne's reins as the horses surged forward, struggling to match pace.

Everynne looked at him, her pale face flashing beneath her hood. Briefly, Veriasse saw the tears moistening her dark blue eyes, saw her struggling to fight off her confusion and grief. She hunched low and clung to her saddle horn as Veriasse pulled her horse over the rise, and soon their mounts were fluidly running downhill, side by side, over muddy roads where one misstep would throw a rider headlong to his death.

Veriasse pulled his incendiary rifle from its holster, gripped it with a cold hand. A wailing sound echoed over the mountains, freezing Veriasse's bones, a keen death cry that could not have issued from the mouth of anything human. Calt had confronted his vanquishers. Veriasse held his breath, listening for more such cries, hoping Calt would be able to fell more than one of the monsters. But no more cries reverberated over the hills.

Everynne gasped, and a wracking sob escaped her as the horses raced through the oncoming darkness between the boles of tall black pines.

Five days. They had known Calt only five days, and already he had sacrificed his life in Everynne's service. Yet of all the places the vanquishers could have attacked, this is where Veriasse least expected it, on a quiet mountain road in a backward place like Tihrglas. This should have been a pleasant ride through the woods, but instead Veriasse found himself hunkering down on his horse, thundering over a muddy road, numbed by cold and grief.

Veriasse was weary to the bone, yet he dared not close his eyes. For an hour they rushed through the darkness and pelting rain until the horses could no longer see well enough to run. Even then, Veriasse pushed the horses as fast as he could, sensing that the vanquishers would soon overtake them, until at last the woods opened up and they clattered over a long, sturdy wooden bridge.

The river below them was a swollen flood. Veriasse shouted, drove the horses forward mercilessly till they reached the far side of the river, then halted.

He leapt from his horse, studied the bridge. It was constructed from heavy logs with planks laid over the top. He could see no easy way to topple it, so he fired his incendiary rifle into the planks. Stark white flames erupted for fifty meters across the bridge. The mare jumped and bucked beneath him in fright. She had never seen the chemical fire of an incendiary rifle.

The cold rain had soaked through his robes, and Veriasse longed to stay a moment, warm himself beside those flames. Instead, he took Everynne's reins and pulled her stallion forward.

"Let's stop here," Everynne said. "I'm so tired."

"There is bound to be another settlement just up the road. We can't stop now, my child. We're so close to the gate!"

He urged the horses on, and Everynne did not answer him, just sat stiffly in her saddle. Ten minutes later, they climbed another small hill. Veriasse looked back to see his handiwork. The bridge was an inferno across its entire length, lighting the muddy river in a dull red, firelit smoke billowing overhead.

Yet on the far banks of the river, Veriasse saw the giant form of a green-skinned vanquisher in battle armor, staring at the swollen river in dismay.

• • •

When Gallen O'Day was five years old, his father took him to the Widow Ryan with the notion of getting the boy a kitten, and on that day, the Widow Ryan said something that saved Gallen's life a dozen times over.

It was a cold morning in Clere, with a dusting of new-fallen snow on the autumn ground. Gallen's father wore a badly stained brown leather greatcoat and a pair of green woollen gloves that had no fingers, and Gallen clenched his father's hand as they went to knock at the widow's door. The Widow Ryan was so old that many of the children in town told stories of her, naming her a witch and saying that the priest had drowned all her babies for being leprechauns.

The widow's house was grown from an ancient, gnarled pine tree, thirty feet in diameter and two stories tall, with assorted black branches poking out like ruined hands. Many houses in town had grown from seeds taken from its cones, but none of the other houses were quite so vast. Often, crows would fly up from the rocky bay and caw in its branches. The widow's husband had been a tinker, and when he'd found a pot that was not worth mending, he had brought it home to use as a planter. Many a blackened iron kettle still hung from branches on that ancient tree, and Gallen imagined they were suitable vessels for a witch to boil children in.

Gallen's father rapped on the heavy door. Moss grew up the wrinkled bark of the tree, and a large brown snail oozed near Gallen's foot. The widow opened the door, hunched beneath a heavy blue shawl. She ushered them into the warm house—a fire crackled in the stone fireplace—and took them to a box by a faded couch. The widow's cat had seven kittens in a variety of colors—one with orange-and-white stripes, two calicos, and four that were black with white faces and boots. Gallen hardly knew which to choose, so the widow allowed that he could sit and watch while she and his father talked.

Gallen looked the kittens over, and he half listened as the widow told stories from her youth. Her father had been a merchant and once bought seven olive presses down in Ireland, thinking to retire. He'd taken the whole family with him, but a storm blew them into uncivilized lands where wild Owens roamed—hairy men who had lost their Christianity and now wore only brass rings piercing their nipples. The wild Owens ate her family, but held the widow prisoner on a rocky isle where they brought their dead along with gifts of food every full moon, leaving the corpses for her blessing. She'd have to feast for days before the food rotted, then she'd starve afterward for weeks. The island's soil was white with the bones of dead Owens. The widow survived for a summer in a haphazard shelter under a leaning slab of marble, teaching herself to swim until she could finally brave the vast waters.

Once she escaped, she traveled the world. She'd gazed on the statue where Saint Kelly had carved the face of God after seeing his vision at Gort Ard, and as she described the statue, neither male nor female, old nor young, she cried at the remembered beauty of it.

She told how she had wandered for days at the Palace of the Conqueror near Droichead Bo, never twice entering the same room, and there she found a small hoard of emeralds that had been overlooked by treasure hunters for two hundred years.

Gallen quit listening, turned back to the kittens. Between his breathing on them and poking them, the kittens soon woke. He watched them stretch and search for their mother's nipples; then he began playing with them, hoping that since he could not make a choice, perhaps one of the kittens would choose him. But the kittens were not used to small boys, so they ran about the house frolicking with one another.

One kitten in particular caught Gallen's eye: the orange-and-white one would glance into a shadowed nook and hiss as if it had seen a ghost, then it would leap up the couch, climbing as if a wolf nipped at its tail, then it would prance along the spine of the couch with all of its hackles raised, its back arched. When Gallen wiggled his finger, the kitten became all eyes and crouched to stalk for the attack.

Despite the kitten's playfulness, Gallen wasn't sure he wanted it: the widow had fed the cats a fish, and its breath smelled bad. A bright calico with blue eyes caught Gallen's fancy. When it became clear that he'd never be able to choose, the widow bent her wrinkled face close and said the thing that saved Gallen's life, "Take the orange one that plays so much. He'll live longest."

"How do you know?" Gallen asked, frightened, wondering if the widow really was a witch and somehow knew the future.

"Clere is a big town," she said, "with tough old tomcats living on the wharf, and hounds on every corner, and many a horse riding through that could crush a cat. But that orange tom can handle life in a dangerous town. Look at the way he practices the skills he'll need in life. He'll do well."

Gallen grabbed the orange kitten in his stubby fingers. The kitten nuzzled into his woollen jacket, and the Widow Ryan continued, "You can learn a lot from that kitten, child. There are many kinds of people in this world. Some live only in the present—moving through life from day to day without a thought for tomorrow or a backward glance. They live only one life. For these people, life is a dream.

"Another kind of person lives in the moment but has a long memory, too. These people often fester under the weight of old slights or bask in triumphs so time-worn that no one wants to hear of them. For these people, the walking dream is spiced with a past that they can't escape.

"Then there is a third kind of person, a person like your cat. This person lives three lives. Such people don't just muck about in the past or drift through the present, they dream of tomorrows and prepare for the worst and struggle to make the world better.

"This orange kitten, he'll likely never get crushed by a wagon or be eaten by a dog, because he's faced all those dangers here." She pointed a crooked finger to her head.

Gallen took the orange kitten. Sure enough, within six months the others in the litter had been tragically massacred by dogs or crushed under carts or thrown into the ocean by mean-spirited boys. But not Gallen's orange tom. It died of old age years later, and by that time Gallen had learned all that the cat could teach.

As a boy, Gallen lived three lives, but by far the life of his imagination was the fullest. Like the cat, he imagined every possible danger and worked to avert it, and like his cat, he was a rangy lad.

So one summer night when he was seventeen, he surprised himself when he and a neighbor named Mack O'Mally were accosted by two highwaymen on a dark road. Both robbers wore loose black flour sacks to cover their faces. The robbers attacked from behind, and just as one was about to plunge a knife into Mack, a screech owl called out. This distracted the felon, making him turn his head. Gallen noticed the small peepholes the robbers had burned into the sack, and realized the sacks must be mighty inconvenient to see out of. So he snatched both flour sacks, turning them so that the robbers were blinded, then he pulled Mack from their grasp. Within five seconds, he had both highwaymen gutted on the ground.

Gallen and Mack made five pounds and three shillings when they rifled the murderers' pockets, and when they got back to Clere, they went straight to the alehouse and bought everyone a round and gave the change to an undertaker to dig a hole for the dead robbers.

In a sense, that was the beginning of the legendary "fantasist" Gallen O'-Day, but that's a far cry from the end of his tale.

No, I suppose that if one were to tell it right—and it's a tale that demands to be told in whole—one would have to continue the story two years later. Gallen had been down south for a year building a name for himself. He had taken up a friendship with a black bear named Orick, and together the two worked as bodyguards for wealthy travelers. In those days, the family clans were strong, and it was hard for a merchant to make a living when the O'Briens hated the Hennesseys and the Hennesseys hated the Greens. An unarmed traveler could hardly ride a dozen miles without someone trying to bloody his nose. But there were worse things in the land.

Rumor said that Gallen himself had rid the countryside of two dozen assorted highwaymen, cutthroats, and roadside bandits. In fact, every highwayman in six counties had learned better than to accost the dreamy-eyed lad with the long golden hair. He was building a grand reputation.

But that fall, Gallen got word that his father had died, and he returned home to Clere to care for his aging mother.

So it was, that one night . . .

An autumn storm kept the rain rapping at the windows like an anxious neighbor as Gallen sat in Mahoney's alehouse with his friend Orick the bear, and as Gallen listened to the rain knocking the glass, he had the unsettling feeling that *something* was trying to get in, something as vast and dark as the storm.

Gallen had come to the inn tonight hoping to ply his trade as a body-guard, but even though the inn was full of travelers and the roads around Clere were rumored to be thick with robbers, no one had approached him. Not until Gallen caught the eye of a fellow at another table, a prosperous sheep farmer he knew from An Cochan named Seamus O'Connor.

Seamus raised a bushy brow from across the room, as if asking Gallen for permission to sit at his table. Gallen nodded, and Seamus got up and tamped some tobacco into a rosewood pipe, went to the fire and removed a coal with some tongs, then lit his pipe. Father Heany, the local priest, came over to borrow use of the coal.

Seamus sat across from Gallen, leaned back in the old hickory chair, set his black boots on the table and sucked at his pipe, with his full stomach bulging up over his belt. He smiled, and at that moment Gallen thought Sea-mus looked like nothing more than a pleasant fat gut with a couple of limbs and a head attached. Father Heany came over in his severe black frock, all gaunt and starved looking, and sat down next to Seamus with his own pipe, sucking hard to nurse some damp tobacco into flame. Father Heany was such a tidy and proper man that folks in town often joked of him, "Why the man is so clean, if you took a bath with him, you could use him for soap."

Together, the two old men blew the pleasant smell of their tobacco all about until they were wreathed like a pair of old dragons in their own smoke.

"So, Gallen," Seamus said, "rumor has it that you'll be staying here in Clere now." He didn't finish the sentence, *now that your father has died, leaving your frail mother a widow.*

"Aye," Gallen said. "I'll not be roaming far from home, nowadays."

"How will you keep yourself, then?" Seamus asked. "Have you thought about it?"

Gallen shrugged. "I've been looking about, and I've got a bit in savings. It should last awhile. I've thought about taking up fishing, but I can't imagine any woman ever learning to love the smell of a fisherman."

"Sure, the blacksmith is looking for an apprentice," Father Heany offered.

"I saw him just today," Gallen said, remembering how the smith would pick up the horse's back foot, leaning his shoulders up against the horse's sweaty rump, "and to tell the truth, I'd rather *be* a horse's ass than work with my head so close to a horse's fertilizing region." Seamus and Orick the bear laughed, and Father Heany nodded wisely.

"Sure," Heany admitted, "a smart man can always find a job that will let him keep himself unsoiled." He frowned as if thinking furiously, then said, "There's the priesthood."

"A fine vocation," Orick cut in with his deep voice. The bear was sitting on the floor, paws on the table, licking out of a bowl. Some milk still stuck to his muzzle. "I've been thinking of joining myself, but Gallen here makes light of God and his servants."

"I'll not make light of God," Gallen responded, "but I've no respect for some who call themselves his servants. I've been thinking on it. Your Bible says God created man in his own image, and it says God is perfect, but then he only made man 'Good,' as in good enough? Like maybe he was lazing about. It seems to me that God could have done better with us, considering that we're his crowning creation: for instance, a day-old fawn can jump a four-foot fence—so why can't a day-old child?"

"Ah, and to be sure, Gallen O'Day—" Father Heany said with a fiery twinkle in his eye "—if God had had you looking over his shoulder on the day of creation to give him a little advice, we would have all been better off!"

Orick lapped at the bowl of milk on the table, and the bear had a reflective look in his dark eyes. "You know, Gallen," Orick grumbled soberly, "God only gave man weaknesses to keep him humble. The Bible says 'man is just a little lower than the angels.' Surely you see that it's true. You may not live as long as a tortoise, but you'll live longer than me. Your mind is far quicker than any bear's. And with your houses and ships and dreams, your people are richer than us bears will ever be."

Spoken like a true priest, Gallen thought. Few bears ever entered the priesthood, but Gallen wondered if perhaps Orick wasn't a natural for it.

"I'm not one for the priesthood," Gallen assured Father Heany. "I still love the road too much. I'm looking to buy some property, then lease it out. Other than that, I plan to continue my work as an escort. There are plenty of short routes hereabouts. I can take some work and still care for my mother." He said it mildly, but it was not the short roads Gallen wanted to travel. He wanted to someday head south to Gort Ard and look on Saint Kelly's likeness of the face of God, or head east and search for hidden treasures. But now he would be stuck here in County Morgan, never more than a couple of days from home.

"Heavens, boy!" Father Heany said. "Why, your reputation has already traveled farther than your foot ever wandered. Every highwayman in the county will clear out in a week, and no one will *need* escorts anymore! Why, you're your own worst enemy!"

Seamus nudged the priest with an elbow, cleared his throat. "Ah, don't give the boy a fat head. He's not that good!" He turned to Gallen. "But, to tell the truth, Gallen, I do want to contract your services. My son's gone ahead to tell Biddy that I'll be home later, but I'm not half as drunk right now as I want to be in an hour, and I'll pay you two shillings if you get me home alive."

"Two shillings?" Gallen asked. It was a low price for a bodyguard, but then it was late of the night—too late and too rainy for robbers to be about. Gallen would only have to escort Seamus over the hills from Clere to the village of An Cochan, a distance of four miles, making certain that Seamus didn't fall off his horse. "Give me four and it's a deal."

Seamus grimaced as if he were passing a kidney stone. "What? Why you've got an inflated notion of your own worth! You're so hot to become a landlord, you're already evicting imaginary tenants!"

"Five shillings," Gallen said. "Four for my services, and one for insulting me."

"Three!" Seamus said with finality.

Gallen held his eye a moment, nodded agreement. The only sound was the wind howling outside and the paddles in the butter churn. The scullery maid, a sweet sixteen-year-old girl named Maggie Flynn, normally churned fresh butter every dawn, but with the stormy night and so many travelers passing through town, she was trying to get a head start. She had dark red hair and darker eyes, a patina of perspiration on her brow. She caught Gallen looking at her and shot him a fetching smile.

Seamus winked at Father Heany and said, "Ah, Father, it doesn't get any better than this, does it? Lazing about after a fine dinner."

"No," Father Heany agreed. "Not much."

"No, not much better at all—unless," Seamus said, exhaling a cloud of blue smoke, "you were in your own house with your own sweet wife sitting on your lap while you were smoking your pipe, and your dear wee children all tucked into bed." Seamus cocked an eye at the priest, as if daring him to disagree—what with the priest being celibate—but Father Heany just sucked on his pipe thoughtfully, seeming to take a cue from Seamus.

"Ah yes, a wife." Father Heany sighed. " 'Tis a fine thing, I'm sure."

"Now, if I were a young man like Gallen," Seamus said, "just moving back to town, getting ready to settle down, I'd be looking for a wife. In fact, I'd almost think it my duty to find some fine County Morgan girl and marry her." Gallen wondered what Seamus was hinting at. Seamus had a couple of young daughters out on his farm, but the oldest was only fourteen. And while it wasn't unheard of for a girl to marry so young, Gallen couldn't imagine that Seamus would be talking about "duty"—unless some boy had filled one of his daughters with a child and then run off into the yonder and now Seamus was desperate to find the girl a husband.

Father Heany must also have been trying to fathom where Seamus was leading, for he said, "Now that you speak of it, there's that Mary Gill down in Gort Obhiann whose husband got kicked by a horse last summer, leaving her with three strapping little boys, all of them fatherless. If I were looking for a wife, I'd certainly pay a visit to Mary. A beautiful girl! Beautiful! And she's guaranteed not to leave you childless."

"Ah, she's pretty enough all right," Seamus agreed. "But dumb as a pine cone, I hear. Like as not, she'll fall in a well or catch a cold from standing in the rain too much, then leave her husband a widower."

"Hmmm?" Father Heany asked, cocking a brow.

"Now, there is Gwen Alice O'Rourke—smart as a bee's sting, and a hard-working girl, too."

"Nooo, no!" Father Heany threw up his hands as if to ward off a blow. "You can't go trying to unload your ugly niece onto the boy," the priest said. "That would be a sin. She's a nice enough girl, but with those buck teeth—"

"You don't say!" Seamus frowned in mock horror. "You daren't talk about my niece that way!"

"I will," the priest said. "God agrees with me on this point, I'm sure. The girl has tusks as dangerous as any wild boar's. Now, if Gallen is looking for a nice young woman, I'm sure others could be found."

Maggie got up from her churn. The cream had hardened to butter, and she could no longer turn the crank. Her face and arms were covered with perspiration. Gallen figured it must be midnight, yet she'd been working since before sunrise. She stood wearily, put a heavy log into the fire, then sat at a nearby table with a sigh that said, "Ah, to hell with it."

"Well, there is Maggie here," Seamus said with a wink, and Gallen saw that he'd been planning this all along. With Gallen and Maggie sitting so close together, it was a perfect opportunity to torment them both. No one in town could have missed the glances they exchanged, and Gallen had just about decided that Maggie was the one for him. "Now, Maggie has it all— she has her wit, she's a charmer, and she works as hard as three people."

"True, true," Father Heany agreed.

"And looks!" Seamus said. "More men come here to look at Maggie than ever came in for a drink! Why, if some boy were to marry her, it would deal a horrible blow to John Mahoney's business. Sure, you'll not find a better catch in all of County Morgan than Maggie Flynn."

"But . . ." Father Heany said with a sigh, "she's too young. The poor girl is only sixteen." He said it with such finality, Gallen knew it was more than a casual thought, it was a verdict. Father Heany was only repeating aloud in front of Gallen the things that others in town had decided in private.

"Too young?" Seamus argued. "Why, she's but two months away from her birthday!"

The priest held up his hands. "Sixteen—even an old sixteen—is marginal, very marginal. Marrying a girl so young borders on sin, and I'd never perform the ceremony!" he declared. "Now, if you ask me—and I'm sure the scriptures would back me up on it—eighteen is far more respectable! But if you make a woman wait until she's twenty, then it seems to me you're sinning the other way and ought to be roundly chastised for making the lady wait."

Seamus raised his brow, gave Gallen a look that said, "You can't argue with a priest," then drained his glass. Maggie got up to refill it, but Seamus shooed her away with a wave. "So, that's how you feel about it, Father Heany," Seamus said as he hitched his pants and strolled to the bar. "Well, all

I can say is that it's growing mighty cold in this corner of the room, so I think I'll sit me by the fire and leave the young ones be."

Seamus filled his mug, then sat at a table nearer to the fire. Father Heany and Orick followed, leaving Gallen alone. Father Heany took up a fiddle and began playing a mournful tune appropriate for a cold night. Maggie sat down next to Gallen. He put his arm around her shoulders, and as soon as Seamus had his back turned, she glanced around the room quickly to make sure no one was looking, then nipped Gallen's ear.

"Gallen O'Day," she whispered fiercely, "why don't you come up to my room? I'll let you play on my feather bolster, and you can undress me with your teeth."

"What?" he whispered, feeling blood rush to his ears. "You've got to be joking! You could have a baby from that. You wouldn't want to get tied down with children so young."

"I'm old enough to cook and clean from sunrise to sunset for a bunch of dirty beggars who give me no consideration and don't know enough to take off their muddy boots before they flop onto a bed. Taking care of a husband and a couple of sweet young ones would be a holiday after this."

"Ah, Maggie," Gallen said, "you heard Father Heany. Give yourself another year or two to grow up."

"I'll have you know, Gallen O'Day," Maggie said, "that most men in these parts think I'm old enough already. You should see my backside: I've been pinched so many times that it looks like I've been sitting in a bowlful of black currants!"

Gallen knew a threat when he heard one. She was saying, either you pay more attention to me, or I'll find someone who will. And she wouldn't have to look far. Gallen took a thick oak stick from his pocket and began simultaneously twisting and squeezing it, an exercise he used to strengthen his wrists. "Hmmm . . ." he said, "maybe I should take a look at your backside." He felt her warm breath on his neck.

"You're not a religious man, are you?" she asked. "I wouldn't want you to think I'm just after fornicating with you. If you would rather have a priest and some vows first—"

"No, it's not that," Gallen assured her, yet marriage was exactly the problem. She was so young that no honorable man would propose to her, yet she couldn't bear the thought of working here for another two years. So, if she happened to turn up with a child in her belly, the whole town would just wink at it and hurry the wedding. It was an odd turn of events, Gallen thought, when the town would view a shameful wedding as somehow being more noble than an honorable proposal.

"If I were to propose right now," Gallen said, "it would hurt us in the long run."

"In what way?"

"I want to have a political career," Gallen said. "Father Heany is right. I'll never make a living by selling my escort services around here. I've killed too many highwaymen. Next year, I plan to run for county sheriff. But I can't do that and go tumbling in bed with you. It would bring shame on us both. I beg of you, give yourself time to grow up."

"Is that a promise you're making me," Maggie asked, her shoulder muscles going stiff in his arms, "or are you just trying to brush me off like a gentleman?"

Gallen looked into her dark eyes, eyes such a deep brown that they were almost black. She smelled of good honest sweat and lilac perfume. Outside, a fierce gust of wind howled and sleety rain spattered against the windows with such startling ferocity that Gallen and Maggie turned to glance at it. The window rattled so loud, Gallen had been sure that someone had pushed against it. He turned back to Maggie. "You're a sweet girl, Maggie Flynn. I beg you, be patient with me."

Maggie pulled away, disappointed, perhaps hurt. He still hadn't promised himself to her, and she wanted a commitment, even if it was informal.

The inn door swung open, and a sheet of rain whipped into the room. At first Gallen thought the wind had finally succeeded in blowing the door open, but after a moment, in walked a stranger in traveling clothes—a tall fellow in riding boots and a brown wool greatcloak with a hood. He wore two swords strapped over his cloak—one oddly straight saber with a strange finger guard on its hilt, and another equally long curved blade. By wearing the swords over the cloak in such a downpour, the stranger risked that his blades would rust but kept his swords handy.

Only a man who made a living with his weapons ever wore them so.

Everyone in the alehouse stopped to stare: the stranger must have been riding in the dark for at least five hours, a sign that he had urgent business. Furthermore, he stood at the door without removing his hood, then silently inspected each person in the room. Gallen wondered if he might be an outlaw. He didn't seem to want his face to be seen in town, yet his roving eyes appraised each person in the room as if he were a hunter, rather than hunted.

At last, he stepped aside from the door so that a slender waif of a woman could enter the room. She stood in the doorway for a moment, erect, head held high with her hood still covering her face. Gallen saw by his tense posture that the man was her servant, her guard. She wore a bright blue traveling robe trimmed with golden rabbits and foxes. Under her arm she carried a small harp case made of rosewood. She hesitated for a moment, then started forward and her hood fell back.

She was the most beautiful woman Gallen had ever seen. Not the most voluptuous or seductive—just the most perfect. She held herself with a regal air and looked to be about twenty. Her hair was as dark as a starless night. The line of her jaw was strong and firm. Her skin was creamy in complexion and her face looked worn, tired, but her dark blue eyes were alive and brilliant. Gallen recalled the words to an old song: "Her eyes kindle a fire for a lonely man to warm himself by."

Maggie boxed Gallen's jaw playfully and said, "Gallen O'Day, if your tongue hangs out any farther, all you will have to do is wag it to clean the mud off your boots."

Maggie got up and greeted the strangers. "Come in and get out of the weather, sit by the fire and dry those soggy cloaks. Would you poor folks like some dinner, a room?"

The tall man spoke with an odd speech impediment, loud enough so that the entire room could hear, "It is said that there is a place near here, an ancient arch with strange symbols carved on it—Geata na Chruinne. Do you know of it?"

Until that moment, everyone in the room had been listening but pretending not to. Now, they cocked their ears and became conspicuous about it.

Gallen wondered if these strangers might not be adventurers, out to see the sights of the world. Geata na Chruinne sometimes attracted such people.

"I know of the place," Maggie said suspiciously, studying the stranger's face, "as does everyone around here."

"Is it easy to reach?" the stranger asked in a thick voice. "Could we make it tonight, after a brief rest and dinner?"

"No one goes to the arch after dark," Maggie said uneasily. "People say it's haunted. You can stand beneath it on a hot day and feel cold air blowing off it like a sheet of ice. Besides, it's deep in the forest, in Coille Sidhe. You can't go there in the night."

"I could pay for a guide," the stranger offered.

"Well," Maggie said, "there are a couple boys in town who know the way, if you're willing to wait till morning."

"No—they can't be boys," the stranger said, standing over Maggie. "I want a man, a seasoned soldier. Someone who can defend himself."

Maggie glanced toward Gallen, lines of worry in her face. Few people in town had actually been to the ancient ruins called Geata na Chruinne, "Gate of the World." And only one had any kind of fighting skills.

Gallen wasn't sure that he trusted these well-armed, secretive people. But he didn't want to miss the chance to make some money. He nodded.

"Gallen O'Day could take you there in the morning," Maggie told them as she jerked her chin toward Gallen.

The hooded stranger glanced at Gallen, said, "Are you a soldier?"

He advanced on Gallen, the hood shielding his face. "He's an armed escort," Maggie boasted, "and he's killed over twenty robbers. He's the best there's ever been."

As the stranger got close, Gallen could see that the tall man had vivid blue eyes, tawny hair going silver. He regarded Gallen with a distant expression.

Without flinching an eye, the stranger drew his sword and swung at Gallen's head. Gallen leapt from his chair and grabbed the stranger's wrist, pinching the nerves between the radius and the ulna, then twisting. It was a painful grip, Gallen knew, and made the victim's fingers spasm open. The stranger's sword stroke went wide, then the sword itself clattered to the table. Gallen twisted the man's wrist painfully in a come-along so that the stranger soon found himself at arm's length, standing on his tiptoes.

The stranger nodded, and said, "Well done. You've the reflexes of a cat, and you must have studied a bit of anatomy to have figured out that trick."

Gallen let the man go, surprised that the fellow had wanted to test him. Gallen's reputation had grown so wide that few employers ever bothered to test his skills anymore.

The young woman in blue looked Gallen over, shook her head. "Not him, he's too small."

"Size is an illusion," Gallen said, catching her eyes. "A man is what he thinks."

"And *I* think that if a foe who outweighed you by a hundred pounds swung a sword at you, you would never be able to parry his blows."

Gallen listened to her words with difficulty, realized that like the man, she too spoke oddly, as if she had a mouthful of syrup. Yet her accent wasn't as thick. He said, "I've been strengthening my wrists since I was six years old, knowing that I'd have to parry blows from bigger men. I believe a man can become anything he puts his mind to. And I assert that by thought, I have made myself bigger than I seem."

"He'll do," the guard said, picking up his sword and shaking the pain from his hand. "He's got a hell of a grip—better than mine."

The woman in blue opened her mouth in mild surprise, then smiled.

"I've already contracted a job for tonight," Gallen said. "But I can pick you up at dawn. The hike to the gate makes for a short trip, only five miles."

The stranger spoke to Maggie briefly. Once he'd purchased rooms for the night and ordered dinner inside, the two began walking up the staircase, and then stopped. The old man said, "We just came from the south, from Baile Sean. There's a large bridge over the river there. Lightning struck it just after we crossed. I suppose you'll want to inform the town." Several people cried out in dismay. By law, the two towns would have to come together and repair the bridge, an onerous task.

Gallen knew that he could not let the young woman, his new employer, go without introducing himself.

He stood and said in a loud voice, "My lady?" The two stopped in their tracks, and the woman glanced over her shoulder at him. Gallen continued, "When you walked in the room just now, and your hood fell back to expose your face, it was as if the morning sun had just climbed over the mountains after a dreary night of rain. We're curious folks hereabout, and I think I speak for many when I ask: may I beg to know your name?" The little speech came out sounding so sweet that Gallen could almost taste the honey dripping from his tongue, and he stood with his heart pounding, waiting for the woman's reply.

She smiled down at him and seemed to think for a moment. Her guard waited cautiously just above her on the stairs, but he did not look back. After a few seconds she said, "No."

They continued upstairs, turned the corner of the hall, and were gone. Gallen O'Day sat down in his chair, staring after them, feeling as if his heart had just turned sideways or he'd died a small death. The last few patrons in the inn looked at Gallen and chuckled. Gallen's face was hot with embarrassment.

Maggie quickly made up two plates and readied them to take upstairs, then came back to Gallen and set the plates on his table a moment and said, "Oh, you poor abused child! To think that she'd mistreat you so." She leaned over and kissed him heavily on the mouth.

Gallen suspected that she was both hurt and angry. He also reminded himself that, wisely, he'd made her no promises. He held her gently as she kissed him, then she slapped his face, grabbed her trays, and danced off, smiling at him over her back.

Gallen put his chin on his knuckles and sat alone, feeling stupid until Seamus O'Connor began to sing and the rain outside quit splattering the windows, then Gallen knew it was time to be off. He helped Seamus to his feet, Seamus snagged the whiskey bottle with his left hand, and they headed out the door.

Amazingly, the storm clouds were scudding by fast instead of lingering like they usually did. Gallen could see pretty well by the slivered moons that shone down like twin sets of eyes, gazing from heaven. Seamus's old mare was across the street, tied in the livery stable with plenty of sweet grass piled before it. Gallen saddled the horse and helped Seamus climb atop, then led the horse out of the stables north toward An Cochan. The mare's hooves clattered over the paving stones. At the back of the inn, in the dim starlight Gallen saw two bears feeding in the rubbish bin and stopped the horse, asking, "Orick, is that you?"

One of the bears grunted in a deep voice, "Hello, Gallen."

"What are you mucking in the slop for?" Gallen asked, surprised that he hadn't seen Orick leave through the back door of the common room. "I've plenty of money. I can have Maggie fix you up a platter." Gallen felt nervous to make the offer. Bears eat so much that they're notorious for always being broke.

"Don't bother," Orick said. "Maggie saved a nice plate of leftovers for me. When I finish here, I'm going up the hill to hunt for a few slugs. It will be a grand feast, I assure you."

"Well, to each his own," Gallen said, appalled as ever at his friend's eating habits. "I'll be back at dawn."

"Do you want me to come along?" Orick asked.

"No, go get some dinner in you."

"God be with you then, for I shall not," the bear said. Seamus hunched over in his saddle and began singing. Gallen shivered at the sound of Orick's cryptic farewell, but pulled the mare's reins, urging her forward.

That night in Mahoney's Inn, the Lady Everynne paced at the foot of her rough bed. The smell of its thick down tick and the soft texture of its heavy red quilts called to her, but even though she was weary, she could not rest. A single dim candle lit the room. She had taken two rooms for appearance's sake. Her guardian, Veriasse, sat at the foot of the bed, head bent in a forlorn attitude.

"Get some sleep, my daughter," Veriasse said. He had slept little in two days, yet she knew he would stay awake at the foot of her bed and keep wide-eyed until they reached safety. His brown hood was pulled back, revealing his weathered face.

"I can't, Father," she said honestly. "Who could sleep? Can you still taste their scent?"

The aging man stood up, shook his head so that his long silver-gold hair spilled down over his shoulders, and went to a basin in the corner of the room. There he poured a pitcher of cool drinking water over his wrists and hands, then toweled them dry. He opened a small window, raised his hands and held them out, long thin fingers curled like claws, and stood for a time with his piercing blue eyes closed as if in meditation. Though the old man could catch a scent with his hands, Everynne could see no sign that he was testing the air. "Yes," he said at last. "I can still taste the scent of a vanquisher. He is distant, perhaps no closer than twenty kilometers away, but I am sure he's here. We can only hope that when we destroyed the bridge, the vanquisher got trapped on the other side."

"Perhaps vanquishers have another reason for coming to this world?" Everynne asked in a tone that was part argument, part plea. "Just because you taste the scent of a vanquisher, it does not mean he has come for us."

"Don't fool yourself," Veriasse said at last. "Tlitkani has sent her warriors to kill us. With only one gate to watch, this world is the perfect spot for an ambush." He said it as one who knows. The Golden Queen Tlitkani had enslaved Veriasse for four years, had forced him to become her advisor. Veriasse was gifted at reading personalities, at studying motives and moods. He could anticipate an adversary's actions so well that many thought him a psychic. No one understood Tlitkani better than Veriasse did.

"The young man downstairs said that the gate is only five miles distant. Could the vanquishers have already found it?"

"It's hard to say—" Veriasse answered. "I feel certain that vanquishers are following, but they could be ahead of us, too. On such a windy night, I cannot even be sure that the vanquisher I smell is twenty kilometers off. It might be ten, or only two."

"Perhaps the vanquishers are searching for the gate, even as we are," Everynne offered.

"Or perhaps Tlitkani wants us to believe that her servants are only searching for the gate—hoping that we will foolishly rush into another trap. I think it best to wait here for the night." Veriasse yawned and rolled his shoulders to keep the muscles loose, clearly uncomfortable. "We should proceed to the gate cautiously. We may have to fight our way through."

Without Calt, Everynne thought, that will not be easy. She felt a pang of grief, hoped that Calt had died painlessly.

Veriasse said nothing for a moment, then asked, "And what of our guide, this Gallen O'Day? Shall we convert him to our cause? He reacts quickly, and he is marvelously strong."

"I won't do it!" Everynne said, perhaps too forcefully. She knew all of the arguments. She needed protectors, she needed an army of men like Gallen O'Day, but what could he know of her world, the weapons that her people used? You could hardly expect a man to battle vanquishers with nothing more than knives, and Veriasse had no weapons to spare. Even if she did choose to persuade the young man to come along, it would be the same as murdering him.

Veriasse sat down cross-legged on the floor, but gazed up at Everynne past heavy lashes. He looked at her knowingly. It was as if he read her mind as she considered the arguments, almost as if he were placing the thoughts in her head. "Then you are decided?" Veriasse said. He smiled secretively.

"What?" Everynne said. "What do you know?"

"I know nothing," Veriasse said. "I can only guess at probable outcomes based on what I know of my associates."

"What do you guess?"

Veriasse hesitated. "I've seen men like Gallen before. He will want to follow you. Regardless of your good intentions, you must allow him to follow you, to fight at your side—if necessary, to die at your feet. So many people depend on you! I would advise you to use this man as your tool. He is only one, but his sacrifice might save many others."

Yet Everynne could not bear the thought of watching another guardian die. Especially not one so ignorant as Gallen O'Day, one so innocent.

"Let's get some rest," she said. Everynne crossed the room, blew out the candle. She closed the window and stood for a moment looking out into the dark streets of Clere. There was a little starlight shining on the town. From this height, she could see over several house-trees and buildings, down to the quay. Small fishing boats lay on the rocky shore, dark, like beached pilot whales. Poles in the sand held twisted coils of fishermen's nets, hung out to dry. Everynne could almost smell the kelp and the sea rime upon them. She had passed those nets only an hour before, as she made her way into town, and the memory of that smell came strong to her.

High on the beach, the seagulls had huddled under folded wings, eyeing her darkly, ominously. Almost, it felt as if they were watching now, through the window.

Everynne shivered, moved away from the window quickly and lay on the bed. Veriasse's heavy, uneven breathing came to her, and she listened to it as she drifted off. Veriasse—with his unwavering devotion, his strong back—seemed somehow more than human. Certainly, by the standards of this world, he would not be judged human at all. Her teacher, her friend. He had guarded Everynne's mother for six thousand years. And during the course of Everynne's short life, he had been a solid presence, always at her side. Sometimes she tried to distance herself from him, think of him only as a warrior, the only one of her guardians to survive this journey. But she could tell that he was weary to the bone, worn through. She could not ask that he continue fighting alone.

The old man sat in the dark at the foot of her bed, wrapped in dark robes—ever faithful, ever determined in the face of overwhelming foes.

With a pang that tore at her heart, Everynne realized what she must do. She needed another guardian, someone to fight beside Veriasse. She knew that men like Gallen O'Day could not resist her. Something in them responded to something in her. It was biological, inevitable. When she had first walked into the inn, she could tell from Gallen's eyes that he believed he had fallen in love. Given an hour in her presence, he would be sure of that love, and within a few days he would become ensnared. Another slave.

Yet there was nothing Everynne could do to dissuade the unyielding devotion of men like Gallen and Veriasse. So Veriasse sat at her feet, waiting to die. Everynne hated her lot in life. But it was her fate. For she had been born a queen among the Tharrin.

Two

Gallen and Seamus had no warning before the attack. The road from Clere to An Cochan was usually well empty by that time of night. Both moons were down. The heavy rains had dampened the dirt road, leaving a thin glaze of water so that the stars reflected off the mud, making the road a trail of silver between columns of dark pine and oak.

They were near the edge of Coille Sidhe, so Gallen moved cautiously. Once, he caught sight of a flickering blue light deep in the wood. Wights, he realized, and he hurried his pace, eager to be away from the guardians of the place. The wights never attacked travelers who kept to the road, but those who wandered into the forest couldn't count on such luck.

Just over the mountain, the land flattened out into drumlins, small hills where the shepherds of An Cochan kept their flocks. Gallen was eager to reach the relative safety of human settlements.

One moment Gallen was walking the muddy silver road, leading Seamus's old nag through a ravine while Seamus hunched in the saddle, singing random songs as a man will when he's had too much whiskey, when suddenly half a dozen voices shouted in unison, "Stand! Stand! Hold!"

A man leapt up from the margin of the road in front of them and waved a woman's white slip in their faces. The horse whinnied and reared in fear, pulling the reins from Gallen's hand, dumping Seamus off backward. Seamus landed with a thud, shouting, "Ruffians, blackguards!"

The nag leapt off up the side of the ravine, her hooves churning up dirt as she galloped through the hazel.

Gallen was wearing his deep-hooded woolen greatcoat to keep out the night chill, but the coat had slits at his waist that let him get to his knife belt quickly. He palmed two daggers, not wanting to show his weapons until the robbers got in close, then spun to get a better view. The robbers surrounded him, swirling up out of the brush. He counted nine: three up the road toward An Cochan, four coming behind on the road from Clere, and one more on each side of the ravine.

Seamus sputtered and tried to find his way up off the ground. The old man was nearly blind drunk, and he yelled in a deep brogue, "Off with you thieves! Off with you varmints," and the robbers all swirled toward him shouting, "Stand and deliver!"

In the starlight, Gallen could hardly make out the soot-blackened faces of the robbers; one of them had curly red hair. They were big men mostly, down-on-the-luck farmers sporting beards and armed with knives, the kind of aimless rogues you often saw sloughing around alehouses in the past two years. Drought one year and rot the next had thrown many a farmer out of work. Gallen made out the gleam of a longsword. Another young boy held a shield and a grim-looking war club.

Old Seamus began cursing and fumbled at his belt in an effort to pull his knife, but Gallen grabbed Seamus's shoulder, restraining him. "Don't be a fool!" Gallen warned. "There's too many of them. Give them your money!"

"I'll not be giving them my money!" Seamus shouted, pulling his dagger, and Gallen's heart sunk. Seamus was the father of seven. He could either let the ruffians have his purse and watch his family suffer, or he could fight and probably die. He was choosing to die. "Now back me, will you! Back me!"

Dutifully, Gallen stood back to back with Seamus as the robbers closed in. That is what Seamus had paid him for. Three shillings, Gallen realized. I'm going to get killed this night for three shillings.

The tall man brandished his sword. "I'll be thanking you to drop your purses, lads." From his accent and curly red hair, Gallen estimated that he was a Flaherty, from County Obhiann.

"I beg you sirs," Gallen said, "not to go making free with our money. I've got none to spare, and my friend here has a wife and seven innocent children."

One robber laughed. "We know! And Seamus O'Connor just made forty pounds while hawking his wool at the fair. Now out with the loot!" he shouted angrily, waving his knife. "An' if you give it to us casual, we won't hurt you so bad." Gallen watched the men close. One of their number must have seen Seamus's money at the fair and waited until the old man got on this desolate stretch of road before setting the ambush.

The robbers had them circled now, but held off a pace. Gallen thought of running. It was only a mile over the hill to An Cochan. A bead of sweat rolled down Gallen's cheek, and his heart was hammering. He glanced around at the circling men in their dark tunics. Seamus was growling like a cornered badger at Gallen's back, and Gallen could feel the old man's muscles, hard as cords, straining beneath his coat. Gallen wanted to stall, hoping that even with his mind all clouded by whiskey, Seamus might see that it made no sense to leave his family orphaned. An owl soared over the ravine.

Seamus began swearing and shouting, "Why do you have your faces blacked, you ugly bastards? I'm not a child to be frightened by a sooty face! Off with you! Off with you!"

Gallen half-closed his eyes and wondered, If I were the greatest knife fighter in the world, what would I do?

In an instant, it was as if a familiar mantle began to fall over him. Gallen's muscles tightened into coils and the world moved into sharper focus. Gallen felt the blood pounding hot in his veins, and his nostrils flared wide, tasting the night air. He sized up the ruffians before him, and though it was dark, subtle shades of light began to reveal details about each man. They were breathing hard, the way men will when they're afraid.

Nine men. Gallen had never fought nine men, but at that moment it didn't matter. He was, after all, the greatest knife fighter in the world.

Gallen tossed his head back so that his hood fell away, letting his golden hair gleam in the starlight. He chuckled softly and said, "I must offer you men fair warning. If you don't back away and give us the road, I'll have to kill you."

One robber gasped, "It's Gallen O'Day! Watch him boys!" The men swarmed around Gallen and Seamus faster, moving warily, but none dared venture in too close. The tallest robber shouted, "Take him, boys!"

Gallen didn't worry about the robbers at his back. Seamus had his knife out, and even though he was drunk, no sane man would try to tangle with him. Instead, Gallen sized up the five men to his front and sides. Two of them hung back half a pace—cowards who didn't want to look it. Another man stood close in, but he was tossing his knife back and forth between his left and right hand, hoping that the sight of it would strike fear into Gallen. Another robber was stocky, with an unsightly bulge under his cloak, and Gallen realized it was a breastplate; this robber breathed heavily and bent low to the ground on legs that were tense, ready to spring. The last of the five closest was their leader—a tall man with a longsword who likely would avoid joining the fray with such a weapon for fear of lopping the head off one of his own men.

Gallen heard the scuffling feet of a robber lunge behind. The robber grabbed Seamus's arm and tried to throw him to the ground, but Seamus twisted away at the last moment and made a stab. The robber yelped in pain, and hot blood splattered across the back of Gallen's neck.

"Take that for your trouble!" Seamus jeered, as if he'd won something, and then more robbers surged behind. A sharp blow from a club sent Seamus to the ground.

Gallen had been watching the man who tossed his knife from hand to hand. The knife was in the air, and Gallen leapt up and kicked it away, disarming the robber. He whirled and kicked an attacker off Seamus, slashed another across the throat. The lad with a club raised his shield to protect his face, and Gallen could have dropped beneath the boy's guard and lunged past, run to win his freedom. But Gallen knew he had to keep the highwaymen from slitting Seamus's throat.

Gallen dodged and came up behind the young robber, grabbed the boy's hair and put a knife to his throat. "Hold where you are," Gallen shouted. "I don't want to have to murder this lad!" The boy struggled, but Gallen was ready for any move he tried. Gallen wrestled him still. "Now, off with you! Give me a clear road."

The highwaymen moved around them, keeping a safe distance. Gallen could see from their determined faces that they didn't value the lad's life. It wasn't worth forty pounds.

The boy cried, "For Christ's sake, Paddy, tell them to back off!" The boy was panting hard, and he began to cry. The sweat pouring off of his neck made him slippery.

Gallen looked up at the tall one with the sword, Paddy. Since it seemed that the boy was a worthless hostage, Gallen decided that Paddy might value his own hide more.

Gallen tossed the boy to the ground. The robber who wore the breast-plate leaned forward, dagger at the ready. Gallen had already slipped beneath one attacker's guard, and the men held their weapons low, preventing any similar moves. One man lunged at Gallen from behind; Gallen side-stepped, slashed the attacker's knife arm nearly in half, then Gallen leapt at the man in the breastplate. He put his toe at the top of the man's throat and let it slide down till it hit the armor, then stepped up and used his momentum to somersault over the robber's head.

He hit ground, swung around and put his knife to Paddy's throat. It all happened so fast that the robbers could barely react. Paddy swore and threw down his sword.

The boy with the club sat on the ground for a moment, crying. Other than the boy, one of the robbers was dead, another was knocked unconscious, and two were nursing serious wounds. Paddy was disarmed. The last three robbers hesitated, not knowing what to do. Paddy said to his men, "All right lads, listen to him! Drop your weapons and give the man the road! Now!"

The three robbers all dropped their weapons and backed away.

"Paddy, you're a lousy bastard!" the boy shouted, still sitting on the ground. "You were going to let him slit my gullet, but you'll save your own? So you think you're worth forty pounds, but I'm not worth a bob?"

The boy got up and held his shield down low like a veteran, and he raised his nasty war club; its metal studs gleamed in the starlight. He advanced slowly, and the other robbers suddenly leered like the greedy thieves they were. As one they reached down and retrieved their weapons.

Seamus moaned and began coughing. Gallen saw that he would have to fight these last four. The men quickly circled him.

Gallen listened for the sound of a scuffing foot behind him, tried watching all directions at once. His senses were overwhelmed: he could smell the wool and sweat and scent of wet humus and ash on Paddy and the other robbers. He could smell the hot blood on his knife. A cool breeze washed through the trees, hissing like the sea. Somewhere over the hill a sheep bawled out, and Gallen wished he was there, safely over the hill, out of the dark Sidhe Forest and into the village of An Cochan.

Gallen slit Paddy's throat and stepped aside to meet these four robbers, hoping that a bold challenge would shake their confidence.

Gallen knew that he stood a good chance of getting killed if he let the men circle him, so he ran head-on into a robber, stabbed the man in the chest, then tried to throw the man behind him as a shield. But the dying robber grabbed Gallen's greatcloak and swung him back into the circle.

For one brief moment, Gallen realized he was in trouble, and then he heard the whirring sound of a club. Every instinct in him, every fantasy he'd ever concocted about such a situation, warned him to duck. He dropped his head to the right as the club smashed into him.

Dozens of brilliant lights flashed before his eyes. There was a roaring in his ears, and the ground seemed to leap up to meet him. Suddenly, the robbers were on him, kicking, and one man shouted, "This will teach you! Never again will you begrudge a man for a friendly knock on the head or for borrowing your purse!"

He looked up and saw a man ready to fall on him with a knife, and Gallen tried to roll away, but his muscles wouldn't cooperate, and he knew he was going to die.

"Hold!" a commanding voice shouted nearby, and Gallen's attackers stopped. As one they looked up the hill to gauge this new threat. The wind was still hissing in the trees, and the muddy road was cold against Gallen's back. He tried to roll over, look up to see his rescuer. The newcomer said evenly in a voice hot with warning, "Those who commit murder in Coille Sidhe shall never escape alive."

One of Gallen's attackers choked in fear, and the others stood up cautiously and stepped back. Gallen heard one robber mutter, "Sidhe."

Gallen's head was spinning so badly, he could only roll over. He'd lived on the edge of Coille Sidhe all his life, and never had he heard rumors that netherworlders might really inhabit the forest. It was said that the sidhe were lesser demons, servants of the devil, and that Satan often sent the sidhe to herald his approach.

"There's only one of them," a robber said, trying to bolster the courage of his fellows. Gallen rolled to his elbows and looked up: above him at the top of the ridge stood a man in the darkness, the starlit sky at his back. He wore garments of solid black, all darker than the night, and his head was covered with a hood. Even his hands were covered with fine gloves. Starlight reflected dully from a longsword in one hand and a twisted dagger in the other. For a moment, Gallen thought it was just a man standing in the darkness, but his eyes focused on the creature's face: its face shone like pale lavender starlight, as if it were a liquid mirror. Gallen's heart pounded in terror, and the sidhe leaned back and laughed grimly at the highwaymen. In that one horrifying moment, Gallen expected the ground to split open and the devil and his legions to crawl forth.

The robbers fled. Gallen urged his leaden arms to move, flailed about while trying to lift himself up, but his head spun and he faltered to the ground. Blackness swallowed him.

Sometime later he woke in a daze. The sidhe was hoisting him into the saddle of Seamus O'Connor's mare. Gallen lurched away from the sidhe's touch, as if it were a serpent, and bumped into something behind him. Seamus was slung over the mare's back, and the wounded man breathed raspily. Seamus's head had been bandaged, and the sidhe whispered, "Hurry, Gallen O'Day. Save your friend if you can."

Gallen's head still spun like leaves in a whirlwind, and he could barely grip the horse's mane to keep from falling off.

The sidhe took Gallen's chin, and Gallen looked into the creature's eyes. The thing looked human in nearly every way—Gallen could make out the fiery yellow hairs of its eyebrows. It was very much a human face, if not for the fact that it glowed like molten metal. "Remember, Gallen," the creature said with great heaviness, "I will hold you accountable for any oaths you make this day."

Gallen had only a moment to wonder at this portentous threat when the sidhe whistled and slapped the mare's rear. She leapt downhill, heading for An Cochan. Gallen dug his heels into her flank and gave her her head.

The night that Gallen O'Day fought off the nine robbers, Orick had been thinking about leaving Gallen forever. A dozen conflicting urges were moving Orick in ways that he did not wish to go.

His love of mankind and his desire to serve God by ministering to others was leading Orick toward the priesthood. Yet Orick knew that he and Gallen were not of the same heart on such matters. While Orick revered the Tome and its companion book the Bible, hungering for the wisdom of the ancient Christ and his disciples, Gallen's attitude toward the books was disappointing. The young man vacillated between grudging admiration for some of the Bible's teachings and open contempt for the Tome. Obviously, Gallen did not have faith in the holy books. Although Orick genuinely liked Gallen, their sharply divergent views on religion were troubling, and Orick believed that soon he would have to leave Gallen, if only to retain some peace of mind.

Furthermore, Orick found other urges beckoning him. He had been spending a great deal of time in the company of humans lately. But such a state of affairs could not long continue. He needed a female bear's company.

So, that night as the two said their good-byes at the back of the inn and Orick watched as Gallen led Seamus away on the mare, Orick's own words rang in his ears, "God be with you then, for I shall not."

The young female bear next to him, named Dara, pawed demurely through the garbage. "Have you decided then? Will you be coming to the Salmon Fest next week?"

Orick imagined the hundreds of bears that would be gathered at the fest, fishing in the day, sitting around campfires and singing all night on the rocky beach on the banks of the cold river. He imagined the smell of wet fur, the pine trees, whole salmon skewered on stakes as they leaned against the fire pits to broil. Though Orick didn't particularly relish the idea of wading in the icy waters of Obhiann Fiain all day trying to catch fish in his teeth, he was nearly four, and certain primal urges were getting hard to ignore. Orick saw that becoming a father would confer upon him a type of immortality, for he would live on through his progeny, and he hungered for that particular blessing.

Yet if he entered the priesthood, he would have to take a vow of chastity, and so he considered that this year he would need to go to the Salmon Fest. At the Salmon Fest many a fair young female bear would be hunting for more than a slimy morsel of fish for dinner, and frankly, as the bears say, "A she-bear in heat is the best kind to meet."

Sure, there would be games at the festival—competitions where the males would go at it tooth and claw, tree-climbing races, the log pull, the pig toss. Orick would have to win the right to breed, but he was becoming rather large, and he'd learned a few wrestling tricks by watching Gallen.

Who knows, he mused, perhaps I'll unseat old Mangan as the Primal Bear. He imagined how envious the other bears would be as he chose the best and brightest females to breed with, then Orick gobbled some cold cabbage and deep-fried clams from the garbage.

"I'm not sure if I'll come or not," Orick growled in response to Dara's question. "I'll think about it." It was possible to find a mate without going to the Salmon Fest, but a saying rang through Orick's mind: "While the common bear shivers in his wet fur, the superior bear builds a fire." So, Orick knew that if he really wanted a quality mate, he would need to make the journey to the Salmon Fest, leaving Gallen O'Day behind.

"I saw some deer up the hill in Covey's apple orchard," Dara said coyly. "I really like venison. How about if we go up there and see if we can kill us a deer?"

Orick grumbled, looked at her askance. He didn't like hunting for deer. The bucks had antlers, and even the females had sharp little hooves to kick with. Orick didn't like undertaking unnecessary dangers. Besides, he was hungry, and being hungry made him grumpy.

"Nah, I never developed a taste for venison," Orick lied. "I know where some squirrels have a midden. Do you like acorns?"

"Well," Dara said, "I'll go catch one myself." She left the garbage to Orick and headed up the north road. Orick watched her longingly. He knew that she expected him to follow. The chances were slim that she'd be able to sneak up on a deer herself. But deer usually ran uphill when frightened, so if Orick were to go uphill and wait for Dara to scare the deer up to him, the chances were pretty good that he could catch one.

Orick imagined a huge six-point buck charging uphill, antlers lowered like pikes, hooves slashing, and decided not to risk it.

He crept beneath the shadows of the pine boughs that sprouted from the inn, then lay down. The clouds were quickly blowing away and stars dusted the sky in a fiery powder while the moons sank lower, staring down like the eyes of God. For awhile Orick watched for falling stars and thought about Dara. She was a flirtatious young thing. Orick suspected that she had no idea how strongly her charms affected him, and he felt as he laid there that he was making a momentous decision: should I follow her to the Salmon Fest and see if I could win the right to mate with her, or should I stay with Gallen for one more season?

Above Orick's head, someone blew out a candle in one window of the inn. Orick suddenly noticed how dark it was. Nearly all the lights in town were out, and only the pale fires of heaven shone in the streets. The shushing whisper of waves breaking on the beach a quarter of a mile away lulled the bear.

Orick closed his eyes and rested his muzzle on the ground. He slept lightly for some time, but a dog's yelp interrupted his dreams. It was an odd bark, the noise a startled dog makes, but it was cut short, as if someone had kicked the dog in the ribs. Orick would have gone back to sleep if he had not noticed a faint, peculiar scent barely distinguishable above the salt tang of the sea air—blood. He blinked and looked down the road south of town, and for a moment thought he was dreaming.

Something was walking up the road. It resembled a human creeping on all fours, but its spindly legs could have been no less than eight feet long, as were its arms, while its torso was very short, perhaps only two feet. It moved jerkily, wary as a mantis, its tiny round head pivoting as it tried to gaze in all directions at once.

It carried something in one hand—the mangled body of a whippet. The creature got to a crossroad and hesitated in the shadows, then dropped the dead dog and bent its elbows so that its forehead nearly touched ground. Orick could hear the creature sniffing. It crept toward Mahoney's stables, keeping its nose to the ground, then suddenly seemed to catch a scent. It swerved back toward the inn.

The monster sneaked to the darkened windows of the inn, not twelve feet from Orick. It stopped, sniffed at Orick and regarded him a moment. The monster had large eyes that showed orange in the moonlight, and Orick saw that its marvelously long hands looked very powerful. Orick didn't move, and the creature must have decided that Orick was asleep and therefore didn't matter. Let sleeping bears lie.

It began inhaling near the small round windows of the inn, tasting the scents. The head was indeed human in shape, but the monster really did not move at all like a human. Its jaunty twitches reminded Orick more and more of an insect.

The thing reached up sixteen feet to a small window, grabbed the sill in one hand, and pulled itself up to sniff at the crack under the window. In performing this maneuver, it seemed to defy gravity, as if it were a mosquito clinging to its victim.

It reached one long arm sideways eight feet to the next small window, swung over to it, tasted the scent there.

Mahoney's Inn, like most structures in town, had grown from a house-pine seed. As with many such homes, the owners were of course obliged to put in windows and doors only where openings for such grew naturally, and new windows and doors had to be fitted every few years as the openings grew larger. So it happened that sometimes the window didn't fit snugly.

The creature must have known this, for it stuck its long fingers into the lintel, scrabbling with heavy claws to pull the window free. Orick heard wood splinter under the force of its assault, and though Orick had never before seen anything like this monster, he knew that this thing was intent on mayhem.

The monster pulled the window free and tossed it away with a flick of the wrist. Its hand shot into the dark cubbyhole of the room.

Orick roared in warning, then lurched from his hiding place, jaws snapping. Though the monster was incredibly long of limb, it looked to be rather flimsy. Orick grabbed a leg and shook his head, pulling the creature down, ripping its sinews.

For its part, the creature slashed at Orick with its long fingers, raking open wounds across the bear's face. In the heat of battle, Orick hardly noticed. He bit into an arm and found it to be much tougher than he'd imagined—indeed, Orick had once bitten into the haunches of a running horse, and the horse was not nearly as tough as this monster. Orick growled in his fury, clamped his jaws down and rolled, then finally managed to snap a bone.

The monster struggled up on three limbs to run. Orick heard shouts of dismay and screaming from the inn, and he worried that if he let the beast escape, it would return to town with murder on its mind.

Orick seized a foot in his teeth, pulled the monster to the ground, then dragged it backward like a sack of onions. Orick's teeth gouged through the thing's flesh, ripping its leg wide open, yet Orick felt as if his own teeth might be yanked out.

The beast raised its head, and Orick saw in the starlight that it had fierce-looking fangs. It blinked its orange eyes and screamed, an odd howling that rang through the city and out over the surrounding mountains like a war horn.

There were words in that cry, and Orick sat in astonishment as he recognized them—"I have found her! Come, fellow vanquishers!" Orick lunged for the creature's throat, trying to silence that call for aid, and with a vicious wrench he tore the beast's windpipes out.

Bloodlust hit Orick then, some primal instinct. He roared and tore at the dying creature, swatting it with his claws, ripping it with his teeth, dancing around it in a red fury until he became aware that a dozen people had poured from the inn.

John Mahoney rushed out with a lantern, and he shone it on the beast, a look of stricken horror on his face. For the first time, Orick saw that the thing had green skin, like that of a toad. "Get the priest! Get the priest!" John Mahoney began shouting. "Och, God, it's a monster!"

And most of the others from town were running around, shouting in dismay and disbelief. But among those who issued from the inn were a beautiful young woman and a hooded man who wielded a sword.

They stood for a moment, gazing at the dead monster, and though fear shone in their eyes, there was not the look of total incomprehension and shock that Orick saw in the faces of his townsmen. Instinctively, Orick knew that these two had battled such monsters before.

Indeed, the man leaned close to the woman, and Orick caught his words. "It called for other vanquishers. We must hurry into the woods. We can't stay."

"What of our horses?" she asked.

"They will do us no good in the forest, in the dark. Better to leave them."

The woman nodded. Her companion rushed back into the inn, came out with two packs. He gave the woman a pack and she immediately headed north up the road.

But for one moment, the warrior stood, pulled out his naked sword gleaming in the starlight. He looked right at Orick, as if to thank him, and raised the sword in a silent salute. Then he spun and rushed into the night.

A crowd gathered around Orick, congratulating him, and men brought out their torches. Orick warned that other such monsters might be about, and soon the men formed up into a militia and set to guarding the edges of town. A boy ran to the parsonage to wake Father Heany, who took one look at the creature and pronounced that it must be some unrepentant sinner, transmogrified by God in retaliation for its unholy deeds.

Many of the townspeople stood by, congratulating Orick, yet Orick himself wondered at what he had done. Who had he helped? What evil plans had the monster harbored? Orick knew so little about the creature—only that the beast's flesh was made of tougher stuff than anything he had ever sunk his teeth into. As townspeople brought their lanterns close to look at the beast, Orick smelled its torn flesh. It had an oily scent, not like any land beast, but more like a fish, yet without the putrid fishy flavor.

When he looked at the ropey coils of torn muscle, he saw that each fiber was like a tiny thread of white. Yet when he looked into the creature's face, aside from the heavy jaws and sharp teeth, it looked to be human, a young boy perhaps.

Orick did not know what the monster was, but others knew. Orick stared up the north road that led to the deep forest of Coille Sidhe, the direction that the two strangers had run. The vanquishers would be there, hunting the strangers, and Orick knew they would need help. He decided to leave as soon as Gallen returned.

Orick looked up at the moonlit sky, wondering what had taken Gallen so long.

Three

An hour before dawn, Gallen urged the mare under the canopy of Seamus O'Connor's house. His home had grown from a great oak, and at this time of the year the dead leaves in the canopy rustled in the wind under the starlight. Other oak houses, planted generations ago, grew near in a cluster, so the O'Connor farm—inhabited by several families of O'Connors—was more like a grove of houses. Here in the wilds, such groves gave one a sense of security, with people all around—though they were really little more than firetraps. Eventually, if the family didn't leave, they'd get burned out.

As Gallen neared the house, a watch owl swooped near his head, shouting "Who are you?" Gallen gave his name, fearing that the raptor might rake him with its talons. A candle burning in the O'Connor window bore testimony that Seamus's wife Biddy had waited up for him.

Seamus was in a bad way. He kept crying out at visions and couldn't answer a simple question.

Gallen slid from the saddle and shouted for help, then lugged Seamus to the house. Biddy unbolted the front door, and soon Gallen had him laid out on the sturdy kitchen table and all seven of Seamus's children got up. Brothers and aunts and cousins poured in from the other houses in the grove. Soon the house bustled with crying children. They gathered around Seamus and hugged his hand, wiping their snotty noses on his sleeve.

Biddy sent her oldest daughter Claire for the priest while her son Patrick fetched the doctor. Gallen watched Patrick make ready to leave. The boy didn't hurry—instead he just skulked away, lazy to go out. Patrick had a likeness to his father, but was still just a gangrel of a boy with long arms and a slouching posture. Word around the county said he was a rowdy and a drunkard that his mother wouldn't be sorry after once he left home.

Seamus woke and called for Biddy but didn't know her when she answered him. The doctor arrived and checked Seamus's wounds—a shallow cut to the ribs and a cracked head that was swollen and feverish.

The priest, a Father Brian who was a second cousin of Gallen's on his mother's side, gave Seamus the last rites even as the doctor drew cold well water to bathe Seamus's head.

Gallen told them the story of the attack, saying only that a stranger had intervened, frightening off the robbers. He was afraid to admit that the stranger was a sidhe. How could he explain that one of Satan's minions had rescued him?

Afterward, Gallen sat on a stool, holding his head in his hands, afraid Seamus would die. He kept replaying the whole fight in his mind, wondering if somehow he couldn't have made it come out better. He recalled one moment, when one of the blackguards had first jumped up from the roadside, waving the white slip to spook the horse, when he had thought to pull his knife. Yet he'd held still, wanting first to gauge his enemies, estimate his chances of winning.

But if he'd only pulled his knives from the start, attacked before the robbers consolidated their forces, Gallen would have stood a better chance. Gallen relived the incident over and over, and within an hour he was sure he could have won. He could have killed all nine bandits and gotten Seamus home safely.

And Gallen wondered about the sidhe. There, in the mountains at night with a spinning head, Gallen had been sure of what he'd seen, but now that he was back in a warm home, with people bustling around, those swirling images of the glowing lavender face seemed—astonishing, impossible. He could not have seen such a thing.

Just before dawn, Seamus lapsed into a deep, uneasy sleep, the kind of sleep that men seldom wake from. Gallen's eyes became gritty and his eyelids heavy. He was in that state where his skin felt as if it slept, as if he were losing the sensations of touch and heat and cold.

Biddy brewed some rose hip tea, sweetening it with honey, and the doctor forced it down Seamus's throat. Gallen watched from a distance, yawning.

Father Brian turned, his black robes swaying grandly, saw Gallen's face, and appeared startled. Brian crossed the room and in a hushed voice said, "You look like hell, my son. What's the matter, did you get all of the heart knocked out of you?" Gallen didn't answer. "Why don't you come outside with me for a walk? The stretch will do your muscles good."

"No," Gallen said, shaking his head. He felt as if leaving Seamus's bedside would be some form of betrayal. He needed to see this through, be there if Seamus died.

"You'll do no one any good here," Father Brian said. "Whether Seamus lives or dies or wakes up an idiot, there's nothing you can do for him."

Father Brian pulled at Gallen's hand, and led him out into the dawn. The sun was rising pink over the green grass of the drumlins. Morning fog burning off the downs crawled up the hillsides in some places like pale spiders of smoke. The raucous calls of crows echoed over the fields. Father Brian took Gallen out behind the O'Connors' barn, to a reedy pond. At their approach, several snipe got up and flew about Gallen's head, uttering sharp cries. A pair of mallards rose from the glassy water, and Father Brian sat with Gallen on a sun-bleached log.

"All right," Father Brian said, folding his hands. "Out with it. Give me your confession."

Gallen felt odd giving his confession to a cousin. Father Brian was only twenty-five, and the man was so fresh that he couldn't grow a beard to save his soul. Still, he was a priest.

"Forgive me, Father, for I have sinned," Gallen said.

"How long has it been since your last confession?" Father Brian asked, folding his hands like a steeple.

"A year."

Father Brian raised his eyebrows, looked at Gallen askance. "So long? How many men have you killed in that time?"

Gallen thought a moment, added his three kills from last night. "Thirteen."

"Business sounds a bit slow," Father Brian mused. "Killing is a grievous thing—a mortal sin under some conditions. I assume that all of them were highwaymen and scoundrels?"

"Yes."

Father Brian folded his hands again. "Hmmm. And how much booty did you find on the corpses?"

Gallen had to think. He hadn't kept a running tally. "Well, if you consider the boots and clothes and weapons I sold, not more than a hundred pounds."

Father Brian whistled in surprise. "That much, eh? A good haul." After a bit of thought, he said, "Say a Hail Mary for each man you killed. That ought to suffice. And of course, I'd thank you to pay a tithe to the church."

"Ten pounds?" Gallen asked, his heart beating hard. He'd spent the money long ago. Sure, he made a lot of money as an escort, but he had to buy his food at the inn, pay lodging—his expenses were equally high.

"Well, you wouldn't want to risk dying with any kind of stain on your soul," Father Brian said. "God delivered these evil-doers into your hand. It's only fair that you offer something to show your gratitude."

"But ten pounds—"

"Och," Father Brian interrupted, "think nothing of it. You'll take more than that off your next couple of jobs."

Gallen nodded reluctantly, wondering how much Paddy and the other thieves might have had in their pockets. Father Brian stared hard at him. "So, what else have you got to confess?"

"About last night. I keep thinking, and I'm pretty sure I could have saved Seamus that knock on the head."

"Ohhh," Father Brian said thoughtfully. "So that's why you look so wrung out. I figured as much. You've never lost a client before. So what makes you think you could have saved him? You said there were, what, nine robbers? You're sure you could have taken so many?"

"I stood fast when they first came at us," Gallen said. "I knew what they wanted, but I advised Seamus to throw them his purse. But—"

"And why did you do that?" Father Brian interrupted. "You're not a coward, are you? I've never heard such talk about you. Think close, and give me the truth."

Gallen considered closely, remembered the men circling him in the dark, big men sporting beards, men who looked soft and flabby from lack of work, men armed with kitchen knives and a relic of a sword that had showed a faint patina of rust even in the dark. "I didn't want to have to fight them," Gallen said at last. "They looked like farmers, soft, down on their luck—not killers. A couple of them were just boys."

Gallen thought back, remembered the two strangers that had hired him last night at Mahoney's Inn. Now, the man who had worn two swords on the outside of his cloak—that man had been a trained warrior. Gallen had seen it in his stride, in the clean way the man had maneuvered through the common room without letting his weapons knock against the stools. His cautious demeanor showed that he'd been a man who lived with battle. Gallen had fought such men before—trained swordsmen out of Darnot who turned to butchery after the war. Gallen didn't mind fighting such men, though they could be more dangerous than a wounded boar.

"So, you took a little pity on some robbers," Brian said. "Christ advocated the same, that we have mercy on our brothers—but only if they are penitent. The men who were robbing you last night didn't merit mercy. They gave you no quarter and asked none in return. Now, if the survivors repent and turn to Christ and ask your forgiveness, then it would be appropriate for you to forgive them, welcome them back as brothers in Christ. In such circumstances, your feelings would do you merit."

"I know," Gallen said. Father Brian sounded as if he were trying his best not to chastise Gallen, make him see things in their proper light. In truth, Gallen was too tired to argue or think on his own. He only wanted to sleep.

"So, perhaps your hesitation did cause Seamus some hurt, and perhaps not. You can't know anything for certain," Father Brian said. "So I'll tell you what. I want you to take a vow before me now. I want you to promise God that when your heart is hot to come to the aid of another, you will never again hesitate."

Gallen glanced over at Father Brian, and in his mind the words of the sidhe echoed: "I will hold you accountable for any oaths you make this day." The morning sun seemed to go cold, and Gallen stood up and looked out over the drumlins at the white spiders of fog climbing the hills. Sheep were bawling in the distance, but otherwise the world seemed quiet, desolate. Gallen felt almost as if the sidhe stood nearby, with his hand cupped to his ear to hear the enunciation of the oath. Somehow, Gallen felt sure, the sidhe had known that Gallen would be asked to take this oath, so the sidhe had warned him that this was a solemn business. But would Gallen be speaking the oath to God, or to the sidhe? To speak an oath to a magical creature would be a sin. "Thou shalt not suffer a witch to live," the Bible said, so how much more wicked was a sidhe, a creature of pure magic? Gallen could not make a vow to the sidhe.

"Well," Father Brian asked innocently, unaware of Gallen's dilemma. "Will you speak the oath?"

"I will," Gallen said. "I'll speak it to God: If ever again my heart is hot to come to the aid of another, I will not hesitate." Gallen said the words, and out over the fields a crow began cawing and flew up into the hills as if to carry the message. Gallen wondered if the sidhe had taken animal form.

"Now," Father Brian said, "before the sun gets any farther up the sky, how about if you and I hike up the road and search those robbers? Maybe we could get a handle on some of that tithe you owe the church."

Gallen agreed reluctantly. He didn't expect much from these bodies, and it seemed rather ghoulish to be searching them in the company of a priest. Still, if they didn't hurry, some early traveler would get there first.

They headed up the road, over the mountain. When they got to the site of the ambush, Seamus's son Patrick was there. He already had the bodies laid out side by side like partridges. He hunched over them, hurrying to get their purses and anything else of value. When he saw Gallen and the priest, he hurried even faster, as if he would take the loot and run.

Gallen stood back and surveyed the scene. He knew he had killed three last night, but there were four corpses. One of the wounded men had bled to death on the spot. All four men looked small and harmless when displayed here on the ground. Their clothes were rough-sewn wool, worn through.

Patrick and Father Brian retrieved the purses and other valuables while Gallen scouted around the ambush site, checking the prints in the soft mud. Eight of the attackers had been from County Obhiann. Gallen could tell by the rounded toes of the boots, a northern style, but the ninth robber was probably a local, for his boots were pointed and soft of sole. Both outer soles on the boots had holes worn through, so that they left distinctive prints. Gallen found where the local had come down out of the brush beside the road, and Gallen tried to recall a face. The prints showed that this local robber had never really come into the fray. He'd hung back.

As for the sidhe, Gallen found his prints, too. The sidhe had worn a boot with heavy heels that cut the shapes of crescent moons into the soft mud.

Gallen went back to Father Brian and Patrick. They were just finishing up, checking to make sure that the thieves didn't have any silver coins in their boots. Gallen watched the priest grunt, struggling to pull a worn leather boot off of Paddy. Patrick—who was economical with effort but not with other people's property—took out his knife and tried to slice open the other boot. Father Brian scolded the boy, saying that the boots still had plenty of wear and could be given to the poor.

As he watched, Gallen saw that Patrick's boots were pointed, with distinctive holes worn in the outer soles. He had a drop of blood spattered on one toe. Now, in the light of day, Gallen could see that Patrick's sparse red beard had a streak of chimney soot on it, smeared down below the right ear.

As Father Brian wrestled Paddy's boot off, two silver coins fell out.

"Well, you old crows." Gallen smiled. "How much did you find on the pitiable corpses? Any meat on them bones?"

"Three pounds, two shillings," Father Brian answered. "Not much of a haul."

"Oh, I don't know about that," Gallen answered. "It sounds like plenty to me. Three pounds? Why, for that much money, I'd sit out all night in the cold with a gang of robbers so that I could point out my own father when he came down the road. Three pounds would be enough to betray my own kin for. Don't you think so, Patrick?"

The gangrelly boy looked up, uncertain. He startled back at the threatening tone in Gallen's voice. He didn't answer.

"You've got your father's blood on your boot, and you've still got a robber's soot to hide your shameful face," Gallen said. Father Brian looked at the boy darkly, saw the betraying marks. The priest bit his lip.

Patrick glanced longingly down the road to Clere, set his muscles as if to run. He wasn't an agile sort. Gallen judged that he could catch the boy in fifty paces.

"The likes of you," Father Brian grumbled at Patrick, "would be only a burden to your widowed mother even if you hung around."

"I didn't mean for anyone to get hurt," Patrick whispered. His face had turned red, and now hot tears poured down over his freckles.

"You thought you could steal from your brothers and sisters, and no one would suffer?" Father Brian asked, shocked. "What were you thinking? Aren't times hard enough with poachers stealing your sheep and wolves in the flocks? You wanted to add another burden to your father's shoulders, all for a few pounds to spend on whiskey?" Father Brian was known to be an occasional whiskey drinker, so he added, "or worse—beer?"

"Get yourself gone, now!" Father Brian shouted at the boy in disgust. "And never return to County Morgan. You're outlawed from here. I'll give you till sundown, and then I'll spread the word. If anyone in County Morgan ever finds you walking the road again, your life is forfeit. Go and make a living for yourself elsewhere if you can, but we won't tolerate you here again!"

"Let me stay a bit," Patrick begged, reaching for the hem of Father Brian's robe. "My father's hurt bad, and my heart is sore for it. Let me stay to see if he makes it through the week!"

"What?" Father Brian asked. "You beg to stay in striking range of a sick man's purse? Aw, to hell with you! I'd rather trust a weasel to guard the chicken coop. Get out of here before I have Gallen O'Day slit your throat."

Father Brian picked up a large stone and hurled it at Patrick as a sign that he'd been outlawed. The stone struck the boy on the shoulder, and Patrick hissed painfully but still looked at Father Brian with pleading eyes, begging to stay.

Gallen picked up a stone of his own and threw it hard, slamming it into the boy's thigh. "Get out of here, outlaw!" Gallen shouted.

Father Brian reached for another stone. If the lad didn't leave, then according to custom, Gallen and Father Brian had no recourse but to stone him to death.

Patrick jumped away up the road and began limping toward Clere, shooting angry glances back at the two. He seemed to be in the throes of trying to conjure some devastating curse, and finally he shouted, "You don't fool me, Gallen O'Day! You consort with the sidhe and creatures of the netherworld, and you're no better than a demon yourself! I saw him, Father Brian! I saw Gallen O'Day with a sidhe last night! He prayed to Satan for help, and a sidhe came to his aid!"

"I'd be pleased," Father Brian shouted, "if you wouldn't make such accusations about my cousin, you damned misbegotten purveyor of patricide! Get, now!" He hurled another rock, and Patrick dodged and hurried up the road.

They watched Patrick climb the winding mountain path, between the blue pine trees and the gloam of the wood. Father Brian kept his eyes on Patrick and asked with clenched teeth, "Was there any truth to his words? About the sidhe?"

A shiver ran through Gallen. He couldn't lie to a priest, even if that priest was only his cousin. "I've never prayed to the devil," Gallen said, "but last night, when those Flahertys knocked me in the head and were hot to skin me alive, some creature came out of the woods. It looked like a man, all dressed in black and carrying swords, but its face shone like molten glass. It warned them that anyone who committed murder in Coille Sidhe would never make it out of the woods alive."

Father Brian caught his breath and looked at Gallen askance. "You're sure it wasn't just a wight or some spirit of the woods?"

"It was flesh, like you or me," Gallen said. "It put Seamus up on the horse, and I looked into its face. It . . . I've never seen or heard of anything like it."

"But it warned men against murder," Father Brian whispered in a tone hinting at something between confusion and awe. "It couldn't have been in league with the devil. Therefore, it must have come from God. The thing that you saw last night," he whispered with desperation, "could it have been an angel?"

"I don't think so. It was dressed in black," Gallen said.

"Then it was an angel—" Father Brian said with finality, "it was the Angel of Death, walking at the right hand of Gallen O'Day and keeping guard over him. That's what we'll tell people. That's what we'll say."

"I'm not so sure—" Gallen started to argue, but Brian spun and grabbed Gallen's collar at the throat. "Don't dispute me on this! I'll not have it said that a cousin of mine consorts with demons. Only you and the robbers saw what happened last night. No one can contradict your testimony! It was God who sent the Angel of Death to stand guard over you—do you understand me? And I'll excommunicate anyone who begs to differ!"

"Yes," Gallen said, confused and frightened. Father Brian's argument made sense, but in his heart Gallen knew that he would not live this down easily. Five other men had seen the sidhe, and they could not but tell what they had witnessed. Somehow, Gallen felt sure, this would come back to haunt him.

Four

At dawn, the townspeople in Clere dragged the dead monster from the inn and dumped its body into the bay. Father Heany said that no creature damned to be so ugly should be buried on hallowed ground, and the ocean seemed the only place big enough to hide such a fiend.

The town militia guarded the roads but still hadn't seen more monsters. Yet Maggie knew they were coming. All over town, dogs sniffed the air and barked, sending up keening wails that troubled Maggie's soul.

"Can you smell them?" Maggie asked Orick just after dawn.

"Aye," Orick grumbled, standing on his hind legs to catch the scent. "There's an oily stench on the wind, not from anything human."

Everywhere, townspeople were rushing about frantically, spreading rumors. But Maggie Flynn just stood, watching longingly up the north road to An Cochan. Gallen still hadn't returned. He was hours overdue.

"I'm going to An Cochan," Maggie said at last to Orick, her voice quavering. "If Gallen doesn't know what's afoot, he'd better be warned." She glanced up the road again. There was a tightness in her stomach, a certain knowledge that Gallen had already found trouble. He would never willingly keep a client waiting, and Maggie suspected that his body lay somewhere on the road to An Cochan. If she was lucky, he might still be alive.

"You're as likely to meet one of those monsters on the road as he is," Orick said. "And he's better prepared to defend himself. Just sit tight."

Orick paced in a circle, rose up on his hind legs and tasted the air again.

Cries of dismay rose from the south end of town. Crowds of people began shouting. Maggie and Orick rushed to the crossroads, looked down the lane: between the shading pine trees, up the cobbled streets lined with picket fences, an ungodly array of giants marched three abreast. Some of them, green-skinned ogres, looked like huge men, eight feet tall. At their head was one of the monsters Orick had slain last night, its too-human head down low, sniffing the ground, blinking at the townspeople with orange eyes.

There were thirty or more of the monsters, and in their center, well protected, walked a creature straight from the bowels of hell. It stood seven feet tall and had a chitinous black carapace. It walked on four extraordinarily long legs, and it held two huge arms before it. One clublike arm seemed to end only in a vicious claw, while the other revealed a small, spidery hand that held a black rod.

The beast's head was enormous, with three clusters of multifaceted eyes in various sizes—two sets of eyes in front, one in back. A long, whiplike whisker was attached to each side of its lower jaw, beneath teeth that looked like something that might have belonged to a skinned horse. Its main body was only about a foot wide across the front, but its ribs would have measured three feet in height. From its shoulders sprouted two enormous pairs of translucent wings, the color of urine. Its bloated abdomen, which was carried between its front and back pair of legs, nearly dragged the ground.

People shouted and ran for their houses, dogs barked and leapt about insanely. Some women and an old man fainted outright, falling to the ground.

Father Heany in his vestments rushed to the street and confronted the black beast. He swung a crucifix overhead and shouted, "Beelzebub, I command you in the name of all that is holy to turn back! Turn back now, or suffer the wrath of God!"

Beneath the black devil's mouth, dozens of tiny fingers drummed over a patch of tight skin.

The ogre guardians stepped aside, and for one moment the devil faced Father Heany. It pointed the short black staff at the priest. Flames brighter than lightning fanned out, catching Father Heany in the chest. For a moment, Father Heany stood, blazing like a torch, and then the flesh dropped from his bones and his skeleton fell in the middle of the road, amidst a puddle of burning skin. Maggie felt as if her blood froze in her veins.

The ogres trampled Father Heany's body and just kept advancing toward the inn.

Maggie backed away, retreating between two house-trees toward the edge of town, and Orick padded quietly beside her.

When the menagerie of creatures reached Mahoney's Inn they stopped, and the doglike leader crouched to sniff the bloody ground.

He turned to Beelzebub and cried, "Master, a vanquisher died here!"

The giants stopped. Beelzebub strode forward and let the whiplike tendrils at his mouth feel the ground, twisting from side to side.

Orick circled behind a tree to hide. Maggie had seen enough. Her heart was pounding, and she struggled to breathe. Every instinct told her to run.

"Let's get out of here!" she said.

"Wait," Orick whispered. "Let's see what they want."

One ogre kicked down the door to Mahoney's Inn and rushed inside. A moment later, it dragged out John Mahoney. The innkeeper screamed, gibbering for mercy.

Beelzebub made clicking noises, and one of the giants translated, shouting, "Where did they go? When did you last see them?"

Mahoney fell to his knees. "I don't know who you mean. Who do you want?"

"You are the owner of this inn?" an ogre shouted. "Two strangers came here last night. A man and a woman."

"I didn't see them," Mahoney begged, crying. And Maggie realized he was telling the truth. He'd already been abed when the strangers came.

But the ogres thought he was lying. One of them growled, and Beelzebub flapped his wings suddenly and leapt into the air. He landed on John Mahoney,

THE GOLDEN QUEEN 45

teeth first. Maggie saw red blood spurt from John's head, like the spray of a sea wave as it washes over a rock, then she turned and ran for her life, Orick barreling along beside her.

They hit the woods, rushing through the trees, leaping over logs. Maggie ran until her lungs burned and she could hardly tell which way to go. Still, no matter how far or fast she ran, it did not seem that she was moving far or fast enough to get away. Always she would look behind her, and the town seemed too close, the monsters seemed too close. She probably would have kept running forever, run like a maddened beast to her death, but Orick growled and caught her by the cloak, pulling her to a stop. She screamed and kicked at him, but the bear only growled, "Stop! The strangers went this way! I can follow their trail. We must warn them!"

The two strangers rushed ahead through the forest, and Orick sniffed at their trail in the early morning, forepaws digging into the thick humus while his hind paws kicked forward in a rolling gallop. Maggie struggled to keep up. Between the towering black trees, the forest was wreathed in mist, with the early morning smell of fog that has risen from the sea. Sometimes Orick would spot a juicy slug as he ran. He would dodge aside and grab it from the mossy ground, flicking it into his mouth with his tongue. Yet mostly as he ran, he dreamed, and not all of those dreams were his own: snippets of racial memories stirred in him, visions from the Time of Bears, glimpses of forests from ages past. As he ran among the silent woods, he remembered being a bear cub, tearing at a log for sweet-tasting grubs and termites. Winged termites fluttered above him in a shaft of sunlight, glittering like bits of amber or droplets of honey. Sunlight shone on the emerald leaves of a salmon berry bush. In the memory he felt a vague longing for his mother, as if she were lost, and he heard something large crashing through the forest before him. A trumpet sounded, and a great shaggy beast suddenly towered over him, curved tusks thrusting out impossibly long. It shook its head, and the tusks slashed through the air, casually scattering the flying termites. The cub turned and ran.

Orick relived tales told by his mother, tales so familiar that he could not separate them from his own memory: how she had loved the taste of squirrel meat until she discovered the squirrel's midden and found that eating its cache of food was wiser than eating the squirrel. He listened to his mother describe tactics for catching salmon—how an old bear should slap the fish from the water with his massive paws while a smaller bear should use his teeth, stretching his head down under the water to gaze open-eyed into the stream. In Orick's waking vision, he dreamed of bright silver fish slicing through the icy foam. He tasted the small scales in his mouth, the juicy salmon wriggling as it tried to swim free of his grasp.

So it was that as Orick ran through the forest, chasing the strangers, he felt as if he were running backward through time, to the heart of wonder.

Surely this morning had already been magic. In solitary battle Orick had defeated a monster, and now he was galloping away from others of its kind, grunting under the weight of his store of winter fat, barreling into the primordial forest of his dreams, into the unknown.

Once, as he passed through a shadowed valley, Orick glimpsed a wight—the flickering green soulfire of someone long dead, a woman with long hair and a frown. She glanced at Orick, and then the wight gazed heavenward. She seemed to recognize that morning had come, and she sank into the hollow of a log.

Orick tracked the strangers' scent. After two hours, the strangers had marched into a bog of briny water and were forced to veer up a mountain and intersect the north road to An Cochan. Orick and Maggie crept to the edge of the road, Orick padding on heavy feet, sniffing the sour mud of the strangers' footprints.

He stopped. The morning sun had nearly cleared the hills now, shining on the road, and it seemed strange that the sun could be so warm and inviting on a day so filled with fear. Orick listened. Kiss-me-quick birds were jumping in the bushes, calling out for kisses.

Maggie was panting from the long run. Orick glanced at the road, inviting her to climb up.

She shook her head violently. "I think I heard something."

Orick tasted the scent of the strangers, looked uphill. They had crossed the road shortly before, heading up under the old pines, into a patch of chest-deep ferns on a knoll. Orick saw the bole of a young house-pine up there, grown from a seed gone wild. Though the house had only open holes for doors and windows, it was the kind of place that made a good temporary shelter for travelers. Orick could not see the strangers, but their scent was strong. He suspected they were hiding inside, resting where they could watch the road.

On both sides of them, the road curved sharply into the deeper woods. The trees provided heavy cover. Orick started to climb, but suddenly heard the shuffling of heavy feet on the muddy road to the south. Both he and Maggie faded back, crawled into the shadow of a twisted pine. From under the heavy cover, Orick watched the road above.

Orick's snout quivered in fear, but the scuffling footsteps had halted a hundred yards off, and everything became silent. Orick wondered if the monster had stopped to wait for passersby, or perhaps quietly slipped off into the woods, or if it had turned around and headed back toward Clere. For ten minutes, he and Maggie waited in silence, and Orick was just imagining that the danger had passed when Gallen O'Day came ambling up the road, heading toward Clere, whistling an old tavern song. Orick moved a bit so he could see Gallen clearly. Gallen looked worn, and his head was wrapped in a bandage. Orick wanted to call to him, warn him of the strangers in town, but at that very moment a deep voice shouted, "Stop, citizen!"

Gallen stopped and stood looking up the road, his mouth hanging open. An ogre hurried down the road to meet him. The ogre's chest and lower extremities moved into view, and Orick got a close look at the thing. Its long arms—covered with bristly hair and strange, knobby growths—nearly reached the ground, and in one hand it held an enormous black rod, like a shepherd's crook. Its fingers could not have been less than a foot long, and they ended in claws that were like nothing Orick had ever seen on a human or bear. The ogre wore a forest-green leine, belted at the middle, and wore enormous brown boots. As Orick watched, the ogre clenched its fists rhythmically, in and out, in and out, flexing those claws threateningly. For a moment, Orick though it would lash out, catch Gallen by the throat.

"Citizen," the ogre growled in a heavy voice Orick could understand only by listening intently. "I am searching for a man and a woman, strangers to your land, thieves. Have you seen them?"

"Thieves?" Gallen hesitated. "Well now, sir, with the great fair just ending at Baille Sean, the road is heavy with strangers. I saw several pass by an hour ago. Yet I must admit that in all my days, I have never seen anyone stranger than yourself. Would you mind if I be asking: do these strangers present as much of a spectacle as you?"

"No," the ogre answered softly, hunkering closer to Gallen. "The two I seek are more of your size, citizen. One man is a warrior, skilled in all arms, and he is a scholar. Yet if you saw the pair, your eye would catch only on the woman: she is of unequaled grace and beauty, and at first you would watch her distractedly, almost unaware of anything or anyone else. But the more you watched her movements, the more entrancing she would become. Her every step is like a dance, every soft word a song, and soon you would fall under her spell. If you stood in her presence for an hour, you would think you loved her. If you were with her for a day, you would become lost, and you would find yourself helplessly worshipping her forever—such is her power."

Gallen's mouth had fallen open again, and he stared at the ogre. Orick bent lower so that he could try to see the ogre's face, but the trees were in the way. Orick was tempted to come out of hiding, if only to see this curious beast, but fear made him stay hidden. Finally, softly, Gallen asked, "What is this woman's name?"

"Everynne," the giant answered.

"I saw her," Gallen said, "late last night, at the inn in Clere. She had dark hair, and a face so sweet and perfect that she seemed then to steal my heart." Orick wanted to shout, dismayed that Gallen would betray the strangers, but Gallen went on. "And I saw her with her companion again this morning, only an hour ago. They stopped in An Cochan to buy fresh horses, and they hurried off north."

Gallen pointed up the road toward An Cochan, and Orick felt his muscles ease in relief. He could always tell when Gallen was lying, and right now the young man was sending the ogre off on a mad quest.

The ogre tensed and rose on his tiptoes, anxious to head off down the road. Gallen said, "Sir, may I ask what they have stolen? Can you offer a reward if I regain the merchandise?"

The ogre hesitated. "She stole a key made of crystal, a key which opens gateways to other worlds. If you recover the key, my master will pay a generous reward."

"How much of a reward?" Gallen breathed.

"Eternal life," the ogre said. The creature straightened its back and shouted, "Vanquishers, all north!" Its voice rang out with such amazing power that the ground seemed to shake beneath Orick's paws. In the distant woods, dozens of other voices bellowed the message, "Vanquishers, all north!"

Orick could stand it no more. He knew that if he did not get a good look at the ogre now, he might never get another chance. He edged lower in his hiding spot, and his heart began pounding and he wished he'd never seen the thing: the ogre's head was enormous, and its hideous face was deeply creased, while a massive chin hung down like the arm on a sofa. Its lips were reddish brown, the color of burnished wood, and its large teeth were as yellow as pears. Its eyes were as huge as a stallion's testicles, and they were a bright orange. Scraggly brown hair hung limp from its head. All in all, the ogre was like no creature he had ever dreamed.

The ogre seemed to realize he had urgent business elsewhere. It loped toward An Cochan, back bent, head held peculiarly low, as if that enormous head were some great burden that it carried.

Gallen stood watching after it for several moments, an astonished expression on his face. He licked his lips and shook his head in wonder. He muttered to himself, "Eternal life, is it? What if I want a bonus? How about eternal life and a pair of laying hens? Or maybe eternal life and a sack of potatoes thrown into the bargain? Would your penurious master go so high?"

Gallen stared down the road. The sunlight still shone on the road, birds were hopping in the brush. A light morning breeze sifted through the trees, and Gallen shook his bandaged head, then stood with his mouth open as if he could not believe what he'd just seen.

Maggie stepped forward from the brush and whispered, "Gallen?" Orick followed.

Gallen saw her, then looked back up the road where the ogre had gone. He began jumping up and down and pointing. "Ah, Christ, you missed it!" Gallen said. "I just saw the most incredible giant! Come here! Hurry! I'll show you its tracks! I swear to God, it had green skin and teeth as big as shingles!"

"I know," Maggie said. "We saw it, too. Gallen, there's a bunch of those things in the wood. They came through town and murdered Father Heany. It was terrible!"

Maggie was on the road by now, shaking her head and grabbing Gallen's arm as if to make sure he was alive. Up here on the road, Orick could smell the strangers more strongly—Everynne and her guard—but he didn't want to say anything, afraid that somehow perhaps one of the giants might hear.

"Father Heany is dead?" Gallen stepped back in shock. "But . . ." He searched for something to say.

"Father Heany tried to drive the monsters out of town. And they burned him up. Then they went to the inn, looking for those travelers. They knew John Mahoney had let them stay in his inn. They killed him for it."

"But, he's an innkeeper, for Christ's sake!" Gallen shouted, looking angrily back up the road. "That's what he does for a living! Ah, hell, where is Everynne and her guard now?"

"They ran off into the forest before dawn," Orick said. "I've been trying to track them."

"You wouldn't turn them in, would you?" Maggie asked. "That beast may sound like he's offering some grand reward, but those creatures are devils! Beelzebub himself walked at the head of their procession!"

Gallen looked sober. "Even if I didn't know that they'd killed a priest, I wouldn't turn anyone over to that thing. I have my honor to think about. I promised to take Everynne to Geata na Chruinne, and I'll do it, even if the woods are full of sidhe. Orick, can you still follow their trail?"

Orick shivered. He had not thought about it, but here they were in Coille Sidhe. The humans told stories of the sidhe—strange and brutal beings from the otherworld. Orick had always thought them to be only tales for children, but suddenly the otherworlders were walking about in the daylight, looking for an enchantress with a key. "I can sniff them out."

"Wait!" Maggie said. "Gallen, we've no cause to get involved in the affairs of the sidhe. Let the devils squabble among themselves. If this woman has stolen something, maybe she deserves to be punished!"

Gallen half-closed his eyes in thought, and his long golden hair shone in the sunlight, the bandage holding it like a bloody headband. Orick wondered why his head was bandaged. Gallen looked down at Maggie and Orick, the sun catching his powder-blue eyes. "I don't believe this Everynne is a thief. Her guard was loyal to her. Thieves are never so devoted to their own. Greed wrings all the devotion right out of them."

"Perhaps he was under a spell—" Orick said, "as the ogre warned."

"Perhaps," Gallen agreed. "But only an hour ago, I swore to Father Brian that if my heart was ever hot to give someone aid, I would do it. And this morning my heart is hot to give aid to Lady Everynne."

"Well spoken," a gravelly voice said from the knoll above them. As one, Gallen, Maggie and Orick glanced up. The hill was covered with pines near the top, but the voice had come from close by, from the fern beds not twenty yards away. Suddenly there was movement, and Orick saw a man standing in the ferns, wearing a deep-hooded robe painted in greens and browns. Images of ferns were painted on it so precisely that if the man had remained still, Orick would never have seen him. Yet as the stranger walked downhill toward them, the robe shimmered and turned a soft brown. The man wore two swords at his hip.

The stranger halted in front of Gallen, and his scent was muted—hard to catch even at ten feet. Of all the wondrous things that had happened today, to Orick this was the most wondrous, the man's lack of scent.

The stranger pulled back his hood. He appeared to be in his late forties, but he was well-muscled, and his skin was ruddy tan. His hair had once been a golden brown, but now was turning silver. "I am Veriasse Dussogge," he said, "Everynne's counselor and protector. Will you guide us to the gate now? We are in great need. It will not take long for the vanquishers to discover your ruse and return in greater numbers."

"I can take you," Gallen said, "but we have not yet agreed to a price."

The stranger licked his lips. "You said only a moment ago that your heart was hot to give aid to the Lady Everynne."

"True," Gallen admitted, "but I didn't say that my heart was hot to give it to her for free!"

Orick looked from Gallen to Veriasse. Veriasse seemed to be weighing his options. Obviously, he could not afford to spend hours searching for either the gate or a new guide.

"You have me at a disadvantage," Veriasse said. "What is your price?"

"Well, that depends," Gallen answered. "Finding the gate is easy enough, but I'm not eager to tangle with one of those ogres. I assume you knew they were following you? That's why you wanted a man-at-arms?"

Veriasse nodded. "The vanquishers are very dangerous. I should warn you that they carry weapons more powerful than any on your world. The vanquishers can easily kill you at a hundred yards."

"Hmmm. . . . Then my price needs to reflect the risk I'll be taking. How about eternal life?" Gallen raised a brow.

"It is not in the Lady Everynne's power to grant that to you now," Veriasse said, "but if she reaches her destination . . ."

"Then she can give it to me if she reaches Geata na Chruinne?" Gallen asked.

"She has other gates to pass through," Veriasse answered. "She must face many dangers. But if she wins through, then, yes, she would return and pay your fee."

Uphill, a whippoorwill called. "Quickly!" Veriasse hissed, urging them off the road. "Vanquishers!"

He grabbed Gallen's arm and leapt downhill into the brush. Orick plunged after them, and Veriasse led them a few hundred feet off the road, into the shadows under a pine.

"Don't stir," Veriasse warned. Orick waited motionless for a moment. A trio of ogres passed on the road, marching quietly, heads swiveling as they searched the forest. Maggie was breathing so heavily, Orick feared the ogres would hear her. But they passed quickly.

After another two minutes, Veriasse whistled once like a thrush. Lady Everynne bounded downhill over the edge of the road, wearing her blue robes and a headdress made of triangular silver bangles fastened with a metal mesh. She bore her rosewood harp case under one arm; a pack was strapped to her shoulder.

Veriasse stood, and Orick saw that his robes were taking on the colors of the wood—deep grays and greens with splashes of yellow sunlight. Veriasse pulled his hood low over his eyes. "Everynne," he said, "this young man asks eternal life as his reward for leading you to the gate. Will you accept his price?"

Everynne looked at Gallen. "He doesn't know what he is asking. How could he? He doesn't know who I am, nor can he understand the limits of our power." She looked into Gallen's eyes. "When you ask for 'eternal life,' it is not what you think. I could change you—make you so that you will not grow old, cure you of all ills and injuries. Perhaps by doing this, I could extend your life—for a thousand or ten thousand years. I can give you new bodies, keep you so that you are reborn at each death. But you could still be killed. Your life will still end, someday."

"You can do this?" Gallen asked. Maggie was looking at Everynne in astonishment, and the young girl backed away as if afraid.

"Perhaps," Everynne said. "At the moment, I am as helpless as you. But I promise: if you take me to the gate and I survive the next few weeks, then it will be in my power to pay your fee."

Gallen offered his hand, and Maggie said, "Gallen, no!"

"Why not?" Gallen asked.

"It's a trick—" Orick cut in. "There's things she's not telling you. If you help her, you might not die of old age, but those giant vanquishers can come back and knock your head in! Listen to Maggie. You've no cause to be concerning yourself in her affairs." Orick's heart pounded, and he stared at his friend. Orick was a practical bear, and Gallen's bargain here just didn't make bear sense. Obviously these were magical creatures, and by bargaining with them, Gallen might win eternal life, but would he have a soul when he finished?

Gallen raised an eyebrow, questioned Everynne without saying a word.

"If I live, the vanquishers will become my servants," Everynne said, "and to my knowledge they will never return to this world to harm you or your family. Gallen, I cannot promise you that all dangers will fade from your life. There are worse things than vanquishers. If I die, I suspect that you and your people will learn more about what lies beyond the Gate of the World than any of you ever wanted to know."

"What do you mean by that?" Maggie demanded.

"We are at war," Veriasse cut in.

Orick looked hard at Gallen, and it was plain that the young man was wrestling with his thoughts. "Then," Gallen said, "I think I know what price I must ask."

"Which is?" Everynne asked.

Orick's nose was dry from fear, so he licked his snout. He waited for Gallen to ask for eternal life, but Gallen said, "I want to come with you beyond the gate into the realm of the sidhe and make sure that you reach your destination."

"No!" Everynne said. "You cannot even guess the kinds of dangers we will face. I cannot take you. You would not be a help—only a hindrance."

"You are a traveler and you need guards," Gallen said. "That is what I do."

Orick thought the man crazy, but Gallen had eyes only for Everynne. It was a case of lust, sure and through. And when Gallen got that set look in his eye, you could more easily pull a badger from his den than deter Gallen from his goal.

"Last night," Gallen said, "you would not tell me your name because you knew that these vanquishers would be following you."

"Yes," Everynne answered. "I didn't want to hurt you."

"Yet the vanquishers came. Inadvertently, perhaps, you have touched our world. Now I want to touch yours."

"It's not that simple," Everynne said. "I could let you come through the gate, but it does not lead to one world, it leads to a maze of worlds, and you are not prepared to enter. Even if you did, you would only want to come home again. In these last few days, I have grown to appreciate this world immensely for its simplicity, its ease of life."

"I don't know about other worlds," Gallen said. "But I suspect that this one is damned boring."

"A boring world is a valuable commodity," Everynne said. "I would that all worlds were so innocent."

Gallen thought a long moment, shrugged. "Then I'll take nothing in return for my aid. Only a scoundrel would extort money from a woman in need."

Orick shook his head, confused by Gallen's sudden turnabout. He wondered if he'd ever understand humans. The Lady Everynne smiled gratefully, raised her brow as if her opinion of Gallen had just raised dramatically.

In the distance was a sound Orick could just barely make out, though none of the others could have heard it. Voices shouting, "Vanquishers, to the south!"

"They're coming back!" Orick said. "Hurry!"

Gallen leapt into the woods, and the others followed.

Five

Everynne raced through the forest, following Gallen and Veriasse while Maggie and Orick brought up the rear. Everynne found it hard to toil through the thick undergrowth of Coille Sidhe. Everywhere, trees grew in a riot: dark pine brooded over the wrinkled hills and valleys. Tangled vine maple and ironwood climbed high to capture the dappled sunlight, their limbs twisted like snakes. Dense undergrowth covered the forest floor. Everywhere, ancient fallen pine trees lay molding.

Everynne wished she could hear the vanquishers' calls in the woods, but the pine needles and leaves of lesser trees muffled all sound. If the vanquishers fell upon them, there would be no advance notice.

Veriasse and Gallen ran side by side, Veriasse carrying his incendiary gun in both hands. Gallen kept glancing at it, but did not immediately ask what it was.

Veriasse hung his shoulders as he ran, weary. Everynne herself felt weary to the core of her soul, and she knew she needed more help. She needed a man like Gallen, and she considered taking him for a servant. She studied him as she ran.

After thirty minutes, Gallen reached a hill where a trio of tall stones hid them. Inside this natural fortress, he called a halt. He stood panting and asked Veriasse, "Those vanquishers, will they try to follow our tracks or are there enough of them so that they can beat the brush and force us out of cover?"

Veriasse heaved for air, said, "They will hunt us both by scent and by track. Gallen, we must take great care. If they have already found the gate, they will be guarding it. We will need to sneak up to it. Yet with vanquishers at our heels, we cannot afford to be timid."

Gallen considered. "You said that the vanquishers can kill from a distance, and they carried rods like the one you have. Is this the weapon they use?"

"It's called an incendiary rifle," Veriasse said. "When you discharge the weapon, it fires chemicals that burn very hot."

"So it's something like a flaming arrow?" Gallen asked.

"Yes, only far hotter. Where we come from, some creatures can only be killed with such a weapon. It has become our weapon of choice."

"How does it work?" Gallen asked. Everynne was surprised at how casually he asked it. She imagined that the young man, being a Backward from such a low-tech world, would find such weapons to be somehow shocking. But Gallen asked in a brusque, businesslike manner.

Veriasse held the weapon up for Gallen to examine. "Down here under the guard is a trigger. When I pull it once, the weapon becomes active and a red beam of light shoots from this lens above the barrel." He pointed the rifle at a stone, and the red dot of a laser shone on the rock. "You will also feel a vibration in the weapon when it's active. Whatever the red dot shines on, that is what you will hit if you pull the trigger a second time."

Veriasse flipped the weapon on its side, pointed to a little indicator light. "These lights show how many more shots you can take with the weapon." His indicator showed ten shots.

"How far can it shoot?" Gallen asked.

"Officially, it can fire about a hundred and fifty yards," Veriasse answered. "But the flames can carry farther if you aim high. You must never fire at an opponent who is too close—unless you want to burn with him. Once the weapon sits without firing for three minutes, it deactivates."

Gallen touched the rifle's stock. "This can kill an ogre?"

"Yes," Veriasse said.

"How tough are they?" Gallen asked.

"There are three main types of vanquisher," Veriasse answered. "Orick here killed a tracker last night—a creature with long legs and arms that walks on all fours. The 'ogre' that you saw is one of their infantry. They are tough warriors, and I would not advise you to fight them in hand-to-hand combat. They are very strong. Still, their vital organs are much the same as ours.

"In days gone by, my people created these creatures as guardians, to keep the peace on many worlds. But things have changed. The dronon warriors conquered our people and enslaved our guardians. The dronon are the third kind of vanquisher, and the most dangerous."

"Dronon?" Maggie asked, panting. Her face was pale, frightened.

"You saw one back in town," Veriasse said. "You called him Beelzebub, Lord of the Flies. He is really a dronon, a Lord Vanquisher from another world. Sixty years ago, his people came among us, and they were wise in the ways of war. At first, we tried to help them. But they envied our technology and sought to take it. They captured many worlds. Now, any guardians who were not slain all serve the dronon vanquishers. On some worlds, even humans serve the dronon's Golden Queen and her empire."

Gallen stood up, seeming to have caught his wind. "We'll need to keep to the trees so that they can't shoot us, and I'll lead them on some trails that will be hard to follow. If we can shake them off our track, we won't have to rush to the gate."

Gallen took off running. He set a path that the vanquishers would be hard-pressed to follow. He zigzagged between growths of jack pine, where the trees grew so close together that their branches formed a nearly impenetrable wall. Twice he made great circles so that his scent would be strong, then led the others over dry logs where no footprints would show, where even their scent would not hold.

When he had done all he could to obscure his trail, Gallen led them to a cave at the base of a mountain. He took the group to the largest opening, then at the black mouth of the cave he hesitated to enter.

"What's wrong?" Everynne asked.

"This cave," Gallen said, "has narrow passages and five openings. If we want to lose the vanquishers, we could go in here. But the cave is haunted by wights. We'll need to light a fire and take torches in to hold them at bay."

"We shouldn't go in," Maggie said. "It's too dangerous."

"Wights?" Veriasse asked. "What is a wight?"

"A spirit. If someone is too curious and breaks the laws of the Tome, the priests give the person to the wights."

"Surely you don't believe in ghosts?" Veriasse said. "There's no such thing. Have you ever seen such a thing?"

"Not ghosts," Gallen said. "These are wights. I've seen them more than once: there was an old woman in our town, Cally O'Brien, who experimented with herbs. One night the wights came and dragged her off screaming, down the road to An Cochan. No one ever saw her again."

Neither Veriasse nor Everynne looked as if they believed Gallen.

"What he says is true," Maggie offered. "Wights are real. At night you can see their soulfires glowing blue and green in the forest."

Everynne and Veriasse looked at each other and spoke simultaneously, "Artefs!"

But Veriasse asked, incredulous, "What would an artef be doing here?"

"Guarding this world," Everynne said. "Keeping its people in enforced ignorance. That is what their ancestors wanted, a world where their children could hide from the problems of a universe too large to control. I'll bet the original settlers downloaded their intelligences into artefs."

"So you're knowing the wights by another name, are you?" Orick asked. "You have them in the realm of the sidhe?"

"Yes," Everynne said. "We *make* them in the realm of the sidhe. They are simply machines that store human thought. We can travel through your cave safely."

"I'm warning you—the sunlight does not penetrate these caverns," Gallen said. "Inside, it is as dark as night."

"Sunlight weakens artefs," Veriasse said, "because the radio waves cast by your sun confuse them, leave them unable to think. But an artef can't withstand an incendiary rifle."

Gallen gulped, obviously still afraid. He led them in through a narrow chasm. He took Everynne's slim hand and pulled her through the dark. She could feel him trembling. She did not know if he feared this place still, or if he simply trembled at her touch. Often, men reacted that way to her. It was a mistake to let him touch her.

Gallen felt his way along a wall until he bumped his head on a rock outcropping, then took a side tunnel. After several hundred feet, he reached a narrow passage, then took another left where the cavern branched; they began climbing a steep slope filled with rubble. Dripping water smacked loud as it dropped to unseen puddles. Everynne struggled to keep from slipping on wet rock. The air had a faintly metallic smell, and Everynne hurried to get out. In the distance, she thought she saw sunlight shining through an exit, but instead a ghostly green apparition began leaping toward them through a large chamber.

It was an old man with muttonchop sideburns and a bushy mustache. He wore a leine without a greatcloak, and short boots. The wight stood quietly, gazing at them in the dark. Its phosphorescent skin let Everynne see the walls of the cave immediately around them, and she was surprised at the jumbles of stone, the numerous stalactites and stalagmites.

The wight asked cordially, "What are you doing in my cave? Don't you know that this forest is haunted?"

"Off with you!" Gallen said. "I'll not have you barring our way!"

"Och, why it's Gallen O'Day," the wight said merrily. "It's been a long time since I've seen you in these woods." But the wight studied Everynne, looking at the silver net she wore in her hair. It made a tsking noise and shook its head. "You're in a tight spot, Gallen—consorting with strangers from another world. Didn't your mother ever warn you against such things? Didn't she ever tell you what happens to curious boys?"

"Get back!" Gallen hissed. "We only want to pass."

The wight studied Veriasse's incendiary rifle. "Oh, I'll leave for now, Gallen O'Day. But it's sure that you can't shake me off so easily." The wight backed into a side tunnel, and ducked around a corner.

They hurried through the cave, climbing treacherous outcroppings, dropping down into crevices. The wight paced along behind them, crawling through the rocks. Soon another joined, and another, until Everynne counted a dozen of the creatures shadowing them through the cave. For a long way, their dim glow provided the only light for Everynne to see by.

The group reached the sunlight, and Gallen fell down to the forest floor, gasping. His face was pale, and Everynne realized that entering the cave must have been a great ordeal for the man, being a Backward who believed the wights to be invincible spirits. Soon Orick and Maggie rushed out behind them. Maggie's eyes were wide. Gallen looked up at Maggie, and he burst out laughing.

"What's so funny?" Maggie asked.

"Nothing is funny," Gallen said. "I just feel good."

Gallen got up and led them south a half mile to a steep slope that descended into a valley. A fire had recently burned the ridge, and large boulders dotted the ground. The soil around the stones had eroded away so that often the slightest touch could send a boulder tumbling downhill, and Everynne saw that Gallen was thinking ahead. A vanquisher, with its enormous feet, would be tempted to step on the boulders, and she imagined how it would go tumbling down in the resulting landslide.

At the bottom of the ravine, Gallen headed west, marching his followers down the channel of a rocky creek. Mosquitoes buzzed around their faces,

and often mallards would fly up from the water. In one place where the channel narrowed and the water deepened, Gallen pulled up a small tree, sharp-
ened it into a stake, and pushed it down into the mud where no one could see.
It took only a moment. So far, they had traveled a little over five miles in
eight hours. Everynne hoped that his tactics would give them more time in
the long run.

They reached the shelter of the forest again at the valley floor, and there
they rested for a few moments. Maggie was gasping, sweat pouring from her
brow. They were all dirty and thoroughly worn. They had to rest.

From the mountain above them nearly half a mile back, a deep voice
boomed: "Vanquishers, to me!"

The vanquishers had already found their exit from the caves. Gallen
cursed under his breath and looked helplessly to Veriasse.

Veriasse studied Gallen's face. "You've done well," he said at last, and Gallen
furrowed his brow, as if struggling to understand Veriasse's accent. "You've set
as difficult a trail for the vanquishers as they could possibly hope to follow, but
we must run now. We cannot afford more delays."

Up on the mountain, there was a rumbling roar and a scream as a vanquisher learned just how treacherous the trail was. Gallen stepped into a clearing where a tree had fallen. Everynne followed and looked up the mountain.
Two humanoid infantrymen were helping a tracker to his feet.

"Veriasse," Gallen asked, "may I try your weapon?"

Veriasse handed Gallen the incendiary rifle. Gallen raised it. The barrel
bounced a bit until he held his breath, relaxed his muscles, pulled the trigger.
He frowned a second, obviously having expected the gun to discharge, then
raised the gun a second time. Everynne could not see the red dot from the
laser scope, but up on the hill, the ogres must have seen it. They suddenly released the tracker and leapt aside. Gallen pulled the trigger. A plume of
white-hot chemical fire soared through the air, splashed over the tracker.
The creature screamed briefly and burst into flame, then dropped in a pile of
melting bones.

Gallen handed the rifle back to Veriasse. "That might keep them off our
trail for a bit."

Gallen raced northwest. He led them on a clear path through deep
woods, yet Everynne knew that the vanquishers would be able to run here
just as easily. With their long legs, they would run even faster.

At last he reached a grove of pine-houses. Centuries before, perhaps, a
town had nestled in this river valley, but it had been abandoned. Seeds from
pine-houses had dropped to the ground, and a veritable city of hollow trees
grew so close to one another that their trunks had fused.

No one could hope to walk through this section of wood. It was virtually
impenetrable.

"We'll go through here," Gallen said.

"We'll never make it through that mess," Veriasse objected.

"I used to play here when I was a child," Gallen answered. "There are paths through the trees, if you're willing to climb a bit. This grove is eight miles long and two or three miles wide in most places, but up here a ways, it's only a quarter of a mile across. We'll go through there."

Like all homes grown from pine-house seeds, the houses naturally formed holes for doors. Always the seeds grew at least one door at the front of the house, and one at the back. In addition, at odd spots on each side, various openings grew for windows.

Everynne knew that the vanquishers would not be able to follow. Gallen skirted the trees till he reached a steep canyon, then walked to that impenetrable wall and entered a door hole.

They moved through the grove of pine-houses with great effort, grunting and struggling from window to window, often climbing up and down.

Perhaps as a child, Gallen had played here as a game, but windows he had squeezed through as a boy were now too narrow to permit an adult, much less a bear like Orick with his winter fat. Everynne was perspiring heavily. When they were halfway through the grove, Gallen suddenly halted, looking at a narrow window. Obviously, they could not squeeze through it, and Gallen furrowed his brow, deep in thought.

"What's wrong?" Veriasse asked.

"We're stuck here," Gallen said. "I used to fit through that hole nicely, and there is a narrow path ahead that we could follow, but we can't make it through here. There's no way to go forward."

"What will we do?" Maggie asked.

"I'll have to go out and scout another way."

"Do you need help?" Veriasse asked, yet obviously the older man was worn through.

"I'll find a way," Gallen said, and he went out the door. Everynne could hear him scrabbling around outside, climbing up a branch. The pine-house was dusty, full of needles and cones, the leavings of squirrels. A soft afternoon breeze blew through the little valley, stirring the treetops, even though down here on the ground it felt hot, sultry.

For the first few minutes, Everynne was glad of the chance to rest. Veriasse reached into his pack, pulled out a small flask and gave it to her to drink. She was terribly hungry—had gone all day without food—but they had nothing left to eat in the packs.

When Gallen had been gone for nearly an hour, Maggie said, "I think I'd better go look for Gallen. Maybe he's lost us."

She headed outside through a window and scuffled about in the tree, climbing limbs. The sunlight filtering through the open doorway had grown dimmer. Night was coming on, and Everynne could hear pigeons cooing from their roosts. It was very quiet, and Everynne began to feel nervous. They had been sitting for a long time, and the vanquishers could not be far behind. She began to wonder if one of the vanquishers might have already killed the young man, but dared not say it. The bear snuffled, looked out a window.

"Do you think Gallen could be lost?" Everynne asked Veriasse.

Veriasse shook his head. "No. As he's said, he played here as a child. I suspect he knows exactly where we are. I've been impressed by his competence. For a Backward, he seems to have grasped our predicament well, and he's led the vanquishers on a marvelous chase. He'll come back soon."

Veriasse said it with such certainty, that Everynne suddenly felt more at ease. Yet the older man also seemed to need to fill up the silence. "As a warrior, I find him . . . intriguing."

"In what way?" Everynne asked.

Veriasse smiled, contemplating. "He carries himself with a deadly grace. If I had seen him on any planet, I would have known he was a killer. He moves with caution, a type of confident wariness that one learns to spot quickly. Yet he is different from warriors on most worlds. Our ancestors relied heavily upon armor until the incendiary guns made it useless. Now, we rely upon our guns and upon tactics downloaded from personal intelligences. We fight battles at long distances and seldom look into the faces of our victims. Even more seldom do we purposely expose ourselves to risk. We have, in effect, become chess masters who've memorized too many classic moves. But this young man relies on quick wits for his survival, and his weapon of choice is the knife. It seems an odd choice."

In the corner of the room, the bear stirred in the shadows under the window. "Oh, Gallen would love a sword," the bear said, "but they're so expensive. You have to pay taxes on the damned things every time you travel through a new county."

Veriasse smiled at the bear, his eyes glittering. "So, even on your backward world," he said, "you practice arms control?"

The bear shrugged.

Veriasse sighed. "I feel fortunate. I have not met a man like him in many thousands of years." He stared at Everynne as if to say, "We need him. You could make him follow you." And a chill went through her. She remembered how Gallen had quivered when he touched her hand in the cave, the way he laughed off his fear of the wights. She, too, found herself intrigued.

"He is taking an awfully long time. . . ." Everynne said.

The bear was watching them intently, and he cleared his throat. "Is there anything you can do to help us find our way out of this wood? Do you know some magic?"

Everynne laughed. "We aren't magic, Orick, any more than you are magic."

"Oh," the bear said, disappointed.

A vanquisher bellowed in frustration. It sounded quite close. The creature had made it partway through the woods. Veriasse stood up, fingering his incendiary rifle, listening.

Ten seconds later, there was a swishing sound as someone leapt down through some upper branches of the tree.

Gallen's shadow darkened the doorway. "Come on. I found a new trail."

"What about Maggie?" Everynne asked.

"She's up ahead, waiting for us."

Gallen climbed up the tree, leading them through limbs with the grace of a marten. Yet the trail was very difficult.

Soon, Veriasse called for a halt and stood in the shadows under a limb. The sun was setting. He rubbed the backs of his hands against his shirt. "Stop a moment, stop," he said. He raised his hands. "I smell fire. The vanquishers have set these woods aflame. How much farther?"

"Not far," Gallen panted. "Not more than fifty yards."

Everynne was nearly senseless with exhaustion. They climbed ahead, and she found herself blindly grasping for limbs. Smoke crept through the forest like a thin fog. Just before they left the grove, Gallen pulled off his sweaty, soiled greatcoat and threw it into a crevice between two trees. Veriasse watched him and did likewise, and Everynne realized the value of leaving behind something strong of scent. She pulled off her own blue cloak, tossed it back. Everynne looked down, caught Gallen staring at her as she perched on a branch. He did not look away guiltily as some men might have. Instead, he just seemed to admire her. She wondered what he saw—a woman in a blue tunic, perched in a tree, silver ringlets in her dark hair. She realized that she was sitting in the last rays of the dying sun, and perhaps so lit, she looked resplendent. She had been bred to look that way to common humans.

She leapt to the ground and raced into the forest, under the tall pines.

Night was falling. Gallen seemed bone weary and had no more tricks in him. Now it was only a race to the gate, and the young man led them over the shortest route.

They reached an old forest at the fork of a canyon just at sunset. Behind them in the distance, Everynne heard an exultant howl. The vanquishers must have picked up their trail. In moments they would be here.

Everynne rushed to the gate and opened her harp case, throwing it to the ground. Gallen stood panting beside Maggie and the bear while Veriasse stepped up behind them. Everynne pulled out her key, a crystal shaped like a horseshoe, then held it up and thumbed a switch that transmitted an electronic code to power up the gate. Her crystal began glowing as the gate transmitted its acceptance signal.

The gate on this world was perhaps the oldest Everynne had ever seen. It was a small thing—taller than a man and two yards wide. It looked like a simple arch made of polished gray stone. On the posts of the arch were carved designs—flowers and vines, images that Everynne could not decipher.

As Everynne held her crystal aloft, the air under the arch began to glow pale lavender.

"My lady," Gallen said, "will you be safe in this next world?"

Everynne looked at him. Gallen obviously wanted to follow, and Everynne had to decide whether to take him. But the vanquishers were coming. The young man would need to guard Maggie and Orick. If Everynne let him follow, the others might die.

"I'll be safe enough for the moment," Everynne answered. "I have the only key to the gate. The vanquishers will have to hunt me in their sky ships. I should get a good lead on them. But for now, you and your friends need to leave here at once. The vanquishers want only me."

Everynne took one last look at this world—tasted the scent of the pine trees, the freshness of the air under the dark forest. On the first part of her journey here, she had seen the clean brooks full of trout, slept under stars where no one worried about dronon. She doubted that Gallen and Maggie understood what they had here, and she hoped that by leaving, the vanquishers would follow. Perhaps in ten years, people here would forget that vanquishers had once passed through a town. And in a hundred years, the account of Everynne's race through these woods would only become a fairy tale, the story of the time that the sidhe were seen walking alive.

Everynne looked at Gallen over her shoulder. The young man was tense, and Everynne could read his intent simply by looking into his eyes. He planned to leap through the gate when she did. She said quickly, "Eternal life, if I reach my destination. I promise. Gallen, will you pick up my harp case for me?"

Gallen bent over, and before he could react, she grabbed Veriasse's arm and pulled him through the gate.

Gallen had not known what to expect. He planned to wait until Everynne was ready to leave, then jump through the gate with her, but he'd wanted to say good-bye to Maggie and Orick first.

Instead, Everynne had taken Veriasse's arm and leapt forward. There was a flash of white, and suddenly the lights under the arch snuffed out like a candle. A freezing chill hit the air. The arch itself turned white with frost, and Gallen walked under it, stood a moment looking up at the ancient runes of flowers and animals carved into the stone. As a child he had brought a hammer and chisel to the gate, but had not been able to chip off any of that stone. Instead, his chisel got blunted and bent, and finally the handle to his hammer splintered. It was like no stone in the world. He looked at Maggie, took her hand.

Gallen felt as if his heart had been pulled from him, and he just stood, staring. He heard a shout from the forest behind, and Maggie tugged on his hand, urging, "Come away from here. Take your legs into your shoes. Run!"

Gallen found that he was shaking, and he ducked beneath the arch, felt a thrill of cold air, but nothing more. For him, the gate led nowhere. It had closed.

"Come!" Orick growled. The bear stood up, sniffed the air nervously.

They ran up a small hill. Gallen stopped near the crest and took cover behind a fallen log. Maggie and Orick lay down beside him. There was shouting below in the glen, and Gallen peeked over the log, the rotting black bark pungent under his nose.

Vanquishers rushed under the dark trees. Two ogres. They were battered, dirty. One ogre cursed and kicked at the arch. "They made it through," he said.

The ogre looked up while the other threw himself to the ground to rest. He spoke to the air. "Lord Hitkani, we've found the gate, but Everynne and her escorts have escaped." He listened for a moment, then answered, "Yes, we'll wait."

Gallen sat watching them for several minutes and heard a rumbling noise over the trees. A black creature with enormous wings dove below the tree-tops, settled on the ground beside the gate. It walked in circles around the gate, touching it with long feelers beneath its mouth. Gallen watched the dronon and could only name it to himself silently—Beelzebub.

The dronon reached into a pouch at its side, pulled out a crystal shaped like a horseshoe. It held the crystal in the air, watching it change colors to a soft lavender. In an odd, guttural voice it said, "They have gone to Fale. When the others arrive, we will renew the chase. You there," he said to one ogre, "see if you can get this key working."

The dronon sat on a thick carpet of pine needles, beating his wings softly, while one vanquisher fumbled with the key. The shadows under the trees were thickening. Gallen wanted nothing more than a bath and something to put in his shrinking belly. This seemed to have been the longest day of his life. He had not slept in over thirty-six hours. Yet he dared not move for fear of making some noise that would alert the vanquishers, and he dared not sleep.

Beside him, Orick and Maggie quietly watched the vanquisher work as the shadows deepened under the trees. An evening wind began blowing in from the sea, hissing through the treetops, making limbs creak.

Orick stuck his muzzle into Gallen's ribs, then looked off behind them to the north. Gallen followed the bear's eyes. In the woods, flitting through the trees, was a pale blue light.

It was said that a man's best defense against a wight was to lie low, hide. Yet Gallen knew the wights would be searching for him this night.

His mouth suddenly felt dry; he licked his lips. He spotted other lights flickering in the forest, pale blues and greens flowing between the trees as fluidly as a deer leaping a fence. By staying where he was, Gallen risked that the wights would catch him. Yet if he tried to make it out of Coille Sidhe now, the vanquishers would take him.

"Got it," the vanquisher muttered, a weary note of triumph in his voice. Gallen turned, saw that the arch glowed brighter. The ogre set the flaming crystal back into its pouch, then sat with the others a couple yards away.

The wind hissed through the trees, and a woodpecker began tapping above them. Gallen toyed with the idea of rushing the giants, grabbing the key and leaping through to another world. Everynne had seemed secure in the knowledge that she had the only key to the gate. She would not expect the vanquishers to follow her so quickly. But Gallen suspected that if he tried to attack, his little knives would hardly trouble the vanquishers.

Gallen put an arm around Maggie's shoulder and whispered, "Lie low and make your way home in the morning," then tapped Orick on the muzzle, stood up and leapt over the log quietly and began running downhill on the soft humus, letting the pine needles cushion the sound. Orick leapt over the log and ran beside him, glancing at Gallen fearfully. Gallen poured on the speed, thinking, by God, they won't see my heels for the dust.

But at that moment, the dronon lifted its head and hissed, making some spitting noise. Gallen had been running up behind the creature, but now he saw that it had a clump of eyes on the back of its head. The dronon pulled out its incendiary gun, but Gallen was too close for the creature to use it.

Gallen whipped out his knives, screaming, "Hold or you die!" and the ogres were so stricken with surprise that they scuttled backward a step.

Gallen was almost to the arch, and he snatched the pouch in one smooth move.

Fast as a striking serpent, one of the ogres grabbed Gallen's wrist, spinning him around. Gallen concentrated on holding onto the key as he slashed the giant's corded wrist. Huge gobbets of blood shot out, drenching Gallen's hand, but the giant held on. Gallen slashed again, jerked backward, and fell to the ground, still holding the key.

He looked up. All three vanquishers had recovered from their surprise. In unison they lunged.

A piercing shriek rose behind them. They halted for half a second, and Maggie rushed between one ogre's legs. Gallen felt Orick's teeth biting into his collar as the bear tried to drag him under the arch.

Gallen scrabbled to his feet enough to kick backward a step, faintly aware of the ghostly lavender light radiating from the arch.

Orick roared in fear and Gallen kicked again and Maggie was with them, dragging Gallen backward. He saw the giants' faces twist in rage, yet suddenly Gallen was swept away through a cold, brilliant light.

Six

When Gallen and Orick took off down the hill toward the vanquishers, Maggie had felt a thrill of fear as she realized they planned to leave her. She buried her face in the dirt, trying to make herself as small as possible, then heard Gallen's shout.

Below her in the woods, she saw the green and blue lights of wights rushing uphill toward her, and she realized she was in the thick of it.

Her fear suddenly turned to anger. She got up, saw Gallen and Orick struggling to get the bag with the key from a vanquisher. She rushed down the hill, screaming, and bowled into Gallen and Orick, pushing them through the gate.

An icy white light took her, and she had a strange sensation of gliding, as if she were a leaf fluttering through the wind.

Maggie fell back and hit the ground rolling, tumbling against Orick's warm fur. Gallen landed on top of her. She was furious, wanted to hit someone. Maggie shouted, "Gallen O'Day, you. . . ." Then she just sat and stared, her mouth open in wonder.

They sat in a meadow surrounded by a lush forest, thick with undergrowth. It felt like summer. A warm evening breeze rushed across her back, ruffling her hair, and in the distance a tiny oblong lavender moon hung on the horizon behind a swirl of clouds.

There was no sign of a gate from this side. Maggie looked around, just to be sure. All around them, broad-leaved trees whispered and rippled in waves under the wind. Locusts sang in the darkness. Overhead was a sky filled with more stars than Maggie had ever imagined.

Gallen got up, folded his arms and stood staring. "What?" he asked, absently. Orick sniffed the air.

"Gallen, is your head filled with nothing but blubber?" Maggie shouted. "You've done it to us bad! I don't like the looks of this place."

"Fale," Gallen whispered under his breath. "The vanquishers called it Fale."

Suddenly, carried on the wind, there were screeching sounds from above. A flock of white birds hurtled overhead in the twilight, creaking like rusty hinges, some diving into the trees as if to catch insects in the air. The birds passed.

Gallen put his hand to his mouth and shouted, "Everynne? Veriasse?" He stood waiting for an answer. None came.

"I can't smell them," Orick grumbled, standing on his hind legs to sniff at the wind. "Not even the faintest trace of a scent. They didn't come out here."

"What?" Maggie asked. "They had to come out here. They came through not five minutes ago!"

"Maybe," Gallen wondered aloud, "it's not like a gate so much as a hall-way. Maybe it branches. Leading to different places. Everynne called it a maze of worlds. Maybe we made a wrong turn."

Maggie looked at the sky full of whirling stars and an odd-shaped moon. The trees smelled strange, and the evening breeze was soft and warm. Nothing like Tihrglas. She couldn't begin to imagine where they might be.

"You mean we got off on the wrong world somehow?" she asked. "Gallen, you reeking bag of fish, I ought to knock you in the head! What did you have to do this for? What were you thinking, going after the key that way? You could have gotten us all killed! I know what you were after—that woman Everynne. You've been hot for her from the moment you first saw her. Why, if someone lopped off your head, it would be no loss. Your gonads would still do all the thinking!"

Gallen shrugged. "The vanquishers had another key. I had to warn Veri-asse. Besides, I didn't ask either of you two to come along."

Maggie glared at him. "You left me! Both you and your dumb bear left me. As soon as those ogres began shouting, every wight in the country rushed up the hill toward us. I had to throw in with you! And if I hadn't come to your aid, we'd have all been killed! We could have all stayed home, hidden safe in the woods, but now . . . !"

Gallen said, "I'm sorry. I would never wish any harm on you. I'd never have dragged you into this."

He had such an expression of grief on his face, and he spoke with such sincerity, that Maggie had a hard time staying angry. She pointed her finger at him and then shook her fist. "Just admit one thing. Just be honest about one thing: don't you dare tell me that you came here to talk to Veriasse. It was Everynne you were after. You've been giving her looks all day, and don't you dare deny it, Gallen O'Day, or I'll beat you with a stick."

Gallen shrugged. "I couldn't just let her get killed."

Maggie figured that was as much of a confession as she'd ever get from him. She got up and looked furiously for the crystal key. She had fallen on it when she rolled through the gate. Its lights were gently fading. Maggie picked it up. She could see little worms of silver inside, bits of wire and small circles made of gold, odd things that looked like a priest's communion wafer.

Orick grunted. "I'm hungry. Is anybody else hungry? Where do you think we could get some food?"

"Aye," Gallen said, "I'm hungry. And thirsty, and tired. And I've no idea which way to go, do you?"

Orick gave a little bawl, bear talk for, "No, and it really makes me mad."

"If we head off on a straight path," Gallen said, "maybe we'll meet up with a river or a road."

Maggie looked toward the falling moon on the horizon. It seemed as good a direction as any to take, and if she left it to Gallen and Orick, they'd never make up their minds. She began hiking through the forest and the others were forced to follow.

The uneven ground featured no real hills but few flat spots. They pushed their way through broad-leaved plants that made the sound of tearing paper, and everywhere she could hear mice or rats running through the dry undergrowth. Often, tumbled white stones protruded from the ground.

Every few minutes, Gallen called Everynne's name, but after nearly two hours, Maggie got angry. "Will you quit that bawling. She's nowhere near here, so you might as well put a cork in it."

Gallen fell silent. Though they walked a long time, the moon still lay in the sky like a glowing blue eye, warm and distant. It had hardly moved at all. They found a small pool of water that reflected night shadows and starlight, then knelt to drink. It tasted slightly salty, but quenched Maggie's thirst. Nearby, several white birds flew up in the night, screeching and circling.

Orick snuffled in the grass and shouted, "Hey, you two, over here!"

He'd discovered some nests. Maggie opened the first egg and found a bird embryo in it, so left the rest to Orick. Maggie was exhausted. They hadn't found anything more impressive than what might have been pig trails—no sign of a house or a road.

Not knowing what else to do, she looked for shelter. Aside from the arching trees, she found nothing.

She went to a large white rock, thinking to huddle behind it. It had been sculpted with strange symbols—as if it were part of a building. She looked about. All the white stones had been shaped by hand. They had been hiking through the ruins of a vast city.

Gallen collected two armloads of grass and leaves to use as a blanket, laid them by Maggie in the lee of the rock. The ground was hollowed like a shallow grave or as if some beast often came there to rest, thus packing the soil. Orick lay with Gallen and Maggie, his thick fur warm and welcome.

Gallen called one last time for Everynne. Only the croaking of frogs gave answer. A wind blew cool against Maggie's skin, like the touch of a silver coin in winter.

Maggie wondered if someone should keep watch, but they'd seen no sign of anything larger than a mouse.

Gallen whispered to himself, "So Father Heany is dead. He was such a clean man. Death is such a small and nasty affair, part of me is shocked he would get involved in it." He said nothing more. Soon, Gallen breathed deeply in sleep.

Orick sang some bear lullaby to Maggie as if she were a cub:

"Through winters long and cold we'll sleep.
Don't you weep, don't you weep.
With hides and fat, warm we'll keep,
Though snow grows deep, though snow grows deep.
So let your tired eyes rest, my dear,
And when you wake, I'll be here.
And when you wake, I'll be here."

When the song finished, Orick sprawled a paw over Maggie's shoulders and licked her face. "I have plenty of winter fat stored," Orick said. "Next time we find food, you eat."

Orick closed his eyes.

For some reason, Maggie stared up at the night sky. Hundreds of thousands of stars shone. Directly above was a great pinwheel made of brilliant points of light. Somehow, when she had stepped into this new world, she had not anticipated that all the stars she had known as a child would also be gone. Yet if they were to be replaced by so many stars, in such wondrous arrays, she imagined that she could grow accustomed to them.

Three stars moved fast, in formation, from west to east then dropped toward the treetops in the distance, and Maggie wondered at them. Were these strange stars flying on their own, or were they perhaps distant birds of light, flapping in the darkness?

Maggie gave herself over to fatigue and began to drift. What kind of world have we entered? she wondered. So many trees, nothing to eat. What will become of us?

When Maggie woke, Orick was gone and the moon had set. Gallen slept soundly beside her. Maggie got up, scanned the landscape in a huge circle. It was especially dark under the trees. Orick was nowhere to be seen, but after a few minutes she spotted him in the distance, running toward her between the trees. Orick raised up on his back legs and called, "Hallooo, Maggie. Over here! I've found something! Food!"

Maggie was painfully aware of her empty belly. While working at the inn, providing three meals a day for strangers, she had grown accustomed to eating on schedule. But now she had been fasting for over thirty hours. She prodded Gallen's ribs with her toe. "Get up. It's time to eat."

Gallen sat up, rubbed his eyes. "It's a little more sleep I'm wanting."

"Up with you, you lout! You'll sleep better with some food in your tummy." Maggie realized belatedly that she sounded shrewish—like her own mother before she died. Back in Tihrglas, John Mahoney often warned her about her mouth: "Your mother grew so accustomed to nagging you kids, that she soon started bedeviling everyone in general. I'll tell you right now, Maggie: I'll not have you shrieking like a harpy at my customers, as your mother did!"

Maggie bit her lower lip, resolved to control her tongue.

When Gallen and Maggie reached the bear, he began loping through the woods. "I caught scent of it as I was sleeping," Orick said. They reached a cliff and found themselves looking over a large valley, lush with trees. A broad river cut through the valley. Lights blazed on the water.

It took Maggie several moments to realize what she saw: the river was enormous, and huge ships sailed down it, each bejeweled with hundreds of lights. On the far side of the river was what appeared to be a single building that extended low along the ground for dozens of miles. Fierce bluish lights shone from thousands of windows. In places the land was clear, leaving bits of open meadow and farm. In other places, the building spanned over the water like some colony of mold growing in a neglected mug of ale.

As she watched, bright globes dropped from the sky and fell toward the city, then settled upon rooftops. Perhaps a mile away, a woman in green robes climbed from a shining globe and walked through a door into that vast building.

Maggie drew a breath in exclamation.

"As I said, I picked up the smell when we were sleeping," Orick explained. "There's good farmland down there. I smell ripe corn and pears." Indeed, Maggie saw a few squares of checkered fields and orchards not far off.

"So," Orick said, "shall we go knock on their door, ask for food?"

"It's better than starving in the night," Gallen said.

Maggie felt a deep sense of disquiet. "Are you sure?" she asked. "How do we know what they'll do to us? What if there are vanquishers about?"

"You just saw that woman get out of her sky coach," Gallen said. "She looked nice enough. Besides, what if *there are* vanquishers about? They won't know us."

Gallen searched for a way down the embankment and found a narrow footpath. Maggie hesitated, but didn't want to be left in the dark. They climbed down. The starlight was not enough to see by, and Maggie found herself feeling her way forward through the shadows with a degree of apprehension.

At the bottom of the valley was a lush orchard where some sweet-smelling, pungent fruit had fallen. Orick licked one. "This stuff is pretty good," he said, and he began eating.

Maggie gave the bear a minute, thinking that if the fruits were poisonous, the bear might start gagging, but Orick showed no sign of dying or taking sick.

"Didn't you say you smelled corn?" Gallen asked.

"Yeah, over there!" Orick pointed toward the city with his snout. "But why eat feathers when there's a chicken to be had?" he quoted an old proverb often spoken by bears. Obviously, he preferred this strange fruit.

Maggie cautiously followed Gallen toward the river. Halfway there, he stepped into some bushes and disturbed a buck that leapt up and bounded through the brush.

Maggie's heart began thumping.

The deer charged uphill toward Orick, and the bear bawled in startlement and ran downhill to pace nervously at Gallen's side.

They found a paved road by the river and followed it. Often through the trees Maggie glimpsed boats sailing the river or sky coaches rising from the city, yet the night remained quiet.

At last they found a field of ripening corn, the tassels shining silver-gold in the starlight. The corn stalks, at twelve feet, grew taller than any in County Morgan; the huge ears were sweet and full.

Maggie shucked an ear, knelt to eat, and Gallen followed.

Maggie was on her second ear, the sweet kernels dribbling down her chin, when Orick roared, "Spider! Run!"

The bear lunged away.

Maggie looked up. Towering above her, its belly just skimming the corn tassels, stood an enormous creature with six thin legs. The spider's body itself was a yard across, and Maggie could discern green glowing eyes. One enormous leg whipped out with blinding speed and knocked the cob from Maggie's hand, another lashed at her.

Gallen shouted and charged, grabbed one of the spider's legs and twisted, wrenching it free from its body.

The spider shrieked and tried to retreat, but Gallen caught another foreleg and wrenched it free.

The leg brushed against Maggie, striking her with a metallic ring. Maggie screamed and backed away. Suddenly Orick was back at her side, standing on his hind legs and roaring, raking the air with his claws.

The spider's torso became unbalanced, leaned forward precariously. In that split second, Gallen used the torn leg to club the spider between the eyes. It crashed to the ground, emitting a loud squeal.

Gallen jumped forward and began bludgeoning it. Orick pounced at the same time, holding it down. The two green lamps of its eyes kept shining, and Gallen had to pound at them for several moments before they cracked and the lights faded. Only then, when the lights were out, did Gallen stop beating the creature.

He stood over the broken monster's carcass, panting. An odd wailing sounded in the distance, a horn that rose and fell, rose and fell.

Maggie turned a full circle, looking for more giant spiders. She wondered if this city, these fields, belonged to the giant spider, or maybe a family of spiders. She was in the magical realm of the sidhe now. Who knew what wonders lay in store?

The wailing continued. Orick growled, sniffed at the spider. He pricked his ears up and said, "Something's coming."

Maggie heard whispering movement among the cornstalks. Gallen took her hand, and they ran. They crossed the road and hid in the brush, watching as ten more enormous spiders came to patrol the perimeter of the field.

The spiders discovered their dead comrade, and one of them dragged the carcass off while the others raced through the field in a frenzy, hunting.

Gallen frowned. The corn might as well have been a hundred miles away. They wouldn't dare try to harvest any more from that field. "Come on," he whispered, pulling Maggie's arm. "Let's get out of here."

Orick crept ahead, using his night vision and keen sense of smell to scout until the spider-infested fields fell behind. The sky began to brighten, turning to a dull silver as it will before dawn.

A spur of the city sprawled across the river just ahead, and the three had to make a choice—forge on into the city, or return to hide in the wilderness.

Orick glanced back at Gallen and Maggie. The sun was rising quickly. Behind him, the colors of the city walls could be seen, vague swirls of green and purple, like a field of alfalfa in bloom. The walls had rounded contours. Tall trees grew in certain clearings, rising above the city. The forest obscured the road ahead.

"I'm going to sneak up on the highway," Gallen said, "just to take a look."

Maggie nodded. Gallen began climbing. As soon as he left, she knew she had to go up there and join him. She hurried to follow. Behind her Orick grumbled, "Damn you for trying to leave me behind!" He rushed after them.

As Maggie climbed onto the highway, it seemed that magic struck. Suddenly, two brilliant lavender suns climbed above the distant mountains, casting a complex network of shadows over the city. As their light touched the highway, it glowed a deep red as if it were made of rubies. The trees at the roadside hissed in the breeze, their long fronds of leaves swaying. Maggie caught the sound of distant music blowing on the wind.

Ahead a shadowed archway led into the city. Several men and women milled about near the arch, seating themselves at tables. The scents of roasting meat and fresh breads wafted from the arch.

"That's an inn," Maggie said. "I know an inn when I see it."

Maggie stood, not quite sure what she saw. Neither Gallen nor Orick dared move forward. Not all of the creatures stirring in that inn were human. A yellow man with enormous spindly limbs leaned his back against one wall near the entrance to the arch. He was bald and naked but for a burgundy loincloth. Maggie suspected that the man would stand over ten feet tall. Other things moving about in the shadowed inn looked like ivory-skinned children with enormous eyes and ears.

Yet there were plenty of normal people inside. Some wore robes in brilliant greens and blues and darkest black, others wore pants and vests of gold with silver headpieces. Yet others were dressed all in silver body armor.

Then the wind shifted and the music swelled with the clear calling of pipes, rumbling drums, and the mellow tones of instruments that Maggie had neither heard before nor imagined. The combination of music and scents and movement of the glittering people in the city called to her, and Maggie knew that if it were the last thing she did, she had to go.

They rushed to the gaping arch, and the yellow spidery man stood to greet them. "Welcome, welcome travelers!" he called in an odd accent. "Food for all travelers, food near the road. Heap a plate to your liking. Enter to eat!"

"How much do you charge for breakfast?" Gallen asked.

The tall man opened his mouth in surprise. "You must have traveled far indeed! Food is such a small thing. Here among the Fale, all eat for free. Please, come in."

They entered the inn, and the shadows felt cool on Maggie's face. The music was louder. Maggie cast her eyes about, searching for the band, but the music came from the ceiling, as if the living walls of the building had broken into song. Overhead, small gems shone from dark niches of the room, glowing like lamps that did not burn. In one corner of the inn, people were pulling trays from a stack and piling on cups and silverware. Gallen got in line, and they followed it to a narrow aisle where a row of bushes hid the sounds of a kitchen. Each person in front of them went to a small opening and ordered food, then stuck their tray into the opening. When they pulled the tray out, food was on it.

Gallen set his tray in, asked for rolls, fried potatoes, sausage, fresh raspberries, and milk. He pulled out his tray and had all that he'd asked for.

Maggie looked into the hole. In a well-lighted room on the other side, men made of gold and porcelain were cooking. Each man had six arms and moved so quickly that her eyes were baffled.

Maggie found her curiousity piqued. She would have stared for hours if more people hadn't gotten into line behind her. Instead, she set her tray into the slot and ordered breakfast. It felt odd, asking for food when she could not see the faces of the metal men. She realized that they must have had phenomenal hearing.

She got her food, and Orick stuck in his tray, ordered quadruple portions for himself. He pulled the tray out a moment later, carrying it in his teeth. He had muffins heaped on a pile of eggs, a string of sausages dangling over the tray, and the whole affair was smothered in honey.

They found an empty table and began to eat. Maggie could not help but watch the strangers around her. At a nearby table sat several people in silk tunics with swirling patterns of green and red and blues. They were talking vociferously and laughing. Beyond them, two other tables were filled with young men and women who wore pants and vests of gold, and silver crowns adorned their heads. Their skin was well-tanned, and they did not speak as they ate. Instead, they looked at each other knowingly and sometimes laughed as if a joke had been spoken.

Those in bright cloaks and those in gold seemed to be of separate castes. The small ivory-skinned men and women who hugged the shadows made up a third group. They wore no clothing at all. As they sat at their benches, the women's breasts were so small it was hard to distinguish sexes. And then there were the machines—a fourth caste, Maggie decided. From outside they had looked like warriors in armor, but now she saw that the silver men were only machines like those in the kitchens. They moved smoothly through the room, refilling mugs, cleaning tables.

Neither Gallen nor Orick had spoken since entering the building. Maggie wasn't sure what to say. Should they talk about the strangers? Discuss the wonders they beheld? Something warned her that neither would be prudent. She did not want to call attention to herself.

Maggie felt ignorant. The people here lived among so many marvels—walls that sang, machines that cooked and could fly. Compared to such people, she was a savage. Maggie had always had a quick wit, and for the first time in her life, she felt profoundly undereducated.

Halfway through breakfast, Maggie realized that people were watching them with furtive glances. She whispered to Gallen and Orick, "People are staring at us."

"Maybe we're not dressed to their liking," Gallen whispered.

"Or maybe I'm the only bear they've ever seen," Orick growled. "I can't smell another anywhere." Maggie was used to seeing bears in Tihrglas—they often would try to panhandle in town. She hadn't even noticed the absence of them here.

Gallen glanced around the room and said softly, "Orick, can you pick up Everynne's scent here? Even the slightest whiff?"

"Believe me," Orick answered, "if I could catch the slightest trace of that dear creature's fragrance, I'd pounce on her like a hound on a hare. She's nowhere near."

The folks at the nearest table left, affording Gallen, Maggie, and Orick a moment of privacy.

"What now?" Gallen whispered. "Do we throw ourselves on the mercy of these townsmen? Do we look for work and try to scratch out a living? Or do we hunt for Everynne?"

"We can't announce ourselves," Maggie warned. "We left those vanquishers behind, but for all we know, they could be on our trail at this very moment. If we were to be going around telling everyone that we were strangers, we'd only attract attention. They might even turn us over to the vanquishers."

Orick said, "By the way folks are staring at me, they must know we're strangers. Yet they seem mighty hospitable. Free food for everyone! If these are Everynne's enemies, then maybe we've taken up with scoundrels."

"Hmmm," Gallen said. "You and Maggie are both right. The folks here seem nice enough, but the vanquishers might be hunting us. We should lie low. Still, there's more to this city than this one corner. Everynne and Veriasse may be here. I want to go look for them."

"And leave us alone?" Maggie asked.

"I'd be less conspicuous that way. It would only be for a bit," Gallen said. At that moment, Gallen caught a startled breath. Maggie followed his gaze. A man stood in the doorway to the dining room, a man in a black robe with black gloves and tall black boots, a man with a face that shone like golden starlight. Gallen got up clumsily.

"What is it?" Maggie asked, taking Gallen's wrist.

"Nothing," Gallen said. "I thought I recognized someone."

Maggie looked at the silver-faced man. "Him? Where would you have met the likes of him before?"

"Not him," Gallen said. "The one I saw was dressed the same, but his skin shone lavender. Besides, the man I met was younger and thinner."

"Where did you meet him?" Orick asked.

"In Coille Sidhe. Last night, a man dressed like that saved my life." Gallen stretched. "I'll be back in a couple of hours—sooner, if I find Everynne." He left the dining room, passed the stranger, and moved into a well-lighted hall.

Maggie watched his back. Right, Gallen O'Day, go chase your mystery woman. I wish you both all the happiness.

The room seemed to close around Maggie. Every few moments, someone would bump her as they tried to get past. The room filled with diners, becoming cramped. She and Orick moved to a table that let her look out over the broad, muddy river. Green barn swallows were skimming over the river, dipping for drinks.

Maggie nibbled at her food and began to think that this place might be heaven. The weather was beautiful, the food delicious, and life here appeared to be simple.

But when Gallen had been gone for nearly an hour, the truth became more apparent: on the ruby road outside the city, six black dronons appeared. They wore odd shoes that let them glide along the road as swiftly as water striders. One of them skated to the inn. Maggie and Orick moved back against the wall, fearing that the creature was searching for them.

The inn became deathly quiet. The dronon was so wide that it could not easily pass between tables, but the gleaming black creature folded its wings and pulled itself slowly under the arch. Its head swayed from side to side as it moved. It held a long, black incendiary gun in one chitinous hand.

It stopped beside Maggie and Orick, and a single long feeler twisted up from beside its mouth. The feeler wrapped around Maggie's wrist. She stood abruptly, wanting to run, but found she was trapped between two tables with her back against the wall.

The dronon's feeler held her like a thick cord, binding her in case she should try to flee. Beneath the creature's mouth was an organ that looked like dozens of small, blunt fingers poised above the stretched membrane of a drum. The fingers began rhythmically tapping, creating an odd thrumming noise not unlike the sound that some deep-voiced locust might make. Yet the thrumming varied greatly in intensity and pitch. Maggie could distinguish words in that music. The dronon was speaking to her.

"You are not from this world. Where are you from?" the dronon demanded.

Maggie froze, not knowing how to answer. She pressed herself farther against the wall. The dronon's grip tightened, and it raised one arm overhead. She looked up—the arm was heavy, like the claw of a crab, and had a serrated edge. The dronon's tiny segmented hand had retracted, leaving a single large hooklike claw. If the dronon struck her, the arm would chop her in half like an axe. The dronon hissed, threatening to strike her into oblivion if she did not answer.

"You are not of this world. Where are you from?"

At a nearby table, the man dressed in black robes, the man with a golden face that glowed like starlight, stood and answered. "Great Lord, she is a Silent One from Pellarius!" He stepped forward. "She cannot speak. The singers there thought her voice lacked beauty, so they cut out her vocal cords and sterilized her so that she could not breed. Still, I have purchased her as a worker so that she might serve the greater glory of the dronon empire."

"What is her function?" the dronon asked.

"She is an aberlain, highly skilled in installing genetic upgrades in the unborn."

"If she is an aberlain, where is her Guide?" The dronon's feeler began probing Maggie's scalp.

"She has been a class-two aberlain," the stranger said, "and is ready to be promoted to class one. I am having a new Guide created for her at this very moment."

"Where is her current Guide?" the dronon demanded.

"Here, in my pocket." The stranger pulled out a wide band of silver, a crown with small lights in it. He held it up for the dronon to see. The dronon warrior abruptly lowered its battle arm.

"May your work prosper the empire," the dronon said, addressing both Maggie and the stranger in the same breath. It regarded Orick for a moment, then hunched and dragged its massive body through the cafeteria. It turned at the hallway and disappeared into the deeper recesses of the building.

Maggie found herself shaking, dizzy. She could not move. Terror held her in place. The dronon's feeler had left a gray powder on her arm that burned slightly.

The people in the cafeteria resumed talking. Maggie sagged into her chair. The stranger with the golden face watched her unabashedly. For the past half hour, Maggie had noticed that he had been studying her and Orick with an intensity that others in the room could not match. She did not know how to thank him.

The stranger came to their table. He took her arm, and poured her mug of drinking water over the skin where the dronon had touched her, then began to sponge it with a cloth napkin. "I don't know where you are from," he whispered, "but you obviously know nothing of the dronon. I envy that." He sponged her face and scalp. "The first lesson you must learn is that the dronon's exoskeleton produces a weak acid. They come from a dry world, and the acid coating is an effective addition to their immune system. But if they touch you, you must wipe off the acid to avoid getting burned."

He set down the napkin and peered into her face, ignoring Orick. The stranger had a strong jaw, penetrating brown eyes. Up under his black hood, he wore a silver headdress, much like the one Everynne had worn. Long silver chains dangled from it with hundreds of small triangles, like some metallic wig. She wondered why he would hide this beautiful headdress under a cloak, but did not ask.

"So," the stranger said, "my name is Karthenor, Lord of the Aberlains."

"I . . . I saw you watching me earlier," Maggie said.

"Forgive my inquisitiveness," Karthenor said. "I did not mean to offend you. But I have never seen anyone dressed like you, nor have I ever seen anyone like your friend." Karthenor glanced at Orick and said with a tone of dismissal as if Orick were a child, "I recognize the species. He is a bear."

"A *black* bear!" Orick grumbled.

"Excuse me," Karthenor said, raising a brow. He looked at Orick with a new degree of respect. "He is a genetically enhanced black bear." He addressed Orick, "I am pleased to make your acquaintance."

Karthenor pulled up a chair. Maggie could sense an eagerness in him, an expectancy she associated with traders who wanted to sell something. "You and your friend have been watching us, too. I suspect that you find us to be as strange as we find you. Am I right?"

Maggie studied his golden face. She could not think of a lie. In fact, she didn't know if she should tell one. She knew only that she wanted an ally, and Karthenor offered help. Gallen's brief mention that another man dressed like this had saved his life inspired her to a degree of confidence that was perhaps dangerous, but on impulse she said, "We came here through the World Gate. Yes, we do find it strange."

Karthenor leaned back in surprise, his voice so neutral that Maggie could not guess what he might be thinking. "You came through a World Gate? What is your name? Where are you from?"

"My name is Maggie Flynn—from the town of Clere."

Karthenor looked at her impassively, then bowed deeply. "I am honored to meet you, Maggie Flynn from the town of Clere. I . . . hope that I am not being too inquisitive, but may I ask what *world* you hail from?"

"Earth," Maggie answered.

The stranger seemed perplexed. He stared at Maggie and Orick with a bemused expression, rested his elbows on the table, and touched a gloved finger to his lips. "Which Earth are you referring to? You obviously speak English, so you've been genetically engineered to remember our language. Yet you speak it with an odd accent, one I've never heard."

"Earth," Maggie said. "Where I live."

The stranger turned his head to the side, thinking. "What continent are you from on this Earth of yours?"

"Tihrglas," Maggie said.

"Ah, that Earth!" The stranger smiled. He folded his hands, looked at Maggie and Orick appraisingly. "Surely you did not find a gate key just lying around on Tihrglas? How did you come by it?"

Maggie felt inexplicably frightened. It had nothing to do with Karthenor's mannerisms. He seemed kindly, hospitable. But Maggie froze, not letting the stranger prod her further.

"Ah, forgive me! I've frightened you," Karthenor whispered, and his golden face crinkled in a beneficent smile. "Obviously, because you are a stranger to our land, you do not know our ways. Here on Fale, we are very open with each other. Perhaps you find this . . . disconcerting. Please, ask me any questions first, if this will put you at ease."

"Are you human?" Orick asked.

Karthenor smiled, touched his own cheek. "You mean the mask? Of course I am human, by most standards."

"Why do you wear the mask, then?" Maggie asked.

"To reveal," Karthenor said, taking Maggie's hand companionably. "It is a style here. The masks reveal our innermost selves. Those who do not wear the mask may hide emotions from one another, but when one wears the mask of Fale, he cannot hide behind his flesh and is ever forced to reveal his true emotions. Those of us who wear masks can practice no deceit. That is why, among all worlds, those who wear the mask of Fale are known to be trustworthy." He smiled gently at Maggie, and in that moment, Maggie felt ashamed for having distrusted him.

Karthenor held her hand, as if she were a child, and smiled as he looked out past the veranda to the swallows dipping in the wide river. Children were out on the water now, riding the backs of giant geese. "If you like, I can give you a tour of our city," Karthenor offered. "If you come from Tihrglas, you will find it quite marvelous. Not at all like your home, I dare say."

"You've been to Tihrglas?" Orick asked.

"Heavens no," Karthenor answered. "I don't travel, but there are records. What do you know of Fale?"

"Nothing."

"Well then, it is time you learned. Our ancestors once lived together on the same world, long ago. A planet called Earth, but not the same Earth that you live on now."

Maggie looked at Karthenor suspiciously but said nothing as he continued. "On that planet, our ancestors had descended from animals, and there they acted the part—always warring, seeking wealth.

"Eventually, they developed space flight and journeyed to distant stars. There was an explosion of knowledge and technology unlike anything ever before. Machines learned to think. Men learned to hold death at bay and extend their lives for millennia. We met new races, new allies who also traversed among the stars.

"Still there were wars, still there was poverty and sadness. So some of our ancestors rejected technology, decided to live on backward planets in rustic settings. They came to be known as Backwards, and eighteen thousand years ago, some of them settled on your world. They took only the most basic tools—a few genetic upgrades that would let them remain relatively healthy and transmit an inborn memory of English. They took seeds for house-trees and plants.

"That is where our ancestors split: my ancestors were Forwards. They embraced technology and traveled to the stars." Karthenor waved his hand in a gesture that encompassed the sky.

"How do you know about our ancestors?" Maggie asked. "I've never heard these tales."

Karthenor touched the silver headdress, the tiny triangles. "My mantle is telling me about it," he said. "The mantle is a teaching machine that knows far more than any human." Maggie studied the ringlets and triangles. "Would you like to learn about such things? I have another teaching device here." His golden face was strangely intense. He reached into his pocket, pulled out the silver crown and gave it to Maggie. She held it, turned it over. The outside of the band showed only a single opening, a small window. But inside were colored lights. Two tiny prongs protruded so that they would push gently into the back of the wearer's neck.

"This is a Guide," Karthenor said. "Here in Fale, it is considered to be a thing of great worth. I want to give it to you, as a gift. You are a beautiful young woman. You will need it if you are to make a living here."

Maggie asked, "What does it do?"

"It is a teaching device, to make you wise," Karthenor said. "It is not only beautiful when worn in your hair, but very valuable. If you wear it, you will learn all of the secrets of how to become an aberlain. You will learn how to create life, shape the human genome into new complexities so that future generations will be wiser, stronger, and better servants of society than they are now. If you choose to wear such a Guide, you would become rich beyond imagination, and in time your wealth and power will rival that of the Lords. Here, let me show you how to put it on."

A hundred questions flooded through Maggie's mind: If it was so valuable, why would Karthenor simply *give* it to her? She realized now that many of the people here in the cafeteria wore similar Guides. They were the ones who ate silently, seemed to have no need to communicate with words. She wondered how long Karthenor would let her wear the thing.

Karthenor lifted the crown. It was bow-shaped and would not fit completely around Maggie's head. Instead, Karthenor began to put it on from behind, so that the ends of the bow touched the top of Maggie's neck. Just as it touched her, another question flooded into Maggie's mind, one that had nothing to do with the Guide: If Karthenor's mask kept him from lying, then how could he have lied to the dronon?

The cool metal Guide wrapped around Maggie's forehead. A faint itching pierced her skin where the prongs touched.

"There now," Karthenor said. "This will be your Guide. It shall teach you all things that you shall do. It will be your comforter and your constant companion. With it, you shall learn many great things."

Maggie looked up. Karthenor's black robes silhouetted his golden face, and Maggie looked into his malicious grin. She clawed at the Guide, trying to pull it free, and a raging fire seemed to sweep through her head. Tears rolled down her face, burning like molten lead. Maggie cried out and fell to the floor, gasping.

"Get that off her!" Orick roared. Karthenor glanced back at the bear, waved his hand. A web of thin gray wires, so small that they could hardly be seen, shot out from a device at Karthenor's wrist. The web struck Orick and the wall, gluing the bear in place. Orick roared in terror and tried to claw his way free, but the tiny net held.

"Help!" Maggie shouted, rolling on the floor, looking to the others in the room.

Karthenor's image swirled, and Maggie watched him through a fog of pain and dismay. He bent low and hissed, "No one can help you. I am a Lord here. Don't try to remove the Guide—it will only punish you for your efforts! Now: tell me how you got through the gate at Tihrglas! Where did you find the key?"

Maggie's muscles went limp, and though she fought to move, she could not control her arms, could not budge a muscle. Yet as Karthenor had promised, the Guide began to teach her.

In an overwhelming instant, knowledge coursed into her like a pure foaming river, filling her with more facts than she'd ever thought she could know. The tide of human learning cascaded over her, drowning her, and she despaired.

In one marvelous moment, Maggie understood the work of an aberlain. With the Guide to help her, she would spend the rest of her life altering the genetic makeup of unborn children, making them into better servants for the dronon empire. In return, each child and their offspring in perpetuity would become indebted to Maggie and her Lord Karthenor. Though they sweated for a thousand generations, a portion of all their earnings would be deducted for payment. The work of aberlains had been illegal until six years ago, had been considered immoral.

But now the dronon ruled, and in dronon society, each creature was born into a caste he could never escape. Images flashed before Maggie's eyes of her dronon leaders: the Golden Queen, Tlitkani, who had so recently seized control of six thousand worlds; the black Lord Vanquishers, her soldiers; the small, sand-colored artisans of dronon society; and the vast oceans of white-skinned workers. Each was born to its place, and the dronons now sought to remake mankind in their own image.

Karthenor, Lord of Aberlains, was one of mankind's greatest enemies on this world. Through genetic manipulation, he hoped to engineer a race of slaves and reap endless profit.

And through the Guide, Maggie would become a slave. The Guide stored information on an atomic level. The silver band housed billions of volumes of data along with transmitters and receivers. Already, the Guide's nanotech components were creating artificial neurons to thread through her cerebrum and brain stem, binding her to the machine. Within hours, she and the machine would be one.

Maggie looked up at Karthenor with undisguised hatred. "I know you!" she growled. The effort caused her great pain.

Karthenor laughed, "Now, see, your eyes are beginning to open already. In your own small way, you are becoming like one of the gods. I want you to think about gods for a moment, and tell me where you got their key."

Karthenor waved his hand. Two silver android servants came to the table, lifted Maggie by each arm, and began dragging her into the recesses of the building. Orick roared and growled in rage, but he could not save her.

When Karthenor said the word "gods," the world went gray as information flooded her senses. Just as Maggie had this small Guide enmeshed in her brain, others across the galaxy were joined to larger intelligences. Karthenor's silver mantle stored far more information than Maggie's Guide, yet some immortals were connected to intelligences the size of an entire planet. They were gods.

In her mind's eye, Maggie saw Semarritte, the great judge who had ruled this sector of the galaxy for ten thousand years. She was a woman of proud bearing and dark hair, very much like Everynne, but older. Semarritte had built the gates at the beginning of her reign as a means of traveling between worlds quickly. Yet to protect herself, she had kept the method for constructing the gate keys a secret.

In one bitter moment, Maggie understood that Everynne was the daughter of Semarritte, and that Everynne had stolen the gate key in a desperate bid to win back her mother's worlds.

Karthenor and his servants dragged Maggie down a long hall. With each jarring step it felt as if the androids would pull her arms from her sockets. They passed shops and hallways and came to a blank wall which turned to mist when Karthenor touched it.

They entered a living room with comfortable sofas and luxurious white rugs. The androids laid Maggie on the floor, and Maggie's lips began to move against her will.

She lay helplessly and listened to herself tell Karthenor of the Lady Everynne, of the dronon that dogged her trail in Tihrglas, and of Gallen's own naive efforts to aid Everynne. With each word, Maggie betrayed Gallen, herself, the Lady Everynne—every human on every world.

Sometimes Karthenor would stop her, ask a question, such as, "And where is your friend Gallen now?" No matter how hard Maggie sought to lie, the whole truth came out. She could not will her mouth to shut.

When Maggie finished, tears rolled down her face. Karthenor said, "Go to your quarters."

Maggie suddenly knew where her sleeping quarters lay in an upstairs loft. She willed herself to run away but could not move her feet. She moved to the rhythm of the machines.

This is your home now, the Guide whispered. You will serve Karthenor. I will teach you what you must do. Stiffly, the Guide moved Maggie's legs and arms, taking her down a sterile white corridor, up a long staircase. Maggie watched, knowing that she was no longer human. She climbed into bed, then lay down, thinking. The Guide was always thinking.

Maggie had one hope: Gallen O'Day.

Seven

Gallen wandered the pale green hallways of the city. The air was warm, moist, like the air inside a house-tree. The very city was alive, growing.

Windows in the roof let in some light, while glowing gems overhead provided the rest. As Gallen moved deeper into this living catacomb, he twice came upon open-air bazaars where merchants in colorful swirling robes sought to sell him fabulous merchandise: a pair of living lungs that could attach to his back and let him breathe underwater; the seeds to a flower that could be planted one day, grow six feet overnight, and break into glorious blooms; a hood that would let him talk to a dead man; a tiny plug that he could place in his ear so that he could always listen to music; a cream that not only removed wrinkles and blemishes from skin but also left the wearer pleasantly scented for a number of years.

Gallen recognized that much of it was junk and gadgetry, trifles for a people who had everything. But still vendors hawked their wares, trying to engage his attention in odd ways. At one shop, a beautiful woman appeared out of thin air. She was tanned and strong and wore only the slightest scrap of clothes. She smiled at Gallen and said, "Why don't you come in here and try me on?" Then she walked into a shop. Gallen followed, and she went to a stack of pants, pulled a pair on and wriggled into them, then disappeared.

Gallen found himself staring at a display of pants, looking about for the woman, but she was nowhere to be seen. Suddenly he realized that she had been created only to lure him into the shop. He left, found that similar devices were at nearly every store. Voices would speak from nowhere, demanding that he buy here and now in order to save. Spirit women would appear, begging him to purchase something from the shop, and always they were so beautiful as to make him dizzy.

A manic glee fell over Gallen, and he wandered the long corridors as if in some intoxicated daze, sampling confections that tasted of ambrosia, yet always declining to buy.

In one square, he found a beast that looked like a huge gray toad sitting in a chair, surrounded by bright containers filled with colorful powders. The toadman wore an immense wig of silver with many ringlets and triangles that cascaded down his shoulders. On his back he wore a number of tubes, and each tube had dozens of tiny appendages rising up from it—some with hairs on them, others with clamps or scalpels. All these appendages rose overhead and by use of various joints managed to converge on a small table in front of the toad. Children had gathered around, and Gallen stopped to look.

The toadman's limbs all pointed to a small object at the center of the table, and Gallen stood breathless, watching. A purple dragonfly sat on a thin reed there, motionless. Dozens of tiny needles, or perhaps hairs, met at the focal point of the device, and Gallen saw that the hairs seemed to be stroking one of the dragonfly's wings. Part of the dragonfly's wing was missing, but the toadman's machines were stroking it, creating a new wing.

Gallen's jaw dropped open, and he walked around so that he could watch over the toadman's shoulders. The old gray fellow was looking at writing that appeared in the air, fiery red letters that blossomed and departed so fast that Gallen couldn't read them. An image of the dragonfly, magnified many times, sat in the air above the toadman's head, and every few moments the toadman would look up at the image whenever a new layer of wing had been placed. He would stare at the image a moment, until new veins and an expanded portion of wing appeared, then glance down. His machines would begin constructing the rest of the dragonfly.

Within five minutes, the toadman finished. "Now, children, which of you would like this dragonfly I have formed?" he asked, and the children clapped and pleaded.

The toadman reached out with one warty gray finger, touched the dragonfly, and it climbed onto his long nail. He held the dragonfly aloft for a moment, then turned to Gallen.

"I think I will give this one to the child who looks like a man." He extended the dragonfly to Gallen.

Gallen touched the toadman's finger, and the dragonfly crawled to Gallen's thumb and sat, wings pulsing. It was vivid purple with touches of red under its belly and in its wings. The children walked away, disappointed.

"Thank you," Gallen said.

"It is nothing. In a few moments, its wings will dry, and it will fly away," the toadman answered.

Gallen studied the toadman. He had yellow eyes, warty gray skin, and a mouth wide enough to swallow a cat whole. His arms and legs were thin, with baggy skin.

"You have never seen a Motak," the toadman said.

"Is that what you are?" Gallen asked.

"Yes," the toadman answered. "And if you knew of us, you would know that you are supposed to avert your eyes and not stare. On Motak, we stare only at those who are ugly."

"I'm sorry," Gallen said. "I didn't mean to imply that you are ugly."

"I know."

"I was simply curious."

"I know that, too," the toadman said. "It has been ages since I have seen an adult so interested in the doings of a creator."

"Is that what you do?" Gallen asked. "You create life?"

"Not true life. Only viviforms, artificial beings. Still, they look true enough, and they don't know that they aren't living creatures."

"Can you create people?" Gallen asked.

"For a price. I can make a viviform that looks and acts any way that you like. Between jobs, I create pets for the children." The dragonfly began flapping its wings.

"Thank you. I'm very grateful," Gallen said, and he cupped the dragonfly into his palms, determined to carry it back to show Maggie.

"I thank you in return," the toadman said. "It is good to see such light in the eyes of an adult again, especially during such hard times. May joy burn brightly in you."

When Gallen returned to the cantina, patrons of the restaurant were freeing Orick from a net, and Maggie was nowhere to be seen.

Orick growled at those who freed him, "Why didn't you stop him, lads? Why didn't you stop him?" No one answered.

"Stop who?" Gallen asked, setting the dragonfly free. He pulled out a knife to cut at the fine webbing. Each tiny thread was tough as a nail and seemed to be glued to the wall.

"A man named Karthenor kidnapped Maggie!" Orick shouted. As Gallen helped cut through the last thread, Orick urged, "This way, Gallen!" and rushed down a corridor toward the heart of the city.

Orick barreled down the hallway, navigating by smell. Sometimes he would come to an intersection and stop, testing the scent in both directions. At other times, he would lunge down a corridor and then come up short, only to test the scent of some side passageway. After a few minutes, they reached a hallway that led to a dead end.

"They came here," Orick said. "They came at least this far." Orick sniffed the creamed-colored wall, stood up on his back legs and smelled the ceiling.

Gallen took Orick by the shoulders. "Now," he said, "tell me everything that happened."

Orick told Gallen of the visit by the vanquisher and how a man named Karthenor, Lord of the Aberlains, put a silver band around Maggie's head and took her captive.

Gallen considered. As in any battle, he took stock of his assets and liabilities. He had his wits, his skills as a fighter, and two knives. Yet he did not know his enemies or their weaknesses. One old sheriff down in County Obhiann had often warned: "When you are confronted by an outlaw, always take stock of the terrain. Look for what cover you can find, watch to make sure he doesn't have a bowman or a couple of lads sitting in the same bush you might want to hide under."

Obviously, when it came to terrain, Gallen was at a phenomenal disadvantage. "Come on," he said. "Let's get you under some cover. If we go hunting for Karthenor together, he'll spot you a mile off. But he's never seen me. I will leg it back here and study the situation."

They made their way back to the highway. The road was filling with people—coaches floated over its ruby surface. Some people had shoes that floated in the same manner, and they skated over the road faster than any horse could run.

Gallen and Orick walked north along the river for a mile until they came to some low wooded hills. Here they slipped into the brush and made camp. Gallen worried about Maggie. Every few moments he would verify some details. "This Karthenor said that Maggie would be working for him? Did he say where?"

"No," Orick answered, yet Gallen felt more easy. If Karthenor needed workers, then Maggie should be all right. Karthenor wouldn't want to harm a servant.

"I'll have to find Maggie," Gallen said. "To do so, I'll need to sneak through the city. You can't come with me."

"But what should I do?" Orick asked. "I don't want to just sit and wait."

"I still need your help. We know Everynne came through the gate before us, but we don't know where she may have come out. I'd like you to hunt for her trail. Maybe you can find her. I want you to make a thorough search, then come back here in two or three days."

Orick agreed reluctantly, headed south. He looked over his back. "You'll get her out all right, won't you?"

"I'll do my best," was all Gallen could promise.

When Maggie woke in the morning, her head burned with a fever. She wondered at the pain. A voice whispered in her mind, "It is I, your Guide. I have been creating neural pathways into your brain and spinal column all night, and this causes your discomfort. By nightfall the process will be complete, and we will become one."

Maggie tried to get up but could not move. Instead, the Guide let her lie abed for a few moments and began feeding her information at an incredible pace. "If you have questions," the Guide said, "ask."

The Guide began by showing her the structure of DNA in all of its intricacy. In brief visions, it revealed the function of each set of genes in the human genome, and how these genes were affected by variations. It showed her machinery and taught her how to run the tools that aberlains used in their work—chromosome readers, gene splicers, tissue samplers, DNA dyes. She learned how to remove egg cells from women and sperm from men, divide them into lots based on desirable characteristics that the cells would transmit, and then infect each lot with tailored genes to ensure that all progeny were properly upgraded to standards set by the dronon overlords. Once a batch of eggs and sperm were perfected, they could be mixed and incubated for sixty hours, then the resulting zygotes would be implanted into a woman's womb.

The lesson lasted for nearly an hour, then the Guide forced Maggie from her bed, had her shower, and let her go down to the dining hall for breakfast.

Maggie sat at a table with other aberlains, men and women who all wore Guides like hers. And though none of them spoke, she could hear their voices in her mind as they discussed the tasks that each would need to complete that day. She ate greedily, but the Guide forced her to stop just before she felt satisfied.

She spent the morning working in a clinic. Couples who had sought a license to bear children were there, and Maggie took egg samples from women, sperm from men. She laboriously tagged and labeled each sample, but since the dronon would allow only people with certain body types to reproduce, she ended up throwing most of the samples away. Instead, the women were implanted with zygotes from approved parents.

Several times during the day, the women asked Maggie, "Will I really be getting my own child? You won't implant me with someone else's child?"

Each time, Maggie's Guide responded by comforting the potential mother and answering, "Of course you will get your own child. We take great care in labeling every sample, and there is no chance that the samples could get mixed. We will simply invest the cells with some standardized upgrades, and you will then have your own embryo returned to you."

Each time she told this lie, Maggie would fight her Guide, try to scream out a warning, and the Guide would respond by doing something that Maggie could only describe as "tickling" her: suddenly her head would itch, and then a sweet feeling of euphoria would wash through her, the greatest contentment she had ever known.

Once, when Maggie was away from the patrons of the clinic in a storage room, she said to her Guide, "How can we lie to them? Why should we lie to them?"

"We do them a favor. Why should we let them harbor ill feelings about a process that they cannot change? Our system maximizes efficiency and insures an even distribution of genetically upgraded offspring."

"But their children will all be brothers and sisters, even though they come from different families," Maggie whispered to her Guide. "They won't be able to marry."

"Within each hive, our dronon masters are brothers and sisters. Each queen bears a hundred thousand eggs, and vanquishers are born brothers to architects, workers are sisters to queens. The new family revels in unity; thus the hive bonds. When our human offspring discover that they are all brothers and sisters, they will revel in that kinship."

The Guide tickled her again. A new and stronger wave of pleasure washed through Maggie. It was a mystical, magical feeling, to be involved in such a great work, a work approved and loved by the Golden Queen and her overlords.

In the late evening, Maggie took a young woman into a back laboratory and had her lie on the operating table. Maggie took out a tissue sampler which she would use to remove egg cells from the patient. The sampler was a long, thin piece of metal with a small scoop at the end to catch a slice of ovary. Maggie was removing its sterile covering when the patient looked up at Maggie and asked, "How free are you?"

Maggie turned to the woman, unsure if she had heard correctly. The woman looked deep into Maggie's eyes. "How free are you? Do you want to escape from your Guide? If so, blink twice."

Maggie tried to blink, struggled until tears formed in her eyes, but she could not blink. The Guide whispered, "Do not be alarmed by this woman, the guards are coming for her."

Maggie stared at the woman. She was small, with mousy blond hair cropped close to her scalp, and a firm chin. She was nervous, sweating, and she whispered, "I'm in danger, aren't I? I think I'll go."

She leapt off the table and opened the door. A green-skinned vanquisher with large orange eyes stood behind it.

The small woman tried to slam the door. The vanquisher shoved it open, grabbed the woman by the throat and one arm. She kicked and screamed, trying to escape, but he held her tight, dragged her away.

Maggie stood, staring out the door, shocked, her heart hammering. The Guide flooded her with pleasant sensations, whispering peace to her soul.

That night, as Maggie prepared for bed, her Guide transmitted a report to Lord Karthenor, detailing her accomplishments for the day. Her Guide reported that Maggie proved to be "culturally retarded," and the Guide had to instruct her in the use of even the simplest machinery.

Karthenor was not concerned by this. Given Maggie's background, it was only to be expected. But the Guide also reported that it had been forced to stimulate her hypothalamus over fifty times during the day, keeping her in a state of vegetative euphoria. Such overstimulation was dangerous. Within a week, it would lead to severe depression, a depression that could not be reversed for months. Under such circumstances, the Guide could still use her, but she would become despondent, an unreliable host. If the Guide temporarily lost control of her under such conditions, she might kill herself.

Karthenor considered the report, called to one of his technicians, a human named Avik whose parents had been integrated into dronon society two generations ago. He was a young man with hair so golden it appeared to be silver, and he had a sleek, well-muscled body. Avik reported quickly.

"My lord?" Avik said when he reached the door.

"The new servant, Maggie Flynn, needs someone to help make her adjustment smoother," Karthenor said. "I would like you to talk to her, befriend her. I'll instruct her Guide to give her free reign during your contact."

Avik nodded. He was a young man, with burning blue eyes. "Would you like me to seduce her?"

Karthenor considered. These dronon-bred technicians mated like animals. Perhaps because they were forced to work under the domination of

Guides, they had become emotionally stunted. They tended to confuse sexual gratification with the more permanent rewards of a committed relationship. "Yes," he said after a moment. "I think the physical contact might be appropriate, comforting for her. However, I would like you to take her slowly, at her own pace. Don't rush her."

"Very well, my lord," Avik said, giving a deep bow as he left.

Eight

Gallen began to canvass the city an hour after leaving Orick. That day, he stopped at numerous shops and studied local merchandise while quietly pumping proprietors for information. He methodically stepped off passageways and learned the ins and outs of the city.

The locals called the place Toohkansay, and Gallen learned about the various housing quarters, the manufacturing sectors, and the business districts. Some of these places denied access to the public, and this left gaping holes in his mental map of the city. For example, with only a few questions he learned where Lord Karthenor's two hundred aberlains worked night and day in some mystic enterprise that a businessman said would "improve mankind," but when Gallen went to the place, he found only a small clinic where men and women waited for some mysterious ministrations to be performed on them.

Gallen surveyed the area around the clinic—studied Toohkansay's exits, found each window and skylight, hunted for likely places to hide.

Most of the city's inhabitants fit within certain categories: those who wore silver bands on their heads either could not or would not speak to Gallen. The merchants with their lavish robes soon became easy to spot. In a dark cafe near one manufacturing district, Gallen sat at a table filled with the small white men and women with enormous eyes and ears. His questions elicited raucous laughter from them, yet they answered good-naturedly. They called themselves the Woodari. Their ancestors had been created to work on a distant planet where the sun was dark. Here on Fale, they worked as miners and built ships to carry cargo from one world to another. The Woodari starfarers claimed that their guild was so powerful that they did not fear the dronon.

Gallen asked so many questions of one little Woodari named Fargeth that the little man said, "Your vast ignorance amuses me, but I have work to do. You are so full of questions, why do you not go to the pidc?"

"The pidc?" Gallen asked. "What is that?"

"It is a place where all the questions you can ask in a lifetime will be answered in moments."

"Where is it?" Gallen asked. "What do they charge for their service?"

Fargeth laughed. "Knowledge carries its own price. Gain it to your dismay."

Gallen wandered the halls until he spotted the creator at work in his stall, making a child. In his past two days here in the city, the old alien was the only person Gallen met whom he genuinely liked. Gallen recalled the sadness in the old creature's voice as he talked of "troubles in the city." Gallen suddenly knew that the old man was an enemy to the dronon.

Gallen said, "A friend of mine has been taken by Lord Karthenor of the aberlains. I need to learn how to free her. Can you tell me where the pidc is?"

The old toadman nodded. "I feared such a thing might befall you. I will take you there."

The toadman unhooked the various mechanical devices from his back, led Gallen down a familiar corridor to a business where young parents took children into little cubicles, set them in plush chairs, then attached silver bands to their children's heads for hours at a time. The bands had a calming effect on the children, and Gallen had thought this was the only benefit the devices imparted.

The creator set Gallen in a white chair, showed Gallen how to strap a silver band to his temples, and whispered, "Good luck, my friend. For most people, this is all they ever learn in life, and a session here becomes the end of knowledge. If you were from Motak, you would know that filling your mind with trivia is only the beginning of study. Right action will lead to greater light."

The toadman left, and Gallen held the silver strip a moment. He placed it on his head as if it were a crown. A gray mist seemed to form before Gallen's eyes. The room went dark, and in the distance he could see a bright pinpoint of light. A voice within the light said, "I am the teacher. Open yourself to knowledge. What do you wish to know?"

Gallen couldn't decide where to begin. "I know nothing of your people or customs. I can't figure out what your machines are, or how they work—"

"I can teach you of people and customs—save those things that each community might consider too sacred to share. I can teach you the basics of all technology, though each industry has its own manufacturing secrets that are private property."

"Teach me," Gallen said. And if Maggie's education was rough and painful, Gallen's was sweet and filled with light. It began with a knowledge of mathematics that coursed into him evenly—beginning with the basics of number theory, moving up through advanced spatial geometry. There, mathematics branched into physics and he learned about subatomic particles, relativity, and Gallen memorized the various equations for the unified field theory and its many corollaries.

Then the introduction to physics moved into applied technologies, and Gallen was given to understand the workings of starships and incendiary rifles and gravcars and ten thousand other items.

He learned how thinking machines developed until they reached the point where they began evolving on their own and now could store more information than any human. The Guides were one form of teaching machines, but they included invasive technologies that let the Guide control the wearer. The chainmail headdresses, called mantles, like the one worn by Everynne were a more advanced type of personal intelligence that did not seek to dominate its wearer, and beyond these were a realm of intelligences that had nothing to do with mankind.

Gallen studied nanotechnology and learned how war machines were built. He learned about the development of viviforms and artefs and genetically upgraded humans—and he learned of some creatures that appeared to be biological in their construction but straddled the line between creature and machine.

He learned how the World Gates tapped into the power of a singularity, a black hole, where time and space were warped to the point that they did not exist, so that those who walked through the gate were whisked in a stream of atoms and recreated at a chosen destination.

At the end of an hour, Gallen's head was sweaty. The teacher interrupted the session. "You are learning too much, too quickly," it said. "Your brain can form only a limited number of neurological connections within a given time. Now, you must rest."

"When can I come back?" Gallen asked.

"You will need to eat, nourish yourself, and return tomorrow," the teacher answered.

Gallen rose from his chair, and the world seemed to spin. He fell down, grabbed the chair to support himself, and waited until he felt steady enough to walk to a cafeteria. He ate heavily and felt gloriously elated for an hour, then found himself slightly nauseated and absentminded.

In three hours, his head began to clear. He walked through the bazaar for a bit and felt a new man. He looked at the vendors with new eyes now, appreciating the craftsmanship of their wares, understanding the utility of items that he could not have fathomed hours before. Indeed, he had become a new man. Before, he had walked through the bazaar shaking his head in wonder, certain that many items worked on principles of magic beyond his ken. Now he saw that there was no magic—only creativity and craft.

He watched the people with open eyes, marking those who wore personal intelligences. Those who wore Guides, he saw now, were often slaves or bond servants. Some submitted to the indignity of wearing a Guide in the hope of earning greater rewards.

Those who wore the chainmail headdresses called "mantles" were vastly wealthy in ways that Gallen had not imagined. Their mantles served them and were far more intelligent than the little Guides.

Merchants were frequently freemen who made themselves useful, but the vast majority of mankind were worthless in this society, and so long as they were free to eat and breed and be entertained, they seemed content.

Here on Fale, there was no need for a man with a strong back or quick wit. There was nothing a human could do that an android could not do better. So those who did not have some type of relationship with a personal intelligence—either as a possessor or as one possessed—were considered only waste, the excess of humanity. And as Gallen studied the peons of Fale, he began to see that behind the well-fed faces, there was a haunted, cramped look.

Gallen went to his camp that night and lay looking up at the stars, smelling the wind. On this world, despite all of his strivings, the people would consider him worthless, and this was something that he had never imagined.

He considered what Karthenor had done. Perhaps in the lord's mind, by giving Maggie a Guide, he had made her a person of worth, bestowed upon her some dignity. Yet such a gift was bound to carry a terrible price.

On the morning of her third day on Fale, Maggie's Guide completed the task of injecting its own artificial neural network into Maggie's nervous system. The Guide now commanded a secondary network of neurons that led through all of her extremities, so that it could control the rate of Maggie's pulse and breathing, feel with her fingers and toes, watch with her eyes, and hear with her ears.

When it finished, it reported its progress to Maggie, flashing a three-dimensional image of the new nervous system to her. A sense of panic rose in her when she saw what had happened, but the Guide did not tickle her, did not send her its calm assurances. Instead, it left her with her fears.

Now that the Guide had extended its control over her, it announced that it was free to begin its greater work of teaching Maggie the intricacies of genetic manipulation. The Guide gave her routine tasks for the day. During one marathon twenty-hour work session, Maggie extracted, sorted, and upgraded over a hundred egg cells from one woman. Afterward, she added genetic enhancements to several hundred thousand sperm. She then mixed the cells and put them in the incubator before she left for the night. Her Guide reported her daily accomplishments to Karthenor, and Karthenor set up a credit account to give her advances on the future earnings of the children she was creating. In time, one hundred children would each pay her one percent of their life earnings. In one day, she had sewn a crop that would in time reap a fortune. The Guide made sure that she understood and felt properly grateful to be so employed.

As she worked that day, there was little to distract her. In the late afternoon, she heard an explosion in a storage room. For a few moments sirens blared and dronon vanquishers rushed through the smoke-filled compound, securing the area. Maggie could hear the screams of a wounded woman. Her Guide merely informed her that terrorists had exploded a small bomb, and one of her fellow workers was injured. The Guide instructed Maggie to continue working.

Maggie was too heavily tranquilized to even consider disobeying. All through the morning, the Guide had been dumping information into her, data gleaned from genetic engineering experiments over eighteen thousand years from a hundred thousand worlds. A thousand distinct subspecies of mankind had been formed in that time, and billions of minor alterations had been tried. Maggie learned how to engineer people to live underwater, in reduced or increased gravities, or to cope with chemically altered atmospheres.

Yet the dronon Guide also taught her the glorious plans that it had for Maggie's people, and as the plans unfolded, Maggie was tickled so that she felt as if she were floundering in a pool of ecstasy. The genes that Maggie inserted into that day's batch of children were specifically designed to decrease a female's infant mortality rate and at the same time engineer a subspecies of future women to become breeders. These breeders would bear litters of ten or more children. The women that Maggie engineered would be tall, languid, wide at the hips, and would spend a great deal of time eating. They would require little in the way of cerebral stimulation—would shun mental exercise, physical stimulation. In effect, they would be sacks to bear children.

In a few days, Maggie knew that she would be allowed to work on a second subspecies of females who would be sterile workers, filled with an incredible amount of nervous energy that would be released in the joyful pursuit of labor. Other colleagues were developing males that would consist of one subspecies of dreamy-eyed artisans and creators, while another subspecies would form a caste of giant warriors with superb reflexes, immense strength, and an instinct for killing. These would burn a path across the galaxies, uniting all mankind under a common banner.

In all aspects, human society would come to emulate the more perfect dronon society, and the worlds would embrace a new, superior order.

That night, Maggie ate a quick dinner and then threw herself on her bed, contemplating the riches she had earned. Her Guide tickled her so that her blood raced at the thrill of it.

A few minutes later, her Guide announced a visitor only seconds before he entered the room.

He was a tall man, perhaps twenty-five years of age, with pale blond hair. The sculpted muscles of his chest and shoulders revealed a body type that Maggie recognized from her studies—the human equivalent of a dronon technician.

He entered her small bedroom and sat in her single chair. He watched Maggie with an intensity peculiar to those raised in dronon society. It was as if Maggie were food, and the man was feeding on her with his gleaming blue eyes.

"My name is Avik," he said. "Lord Karthenor asked me to speak with you. He feels that you are not adjusting well to your new assignments. You've been distressed, and your Guide is devoting considerable resources in an effort to make you happy. Is there anything I can do to make you happy?"

Maggie stared at him, and it was as if suddenly her Guide shut off, and she was falling, swirling toward ruin. The false euphoria left her, and she felt helpless, abused, physically exhausted. Her head was spinning with visions of the children she was creating, the mothers with their vast wombs, the legions of sexless workers, the deadly warriors with their quick wits and killer's eyes.

Maggie found herself sputtering, trying in one quick burst to express the rage and horror that the Guide had been suppressing for two days now.

"I can't . . ." she cried helplessly. She wanted to launch herself at Avik, claw his eyes out, but the Guide would not let her.

Avik took her hands, held them. "What you need," he said softly, "is another human to help you cope with this change."

Maggie glared at him and thought, *If there were another human in this room, I would* do *that.* She was painfully aware that Avik's enhancements made him unlike other men. He had a dreamy look in his eyes, a soft-spoken nature, a predisposition to move his hands as he spoke. In every way he was a dronon technician, as distinct in his characteristics as a bloodhound would be among mongrels. Yet Maggie could not hate him for something he could not change.

"Set me free," Maggie pleaded. "I can't live the way you want me to."

"Of course you can," Avik said. "It takes time, but you can become dronon. In fact, you have no choice in the matter. Believe me, you will find peace among us."

"I can't," Maggie said. "Don't you see how different they are from us? We weren't meant to live like the dronon."

"The differences between us and the dronon are superficial," Avik said. "They have chitin, we have skin. But we are both a species of conquerors, and both of us found the need to overwhelm nature, expand our domain to the stars. Do you realize how few sentient species have done this?"

"We are nothing like them!" Maggie shouted. "If we were, they wouldn't need to force us into their castes. . . ."

Avik smiled, sat back smugly. "They are not forcing us into castes. Don't you see what they are doing? They are merely enhancing the differences that already exist between us. Even in the natural state, some of your men are born to be warriors. The urge to compete in them is so overwhelming that they can hardly control it." Maggie suddenly thought of Gallen. "And others of your men are like me, dreamers and creators. Some of your people are workers—unable to stop, unable to enjoy any other facet of life but the workplace. And some of you are nurturers, breeders who find comfort in sprawling families and take joy in raising children. And some of you are born to become leaders. In every age of humanity, it has been this way. The hive mind is within us, just as it is within the dronon. Believe me, once your people make the transition to our order, your children will enjoy greater peace and prosperity than they have ever known."

It was disconcerting in a way to watch Avik, so human in form, talk about humans as if they were alien. But she could see the alienness in his eyes, in the hungry way he watched her.

"But you have no freedom. Our children will have no choice in their decisions," Maggie shouted. She found herself shaking with rage, her muscles spasming.

"Perhaps we lose a little," Avik countered, "but we gain much in return. We have no crime on dronon worlds, for the Guides do not allow it. We have no confusion over making simple choices. We don't spend vast portions of our youth uselessly vacillating as we struggle to learn what we shall become. Among the hives, each child knows what he or she will do as an adult. We are bred to our positions, and we *do* find peace, a peace that is greater and more profound than any you can imagine. It may appear to be a contradiction, but though our laws seem restrictive to you, they free us to find that peace." Avik spoke evenly, a thin sheen of sweat on his forehead. Maggie looked into his wild eyes, wanted to shout him down, yet he so obviously believed in the dronon order, she realized that to argue would be futile.

Still, she could not resist the temptation to say more. "Avik, don't you see—your order doesn't really free you, it merely limits you. You could choose to be more than an architect—you could become anything you want: a father, a leader, a warrior. The dronon haven't freed you. They've merely made you comfortable. You have become content slaves, when you could be gods."

Avik's nostrils flared. Maggie could see that she'd struck a chord. He backed up in his chair, looked at her appraisingly. "You will never speak against the order again."

Maggie tried to argue, but the Guide stopped her tongue and would not let her speak, so that his words seemed to carry the weight of a prophecy.

Avik got up from his chair, put his hands on her shoulders and looked into her eyes. "I will instruct your Guide to continue tutoring you in the ways of the dronon, and in your job. Each time you think of the order, your Guide will give you comfort, and perhaps in this way, over time, you will learn to love the order. Tomorrow you will begin working on the Adoration Project, and as you learn to love our order, you will in turn be teaching others to love it. Maggie, don't fight us. You can't win, and you might get hurt in the struggle."

He cupped her chin in one hand, and her Guide sent her a spasm of lust that knotted her stomach and made her face burn. She tried to fight it, to give vent to her anger, but she realized that Avik was controlling her Guide, forcing this emotion on her. "You're such a pretty thing. I like red hair. Lord Karthenor has asked me to give you physical companionship. You will find that having sex while wearing a Guide is more compelling than anything you have ever dreamed. No beast in heat will ever find greater satisfaction than you will find with me this night."

Maggie locked her legs together and curled up in a ball on the bed. She knew that fighting would be no use. Her Guide could take control of her muscles at any moment, force her to open her legs and give herself to him. But she needed to do this, to commit one small act of defiance.

Avik grinned. "So, is that to be the way of it? Then I'll leave you to this lust, and it shall keep you company tonight. Tomorrow, when I return and make the offer again, you will be grateful."

Avik left the room. The lights dimmed as he exited, and Maggie was left in pain, screaming inside, aching for Gallen.

• • •

Gallen returned to the pidc that morning, put on the instruction hood. "Teach me about mankind," he said. The teacher began with genetics and showed the path of evolution, including ancient species of mammals and dinosaurs whose DNA had been salvaged and reproduced on many worlds. The teacher taught him the genetic structure of man, showing how genetic engineers had developed mankind into over a thousand distinct subspecies, each bred to a specific purpose, to live in a specific environment.

He learned the schemes humans used to achieve life extension. Thousands of drugs and procedures had been developed to cheat death. Most who died had their consciousness transmitted to virtual heavens that existed within computers. Some had their memories downloaded to machines, like the artefs, which were simply colonies of self-replicating nanotech devices. The most ambitious plans to beat death involved life extensions coupled with downloading memories into clones. Such plans culminated in virtual immortality—a commodity that had once been reserved for the most deserving but now available only to the wealthiest.

Last of all, the teacher showed Gallen the crowning achievement of genetic manipulation, the Tharrin, a race fashioned to embody nobility and virtue, a race designed to integrate fully with personal intelligences without losing their humanity. The Tharrin were to be the leaders and judges of mankind, a subspecies that would control the naval fleets, the police forces, and the courts of a million worlds.

The Tharrin's physical features embodied strength and perfection. Certain glands secreted pheromones that attracted other humans so that the Tharrin constantly found themselves at the center of attention. Yet the Tharrin seldom became conceited. They did not see themselves as leaders or judges, but as the servants of mankind.

Gallen was not surprised when an image of a Tharrin formed in his mind, and he recognized Everynne in a thousand details.

Yet the Tharrin represented only half of a human/machine intellect. The machine half, the planet-sized omni-minds, stored information on the societies, moral codes, and political factions of tens of thousands of worlds. All such information was used when debating criminal and civil suits, but the data was all considered to be obsolete when passing a judgment. When a Tharrin passed judgment, it did so based on information stored in its omni-mind, but human empathy and understanding were meant to vitiate judgment. In the end, the wise and compassionate Tharrin ruled from the heart.

In his lessons, Gallen learned the brief history of Fale, how here the Tharrin ruler Semarritte had been overthrown by the alien dronon.

For decades, the dronon had presented a threat to mankind, but Semarritte and her Tharrin advisors refused to go to war. Semarritte had created more guardians to protect her realm—creatures who were as much nanotech machine as flesh, creatures who could be controlled only through her omni-mind. Yet always Semarritte and the Tharrin had hoped that the humans and dronon might someday learn to live together in peace. They could not reconcile themselves to the horrors that would result from an interspecies war.

But in a surprise attack, dronon technicians won control of Semarritte's omni-mind, then manipulated her fleets and guardians, sending them to war against their human creators. Then the dronon killed Semarritte herself and murdered every Tharrin who fell into their hands.

Gallen had to rest and eat again, but he came back late that night and questioned his teacher on matters of law, hoping that he would find some legal means of freeing Maggie. Under the old Tharrin law, slave-taking had been criminal. But under dronon law, Lord Karthenor could capture or buy servants who were not claimed by more powerful lords. Since his work ranked as a top priority among the dronon, he was free to choose servants from ninety percent of the population.

Seeing that he had no legal recourse, Gallen sought information on current war and battle techniques, but the teacher let him study only some very basic self-defense. Obviously, the dronon controlled this teaching machine to some degree, and they would not let it teach tactics that might be used against them.

In his last session that evening, Gallen downloaded a map of Toohkansay. That night, he dragged himself back to the woods late. Orick had returned to the camp.

"I searched all around the spot where we entered," Orick said. "I couldn't smell Everynne anywhere. I couldn't find any other cities."

"I know." Gallen sighed. "Toohkansay is the only city for—" he converted kilometers to miles in his head "—eighty miles."

"I don't understand," Orick said heavily. "We all went in the same gate, but we didn't come out at the same place."

"The making of gate keys is hard," Gallen said, "and our key was stolen from someone who may have fashioned an imperfect key. Obviously, it dropped us off in the wrong spot. Each gate leads to only one planet, so I'm certain we are on the right world, but Fale is a big place. We might be two miles from Everynne, or ten thousand. There is no way to tell."

Orick studied Gallen. "You're certain of this, are you?"

"Aye, very sure," Gallen said.

"What else did you learn in the city?"

Gallen could not begin to answer. He had studied handwritten books in Tihrglas, but in only a few hours here on Fale, the equivalent of a thousand volumes of information had been dumped into his head. How could he explain it?

"I went to a library," Gallen said. "I learned some things from a teaching machine, like a Guide—but this machine doesn't control your actions. I learned so much that I can't begin to tell you everything. But I can take you there tomorrow, if you have a mind to learn something."

"I'll not have one of their devices twisting my brain, thank you!" Orick growled. "I saw what it did to Maggie!"

"It's not the same," Gallen said. "This is a different kind of machine. It won't hurt you."

"Won't hurt me, eh?" Orick said. "What have they done to you? There's a new look in your eyes, Gallen O'Day. You're not the same man who left here two days ago. You can't tell me that you're the same, can you?"

"No," Gallen said. "I'm not the same." He reflected for a moment. Only a few days before, Everynne had told him that she found the naivete of his world to be refreshing. She'd wished that all worlds could be so innocent. And now Gallen lived in a much larger universe, a universe where there was no distinct boundary between man and machine, where immortals wielded vast power over entire worlds, where alien races battled the thousand sub-species of mankind for dominance in three separate galaxies.

Gallen could have described the situation to Orick, but he knew Orick wanted to be a priest. He wanted to sustain the faith of those in Tihrglas, ensure the continuation of the status quo, and Gallen saw that this too was a valuable thing. In one small corner of the galaxy there could be sweet, bliss-ful ignorance. In one small corner of the galaxy, adults could remain chil-dren. Knowledge carries its own price.

"I have learned some of the lore of the sidhe," Gallen said at last. "Not a lot, but perhaps enough. I'm going to try to steal Maggie back."

In a darkened room in the city of Toohkansay, nine lords of Fale sat around a table in their black robes and boots. Their masked faces shone in shades of crimson starlight. Veriasse and Everynne sat with them, both masked and cloaked as lords, Everynne in a pale blue mask, Veriasse in aquamarine. Though they had been on the planet for less than an hour, Veriasse had set up this meeting nearly five years earlier, and as Everynne watched her guardian, she could see that he was tense to the snapping point. His back was rigidly straight, and his mask revealed his profound worry.

All their years of plotting came to this. If anyone down the long trail of freedom fighters had betrayed them, now was when they would be arrested. And everyone in the room expected to be arrested: one of their number had not been seen in two days. Surely, the dronon had captured him, wrung his secrets from him. Because of this, they had been forced to change the meet-ing place at the last moment.

One crimson lord, a woman whose name Everynne did not even know, pulled from the depths of her robe a small glass globe, a yellow sphere that could easily fit in Everynne's palm or in a pocket. "As Lord of the Techni-cians of Fale, I freely give you this in behalf of my people," the woman said. "Use it wisely, if you must use it at all."

Everynne took the globe, held it in her palm. It was as heavy as lead. In-side, was a small dark cloud at the machine's core—a housing where the nanotech components were stored, along with a small explosive charge designed to crack the globe and set its microscopic inhabitants free. In ages past, only a few weapons like this had ever been used. People called it "the Terror." It seemed only right to Everynne that something which could destroy a world would be so gravid, so weighty.

"How fast will it work?" Everynne asked.

The crimson lady's mask showed sadness. "The Terrors reproduce at an explosive rate. We designed them to seek out carbon molecules and form graphite. On a living planet, every animal, every plant, the atmosphere itself will be destroyed. Only the Terrors will survive for more than a day. They will appear as a blue shimmering cloud, moving outward through the sky at two thousand kilometers per hour. On the ground and in the sea, they move somewhat faster. The Terrors would destroy most worlds within a matter of twelve to eighteen hours."

Everynne watched the woman's face. The crimson lady was old, centuries old, and in that time she had probably learned to control her emotions exquisitely, yet her voice cracked as she spoke of the machine's capacity for genocide.

"And how fast could this destroy Dronon?" Veriasse asked. "Will the Terrors be slowed significantly by being forced to reproduce on such a dry, desolate world?"

Even as Veriasse asked the question, Everynne cringed. The thought that the weapon might actually be used disturbed her. Time and again, she had begged Veriasse not to fashion such a weapon, to create only a simulated Terror. If the glass case broke, an entire planet would be destroyed. But Veriasse would not hear her arguments. He planned to take the Terror to the planet Dronon itself. He wanted the Golden Queen to fear him, and the only way he could arouse such fear was if the dronon knew that a working Terror lay hidden on their world.

But sometimes at night, Everynne wondered if he had a hidden agenda. If the Golden Queen refused to concede to his demands, she wondered, would Veriasse hesitate to lay the planet Dronon to waste?

"Dronon's atmosphere is heavier in carbon dioxide than most. The Terrors will find it to their taste."

Another of the masked lords smiled cruelly and said, "I designed the package with Dronon in mind. The planet can be terminated in six hours and fourteen minutes. Just make sure that you are near the imperial lair when you set it off."

Everynne was disturbed by the man's maleficent air. It pained her to see her people given over to such hatred. Though she knew that the dronons had killed her own mother, Everynne did not hate them. She understood them too well, understood their need for order at any cost, their instinctive desire to expand their territories and control their environment. "Let us have no more talk of genocide," Everynne said. "Even if we tried to fight the dronon on such terms, they would be forced to retaliate. In such a war, there can be no victors."

"Of course, Our Lady," the crimson lords agreed, and almost as one they breathed a sigh of relief. They had spoken treasonous words and had not been arrested. Everynne could feel the clouds of doubt and fear lifting from her. For a long moment, they all sat and simply looked at one another around the table. For five years the crimson lords had worked, and now their part was done. Everynne watched them relax and wanted only to relax with them, take one last rest before her part in the great work began.

"We must go now," Veriasse said. Everynne knew he was right. They had left Tihrglas only an hour ago. The vanquishers could transmit news of their escape over tachyon waves. Within another few hours, word of their escape would reach Fale, and the vanquishers would seek to block all of Everynne's escape routes.

"Wait, please," the crimson lady begged. "I have one last favor to ask before you leave."

"Which is?" Everynne said.

"Your face," the crimson lady asked. "Once, before you leave, I want to see your face."

On Fale, the lords never went unmasked in public. It was a tradition millennia old. The crimson lady would never have asked such a favor of one of her own neighbors. Everynne had little time to spare, but these people had risked so much for her that she could not resist.

She peeled off her pale blue mask, and the lords stared at her in awe for a moment. "You are truly a queen among the Tharrin," the crimson lady said. Everynne felt sick at the words. After all, what was a queen among the Tharrin but a specific set of genetic codes given to those who were born to be leaders? It was nothing she had done, nothing she had earned. Her genetic makeup gave her a certain sculpted beauty, a regal air, a measure of charisma and wit that probably would never have been duplicated in nature. Yet Everynne saw all of this as a sham. It was simply a station she was born to. Her flesh was the clothing she wore.

The crimson lady peeled off her own mask, showed herself to be a handsome, aging woman with penetrating gray eyes. "My name is Atheremis, and it has been my pleasure to serve you. I will never betray you," she said.

One by one, the other crimson lords around the room also peeled back their masks, spoke their names and their gratitude.

That is when Everynne knew for sure that they would kill themselves. If they had not been planning suicide, Everynne was sure that they would not have revealed themselves. But one of their number was missing, so they were choosing to die now by their own hands rather than risk that they might be captured and forced to reveal damning evidence.

The crimson lady cried; tears rolled down her cheeks. Everynne wanted to stay with them a little longer, hoping to keep them alive. If looking into her face gave them pleasure, then she would stand here for hours. But Veriasse took her elbow, and whispered, "Come, we must hurry."

Together they walked from the darkened chamber and headed down a long green corridor past the shops and apartments of Toohkansay. Only Everynne's mask hid the fact that she was sobbing inside.

They had hardly gone a hundred meters when a blinding flash of light erupted behind them, and the blast from the explosion buffeted their robes like a strong wind. Sirens began to wail, and citizens of the city rushed toward the blast, searching for victims. The living walls of the city did not catch fire, but the distinctive smell of cooked vegetable matter filled the smoking hallways.

They hurried to a cantina on the edge of town where the scent of food beguiled them. Everynne had not eaten for nearly twenty hours, so they went through the dispensary line and grabbed some rolls, then hurried out to a waiting shuttle, a beat up old magcar that would not draw undue attention.

They hopped over the doors, and Veriasse unfolded a thin map and pushed a button until *Fale* appeared on the legend of the world. The map showed them at the edge of Toohkansay, and a three-dimensional image showed the land around them for hundreds of kilometers. There were three gates within that range, but only Veriasse had traveled the Maze of Worlds enough to know which planet each gate would lead to. "This gate here," Veriasse said, pointing to the most distant of the three, "leads to Cyannesse. We will be safe there."

Everynne took the stick and gunned the thrusters. The car raised several inches on a magnetic wave, and she piloted the vehicle slowly at first, fearing that foot travelers might be on the road so close to Toohkansay.

For ten minutes they drove past the yawning farms that sprawled along the calm river. Huge, spiderlike harvesters were at work, cultivating the fields. They turned a wide bend, and Everynne was just ready to raise the windshields so that she could speed up when she saw a bear ahead. It leapt from the road into the woods.

"That's Orick!" she said, reversing thrusters.

"It can't be," Veriasse said. "It's just a bear."

"I'm sure of it." The magcar slowed and idled beside the trees. She gazed into the woods, up a slight rise where white rocks lay in a jumble. There was no sign of Orick—only prints among the fallen leaves that the bear had made as it bowled through the trees. Everynne wondered if it had been a trick of her imagination, yet she let the magcar hover on the road. Uphill, the nose of a bear poked cautiously over some bushes to watch her.

"You're right," she said, distracted. She had last seen Orick only slightly more than an hour ago on a planet nearly six hundred light-years away. Somehow, that recent image must have burned into her subconscious so that she imagined that this bear looked just like Orick.

She gunned the thrusters and the magcar rose and began to move forward slowly. She glanced back, and the bear stood up on its hind legs, sniffing the air.

It yelled, "Everynne? Is that you?"

She slammed on the reverse thrusters.

"Orick?" Veriasse called. The bear dropped to all fours and ran toward them with astonishing speed.

"It's you!" Orick shouted. "Where have you been? I've been searching for you everywhere! It's been days!"

Veriasse and Everynne looked at each other. "What do you mean, 'days'?" Everynne asked. "We left Tihrglas less than two hours ago. How did you get here?"

"Gallen stole a key from the dronon. He was afraid they would use it to catch you. When we got here, we couldn't find any sign of you. Maggie's been kidnapped, and we can't get her back. Gallen and I have been here for nearly four days!"

"The dronon tried to make a key?" Veriasse asked, incredulous. "Only a great fool—or a very desperate person—would try to make his own key to the Maze of Worlds. That explains how you got here before us. Your key is flawed."

"You mean to say we got here four days early because of a busted key?"

"Of course," Everynne said realizing what had happened. "The gates move us from one planet to another faster than the speed of light—but any method of locomotion that can do that can also be used to send things into the past, or the future."

"Still," Veriasse said, "it's a wonder that they broke our access codes at all. We will have to re-tool the gates." Veriasse looked down at the chronometer on the magcar. "We have to go, Everynne."

"Wait a moment," Everynne said. "They need our help."

Anger flashed in Veriasse's eyes. "Many people need your help. You cannot risk staying in enemy territory for *these*."

Everynne looked at Orick. The bear was dirty, had lost a little weight. The whites of his eyes were wide. "I was born to be the Servant of All," she said. "I will take care of these three now, because they need me now."

"Nine people just sacrificed their lives for you back in town!" Veriasse countered. "You can't stay here and risk making that sacrifice invalid. Leave these three. What's the difference? It is an acceptable loss."

"Acceptable to who? To you, perhaps, but not to me. Those nine gave their lives voluntarily for something they understood—" Everynne answered. "These three want to live, and they serve us with innocent hearts. We must give them a little time—fifteen minutes."

Everynne turned to Orick. "Where is Gallen?"

"Hiding in the woods," Orick answered. "I'll get him." He spun and galloped uphill.

"We don't have time for this," Veriasse told Everynne after Orick hurried into the brush. "Every second of delay places you in greater jeopardy. Can't you feel the worlds slipping from your grasp?"

"Right thoughts. Right words. Right actions. Isn't that the credo you taught me?" Everynne said. "Right actions. Always do what is right. That's what I'm trying to do now."

"I know," Veriasse said more softly. "When we win back your inheritance, you will truly be worthy of the title Servant of All. But think: at this moment, you must choose between two goods. The right action is to choose the greater good."

Everynne closed her eyes. "No, you cannot prove to me that fifteen minutes will make a difference. I'll serve my friends here to the best of my ability, and afterward I'll serve the rest of humanity.

"Veriasse, if not for Gallen stealing that key, we would have jumped out of the gate and found the whole planet mobilized against us. We must help them—you must help them. See, here comes Gallen now."

Gallen and Orick raced through the trees. The young man was dressed in the swirling greens and blues of a merchant of Fale, yet his garments were stained from the camp and his hair was unkempt. He breathed hard as he rushed up to the magcar.

"Orick says that Maggie has been kidnapped," Everynne said. "Do you know who took her?"

"A man named Karthenor, Lord of the Aberlains," Gallen panted. "I've scouted the city. I plan to get her back."

Everynne marveled that such a simple man could have so much faith in himself.

"If Maggie has been taken by Karthenor," Veriasse said, "she is in the hands of a most unscrupulous man. For enough money, he might sell her back to you—or he might become curious and send you to his interrogators to find out why you want her. With the right equipment, you could free her from her Guide and steal her back, but that would be very dangerous to attempt. Both plans carry their risks, and it seems to me that in any event you are likely to fail."

Everynne hesitated to tell them the most logical course of action. She wetted her lips with her tongue. "Gallen, Orick," she said slowly, "would you be willing to leave Maggie behind, come away with me through the Maze of Worlds?"

"What?" Gallen asked, incredulous.

Everynne tried to phrase her argument as succinctly as possible. "I am going to try to overthrow the dronons. If I succeed, then we can rescue Maggie. If, on the other hand, I do not succeed, she will become a valuable member of dronon society, and in the long run she will be better off where she is. So, I ask you again: do you two want to come with me?"

Gallen and Orick looked at each other. "No," Gallen said. "We can't do that. We'll stay and see what we can do to get Maggie free."

Everynne nodded. "I understand," she said heavily. "Then we will both do what we must, even though it takes us on different paths." She turned to Veriasse. "Do you have allies here that might help him?"

"I had few allies here," Veriasse said. "And all of them are dead now. Gallen must forge ahead on his own. The first thing he should do is go learn all that he can about our world."

"I've already been to the pidc," Gallen said. Everynne looked into his eyes, saw that it was true. There was a burden in his eyes, as if he knew too much.

"The pidc can teach you many things, but it is still under dronon control," Veriasse said. "Much of our technology is kept secret. Gallen, if you want to free Maggie, you will have to do it without her knowledge. The Guide sees through her eyes, hears with her ears, and it can transmit messages to other Guides. It will be your greatest enemy, and since it controls Maggie, she will fight you herself if you try to rescue her while she's still connected to the Guide. You will need the help of a Guide-maker to learn how to dismantle the thing.

"At the same time, security around the aberlains will be very tight. Microscopic cameras will be hidden in the main corridors, and motion detectors will be at every window. I doubt that you can make it into the compound undetected. Dronon vanquishers themselves will probably patrol the compound, and they are very dangerous. You will need weapons and an escape plan.

"Gallen, don't be in a hurry to rescue her. This will require careful planning and research."

Veriasse looked down at the chronometer on the magcar. "Everynne, my child, we really must go now, before the vanquishers block our exit."

Everynne gritted her teeth. Veriasse had just outlined an impossible task for Gallen—a task that only Veriasse himself could pull off. She glanced at Gallen, ashamed to be leaving, and said, "Good luck."

"What world will you be going to next?" Gallen asked. "Maybe we will follow you there?"

Everynne considered lying. She had to protect herself from possible danger, yet she knew that Gallen must be feeling lost and alone. As a Tharrin, her presence gave him a sense of comfort that he could not find elsewhere. And the world she was going to was beyond enemy lines.

"Cyannesse is its name," she said. "The gate lies nearly three hundred miles north of here, about a quarter of a mile off the right-hand side of the road. When you put your key up to the gate, it will glow golden. That's how you know you have the right destination."

Gallen looked at her longingly, and Everynne could not bear to watch him any longer. "Take care of yourselves," she said. She gunned the thrusters and headed out.

Nine

Gallen watched Everynne and Veriasse glide off through the forest in their magcar. Orick grumbled and pawed the ground, raking leaves as if he were frustrated. "What now?" he asked. "Do you have a plan to save Maggie?"

Gallen considered. He had few resources: a couple of knives, a key to unlock the Maze of Worlds. A few days before, he'd told Everynne that imagination was the measure of a man, but now he wondered if that were true.

"You heard Veriasse," Gallen said. "If we try to rescue her, the Guide will warn Karthenor. Our only hope is to take her without her or her Guide knowing of it."

"Can we trick the Guide?"

"I doubt it," Gallen said. "It's probably smarter than we are. But I may be able to figure out some way to lure Maggie out of the city at Karthenor's request, so that the other Guides can't hear her talk."

"Och, this sounds like a *grand* plan!" Orick said. "Why, it's no plan at all, that's what it is."

Orick was right, at least for the moment. "We'll have to find a way to disable the Guide," Gallen said. "I'll have to find a Guide-maker."

"So, what are you going to do," Orick asked, "walk right into a shop and ask the fellow, 'By the way, how can I break one of those things?' and then hope he answers you square?"

"No," Gallen said. He knew the means had to be close by. He thought, If you were the most creative bodyguard in the world, Gallen O'Day, what would you do? He waited for a moment, and a familiar thrill coursed through him. He knew the answer. "I'm going to go speak to a past employee of the company that makes the Guides. A dead employee, to be precise."

"What?" Orick shouted.

"When we first went into town, and I was wandering around on my own, I met a merchant who sells a machine that lets you talk to the dead, so long as they're properly embalmed and haven't rotted too much."

"And what if you can't find a dead employee handy?" Orick said. "What then?"

"Well, then I'd stick a knife in an employee and make him dead!" Gallen shouted, furious at Orick's exasperating mood.

"Fine!" Orick growled. "That's fine. I was just asking."

It was early morning. Kiss-me-quick birds sang in the trees, hopping from bush to bush, their green wings flashing.

"I think I'll go ask about this now, in fact," Gallen answered.

"What about me?" Orick asked. "You can't leave me here again."

"And I can't take you with me. Orick, there are some things we'll need—food, shelter, clothing, weapons. You're in charge of finding them and setting up a proper camp. We might be stuck here awhile."

"Right," Orick said.

Gallen hunched his shoulders. His muscles were tight from the tension, and suddenly he longed to be back home in Tihrglas, guarding some merchant's wagon. Hell, on any day of the week, he'd rather take on ten highwaymen single-handed. Ah, for the good old days.

He ambled back to Toohkansay and made his way to the merchant quarters. There, he sold the shillings from his purse along with a bead necklace to a dealer in exotic alien artifacts.

Then he went to the merchant who sold "Bereavement Hoods," and began to haggle. Gallen didn't have enough money to buy the thing. The hoods were designed for those who wanted to "Share those last precious thoughts with the recently departed." Gallen cried and put on a show, talking about his dear sister who had died, until he finally convinced the merchant to rent him a hood.

"Now you understand," the merchant warned, "that your sister is dead. She'll know who you are, and she'll be able to talk through the speaker in the hood, but she won't gain any new memories. If you visit her once, she'll forget all about it, even if you return five minutes later."

Gallen nodded, but the merchant drove the point home until Gallen finally asked, "What are you really telling me?"

"Well," the merchant finally admitted, "it's just that the dead are always surprised and happy to be visited, and they'll tell you about the same fond memories time and again. They tend to get . . . repetitive."

"So they get boring," Gallen accused.

"Most of them, yes," the merchant admitted reluctantly.

When Gallen finished, he went to the pidc, accessed the public records to find out who in Toohkansay made Guides, and found that they were made under the auspices of a Lord Pallatine. Gallen accessed Pallatine's files, got a list of his workers for the past ten years. By checking vital statistics for each worker, he found that sure enough, a fellow named Brevin Mackalrey had been a corpse for less than three months, and poor Brevin was down deep in the crypts under the city, kept in cold storage so that his widow could speak to him on occasion.

Gallen hurried down a long series of subterranean corridors to pay a visit to poor old Brevin. The crypt was a dark, desolate place, with only a few visitors. Corpses were stacked in long rows, sleeping in glass coffins that could be pulled out for display. The temperature in the crypt was near freezing, and perhaps that tended to keep the mourners' visits short. The bodies were stored for a year before final interment. Still, Gallen was surprised to see hundreds of bodies and only five people visiting them. Gallen searched alphabetically until he found Brevin Mackalrey, pulled the man out.

The glass coffin was fogged; icy crystals shaped like fern leaves had built up under the glass lid. Gallen opened the lid. Mr. Mackalrey did not look so good. His face was purple and swollen. He wore only a pair of white shorts. He had dark hair, a scraggly beard, and legs that were knobby and bowed. Gallen decided that this particular fellow probably hadn't looked so good even when he was alive.

Gallen pulled up the fellow's near-frozen head and placed the hood on. The hood was made of some metallic cloth, and electromagnetic waves from the hood stimulated the brain cells of the dead. As the dead man tried to speak, the cloth registered the attempted stimulation of the cerebral cortex and translated the dead man's thoughts into words. The words were then spoken in a dull monotone from a small speaker.

Gallen activated the hood, waited for a few moments, then said, "Brevin, Brevin, can you hear me, man?"

"I hear you," the speaker said. "But I can't see you. Who are you?"

"My name's Gallen O'Day, and I came to ask your help on a small matter. My sister has a Guide on, and she can't get it off. I was wondering if you could tell me how to get one of them buggers off."

"She's wearing a Guide?" Brevin asked. A mourner passed Gallen, heading down the aisle of coffins.

"Aye, that's what I said," Gallen whispered, hunching low. "Is there any way to get it off?"

"Is it a slave Guide?" Brevin asked.

"Of course it's a slave Guide," Gallen hissed. "Otherwise, we'd be able to get it off."

"If she's a slave, it would be wrong for me to help you. I could get into trouble."

"Well," Gallen drawled, "how much trouble can you get into? You're already dead!"

"Dead? How did I die?"

"You fell off a horse, I think," Gallen said. "Either that, or you choked on a chicken bone."

"Oh," Brevin said. "I can't help you. I would be penalized."

"Who would know that you'd told me?" Gallen said.

"Go away, or I'll call the authorities," Brevin's microphone yelped.

"How are you going to call the authorities?" Gallen asked. "You're dead, I tell you."

Brevin went silent for several moments, and Gallen said, "Come on, answer me you damned corpse! How do I get the Guide off?"

Brevin didn't answer, and Gallen began looking about, wondering what kind of barter chip he might use. He whispered, "You're dead, do you understand me, Brevin? You're dead. You got no more worries, no more fears. If there was one thing in the world I could give you, what would you want?"

"I'm cold. Go away," Brevin retorted.

"I'll give you that," Gallen said. "I'm going away. But first I want you to tell me how to take a Guide off of someone without setting off any alarms."

Brevin didn't answer, and Gallen decided to bully him into it. "Look," he said. "I hate to have to do this to you, but you've got to answer me."

Gallen took the dead man's pinky finger and bent it back at an excruciating angle until he feared it might snap. "There now," Gallen said. "How does that feel?"

"How does what feel?" Brevin asked.

Gallen saw that torture was no use. The dead man couldn't feel a thing.

Gallen scratched his head, decided on another tact. "All right, you've pushed me too far. I didn't want to have to tell you this, but the reason you're so damned cold is because you're lying in this coffin naked. Did you know that?"

"Naked?" Brevin asked, dismayed.

"Yes," Gallen assured him. "You're bare-assed naked. At this very moment, I'm looking at your penis, and I've got to tell you that it's not a pretty sight. You were never well-endowed in the first place, but now you're all shriveled down to the size of a pinhead. Did you know that?"

Brevin emitted a low moan, and Gallen continued. "Now, not only are you bare-assed naked," Gallen said, "but I'll tell you what I'm going to do. I'm going to drag your naked carcass upstairs and leave you in a hallway tonight, and every person who walks by is going to see what a shamefully inadequate organ you have. It will be an embarrassment to your whole family, I'm telling you. Everyone in Toohkansay will see your shrunken pud, and when they do, they'll look at your wife and smile in a knowing way, and wonder, 'How could she have stayed with that fellow all those years, what with him being so sorrowfully lacking?' So tell me, my friend, what do you think of that?"

"No," Brevin said. "Please!"

"You know what you have to do," Gallen said. "Just a few small words is all I'm asking. Give me those words, and I'll put your pants on and leave you with your dignity intact. What do you say? You do me a favor, and I'll do you a favor."

Brevin seemed to think for a moment. "A universal Guide extractor can take off the Guide. Simply point the rod at the slave in question and press the blue button. Lord Pallatine has three of them locked in the security vault."

"Tell me about this vault," Gallen said. "How would I get into it?"

"You can't. Lord Pallatine has an electronic key, but the vault is equipped with a personal intelligence that will only open when it recognizes that Pallatine alone has come to open it."

"So I don't have access to all that fancy equipment," Gallen said. "I just want to free my sister, quick and easy, and I don't want to get caught. Surely you know how to do it."

Brevin's stomach muscles twitched, and for a moment Gallen feared that he would sit up, even though he was stiff as a twig. But the dead man said quickly, "First, you will need to catch her unawares. You should take her when she's asleep. If you can't take her in her sleep, you need to immobilize her so the Guide can't fight you. It will take control of her body at the first sign of danger. If you can, perform the abduction in a room that has metal walls to block any transmissions the Guide might send. Then insert a knife at the back of the Guide near the base of the skull. You will have to cut through two small wires. This will sever the Guide's neural connection to the victim. When you're done, destroy the Guide."

"What do you mean destroy it?"

"Put it in acid, or crush it, or burn it. It must be thoroughly pulverized on the atomic level."

"What if the Guide isn't thoroughly destroyed?" Gallen asked, half certain of the answer.

"If the Guide is retrieved, its memory will identify you."

"Thank you, Brevin. May you rest in eternal peace. I've already got your pants back on you, and all your secrets are safe with me," Gallen said. He sat back and thought. He knew where Karthenor's aberlains slept, in apartments near the cantina with windows over the river. He would have to work quickly—get in through the window and remove the Guide before the vanquishers responded to the alarm from the motion detectors at the window. Afterward, a simple toss could send the Guide off into the muddy deep. It would take the vanquishers some time to retrieve the Guide from the water. By then, Gallen imagined he could be well away from Toohkansay, on the trail to another gate and a new world.

He removed the bereavement hood, closed Brevin's coffin, and shoved it back into its chamber. He knew that he couldn't leave poor little Maggie any longer than necessary. He stared at the black bereavement hood. Its metallic cloth was of a heavy weave. Perhaps not as thick as the walls of a room, but it might block radio transmissions from a Guide.

Gallen could only hope.

The road from Toohkansay to the Cyannesse gate was clear most of the way, yet Everynne drove with a heavy heart, a sinking feeling of guilt. She had left nine ardent supporters dead behind her and had left Gallen, Orick, and Maggie to fend for themselves in matters beyond their understanding.

Yet she drove on. Everynne skirted two smaller towns in an hour, barely slowing the magcar. When she was four hundred and eighty-one kilometers north of Toohkansay, the land began turning to desert, a sandy plain where only a few volcanic flows marred the surface.

This gate, unlike most, was in open view of the highway. Perhaps ten thousand years earlier, when the gate was built, the landscape had been different. The gate may have been hidden in a forest or swamp, but now it was in open view of the road. Even though the road was nearly empty of traffic,

Everynne did not relish the idea of entering from a place where she would be in view of prospective witnesses.

She began to slow the magcar, but Veriasse waved his hand and whispered, "Keep going! Keep going! Don't stop. Don't even slow!"

She engaged the thruster to speed up, and on her rearview display saw six giant humanoid figures rise up from some camouflaged pit out near the gate. Vanquishers had been hiding, and now were watching them pass, perhaps wondering if they should give chase. If six of them were secluded there, many more would also be hiding.

"How did you spot them?" Everynne asked when they were far down the road.

"I didn't," Veriasse said. "I just felt uncomfortable. If Maggie was captured three days ago, then the authorities may have been expecting us. They've had plenty of time to seal off the gates and prevent our escape. In another hour, they will simply receive confirmation of our escape from Tihrglas, and matters will be worse."

"What will we do?" Everynne asked. She looked over to Veriasse. He had been her mother's protector for six thousand years. He was used to intrigue and danger in a way that she hoped she never would have to be.

"We will need to form some new allies here. We won't get through that gate without an armed conflict." He sighed. "I'd say that the city of Guianne is our best hope. It's about five hundred kilometers south and ninety kilometers east of here."

"Where Mother was killed?" Everynne asked.

Veriasse nodded slightly. "There is a shrine to her memory. We shall go and see if anyone tends it. Perhaps our allies will make themselves known to us."

Everynne swallowed hard, trying not to cry. She had never seen her mother's resting place. Of all the worlds they had visited, Everynne had harbored only one secret wish: to see her mother's tomb. And if Everynne died on this journey, as long as she saw her mother's tomb first, then she would feel that she had accomplished at least one significant act.

"I know where three allies are," Everynne said. "They're right on our way, and at this moment, they need our help."

Veriasse sighed deeply. "You are right, of course. We'll stop and get them. But I won't let you put yourself in jeopardy. If they are in trouble, I will try to rescue them. And if I fail, you must promise to go on without me."

"I promise." Everynne's heart leapt. She had not felt right about leaving Maggie in captivity. She turned the magcar around, and as she soared over the highway toward Toohkansay, she felt light and free.

Two hours later, Veriasse crept over the hill to Gallen's camp. The early afternoon sunlight slanting through the trees dappled the leaves in purple and scarlet. Veriasse had pulled the magcar off the highway, hidden it in the brush. He was skilled at moving quietly. In his cloak of concealment, wearing a specially designed scent from the planet Jowlaith that neutralized his body odors, Veriasse could pass through the woods unnoticed by all but the most wary forest animals.

Thus he came upon Orick unawares. The bear had retired to a glade, and there he had been busy making a small shelter by leaning broken pine branches up against a tree. The shelter was finished, and now the bear sat beside it, engaged in fervent prayer. "Holy Father," Orick grumbled, shaking like a cub, "spare Maggie and Gallen. Bring them alive and safe from the realm of these damned sidhe. They are innocent of everything, innocent of any desires to do evil. I brought them here by accident, because there was no other way to save their lives, and I did not mean to break your commandments in doing so. If we have sinned ignorantly, I pray that the sins will be upon my head, and that Maggie and Gallen will be found guiltless—"

"I am sure that your friends will be found guiltless," Veriasse said, startling Orick. The bear tried to stand, and twisted around so fiercely in his panic that he fell over.

"You!" he roared accusingly. "What are you doing here?"

"The gate we sought was guarded by vanquishers," Veriasse said. "We have been forced to make new plans. I came to see if I could be of any help to you and your friends."

The bear gazed from left to right, scanning the woods behind Veriasse. "We don't need your help. Gallen will handle things."

"So, you don't need the help of any 'damned sidhe'?" Veriasse smiled. "Your friend Gallen may be a fine man, but he is a stranger to our world. I doubt that he will be able to bring your friend out."

"Ah, keep your misgivings to yourself," Orick grunted. "Gallen got himself a bit of book learning. He knows plenty."

"At the very least, I can expedite his plans," Veriasse offered. "What were his plans?"

"I'm not sure he has any," Orick said. "Gallen doesn't work that way."

Veriasse considered. "I'll leave Everynne to your care. Right now, she is down by the road. I want you to take her deeper into the woods, then come back here shortly after dawn. I don't want you here to meet Gallen if he comes back."

"Why?"

"Because if he is captured by the vanquishers, then he will lead them here."

"Gallen would never do that!"

"If they put a Guide on him, then he will have no choice," Veriasse countered. "Please, take her with you, and I will see what I can do for Gallen and Maggie."

Veriasse watched Orick head down the valley toward the road. He rummaged through his pack, put on a mantle as a disguise, then walked to

Toohkansay. Since he was already dressed and masked as a lord of Fale, no one challenged him. Even if they had, they would find that Veriasse, Lord of Information Managers, was registered as a citizen of the world. His forged records included computerized documentation that detailed much of a fictional life, down to his bathing schedule and the content of meals purchased during the past seventy years.

Veriasse went to the northwest quadrant of the city where the aberlains worked. He found the place to be heavily guarded. Green-skinned vanquishers on roving patrols were a sure sign that dronon guards resided within. In some places, he found that the living walls of the city were blackened by fire. Obviously, resistance bombers had been at work here within the past few weeks, and Veriasse suddenly became very concerned about Maggie.

He had worried before about her treatment by the dronon and her lord, but he had not considered the very real possibility that her greatest threat came not from her captors but from the local freedom fighters. Before, when he'd heard that Maggie was captured, he'd wondered why Karthenor had made such a poor choice of worker, but now he saw that indeed Maggie might have been exactly what the lord needed—someone who was alone in the city, someone who would not be missed. By taking slaves who were well tied to the community, Karthenor would only have earned further resentment.

Veriasse cursed himself, wondering if he might be able to get in touch with some of these freedom fighters. But he had to find Gallen first.

As he had imagined, the exterior of the compound was well secured. In sensitive areas, the dronon had installed heavy doors that would resist bombing.

Veriasse finished his scouting expedition and went down to the pidc. There he requested to view all documents that Gallen had studied. The teacher gave him the information, and Veriasse was impressed. Gallen had tried to retrieve data on Maggie's rooming situation, but the computer had not given him such sensitive information, nor would it supply a map of the interior of the compound. So Gallen had requested information on all areas where the aberlain compound did not extend, and had thus retrieved a negative image of the compound. By requesting maps of the laundry chutes which went through the floors below, he had been able to decipher the location of the living quarters for the aberlain workers. Veriasse studied the map, saw that most of the rooms had exterior exits. But Gallen went one step farther. He had requested computerized readouts on the electrical output for each room. One of the apartments had been left idle for three days, then suddenly recorded a tenant who turned on the lights each evening for a moment before retiring.

Gallen had taken his questioning one final step. The room had a southern exposure, and Gallen had asked the city computer to study the temperature records for the room and then determine whether the occupant left the windows open at night. The computer responded by showing that for the past two nights, the windows were left open, but the computer shut them when the temperature dropped below a certain threshold.

Veriasse smiled, impressed that some rustic could negotiate through the city's information system so smoothly. At the same time, Gallen showed some gaping holes in his education. For one thing, the boy didn't know that he'd left a data trail that would indict him. Veriasse asked the computer to run a credit check on Gallen, found that the boy was attempting to purchase clothing, ropes, and air exchangers—items he would need for his rescue attempt. Yet Gallen was broke. Veriasse used his credentials as a Lord of Information Managers to have the computer transfer credits from his personal account into Gallen's account, then he ran a security-delete on most files that mentioned Gallen's name.

He sat for a moment, thinking. Before Gallen tried to climb in that open window, he would need to neutralize the motion detectors. One could build a simple jammer that would disable any warning the motion detectors might send.

Veriasse would have to work fast, if he were to complete the jammer before Gallen tried to rescue Maggie.

Maggie tried to sleep, but after Avik left her, her lust kept her awake. Near dawn, her Guide quit stimulating her sexual appetites, and Maggie was free to dream: she dreamed of Tlitkani, the Golden Queen of the dronon, and in her dream Maggie's heart stirred with passion. The queen walked across a plaza of white stone, and her chitin flashed gold in the sunlight. She was perfect in every respect—without a flaw or blemish, not so much as a nick in her exoskeleton, and all around her was a great celebration. Dronon warriors with their heavy front battle arms knelt at her feet, battle arms crossed and extended in a sign of reverence. Tan dronon technicians with thin little segmented hands stood by to adore her, too, along with the small white workers. But among the insect hordes were many humans in all manner of clothing and attire, worlds of them, dancing and capering about, gazing at the Golden Queen with adoration shining from their eyes. Little human children had made garlands of flowers and strewn them at her feet, and a song rose up from humans and dronons alike, their voices raspy with fervor, praising the Golden Queen.

In her dream, Maggie felt such a profound respect for the golden one that tears streamed from her eyes. To simply gaze upon her caused a height of religious feeling unparalleled in all Maggie's life.

Maggie woke, eyes still streaming with tears, and her Guide whispered to her, "This is a vision I have given you of the future you shall help bring to pass. When a dronon looks upon its Golden Queen, it feels the ineffable sense of awe and wonder I have shared with you. We shall insert the genes that cause this condition into the fetuses of your children, so that they will no longer view the dronon as aliens, but will see them as brothers. Today you begin laboring within the inner sanctum of our compound, and you will help in the great work of bringing to pass the Adoration."

Having said this, the Guide had Maggie rise from bed, shower, and go down to eat. She was dead on her feet with fatigue, and after breakfast, the Guide had her walk into a part of the aberlains' working compound that she had not visited before. On her previous days, Maggie had worked only at the reproduction labs, but far more of the aberlains' labors were spent here in the research department, the inner sanctum of the aberlains' lair.

Here, she joined Avik's research team, which was supervised directly by Lord Karthenor. Here, Karthenor engaged in decoding dronon DNA so that the genes that carried Adoration might be discovered. To work here was a great honor, and the Guide stimulated Maggie's emotions so that she approached her task with a proper sense of reverence.

The research department was dark and warm, with dim red lights to simulate conditions on the planet Dronon itself. Black-carapaced dronon vanquishers patrolled the corridors while dronon technicians worked side by side with humans in their sterile white coats.

Maggie was put to work on a gene scanner, dyeing and scrutinizing dronon DNA. Thousands of healthy dronon specimens had given tissue samples over the past six years, and all of these were well catalogued. Now, Maggie and the aberlains studied samples from unhealthy dronon.

So it was that Maggie spent her day encoding the DNA of dronons who were born with lung defects. Genetic aberrations that led to weaknesses were never tolerated in dronon society. The congenitally insane, retarded, and deformed were always killed when their abnormalities were discovered. So Maggie found herself working with tissue from dronon infants. The workers who had shipped the specimens from Dronon had not taken great care to clean and prepare the tissues. Instead, they had shipped crates filled with pieces of the dead. The whiplike sensors had been ripped off the young dronon mouths. The feelers were then placed in refrigerated boxes and labeled according to deformity.

Maggie's job was to carefully unwrap the feelers, remove small samples from each and label them according to specimen, then place each in a gene decoder. Computers would then store information on the mutant DNA, match identical genetic structures from different samples of mutants, and thus by defining the areas of aberration, learn which genes controlled which functions.

Maggie worked at her grisly task all morning. For days she had been fighting her Guide as it attempted to stimulate her emotions. When she was angry or frightened, the Guide continually sought to calm her, send feelings of bliss. Maggie had found herself nursing her anger, trying to overwhelm the Guide. But now she was so weary that she could not fight it any longer. If not for the Guide, she would have collapsed from exhaustion. But the Guide kept her awake.

The Guide carried her about the room, fed her comfort and information.

She knew that her work was important, and Maggie found herself wishing that she could do more, hoping she would discover the actual genes that led to Adoration.

But the most important work was left to others, to aberlains with greater skill. They worked with tissues from the criminally insane, decoding genes from those few dronons who did not adore the Golden Queen.

Few such specimens had ever been born in dronon history, and they had been completely eradicated. Since the dronon used their own dead to fertilize their fields, the tissue samples of these insane individuals were rarely available. Still, a great search of the dronon worlds would eventually turn up a few new individuals. Maggie could only hope that when such samples became available, they would be sent here to the laboratories on Fale, so that she might have the honor of decoding them.

The tissue samples that Maggie used came from dronons who were born with a disorder that caused the chitin around their breathing orifices to form scarred nodules that could block the air passages. The breathing orifices on a dronon consisted of a row of nine holes located on the back upper hips of the dronon's hind legs. The orifices led to small lung sacks between the inner wall of the exoskeleton on the hip, and the hip muscles themselves. The dronon could not properly be said to have hearts. Instead, a rhythmic movement of the back legs caused the hip muscles to pump oxygen through the lungs and oxygenated blood through the rest of the body. For this reason, a dronon actually pumped blood more efficiently when it walked or ran. When it stopped walking, it would be forced to crouch and rhythmically bob up and down to keep its circulation going.

By evening, Maggie's work allowed her to isolate a defective gene and thus learn the gene's purpose in the great act of controlling the development of dronons.

The dronon technicians congratulated her and rewarded her by letting her work late. Her Guide fed her a sense of rapture, and she felt thrilled to be engaged in such a great and noble cause. Thus it was that she finally stumbled to her cubicle.

She opened the window, smelled the fresh night air, listened to the sound of the river lapping against the living walls of the city. A hundred thousand stars filled the night sky like white sand, and she looked up at a great swirling galaxy, wondering at its beauty.

She set the temperature of her bed higher, took a quick shower, then put on a thin robe and lay down to sleep. Out in the hall, she could hear the comforting sound of a dronon vanquisher's feet clicking as it patrolled the hallways of her sleeping quarters.

In the middle of the night, Maggie woke to a consuming lust that rolled over her in waves. She knew Avik was coming, and she did not think she could fight the Guide's commands anymore.

She was lying on her stomach, and the air stirred behind her. She realized that Avik must already have entered the room; the light did not go on, but she felt the weight of his body as he climbed on the bed. He moved quickly. She could hear his heavy breathing, and feel his weight as he straddled her back.

She whimpered softly. He pulled at the Guide on her head, thrust what felt like a chisel against the base of her neck. There was a searing pain, and hot blood spurted down her neck, and suddenly she was free from the Guide.

Maggie's only thought was that Avik had decided to kill her. She screamed, twisted to her side so that she could wrestle the knife away.

Gallen sat atop her, knife in hand, lit only by the starlight shining from the window. He thrust the Guide in a sack, then hit the sack sharply against the wall so that it made a sickly crunching sound, like breaking bones.

Maggie's head was reeling from fatigue, from a sudden overwhelming sadness. She couldn't think what was happening. "Get out," she whispered. "Avik is coming."

"Who is Avik?" Gallen whispered.

"A rapist," Maggie said, and behind Gallen the door whispered open. Light from the corridor shone in. Gallen surged from the bed so quickly that Maggie hardly saw him move. He seemed almost to fly across the room, a black shadow in his robes, a gleaming silver knife in his hand.

Gallen's knife fell just as Avik began to cry out. Gallen tossed the body to the floor with a thud.

In the corridor outside her door, the dronon guard shouted and scrabbled to come to Maggie's rescue.

Gallen slammed the door and locked it, saying, "Quick! Out the window! Jump in the water!"

Maggie staggered off the bed; horror overwhelmed her—not just horror at the thought of the dronon guard racing to the door, but a horror at all that had happened here.

In one instant, she realized what kind of work she had been engaged in, and an image flashed in her mind—a vision of the bloated sacklike mothers she had helped engineer, the remembered smell of dronon body parts stacked like cordwood in bins.

Her hands felt filthy; her entire skin felt filthy, and Maggie dropped to her knees and simultaneously cried from the core of her soul and tried to keep from retching up her dinner.

With a squeal of rending metal, the dronon guard hit the door, peeled it back with one chitinous claw, tearing it from its hinges. It held its black incendiary rod forward, pushed it through the door, and Maggie could see the wicked serrated edges on its forward battle arms. Gallen and the beast were dancing shadows in the light thrown from the corridor. As Gallen rushed to the torn door, the dronon's wings buzzed in anticipation.

Gallen grabbed the dronon's incendiary rod, twisted it away and spun, firing through the rent door. He was far too close to shoot the weapon, and Maggie hoped that the thin metal door would shield them from the heat.

The chitinous black flesh of the guard squealed as its body temperature rose above boiling, and smoke roiled from its carapace and crawled along the ceiling. It became a blazing pillar of white fire. Intense heat filled the room, and the broken door caught flame. Gallen threw up his arms and staggered back to her.

Somewhere in the building, an alarm sounded. Gallen threw his robe over Maggie's face. She struggled up, thinking that they would die any moment, but Gallen scooped her into his arms and staggered to the window.

"I can't . . ." Maggie cried, weeping bitterly.

Gallen pushed her out. The building was sloped, and for a moment she slid out in the darkness through air that felt pleasantly icy, then hit the black water. It was far colder than she would have guessed. She thrashed vigorously and floundered for a moment, found herself underwater. She bobbed to the surface again and called for help. She looked up. Gallen was clinging precariously to the windowsill like a spider, and she wondered if he had somehow gotten stuck, then he splashed into the water ten feet away. Maggie thrashed her legs, went under again. A moment later, Gallen grasped her neck.

He pulled her to the surface, holding her head up from behind. She kept struggling and tried to spin, grab him. "Help! I can't swim!"

"Can't swim?" Gallen asked. "Your father and brothers all drowned. I'd think you'd learn to swim."

Maggie gasped, part from the cold, part from the fear that she would slip under again. Gallen reached around, put something in her mouth. It felt like the mouthpiece to a flute, but it was attached to two small bottles.

"Breath in and out through this," Gallen panted. "It's an oxygen exchanger. It recycles air. As long as you breathe through this, it doesn't matter if your head goes underwater. In a minute, I'll start pulling you to shore. We will have to dive underwater. Don't fight me." Maggie tried breathing through the machine. She had to exert extra force to inhale, as if she were breathing through heavy cloth.

Gallen fumbled to put on his own oxygen exchanger, then dove and began pulling her toward shore. He did not try to hurry, just made a leisurely swim of it, so that by the time they came up, they were far downstream from Toohkansay and had rounded a bend in the river. The lights from the city gleamed over the water, and a lighted barge sailed past them, heading downriver. Gallen swam to the mouth of a small creek, and they waded upstream till they reached a bridge that arched above them darkly, shutting out the powdered light of the stars.

Under the bridge, Gallen stepped from the water, pulling Maggie after him. He bent and opened a cloth sack that was lying in some tall grass, pulled out a single blanket. Maggie was shivering vigorously, shaking from more than the chill night air. Everything that had happened to her over the past few days slammed into her like a giant fist.

"I'm sorry," she cried, feeling ill to the core of her soul. "I'm so sorry." She wanted to explain why she was so sorry but did not know where to begin. She was so cold, she could not feel her fingers. Gallen wrapped the blanket around her; he was shivering violently. She wrapped her arms around him so they could share the blanket.

"You—you had this planned?" she asked between chattering teeth. His golden hair gleamed in the starlight, and she could make out little of his features. The brackish odor of the river was heavy on them both.

"Aye," Gallen said. "I've got some food in the pack, dry clothes. I found a trail along this creek. We can follow it up into the hills, then circle back north of town to where Orick and I set camp. I think we should stay off the road."

The blackness still hung over Maggie, and every few moments the images of her work over the past few days would flash in her mind. The demented gleam in Avik's eye. Sorting the tagged feelers of the dead dronons, the images of the twisted people she had built.

There were no signs of pursuit, but she was sure that the dronons would come after them soon.

The cold, the fear, the darkness of it all was too much for Maggie, and she sank to her knees. Wild vetch grew in a tangled mass here in the shadow of the bridge.

Gallen knelt, hugging her to keep her warm.

"Everynne?" Maggie stammered, and it seemed to her that her thoughts were now unnaturally clear, bright and well-defined, like the chemical fire from an incendiary rifle.

"We found her this morning," Gallen said. "She was heading north for another gate. The dronons were on her trail. She plans to fight them. She asked us to come with her, but . . ."

Maggie looked up, studied his face. It caught only the slightest touch of starlight, and she could not see his eyes. But one thing was clear: he could have gone with Everynne, but Gallen had chosen to stay and rescue Maggie.

She leaned her shivering body against Gallen, felt the firm muscles beneath his wet shirt. His breath warmed her neck. She realized he'd planned the escape in every detail: two sets of dry clothes, two oxygen exchangers. But only one blanket. He'd planned to share this moment with her.

The residual emotions stimulated by the Guide were still affecting her somewhat. The night before, she'd staved off Avik's advances by fantasizing about Gallen, and now she found that an edge of lust still lingered.

Maggie was painfully aware of her thin nightgown, her nipples tight, protruding against the hairs of Gallen's chest. He shivered. She wrapped both hands around his neck, kissed him firmly on the mouth. Gallen pulled away slightly, gasped as if surprised by her action.

"What's wrong?" she asked, aware that he was shaking harder. She recognized it for what it was. He was shaking with desire. "Don't you want this?"

"You're still too young," Gallen said, his voice husky.

She grew so angry, she wanted to hit him. "We don't all age at the same rate, and some things make you old before your time," she said. "Watching your family die, that ages you! Working—working day and night just to stay alive, that ages you. Wearing a Guide—hell, Gallen, I, I can't even begin to tell you what that thing did to me. It's like a vice, crushing you. It teaches you and it rapes you all at the same time, because the things it teaches you shatter all of your deepest hopes—and if it didn't play games with you and make you feel like you were in heaven, you would gladly cut your own head off to be rid of it!"

Maggie began sobbing and trembling. She imagined that she could feel the dronons' black sensor whips on her arms, cold and rough like cornstalks, fouling her. "Gallen, you don't even begin to understand what kind of place we live in—"

"I know—" Gallen said. "I put on a teaching machine in the city. It taught me."

"Did it teach you about the dronon, about their plans?"

"No," Gallen admitted. "The teacher only showed me how the dronon conquered this world."

"In other words, this teacher taught you only what the dronon want you to know!"

Maggie was shivering and angry. Gallen put his arm around her, and she desperately wanted to be loved, to be comforted, for at that moment, it seemed that love was the only token that could be put on the scale that might balance out all the pain and despair that threatened to overwhelm her. Even then, she wasn't certain that love would be quite enough.

At that moment, something touched her back, and Maggie realized that Gallen held something long and hard in his hand. She reached around with her palm and touched the incendiary rod. Amazingly, he had managed to carry both it and her through the water.

And in that moment, she knew what else she needed to balance out her pain. Revenge.

"You said Everynne plans to overthrow the dronon," Maggie whispered. "Do you have any idea what her plans are?"

"No," Gallen admitted, "but I know where her gate is."

Maggie nodded softly and whispered, "Let's go."

But at that moment, a great circle of light shone on the bridge above them. The bridge rumbled and shook, so that bits of dirt rained down.

In horror, Galled clapped a hand over Maggie's mouth. She could think only one thing: they found us!

Overhead, a voice sounded from the sky. "You there: put up your hands!"

Ten

The light shined all around the bridge, bathing every grass blade in a brilliant glow. Gravity waves shook the bridge, making it thunder and vibrate so that bits of dirt and paint rained down. Maggie hugged Gallen. Overhead, Gallen heard someone shout, "I'm not armed! I'm not armed!"

Someone's up there, Gallen realized.

"I was only out for some exercise," a man called. "There is no harm in that." Gallen recognized the voice. Veriasse.

The flier hovered nearer. "Citizen, have you seen anyone pass you on the road?"

"Indeed," Veriasse said. "A magcar flashed past me not five minutes ago."

"Can you describe its occupants?"

"It carried only two—one was a woman. I cannot be sure of the sex of the driver."

Without another word, the flier darted south. Gallen peeked out and saw a second white, saucer-shaped flier that had been zigzagging over the far side of the river do likewise.

Veriasse whispered, "Gallen? Maggie?"

"Down here." Gallen started to climb up. "What are you doing back? I thought you were gone?"

"Shhh . . . talk softer. The gate we sought was guarded, so Everynne and I were forced to retreat. Don't climb up here. The night scopes on the vanquisher's flier can spot a man at forty miles. It is likely that I am being watched. Stay hidden and speak softly. The fliers can discern loud sounds, but softer sounds are masked by the fluctuation of air molecules that are disturbed by the fliers' gravity waves. I'll meet you at your camp at dawn. For now, follow the creek, keeping under heavy cover, then circle back through the woods. As an information manager for Fale, I've taken the liberty of issuing you false identifications. If you are captured, feign innocence. You will not be harmed."

"I wondered how I got credits on that empty chip," Gallen whispered. "I knew I had a hidden ally."

"Good luck," Veriasse whispered, and he hurried away.

Gallen led Maggie through the ravine into the hills. They crept under the starlight, more anxious to keep under cover than make good time. They reached camp before dawn, so they took shelter in a deep grotto to sleep.

At dawn, Veriasse woke them with a whistle. He stood at the top of a small rise, holding three bundles tied with string. He was gazing north. It took Gallen a second to realize that Veriasse was calling to Everynne and Orick. Gallen got up and stretched. In the distance, he could discern

Everynne and Orick making their way through the woods. He wondered at the old man's uncanny ability to walk softly in such heavy growth, to find them no matter where they hid.

Gallen shook Maggie awake, then walked up the rise. "Thank you again for your help last night, Veriasse. How did you know we were under the bridge?"

"I watched you from a distance," Veriasse said. "I saw you enter Maggie's room and effect her escape. I was impressed at the last, when you closed her window as you leapt out. I'm sure that it confused the guards, forcing them to search for you within the compound. In fact, they are probably still concentrating their main search inside. Anyway, I saw you leap into the river, and by gauging the flow of the current was able to guess where you would exit. I would say that you planned your escape fairly well, although your lack of education was almost your undoing."

"In what way?" Gallen asked, perplexed.

"You didn't know about the capabilities of modern pursuit vehicles. That was my fault, for not warning you. But you also tried to beat the motion detectors. I suspected you would, so I went to Maggie's window and put jammers down before you arrived."

"You mean you were there?"

"Just for a moment."

"Why didn't you rescue Maggie yourself?"

"And expose myself to unnecessary hazards? As long as you were willing to take the major risk, it seemed reasonable to let you. Besides, if you had failed, you would have needed me to rescue you both."

Gallen stared at the ground, annoyed. Veriasse's argument made sense, but an hour ago Gallen had felt like a hero. Now he felt like a child who had been caught doing something stupid. The older man must have guessed what he was thinking. "You are a talented and courageous young man. I'd like to imagine that I was as good when I was your age, but I was not. I have trained many guardians in my time. Would you like to be one of them?"

Gallen nodded.

Veriasse began unwrapping his bundles. He had brought a black cloak for Gallen, with black boots and gloves and a lavender mask. The outfit bore two scabbards, one for a sword, one for an incendiary rifle. Gallen stared at them in awe, for it was the attire he had seen worn not five nights ago by a man he had thought to be a sidhe.

"Those are the clothes of a Lord of Fale, but who wears these colors?" Gallen asked.

"I wore these colors when I was young," Veriasse said. "They were my colors as Lord Protector. Lord Oboforron purchased them from me a few years back, but he was executed by the dronon recently, so I bought the title back last night. I told you I had issued you a new identity. You will need clothes to match the part. Put on the robe."

Gallen put on the outfit. The boots shrunk around his feet as soon as he pulled them on, and the robe seemed massive, thick enough to foil a dagger blow, but was actually very light and comfortable. There was some type of metal padding in the gloves on the knuckles and at the palm and edge of the hand. Gallen imagined that if he landed a blow while wearing the gloves, it would be devastating. He strapped on the weapons.

With the outfit was a personal intelligence, a fine net with many triangles of silver. Gallen hesitated to put it on, for he had never worn a mantle. He was becoming familiar enough with personal intelligences that he did not know if he wanted to trust this one, but Veriasse urged, "Go ahead. It will whisper the intricacies of the protector's art for you, and it can teach you much that will be of value."

Gallen put on the silver mantle, felt the now familiar thrumming in his head as the intelligence established communication. Yet his mind did not flood with images like it had at the pidc. Instead, his muscles seemed to tighten involuntarily, as if he were preparing to leap into action, yet there was no tension. He felt almost relaxed, and his senses became heightened. Gallen almost felt as if . . . he listened, and in the distance to the south, perhaps twenty miles away, he heard a flier approaching. The vanquisher pilot was giving a report over the radio, telling his supervisors that he had found nothing in his search of the area.

"What?" Gallen said. "What is this thing doing to me?"

"This mantle has many sensors built into it," Veriasse said. "It hears, sees, smells. It detects motions and weaponry better than any mere human ever could. If you want to see something in the distance, close your eyes and think of the thing you want to see. As long as the object is within your line of sight, its image will appear in your mind, in expanded form. Over time you will learn to access the mantle's higher awareness without conscious thought."

"How does this thing teach?" Gallen asked.

"When you are safe, away from harm, in quiet moments it will begin training you in earnest. But for now, you are in danger. The mantle will simply be prepared for whatever comes our way. In the early decades of your training, should anything put you in danger, just let yourself go, follow your instincts. Wisdom will flow to you in your time of need."

Gallen picked up the mask. It looked like a thin layer of gel, but when he put it on his face, it stuck with an adhesive quality. He hadn't fitted the mask perfectly, but like the boots, it flowed to fit the contours of his face.

For Maggie, Veriasse had a yellow-ocher robe with a pale green mask. Her mantle was large indeed, with dozens of round silver icons that flowed down her back to her waist. "I have decided to dress you as a Lady of Technicians," he said. "You will find that this intelligence knows far more than your little Guide did, but it is a gentle servant, not a cruel master. You can remove it any time you wish."

"I don't understand," Maggie said, pulling the yellow robe over her thin nightgown. "These mantles must be expensive."

"Indeed," Veriasse said, "but I have been very wealthy for a very long time. And, so, I am free to give you these."

"You were Semarritte's husband before the dronon overcame her?" Gallen asked.

"Husband?" Veriasse said. "An odd word, and a very old one, and I was not her husband in the way that you think, though I husbanded her. I nurtured her and protected her as much as any man could, and I made a career of it. Indeed, Gallen, I once thought of myself as being very much like you—a bodyguard, a protector. But I think the dronon have a clearer view of what I am.

"I played the part of Semarritte's Lord Escort, the Waymaker. Among the dronon, the escorts battle for the right to become the Golden Queen's personal honor guard. The winner takes the title of Lord Escort. The Lord Escorts from different hives then engage in ritual combat, and the winner's Golden Queen takes the high throne, making her Lord of the Swarm. Thus her Lord Escort is also called the 'Waymaker,' he who secures the path to the throne.

"It was my job to fight Semarritte's battles when needed, to protect her from other powerful lords. But I could never have been Semarritte's husband in the sense that you mean. Only her caretaker. Now, I am the Waymaker to her daughter, Everynne."

"You mean Everynne isn't your daughter?" Maggie asked.

"Not my biological daughter," Veriasse answered. "She is a Tharrin, from a race born to rule. I am from less elegant stock. She sometimes calls me father from affection, and I call her daughter perhaps because I raised her as my own. She is, in fact, a duplicate of Semarritte, cloned from her cells."

As Orick accompanied Maggie to the top of the rise, Veriasse said, "Our magcar can carry all five of us, but I'm afraid that you, Orick, will be easily noticed. We will simply have to take our chances, keep you out of sight. I purchased a cloak to disguise you on our drive to the city of Guianne."

Orick hugged Gallen and Maggie, and his heart swelled with joy. "My prayers have been answered. You are safe."

"You should also thank Veriasse," Gallen said. "The rescue went smoothly because of him."

Orick wondered at this. It seemed to him that they were in trouble precisely for trying to help Everynne and Veriasse. It was only fit that Veriasse should help them in return.

Yet as he watched Maggie and Gallen, Orick realized that this adventure was not over. It had only begun, yet by Maggie's pale features, the lines in her haunted face, he could tell that they had already suffered casualties. Gallen, in his mask of lavender starlight, looked as if he were fast becoming a sidhe. Maggie and Gallen would never recover from this trip. And Orick felt cast off, alone. Of them all, only he had had the strength to refuse to accept this world, preferring to suffer the consequences of that decision.

From his last bundle, Veriasse brought out a cloak in colors of forest brown, then began fastening it around Orick's neck. But the fastener would not let Veriasse stretch the cloak around Orick's neck completely. Orick was forced to stand for several minutes, and he grumbled at being compelled into an uncomfortable position for so long. Veriasse did not hurry.

Orick looked into Veriasse's deep blue eyes as the old man worked at the fastener, and saw in them an intensity, a deliberateness that few men carried. Here was a man, Orick decided, who had become a fanatic, a man who could be driven beyond mortal efforts.

Veriasse managed to fasten the cloak, then led them to the magcar and drove south for an hour through a winding mountain pass. In that time, they had to stop at two inspection stations where green-skinned ogres questioned them. Yet after checking the false identification for Maggie and Everynne, the ogres let them pass.

As the magcar climbed over a last mountain, Orick could taste the scent of sea air even before they saw the water beyond. The city of Guianne gleamed white below them, a collection of exotic domes that rested on a sandy beach like broken eggshells from some giant bird. Above the city, people flew lazily in the air currents, clear wings strapped to their backs flashing like giant dragonflies.

It was only as Veriasse descended toward the city that Orick began to realize how large it must be. He drove for five minutes, and though the buildings loomed larger, they were still very far away.

Just as Orick began to get used to the idea of those enormous buildings, the winged people scattered away from one quadrant of the city, then one round building lifted into the air, defying gravity, and continued climbing straight up into the morning until it vanished behind a layer of clouds.

"By Saint Jermaine's wagging beard, you'll not get me in one of those buildings!" Orick shouted.

"That isn't a building," Maggie said. "It's a starship. All of the domes are starships." Orick looked over at Maggie. She wore a strange expression, one of both profound awe and conquest. He had never seen her so happy, so transformed by wonder. "And I know how they work."

Orick crossed himself to ward off bad luck. He muttered under his breath. "I don't know why I came here. Nothing good can come of it, as I've said all along. You stay right where you belong, Orick. Bears need the woods like birds need sky."

The car skimmed over the highway, then turned onto one of many branching boulevards. When they neared the city, the egg-shaped ships loomed above them. Beneath the ships was a sprawling conglomeration of tunnels and passages that seemed to wind about in meandering patterns like veins in a leaf.

Veriasse pulled up to one huge tunnel-like opening and passed under an arch. The presence of the dronon vanquishers was heavier here than it had been in Toohkansay. A dozen vanquishers manned an outpost at the gate, brandishing oversized incendiary rifles. Veriasse stopped to give his identification.

The vanquishers let the car pass. Veriasse drove down a broad boulevard beneath the covered city, a vast arching tunnel whose ceiling could not have been less than three hundred feet high. Everywhere along the sides of the street were shops with exotic displays. The scent of foods unfamiliar to Orick wafted through the tunnel. Smaller side passages led off to living areas and uncovered parkways. Veriasse drove slowly, for many pedestrians and other vehicles also negotiated the great boulevard. A dozen times, Orick was tempted to ask Veriasse to stop so that he could try out some pastry or other dish sold by vendors, but the old man kept driving for nearly an hour, heading down at a slight angle.

It was getting darker. Orick glanced up at the huge skylights, saw that they had descended below the ocean. Schools of fish swam in the green waters above them.

Far from the gates of the city, Veriasse halted the car in front of a building whose strange facade attracted Orick. The building displayed no markings to explain its purpose to passersby. Lampposts in front had glow globes attached, but the muted lights gave the place a somber appearance. To heighten the solemn atmosphere, Orick saw that there were no businesses nearby for hundreds of yards. The building was silent. A few people hurried in, some away, but all of them kept their heads low, as if to hide their identities. The building's facade showed in bas relief an image of a woman standing with arms outstretched. Behind her glittered a field of gold stars. The handiwork was astonishing, beautiful, but something more attracted Orick: the woman herself.

"Hey, that's a picture of Everynne," Orick said.

"Shhh," Veriasse muttered. "It's not Everynne. That is an image of Semarritte, Everynne's mother, who was once our great judge. This is her tomb."

Now Orick understood why the place was so quiet, so solemn.

"Why are the lights so low?" Everynne asked. "It looks as if the building is closed." Indeed, beside the doors were two burly vanquishers, watching the entrance like ogres.

"The dronon would close the tomb, if they dared," Veriasse said. "They want the memory of Semarritte to die with her. But too many remember her still. Too many revere her, and this confuses the dronon. Reverence for the vanquished is a concept that is alien to them."

Orick didn't say anything, but he doubted that anyone would revere a mere woman as much as the old man said. Semarritte was, after all, only human, but Veriasse spoke of her with an awe that Orick reserved only for God and his servants.

They got out of the car. Both Everynne and Veriasse refused to slouch and scurry to the entrance as others had. Instead, they walked tall and proud up the broad steps, toward a large ornate door. The green-skinned ogres stood silently, but when they saw Gallen, one of them reached out a hand to Gallen's shoulder, stopping him. The guardian said, "There was a time when I served one who wore those colors."

Gallen turned, looked up from beneath his black hood, and his lavender mask of starlight twisted in rage at being stopped, as if the ogre were some gnat that Gallen would squash. "Many things are changing," Gallen said. "I hope you served him as well as you do your new lord."

The ogre removed his hand from Gallen's shoulder, and the group passed through the doors into what Orick recognized as a cathedral. The room was silent, heavily carpeted with red fabric, and the sound of a muttered word or cough did not echo back from the ceiling. They walked up an aisle between rows of pews, where a few mourners sat quietly. Most of the mourners were lords, with their glowing masks and somber robes, and Orick wondered at this. Apparently, the inside of this building was off limits to common folk. Or perhaps commoners feared to worship here.

Ahead was a great stone pulpit with what looked to be an image of the stricken Christ carved upon it. Upon the stone pulpit stood a ghostly apparition of Semarritte, speaking softly to the crowd. Her clear voice seemed to issue from her lips, saying, "The rightful duty of one who would be your leader is to become the Servant of All. We Tharrin believe that those who serve must do so in both thought and deed, subjugating all selfish desires. Any leader who does less is not worthy of either position or honor. . . ."

Orick listened enrapt, for the Lady Semarritte's teachings were not like those he had ever heard from any puffed-up mayor or clan chieftain back in County Morgan. These words recalled to Orick's mind the teachings of Christ to his disciples when they argued about who would become the greatest in the kingdom of heaven: "Let him who would be greatest among you, become the servant of all." The hair began rising on the back of Orick's neck, for here among the sidhe, this was indeed their church, and the Lady Semarritte had been their god.

As Orick got closer, he saw that it was not Christ at all carved upon the pulpit but a blackened skeleton fused against the stone. Here were the remains of Everynne's mother. The flesh had burned from her bones and turned into a black, oily substance, but the whole skeleton was intact, hands clawed out protectively as if the dead woman had raised them to ward off a blow, legs tilted askew. Bits of dark hair and the chainmail netting of her mantle were fused into the stone, along with a necklace and other metal items.

This is what someone looks like after getting shot with an incendiary rifle, Orick realized. He'd seen Father Heany go down in flames back in Clere, but he had not realized the full magnitude of what the weapon could do.

The five of them lingered before the blasted remains. Veriasse knelt on one knee, and Everynne got down on both knees and wept softly over her mother's body. Above them on the pulpit, the image of the dead queen continued her sermon for several minutes, detailing the rightful duties of a judge, pledging to fulfill those duties for as long as her people wanted her. When she finished, the image faded, and a voice floated through the hall, saying that the dead woman's oration would be repeated in five minutes.

Veriasse touched Everynne's shoulder and whispered, "It's time, my daughter, my lord." Several people got up to leave, but Veriasse walked to the back of the room, closed the inner doors to the chapel while Everynne went to the podium. When she reached the top, she pulled back her robe to expose her face, peeled away the pale blue mask.

She began speaking, reciting what Orick was sure must have been the beginning of Semarritte's oration. "Through all the heavens, at all times, among all peoples, the greatest treasure of a nation has always been the quality and number of its good leaders. No abundance of wealth can quell the rapaciousness of a tyrant. No nation can count itself fortunate while groaning under the iron foot of war. No people can afford to tolerate corruption at the hands of a governor, whether that governor was chosen in free election or has maneuvered himself into position through influence."

Orick's hair bristled, and he wondered that Everynne would dare to speak so with the vanquishers out at the gates of the cathedral, but Everynne did not shrink from her duty. Instead, as she spoke she seemed to grow in size and power and majesty. She pulled off her outer robe, and beneath it she wore a pale blue gown. The light that had been shining upon the skeletal remains of Everynne's dead mother now shone fully on her, and Everynne stood in the darkness, shining like a bolt of lightning.

Orick looked back at the pews, and these handful of mourners who had come to pay homage to the dead Semarritte now all stood, mouths agape, to see their great judge standing before them, as one raised from the dead. Some of them wept openly, and Orick watched one woman put her hand to her mouth and repeatedly cry out in astonishment.

Everynne continued. "And so you have fashioned us Tharrin to keep the peace among you, to establish order and ensure that every person is granted the right to life, liberty, and the freedom to prosper according to their best abilities.

"The rightful duty of one who would be your leader is to become the Servant of All. We Tharrin believe that those who serve must do so in both thought and deed, subjugating all selfish desires. Any leader who does less is not worthy of either position or honor." At this point she cut the oration short, and said, "I stand before you, offering to become the leader you have sought. I am Everynne, the daughter to Semarritte, and I was born Tharrin. I seek to cast the dronon from the midst of our realm, but I cannot do it alone. Who among you will come to my aid?"

From every corner of the room, the people erupted with shouts of "I! I! I will help you!" and the proud lords in their gleaming masks rushed forward, weeping in glee like children to fall at Everynne's knees. They knelt at her feet, reaching up their hands in adoration so that she could touch them, not daring to touch her on their own, and Everynne grasped each person's hand firmly and thanked each lord.

And somehow, Orick the bear, who had always believed that he would become a servant of God, found himself rushing forward into the small crowd. He sat down and raised his paw, and Everynne smiled at him in surprise, tears filling her pale blue eyes. "Orick!" She laughed. "Even you?"

"I will aid you, lady, though I be the humblest of your servants," he said firmly.

"No doubt you shall be among the most valiant," Everynne said as she knelt to kiss his paw. And even though she had not asked it, Orick felt as if he ought to take his priestly vows of poverty and chastity.

Eleven

That night, Gallen could not sleep. All night long he lay in a fever, waking in a sweat. For a time he worried about his health, but then he lay back calmly, realizing that the mantle had begun its instruction. He had been dreaming, and the dreams were memories of things that had happened to Veriasse.

He dreamed first of Fale. He had been escorting Semarritte on this world when the dronon warships fell from the sky in dark clouds. The dronon came in vast numbers, sealing off Guianne so that its residents were trapped in tunnels beneath the ocean. Guardians tried to fend them off, but the dronon were too numerous; like dark grains of sand they swept over the land.

Veriasse and Semarritte had become trapped here in Semarritte's judgment hall. Dronon by the hundreds of thousands had surrounded the building, a black wave of warriors clambering over one another's bodies, until at last they cleared a path so that the Golden Queen and her Lord Escort could enter.

In his dream, Gallen struggled fiercely with the Lord Escort—landing blows on the beast's chitinous body, ripping off one of its feelers, smashing eyes with a leaping kick. But in time he wearied, and the Lord Escort lashed forward a wing—an unprecedented move that would have availed the creature nothing in a battle with one of its own kind. But the dronon's wing slashed through Veriasse's belly like a saber, and suddenly he was reeling away from the battle, his entrails spilling across the floor.

The Lord Escort then rattled its wings in a thunderous roar, leapt into the air, and in one swift kick disemboweled Semarritte while Veriasse watched. The dronon vanquishers who encircled the room raised a rattling howl of congratulations. Then the Lord Escort cried to his people that Tlitkani of the dronon had become the new Lord of the Swarm, queen over all peoples both human and dronon.

Afterward, a dronon vanquisher rushed forward with an incendiary rifle, firing into Semarritte's body.

Smoke and the scent of chemical fire rose through the building. Veriasse pulled his intestines in as the world faded to gray, pinching the skin closed, unsure whether the nanodocs in his body could heal such a massive wound.

In the dream, Gallen could not feel Veriasse's pain. He could discern the man's thoughts, observe his actions. But the dream carried no emotional weight.

Gallen woke and thought long about the dream, wondered if there were any way that Veriasse could have defeated the dronon, and suddenly images of the planet Dronon filled his mind. He saw a brown world filled with odd plants, where insects had developed interior lungs that allowed them to grow in size far beyond anything on Earth. Dronon was a vast world, and it orbited its sun once each four Earth years. Its axis tilted at a forty-two degree angle, with the result that each year, each polar icecap would melt. During a summer, one hemisphere would bathe in perpetual daylight while the other suffered perpetual night.

As a result, the dronon were forced to migrate over vast continents with each changing season, foraging for shrublike fungi. Each hive continually competed with others for food and space, for the finest nesting sites, for water that became scarce during the dry seasons. The order of their universe was clear: expand your territory or die.

In each hive, as the first few females hatched, they would battle among themselves, fighting in order to remove the exterior ovaries from one another. The female who managed to keep her ovaries established her dominance as a future queen, and soon the others recognized her authority as a princess. She would bide her time until a Lord Escort flew in from another hive, one who would kill the reigning Lord Escort and queen, making the princess the new queen of the hive.

Those poor females who were neutered could never form the secondary sexual characteristics of a queen. They grew only to a small size, and their color remained as white as that of any grublike larvae. Their boundless energy was channeled into work, rather than procreation, and they became the most menial servants of the hive.

Among the males, a similar battle would take place, but only after the larvae had exited their cocoons as adults. Adult male vanquishers, with their flashing wings and huge battle arms, engaged in ritual combat, seeking to remove one another's testicles, until only six males remained. These six princes would then fly to new hives, hoping to win their own kingdoms, while the neutered vanquishers remained with their hive.

A third sex often hatched without functioning sexual organs—neither male nor female. These had deformed wings and less energy than workers, but often had facile minds, suitable for solving problems. These become the technicians of the hive, the architects, counselors, and artists.

Over the eons, the queens had evolved to become more and more virile—laying more eggs, living longer lives. Only the strongest survived, and it was in the interest of the queens to root out the weak, destroy competing hives.

But among the queens, one great lady ruled each swarm. She could not begin her rule until she reached the age of one hundred and fifty dronon years. At that point, her exoskeleton would change color, bleaching from its pale wheat to a beautiful gold. If the queen survived to this age without injuries—broken appendages or a cracked exoskeleton—her offspring would gather near, carried into ecstasy at the sight of a new Golden Queen.

The Lord Escort of the hive, stricken with adoration, would pilgrimage with his Golden across the continents, seeking out the reigning Golden Queen.

The Lord Escorts for each Golden would then battle for the right to rule a swarm of one thousand hives. When one of the escorts was killed, his foe would attack the opposing queen and maim her, damaging her so that she would lose the adoration of hives. Such a queen was often allowed to cower back to her own hive and continue laying eggs until she died.

But the Lord Escort and the vanquishing Golden Queen became Lords of the Swarm. They would choreograph the great works of the hives—the migration across the vast plains of Dronon and through the reaches of space; they would choreograph battles with legions of the vanquishers as they sought to enlarge the swarm's territory.

Gallen lay in a half sleep, and the mantle displayed battles that had been filmed between Lord Escorts. Veriasse had made a great study of the battles—had noted the various fighting stances, attack forms, the use of feelers, mandibles, serrated battle arms, and the clawed legs as weapons. He had performed autopsies on dead dronon vanquishers—had determined how much force was necessary to crush their faceted eyes, to pull off the hooked claw of a forearm, to rip out a feeler, to pry off a head. He had measured the thickness of their chitinous exoskeletons, searching for thin spots.

The dronon had few weaknesses. Their exoskeletons offered superb protection for the head, belly, and back. They were most vulnerable on the hind legs, where their respiratory orifices weakened the hip, but reaching those legs was a task—the dronon could protect themselves well from a frontal assault, and with the dronon's flight and leaping capabilities, it was nearly impossible for a human to attack from behind.

Gallen lay for a long time, thinking about how one could engage a dronon in hand-to-hand combat with the hopes of winning. Sometimes, he would doze and wake to find himself sleepwalking, performing arcane exercises, stretching muscles he did not know that he had, leaping and kicking at imaginary foes in the quiet halls of the temple.

In one such session, Maggie came to him, half asleep herself. "What are you doing up so late?"

"I can't sleep," Gallen said. "Veriasse said this damned mantle would teach me when things were quiet, but it's kept me up all night."

Maggie simply said, "Have you tried talking to it? Just tell it to let you rest for the night."

Gallen gave the command, and immediately the mantle relinquished its lessons. He went back to bed, found himself compelled to lie next to Maggie, recognized that the mantle was whispering for him to lie beside her.

"Why?" he wondered, and the answer flooded into his mind. "You are a Lord Protector now. You must have someone to protect."

Over the next few days, Orick became inseparable from Everynne. He would disappear into his room for a few moments, and then while Everynne was speaking in a secret meeting with the masked Lords of Fale, she would suddenly turn and find him lying on the floor near her foot like some great hairy dog.

She did not mind his attentions. Few men could best a vanquisher in single battle, and she did not forget that the bear had already saved her life once. More than that, she found his presence somehow morally calming. Everynne was acutely conscious of the fact that she had been born to lead, that every facet of her appearance, even the chemical combination of her pheromones, had been designed to make her appealing to other humans.

From childhood she had been keenly aware of how easily she could manipulate people through a thousand seemingly insignificant things—by sitting when making a request of a man, she could appear more helpless and in greater need. By standing with head erect and back straight, she could more easily seem in control of any situation. By holding eye contact and softly making requests when someone hesitated to give allegiance, she could force the person to make a choice. By taking great care of her clothing and her appearance, she could make herself more desirable to men. By emphasizing the things she held in common with other women, she could convince a woman that they were sisters rather than competitors. The list was endless, and Everynne knew that her very ability to learn the art of manipulation was bred into her. Billions of people had none of her talent and as a result were born destined to become socially inept.

Orick, by not being human, should have been immune to her charms. Yet he stayed at her side, seemingly for his own purposes. Everynne wondered at his motives. Perhaps it was only the crowd. In the past two days, each of the Lords of Fale had come to her, detailing some startling atrocity committed by the dronon. A merchant told of vast assets the dronon had seized for war efforts, so that now he was poor. A mother told of a son who had disappeared. A builder told of a mass grave he'd discovered, filled with the corpses of handicapped children, or "defectives," as the dronon called them. The tales of horror were far-reaching and personal, and Orick listened in startled silence, then would listen even more keenly as the lords told of their fondness for Everynne's mother, told how they dreamed of her return. And though Everynne knew that her mother had never been a perfect governor, she had truly sought to be a Servant of All. There had been peace in the land, honest strivings for justice. But the dronon did not value peace or justice. Their biological imperative told them to vanquish all, then reap the spoils. To them, human lives were simply merchandise for the taking.

And if the tales that Orick heard were his motive for staying by her side, then she worried what he would think when he discovered her inadequacies.

On their first day in Guianne, Everynne collected her confidantes, and together they had devised a plan to escape from Fale. The dronon had been systematically sealing off the planet. Guards were at every gate to the Maze of Worlds, and warships were being diverted to block the skies above.

Right now, the beleaguered vanquishers were spread too thin. They could hinder Everynne from escaping, but they lacked the manpower to effectively search for her. But once their warships arrived, they would form a picket, reinforce the troops, and begin searching Fale in earnest. Everynne had to leave now.

In order to escape, Veriasse had designed a system of thrusts and parries that included three attacks: first, they would feint at another gate, forcing the dronon to send for reinforcements. Everynne's forces would then attempt to hijack a starship. If the starship made it to hyperspace, the dronon would think she had escaped the planet. If it was destroyed, the dronon would believe she had died in the attack. In either case, they would be off their guard.

While the dronon had their support drawn off and were reeling from the belief that Everynne was on a spaceship, her forces would begin an aerial assault against the gate that led to Cyannesse. If that attack succeeded as it should, Everynne could leave.

Now, the morning of the assault, Veriasse drove up the highway in an ancient hoverbus. It was an old model—a long aluminum cab suitable for ten people, with flaring wings where the exhaust vented.

Beneath them, the highway rolled flat and smooth. For the moment, they simply looked like tourists, floating along the highway. Everynne glanced at her chronometer. It was nine in the morning, and three hundred kilometers to the south, the Lords of Fale had mobilized their workers in a ground assault at the gate to Bilung. The gate served well as a diversion, being close both to the city of Guianne and to the gate to Cyannesse.

Everynne closed her eyes and let her mantle connect to Lord Shunn's personal intelligence via telelink. She watched his attack progress—silver fliers swept through the sky in a wedge, shooting low over the forest toward the gate, dropping a barrage of explosives along with canisters of chlorine gas, which was particularly toxic to dronon. As soon as the fireballs began erupting over the treetops, Lord Shunn's attack force moved in.

Under cover of the trees, long-range laser weapons were nearly useless, so Shunn's forces all wielded only incendiary rifles. No human could bear the weight of the armor needed to ward off an incendiary blast, so Shunn's men were protected only by gas masks and lightweight heat-resistant combat fatigues. The men ran forward in loose formation, moving cautiously. Since the battle was meant only as a diversion, they were not in a hurry to engage the vanquishers.

Lord Shunn himself flew in behind on his hovercar, with its hood down, observing the battle. He glided through the trees, and only the distant smell of smoke signified that a battle had been launched. For fifteen minutes, Everynne watched the battle progress, until Lord Shunn's troops met several dozen vanquishers. Suddenly the woods filled with fire as incendiary rifles began discharging. Flaming balls of sulfurous white whipped through the air with incredible speed.

She watched a civilian try to dodge behind a tree in hopes of eluding a ball that flamed toward him, growing in size. The chemical charge from the rifle splattered across the tree and across the man's arm, erupted into flames hotter than the sun. He screamed and held out his arm, spinning once, kicking up detritus from the forest floor. In less than a second, he succumbed to the heat and lay burning.

The sight horrified Everynne to the core of her being. As a Tharrin, she was bred to be empathic. She detested violence. Somehow, knowing that Lord Shunn and his workers had volunteered to die in the woods this day made Everynne feel ashamed, weak. She only wanted the killing to stop, everywhere, but she was forced into a deadly contest and could not escape.

Suddenly on the highway ahead of Everynne, sirens began blaring as army hovertrucks approached. Veriasse pulled his own old bus off the highway to let them pass. Everynne disengaged the telepresence link and looked up. Three truckloads of vanquishers were heading south at full speed, perhaps sixty green-skinned giants. Ahead of her, Veriasse relaxed in his seat for a moment, breathed easier. The soldiers could only have come from the Cyannesse gate. Their ruse was working.

Veriasse let the soldiers pass, gunned the throttle. Everynne engaged her telepresence again, saw how the battle was progressing.

For four more minutes, the battle continued. Suddenly, far to the south, a spaceship lifted over the horizon, a distant white sphere that floated higher and higher into the morning sky. Lady Frebane began broadcasting urgent messages to Shunn and his troops. "My lord," she called, "the lady's ship is away! Repeat, the mission has succeeded. The lady's ship is away. Break off your attack!"

Lady Frebane continued broadcasting for two minutes. The dronon vanquishers sent low-altitude fliers to intercept the ship, but they did not make it in time. Lady Frebane jumped into hyperspace before the fliers got into range, and Everynne was filled with a deep sense of regret. If she'd been on that ship, she would have made her escape already. But Veriasse had insisted that the ship was too dangerous, too large a target. He had opted for the double feint. The real battle lay ahead.

"We're about sixty seconds from our gate," Veriasse warned. "Gallen—" he began to say, but the young man was already playing his part. He lowered the hood to the hovercraft and got out his incendiary rifle, flipped it on so that its indicator glowed red.

For a moment, as Gallen's black robes flapped, Everynne caught glimpses of the silver bangles of his personal intelligence, the lavender of his mask, and Gallen reminded her of Veriasse. But he turned and she caught the profile of his face, and the illusion dissipated. Everynne gazed across the desert. Three kilometers north of the gate was a line of low yellow hills. At any moment, three phalanxes of fliers would stream over the hills at four thousand kilometers per hour. The vanquishers would have less than three seconds to take cover.

Veriasse focused on the gate. The hoverbus hummed, bouncing as it hit small thermals. In the distance, Everynne spotted a flash of sunlight reflecting from the flier's windshields, and she began counting: three, two . . . one. The saucer-shaped fliers were in a tight *V*, fifteen of them; suddenly the formation split and the fliers veered east and west. Antiaircraft fire erupted from the vanquishers' outpost at the gate; Everynne watched gray pellets rain from the fliers, beacons designed to fool intelligent missiles.

Then the incendiary bombs landed. They were so small that Everynne did not see them drop. Instead, the ground around the gate erupted into a wall of flame that leapt thirty meters into the air. Everynne found it hard to believe that anyone or anything could survive that inferno, but Veriasse had insisted that the fliers make a second pass, and then a third.

By now, their hoverbus had reached the turn where the highway veered west, but Veriasse simply kept his northern course, slowing dramatically; the hoverbus leapt from the shoulder of the highway.

The engines roared, straining as they raced down a small ravine, throwing up clouds of dust. The second wave of fliers was sweeping over the hills now, sooner than Everynne had anticipated, and they dropped a barrage of conventional explosives. Dust and burning bodies pitched into the air, twisting in a great whirlwind. Smoke and fire obscured the nearly indestructible gate, but Everynne pulled out her key and pressed the open sequence. The light under the arch shimmered.

Already the flames from the incendiary bombs were beginning to die. The third and final phalanx of fliers closed over the hills, spraying out their ordnance, an oily black substance that civilians referred to as "Black Fog." It had no toxic properties, but absorbed light so completely that in seconds the sky turned black.

A black cloud boiled toward them, and Veriasse stared in concentration as they hit the wall of darkness. Everynne felt as if her eyes had been painted over. At first she could see no light at all, yet they were hurtling toward the gate; she feared that Veriasse would crash into a post.

Some vanquishers must have heard their hoverbus, for two balls of white fire whizzed over Everynne's head. She screamed and ducked. Gallen returned fire at the unseen targets. Veriasse shouted, "I can't see the gate!"

Gallen fired his incendiary rifle; a fireball of actinic light spattered one gate post, only twenty yards ahead. Veriasse hit the reverse thrusters, shouting, "Run for it."

Everynne leapt from the hovercar. It was so dark, she could see only the fiery light above the gate. Orick tried to leap out of the hovercar but slipped. He yelled, "Damn!"

Everynne turned but could not see the bear. Maggie, Gallen, and Veriasse could be detected only by the faint shimmering of their masks; they floated above the ground like wraiths. Maggie grabbed Everynne's hand, urging her to hurry forward, but they tripped over the body of an ogre. Everynne was just struggling up when the creature grabbed her ankle. She screamed and simultaneously the thing shouted weakly, "Vanquishers to me!"

"Gallen, help!" Maggie cried.

Everynne tried to kick free, but the ogre held her tight. Orick, hidden by the inky blackness, roared and pounced on the creature. The vanquisher let go, and Everynne heard more than saw the ensuing scuffle.

Suddenly the vanquishers surrounded them, too close to use incendiary rifles, faintly visible in the light from the arch. Gallen and Veriasse pulled out their swords and began swinging, but the vanquishers were armored. By the time Veriasse and Gallen brought one down, three more had taken its place.

Everynne had no choice. She reached into her pocket, pulled out a ball of glowing light. "Stop!" She stood defiant, holding the ball high, though her heart was faint.

"You vanquishers, do you see this?" she asked. "You know what it is?"

"A Terror," one vanquisher said, a sergeant in heavy armor.

"If you don't surrender now," Everynne said, "I'll destroy this world. My mantle is linked to eighty-four other Terrors spread across the galaxy, including one on Dronon itself. I've already initiated the arming sequence. They will begin detonating in three minutes, unless you surrender now! You will not have time to issue a warning. You will all die!"

Everynne gasped for breath. She did not know if the vanquishers would fall for her ruse. She was a Tharrin, dedicated to peace. All her training, all the engineering her ancestors had built into her, screamed that even to risk destroying a world was wrong. Yet she held a Terror aloft, hoping the dronon would treat her threat seriously.

From the darkness, a dronon limped forward. The fire had burned its wings, and it dragged one hind leg. A familiar clicking began as mouthfingers tapped its voice drum. "I am broadcasting your demands to Lord Annitkit, our supervisor on this world. He will contact the Golden Queen, Tlitkani, and learn her will in this matter. It will take several hours to learn her reply."

"You don't have that long," Everynne said. "We're leaving." She turned to the others. "Get through the gate, now!"

She began inching backward through the crowd of vanquishers, moving carefully. It might be that Lord Annitkit would order them to kill her, risk losing eighty worlds in order to keep the thousands they had gained. But Everynne had to hope that he would take her threat seriously. The dronon were often as paranoid as they were violent, but they loved their queen. She did not know of a dronon who would risk the chance that his queen would be killed.

The dronon vanquisher rushed forward, and a segmented hand erupted from the hidden compartment in its battle arm, grasping her arm, pinning Everynne to the spot.

"I do not believe you will detonate the Terror," the dronon said. "A Tharrin would not destroy a world."

"Can you be so certain?" Veriasse shouted from behind the dronon. "Others of our people have detonated Terrors on your worlds. My mantle, too, has the access codes for these weapons, and I am not a Tharrin. Believe me, if you do not let us go, we will kill your precious Golden Queen."

The dronon hesitated. He seemed to be stalling as he waited for further orders. "If you have a Terror on Dronon, why have you not used it? I do not believe you have another Terror."

Veriasse strode forward, put his face close to the vanquisher's, and looked into its eye cluster. "Perhaps we only take our orders from a higher source," he whispered threateningly. "Perhaps we do not completely comprehend their plans for your queen. I only know that I am not free to contravene those orders. Friend, take your hand off the woman's arm. If she drops the Terror, it could break open. We wouldn't want any accidents. . . ."

The dronon held Everynne's hand. It had a tiny metal device clipped to one of its feelers, and the device buzzed. The dronon addressed Veriasse and Everynne simultaneously.

"Lord Annitkit demands your word of honor that if we release you, you will relinquish your attack on Dronon!"

"Once I pass through the gate, I will initiate the disarming sequence. I will spare your queen, for now," Veriasse said.

The dronon began walking, wrenched Everynne toward the gate. Maggie and Orick leapt through ahead of her, but Gallen and Veriasse stood on each side of the gate. The chemical fire of the incendiary rifle burned white across the arch. With their dark robes, weapons drawn and faces masked, Gallen and Veriasse looked like doormen to some hell.

They each took one of her hands. Together they leapt into the light.

Twelve

Gallen stood up to his knees in the warm water of a new world, panting, holding onto Everynne's hand. He spared the world a quick glance: twin white-hot suns spun on the horizon. In every direction, a shallow sea reflected the yellow sky, and fingers of vapor climbed from the water. The sea was calm, with only tiny lapping waves, and when Gallen looked toward the distant suns, a strange prismatic effect caused the waves to sparkle in a rainbow. Maggie and Orick were searching about, unable to spot land. But to the southeast, Gallen's mantle showed him distant bluffs of coral, rising from the water.

"Where the hell are we?" Gallen asked angrily. He was shaking—they'd come close to getting butchered on Fale, and Gallen didn't like that. Even worse, he didn't appreciate Everynne hiding things from him—like the fact that she carried a weapon that could destroy a world. She put the Terror into a fold of her robe. Veriasse opened his map.

"We're on Cyannesse, of course," he said. The map showed them as a fiery dot of red, but showed no gates. Veriasse pushed a corner of the map, and its scale expanded to display a continent—if continent you could call it. Cyannesse was mostly ocean, and the land here looked to be only a rough archipelago. "Ah, here is the gate," he said, pointing to a blue arch. "Only about a thousand kilometers. We're not far from a city." He pointed southeast, toward the cliffs. "Let's go."

"I don't get it," Orick bawled. "Why don't we see the gate from this side? Why did we get dumped in the water?"

"You don't see a gate from this side," Veriasse explained, "because the gate doesn't have two sides. Each gate on a planet is like a bow, shooting you toward a single destination, and you are the arrow. You simply land where you are pointed, within reason. An intelligence is built into each gate, and that intelligence continually tracks the destination planet. There is a beacon buried beneath us that tells the gate how deep the soil is, so you don't land in a bed of rock. When this gate was built, this spot was on land, but now the oceans have risen. Still, I've been through this gate before—this spot is only underwater during high tides. We can make it to shore easily enough." Veriasse made as if to depart.

"Wait!" Gallen said, looking first to Veriasse, then to Everynne. Gallen still had not sheathed his sword; it dripped blood into the clear, warm water. "Neither of you are going anywhere until I get some answers."

"What?" Veriasse said. "You wear the mantle of a Lord Protector for two days and think you can beat me in combat?"

Gallen stuck his sword into the sand under the water, swiftly pulled his incendiary rifle, aimed it at Veriasse. "I've known you less than a week, but I have heard two very different stories about your plans. First, you said you planned to start a war to win back your realm. But a minute ago, you said you plan to destroy nearly a hundred worlds. I may be a Backward, but I've learned a few things in the past week. If that Terror breaks, it will destroy this planet. You are jeopardizing every world you set foot on. No one has that right! You've been traveling between the Maze of Worlds, and by your own admission you have sabotaged world upon world. Though you may be a Tharrin, Everynne, I have yet to see evidence of the compassion that you claim as your birthright."

Maggie and Orick kept still, not daring to interrupt. Veriasse held back. Everynne watched Gallen and licked her lips.

"You are right, of course," she said. "I'm not what I seem. On Fale, they so wanted a new incarnation of their great judge that they were willing to believe I was her without any evidence. But I am not so certain that I am my mother's daughter."

"Don't say that!" Veriasse interrupted. He said to Gallen, "How dare you! How dare you set yourself up to judge her, you miserable little piece of filth!"

"And how dare you create a god to judge me without my consent!" Gallen shouted. "I'll not aid you further. In fact, I'll kill you both dead right now, unless I get some answers!"

"Don't, Gallen—" Orick growled.

"If he must know the truth," Everynne said to Veriasse, "I prefer to answer his questions." She held her head high, gazed evenly into Gallen's eyes. He could detect no fear in her, no deceit.

"You're right about me. I don't feel that I deserve to be the Lord Judge of your world or any other. I haven't earned that right, and I doubt I'm worthy of it. Certainly, I'm not sure that my people would approve of me. The Tharrin do not just insert a Lord Judge as a ruler. They breed and train and test tens of thousands of candidates for every position that is filled—and I fear that if they knew me, they would be horrified by me. Yes, I carry a device in my pocket that could destroy this world! Yes, I've let hundreds of people throw their lives away so that I can win back my mother's place. I—I don't even want the position! Maggie—" She looked at the girl. "You told me the other day about how you hated working in your little inn, scrubbing dirt from the floors, washing, feeling like a slave. Yet can you imagine being asked to clean the filth from ten thousand worlds? Can you imagine being the sole arbiter in a hundred thousand disputes per day, sentencing thousands to die every hour? I—I cannot imagine any post that would make me feel more corrupt!"

Tears filled her eyes, and Everynne began coughing, heaving in great sobs. She fell to her knees in the water, folding her arms over her stomach. "Did you see how many died for me today? When I look at the things I've done . . ."

"Shhh . . ." Veriasse said, sloshing through the water to comfort her. "No matter, no matter. You must only take the post for awhile—long enough for the Tharrin to send a replacement."

Gallen studied them. It was said that the Tharrin were bred for compassion. He could now see how Everynne suffered. She carried weapons to destroy a world, yet those weapons tore at the very fabric of her sanity, and as he watched her sobbing, saw her self-loathing, part of him realized that if he were to be judged by a god, she was the one he wanted.

Veriasse held Everynne, but he stared up at Gallen with angry, brooding eyes.

"What are your plans?" Gallen asked, "I want every detail."

"We are going to make war with the dronon," Veriasse answered. "The Terrors are set on their most heavily occupied worlds. We will only detonate them if we are forced to."

"Father, don't!" Everynne said. "No more lies! They've earned the right to learn the truth."

"You can't—" Veriasse urged, but Everynne said, "Veriasse and I are going to Dronon, to battle the Lords of the Swarm in single, unarmed combat. If Veriasse can defeat them, then by dronon law we will become their lords, and I can order the dronon to retreat from human territory. It's the only way to save our worlds. It is what my mother wanted. Everything we've done— the Terrors, the talk of war, all have been a ruse."

Gallen considered—his mantle carried a great deal of battle information, and he recalled the dreams it had been sending. Veriasse had made detailed studies of how to fight the dronon in unarmed combat, and Gallen pondered upon the possibility. Nature had gifted the dronon vanquishers with armor. They were larger, stronger, and more mobile than a human, and had an array of weapons that was frightening. A human could hardly hope to win against one in unarmed combat.

"Why not a full-scale war?" Gallen asked. "You could win a war like the one you described on Fale. Destroy Dronon and the occupied worlds. A few fleets could then clean up the mess."

"We could win a war temporarily," Veriasse said, "but we would weaken this entire arm of the galaxy. The dronon despise weakness. They try to root it out, destroy it. We would open ourselves to certain attack by other swarms. In time, we would lose. The only way to defeat them with any hope of retaining our territories for an extended period is to beat them decisively while retaining a strong navy. This means that we cannot risk destroying our old guardians, the ones you call "ogres." Each guardian takes orders through the omni-mind. We have to win Everynne's omni-mind back and regain control of our navies. We must make the dronon fear our species more than they already do."

"What do you mean, fear us more than they do? I have seen no evidence that they fear us."

"The dronon rule by a rigid hierarchy," Veriasse said. "When a Golden

Queen takes over as Lord of the Swarm, then the lords of her defeated enemy do obeisance, accepting her as their rightful leader. But it has been six years now since the dronon conquered us, and few of our lords have subjugated themselves to dronon authority. Instead, our resistance fights the dronon continually, while our lords publicly apologize to the dronon for the 'madmen' in our midst who have not yet accepted their queen. But the dronon are not stupid—they see the pattern. Although it goes against their very nature to destroy all members of a defeated hive, they have resorted to xenocide on dozens of our defeated worlds. They fear that, as a species, we are insane."

"Why do you keep your plan a secret, then?" Gallen said. "If you plan to challenge the Lords of the Swarm in combat, why not be more forthright?"

"Some factions would try to stop me," Everynne said. "The aberlains, for instance, hope to reap great profits under the Dronon Empire, and they would sabotage our efforts. But there is a more compelling reason to keep this a secret: by dronon law, those who do battle against the Lords of the Swarm must earn 'Charn'—the right to pass through hive territories—by battling each lesser queen and her escorts."

"We've had to pass through fourteen occupied worlds so far," Veriasse said. "If we had kept dronon law, I would have had to fight the ruling Lord Escort on each planet. You are wearing my mantle, Gallen. You know how difficult it will be for a mere human to win against dronon vanquishers in unarmed combat. I can't risk fighting many Lord Escorts. In any given battle, if I lost, then the Lord Escort would try to mar Everynne by wounding her. If Everynne is wounded, she would forfeit her eligibility to succeed the Golden Queen."

"What do you mean?" Maggie asked.

"Among the dronon, the Golden Queens must be unblemished," Veriasse answered. "And though some humans have been integrated in dronon society for sixty years, we are not even sure that the dronons will accept a human as Lord of the Swarms. But if they will even consider her as a contender, Everynne can have no visible defects, no scars. I hope the dronon will accept Everynne as an example of one of our own Golden Queens—one who is flawless. One born to rule. For her entire life, we have managed to keep Everynne from ever taking an injury that would leave a scar. That is why I work so hard to keep her from jeopardizing herself."

"I have one question more," Gallen said. "You carry a Terror. If you plan only single combat, why do you need such a device?"

"In case we lose totally," Veriasse said. "Everynne and I are going to the planet Dronon itself. If they reject our suit for the right to engage in ritual combat, they may try to kill us outright. Under such conditions, we have no choice but to begin the fruitless war that we have tried so hard to avoid. We hope that the very presence of the Terror will force the queen's hand, so that she will have to let us challenge. But, if necessary, Everynne's mantle will detonate the Terror. When the Golden Queen dies, the dronon will lose contact with the omni-mind. Their automated defenses will close down, and our freedom fighters will attack."

Gallen did not need to ask what would happen next. His mantle whispered the answers. If Dronon was destroyed, forty percent of the hives would die with it. Lesser queens might take over their own realms on distant worlds, but a long and bitter civil war would begin as hives battled to determine who would become the new Lords of the Swarm. Other dronon swarms around the galaxy would be tempted to invade during that time. Even if new lords were found, the inexperienced leaders would be weak. Leadership might turn over several times within the first few months. During such turmoil, the humans would be given time to win back lost territories, gain a stronger foothold. But as Veriasse had said before, it would pose a terrible risk in the long term.

"There is one scenario that you have not described," Gallen said, "and I am afraid it is the most likely. What if the dronon let you battle for succession and you lose?"

"Then we will at least have established a precedent that would give humans *the right* to battle for succession," Veriasse answered. "I have provided key people on several worlds with tissue samples from Everynne. Thousands of clones could be made. In time, one of her escorts could win the battle."

"Would you then detonate the Terror on Dronon?"

Everynne shook her head. "We couldn't. Our best hope for success in this contest is to fight the dronon within the bounds of their laws. My mother and the Tharrin considered this course of action for many years. This is the best way to win back our worlds. Otherwise, billions of innocent people will die on both sides of the battle. Surely you see that this is how it must be?"

"But if you don't win," Maggie said, "you will be subjecting your people to years of domination by the dronon. You can't let that happen. The aberlains are making such far-reaching changes that in another generation, our children will no longer be human. You can't let that happen!" Maggie's eyes went wide. Though she had appeared calm over the past two days, Gallen could see how her experience on Fale had devastated her.

Veriasse sighed, and Everynne tried to comfort her. "It will be a sad day, even if we win," Everynne admitted. "Under Tharrin law, we also permitted upgrades on humans—but only within the limits agreed upon by their parents. We wanted all people to be decent and free, and earn the right to immortality. Sometimes we allowed upgrades of whole civilizations so that a people might become better adapted to their own world. But these sad creatures the dronon are forming—my heart bleeds for them. I fear that there will be little place for them in our society. We will give them the opportunity to go to Dronon, if they so desire, carve a niche among the hives. Those who choose to remain with us may have their children reverse-engineered. And I promise you, the aberlains will be punished."

Gallen could see that Everynne was not gambling with the future of her people. She would either win and live, or she would die and give her people new hope in the process. In either case, Gallen suddenly yearned to go to Dronon to see what would happen—even if it meant dying in the nanotech fire of a world-burning Terror.

Gallen thrust his incendiary rifle into its sheath, pulled his sword from the sand, and began to dry the dripping blade by whipping it over his head in complex patterns.

"Veriasse," Maggie said, "I have been wondering. Even in my short time working for the aberlains, I concluded that your guardians could have been engineered better. They could be more heavily armored, could be virtually invincible. Since they were Lady Semarritte's only police force, I find it odd that they are this weak. Orick killed one with his teeth."

"Lady Semarritte did not rule with an iron hand," Veriasse said. "The Tharrin rule by the will of the people. Yes, the guardians are imperfect. Part of their weakness stems from the fact that they are based upon models that are very old. But we have always known that someday, someone like the dronon could gain control of an omni-mind. Since guardian officers wear Guides and receive orders directly from the omni-mind, any usurper who controls the omni-mind also controls fleets and armies with billions of warriors spread out across ten thousand worlds. Isn't it a comfort to know that a human has some hope of beating them?"

Gallen thrust the blade into his sheath. "Let's go," he said as he turned and began walking toward the distant shore.

They chugged through the warm water for the next three hours with only one brief rest. The sea had little salt in it and remained marvelously clear. By picking a trail through shallows, they spent most of their time in water that didn't reach their hips, though they could often look out into deeper pools. In places, rock formations thrust up to create submerged islands. Here, fish swarmed in great silver schools that darted out to the depths and then raced back to the shelter of the rocks. Twice they saw great beasts swimming in the depths, chasing fish. Veriasse warned Gallen to watch for the creatures. "Puas, they are called," he said. "They feed on fish and anything else they can swallow."

At last they reached dry land—a beach that extended for miles. The beach was home to sand flies and some soft creature that reminded Gallen of a pine cone with eight legs. Small reddish black spiders fearlessly scuttled about carrying small rocks. If anyone got too close to the spider, it would toss a stone, flipping it over its back with its hind legs. They were fearless spiders, lords of the sand. Gallen saw no birds.

A stiff gale blew from the sea; soon it began driving water over the beach. At last they reached a stony ridge—a metallic green expanse of sculpted limestone like a chimney, flat on top. The ground here was rocky, thick with tide pools.

Gallen and Orick climbed one steeple of pale limestone, looked south-east. In the distance they saw a city built on stilts, but just below them a group of four children were hunting in the tide pools. The children had red skin and were so long of leg that they looked like cranes as they waded through the pools. They had tied colorful rags into their hair, and they wore bright tunics.

With them was a beast, striped with gold and brown scales. It had large carnivorous teeth and used its tail to balance on its strong back legs. Its front legs were small and heavily clawed. Gallen recognized the creature as a dinosaur, some type of raptor. On its back was an ornate leather saddle. Gallen watched the children and their dinosaur hunt. The beast would run through tidal pools, splashing, using a bony crest near its nose to push over heavy rocks. The children would then leap in with capture sticks and scoop up large, yellow lobsters. Some of these they put in a sack, others they fed to their pet.

At last a small child noticed Gallen's shadow on the ground and looked up. She smiled and waved, pointed at Gallen. The other children glanced at him, then returned to hunting lobsters.

Gallen and Orick climbed back down, and the group made their way around the ridge. The children were just fishing their bag of lobsters from the water. An older boy, perhaps ten, greeted them and asked their destination. Veriasse said that they were heading to the city, and the children seemed happy to see visitors.

The two smallest children were eager to announce the strangers. The children mounted the dinosaur and headed toward the city in the distance, letting the dinosaur run in a long, loping gait. Soon they had nearly raced out of sight. The city, six miles distant, rose from the ground like some vast collection of mushrooms.

Gallen and the others walked through a maze of stony tide pools as an afternoon thunderstorm brewed, until they reached the city. They climbed a wide, winding stairway, like the stem of a mushroom.

When they reached the top, the terrain was uneven, like rolling hills. Small clusters of cement domes made up the homes. No glass was in the windows, no doors in the doorways. Apparently the temperatures here remained warm all year, and no annoying insects flew about. Each doorway led out to a wide parapet where people sat and cooked at communal fires and listened to music. Atop the dome houses were lush gardens.

Everynne removed her mask and pulled back the hood that veiled her face, walking into the city undisguised. The people came out on their verandas to cheer her entrance to the city with loud whistles. Gallen looked at Veriasse, wondering why Everynne was so bold here, and Veriasse explained. "Here on Cyannesse, the dronon are but a distant threat. We are over forty thousand light-years from the world of Fale, well behind our battle lines with the Dronon Empire. Their warships will not reach here for many years.

Still, the people here have heard of our long war, and they know Everynne for what she is."

So it was that by early afternoon, Gallen found himself in the ancient city of Dinchee by the Sea of Unperturbed Meditation on Cyannesse, and there tasted the peace that had once been the rule among Everynne's people.

That evening there was music and feasting in the city of Dinchee, on the city's uppermost tier. The suns went down in a blaze of gold, and a cool wind blew thunderheads across the wide ocean. Children roasted whole lobsters over cooking stones and brought them to the guests on great heaping trays, along with melons and roasted nuts and tubers. Gallen could not identify all that he ate, but he ate to his fill, then lay back on the grass with his mouth open, letting the wind play over his face.

Out over the gardens, three youths played mandolins and guitars while a young woman sang. Everynne sat beside them listening, while Veriasse sat beside an old Tharrin woman who insisted on being called only Grandmother, a silver-haired matriarch with small bones and a beauty undiminished by age. She sat on the stones, her long legs folded out to the sides. She wore an ancient mantle that was made of brass-colored plates with ornate symbols of knowledge. The young people of her city served her with great deference.

As Gallen sat under the oncoming night, he saw that these people were not rich. They did not have great stores of food, but instead harvested from the sea and from their gardens. Their entertainment was simple. Shops did not crowd the plazas, as they had on Fale. Everyone wore tunics in bright colors. But if they were not rich in worldly goods, they had enough, and they seemed rich in peace. Their children were strong and smart and happy.

Veriasse talked softly with Grandmother, asking for a couple of airbikes and provisions. The old woman smiled and nodded, saying that they had few airbikes. Yet she granted all of his requests.

Veriasse stopped talking for a moment, looked at Gallen, Maggie, and Orick. "Our three friends," he told Grandmother, "would like to rest here, taking refuge with your people until they can return home."

"They will be welcome," Grandmother said. "As friends of the Grand Lady, we will be glad to attend to them."

"Pay no attention to that old rooster," Gallen said quickly. He nodded at Veriasse. "I'll be going with Everynne when she leaves."

Veriasse shook his head. "I have given it some thought, and I've decided that you shall not come. The dronon control the next two planets we shall visit, and frankly, Everynne and I will be less conspicuous without you."

"Have you asked Everynne about this?" Gallen asked.

"No," Veriasse said softly. "I don't think I need to."

"Then I will," Gallen said. He glanced over at the singers. Everynne had been listening to them, but now she had gone. He spotted a flash of blue in the twilight, saw her walking over a small hill among the trees. He got up, made his way through the crowd until he found the trail she had taken. It led down a small gully and off into a miniature woodland where crickets sang in the evening. Of all the things on this planet so far, only the crickets reminded him of home. The path was broad and well-maintained.

He couldn't see Everynne, so he let his mantle tweak his hearing and vision. He moved as silently as a mist down the trail, passed a pair of naked lovers rolling in a deep bed of ferns.

After a hundred yards, he reached a railed balcony at the edge of the city. There he found Everynne on a parapet at the forest's edge, watching the suns set. The tide was rushing in over beaches they had negotiated a few hours earlier. The sea had turned coppery orange, and huge white breakers smashed against the limestone rock formations. Beneath the wild, tormented waves, he could see a vast line of green lights.

Everynne stood very quietly. Though she held herself erect, proud, she was so petite that he could have lifted her with one hand. Though her back was to him, he saw tears on her cheek. She shook softly, as if she tried to hold back a wracking sob. "Have you come to watch the torchbearers?" she said, jutting her chin toward the waves and the green lights beneath. "They're beautiful fish. Each bears its own light to hunt by."

Gallen walked up behind her, put his hands on her shoulders. She started a bit, as if she had not expected his touch. Beneath his hands, her muscles were tense, strung tight, so he began kneading them softly.

He wanted to ask permission to follow her, but she seemed so troubled, he could not bear to do so. "I don't want to talk about fish. They aren't important. What are you crying about?" Gallen waited a long moment for an answer.

Everynne shook her head. "Nothing. I just—" She fell silent.

"You are sad," Gallen whispered. "Why?"

Everynne looked off, staring at the sea. "Do you know how old my mother was?" Her voice was so soft, Gallen could hardly hear it over the crashing of breakers.

"A few thousand years," Gallen guessed. She had, after all, been immortal, and Veriasse claimed to have served her for six thousand years.

"And do you know how old I am?"

"Eighteen, twenty?" Gallen asked.

"Three, almost," Everynne answered. Gallen did a double take. "Veriasse cloned me after my mother died. He raised me in a force vat on Shintol, to speed my growth. He couldn't risk that I might have a normal childhood—couldn't take a chance that I might cut myself or break a bone. While I grew in the force vat, he used mantles to teach me—history, ethics, psychology. I feel as if I have learned everything about life, but experienced none of it."

"And in a few days, you fear that your life may end?"

"No—I *know* it will end," Everynne said. "My mother was far older and wiser than I. The dronon had been lurking on her borders for thousands of years. She had millennia to prepare for her battle with them, and still she died. I think my chances of winning are nil. But even if I win, I will be changed. You know what it is to fuse with a personal intelligence, the wonder and pain that all burst in on you in a moment. But an omni-mind is the size of a planet and stores more information than a trillion personal intelligences combined. I am . . . less than an insect compared to it. My mother and it grew to become one, and when her body died, it would download her personality into her clones. It stores everything that was my mother—all her thoughts, her dreams, her memories. And if I fuse with it, I will no longer be me in any way that matters. Her experiences will overwhelm me, and it will be as if I never existed."

"You would still be you," Gallen said, hoping to comfort her. "You wouldn't lose that." But he knew he was wrong. As far as the omni-mind was concerned, Everynne was just a shell, a template of the Great Judge Semarritte, waiting to be filled. In the space of a moment, Everynne would grow, learn more than he or billions of other people could ever hope to know. Yet her personality, her essence, would be swept away as something of no importance.

She turned and looked into his eyes, smiled sadly. "You're right, of course," she said, as if to ease his mind. The wind blew her hair; Gallen looked into her dark blue eyes.

"Maybe," Gallen offered, "someone else could take your place. There are other Tharrin. Perhaps Grandmother would reign in your behalf."

Everynne shook her head. "She is a grand lady, but she would not take my place. A Lord Judge must earn that position, but Grandmother could not earn that title. All of the Tharrin knew of Semarritte's plan to return as a clone. I sometimes wonder if I am worthy to become a Servant of All, but the Tharrin treat me as if I am but an extension of Semarritte. They say that once I join with the omni-mind, my own short life will have meant nothing. I will be Semarritte." She paused, took a deep breath. "I want to thank you for what you did today."

"What do you mean?"

"When you pulled the incendiary rifle on us. I'm glad that you're not the kind of person who would follow me blindly. Too few people question my motives."

"Do you feel that your motives need questioning?"

"Of course!" Everynne fell silent for a moment; Gallen heard someone laugh in the distance. It was growing dark, and Gallen felt he should go, but Everynne was standing close to him, only a hand's breadth away. She gazed into his face, leaned forward and kissed him, wrapped her arms around him.

"Question my motives," she whispered fiercely. Her lips were warm, inviting.

Gallen took her request literally. "You're afraid that you will die soon,"

Gallen whispered, and he kissed her back. She leaned into him, her firm breasts crushing into his chest.

"I think I'm falling in love with you," she whispered. "I want to know what it's like for *me* to be in love."

Gallen considered the way that she had said it, pulled back. "Veriasse was your mother's escort. Was he also her lover?"

Everynne nodded, and suddenly Gallen understood. Once the omni-mind downloaded its memories, Everynne would become Semarritte in every way. Veriasse was not just trying to restore the Great Lord Judge to his people. He was rebuilding his wife. "He has never touched me, never made love to me," Everynne said. "But I can see how I torment him. I'm but a child to him, a shadow of the woman he loves. Sometimes he watches me, and I can see how his desire tears at him."

Everynne leaned close for a long moment. Gallen could feel her heart hammering against his chest. "Give me this night," she said. "Whatever comes later, let me stay with you tonight."

Gallen looked into her wide eyes, felt the heat of her body next to his.

"I know you want me," she said. "I've felt the intensity of your gaze from the moment we first met. I want you, too."

Gallen found himself shaking, stricken. She was indeed the most beautiful, most perfect woman he had ever seen, and it hurt to know that they could never be together. He could not deny what he felt. If she asked him to become her Lord Escort, fight the dronon in her behalf, he would gladly do so, lay his life on the line day after day, hour after hour.

Yet she could only promise him one night of love. Everynne pulled off her own robe and undergarments, stood in the dusk and let him hold her. Her breasts were small but pert. Her hips were shapely, strong. She began breathing deeply, pulled off Gallen's robe, then pulled him down to the deep sweet grass there on the parapet, and together they made love long and slow.

Afterward, they lay together naked. Down in the sea below, the waves covered the limestone and the torchbearer fish lit the ocean in pale green. Above them, the clouds passed and stars sprinkled the sky, until everything was light. The warm winds blew through the trees, and Gallen felt peace inside.

Everynne cuddled closer, and they slept awhile. When he woke, the winds were beginning to cool. The great school of torchbearer fish had departed, and the night draped over them like a tent. Gallen kept his arms wrapped around her protectively. He could not help but think that this was the beginning and the end of their love. They had sealed it with one, small, nearly insignificant act. Now, the future lay before them, and no matter what happened, tomorrow the winds of change would blast them apart like two leaves scattered in a storm. The sky above them was so vast, so nearly infinite in size, and it seemed to Gallen that they were lying naked while the infinite, appalling darkness prepared to descend.

Thus it was that at last Gallen looked up to see Veriasse standing in the shadows at the head of the trail. Gallen startled, tried to sit up and throw his clothes on in one move, but Veriasse raised a finger to his lips.

"Careful, don't wake her," he said, his voice ragged. "Throw her robe over her, keep her warm."

Gallen did so, slid into his undergarments, then his own robes. He watched Veriasse from the corner of his eye, half afraid that the older man would attack him, but Veriasse seemed more hurt than angry. He kept his arms protectively folded over his stomach and turned away, began walking slowly up the path.

Gallen finished dressing and followed Veriasse. The old man walked with his back straight, tense. Gallen needed to break the silence, so he said softly, "I'm sorry, I—"

Veriasse whirled, stared hard at Gallen. "No apologies are necessary," he said at last, with hurt in his voice. "Everynne obviously has chosen you over me. I suppose it is only natural. She is a young woman, and you're an attractive man. I, ah, ah . . ." He raised his hands, let them drop in consternation.

"I'm sorry," Gallen said, unable to think of anything more.

Veriasse advanced on him, pointed his finger. "You shut your mouth! You know nothing of sorrow! I've loved her for six thousand years. I love her as you could only hope to love her!"

"No!" Gallen shouted, and suddenly a rage burned in him. "You loved her mother, you miserable bastard! Everynne is *not* Semarritte! Everynne may be willing to do your will, she may be willing to wear the omni-mind for the good of her people, but if she puts it on, you will have destroyed her. You will have murdered your own daughter in order to regain the woman you love!"

Veriasse's eyes blazed and his nostrils flared. Gallen realized that his mantle was heightening his vision. Gallen's own muscles tightened and when Veriasse swung, Gallen ducked under the attack, sought to remain calm, emotionally detached. He punched at Veriasse's belly, but the old man dodged, kicked at Gallen's chest.

Suddenly they were both moving, spinning in a blur of fists and feet in the darkness. Veriasse was like a ghost, impossible to touch. Guided by his mantle, Gallen swung and kicked in a steady barrage of attacks that would have overwhelmed any dozen ruffians back on Tihrglas, yet never did a blow land with any force. Sometimes Veriasse would turn a blow, and in one brief portion of a second, Gallen's hopes soared. But after three minutes, he had not landed a blow, and he was beginning to tire. He knew that Veriasse would soon attack.

Gallen stepped back from the fight, took a defensive stance. Veriasse was not winded. "I wore that mantle for six thousand years, and would be wearing it now if I didn't fear that it would jeopardize my right to fight in ritual combat," he said. "I taught it most of what it knows."

Then he leapt for the attack. Gallen dodged the first few swings and kicks, but Veriasse threw a head punch that Gallen tried to deflect with his wrist. The old man was far stronger than Gallen had ever imagined, and the blow felt as if it would snap Gallen's arm. The punch grazed his chin, sent him sprawling.

Gallen leapt back to his feet, let the mantle guide his actions. Veriasse began a deadly dance, throwing kicks and punches in combinations that were designed to leave a victim defenseless. Gallen's mantle began whispering to him—this is a fourteen-kick combination—flashing images of what would happen in his mind quickly so that Gallen could escape the final consequences.

After forty seconds, Veriasse leapt back, apparently winded, studied Gallen appreciatively for a second, then leapt into combat once more. He swung and kicked in varying combinations so fast that Gallen's mantle was overwhelmed; Gallen had to fend blindly, retreating through the woods. Veriasse was swinging and leaping, his fists and hands in Gallen's face so much that Gallen was sure he would go for a low kick. But suddenly Veriasse vaulted into the air and kicked for his chest. Gallen reached up to turn the kick with his arm, but the old man shifted in midair, aiming the kick at the blocking arm.

The blow landed with a snapping sound on the ganglia in Gallen's elbow, numbing the entire arm. A second kick landed as Veriasse dropped, hitting Gallen's ribs hard enough to knock the wind from him. Veriasse twisted as he fell through the air, and a third kick grazed Gallen's head, knocking off his mantle.

Gallen hit the ground, gasping for breath, and glared up at Veriasse. He would be no match for the old man without a mantle. Even with a mantle, he'd been no match for the old man.

Veriasse stood over him, gasping. Sweat poured down Gallen's face; without the mantle, he could see little in the darkness, but he could make out Veriasse's blazing eyes. Gallen held his aching arm, found that he could only move his numb fingers with difficulty.

"I don't need you," Veriasse said. "You are not coming with us."

"I'm sure Everynne will have something to say about that," Gallen said.

"And I'm equally sure that I will not listen to her."

"Just as you've never listened to her?" Gallen asked. "You send her to her death and think you can ignore her cries?"

"You find that appalling?" Veriasse said roughly, his voice suddenly choked.

"Yes," Gallen said. "I find *you* appalling."

The old man nodded his head weakly, stood by a tree and suddenly grabbed it for support, looking about absently as if he had lost something. "Well, well, so be it. I find myself appalling. There is an apt saying among my people, 'Of all men, old politicians are the most damned, for they must live out their days in a world of their own creation.'"

Gallen was surprised that Veriasse did not argue, did not defend his actions. "Is it so easy for you to be appalling?"

"What I'm doing," Veriasse said, straightening his shoulder, "appalls even me. . . . But, I can think of nothing else to do. Gallen, an omni-mind takes thousands of years to construct. Once it is built, it is meant to be used by only one person throughout the ages. If another person tries to wield it, the intelligence cannot function to full capacity. We *must* win back that omni-mind! And though I wish it were not so, whoever deigns to use it will be consumed in the process. I knew this when I first cloned Everynne. I knew she would be destroyed. Somehow, the sacrifice seemed more . . . bearable at the time." Veriasse turned away, his breath coming deep and ragged. "Gallen, Gallen—how did I get into this mess?"

Veriasse needed a way out of his predicament. He stood for a moment, his back turned to Gallen. "What if you get killed in your match with the dronon?" Gallen asked. "What will happen to Everynne?"

"She may be killed also."

"But, if I remember your words correctly, that is not what the dronon do to their own Golden Queens who lose the combat. Instead, the losing queen is only marred and may never compete in the contest again."

"True," Veriasse agreed, "sometimes. But the decision whether to mar or destroy the queen comes at the whim of the victor. I fear that the dronon would not spare Everynne. They murdered all of the Tharrin they could catch in this sector after the invasion, then obliterated their genetic matter."

"I am coming with you to Dronon," Gallen said. "If you lose, perhaps I can convince the dronon to only mar Everynne. Of all possible outcomes, this one alone gives her some hope. She would be free to live her own life."

Veriasse looked down at Gallen, raised an eyebrow. "You would risk everything on this one chance to save her? It sounds like a noble gamble," he admitted. Veriasse paused, drew a breath, and he suddenly straightened, as if a load had been lifted from his shoulders. "I will welcome your company, then. And if I die in the contest, I can only hope that you will succeed in bringing Everynne away safely. She is a great treasure, the last of her kind in this part of the galaxy."

Veriasse helped Gallen to his feet. Gallen's arm and ribs ached. Veriasse said heavily, "I would like to ask you an important favor. When I gave you my mantle, I did so with ulterior motives. Gallen, I have seen tapes of the Lord Escort's battles. His name is Xim, and among the Lord Escorts, he is the most capable warrior in many generations. I do not think I have a great chance to survive this fight. If I die, I want you to be my successor. Would you become the next Lord Escort?"

"Me?" Gallen asked, suddenly aware that Veriasse had made a complete turnabout. "But I'm no one. Certainly you have better warriors than me."

"We created the guardians to fight for us," Veriasse said, "and so we have not needed human warriors. You wear my mantle, and in time, given a few years, it will teach you. You could become as great a warrior as any I might hope to find."

Gallen considered the request. He was tempted to say yes. If Everynne died, another like her would be created, and her need would be just as great. Yet if he promised to do as Veriasse asked, he would be bound to labor for many years with perhaps nothing but an ignominious death as a reward. He recalled his oath, that when his heart was hot to aid another, he would always do so.

"As you wish," Gallen said.

Thirteen

As night fell, Maggie and Orick sat talking to Grandmother. The old woman let the children build a bonfire with branches from the nearby woods, and Grandmother asked Maggie many questions about her home in Clere.

Maggie told Grandmother of her work in the inn, how she cleaned and scrubbed and cooked all day. She told how her mother died of sickness after giving birth, and of her father and brothers, who had all drowned when their small fishing boat capsized. It seemed to Maggie that Tihrglas was a cold and bitter place, where she had felt cramped, forced into a corner, and as she talked, Maggie realized that she did not want to go back. To live here on Cyannesse, even to live on Fale as a free woman, would be better.

Yet when she finished telling Grandmother about Tihrglas, the old woman smiled and nodded sagely. "We are like you, in that we keep no android servants. This lets us serve one another and take pride in our work. A simple life is best," she said, as if she were agreeing that, yes, life on Tihrglas must be peaceful.

Maggie wanted to growl and scream in the old woman's face, but Orick chimed in with, "Och, well said! I'll drink to that!" and he lifted a goblet of wine in his great paws and poured it down his throat.

The wind was blowing through the trees, and it sounded like the wind that blew through Tihrglas on a summer's night, warm and comforting with the taste of the sea in it. It was the same kind of wind that had lulled Maggie to sleep as a child, and she felt a pang of longing, not for that damned Tihrglas, but for her childhood, for the blissful ignorance she felt before she'd heard of the dronon, and Maggie realized that if she had never heard of the dronon, even if she'd never left home, she would probably have grown old and been content. "Yes," Maggie agreed at last, "a simple life is best."

Veriasse had gone out to look for Gallen and Everynne quite awhile ago, and Maggie was growing worried. Veriasse had said that there were factions who would fight Everynne. Maggie wondered if such factions existed here on Cyannesse, among these seemingly peaceful people.

"I think I'll go look for Gallen," Maggie said, and she went uphill, past the singers who sat around a small fire.

By now the stars were out. A red moon was rising and the ocean had slid in under the city. With the wind, Maggie felt pleasantly cool, and she strained her senses as she entered the woods. She found dozens of trails and had no idea which to take, but soon she found one that led to the railing looking out over the ocean. There were benches by the railing, and a path that followed the rail around the city. Maggie imagined that if she just followed the path, she would find Gallen and the others sitting on some bench, talking quietly.

She grabbed the iron rail and used it as a guide, walking through the forest. At the third intersection to another path, she still had not found Gallen and Veriasse, but just as she was ready to pass, she looked down in the cinnabar moonlight, saw Everynne lying in the grass, dead. Her robe was draped over the body, as if to hide it.

Maggie gave a startled cry, rushed to Everynne's side and pulled off the robe. Everynne was naked. She opened her eyes, looked up.

"What?" Everynne said, sitting up. She looked around in a sleepy daze. "Where's Gallen?"

Maggie could think of nothing to say. Her heart was hammering and her head spun. "You slept with him, didn't you?"

Everynne crawled through the grass, picked up her underclothing and put it on, watched Maggie without saying anything. She began to put on her robe.

"You took him, just because you could!" Maggie said.

"On many worlds," Everynne said, "men and women sleep together whenever they want. It means nothing."

"Yeah," Maggie said. "Well, where I come from, it means something, and you knew that!"

"I didn't *want* to hurt you," Everynne said.

Hurt me? Maggie wondered. You've crushed me. Maggie found her heart pounding. She didn't know who to be maddest at, Gallen or Everynne, but she knew they were both to blame. "Maybe you didn't want to hurt me," Maggie said. "But you knew that this *would* hurt me, and you did it anyway. You bought your pleasure by giving me pain. Think about that when you're the Servant of All."

Maggie turned and stormed away.

Maggie did not sleep well that night. She returned to the fire, stayed up late listening to the music of this world while waiting for Gallen, but he didn't return. Veriasse ambled from the woods later. Maggie asked if he had found Gallen. He nodded soberly, saying only, "Gallen and Everynne are talking. They wish to be alone."

When the music ended and the crowds dispersed, Grandmother conducted Maggie to a large but modestly furnished room, where Maggie bathed in warm water and lay on a soft bed to sleep, with Orick sprawled at her feet.

The longer Gallen and Everynne stayed away together, the more despair tugged at Maggie. She knew she had no claim on Gallen, they weren't promised to one another, yet she could not help but feel stricken to the core. Two years earlier, when Maggie's father and brothers had all drowned, a horrible sense of loss had overwhelmed her. But somehow it was less than what she suffered now. To watch family die caused more grief than Maggie had ever believed she would suffer again.

But when Gallen slept with Everynne, Maggie didn't just grieve from the loss but agonized with the numbing realization that no matter what she did, she could never match up to Everynne. Maggie could love Gallen, serve him, offer everything she was and ever hoped to become, but she wasn't good enough.

Part of her wanted to be angry at Everynne, to hate the woman for stealing Gallen. But the more she thought about it, the less Maggie found that possible. She had been jealous of Everynne from the first. Everynne was beautiful and kind, and in her own way she bore an air of profound loss and loneliness. It was hard for Maggie to resent someone who was in such pain.

A part of Maggie wanted to be angry with Gallen, but she kept reminding herself that he had never promised her anything. In the end, his loving Everynne seemed inevitable.

In the morning, Maggie stayed in bed late, hoping to get some sleep. Orick left for breakfast quietly, then returned.

"Grandmother and Everynne want to see you," Orick said. "They have gifts. Everynne and Veriasse are planning to leave. They want to say good-bye."

Maggie lay on the bed, her eyes gritty from lack of sleep. She could not think straight. "No. I'm not coming."

"Are you sure?" Orick asked. "They have some nice gifts." Maggie's curiosity was piqued, but she didn't want to let it show. "And there's something else. I guess I'd better break the news to you myself. Gallen is going with Everynne and Veriasse."

"He is?" Maggie asked, pulling the covers down so that she could look at Orick. The bear stood on all fours at the head of the bed, his nose only inches from her face so that he could sniff her as he spoke, the way that bears will. She could smell fruit and dirt on his moist breath.

"No, I can't go," Maggie said.

"That's a shame." Orick turned away. "Gallen will be hurt that you didn't say good-bye."

"He doesn't know what it means to hurt," Maggie said.

"Hmmm . . ." Orick grumbled. "I suppose you're referring to what happened last night? There's a lot of folks out there giving guilty looks and shuffling their feet. Even a bear can figure out what's going on." Maggie didn't answer. "Och, what are you thinking, girl? Gallen loves you! How can you believe otherwise?"

"He loves Everynne," Maggie said.

"You humans are so narrow!" Orick replied. "He loves you both. Now, if you were a bear, you wouldn't get so all bound up in trivial affairs. You would come into heat, go find some handsome young man if one was available—or an ugly old geezer if nothing better could be had—and you would invite him to perform his favorite duty in life. Then you would be done with it. None of this moaning and moping and wondering if someone loves you."

"And what if someone else wanted your lover?" Maggie asked.

"Why, that's easy!" Orick said. "You wait until he's done, then invite him over. Just because a bear is interested in one female today, doesn't mean he won't want another tomorrow."

Maggie found herself thinking of evolution, such a new concept, yet one her Guide had taught her much about. Human mothers and bear mothers had different needs. A female bear didn't have to spend twenty years raising her cubs the way a human did, and bears ate so much that having a male bear around to compete for food just didn't make sense.

"Of course," Orick offered, "if you're in a hurry to get a lover, you could just go bite the competition on the ass, chase her away."

"I can't do that, either. They're leaving together. Besides, it's not that easy with people."

"Sure it is," Orick said. "If you love Gallen, you'll fight for what you want. Get mad! Oh, hell, what am I talking to you for? Don't you realize that Gallen made his choice long ago when he rescued you from Lord Karthenor?"

Maggie watched the bear trudge away, his belly swaying from side to side. "Stupid people," he grumbled. "Sometimes I don't know why I bother. Maybe I've had things backward. Did my mother tell me to eat sheep and talk to people, or was it eat people and talk to sheep?" He wandered off.

Maggie tossed on the bed, angry at herself. Everynne, Veriasse, and Gallen would be leaving, and there was a strong possibility that they would be killed. Yet Maggie was lying here pouting. She steeled her nerves, threw off her covers.

Outside, the bright morning suns rose in an amber haze. The water had dropped during the night, revealing a vast beach, wet and gleaming. Already, the children were running out over the sand toward the rocky tidal pools to hunt.

Maggie found Gallen and the others just outside her door, sitting on stone benches in the plaza. Grandmother had three airbikes sitting in the open—machines that were all motor and chrome with a set of stabilizing wings both fore and aft. At Grandmother's feet sat several packages wrapped in silver foil.

"Ah, Maggie, I am so glad you made it," Grandmother said, clapping her wrinkled hands. "You are just in time for gifts." The old woman smiled so graciously that Maggie could not help but believe Grandmother took great pleasure in her company. Indeed, they had spoken together for a long time the previous evening, but Maggie had become so distracted afterward that the pleasantness had been driven from her mind.

Grandmother looked through her packages. "First," she said softly, "I have a gift for Lady Everynne, who is already rich beyond anything I can offer. Still, I was thinking last night that you will be going to fight the dronon, who esteem their Golden Queen higher than any other." Maggie looked at the old woman in surprise. She had forgotten that, as a Tharrin, Grandmother had been apprised of Semarritte's plans. "Since you will be our Golden Queen, you must look the part. I have for you some golden clothes and a mantle of gold." She brought out two packages. Everynne unwrapped them.

The outfit included long gloves and boots, stockings and a tunic, all in brilliant gold. The small mantle was made of golden ringlets and fit over her hair. "You will find that the gloves and clothing are very tough," the old woman said. "Almost as tough as symbiotic armor. Often, a dronon queen will defend herself if a Lord Escort chooses to do more than mar her. If you are forced to defend yourself, these clothes will help protect you. In addition, we have bonded a selenium matrix into the fists of the gloves and toes of the boots. A solid blow to a dronon body will let you crack its exoskeleton."

Everynne thanked Grandmother, and the old woman turned to Veriasse. "For our Lord Protector, I doubt that we have anything on our world that could match the weapons you already bear. And so, I give you a special hope. It is a small thing, but perhaps it will carry you through a dark time." She handed him a small package, and he opened it. The package contained a crystal vial. Veriasse took out the glass stopper.

Immediately a heavenly scent wafted through the air of the open courtyard, and Maggie was filled with such enthusiasm and a boundless sense of strength that she wanted to leap from her seat with a battle cry. Veriasse suddenly seemed to become a younger man—all the cares and worries that so creased his brow melted away. He threw back his head and laughed deep and easy. In that moment, Maggie had no doubt that Veriasse would slay the Lords of the Swarm. He was a powerful man; he could not fail.

Veriasse stoppered the vial, yet Maggie's sense of boundless fervor was slow to diminish. From Maggie's work with the aberlains, she knew that the vial must contain an extract of simple proteins—the chemical components of enthusiasm to act upon the hypothalamus, along with some type of airborne delivery system so that "hope" could be absorbed through the sinus membranes as a person breathed.

And yet, even having some idea how the hope was borne, she couldn't help but admire the craftsmanship inherent in the gift. The artist had combined the hope with some exotic perfume and had probably taken great pains to mix the right proteins so that he could elicit the perfect response.

Grandmother looked over the little group. "For Gallen, the Lady Everynne has asked a special thing. He once asked for eternal life in return for his service. And even though he rescinded his request, he has more than earned his reward. She would like to begin payment." She lifted a small packet from the ground, handed it to Gallen. "Inside, you will find six tablets containing a full set of nanodoctors. They will help heal your wounds, slow your aging, cure all ills. You have only to swallow the tablets. You will not be immortal, of course. You can be killed. But before you leave here today, we will take a template of your intellect and gather gene specimens. Then, if you should die, we can build you again."

Maggie knew something of how valuable a gift this would be. Even in Everynne's world, such things were reserved only for the most deserving. Yet Gallen took the small package, hefted it, then glanced into Maggie's eyes. He tossed the package to her. "I want you to have this. I wanted it for you all along."

Maggie sat with the package in her lap, too surprised to reply.

"Ah, a gift of true love," Grandmother said, and Maggie realized that she was right. Gallen would only give such a treasure to someone he cherished.

"I don't know what to say," she offered. "Thank you."

Grandmother patted Maggie's knee. "I have something for you, but it will not be ready until tomorrow."

Maggie thanked her, and Grandmother turned to Orick. "And now, for the bear. I have considered many things, but as I talked to you last night, of all the people I have ever met, you seem to be the most self-sufficient. You yourself admit that there is nothing you want or need, although you grumble more than anyone else I know. So, I put the question to you: what one thing would you ask of me?"

Orick stepped forward and licked his lips. "Well, you have a lot of nice things here. The food is good, the music and the company is even better— but I'm just a simple bear from the woods, and the land provides for my needs. I think if there were one thing I'd ask for, it wouldn't be yours to give." He looked at Veriasse and Everynne. "I didn't start this journey because I wanted to, but I'd sort of like to tag along with Everynne and see it through to the end."

Gallen and Veriasse looked at Everynne, letting her make the decision. Maggie suspected that even Everynne had no idea how much this would mean to the bear. For days now, Orick had been showing her a special kind of devotion, and Maggie suspected that as unseemly as it might appear, the poor bear was as lovesick for the woman as he could get.

"You've been a good friend, Orick," Everynne said. "But if I were to be a true friend in return, I would deny your request. I've tried to put a calm face on when speaking of it, but this last portion of our trip will be extremely dangerous."

"Gallen and I have been in a few tight spots before," Orick said. "And I've always been right there at his side."

"Please, don't ask this of me." Everynne's eyes misted over. "Orick, I love you. I couldn't endure the thought that you might get hurt on my account."

Orick watched her with longing in his brown eyes, turned away. "All right, then," he said. "If you don't want me. I'd probably just get in the way." He turned and began loping back toward Maggie's room.

"Wait!" Everynne said, and she rushed to him. She got down on her knees and scratched the thick fur under Orick's ears, then looked into his eyes and said lustily, "If you were a human, or I were a bear, wouldn't we have a *fine* time?"

She kissed him on the snout, and Orick's red tongue flicked out, licked her forehead. Orick gave a sharp little roar of grief and lunged away to Maggie's room.

Everynne stood watching after him a moment.

Veriasse said, "He'll be okay. Male bears get used to being sent away by females." He did not say it to be unkind, merely stated the fact. Young cubs never left their mother voluntarily. Instead, she chased them off. And later, when a male mated, he would usually run with the female until she chased him away.

Everynne nodded wistfully while still watching after Orick.

Grandmother glanced at Everynne. "Do not feel bad. You've given him the thing he most wants: your love. It is something I could not give him, and he will treasure it always."

"Can you give him something more?" Everynne asked. "Will you make him a locket with my image inside? Something to remember me by."

"Of course," Grandmother answered.

Everynne and the others prepared to leave. Veriasse began teaching Gallen the basics of riding an airbike. Maggie found it odd that Gallen didn't know how to ride the thing. She realized that the mantle she wore must have been teaching her in her sleep, for Maggie understood the most intimate workings of the bike, and as she listened to Gallen rev the thrusters, she heard them whine just a bit, suggesting that a turbine wasn't properly lubricated. She considered pulling out the toolkit stored under the airbike's seat, just to tinker.

Everynne went to get her pack, and Maggie went to get Gallen's. Orick was lying at the foot of the bed. Maggie rummaged through Gallen's pack until she found Gallen's defective key to the Maze of Worlds. He'd placed it in his old black leather money purse, drawing the string tight. Maggie removed the key, glanced around the room, looking for something of similar size to put in the key's place. In one corner was a potted plant with purpling flowers. She removed a flat stone from the plant's container, placed it in the purse, and returned the purse to the pack.

Orick watched the whole affair, then said, "What are you doing?"

"You want to go with Everynne, and I want to go with Gallen. All we need to follow them is a key."

"Do you know where they are going?"

"Veriasse was looking over his travel plans last night at the campfire. I watched over his shoulder. My mantle has stored the coordinates of all the gates but the last. We should be able to find them easily."

"But Veriasse said that using a defective key is risky," Orick warned, shaking his head.

"Everything we've done has been risky," Maggie shot back. "I'm not going to let that stop me now." Her mantle could not tell her specifically how the key worked, but obviously an electronic signal unlocked the gate and gave it the coded information on how to make a jump. True, the key was defective, but they hadn't been hurt in that first jump. Maggie decided that the key time/location send coordinates were probably out of synch with the gate destination decoder. The gate key would simply perform as it had before—sending them back in time as they traveled.

She looked at Orick sharply. "We both know that Gallen and Veriasse think we've been as helpful as a pair of mallards on this trip, but even they might need our talents. Are you coming with me, or are you just going to let the woman you love walk out of your life forever?"

"I'm with you," Orick answered.

"Good," Maggie said. "Now do me a favor and get out of here. Gallen is going to be coming in for his pack in a minute, and I want some time alone with him."

"Always being nagged by women," Orick grumbled as he left the room. "Doesn't matter if they are human or bears, they're all the same."

Maggie stood by the foot of the bed, waited for Gallen to come in. She found her heart pounding, tried to compose something to say, but nothing came to mind. All too soon, he stood in the doorway, a circle of morning light silhouetting him. In his black robes, weapons at hand, the mantle of a Lord Protector on his head, he looked somehow different, strange. No one on Tihrglas had ever worn such clothing, and Gallen seemed to stand taller in his costume, walk in more of a rolling gait. This trip was changing him, leaving an indelible mark, just as it was changing her.

"I'm surprised that you, too, didn't ask to come with us," Gallen said after a long moment.

"You wouldn't have let me," Maggie said.

"How do you know?"

"You protect people for a living. You're always watching out for others. You must know that the best way to protect me is to leave me out of harm's way."

Gallen smiled weakly. "I'm glad you understand." He walked over to her, took her by the shoulders and kissed her firmly, passionately. "Everynne told me that you know what happened last night. Can you ever forgive me?"

Maggie was confused, unsure how to answer. She thought—or at least she wanted to believe—that he really did love her. Some things pointed to it—his protectiveness, his tenderness to her now. Yet she couldn't accept that he would sleep with Everynne one night, then come to her in the morning and try to pretend that nothing had changed. She slapped his face, hard, and it barely moved him, so she punched him in the stomach. "Don't you ever do that to me again!" she hissed. "Do you understand me? Don't you ever put me in second place again!"

Gallen nodded, the lines of his face set in hard angles. She couldn't read what he was thinking. "I know that an explanation will just sound like an ex-cuse, but in all likelihood, by tomorrow night Everynne will either be dead or else so . . . changed that she will be at least as good as dead to me. She wanted something last night that only I could give. I cannot be sorry for what we did, though it pains me terribly to know how it must hurt you. What Everynne and I did last night—that was just saying good-bye." He considered for a moment, then said, "I will never put you in second place again."

Maggie studied his face. When Gallen O'Day took an oath, he'd keep it or die trying. She knew that much about him.

"Just promise to come back to me," she said. Gallen reached out to her, stroked her jaw with one gloved hand. He made no further promises. She fell against his chest and began weeping. Gallen wrapped his arms around her and hugged her until it was time to go.

Orick spent much of the day sleeping, worrying about Everynne. He wanted to leave immediately, but Maggie insisted that they wait until dark to sneak away. Maggie and Orick were both exhausted, so he tried to rest.

In spite of his nervousness, he enjoyed the hospitality of the Cyannesse that day. Once again, the day ended clear and beautiful. He and Maggie ate a sumptuous dinner, and Grandmother announced afterward that an actor wanted them to watch a play he had written in their honor.

So when the campfires had burned low, they watched the actor perform the story of an old man who became lost in a magical wood filled with wise beasts.

The old man worked for a long time, searching for a path home, but by the time the beasts helped him discover that path, he desired only to stay in the forest forever. The old man was tremendously funny, and Orick enjoyed his performance, but the thing that impressed him most was the scenery. The play was set in an open amphitheater, and when a scene changed, an entire forest would grow up as needed, or a moon would rise and shine down on a glen, or a pool of water would begin lapping where only a moment before there was solid ground. The animals, too—the gossiping deer, the overbearing badger—would appear or disappear as needed.

When the play finished, Orick thought longingly of the woods at home, the sweet mountain grasses, the trout-filled streams. Yet when they got back to their room, Maggie asked Orick, "Did you enjoy the play?"

"Och, it was a grand play," Orick said honestly. "My favorite character was the fox, most amusing."

"But what of the message of the play? What did you think of it?"

"There was a message?" Orick asked, perplexed.

"Of course there was a message. The actor was asking us to stay. We are the people lost in their magic woods."

"Oh," Orick said. "Are you sure? It only made me homesick, thinking of the woods."

But Maggie seemed sure. She sat on her bed, looking at the box of nan-odocs that Gallen had given her, as if wondering whether or not to pack them. Orick asked, "Are you going to eat those?"

"Not yet," she said firmly.

"Why not?"

"Gallen might need them still."

Orick studied her. She seemed deeply occupied. "If he died, would you take them?"

"No. I don't think so." She shoved them into her pack. "You had better get some rest. When the others are asleep, we can go borrow an airbike. There's got to be one somewhere in town."

"That would be stealing," Orick said.

"We'll bring it back, if there's any way we can."

Orick grunted, sniffed the floor, and lay down. He envied Gallen. Not every woman would choose to die if her lover died. No bear would ever do such a thing. The sense of romance behind it overwhelmed him until he almost wanted to laugh with glee. Instead, he lay down and rested.

Half an hour later, Maggie grabbed her pack and whispered, "It's time to go." She led him out into the night, under the red moon.

Grandmother sat outside the door, in the moonlight, wearing a deep robe to keep out the night air. "So, you are leaving us so soon?"

"I—" Maggie started. "Please don't try to stop us."

Grandmother smiled, her face wrinkling in the dim light. "I was once young and deeply in love," she said. "And I could never have left the man under these circumstances. Gallen gave me this before he departed." She handed Maggie the black coin purse. "He said there was a gate key in it, so that you could go home, but I found only a rock. It was not hard to guess who had taken the real key."

"What are you going to do about it?" Orick asked.

"Veriasse made a map, telling you how to get home, but I am a Tharrin. I cannot stop you from going where you will, so I shall give you your gifts now," Grandmother answered. She waved toward the shadows of a nearby home. An airbike sat beside the wall, and Grandmother escorted them both across the plaza.

Grandmother hugged Maggie, gave her a piece of bent metal. "I don't have much in the way of weapons," she said. "You are going into dangerous territory, and though I abhor violence, this gun might come in handy. Keep it hidden. Also, I have packed some meals for you to eat on the road. They're in the container under the seat of the airbike."

Maggie stifled her tears, thanked Grandmother graciously.

The old woman reached into the pocket of her robe and pulled out a large golden disk, perhaps a foot long. "And this is for you, Orick," she said. She pushed on a latch. The disk opened, and Orick felt as if he were gazing into another world. Everynne stared out at him, and she smiled and said,

"Remember, I'll always love you." Behind her, the oceans of Cyannesse lapped in early morning amber light. Orick could see Everynne perfectly, smell her. He reached up his paw, touching the image, but some soft gel would not let his paw through.

"Everynne had us record this just before she left," Grandmother said. "This memento has captured her voice, her image, her scent. It will stay good for many centuries, and I hope that when you look at it, you will not only be reminded of Everynne, but of all of us here on Cyannesse."

Grandmother closed the disk, and handed it to him. It was slippery in Orick's paws, but he wanted to hold it for awhile. Grandmother hugged him and Maggie goodbye.

Maggie got on the airbike, asked Orick to straddle it. The airbike was obviously not designed for a bear. His legs were too short to reach the foot pads and his tail was crushed at a very uncomfortable angle. Still, he managed to get on, rest his front paws against Maggie's shoulders. But he had to have Maggie put the huge locket in her pack.

Maggie pushed some buttons, and the thrusters roared to life behind his feet. He could feel the heat of the engines, and he feared that his fur would catch fire, but Maggie pressed a throttle and the airbike bucked under their combined weight, then lifted with a kick.

Orick looked back one last time at Grandmother, who stood straight in the darkness and waved good-bye. Maggie applied full acceleration. The airbike whizzed into the night, along the streets of Cyannesse until they reached the winding stair that led down to the beach, then she slowed. Still, the bike seemed to slide down, going faster and faster until they hit the sandy beach, bounced once, and then were off.

They drove straight through the night mists, out over a wide sea. The wind whipped in Orick's face, and lantern fish with their luminous backs lit the water. In some places, it seemed that Maggie and Orick whisked over a road of green light. Tiny silver fish sometimes jumped toward the headlamps of the bike.

After a while, Maggie relaxed, and the machine carried them on until they reached land near dawn. There, Maggie stopped and they ate a short meal, stretched their legs, then rode the airbike up onto a large island, through some rough terrain.

Soon they spotted a gate gleaming gold in the morning. Maggie pulled out the key, thumbed some buttons. Orick was amazed that she could learn how to work such a thing, but ahead of them the gate began glowing white between the arches.

"Where are we going?" Orick asked.

"The planet Bregnel," Maggie shouted. She slowed the airbike until they hit the light wall and were swallowed in the mists.

The airbike skated into profound darkness, into a world where the very air burned Orick's lungs, then lay in them like a clot. The ground was thick with ash, and dead trees raised tortured black branches to claw the sky. Buildings towered above them on every side, like squatting giants, and the buildings too were blackened over every wall.

Maggie coughed, hit the throttle, and the airbike whipped through the night, raising a cloud of ashes as it roared down the empty streets. Here and there on the ground, Orick could see blackened skeletons of small gnome-like humans among the ash, many still wearing their mantles, some holding weapons. It looked as if they had been caught and burned in the midst of a battle. There was no clothing left on the skeletons, no flesh on the ebony bones.

There were no lights in any window, no footprints among the ashes. The world was dead, uninhabited, and by the smell of the air, perhaps uninhabitable.

As bad as the air was, a certain heaviness fell upon Orick as well, as if he weighed more here than he had elsewhere. Upon reflection, he realized that he had felt somehow lighter and stronger upon Cyannesse, but had not noticed it then.

As they hurried forward, Orick saw a corpse on the ground, half covered with ash. Its arms were curled close to its ribs, as if the person had died protecting some great treasure. Orick almost called for Maggie to stop, but as the airbike rushed over the corpse, scattering ashes, Orick looked back. In its hands, the corpse held the bones of an infant.

"What happened here?" Orick bawled, the air burning his lungs.

Maggie shouted back, horror in her voice. "Someone released a Terror on this world."

"Did you know about this?"

"Veriasse told me that the people here were fighting the dronon."

"You mean the dronon killed them?"

Maggie shrugged.

The headlights on the airbike cut a grim alley through the darkness, and Maggie soared over winding roads through a maze of stone buildings. Up ahead, the lights shone over a pair of footprints in the ash.

Someone had lived through this catastrophe. Maggie veered to follow the trail a short way. After two blocks, they came to a dead end in an alley. There, lying in a heap on the ground was the corpse of a small man, his mouth open and gasping. Above him on the wall, he had scratched a message in the ash: "We have won freedom, not for ourselves, but for those who shall follow after."

Maggie stared at the message a moment, then hit the bike's thrusters and rode away. The airbike raced through the city, left the sprawling wastes. The countryside was no better. Fields and crops had been transformed to blackened ash. On the outskirts of town, they saw a red light up the road ahead, and Orick's heart lifted a little, hoping that someone perhaps had survived this devastation.

Instead they came upon a vast machine, a walking crablike city with eight legs and hundreds of gun emplacements sprouting from its back and head. In one lonely turret on the head, a red light gleamed like a malevolent eye. The machine reminded Orick of some giant tick, bristling with strange devices, and Orick knew instinctively that the dronon had created the thing— for no human would have built such a monstrosity.

"What is that?" Orick shouted to be heard above the roar of the airbike, hoping that Maggie's mantle would give them some clue.

"A dronon walking fortress. They built them on their home world to carry their young during their migrations."

"How long must we endure this?" Orick asked. "I can hardly breathe."

"We'll get out fast," Maggie wheezed.

"Maggie, can the Terror still hurt us?"

"If it were going to burn us up," Maggie said, "we'd already be dead by now."

After that, they did not speak. Maggie revved the thrusters, giving the bike its full throttle, and they plowed ahead. It took a great effort to breathe. Orick began gasping; his lungs starved for fresh air. He felt insufferably hot, and the world began to spin. He feared that he might fall from the bike, so he clung to Maggie. She reached up and patted his paw, comforting him. Orick closed his eyes, concentrated only on breathing. He tried holding his breath to save his lungs from the burning air, but then he would become dizzy and have to gasp all over again.

It became a slow torture, and he kept wishing that he would faint, fall from the bike and just die in the ashes.

They crossed a long bridge over a lake, and muddy ash floated on the water, creating a thick black crust. The water bubbled. Dark billowing clouds obscured a pale silver moon, and ahead was a black wall of rain. Orick imagined how the air would be cooler and fresher there in the rain, imagined tasting the water on his tongue. But they hit the wall and found that the sky rained only ash.

An hour later, they reached another gate, and Maggie got out the key, pressed some buttons until the gate glowed a soft orange, the color of sunset, then she gunned the thrusters and the airbike plunged through the white fog found between worlds.

At first Orick wondered if it would stay white forever, for the cool fog gave way only to more white mist, but then they were roaring down a snowy mountain trail through the mist, passing between large pillars of black rock.

As soon as Maggie saw that it was safe, she turned off the thrusters. The bike skidded to a halt. Maggie crawled off, fell to the ground gasping and coughing, trying to clear the foul air of Bregnel from her lungs. Orick climbed off, fell to the ground. Bears rarely get sick to the stomach, but Orick found that the brief trip through Bregnel had left him both wrung out and positively ill.

He lay in the snow and vomited, and though it was freezing, he could not muster the strength to move. After twenty minutes, Maggie got up, rubbed herself.

"Are you all right?" Orick asked.

She shook her head. "That air was too foul. Another few minutes, and I would have fallen off the bike. I'm not sure I could have gotten back up."

Orick understood. He felt grateful to be alive and offered up a silent prayer of thanks. When he finished, he asked, "Where are we?"

"A planet called Wechaus," Maggie answered. "I didn't get time to ask Veriasse about it. He said there was some danger here, but the only gate to Dronon is here, somewhere on Wechaus."

"Are any towns nearby? Someplace we can get a bite to eat, a beer maybe?" Orick looked about in the fog. If a bear could eat rocks, he'd never fear starvation on this world, that much was certain. But other than the rocks, Orick could not make out any sign of trees here, just a few small bushes.

Maggie shook her head. "I'm not sure. We still have some food in the pack. If my guess is right, we should be four or five days ahead of Gallen and the others. I thought we could find a place to stay, then follow them to the Dronon gate."

Orick looked around. It was getting darker out, and he could not see far. He wondered about things: right now, back in Tihrglas, he and Gallen were most likely lazing about at John Mahoney's Inn in Clere, drinking a beer and dreaming about tomorrow, totally ignorant of Everynne or the Maze of Worlds. At the same time, he and Gallen were on the planet Fale, trying to rescue Maggie from Lord Karthenor. In a couple of days, he would reach Cyannesse, and he didn't know when he'd be on Bregnel. Somehow, the idea that he was simultaneously mucking about on at least three different worlds at once left him shaken, and if they kept walking through the Maze of Worlds, things would get even more confusing.

It all seemed sacrilegious, as if they were playing with powers not meant to be comprehended by either men or bears. It reminded Orick of an incident when he was a cub. He and his mother had gone hunting for nuts and had climbed to the top of Barley Mountain. There, under an evergreen, they sat munching at pine nuts and looking out over mountain peaks that seemed to go on forever, fading to blue in the distance. To a small cub, it seemed as if they were viewing infinity, and Orick had asked his mother, "Do you think I'll ever get to see what's on the other side of all of those mountains?"

"No," his mother had answered.

"How come?" Orick asked, thinking that perhaps this would be his life's work, to travel far roads and learn about the world.

"Because God won't allow it. No matter how many mountains you cross, he has always made more."

"How come?"

His mother rolled her eyes at him and sighed. "Because that is how he stays God. He knows what is on the other side of every mountain, but he doesn't tell all of his secrets to others."

"How come?" Orick asked.

"Because if everyone knew the answers, everyone would be gods, even people who are evil. So in order to keep evil people from gaining his power, he hides the answers to the most important questions."

Orick had gazed out over the purpled hills and felt a rushing sensation of awe and thankfulness. God had willed him to be ignorant, and for that Orick felt profoundly grateful.

Yet now he was trying to help Everynne steal the powers of the gods. It seemed only just that he should be punished.

Maggie got a blanket from the pack and wrapped it around herself. A cold wind was stirring.

Orick sniffed the air. "Maggie, child," he said, "I think we'd best get back on that flying scrap pile and see if we can't find some shelter. Something tells me this place gets colder than a lawyer's heart at night, and you shouldn't be out in such weather."

She nodded wearily, got back on the bike, and Orick climbed on behind her. They slowly drove down the mountainside through the rocks and mist. After a few hundred yards, the fog cleared and they got their first view of Wechaus: a rocky, barren world for as far as the eye could see. Off in the distance several miles, Orick could make out one of those sidhe highways.

Maggie made her way down a steep canyon, then wound through it until they reached the highway. Once they hit the highway, the airbike seemed to know the path, and Maggie quit steering. By then, the cold and the wind were having their way with Maggie. She wrapped the blanket tighter around her and kept her head low so that the bike's windscreen protected her somewhat, but within minutes she was shaking fiercely from the chill, sobbing in pain. Orick did not know what to do: should he tell her to stop and try to get warm? It was already so cold that if he stopped, he might never get her going again. On the other hand, the poor little thing could hardly travel farther in her current condition.

So it was that they topped a mountain and looked across the line of the highway to a distant valley and saw a small village. It was an outpost of some kind—a collection of stone huts shaped like domes, well lighted with pale green lights. Orick could discern several emerald pools. Smoke was pouring from them, filling the night air.

Maggie redoubled her speed, and in five minutes they closed in, and Orick saw that it was not smoke filling the night at all, but steam. The buildings sat alongside a natural hot spring, and he could see the dark shapes of people splashing in the waters, swimming in the deep green pools. As they neared, Orick let out a whoop of delight, for among the many swimmers, he saw dozens of bears.

Fourteen

Everynne led the others through the gates on the way to Dronon. After making love to Gallen last night, it seemed that everything was ruined. Both Veriasse and Maggie knew of the tryst, and somehow it had all turned into a fiasco. Now, as she drove, she thought that perhaps it would all end. Perhaps today she would die, and thus put to death her guilt.

The vibration of the airbike mirrored her shaking. Her nerves were frayed, jangled, and she found that her teeth chattered even though it was warm.

She drove the thousand kilometers through Cyannesse at top speed, hit the gate and roared through Bregnel into the early afternoon. Veriasse cried out in shock when he saw the devastation, and all of them drove through the place in horror.

In the daylight, everything was gray and foul. Blackened human bones rotted in the streets, and dronon war cities squatted all across the countryside like dead beetles. Everynne counted twenty of them in the distance.

The air was so foul, that Gallen stopped beside a bubbling lake, got a pair of oxygen exchangers from his pack. He gave one to Everynne.

Veriasse gazed out over the countryside. His eyes were glazed with tears. "Look at all the hive cities. The dronon were building a vast military presence here."

"It looks as if the people of Bregnel decided to wipe them out at any cost," Everynne said.

Veriasse shook his head sadly. "I feared this was coming. The battle to free Bregnel was not going well. They could not have loosed the Terror more than two or three days ago. If they had only waited, perhaps this could have been avoided."

"Let's go," Everynne said. "Let's get to Dronon today." She gunned her thrusters, sped away.

Everynne let her mantle switch through open radio frequencies, trying to catch a clue as to what had happened. She locked onto only one dim channel, far away, probably a transmission beamed from satellite. It broadcast the warning, "Resistance fighters have loosed a Terror. Please take appropriate measures."

The only appropriate measures were to take flight and leave the planet.

Everynne looked out over the wastes in horror, thinking, If we go to war against the dronon, this is what it will be like. Terrors loosed upon hundreds of worlds. Fleets of starships bombarding planets with viral weapons.

Veriasse and Gallen drove side by side, sharing an oxygen exchanger from breath to breath. An afternoon wind kicked up, raising black clouds of ash that swept over the plains. Everynne hurried down the road, passed three skeletons that were half standing, half kneeling, fused together as if they had held each other for comfort in that last moment just as the burning wall of fire swept over them and the invasive nanoware burrowed through to their bones.

Everynne knew that as long as she lived, the images she saw on Bregnel would haunt her.

They broke through the next gate to Wechaus, headed down a snowy trail in the mountains. It was early morning here. They had not gone a hundred meters when they rounded a corner, spotted bloody paw prints in the snow, and Gallen shouted, "Halt!" raising a hand.

He idled his airbike, sat looking at the prints: a bear had rolled on the ground, leaving behind marks of blood and mud, compacting the snow except in one small circle. Within that circle was one firm red print with two scratch marks beneath it.

"Bear tracks," Gallen said. "Orick's here! He left a message."

"Orick?" Veriasse asked. "But I didn't show them how to get to Wechaus."

"Maggie's a smart girl," Gallen said. "And you spent enough time looking at routes on your map that she could figure it out." He pointed at the paw print. "The marks are a code. Back home, when I guard clients, Orick walks up ahead. No one ever bothers a bear, and he can smell an ambush better than any human. He leaves a print by the roadside if the path ahead is clear, but he leaves scratch marks under it if I'm to take warning. One scratch means something has him spooked. Two scratch marks means he is certain that an ambush waits ahead."

Everynne studied the bloody marks, worrying. The poor bear had to be terribly wounded. "But who would be lying in wait?" she asked. "The dronon?"

"Perhaps," Veriasse said. "When last I was here, their numbers were not great on this world, but after our escapades on Fale, they will be more wary. We should move forward cautiously." He pulled out his incendiary rifle, and Gallen did the same.

They followed Orick's footprints down to a small valley; among the snow-covered rocks they found evidence of a great battle—scorch marks from incendiary rifles, bloody tracks.

The torn body of a vanquisher lay in the snow, his naked green flesh ripped by teeth, clawed by strong paws. His incendiary rifle lay nearby, yet Everynne searched the ground with growing discomfort. The signs seemed to indicate that more than one vanquisher had fought here. Everynne could make out tracks of at least three of the giants. But if there had been only one casualty, then it seemed that Orick had fought in vain.

Veriasse looked up at Everynne. His face was rigid, fearful, and Gallen seemed equally disturbed.

Veriasse powered down his airbike, leapt off, and surveyed the site. "The dead vanquisher was taken off guard," he said after a moment. "Orick ripped out his throat, and the vanquisher pulled his incendiary gun and tried to club the bear off, perhaps fired in hopes of attracting attention. Then the vanquisher pulled a knife and drew blood, but by then it was too late." Everynne looked at the frozen corpse. There was a certain look of surprise in the creature's dead face, a blankness in his orange eyes. Veriasse took up the vanquisher's bloody knife, cut open the creature's belly, then stuck in his hand. "The corpse is still warm in the bowels. He can't have been killed more than a few hours ago."

"These tracks are crisp around the edges," Gallen said, pointing to the tracks in the snow. "They had to be made last night." He got off his bike, studied the site.

"It looks as if the vanquishers set an ambush here. They waited several hours, then Orick came up behind, killed this one. The other two ran that way!" He pointed north, shook his head. "But I can't imagine them running from an unarmed bear."

"They didn't," Veriasse said. "Those tracks are too evenly spaced, too confident. They're not the tracks of someone sprawling headlong in fear. I think those two left before the battle took place. Perhaps they were drawn off, or were redeployed. In any case, they left their companion alone, and Orick attacked the vanquisher from behind."

Everynne searched the hills above, scanning for more signs of the enemy; thick snow covered the rocks. The vanquishers could not travel through this terrain without leaving a clear trail, but Everynne could see no other footprints—only the one trail coming up from the road, and the vanquisher prints heading north parallel to the highway.

Gallen said, "After the battle, Orick didn't bother to follow these other two. Instead he left us his message, then headed back down the trail."

"Of course," Veriasse said. "Orick knew he couldn't win a battle against two vanquishers, but felt he had to leave us a warning."

"What are these vanquishers doing here? How did they anticipate us?" Gallen shook his head in disgust.

Everynne was not surprised to find the vanquishers so alert. She and Veriasse had used their key to travel to over twenty worlds in the past six months, and many of those worlds had been under dronon control. It had seemed only a matter of time until the dronon caught them.

"You know," Veriasse said as if to himself. "Maggie stole Gallen's key and experienced a temporal loss on her travels once again. Given this loss, the vanquishers who met us on Tihrglas can only have come from our own future. Which explains why they are obviously searching for me and Everynne. Somehow, the dronon learned our identities. We will have to be doubly cautious."

Veriasse wiped his bloody hand on the snow, put his gloves back on. "We'll have to disguise you," Veriasse said to Everynne. "On Wechaus, the lords do not wear masks, and this will make it difficult. Unpack your blue cloak, and tie the hood up to cover your face."

Everynne dutifully pulled the clothes out of her pack, did as Veriasse said, even though with the bright sun the morning was not terribly frigid. When she finished, they started the airbikes, followed Orick's bloody trail down to the highway and headed north.

They had not gone more than a few hundred meters when they saw bear tracks leave the road again to the east; other tracks showed where vanquishers had pursued Orick across the road from the west.

Gallen shouted when he saw the prints and took off following the trail with Everynne close behind. Not fifty meters from the road, they found the site of the last battle, and Everynne cried out in horror.

A heap of blackened bones was all that the incendiary blasts had left of the bear.

Fifteen

Maggie and Orick got off their airbike. Maggie's legs were so cold she found it difficult to walk, and for a moment she just stood shaking in the snow outside the hot springs, wrapped in her blanket. The place was obviously an inn of some kind. Bears and humans were playing in the water, leaping and splashing, while androids manned dinner tables in a large common room. But it seemed to Maggie to be an odd inn, a relic.

The inn was not a living thing like the trees on her home world or like the city of Toohkansay on Fale. Instead it was made from some poured material, perhaps, Maggie considered, so that it could retain the organic lines of a living hostel even in such a cold environment. It was designed much like the buildings found on other worlds, and if Maggie had not been wearing her mantle, she wouldn't have recognized that Wechaus was Backward. The androids waiting on tables were ancient models, a few thousand years behind the times. Few human patrons wore personal intelligences, and even those who did wore unsophisticated models. Perhaps it was the atmosphere of the inn itself, but Maggie imagined that if people here were any more relaxed, they'd have to be dead.

There was no sign of dronon or vanquishers on the premises, and Maggie took that as a good omen.

Maggie opened the front door for Orick. A golden android hurried up with a jaunty gait and said in a prissy voice, "Welcome to Flaming Springs! We're so glad you could join us!" He eyed Maggie's mantle and said, "May I set up an account for our honored guest in the name of . . . ?"

"Maggie Flynn," Maggie answered, somehow surprised that these people would require money for their services. This was new. She immediately began to wonder how much they would require, but knew that when Veriasse came, he would be able to settle the debt. At the very least, she could sell a knowledge token from her mantle. Each of the metal disks stored thousands of volumes of data, and would be valuable to anyone who wore a mantle.

"Of course, Maggie Flynn," the android said, feigning that he recognized the name. "Let me show you to a room. You may order food at any time, and the pools are always open."

He led them through a complex of small huts scattered like hills over the ground. Maggie guessed that steam piping kept the area free of snow. Around the grounds, alien treelike plants with purple fruit lived in containers.

The android opened a door, and Maggie suddenly saw why the rooms appeared so small from the outside. The upper room served as entryway to a luxurious submerged apartment below.

"Will this be adequate?" the android asked.

"Yes, thank you," Maggie answered. "Do you have the time? And the date? Galactic standard."

The android told her the time. They were one day and sixteen hours ahead of when they had left Cyannesse. Maggie made some quick calculations, realized that the temporal distortion was inversely proportional to the distance they jumped between gates. The shorter the jump, the more time they lost.

The android left, and Orick went out to the hot pools to swim. Maggie had had enough of the cold and darkness outside. A side room contained its own small pool where mineral waters cascaded down some falls. The room was decorated to look like a forest, with deep mosses and beds of ferns. Maggie retired there and lay in the water for a long time, letting the warmth seep into her bones. A startling thought struck her: she had left her pack out on the airbike, where it might get stolen.

She climbed from the pool, toweled dry, then dressed and ran out for her pack. It was still sitting in the dark, nearly frozen to the seat. She pulled it free, walked back into the common room of the inn. She had eaten a bite an hour before, but the smells were so enticing that she took a seat, asked an android for a steak dinner with mushrooms and wine.

While she waited, she took out a brush from her pack and brushed her hair. She could not resist the urge to check her pack, make sure that nothing of value had been taken. She opened it a little, dug through. Her gate key was there, and she rummaged for a moment, pulling out clothing, looking for the gifts that Grandmother had given Gallen and Orick.

Dinner came soon, and Maggie tried to enjoy the food but kept glancing up furtively.

Someone was watching her. Most of the guests at the inn were couples—young men and women out to celebrate, frequent pairs of bears. But not all of the couples looked so innocent. A thin man with a hawkish nose, long dark hair, and a thin goatee sat at a nearby table, hands folded under his chin. He did not hide the fact that he was watching her.

Yet he kept glancing toward the doors—both the front doors and those that led to the pools and the rooms at the side. Maggie lost her appetite.

She got up to leave, but the dark stranger came and discreetly took her arm, forced her to sit again, then sat next to her. "By any chance," he asked, "have you been to Fale recently?"

"Yes," Maggie said, then realized that because of the way her gate key sent her back in time, she was currently on Fale, held captive among the aberlains. "I mean, no."

"I thought so." He smiled. "Eat with me."

"No, I have to be going," Maggie said.

But the man gripped her arm, holding her, pulling her back to her seat. "Come now, you've hardly touched a bite," he said, a gleam of excitement in his eyes. "Besides, you've only had the main course. You must try the desserts."

"No," Maggie said, trying to pull her arm from his grasp. "I must be going." She yanked free.

"You won't get far," the stranger warned in a whisper, "not to the next gate."

"What?" Maggie asked, her heart hammering.

"Come follow me to your room. We must talk in private, before it's too late," the stranger said. He rose from his seat, walked out the back door. Maggie didn't know why, but the man terrified her. There was a certain calculated power in his gestures, a toughness about him, and she imagined that if he got her alone, she would not be able to protect herself. She tried to still her heavy breathing, looked around the room for some sign of help. He expected her to come, but she couldn't follow him out into the dark.

She stayed at the table, pretended to eat for an hour. She wanted to go to the pools, find Orick, but the pools were too close to her apartments. So she sat, hoping the stranger would leave. A patina of sweat broke out on her forehead, and she kept worrying that people were watching her, until Orick came in.

"Hey, Maggie!" Orick called loudly from across the room. "You should try these pools—they're great!" He swaggered over to her table, his fur still wet. "Maggie," he said with uncontrollable excitement, "half of these she-bears are in heat! I tell you, I can hardly believe my luck. Why, I met this she-bear named Panta, and she's panting for me, the dear girl, I assure you. She's invited me to her room tonight—"

"Good, good," Maggie said without enthusiasm. She didn't know how to tell him that something was dreadfully wrong. She especially did not want to talk here where every word could be overheard. Right now, she only wanted Orick to get away from her safely, keep him out of danger. "Why don't you go with her?"

"Well, I don't know," Orick said. "Do you think I should? Are you all right? You look sick."

"I'm afraid," she whispered, hoping none of the other diners could hear. "This world may be more dangerous than we thought."

"Oh, nonsense," Orick growled too loudly. "This place is grand!"

"Yes, of course it is," she said, hoping to quiet him. "Please, just go. I'll be all right."

A female bear came to the side door, stood up on her hind legs, sniffing the air. She saw Orick, walked over on all fours, and stood at the side of the table, demurely watching Orick with big brown eyes that fairly shouted her desires.

"It's nice to meet you, Panta," Maggie said. "I'm afraid I'm feeling tired. Why don't you two take this table. I'll see you in the morning, Orick." She got up, realizing that she needed to go out the side door to reach her room, see this thing through on her own. If the stranger was waiting in the darkness to accost her, she would have to face him sooner or later. She did not want to place Orick in jeopardy.

She stalked back through the night. The hot pools had raised a cloud of steam that lingered in the air between buildings, shrouding everything in heavy fog. The faint green footlights set by the sides of the trail and under the trees gave the only illumination, and they seemed inadequate as she walked back through the maze of apartments.

But the stranger was not waiting for her in the shadows. She reached her own room, glanced skyward before entering. A line of fire ringed the sky, arching from horizon to horizon, and Maggie could just see it through the fog. Her mantle whispered that this planet had a ring around it.

Maggie spoke to the door. It registered her voice and opened. She walked into the room, looked down the broad staircase to the apartments below. There was no sign of the stranger. She closed the door behind her, crept downstairs. The apartment was empty.

She was just feeling safe when the door chimes rang, startling her. She opened the door. A short, bald, fat man stood at the door, his broad arms sticking deep in the pockets of his cloak. Both his leather cloak and his deep frown looked as if they had been worn constantly for years.

"Excuse me," he said. "Maggie Flynn, is it? My name is Bavin. I own this establishment. May I speak with you for a moment?" He looked up at her with sad, baggy eyes.

She nodded. He glanced back nervously, closed the door. "The, uh, the thing is—" Bavin explained, "is that I want you to settle your bill and clear out before morning. I won't have you bringing any trouble down on my inn."

"I don't understand," Maggie said. "What are you talking about?"

"I'm talking about that *thing* you're carrying in your bag," Bavin said, wringing his hands. "I'm not the kind of man who would turn you in for the reward, but there's others who will. I won't have you bringing any trouble down on us poor folks."

"What are you talking about, 'reward'?"

Bavin looked about cautiously, as if someone in the room might be listening. "The dronon—" he confided, "they're looking for a beautiful woman who is traveling the Maze of Worlds. She's rumored to be accompanied by several protectors. When you first came in, I wasn't sure you were the one, because you rode in with only that bear. That cast some doubt in my mind. But you rode an airbike that no one would ever bring down this far south in the cold, and that seemed strange. Then you pulled that key from your bag at the table, and you had the planetary police asking about you. . . ."

"I don't understand," Maggie stuttered. "Are you sure they are looking for me?"

"The dronon sent more vanquishers just a few days ago, using the gates, same as you," Bavin said. "Oh, they've got people scared—scared evil. Good people that would never have thought of doing business with their kind are scrambling now, and there's some that would turn you over in a second, thinking it might give them some leverage in the future. But not me—not me!" Bavin was shaking his head, and Maggie realized that he denied any possible turpitude simply because he was tempted to turn her in himself. "So like I said, I want you to settle up your account and get out of here."

"But where will I go?" Maggie said. "What will I do?"

"Don't go to the gates, whatever you do. They're watched. Beyond that, I don't care what you do. Just settle your account."

"But, I don't have any money," Maggie said.

The little man looked at her, a dangerous gleam in his eyes. "What do you mean, you don't have any money? How did you plan to pay for this?" He spread his arms wide, indicating the luxurious apartment.

"I planned to work, make some money," Maggie said. Maggie reached up to her mantle, pulled off a small silver disk with the emblem of an android on it. Regretfully, she handed it to the man. She would be giving up all her knowledge about androids.

"I—I can't take this," Bavin argued, apparently having an attack of conscience. "It's too much!" The little man grumbled under his breath, looked about the room. "Get out of here. Just get your things and sneak away."

Maggie still had the pack she'd carried in. She went to her bedroom, got her blanket and robes. The soil of the day's travel was still on them, and she was loath to wear the dirty robes, but she slipped into them quickly, wrapped her blanket around her shoulders. When she was ready to leave, she returned to the living room. Bavin was gone. He'd left the front door open for her.

She followed the little footpath through the fog toward the common room, thinking to warn Orick. But as she reached the corner by the pools, she could see the front of the inn.

Three green-skinned vanquishers hunched over her airbike. Two were ogres—typical military grunts—the third was a tracker.

The tracker leaned down, sniffing the airbike, his flat orange eyes tilting about like those on a fish. "This bike was driven by a woman and a bear. They traveled through two worlds in a matter of hours."

"Then we've found her?" one of the soldiers asked.

"Yes," the tracker said. Maggie began fading back into the shadows, looking for a way to escape. She wanted to circle the inn, approach the bike from the other side. Orick was eating in the common room and he needed to be warned, but she dared not go back into the inn. She thought that, instead, perhaps the vanquishers would go into the common room searching for her. If she reached the far side of the inn without being seen, she could hop on the airbike and speed away, creating enough of a diversion so that Orick could also escape.

She ran down the trail and circled to the back of the inn where there were no lighted trails. One moment she was rushing around a building, and the next someone leapt from the shadows, knocking her to the snowy ground.

Maggie screamed, tried to leap up and get some footing. But her captor held her arm, hissed, "Quiet!" then pulled her to her feet with great haste.

She stood in the darkness, looking at the thin man she'd seen earlier in the dining room.

"Hurry—they're after us!" he said, pulling her arm. She heard shouts at the front of the inn, and Maggie didn't need coaxing. They ran over frost-crusted snow to a small field at the back of the inn, where dozens of aircars hunkered in the cold night.

Maggie looked back, saw vanquishers rushing toward them past a green footlight. One pulled out an incendiary rifle and fired.

The actinic chemical light shot out in an expanding ball, and the thin man pulled her down to the right. The fireball whooshed overhead, singeing Maggie's face as it passed, then splattered against an aircar.

She and her benefactor weaved between several cars. Maggie spotted one with an open hatch. A guard dressed in black stood at the door, carrying an incendiary rifle.

Maggie glanced at the man, caught her breath. He was a twin to the thin man. She froze at the sight of him, but her companion urged her forward. As she lunged into the back seat of the aircar, the guard leapt away into the shadows.

The thin man started the ignition, began firing the thrusters, and Maggie looked out the window. His twin took cover behind another aircar and fired his incendiary rifle at the vanquishers. The tracker burst into flame, burned like a pillar in the night, his huge spiderlike body twisting in pain. From around the far end of the buildings, three more thin men rushed from the shadows, and two loped around from the front of the inn.

The vanquishers dove for cover behind some planters and began laying down suppressive fire while shouting for help.

The aircar rose, began sliding away into the darkness, and Maggie cried, "Wait! I've left a friend down there!"

"I know!" the thin man said, though he did not slow the aircar. "I was try-ing to warn him when the vanquishers arrived. They sent for reinforce-ments, so we had to move fast. We hope that by killing the tracker, it will give your friend a chance to escape."

"We?" Maggie said.

"My doppelgangers," the thin man said.

Maggie had never heard the word *doppelganger*, so her mantle filled her with understanding. Some people chose to become immortal by cloning themselves and downloading memories into the clones. Among those im-mortals were people who often kept multiple copies of themselves running at the same time so that they could work toward a common goal. Their leader was called the primary, while the copies were doppelgangers.

The aircar slid smoothly up into the sky, and Maggie looked down. White volleys of gunfire were whipping through the air. The hot springs looked like cloudy green gems from up here, and she watched another vanquisher turn into a living torch, then saw a doppelganger take a hit to the left leg and stagger. He managed one last shot before he toppled; the shot went wide and torched one of Bavin's apartments.

She looked down at the dying man and felt peculiarly detached. Though he was human, he was, after all, only a copy of a man, and therefore not real. But she knew that the man had felt pain and desires like any other person; he had hopes and dreams, and he'd just chosen to give his life for her.

Maggie looked up at the thin man who piloted the aircar. Somehow it was comforting to know that he was the kind of man who would be willing to die for her.

Sixteen

Maggie leaned back in the padded seat as the aircar roared out over snow-fields. The cabin was pressurizing, and her ears popped. She took her eyes off the green gems of flaming springs, hoping Orick would escape.

If I get through this alive, she thought, I'll never go near another inn again. She twisted some hair around her finger, chewed the ends nervously.

The thin man glanced at her. "Your bear friend will be all right. My men just took out the last vanquisher. As one would suspect, the guests of the inn are checking out in record time."

The thin man appeared to be thirty-five years old, though appearances would mean nothing on this world. He did not wear a mantle or guide. He wore a work suit of nondescript brown. He was not particularly handsome. "How do you know that your men killed the last vanquisher?"

"Implants." He pointed to his ear. He sighed and leaned back. The aircar was piloting itself now. He glanced at Maggie. "I must say, I'm disappointed. I had been informed that a Tharrin was traveling between worlds, Semarritte reborn. And the man accompanying her fit the description of Semarritte's Lord Protector. Yet I risked my life and the lives of my doppelgangers for what, a bear and . . . ?"

Maggie shrugged. There was something more in the question than mere curiosity—a demand. His face remained impassive as he waited for her answer. "My name is Maggie Flynn."

"My name is Primary Jagget," he offered, stroking his goatee. "So why are you on Wechaus, and where is Semarritte's clone?"

Maggie did not know if she trusted Jagget. Her first impulse was to lie. Yet she suspected that some of his men were searching for Orick, and in time Jagget might question the bear. She had to make the lie plausible, so she forged ahead.

"Everynne was her name," Maggie said. "She came to my home world of Tihrglas two weeks ago with her escort, an old man who didn't mention his name. They hired me and my bear to lead them through the woods to an ancient gate, but there were some vanquishers and dronon after them. The old man fell behind to slow the vanquishers, sent us up ahead to the gate. We were at the gate when we heard his death scream. Everynne gave me the key, showed me how to use it, then rushed back through a clearing to help the old man. Just then, the vanquishers came out the far side of the clearing and shot her. The bear and I saw that our only chance for escape was to jump through the gate. We've been traveling ever since, trying to find our way back home through the gates."

"What of your mantle?" Primary Jagget asked. "Surely you did not get that on Tihrglas."

"The woman—Everynne—had it in her pack. She handed me her pack before she got killed."

Primary Jagget studied her with dark eyes, his face lit only by the running lights of the aircar. He sighed deeply, closed his eyes. "So, Semarritte's clone is dead," he said. "What a loss. What a tremendous loss!"

"Was she a friend of yours?" Maggie asked.

Primary Jagget shook his head. "I've never actually seen her, but yes, she was a friend of mine."

He fell silent for a long moment. "What shall we do with you? The dronon have offered a reward for the woman who is traveling the Maze of Worlds."

"I've done nothing," Maggie said, realizing that she had a hole in her story. If Everynne was already dead, the dronon wouldn't still be searching for her. "Why should they want me?"

"Isn't it obvious? They want your key."

Maggie breathed a sigh of relief. "Of course." She looked out the window. There were no moons above this planet, only a ring of light, and that was partly in shadow. The aircar sped over a frozen ocean.

"So, you and your friend want to get home," Primary Jagget said. "I can help you—in return for the key." Maggie did not know what to answer. She didn't really want this stranger trying to escort her back to Tihrglas. "Of course, if you think the price is too high, I could sweeten the bargain."

Maggie listened to the tone of his voice, realized that she might have just stumbled upon a universal trait for the inhabitants of Wechaus—they all seemed greedy.

"I will think about it," Maggie said. "When your men find my friend Orick, I'll discuss your offer with him."

"Fine," Primary Jagget said. "I'll take you to my compound. You'll be safe there. I personally can vouch for the character of every person on the premises. It's secluded, well defended. The dronon won't find you there."

"Thank you," Maggie said. She leaned back in the comfortable cushions of her seat, watched the land go by. They were flying very fast. They were in a Chughat XI, an expensive car used by diplomats, and her mantle whispered that its top speed was Mach 12. She guessed that they were nearing Mach 10 when the car suddenly began slowing and dropped toward a city of stone. Bright lights ringed one large building, and Maggie could see dozens of people driving along streets, standing on corners. They all moved with a common gait, stood with a familiar stance. They were all clones of Primary Jagget.

"How many copies of you are there?" Maggie asked.

"All told, right now I would estimate about nine hundred thousand," Primary Jagget answered.

"Why so many?"

"I am a man of great ambition, but I have too little time. So my doppelgangers and I work together."

"And what is your great ambition?" Maggie asked as the aircar slid to the ground.

Primary Jagget didn't hesitate to answer. "To keep my homeland free. That is my sole desire."

The car skidded to a halt, and Primary Jagget climbed out his door. Two doppelgangers hurried up to Maggie's door, opened it for her. One reached out to give her a hand from the car. She took it, stepped onto the pavement.

Primary Jagget said, "I'm sorry that I can't see you to your room, but I have urgent business elsewhere." Maggie turned to glance at him, and there was a soft whispering sound of wings.

Primary Jagget turned into a swarm of cream-colored butterflies that flew away in a cloud.

The butterflies vanished into darkness just beyond the streetlights. Maggie stared at the butterflies, astonished, for Jagget's body had not been flesh and blood but an artifice created through nanotechnology.

Maggie felt something poke her back. Her muscles spasmed and her legs went numb. She saw lights and whirled, staggering. She grabbed a doppelganger's shirt to keep from falling. For a moment the world spun, and she hung on precariously. She twisted and looked down at the doppelganger's hands, saw a blue arc of light issuing from a small grip. She smelled burned cloth and ozone.

Maggie blinked, looked at the arc, and her mind suddenly registered that it was an electric stun gun. The doppelganger shoved the gun into her belly, and the world went white.

Orick had been sitting with Panta in the dining room at Flaming Springs, enjoying a salmon dinner that was more feast than dinner when he looked out the window and saw three vanquishers outside the front door, their breath steaming in the cold as they examined Maggie's airbike.

"I think we'd better haul our tails out of here," Orick told Panta. The young she-bear glanced out the window.

"I think you're right," she said, wiping her greasy paw on the tablecloth.

Orick wanted to leave quietly, but it appeared that Panta had a greater distaste for the vanquishers than he did. She hurried to the side door, making for the apartments, and broke into a run. The front door to the inn opened behind them, and a vanquisher shouted, "Stop!"

Orick halted, but Panta hit the door full tilt, knocking it down. Out by the pools, Orick saw Maggie beside a lighted tree, her back turned as she raced around a building. Two vanquishers rushed through the dining room, ducking their heads to keep from scraping the ceiling, dashing over tables.

When they tried to pass Orick, he veered left as if to avoid them, then swerved right to trip them. He roared an apology as they tumbled to the ground, then backed against the wall as if he'd only been trying to get out of the way. The vanquishers leapt to their feet, dashed into the night.

Panta had disappeared into the fog beyond the buildings, and the vanquishers turned the corner, rushing toward Maggie, apparently determined to capture anyone who tried to run from them. Orick looked out the row of windows behind him. One of the vanquishers—a tracker—was racing around the building in the other direction, as if to cut Maggie off.

Orick didn't know how best to help, so he roared a challenge and rushed out the door, following the two largest vanquishers, hoping that if need arose, he could jump them from behind, gain an element of surprise.

He reached the corner apartment by the pools, and three identical men carrying incendiary rifles rushed past him. He stopped to give them the road, wondered who they were.

Behind the cluster of apartments, the white fire of incendiary rifles broke out with a distinctive whooshing sound followed by a pop as each round ignited. Orick passed the last buildings, saw a battle in progress. Several men were shooting it out with a vanquisher. Tracers of white flame filled the sky. Two other vanquishers were already in flames.

A bunch of cars were parked in a field, and an aircar shot up into the sky. Panta sat cowering behind another aircar. When she saw Orick, she ducked low to the ground, roared for him to stay down.

Orick watched one human defender then another take hits with incendiary fire, but the vanquisher was surrounded. Within seconds, the ogre burst into flames.

The human defenders raced through the parking lot for a moment, shouting to one another, then leapt away north through the darkness and fog. The parking lot was well-lighted by vanquishers and vehicles blazing in raging flames.

Panta rushed through the smoke to Orick. "Let's get out of here!" she shouted. She ran toward an oversized magcar.

"I can't!" Orick said. "I've got to find Maggie!"

"She left in an aircar!" Panta said. "Let's go."

Orick stopped a moment, astonished. It had never occurred to him that Maggie would leave without him, but it only made sense. If it hadn't been for his lust, he would have listened more seriously to her warning. He simply felt grateful that she'd escaped.

"Did you see those men?" Orick shouted at Panta's back, running to catch up with her. "Are they brothers or something?"

"No!" Panta said. "They're Jaggets. If there's anyone I distrust more than the dronon, it's a Jagget. And your friend is with them."

Panta leapt up onto the oversized magcar, and Orick climbed in beside her. "Car," Panta said, "put up the hood, and take me home. Hurry!" A glass hood slid over the top of Orick's head, and the magcar's thrusters revved.

"What's wrong with a Jagget?" Orick asked as the car surged forward, weaving among the flaming wreckage.

"It's hard to put it into words exactly," Panta said. "They used to be the protectors of this planet, but now that the dronon have taken over, the Jaggets have all gone crazy. They've been cloned for too many generations. Their DNA is breaking down, and each new generation is more unstable than the last."

Orick didn't understand what she'd said. Right now, he felt just a bit giddy. He sat in a closed vehicle with a handsome young she-bear who was in estrus, and the scent made him dizzy. Add the excitement of the past few days, the element of fatigue, and the poor bear could hardly think straight.

Panta's vehicle whizzed south over the highway Orick had traversed only a couple of hours before. Orick felt nervous, vulnerable, and wanted to get under cover. After what seemed like a long drive, the car turned abruptly and headed into the hills on a winding road until it reached a small stone house on a knoll. Lights shone warmly from the window, and Orick could see a nice stone fireplace inside, a dining room with a large table, bright flowers growing from pots that hung above the windows. He stared in awe. In all of Tihrglas, no bear had ever owned such a fine home.

He felt nervous. The car stopped and the glass hood rolled back.

Cold air hit him, and he sat for a moment, breathing deeply, steam coming from his breath. Panta looked at him, made a soft whining noise. "Will you come in with me?"

For no reason he could discern, Orick's mouth began to water. He knew that if he went into the house with Panta, he would lose his virginity. Only days before he had been tempted to take his vow of chastity, but now temptation was sitting here beside him, batting her brown eyes and filling the car with the scent of desire.

In the past few days, Orick had seen a lot. He'd let the peace of Cyannesse seep into his bones, and he'd thought it heaven. He'd seen the bones of dead children and tasted the poison air of Bregnel. He'd seen Everynne's powers nearly unleashed on Fale, and he wondered at it all. Was God letting him see beyond hills that no other bear had ever seen? Was this his reward for seeking to serve God, or was God showing all of this to him for his own purposes? Could it be that he was meant to make a difference? And how did Panta fit into God's scheme?

Some priests in Tihrglas held that God's commandment to Adam and Eve to "go forth and multiply" was given to all. But Orick had always believed that only by taking a vow of chastity could he give his full devotion to God.

Oh God, Orick whispered in prayer, you're the one that led me here. I would have resisted her advances, but you brought me here. I swear that after this one night, I'll come crawling back to you on my knees, and I'll take my vow of chastity then.

Panta waited for Orick's answer and asked huskily, "Orick, were those vanquishers hunting for you?"

"I think so," he admitted.

Her eyes grew wide. She licked her lips and said, "I find that soooo exciting!"

Orick trembled with anticipation as she led him into the house.

Maggie woke to a yellow haze. She heard a voice speaking, realized it was her own. But someone else's questions were running through her brain: Where is Semarritte's clone? Why did you lie to Primary Jagget? Where did you expect to meet Semarritte's clone? How many Terrors is Semarritte's clone carrying? You testified that Veriasse and the clone have told you several conflicting stories about their plans; how do you know that they have not planted bombs on each world they have visited?

The questions were all ringing through her mind, and Maggie willed herself not to answer. Her voice quit speaking.

Maggie's head felt as if it would split. Some viselike instrument was crushing her temples. She tried to move her arms and kick, but could not move.

Nearby, Jagget or one of his clones said, "Sedate her again, quickly."

"No!" she shouted, and was swallowed by the cold.

She woke, perhaps hours later, with a headache. She was in a small, cold room made of stone. It had one light, no windows, no furnishings. The white walls were cracked, like rough skin. Maggie felt her head. Her mantle was gone. From the cold seeping to her bone, she realized so were her underwear and her shoes. She had only the pale green robe she'd worn for the past few days. The place was empty, except for some dirt on the floor and her own ripening scent.

There was one door in the room. Maggie got up off the floor, approached the door. It slid open. Two Jaggets stood against the far wall of a corridor, and they smiled at her. They wore crisp, identical tan military fatigues.

"Are either one of you Primary Jagget?"

As one, the Jaggets shook their heads. One answered, "He's asked you to join him for lunch."

"Lunch? Was I out all night?" Maggie asked.

"Yes," the Jagget answered. "We found it desirable to sedate you. We don't like strangers walking around our compound." Maggie looked deeply into the Jagget's dark eyes, saw them glittering with something that might have been madness. She'd reacted to it instinctively the night before.

"I see," she said softly.

"Shall we go to lunch?" the other Jagget offered.

"Please." Maggie nodded so that one of them would lead the way.

"We don't like to walk in front," one of the Jaggets said. "Please, you lead."

"But I don't know where we're going."

"Just walk," the Jagget offered. "We'll tell you when to turn."

Maggie shrugged, headed down a hall dirty with disuse till it reached a side passage. "To the right," a Jagget said. He guided her through an underground construction facility, and everywhere Jaggets in dull brown coveralls hauled containers, worked at monitoring stations, or stood supervising others. She could not guess from the odd components what they were making. It looked to be some type of personal flier in a new design.

They climbed some stairs that led to the surface. It was a cool day with blue skies and fresh snow on the ground. Once she saw the compound in the daylight, Maggie saw that this was a military installation. Several towers held gun emplacements, and on the perimeter of the city she spotted heavy generators that powered energy shields. Only then did she notice the faint shimmering in the sky above as sunlight refracted on the shields.

They climbed a stair that zigzagged uphill to a large house, a stately affair with marble columns. Primary Jagget sat under the portico at a table covered with a white cloth. Sunlight splashed down upon him. The day seemed cool to Maggie, with snow on the ground in most places, but Jagget luxuriated in the thin sunlight, as if it were a warm and pleasant day. Lunch waited on the table. Wine goblets were filled, and an assortment of silver platters held steaming foods. Two Jaggets busily served vegetables onto plates.

Primary Jagget stood as Maggie climbed the last few steps, smiled warmly. "Greetings, Maggie! Well met! Well met! Are you thirsty after your little climb?" She wondered why he didn't ask if she was thirsty after her interrogation.

She was both thirsty and had to urinate, but she didn't want to admit it to Jagget. She was mad, but in control of her anger. Still, he grabbed a wine goblet, handed it to her.

A cool wind blew out over the fields of Wechaus, and Maggie drew her robe tight. Primary Jagget raised his glass in a toast and said, "To my kingdom." He waved in an expansive gesture, indicating the countryside around them.

She didn't want to toast with him and wondered how offended he would be if she declined. Primary Jagget noticed her hesitancy and said, "You don't have to pretend that you like me. I assure you, it is quite uncommon for a woman to take any kind of romantic interest in a Jagget. When I was a lone man, women seemed willing to give their hearts. But now that I am an organism, with hundreds of thousands of individuals acting as cells, people are more . . . reluctant to accept me. Indeed, as a young man they hailed me as an idealist, but now that I am old, they ridicule me as a fanatic—even though my notions have never changed. Believe me, I have grown accustomed to scorn."

"I . . . don't scorn you," Maggie said.

"Ah, you feel pity," Jagget said. "A far more noble emotion. Or is it fear? A far more reasonable emotion."

Yes, both, Maggie thought, but she would not speak it. She wanted to change the subject. She looked out over the valley. A mine shaft sat off to her left, and four Jaggets drove a car up to the edge of the mine. The car had a trailer, and the trailer carried a large white ball. When they got to the mouth of the mine, the car stopped. The Jaggets exited the car, and one of them climbed up on the trailer and opened some fastenings to the white ball. The ball flipped open, revealing a hollow interior like an egg. One Jagget stood talking to the others for a moment, laughing and slapping their backs, obviously saying good-bye, then he climbed into the egg, flipped down the lid. The others got up, made sure the egg was fastened securely, then drove the car on into the mine shaft.

"What are those men up to?" Maggie asked.

"Ah, we are storing some of our personnel for future use," Primary Jagget said.

"What do you mean, storing?" Maggie asked, wishing that she had her mantle back.

"In stasis chambers. We are a defeated planet, you understand. We could choose to flee in starships before the Dronon Empire, but the costs would be prohibitive even for me. So, I am storing some of my clones so that I can wake them when the political climate is more favorable."

Maggie shook her head, wondering at this man. She downed her wine, thinking it might be advisable to be drunk for this encounter.

"I'm sorry for having to take you captive and drug you," Jagget said. "I needed to check you for weapons, and I couldn't have you conscious for the procedure. Aren't you going to ask how I knew you were on Fale in my future?" The smirk on his face assured her that she would have to find out sooner or later.

"How?" Maggie said.

"I learned it from the dronon," Jagget answered. "A huge number of reinforcements landed on the planet through a gate last week. They bore holotapes showing how you and your friends blackmailed them during your escape from Fale. I found it intriguing to watch a newscast from our own future. But the dronon must also have some earlier news, for they suspected that Everynne and Veriasse might have traveled here alone. Anyway, the images of you and your bear friend were not clear in the videos, but I managed to enhance them. The dronon had a gate key that would take them into the past, so they were moving back in time, searching frantically for Terrors on all of their worlds. Since Wechaus is a conquered planet, and since it is rumored to have a gate that leads to Dronon, we received a great deal of attention from the Lords of the Swarm." Primary Jagget stood posed with his wineglass in hand, obviously pleased with himself.

"So, what will you do with me?" Maggie asked.

Primary Jagget shrugged. "In a few moments, we should be receiving a live broadcast of your exploits on Fale. The dronon have been searching for you all night, and they're trying to mobilize the public against you. If the people here believe that Everynne will leave a Terror on this world, I fear that she will receive a typical Wechaus welcome—a cold welcome."

"But you know that's not true!" Maggie said. "Everynne wouldn't destroy a planet."

"I know nothing of the sort!" Jagget snapped. "Everynne has told different stories on at least three different worlds. All I know about her is that she is a talented liar who seems to practice her art at every opportunity!"

"What will you do to her?" Maggie asked.

Primary Jagget smiled, stroked his goatee. "I will decide once I have her in my hands."

Seventeen

Orick woke in Panta's home. The fire in the fireplace had burned down to ashes, and he and Panta sprawled exhausted on the floor like a pair of rugs.

The night had turned into a heavenly ordeal. Like most species of animal that mated only every few years, bears tended to try to make up for lost time. Panta had exhausted Orick after three hours, but demanded his services for two more. Orick was beginning to see that the ritual battles between male bears back on Tihrglas might have served a real purpose. The winners of such battles tended to be the males who had the most stamina, and servicing Panta had certainly tested Orick's stamina to the limits.

He lay staring at the female. She was beautiful—a soft, thick pelt; sensual snout; claws polished to a bright shine. Orick roused himself, went into the kitchen. A bowl of fresh fruit sat on the table, and as he helped himself, he began wondering about Maggie. He felt guilty for not following her, trying to help her. He'd let his gonads do all the thinking last night.

Panta stirred in the other room, and he called out. "These brazen fellows that Maggie went off with—"

"The Jaggets?"

"Aye," Orick said. "Where would they have her?"

"Just about anywhere," Panta said, padding into the kitchen. She stood in the doorway on all fours, put her front paws out and stretched seductively, her rump in the air. "There are Jaggets all over the country. Perhaps before saying where they might take her, I should ask you why they might take her."

Orick had already explained to Panta that he was from Tihrglas, so now he told her all about their exploits on Fale and other worlds. He had no reservations in telling her things that he might never mention to a human. Though many a bear will grow grumpy and irritable, there never was a bear with an ounce of avarice, and avarice is what led humans into so many errors.

"If the Jaggets have taken her to keep her away from the dronon," Panta said, "they'll have her at one of their fortresses. It's beyond the power of a bear to get into one of those places, and I wouldn't try, if I were you."

"The poor child," Orick said, "she's had such a rough life, I wouldn't want to add to her burdens. I'm worried sick over her."

"Perhaps your friends can help when they get here," Panta said. Orick grunted in appreciation, and Panta licked his face.

The door chimed. Panta went to the corner, looked out the window. "Vanquishers!" she whispered. "Stay out of sight."

She hurried to the door and opened it. A deep voice said, "Citizen, records indicate that you were at Flaming Springs last night."

"Yes," Panta said. "I had dinner and swam with a friend."

"Were you there at the time of the shootings?"

"There was a shooting?" Panta asked in mock horror. "I had no idea. I left early."

"It is strange how many people left early," the vanquisher said.

"I was only there for a short time," Panta said. "I went only to choose a mate. It's that time of year."

"Did you find someone?"

"Yes, an old friend named Footh. He left just an hour ago. He can verify my story."

"We shall speak to him, citizen," the vanquisher grumbled.

Panta closed the door, walked swiftly back to Orick and spoke to a grill on the wall. She talked to it for several moments before Orick realized that she was talking to Footh, using little code phrases to make sure that he would verify her story.

"Stay home," Footh told her. "The vanquishers are all over the highways. The holovid networks say that someone carrying a Terror escaped from Fale. The vanquishers tried to arrest her here last night."

She thanked him, and said, "Off." The box quit speaking. Orick had seen so many wonders over the past few days it only made sense that folks who could walk between worlds could talk to each other while miles apart.

"Well, you heard him," Panta said. "We need to stay inside today. We could try calling the Jaggets, ask to speak to your friend, but the dronon will be monitoring all the phones. I don't think we can do anything until your friends get here."

Orick looked around the house forlornly, wondering what a simple bear could do. "The fool rushes blindly down the rocky trail, while the superior bear makes sure of his path," Orick said, recalling the only bit of wisdom he could dredge up. "I should never have come here. I'd quit the place if I could. I'm afraid I've made a mess of this."

"You've made a mess of nothing," Panta said. "Why, your friends are all over the news. They're just as likely to get caught with you as they would have been without."

"That's not true. Maggie and I stirred up a hornets' nest, and now Gallen is going to walk through the gate and get stung. I have to fix this if I can, Panta. Once it gets dark, I have to go warn Gallen."

Panta watched him for a long time. "Do you really believe that this Everynne is a good person?"

"Och, the woman's nothing but cream, as we'd say back in Tihrglas," Orick assured her. "I'd bet my life on it."

"You're betting all of our lives on it," Panta said.

"I'd do that, too."

"Then I'll come with you," Panta offered. "You'll need a cover story, and two bears out for a ride isn't uncommon."

Orick smiled, and they spent the day in the house, eating what they would, frolicking when the mood took them. Panta worked for a textile company, designing prints for cloth. She showed Orick her samples, and Orick found that her art spoke to him like nothing he'd ever seen. She wove cloth in the colors of the forest, greens and grays and the shades of the sky. She wove pebbles under rushing water, sunlight streaming through leaves. Many of her patterns featured bears, cubs running through fields of tan, an old bear staring at the moon. Orick could look at the cloth, and sometimes he would hear sounds, bear voices talking, the grunting of a sow as she dug for tubers. The pictures awoke his racial memories, and when he looked at the pictures, he looked through them into the dimly recalled dreamtime of bears.

Though Panta's people had left the wilds, the wilds had not left her, and Orick saw that he would miss Wechaus, would miss Panta when he left.

That night, after dark, Orick could not sleep. Gallen and the others would not drive through the gate until near dawn, but he was eager to get to the hills, prepare a message to warn Gallen.

He paced through the house on all fours, his claws raking the hardwood floors. Finally, near midnight, Panta said, "Let's go," and they went to her car.

She drove along the highway in the darkness. Once they passed a convoy of magtrucks filled with vanquishers. They appeared to be moving large numbers of soldiers. Another time they passed a roving patrol, and Orick felt nervous. He watched the snow-laden hills until he spotted the beaten path where he and Maggie had driven down from the gate. He told Panta to slow the car and lower the hood. As soon as she did, he smelled vanquishers.

"Drop me here, then off with you," Orick growled. He could not take a chance that she would linger near this spot—not with the vanquishers patrolling the area.

"I'll come back for you," she said.

Orick studied her profile in the darkness, and he longed to stay with her forever. "Do that," he said. He leapt from the moving car, and Panta sped away.

Orick sniffed the ground. The vanquishers had walked up the path. A cool wind drifted down from the hills, carrying their scent. Orick began stalking, his head low to the ground.

He took nearly an hour to reach a small hilltop. The light was faint—the stars were thin here, but a fiery ring ran up the sky at the horizon, giving almost as much light as a moon. Orick looked down into the glade, smelled vanquishers for a long time before he finally spotted them.

Three of them sat as still as stones in the snow, hidden beneath a white sheet, watching up a small draw. Orick was surprised to find so few of them and wondered why they kept so far from the gate. Apparently they had followed the trail a ways, saw that the airbikes had materialized from thin air, but perhaps they just couldn't believe their luck, or maybe they did not realize that the beaten snow led to a gate opening.

Orick watched them for awhile, studied the hills. He could see the forbidding snow-covered top of the mountain, the slopes along two arms. The problem was that he could not circle up to the gate opening without being spotted. The vanquishers had set their surveillance post here precisely because it did allow them to view the area on all sides.

So Orick waited. Given the circumstances, he had no option but to stay through the night. When Gallen and Everynne came downhill, he could roar, warn them of the ambush, and then wade into battle. But until then, he could do nothing.

After nearly an hour, two of the giant vanquishers stood, then headed uphill, running along a ridge. Apparently they had been redeployed. Orick decided to strike.

He crept downhill, his feet padding through the snow. When Orick closed to within a dozen yards, the lone vanquisher turned and glanced at him for a moment, but Orick had bear-sized boulders behind him. He merely stood still in the shadows until the vanquisher turned away again.

Orick raced over the snow, leapt at the vanquisher's back, climbing over its shoulder to rip at its throat. The vanquisher tried to stand, raised the butt of his incendiary rifle and smashed it against Orick's face, but Orick merely wrapped his arms around the ogre, ripping at the green skin.

The vanquisher fired his rifle, then threw himself on the ground, and for a moment Orick rolled free. He twisted and leapt at the vanquisher, grabbing the creature's Adam's apple. The vanquisher unsheathed a knife and plunged it into Orick's shoulder, slicing through tendons.

Orick slapped the vanquisher's head with a paw, knocking it down, then tore out its throat.

When the vanquisher lay dead in the snow, Orick turned and rushed uphill till he found the end of the trail where he and Maggie had first materialized. Orick and Gallen had long ago worked out a system to warn one another of dangers on the road. Orick left his paw print and scratched twice beneath it. Since Orick was not sure if Gallen would enter this world before or after dawn, Orick rolled in the snow, beating it down so that his message would be more likely to attract attention. Then he rushed downhill, heading back for the road.

Halfway there, he discovered that his right shoulder hurt, and he began to limp. Blood was pouring from the wound, but he had not noticed it in the heat of the battle.

He licked at the blood, made his way down to the highway. Panta was nowhere to be seen. Orick grumbled under his breath and began limping down the road, watching for signs of movement in the hills, hoping he did not meet a patrol.

The cold night air sapped his warmth. His blood was leaking away, and he felt small, helpless out here in the wilds, so far from home. Once, he heard voices and raised his head in fear. He did not think he could outrun trouble, but after a moment, he realized that he had been dreaming voices. Another time, he found himself feeling weak, and he just sat on the roadside for a moment. A passing vehicle roused him from his sleep, and he looked about, headed north again, wondering what had become of Panta.

He felt like a cub, lost in the deep woods. For a time he walked, thinking that he could hear the mesmerizing sound of wind rushing through trees.

He had not gone far when he heard the deep voices of vanquishers shouting up ahead to his right. His head spun. He was so weak he didn't know if he could leap from the road.

Gallen looked down at the ruined body of the bear. Many of the bones were burned all the way through, and it looked as if the bear had died while trying to paw fire from its face. Gallen could not cry. The pain went too deep for that, tasted too bitter. He felt only a hardness, a cold anger that demanded vengeance.

Veriasse shook his head. "We must go. Our friend gave his life trying to warn us. Let us heed that warning."

Veriasse powered up his airbike, turned and headed back down the trail to the highway. Everynne pulled her bike up beside Gallen, touched his shoulder. "I don't know what you are thinking, what you might be planning. But there is nothing we can do for Orick now."

"I know," Gallen said. He squinted at the morning sun, pulled his robe tightly about him to keep out the cold. They rode their bikes downhill, hit the highway, and turned north.

They drove for twenty minutes in silence. A creepy sensation stole over Gallen, as if he were being watched. Once, the feeling was so powerful that when they entered a valley, he was forced to stop and gaze out over the white, empty hills. There were no trees, just small bushes and rocks to give shade. No birds sang from the bushes; nothing moved. Even the wind was still. Yet Gallen felt watched.

Veriasse stopped beside him. "Do you feel it, too?" he said. "My bones are trembling in anticipation."

"I haven't seen anything. Nothing has moved," Gallen answered.

Veriasse glanced slowly from side to side, only his fierce blue eyes moving. "That is what bothers me. Gallen, listen with your mantle. See if you can hear any radio conversations. Let it scan for military channels." Veriasse pulled off his gloves, raised his hands in the air as if he were surrendering.

Gallen closed his eyes, freed his senses. The thrusters on their airbikes sounded suddenly loud, but Gallen listened beyond that, began picking up radio frequencies. Images flashed through his mind from commercial holo broadcasts, music played from radio stations. Beyond that, he could pick up some chatter—pilots to the north seeking landing clearance in a city.

"Nothing," Gallen said at last.

Veriasse put his hands down, shook his head. "The same here. I smell nothing. Last time I was here, the dronon had a fairly strong presence on Wechaus. Don't you think it odd that you would hear no military calls at all?"

Gallen agreed. Yet there was nothing they could do but go forward. He hit the thrusters. The bike lifted and hummed down the highway, until at last in the distance he saw smoke rising from a small compound of buildings.

Veriasse pulled beside Gallen. "There's a good inn ahead. Let's stop and see if we can get some news."

As Gallen neared the inn, he could discern white limestone buildings around green pools of steaming water. There were many swimmers near the pools, shivering in the cool air, eager for the water. Gallen had not bathed in several days. He felt grimy, tired. It looked like a good place to stay.

They pulled up to the front, stopped their airbikes, looked through the windows. The dining room was nearly full, dozens of young couples eating breakfast, smiling, some of them laughing.

Gallen felt disconnected from them, found it somehow abhorrent that these people were laughing when he felt such profound pain. Orick was dead, and Gallen wanted the world to mourn with him.

Everynne and Veriasse got off their bikes, but Gallen just sat for a moment. There was an odd smell of smoke in the air, as if something had burned nearby.

Veriasse went to the door, and it slid open at his approach. A golden serving droid rushed to greet them, and Veriasse looked back at Gallen questioningly. "Are you coming?"

Gallen shook his head. "You eat. I'm not hungry. I'll keep watch out here." Gallen arched his back to loosen muscles tightened by too much driving.

Everynne said, "Are you sure? You'll feel better if you come inside where it's warm. Please, come in with me."

"I want to be alone," Gallen said.

Everynne squeezed his hand, went inside. He watched Everynne and Veriasse through the windows, saw them take a seat. A soft breeze stirred, and Gallen used his mantle, listened to the swimmers laughing at the pools. Yet there was something odd, a sound of whispering in the back parking lot. Gallen could not be certain. It might only have been reeds rattling in the wind, but he needed to stretch, get off the bike, so he climbed off and walked nonchalantly around the left side of the building.

The back parking lot held several dozen aircars and magcars. He stared at them a moment, wondering. It seemed that the lot held more cars than the inn could warrant.

His mantle picked up whispering ahead and to his right, at the back of the building. Gallen crept around a small potted tree, looked at the back of the building. Fifty feet away, three men hunched over a box that was linked to an absurdly large transmitter antennae. They wore white cloth combat armor. One of them looked up at Gallen guiltily.

Gallen did not have time to think. His mantle did it for him. He pulled out his incendiary rifle and fired. At this range, to hit one was to hit all. The chemical discharge slapped over two men. They blazed white as the sun. Gallen flinched, looked away, and found himself running to the front of the building.

Just as he rounded the corner, he met four men in cloth combat armor. He holstered his rifle and pulled out his sword in one move, whipped it overhead and decapitated the first in line. He leapt in the air, kicked one man in the face and sliced through two others, then bellowed as he reached the front door of the inn.

He could see Veriasse inside, sword in hand, swinging like a madman. A dozen "patrons" of the inn had him surrounded, and they held small stunners. They were trying to knock him down, but their weapons had no effect. Everynne was down, half sprawled across a table, blood pouring from her nose, apparently unconscious. A dozen warriors with heavier arms were rushing from the back apartments beside the pools.

Gallen leapt through a large glass window, landed on a table. He pulled his incendiary rifle, fired at the side doors, hitting a droid that had scrambled for cover. The resulting fire effectively sealed the door, and Gallen jumped, giving a flying roundhouse kick to the back of the head of one of Veriasse's opponents.

Within seconds, Veriasse's sword put down the nearest attackers, and he scrambled for Everynne's pack, pulled out the Terror and tossed it to Gallen.

"This is what they want!" he shouted. "Gallen, send the arming code."

Gallen held up the Terror as if it were an icon, and every eye in the room fastened on him. People froze at their tables. No one moved.

"All of you get back!" Gallen shouted. "I've instructed my mantle to detonate this if you don't give us the road!" Gallen could only hope that his ruse would work.

"We've got jammers! We've got jammers!" one soldier yelled.

"You mean the jammers that were out back?" Gallen shouted. "I fried them."

"We have a backup!" the soldier shouted, trying to rally his people.

"Are you willing to bet the lives of everyone on this world that your jammers will work?" Veriasse asked.

That seemed to cow them. The soldiers hesitated. None dared step forward.

Veriasse pulled at Everynne's arm, turned her on her stomach and lifted her, cradling her like a child. He began walking toward the door, and Gallen stalked behind them, holding the Terror high.

Outside, Gallen got on his bike. Dozens of infantrymen in white cloth body armor were rushing from the back apartments. Gallen began counting. There had to be over two hundred of them. He looked at the patrons in the dining hall. None had shock on their faces, no expressions of horror. Only anger, disappointment. He suddenly realized that all of them were military personnel.

Veriasse got Everynne on her bike, and one man walked forward. Gallen could not mistake his stride. He carried himself with dignity and a calm as-surance. He had been in charge of this operation.

He was an older man, with long dark hair and eyes as black as obsidian. He wore a small goatee. "Well done, Veriasse," the stranger said. "We meet again."

Veriasse nodded at the man. "Jagget."

"Yes, Commander Jagget, of the planetary defense forces. To tell you the truth, Veriasse, I was not sure I would be able to take your Terror away, but I had to try. No offense, I hope."

"Of course not. But I am curious—why do you call yourself planetary de-fense forces when this is a dronon world?"

"I work under their direction now," Jagget said, "The dronon appreciate competence, even if it does come from the hand of an old enemy. I was able to convince them that we could handle this situation better than their green-skinned oafs. The element of surprise, you know."

"I find your wavering loyalty unsettling," Veriasse said. "In fact, I cannot believe it. Primary Jagget would never give his loyalty to an alien usurper. I would expect more from even one of his mad clones."

Jagget shrugged. "Believe as you will. I caught your act on Fale, Veriasse. The incident is being broadcast all over the galaxy." He looked at the Terror, licked his lips, glanced at his men, as if trying to make a decision.

Then he gazed deep into Gallen's eyes. "Young man, if you really are linked via ansible to Terrors on eighty-four dronon worlds, detonate them now, this very second. And if you feel you must, destroy this world, too!"

Jagget stepped forward threateningly, walked several paces toward Gallen. Jagget's eyes went wide, and Gallen could tell that he planned to die. He was trying to force Gallen's hand. He wanted to start the war.

"Stay back!" Veriasse shouted, pulling out his incendiary rifle.

Jagget raised his hand in a commanding gesture. Three men among the crowd shouldered their own weapons. Jagget clones.

"Young man," Jagget said, walking up to Gallen, looking deeply into his eyes, "ignite it, now! Other worlds have burned themselves down in order to keep from falling to the Dronon Empire. It is a worthy trade. Release the Terrors, and someday this sector of the galaxy will remember your name in honor!"

Gallen held the Terror aloft, looked out over the warriors. These were humans whose genes had not been twisted by the dronon. They could not have been subjugated long enough even to feel any loyalty to their con-querors, yet for the most part, they had sided with the dronon. They would have captured Everynne if they could, would have turned her in. As it was, she was unconscious, and Gallen could not tell how badly hurt she might be. And they had killed Orick.

Even now, only their fear of Gallen held the locals at bay. Except for Jagget. Jagget alone seemed to be a true patriot, and he was begging for

Gallen to end it all. Set this world afire rather than leave it in the hands of the Dronon Empire. Perhaps he knew the hearts of his people too well.

In that one moment, Gallen would have freed the nanotech warriors within the Terror, if he had had the ability. Jagget walked up to him, grabbed Gallen's wrist, shook it so that the Terror fell to the ground. He stared into Gallen's eyes.

"You can't do it, can you?" Jagget whispered fiercely, as if Gallen had just betrayed all of his hopes. "You've got only one Terror, and you're trying to get it to Dronon—just as Maggie said."

Jagget spun, spoke to his soldiers. "I'll be escorting these people to their destination."

"Sir," one young woman objected, "shouldn't we report their capture to Lord Kintal?"

"You may report it to the dronon bastards if you wish," Jagget said calmly with just the slightest hint of a threat. "But of course, our orders to stop these people were based upon the false assumption that they had many Terrors in their possession. Since that report is obviously spurious, we have no reason to detain them."

The woman looked at him warily, took a step back. "I'll report that everything was quiet on my shift," she said. "May I take a car thereafter, along with my personal leave?"

"Yes," Jagget said. "I think that would be wise."

"You mentioned Maggie," Veriasse said to Jagget. "Where is she?" Veriasse had Everynne on the bike, his arms cradled around her. Everynne's eyelids fluttered. She tried to raise her head, struggled to regain consciousness, then fell back.

"She will join us shortly." Jagget unclipped a small commlink from his belt, spoke swiftly in some personal battle code.

"We'll need a room for a few minutes," Veriasse said. "And some hot food."

"Very well," Jagget agreed.

Veriasse lifted Everynne, carried her to the back of the compound, down to a small apartment. There he laid her on a bed, lightly tapping her cheek as she struggled to awaken. A dozen soldiers followed them into the apartment. Veriasse turned on them, shouted for them to leave.

Only Gallen, Veriasse, and Jagget stayed to nurse Everynne. Veriasse removed her robe, turned her on her back. She had two burn marks from the stunners, a light one on her lower back, a severe wound on her neck.

Veriasse caught his breath, pointed to the neck wound. "This one may leave a scar." Jagget went to a sink, returned with some water and began spooning it over Everynne's back. Meanwhile Veriasse took out his sword, nicked his wrist and let the blood flow over her wounds.

"What are you doing?" Gallen asked.

"The nanodocs in my blood will help heal the skin," Veriasse said. "Unfortunately, the burn has seared the blood vessels at the subdermal level. The nanodocs in her own system will not be able to combat the wound very effectively. I am hoping to prevent a scar."

Gallen sat, and together they watched the wound. Over the next fifteen minutes, much of the burned and blackened skin dissolved; the swollen red welts reduced in size. Everynne finally woke during that time and whimpered at the pain. Veriasse bid her to be still.

At the end of the fifteen minutes, fresh new skin began to grow over the wounds, but there was a distinct red mark on the back of Everynne's neck, shaped like an *I*.

Veriasse put his head in his hands, sat still for a long time. "I fear," he said heavily, "that all my years of preparation have been jeopardized. Now that the nanodocs have finished knitting the tissues together, we can do nothing to speed the healing process. The blemish should clear in a few days but . . . We must delay our trip. Everynne's blemish makes her ineligible to challenge the Lords of the Swarm."

"How long of a delay do you need?" Jagget said.

Veriasse shook his head. "A few days."

"Veriasse," Jagget said, "the dronon have been sending in troops all week. They know you're here. I could try to hide you, but I don't think I could hold them off that long. At this very moment, the vanquishers have this entire area surrounded. The sooner you leave here, the better your chances of making a clean escape."

"It's only a small mark," Gallen said. "Her clothing might hide it."

"The dronon wear no clothes," Veriasse said. "They will have the right to inspect her without clothing."

"Cosmetics," Jagget said. "Body paint?"

Veriasse looked up, skeptical. "If the dronon discover our deception, they will kill her outright."

"It's worth a try," Jagget said. "You can't wait for her to heal. The dronon have already built one gate key. They can build another. In a week's time perhaps, none of the worlds will be closed to them."

Gallen studied the two men, feeling trapped. Their inability to make a choice galled him. He wished the scar was permanent. Everynne had never wanted to come on this trip. She had been chosen as a sacrifice, and only her generosity let her continue the journey. The only way she could hope to win this battle was to walk away. At least, then, she could live her own life. A scar on her neck would have been a ticket to freedom.

"It will have to be some form of makeup that will not leave a detectable scent," Veriasse said. "At least nothing the dronon can smell. And it must match her skin color precisely."

"I don't know," Jagget said. "That will be a hard order to fill on such short notice."

Everynne turned over, looked at Gallen for a moment, considering her options. "Please, do what you can," she said to Jagget. "I must challenge the Lords of the Swarm quickly."

"Are you sure?" Jagget asked.

"Yes," Everynne said.

Jagget nodded. "I'll be back in fifteen minutes."

Gallen lay down on the floor, weary to the bone, thankful for a few minutes' rest.

A moment later, the door opened again. Gallen did not bother looking up, thinking that one of the Jaggets had entered the room. Suddenly Orick was beside him, licking Gallen's face. "Top of the morning," Orick grinned. "I see you ignored my warning and blundered right into the trap anyway."

"Orick!" Everynne shouted, rousing up in her bed. Gallen threw his arms around the bear. There was a white bandage on Orick's shoulder, a look of pain in his eyes.

"We thought you were dead," Gallen said. "We found bones by the roadside."

"A friend," Orick said soberly. "I left my message and was on my way home, dodging vanquisher patrols. My friend, Panta, stopped to pick me up on the highway, and the vanquishers caught us. She lost her wits and ran for cover. I was too weak to follow. Afterward, they brought me here for questioning, then left me with the Jaggets."

Gallen could tell that there was more than casual friendship involved with this she-bear. He could hear the hurt in Orick's voice. "I'm sorry, my old friend," Gallen offered. Orick limped over to Everynne, gave her a hug. They sat and talked quietly.

Two soldiers brought in some plates of food. Gallen and Everynne sat on the bed and had a bite to eat. Veriasse paced, looking at the wall clock as he waited for Jagget.

Minutes later, two Jaggets came into the room, escorting Maggie. She looked tired, worn, but she smiled in relief to see Gallen. She hugged him and whispered, "I am glad you're well."

One of the Jaggets, an older man, was better dressed than the others Gallen had seen. Captain Jagget introduced him with great flourish as Primary Jagget.

Veriasse stood in deference and said, "Primary Jagget, I thought you were dead." Gallen could not miss the tone of respect in Veriasse's voice. Veriasse glanced at Gallen and explained. "Primary Jagget is one of the great Lord Protectors of our time. He was a Lord Protector three thousand years before I was born."

Primary Jagget said softly, "I *was* a Lord Protector, Veriasse. Now, the dronon have conquered my world, taken my title and position. I have worn out my flesh and been forced to download myself into an artifice. The dronon would not even have allowed that, but for my clones. They have retained enough power to force an uneasy truce."

Primary Jagget clapped a hand on Veriasse's shoulder. "I regret having detained you and your friends, and I regret the harm I've caused here. What I have done, I have done in order to protect my world and my people. I had to be sure of your intent."

Veriasse hesitated a moment. "I suspect that I would have done the same in your position."

Gallen sensed that much was being left unsaid between the two men, and he wondered what kind of relationship they had. They were both Lord Protectors, and though their interests ran afoul of each other, they shared a mutal respect.

Primary Jagget begged them to be at ease, then knelt over Everynne, applied a flesh-colored salve to her neck, and rubbed it in until Gallen could hardly see the scar. When he finished, he stepped back and looked at Everynne admiringly, then bowed. "You are the exact image of your mother Semarritte. I had to come see you for myself. May you grow in power and grace and beauty. I wish you could stay and enjoy my hospitality, but I am afraid that I have just started a war in your behalf, and it will not be safe for you to remain."

"A war?" Veriasse asked.

"The vanquishers must have learned you are here. They began moving in just moments ago. I've ordered my men to wipe out every vanquisher within three hundred kilometers," Primary Jagget answered. "It has long been rumored that you built a gate to Dronon. I know the location of every gate on the planet. Tell me where you must travel, and I will clear a path for you."

"North, sixty kilometers," Veriasse said.

Primary Jagget raised a brow. "There isn't a gate in that region."

"I disguised it so that it does not look like a regular gate," Veriasse said. He glanced at Everynne. "We must go now."

"Wait a moment more," Primary Jagget said. He reached into a fold of his brown jacket, pulled out a mantle. "This is the mantle I wore as a Lord Protector," Jagget said. "I do not want it to fall into enemy hands. I would like you to take it. You have long been a Lord Protector yourself, and I doubt that there is much it could teach you. Still, when you battle the Lords of the Swarm, I would ask that you wear it. Perhaps it could be of help."

Veriasse took the gift. It was an ancient thing of black metal, not nearly so elegant as the mantle Veriasse had given to Gallen. Still, Veriasse took it for what it was, a symbol of hope.

Eighteen

Primary Jagget took a quick survey of the room at the inn, as if he were checking to be sure he didn't leave something when he departed. "We must hurry," he said. "Are you ready to go?"

"Five minutes," Veriasse answered. "When we jump out of the gate, we will be on Dronon. Everynne should be dressed appropriately."

"A couple more minutes, then," Primary Jagget said. "But hurry. Time is of the essence."

Everyone left the room but Veriasse and Everynne. Veriasse opened his pack, unfolded Everynne's golden attire. The metallic robe was made of a flowing material that felt cool, almost watery under his touch. It had an odd sheen to it and was peculiarly heavy, as if it were actually made of microscopic ringlets of pure gold.

Veriasse let his fingers play over the robe. It seemed somehow appropriate that Everynne should wear it this day. She truly was golden, the human equivalent of the dronon's great queen. He had seen it in people's eyes a thousand times: they would look at Everynne and respond with adoration. And though there were physiological reasons for their devotion, something in his bones whispered to Veriasse that mere science could not explain Everynne's power over him. Everynne was sublime. Some said that she was perfect in figure, that the proportions of each bone in her body were designed to conform to some racial dream, an image of perfection shared by all. Others claimed that it was only a combination of scents that she exuded, a carefully selected range of pheromones that turned men into mindless creatures, willing to sacrifice themselves at her feet.

But Everynne's beauty seemed to him to be more than perfect. When she touched him, he shivered in ecstasy. When she spoke, something in her voice demanded attention, so that the softest words whispered in a noisy room would hold him riveted. Everynne transcended the hopes of the scientists who had created her, and in his weaker moments, Veriasse would have admitted that he believed she was supernatural. There was something mystical in the way she moved him, something holy in the way she could transform a man.

And so, today she would wear gold, an appropriate color for the last Tharrin alive on the conquered worlds, the sole child of a race dead in this sector of the galaxy.

When all was ready, he left the room. Everynne dressed quickly in her golden robes, boots, and gloves, then put on her mantle of golden ringlets. Though she was a woman, and fully as beautiful as any of her previous incarnations, Veriasse looked at her and thought that there was something special about this incarnation of Semarritte. Perhaps it was only her youthfulness. By having been force grown in the vats, she had attained the appearance of being twenty years old by the time she was two. Perhaps that was part of it: there was an innocence, a freshness to this incarnation that had been missing in the previous generations.

When she finished dressing, she sat on her bed and smiled up at Veriasse, weakly, her face pale with fear. But for her expression, she looked the part of a queen. He said, "You look wonderful. You look radiant. Are you afraid?"

Everynne nodded. Veriasse himself had great doubts about this plan. "You will do well today, my love," Veriasse assured her. "Never has there been a woman more worthy to represent the human species in such a contest. I can only hope that I shall be as worthy."

Everynne took his hand, looked into his eyes. "I trust you," she said. "If your devotion for me can grant you power, then I know you cannot be beaten today."

Veriasse kissed her hand, then they went outside to meet the others. Gallen, Orick, Maggie, and Jagget sat in front of the inn, straddling their airbikes. Far to the south, Veriasse heard a dim concussion, the sound of heavy artillery.

"Hurry," Primary Jagget whispered. "Every minute is costing the lives of my men."

Veriasse hopped on his bike, and Everynne climbed aboard hers. She was shaking, unsettled, and Veriasse would have reassured her, but she twisted the handlebars, revving her thrusters, and the rest of the group was forced to hurry to catch her.

They roared over the highway, which was ominously devoid of traffic. Ten kilometers up the road, they came upon a magtruck that had exploded, throwing out the corpses of dead vanquishers, and two kilometers farther along, they whipped past a score of Jaggets lying dead by the roadside.

Primary Jagget held his commlink to his mouth, shouting orders in his personal battle language, a code that was thick with nasal tones and grunts.

Forty kilometers from the city, a wall of scintillating lights blossomed ahead to his right—portable shielding. Just beyond the shields, a curtain of flames and black smoke erupted.

Dronon fliers—swift, saucer-shaped craft—whipped through the air at Mach 15, dropping ordnance on some unseen front. The very ground shook and buckled under the force of the assault, and Veriasse hoped that the saucers wouldn't target them. Jagget screamed into his commlink, and a squadron of slower V-shaped fighters piloted by humans swerved from the north, perhaps forty strong. They would be no match for the dronon. They could only serve as a diversion.

Veriasse and the others continued north for five kilometers, heading toward the front until a vast pall of smoke hung over the little party. It was nearly dark as night, yet Veriasse did not turn on his airbike's headlights.

They had not gone far into the cloud when Primary Jagget shouted to them, "Our front is collapsing ahead. My men can't maintain it. Can we veer off the road?"

"Yes," Veriasse shouted. "There is a river to the right. We can follow it north."

Veriasse alone knew where the gate to Dronon lay. He wondered if he should tell the others its location. Two hundred years ago, he had ordered his men to build the gate. In trying to plant the destination markers at Dronon, he had lost three complete technical crews. Afterward, Semarritte had forbade him from trying to put more gates on Dronon, just as she had always forbade him from building a gate that would lead to her omni-mind. She said some risks were not worth taking. But unlike the gates of old, constructed in simpler times, this one was hidden. He had built it into the arch of a small bridge that spanned the river.

He pictured the location, sent the thought to his mantle, ordered it to transmit the knowledge to Gallen. Gallen suddenly turned, caught Veriasse's eye, then nodded.

Two kilometers farther, the black clouds of soot began to thin. Suddenly light flashed across the sky far behind them, brighter than the sun, followed by a second blinding flash nearby. The light continued to glow redly through the sooty sky.

"They're using atomics!" Jagget shouted, and Veriasse glanced back. Mushroom clouds were forming where the inn had been, and again at a point perhaps nine kilometers behind. "Open your speed up."

Veriasse's heart raced. They were still ten kilometers from the gate. The atomic bombs would raise a wall of dirty, swiftly moving air as the air superheated. The dust storm would rush away from the bomb site at over a hundred kilometers per hour—a speed impossible to match in such rough terrain. Yet if they did not beat that surging storm of radioactive dust, it would kill them all.

"Vanquishers ahead!" Jagget shouted. On the highway ahead, two kilometers away, a convoy topped a steep hill. Veriasse swerved from the road into a snow-filled ravine, and the others followed. The airbikes kicked up rooster tails of snow, millions of tiny motes that glittered like slivers of ruby, reflecting the atomic fires behind.

Veriasse began counting the seconds, listening for the blast, trying to discern exactly how far they were from the detonation site. Fifty seconds later, the air filled with a high-pitched shriek, indicating that the Jagget's shields had collapsed, followed by a deep booming.

The ground rumbled and rolled in waves. To the northeast, a volcano began to spit a sluggish flow of lava down its sides.

The airbikes raced over a rise, down a rock-strewn gully, then swept onto a river, skating over flattened stones and lead-gray water that reflected the winter sky and the towering mushroom clouds that filled the heavens behind them like elementals of flame.

Veriasse glanced at his speedometer. They were traveling at only seventy kilometers an hour—fast over such uneven terrain, but not fast enough. He opened his throttle. "Faster," he shouted.

The river was an old one, and canyon walls soon rose around them as they surged through a narrow gorge. Veriasse's speed hit a hundred and twenty. Everynne pulled ahead of him. She had her head low to combat wind resistance. She threw a trail of icy water in his face, and he only hoped that she could make it as she raced ahead.

Time and again she flirted with death, weaving through the rocky gorge, taking corners so fast that she was only a hair's breadth from destruction. For eight more minutes they raced, and whenever they reached a straight portion of the river, Veriasse would glance back, each time hoping anew that the others had negotiated the last turn. Maggie's bike was both slow and dangerously unstable with the bear on it. Jagget stayed at the far end of the train, bringing up the rear.

The gate to Dronon waited for them somewhere ahead at the end of a wide bend. Through his mantle, Jagget transmitted a message: "We have pursuers behind me." Veriasse glanced back, thinking the saucers would be shooting overhead. He saw no saucers—only a great black wall of dust rushing toward them, the frontal tide of the nuclear storm.

Veriasse rounded a corner. Ahead, the river stretched straight for a kilometer, its troubled waters winking in the sunlight. At the far end spanned a bridge, a simple monstrosity of gray plasteel arching over the river. Veriasse looked at it, and his heart fell. The gate was built into a bridge, but he could not remember ever having seen this one before. Was this the bridge?

"Everynne," he shouted, "initiate your key."

Everynne reached into the pack behind her, fumbled for a moment, and slowed her bike as she grabbed the key.

Veriasse slowed, pulled beside her, glanced back. Gallen whizzed past them, followed by the bike with Maggie and Orick on it. Orick's eyes were wide in terror, and the bear's tongue lolled from his mouth.

Jagget held up the rear, and as he rounded the corner, he looked at Veriasse and Everynne in surprise, slowed his throttle at the mouth of the narrow bend. He whipped out his incendiary rifle with one hand, raised it in salute to Veriasse.

Everynne took the key firmly in hand, opened up her throttle, and Veriasse followed directly behind, drenched by plumes of freezing water.

Everynne thumbed the unlocking sequence. Ahead a silver light began to glow beneath the bridge. Behind them, Veriasse heard vanquishers whoop in delight as they rounded the corner. He glanced back.

Three vanquishers in aircars whipped down the river channel, negotiating the tight turn.

Primary Jagget fired his rifle, and pure white light shot down the river. A vanquisher burst into flame, and his burning car screamed toward Jagget.

Another vanquisher swerved to avoid the explosion, and his car erupted into a fireball as it smashed against the canyon walls. The last in line killed his throttle, and his car slowed and bogged down in the water.

Jagget did not have time to avoid the burning car that hurtled toward him. In less than a heartbeat, his body transformed into a swarm of butterflies that lifted above the collision.

Overhead, the nuclear winds roared toward them all, a black tumult. Veriasse turned to face ahead. Maggie, Orick, and Gallen plunged through the gate while Everynne slowed to match Veriasse's speed. As he hurtled toward the gate, Veriasse spared one last glance back. The last hapless vanquisher had stalled his aircar. He frantically struggled to restart it as the black storm swept over him.

Then came the white and the void, and Veriasse felt the kiss of the cold breeze that blew in this crack between time and space. He could feel the fabric of his robes whipped by the gale, but there was no sound, no seeing here. Instead, there was only a rushing sensation. The hand of a god lifted him to a distant place.

When his vision cleared, a drab plain sprawled before them, filled with pockmarks and covered with rocks. Thin clouds made the sky a dim reddish gray. The air was hot and sticky. He could see no buildings, no roads or any other signs of habitation—only desolation.

A soft wind sighed over the ground, and Veriasse began to recognize that there was some plant life around, a deep gray-brown fungus that grew in tight knots like rosebuds. Things that he'd first taken to be pale rocks also proved to be fat, fanlike plants of palest blue, and the pockmarks in the ground were so numerous that they could not have been formed by any natural means that he knew of. They could only have been formed by the walking hive fortresses of the dronon.

"Where do we go now?" Maggie said.

Veriasse turned to Gallen. "Which way is magnetic north?"

Gallen consulted the sensors in his mantle, nodded to his right. The sun lay to their southeast. Obviously, winter was coming to this section of the world. The walking hives would be migrating.

"North," Veriasse said. "Look for fresh pockmarks in the ground. Maybe we can track a hive."

They hit the thrusters, let the airbikes carry them over the gloomy terrain. They saw only a few animals—often things that looked like a conglomeration of sticks could be seen sunning themselves or dragging pieces of vegetable matter to their burrows.

Once they came to a cloud of round, slightly opaque gray leaves that fluttered slowly over the landscape; it wasn't until the leaves splattered against the windscreen of his bike that Veriasse saw that they were some kind of winged insect, with tiny red heads attached to a single wing. He could not imagine how the creature sustained flight.

After two hours, Dronon's sun set, rolling quickly, a dull shield dropping before the onslaught of darkness. In the distance ahead, they spotted a huge black saucer. Massive legs rose in the air around the saucer like hinged towers.

They drove to it, found a deserted hive city with gaping rust holes in it. The armor was pitted from incendiary fire. The city provided the best shelter they had seen all day, so they stopped to camp. They laid out a few blankets beneath the crook of one towering leg, built a cooking fire, and began heating some food bags.

Then they sat, listening to the night sounds of an alien world: something on the horizon kept making a noise like a popping bag. Elsewhere, a creature called out, "wheeeee," in a high, buzzing voice.

Veriasse felt disappointed at not having found a hive, and after he checked the back of Everynne's neck to see how the wound was healing, Everynne lay down on her blanket just staring up, as if deep in thought. Orick grumbled about the inconvenience of always finding dronon where you didn't want them, but not being able to find them on their own home world, then lay down protectively beside Everynne. The poor bear had been listless all day, and his stab wound, although slight, had cost him much. He fell asleep within minutes.

"Don't worry," Veriasse said to the others. "The chances are good that our fire will attract some attention in the night. Perhaps by morning we will meet the dronon, and then we'll find out how they feel about our intrusion on their world." He lay back and thought. Everynne's scar was mending well, but he somewhat hoped that they could wait a few more days.

Gallen and Maggie were restive. Maggie wore her mantle, and she fairly buzzed with excitement as she studied the legs to the hive city, talked about the engineering feats of the dronon who had made such a thing. At last Maggie took a torch, led Gallen up into the body cavity of the dead city. There they stood on the black metal of a turret mount and gazed into the deep shadows.

To Veriasse they looked as if they were peering into the shell of a huge turtle. Maggie shouted and whistled to hear her voice echo.

The two climbed inside to explore.

Veriasse watched the light from their torch dim as they entered the recesses of the city, and soon he was alone with Everynne and Orick. Veriasse felt weary, tense, and he laid down beside Everynne. Orick snored; it was getting very dark.

He had thought Everynne slept, but she said softly, "Well, here we are."

"At last," Veriasse said, trying to sound hopeful.

Everynne laughed, not the musical sound of joy, but a derisive chuckle. "At last."

"Do you regret having come?" Veriasse asked.

It was an unfair question, he knew, but Everynne answered, "This is the planet where I will die, one way or another. I guess I'm disappointed that it is taking so long. I had myself braced for a battle today."

"I know that you think you will lose something if I win this battle," Veriasse said, "but I promise you—when your consciousness is subsumed into that of Semarritte's, it will not be a death for you. Instead, it will be a wonderful awakening. I have seen it happen with clones before. It will be such a powerful experience that it will overwhelm you, and you will fall asleep for a few moments. But you will awaken a much wiser and more powerful being. Trust me, my daughter, trust me."

Veriasse looked at Everynne's face, lit only by the campfire. She was more frightened than he'd ever seen her. She trembled violently. Her lips pulled back in terror, and a heavy perspiration lay on her forehead.

Veriasse took her hand, caressed it, but Everynne did not turn to him. Instead, she laughed coldly and said, "Father, if I turned around and walked away from here, would you hate me?"

This was a subject that Veriasse had hoped to avoid—a discussion about other options, other plans for defeating the dronon. He had already considered all of his options, discussed them in depth with Everynne and Semarritte before her, rejected them one by one. She couldn't walk away from this, and Veriasse could not afford to let her be weak. He wanted to warn her against trying to take the easy path, remind her of billions of others who would suffer and die under dronon rule if she quit now. Instead, he only spoke the truth. "I would love you, even if you turned away. You are as much a daughter as I have ever had, and I've watched you learn and grow these past three years with great joy and a great deal of pride."

"But you will love me more when Semarritte fills me, won't you?" she said bitterly. "I'll bet you can't wait until she succeeds me. How long do you think it will take before you bed her?"

Veriasse had rarely seen Everynne angry. Never had he heard her say an unkind word, yet he had to remind himself that emotionally she was still a child, and he had to make allowances for that. "Everynne, don't torture yourself this way. No good will come of it."

"I'm not torturing myself," she said. "You're torturing me. You're killing *me*!" She rolled away from him and began weeping.

Veriasse wanted to say something to comfort her, but there was so little he could say. At last he whispered, "If you want to walk away from this, then tell me, and I swear I will do everything in my power to get you home safely. If this is what you want, we can raise armies, take our keys and open the gates. People everywhere love you. They would fight if you asked them to, and in a matter of days I swear I could raise an army of billions to fight in your behalf. They would scream across the worlds in a rampage of blood and fire. Terrors could be unleashed on a thousand worlds. If this is what you want."

He did not have to tell her that the losses from such a war would be immeasurable. The dronon would begin destroying those worlds they had already captured. The images of mushroom clouds were still fresh in his mind from this afternoon, and images from the terror-burned world of

Bregnel lay in his mind like a black clot, but this war would be far worse than anything that had occurred before. The dead would pile up quickly, mountains of corpses so vast that no one could ever begin to count them.

But Everynne already knew that. She could not turn away from so many in need. She lay crying, and said at last, "Hold me, Father. Please?"

Veriasse put his arm over her shoulder and snuggled against her back. She gripped his hand, hard. He held her until she stopped shaking, nearly an hour, and at last he whispered, "Are you all right? Do you feel better?"

"I'm all right," she said firmly. "I just wish it were over. I was frightened for a minute."

"There's my brave girl," Veriasse said, and he lay with his body cupped around hers, smelling the sweet scent of her hair. After awhile she began to breathe deeply, as if she would soon fall asleep, and he wondered about Maggie and Gallen. Though they had been in the dead hive city for a long time, he reminded himself that it was a huge place. He imagined that they might keep exploring for hours. He gave himself permission to sleep, and soon fell into a fitful dream.

Maggie rushed through the dead dronon hive city, feeling wild and free. Her nerves jangled in anticipation, and Gallen ran behind her. They would meet the dronon soon, and she fully expected to die, but for the moment, the mantle she wore wanted images of this city. It drove her forward in a mad rush through the beast, gleaning images of an engine room where monstrously large hydraulics assemblies had once driven the massive legs. She studied the power system and the exhaust nacelles.

Though the city was dead and much of the equipment had been scavenged, the dronon took great care of their equipment; they had even protected the abandoned machinery by coating it with oil.

The heavy odor of rusting iron and dust filled the city. The corridors were dark. Wind whistled through the hallways high overhead.

For an hour Maggie and Gallen studied the engine rooms, then found what could only have been egg warmers in a huge nursery. But Maggie's mantle drove her on, ever curious. It fed its discoveries to her in a constant barrage, so that she felt as if she would burst at the wonder of it all.

She ran laughing into the bowels of the city, and Gallen ran beside her, bearing the torch, sometimes touching her shyly.

At last they reached a storage chamber and walked down a long corridor. Various implements of unknown intent had been piled along the walls, the machinery of a forgotten age. Enormous capacitor coils rose up for ten meters, sitting like huge thimbles. Spare legs for the hive city were strung from the ceiling. Bits of round, antique flying message pods lay heaped in a pile, and Maggie's mantle warned her to fill her pockets with them so she could disassemble them later. Things that looked like dronon heads made of glass—with three sets of compound eyes—lay in a heap, as if in some distant past the dronon had tried creating androids. Or perhaps, Maggie wondered, there were even now dronon-shaped androids running about in the hive cities. But her mantle whispered that if such things existed, they had never been seen on any world.

Much of what she saw her mantle could understand—bits of cabling, servomotors, a shelf heaped with mechanical brains, outdated egg-warming chambers. These things she would explain to Gallen. Yet much of it was equally mysterious to her. Most of the dronon equipment was bulky, five times as heavy as anything a human would use. The dronon seemed to prefer their machinery to be durable rather than lightweight or convenient.

In one vast chamber, they found what could have only been a spaceship. It was a small vessel, eighty feet long, forty wide, shaped like a Y. Maggie didn't know if she could fly it.

She opened the hatch, went inside, and her mantle whispered to her as she studied the engines. She told Gallen, "This has a gravity-wave drive. We couldn't take it out of the solar system. Still, I'll bet it's fast." She went to the control board. The chairs before the panel were saddle-shaped affairs meant to hold a dronon body, and various foot pedals on the floor looked too intricate for any being with less than four legs to operate. The hand controls were set on a dashboard nearly five feet away and could only be manipulated by something with long arms. Maggie grinned, realizing that this must be an ancient dronon warship, for only the vanquishers with their long battle arms could have worked those controls.

She was giddy with excitement, grinning in wonder. She laughed, then laid back on one of the saddle-shaped chairs and stretched.

Gallen set the torch in a groove on the ship's control panel, then turned and looked at her, perplexed. "I've never seen you in this kind of mood before."

"What kind of mood?"

"So ecstatic. So free."

Maggie laughed. "That's because I've never been happy or free before," and she realized that there was more truth in it than she would have dared admit to herself.

"Your smile looks good on you," Gallen said. He swung his leg over the saddle, sat facing her, his legs wrapped around hers. He lay back with his arms folded behind his head. His half-closed eyes looked tired, and the flames from the torch flickered, showing only half of his face. She felt electric, wanted to kiss him now, make love, but Gallen only studied her a moment.

Maggie's mantle whispered for her to get up, look deeper into the storage chambers. She took it off and held it in one hand, not wanting to be distracted by its insistent promptings.

Gallen leaned forward, stroked her jawbone tenderly with his fingers, and kissed her. It was an odd kiss, she thought. It wasn't insistent with desire, nor was it one of the guilty little pecks that Gallen had given her back home. It was slower than dripping honey and tasted just as sweet. It spoke to her, saying, "I love you just as you are, and right now I am content with that."

They held each other and kissed for a few minutes, then Gallen leaned back again, pillowing his head with his hands.

"Damn you, Gallen O'Day," Maggie said. "It took you long enough."

"I suppose it did," Gallen smiled, self-satisfied. "When we get back to Tihrglas, will you marry me?"

Of course I'll marry you, she thought. But then her heart fell. "I'm not going back to Tihrglas."

"Not going back?" Gallen asked.

"Why would I want to go back? What's for me there? You said it yourself not a moment ago. In all my life, you've never seen me so happy. Gallen, how can I begin to explain this—right now, I want to tear this city apart," she said, waving toward the ship and the dronon city around her, "and discover exactly how it works. Like those little dronon message pods. Until two hundred years ago, that was the only form of communication the dronon used. They hadn't discovered radio waves at all, until we showed them. The pods have miniature antigravity drives in them, and no technician that I've ever heard of has disassembled one of the buggers and figured out how it worked. Gallen, I've got a pocket full of dronon technology, and right now I feel as rich as can be. It's amazement and discovery. Here I'm free to learn and grow. I can't get that on Tihrglas. Pick any other world we've been to. I don't care which. I could go back and be happy, but you'll never see me smile again on Tihrglas."

Gallen stumbled over his words. "Maggie, I—we don't belong here. I can't protect you here."

"I don't want your protection," Maggie said. "You asked to be my husband, not my bodyguard."

Her flippant words didn't answer his real concerns, she realized. He was a bodyguard. It came naturally to him. Part of him cried out that at all costs he had to protect those around him, maintain a semblance of order. But in these past few days, they had staggered through so many worlds that he was left confused, overwhelmed. He had not been able to discern the underlying order in the worlds around him, simply because the human societies they had visited were all experimenting and growing, twisting away from any predefined shapes.

"You have your mantle," Maggie said. "It has to be teaching you something. In time, you'll become a Lord Protector, like Veriasse." Or perhaps a frustrated fanatic, like Primary Jagget, she wondered. When Jagget's world had twisted out of shape on him, he had not been able to adapt. He kept calling Wechaus "my world," but it was peopled by folks who over the millennia had become strangers to him.

And suddenly Maggie understood. In his way, Gallen already *was* a Lord Protector. Back in Tihrglas, he'd planned to run for sheriff of County

Morgan, and in a few years he'd have become the Lord Sheriff of all the counties. He'd been born to become the Lord Protector of Tihrglas.

Gallen's eyes misted. After a moment he said softly, "Maybe, maybe I can find a world we could both live with."

Maggie took his hand in hers. "Maybe we can find that world together."

In his dream, Veriasse rode his airbike, speeding over the dull plains of Dronon with Everynne beside him. Ahead were dark clouds, gray as slate. He could hear the distant rumble of thunder. They drove hard toward the sun as it prepared to dip below the clouds, and he passed under the sprawling leg of a dronon hive city. There was so little daylight left that Veriasse despaired of ever making it to the horizon.

The sun dipped below the distant hills, and Veriasse gasped. Grief passed through him as the night descended. Yet suddenly the white sun flared out on the horizon as if it had reversed in its course, blazing across the blasted land, filling him with hope.

The dream was so real that Veriasse stirred, heard a distant rumble, and realized that thunder was brewing on the horizon. He would have gone back to sleep, but Gallen shouted, "Over here! Come over here!"

Everynne stirred from his arms.

Veriasse sat up. Gallen had fired his incendiary rifle into the air. White chemical fire streamed in the sky like a brilliant flare, then arced toward the ground. Gallen and Maggie had come out of the dead hive city and were now standing on a gun mount. They shouted and waved, and Veriasse looked out over the horizon. In the distance, something massive and black moved in the darkness, crawling over the plains, heaving its bloated body along like a gigantic tick. Veriasse could only see it by the lights at its battle stations, lights that glowed in the night like immense red eyes.

The ground shook and rumbled in pain. Veriasse had not heard thunder in his dreams but the sound of a dronon hive city groaning as it pulled itself over the broken earth.

Gallen hooted and shot another round from his rifle, shouting in an exaggerated brogue, "Come on, you lousy bastards! Drag your ass on over here! We're tired of chasing after you!"

The dronon city changed course and began moving toward them, its turrets swiveling as the dronon searched for sign of enemies. Veriasse's heart pounded in his chest. His breath came ragged. They had found the enemy.

Nineteen

Veriasse could almost not believe his luck. Of all the scenarios that he had imagined, this perhaps was most ideal—to spot a dronon hive city in the distance at night. He went to his pack, pulled out his various paraphernalia. Some of it had taken him years to acquire. A translator he clipped to his mantle was equipped with a microphone that he could speak into, loudspeakers that would throw his voice, and a tiny speaker that plugged into his ear. With it, he could speak his native English softly and have his words translated into dronon in a commanding roar. Meanwhile, the device would translate the dronon's own clicks into English and feed them into the earpiece.

Veriasse plugged in the earpiece, then flipped on the translator, noticed that Everynne was doing the same with her own translator.

He also pulled out some protective goggles that would keep acid from his eyes, in case a dronon spit at him.

Under dronon law, those who engaged in ceremonial combat were not allowed any weapons to fight with, but for his own defense, Veriasse had brought a small holo projector. He got it out, set it on the ground before Everynne, turned it on: the air above her shivered for a moment, then blazed with an image of a Golden Queen, a hive mother whose abdomen was a great saucer-shaped, bloated sac. Her small useless wings were neatly folded over her back, and she stood regally, her clublike forearms raised as if to do battle, her head held high so that the uppermost of her three eye clusters allowed her to look behind her back while the other two arrays scanned the horizon at one hundred and twenty degree angles. The whiplike sensors under her mandibles swung about wildly, as if she were trying to catch an elusive scent.

Out on the horizon, the great city would drop, then rise on its legs and shudder forward, like a hive mother dragging her egg sac behind her. The earth protested under its weight, and a cloud of dust and heated exhaust poured from behind. Light glowed from the archways above the forward turrets.

Veriasse looked at Everynne. She was tense, standing with arms folded, her face pale. Orick stood beside her on all fours, the hair on his neck raised, his fangs showing as he gazed on.

Gallen and Maggie shouted as they climbed down rungs built into the dead city's huge legs. In less than four minutes, they made it down. Gallen shouted, "Veriasse, watch out! There's a sea of dronon warriors swarming out of that thing!"

"I know," Veriasse said calmly. "They will come inspect us to make sure that their hive queen is not in jeopardy. Then I will battle them for Right of

Charn. If we win Right of Charn, then they will lead us to the Lords of the Swarm, so that I can battle one last time. I can only hope their queen grants us the opportunity to battle."

"And if she doesn't?" Maggie asked, coming up behind him.

"Then likely we'll all be killed," Veriasse answered calmly. He glanced back. In the golden light thrown by the holo he saw the stricken look on Maggie's face. "I kept trying to warn you," Veriasse said. "The dronon are highly territorial. If we lose any step of the way, by their own law, the dronon may kill us all." He didn't want to have to tell them this, but knew that he had to tell them how to save themselves. "If I'm killed, fall on your knees and lay your arms out in front of you, with your wrists crossed and your head facing the ground. This is the dronon pose of ritual oblation. A dronon who assumes that posture is both defenseless and unable to see the leaders before him. The dronon vanquishers may spare your life if you maintain that pose, although they might strike you lightly with their battle arms. Given our thin skins, even a light blow might kill us. Still, it is your best chance."

"Are you sure it will work?" Maggie asked.

"It is a part of the order," Veriasse answered. "The dronon crave order. Yes, I believe it will work."

The hive city had approached to within two kilometers now, and by its lights, Veriasse could see the black shining carapaces of countless dronon vanquishers scurrying like cockroaches before the great city. At any one time, dozens of them would rise up on their back legs, sensor whips lashing as they gazed forward and tasted the air. Beneath the rumbling and squeaking sounds of the moving city, a dull roar arose, the clacking of arms and legs slapping against the carapaces of the dronon, the clicking of mouthfingers against the dronon vocal drums as they spoke amongst themselves. The city and its racing warriors moved far faster than Veriasse had imagined.

Veriasse took out his incendiary rifle, fired two shots in the ground in order to give them more light. The chemical fire burned in white-hot pillars, and Veriasse threw off his cloak, stepped forward between the pillars of light, raised his arms over his head and crossed them at the wrists, signaling that he wished to engage in ritual combat. He was dressed all in black—shining black boots, supple black gloves, a vest of black battle armor. Even his mantle was a glossy black, and he hoped that in this light he would look enough like a Lord Escort that the dronon would recognize him as such.

The dronon hive lurched its last few steps, then squatted. The saucer section of this hive was perhaps twelve stories tall and seven hundred meters wide. Each of its eight legs towered a hundred meters in the air before reaching the first of its three hinged joints. The lights from the city showed dronon vanquishers at the gun emplacements, and smaller white workers rushed around them, bringing food and drink. Veriasse wondered if the dronon frequently fed during battle, or if perhaps the dronon were assuming some brave pose.

A dark wave of vanquishers swarmed forward to within a hundred meters of Veriasse's small band, then climbed one atop another, forming a wall of bodies that bristled with incendiary rifles. The thrumming of their voices rose, sounding like a vast sea of reeds rustling in the wind. The translator speaker plugged into Veriasse's ear was so overwhelmed by their derisive shouts that it seldom attempted to translate, and Veriasse silently cursed his luck, fearing that he would not be able to hear anything a single dronon might say to him.

Veriasse shouted the formal words of challenge, praying that his translator would phrase them correctly. "This land is ours! All land is ours! A Great Queen comes among you. Prostrate yourselves in adoration, or prepare to do battle!" He waited a moment, and his translator began clicking loudly.

Every dronon suddenly fell silent, and from the top of the wall of living bodies, a single dronon vanquisher raised on its back legs, crossed its battle arms overhead and shouted: "You dishonor us! This is no true Golden Queen before us, merely a projection! Are your minds so simple that you think to trick us?" In the darkness, Veriasse could not see if this dronon wore the facial tattoos of a Lord Escort, but the creature spit acid, as if to say, "You are food." Veriasse guessed that only a Lord Escort would dare offer such an insult.

Obviously, this would not go as smoothly as Veriasse had hoped. His stomach knotted. "This holograph is only a banner that we carry," Veriasse shouted. "Our Golden Queen stands behind me! She is not a dronon like you, but all among us humans worship her form. She is flawless and worthy of adoration. A Great Queen comes among you! Prostrate yourselves in adoration, or prepare to do battle!" Veriasse threw his arms out forward in a battle pose and spit on the ground.

The dronon cringed at his insult.

Silently, Veriasse looked backward at Everynne. She held her hands knotted in a fist, and he saw a faint light shining golden between her fingers, showing that she held the Terror in her hand. If these dronon attacked, she would have only a portion of a second to activate the weapon and begin destroying this world. Almost, he hoped that she would activate it now.

The Lord Escort shouted, "I will perform a rite of inspection on this Golden!" Suddenly its wings unfolded and it leapt from the wall, landing within an arm's length of Everynne. Veriasse could see tattoos on its face— golden waves like rods of lightning striking from each eye. The Lord Escort's sensor whips waved over Everynne's head, flashed around her hips. It hesitated a long moment. Veriasse prayed that it would not make her strip, search for flaws.

The Lord Escort pulled at her clothes, but did not remove them. Apparently, it seemed more pleased by the color and texture of the golden material than by Everynne's pale skin. At last the dronon clicked, "I do not find this one worthy of adoration."

"She is worthy," Veriasse said. "She is Golden among mankind, perfect in form, without blemish."

"She is soft, like a larvae. She is disgusting, unworthy of adoration."

"All humans are soft," Veriasse said. "And we find your bodies to be disgusting, unworthy of adoration. Yet we honor your Great Queen despite the differences in our forms. We ask you to do the same. I assure you that you will never see a more perfect human than this Golden Queen, and I challenge you to battle for Right of Charn."

By battling only for the Right of Charn, Veriasse felt that he was making the decision easier for the creature. If Veriasse should win, there would be a second inspection by the Golden Queen and her Lord Escort. In effect, Veriasse was asking for a small thing. The dronon said, "I reject your right to challenge. This is not a Golden."

"If you reject our right to challenge," Veriasse said, "then you will dishonor the Golden Queen of our kind. If you will not honor our Goldens, then all mankind on all worlds will reject your queen's right to rule over us. You will start a war unlike any that you have ever known."

"You threaten us?" the Lord Escort asked. He looked at Everynne, at the Terror glowing in her hands.

"I do not want to be forced into threatening you," Veriasse said. "But you know what we carry. You've chased us across the worlds. If you do not let humans battle for the right of succession, you leave us no alternatives."

The dronon hesitated. "I speak the truth," Veriasse said. "Let us battle for the Right of Charn."

The dronon studied Everynne a moment longer, backed off two steps. "I will go and consult with our queen." It turned, flew up to the hive city and entered. By now the chemical fires from the incendiary rifles were beginning to die, and in the light thrown from the twisting flames, it almost seemed that the wall of dronon bodies wavered.

Neither Gallen, Orick, nor Maggie moved or spoke, and Veriasse was silently thankful for their good sense. The negotiations were at a critical point. If the queen ruled against them, the dronon would attack in a great wave. If she decided to grant the Right of Charn, Veriasse assumed she would come out with her Lord Escort to do battle.

Ten minutes passed, twelve, and then the Lord Escort flew from the battlements of his hive city, landed on the bodies of his own men.

The Lord Escort raised high on his hind legs, crossed his battle arms over his head. "We have consulted with our Golden. She instructs us to honor you by letting you battle for Right of Charn. I am Dinnid of the Endless Rocks Hive. For ten thousand years we have ruled this plain. Our larvae shall eat your corpses. Our vanquishers shall claim your domain. Your hive shall submit to us!"

As one, a hundred thousand dronon vanquishers raised their battle arms and slammed them together with great clashing sounds.

• • •

Veriasse shrugged, tried not to show his concern. Until now, he'd had no idea where on Dronon he might be, but the name of the Endless Rocks Hive was known throughout the worlds of mankind. Dinnid was relatively young and powerful, a son of the Golden Queen and her Lord Escort. Rumor named him "The Cunning" for his prowess in battle. It was said that he was the finest strategist among the Lord Escorts, and many claimed that he and his queen would become successors to the current Golden. It was said that Dinnid was only biding his time until his nemesis grew older and more feeble.

Dinnid's wings flashed, and he darted high into the air, entered the maw of the hive. Ahead of Veriasse, the dronon vanquishers began clacking and mumbling, readjusting their bodies so that an opening appeared in the wall. Veriasse looked back at Everynne, telling her with his eyes to follow. Gallen, Maggie, and Orick followed, too, and they walked through a tunnel formed by the black bodies of dronon warriors.

When they reached the saucer-shaped belly of the hive, the dronon lowered a ladder much like any that a human might use, except that the rungs were spaced inconveniently far apart. Veriasse climbed, noted the thin gray powder of dried dronon stomach acids on the rungs but decided that his gloves would be ample protection. Only poor Orick among the group did not have gloves, and Veriasse hoped that the padding on the bear's paws would prove adequate insulation.

When they reached the lowest level of the hive city, they came to a security station where strange, gleaming, three-eyed cameras photographed them. Message pods, like tiny balls, whizzed through the air, flying between various levels with a hiss. Small white female dronon workers scurried through the hallways like lice, infecting him with their tremendous energy. They seemed incapable of moving at anything less than breakneck speed.

The group climbed more ladders, and everywhere were tan dronon technicians with green tattoos and long segmented fingers growing from small battle arms. Vanquishers lined the halls. When they reached the mid-level of the hive, Veriasse glanced down one corridor, saw a vast incubation chamber. Thousands of white workers scurried among eggs, adjusting heating devices, catching the grublike newborns as they hatched, regurgitating acidified food into the gullets of grubs.

At last Veriasse climbed to the highest level of the great city, stopped to catch his breath. Dronon vanquishers lined the passage. He stared down the dimly lit hall for a moment, waited for the others to catch up with him. The air here was thick with the acrid scent of dronon, warmed uncomfortably by the heat of hundreds of thousands of bodies. Everynne breathed heavily but tried to stand tall and regal. Orick was panting from the effort of climbing, and Maggie was drenched with sweat when she reached the landing platform. Veriasse let them catch their breaths, then led the way down a long corridor lighted dimly by golden globes.

Some dronon vanquishers raised their battle arms over their heads, crossing them as a sign of respect for Everynne and her retinue, but most of the vanquishers refused that honor.

The air grew hot and fetid as they neared the belly of the city, until at last they came to a wide, circular room two hundred meters across.

Around the room, thousands of dronon lined the walls. Black Lord Vanquishers with their enlarged forelegs and flashing wings seemed to make up the majority of the audience, but as his eyes adjusted to the dim light, Veriasse saw that they were really outnumbered by small whitish workers, plump as lice, who ran about under the feet of the warriors. Dozens of the large tan technicians with their green facial tattoos had also come.

At the far end of the arena, the Lord Escort Dinnid sat beneath the lights beside an enormous young queen. She was a light cream in color, but gold highlights on her upper thighs and battle legs indicated that she would soon develop into a Golden. The queen was perhaps six meters long and three meters tall. Her saucer-shaped egg sac looked as if it were ready to burst, and indeed as he watched, a translucent egg about two decimeters across fell from her sac. A white worker rushed forward and carried it away.

Dinnid raised his battle arms over his head, crossing them as a sign of a temporary truce. Veriasse stopped at his side of the arena and raised his arms in the same token, crossing his wrists.

"You stay here," he whispered to Everynne and the others, indicating a red box drawn on the floor.

As one, he and Dinnid advanced to the center of the arena.

Veriasse studied the battleground—the light in the room was diffuse and came from yellow globes set in the walls all around the arena. The metal floors seemed to be of heavy steel and were uneven, curving slightly like a bowl until they reached a low point in the center of the room. The ceiling was perhaps fifteen meters high—enough so that if Veriasse were the Lord Escort from another hive, he and Dinnid would be able to fly about the room, engaging in aerial combat. Indeed, it was the preferred method among dronon. The males flew at tremendous speeds, batting one another with their heavy forearms, lashing out with their hind legs, grabbing with their sensor whips. The battles tended to be fast-paced and ended quickly.

As Dinnid marched forward, Veriasse studied him. The big male was perhaps two meters tall as he walked, and he bore scars from a recent fight. His right sensor whip had been ripped off near the mandible and had not yet grown back. The right front array of eyes had been damaged. Of the seven faceted eyes of various sizes, two of the larger ones were broken. An ugly white ooze dripped from one mandible.

Yet the dronon lord had impressive forearms. The serrated edges at the bottom of these arms were exceptionally well developed, so that it looked almost as if he had triangular axe heads emerging from those arms. One blow would crush the exoskeleton of nearly any dronon. To be hit with those arms would mean Veriasse's death.

Around him, the dronon began to sing a slow dirge, their mouthfingers tapping rhythmically upon their voice drums. Veriasse looked to the far side of the room, saw that beneath the queen, several white things that he had thought to be workers were in actuality larvae—royal grubs with six small legs and poorly developed eyes.

When the two were forty paces apart, Dinnid uncrossed his battle arms, began to wave them threateningly. Veriasse knew that as soon as he uncrossed his own wrists, the battle would begin. The dronon always considered it a good strategy to strike first, and Veriasse suspected that the Lord Escort would leap into the air, try to strike while flying past. Indeed, the dronon's superior aerial troops had always devastated humans, who relied too heavily on ground-based operations.

Veriasse took a deep breath, uncrossed his arms. Almost before he could see it happen, Dinnid leapt into the air, wings buzzing.

Veriasse dodged right. The Lord Escort twisted his abdomen, tried to kick with a rear leg. Veriasse considered grabbing it, but elected instead to simply avoid this first blow.

Dinnid flew past, circled like a great black fly. It took him several seconds to cross the arena, then return.

Dinnid flew up near the top of the ceiling, then swooped low at the last possible second. Veriasse dodged right again, but the dronon anticipated his move, turned his head, and spat the contents of his stomach into Veriasse's face. The acid splashed out in a wave, and Veriasse saw that he would not be able to dodge it. He leapt up in frustration, kicked the forward edge of Dinnid's lower right wing and heard a satisfying crack.

The lord spun, crashing into the metal floor, then rolled upright. He raised his wings and flapped them madly, apparently terrified on some instinctual level at the thought of being grounded. He lifted himself in the air, but moved slower and was forced to flap his wings much harder to fly at all.

Veriasse pulled up his tunic, wiped the acid from his face. The goggles he wore were dirty with the fruits of the vanquisher's stomach, and Veriasse only managed to smear the glasses. He threw them off in frustration, gambling that Dinnid had emptied his stomach and would not be able to spit any more acid in the course of this battle.

Dinnid circled the vast arena, building up speed, and Veriasse clenched his fists. The metal studs sewn into the fingers of his gloves felt heavy, comforting.

He watched the vanquisher circle, saw that Dinnid was breathing hard. His rear thighs flexed and unflexed rapidly, the air holes expanding as he sought to draw air into his lungs.

Suddenly Dinnid swerved and came straight at Veriasse, battle arms thrust dangerously forward, his head tilted back so that his mandibles were extended down and out. It was the perfect posture for a ramming attack.

Veriasse dodged right early, and the dronon veered to intercept, then Veriasse dodged left at the last moment, grabbed for Dinnid's sensor whip. Dinnid responded by smashing with his left battle arm, but Veriasse was already on the floor, rolling beneath the attack. He felt the cordlike sensor whip in his grasp, tugged it with all his might, hoping to pull it out.

Instead, the dronon flipped onto his back. At that angle of descent, Veriasse's added weight was too much for the creature.

In that moment, Veriasse leapt and kicked Dinnid's right front eye cluster with a cracking sound. Veriasse danced backward while the dronon scrambled to his feet.

Veriasse expected Dinnid to retreat, regroup for a moment, but apparently the creature went berserk. It leapt forward, thrashing blindly with its battle arms, trying to chop Veriasse in half. Veriasse staggered back to avoid its blows. Yet the vanquisher kept advancing.

Veriasse dodged right beneath the creature's blind spot and struck the dronon full force in the right thigh of his rear leg, crushing the lord's exoskeleton so that bits of carapace fell into its air holes.

Dinnid spun to attack, but Veriasse leapt under his blind spot and smashed the dronon's left front eye cluster, then staggered back a step.

Orick shouted, "Get him! Kill him!" and Veriasse suddenly became aware of the noise around him. The dronons too were shouting, but he had been so focused during the fight, that he had blocked out all such mundane sounds.

Lord Dinnid was blinded in both front eye clusters. He responded by rushing forward, lashing out with roundhouse swipes of battle-arms. He twisted his head to the left and right, trying to spot Veriasse with his back eyes. After several seconds, he buzzed his wings, flew overhead.

Veriasse's face burned painfully from the acid. He was sweating heavily, pouring salt into the wounds. He could feel the acid eating into his cheeks and neck like fiery ants.

Veriasse gasped for breath. The room was so damned hot, and his head began to spin. Lord Dinnid landed on the far side of the room, turned his back to Veriasse so that he could watch him, then Dinnid began the dronon equivalent of coughing. His right thigh convulsed rapidly, and bits of exoskeleton came flying from his air holes.

Veriasse considered rushing to attack, but he realized that Lord Dinnid would probably like him to try. The dronon would only fly away, forcing Veriasse to tire himself.

Veriasse began walking toward Dinnid. "Surrender now," Veriasse offered. "I do not wish to destroy you!"

"I will not surrender to a soft creature like you," the dronon answered. "You have been fortunate in this contest, and I have been incautious."

The dronon vanquishers who circled the arena were still singing, their mouthfingers clicking softly. Dinnid shouted for silence, and they obeyed.

Dinnid turned, waved his sensor whip high, then stood tall on his hind legs.

In such a position, he could not launch into flight, but he raised his battle arms overhead like vicious clubs. He stood silently, waiting for Veriasse to advance.

Veriasse watched the creature warily. The sensor whips collected information in three ways: they were chemoreceptors that the dronon used to smell with; they felt vibrations; and they acted as enormous ears. Time and again, the dronon proved to be more sensitive to sound than humans. Veriasse vowed not to be taken in by Dinnid's apparent vulnerability.

Veriasse's face felt as if it were on fire. He closed on Dinnid. Gallen and Maggie must have recognized the danger, and they began shouting loudly, "Get him! Kill him!" making as much noise as possible so that they could cover Veriasse's approach. Dinnid twisted his head in frustration, slowed, then seemed to center on Veriasse and began stalking.

Veriasse waited. The air in the room was suffocating, and he had to focus, try to forget the pain in his face, the strangling air.

Lord Dinnid began coughing again, stopped to clear his air passages. Veriasse looked for a weakness. There were few places to attack. The dronon's exoskeleton was so thick that even a heavy kick to the head would do no good. Veriasse considered the mouthfingers down beneath the mandibles. He might be able to crush its voice drum—which would have much the same effect as putting a hole in its lungs—but the mouthfingers were too close to those heavy mandibles.

There were only a few places he could strike with much effect. The air holes on the thighs were one target. The wings were another. The sensor whips were a third. Yet he looked at the huge lord, a consummate warrior, and he despaired of winning this battle. Dinnid was too powerful.

Veriasse backed away a step, gasping for air, and caught a sweet scent of flowers. He laughed as he realized that Everynne had opened the bottle of Hope he had received on Cyannesse. An adrenaline surge poured through him, filling him with light. And then Veriasse considered ways to use the dronon's own power against it.

Dinnid stalked closer, and Veriasse jumped forward and shouted, causing the monster to swing both battle arms down, slamming into the metal floor. Veriasse leapt, kicked Dinnid's voice drum. His foot connected with a sharp thud. Dinnid raised his battle arms protectively, hitting Veriasse in midair, knocking him away.

Even that minor touch was too much.

Veriasse hit the floor on his back. Some ribs cracked on impact. For a moment, he lay gasping in pain, unable to move. Dinnid swung his head from side to side, biting down with his mandibles in case Veriasse tried to kick his voice drum again.

Veriasse didn't move, didn't stir a muscle, forced himself to still his breathing. Lord Dinnid was so fond of pointing out the weaknesses of the human's soft body that Veriasse decided to let the creature think he'd done some damage.

Dinnid shouted, "Human? Human?" His voice garbled. Of the dozens of voice fingers under Dinnid's mandibles, half were crushed.

Veriasse didn't answer, and the dronon decided that now was his opportunity to strike. He leapt forward, waving his sensor whip and chopping down with his right battle leg. In that moment, Veriasse leapt up, grabbed the sensor whip, and pulled it in front of the swinging leg.

The serrated chitin of the foreleg sliced through the whip. Dinnid groaned in pain, spun away so that his back eye was on Veriasse, then buzzed his wings, lifted off in flight.

Veriasse picked up the sensor whip. It was over two meters long and very heavy. Veriasse snapped it overhead as if it were a bullwhip, cracking the air.

Everywhere, the dronon in the audience hummed in disapproval.

Veriasse imagined how he would feel if a dronon were to pull the leg off a human and use it as a weapon. He imagined how it would anger him and hoped that Dinnid too would be appalled. Perhaps it would break his concentration.

Dinnid buzzed forward, hit the far wall and fell. He turned, leapt into the air again and rushed toward Veriasse. Veriasse cracked the sensor whip, and Dinnid veered toward him.

Veriasse crouched low, and Dinnid swooped over. Veriasse dodged and swung the whip with deadly ferocity, hoping to get the creature's back leg. Instead, the whip cracked against the stub of Dinnid's damaged sensor. The dronon flapped his wings so rapidly that they buzzed, creating a keening that was the equivalent of a dronon scream of pain. He doubled his speed and crashed into the far wall with a tremendous smack.

Dinnid fell to the ground, tried to get up, but his legs wobbled. He turned in a semicircle as if dazed, and Veriasse watched in horror. Dinnid's skull had cracked. White ooze seeped from the wound.

Somehow, even though Veriasse had struggled from the outset for a clean kill, now that the moment was upon him, he was repulsed at the task.

He ran to Dinnid, and the dronon vanquisher wobbled about feebly, trying to prop his massive battle arms so that he could support his own weight. Dinnid was not thinking of fighting now, only of crawling to safety.

Veriasse leapt into the air, aimed a flying kick at the crack in the dronon's skull. He hit with a thud, managed to open the crack a bit wider. Dinnid wobbled feebly on his front legs, and Veriasse leapt again, was forced to kick a third time. His foot entered the skull, and he pulled it away in disgust.

Lord Dinnid shuddered and fell. For a moment there was silence. Veriasse crawled back a pace and sat, gasping, horrified by what he had done.

All around him, the dronon began thrumming their mouthfingers against their voice drums loudly, creating a deafening roar.

Veriasse turned, looked across the room to the young queen of the hive. She was little more than a bloated sac for laying eggs. Her battle arms were small, unformed, and with her great egg-filled abdomen she could not fly, could hardly walk. Yet by dronon law she could defend herself against his attack.

Veriasse walked to the queen, panting. He was exhausted, ready to faint, and could not take any more of the hot air. "I do not want your death, Great Queen," Veriasse said. "We came here seeking only the Right of Charn. We wish to pass through your land, so that we might do battle with your Golden."

"You have earned Charn," the queen said. "If you promise not to kill me, you may mark me. I will not resist."

Veriasse could not escape this symbolic act, the maiming of the queen. He went to her side, made a fist and swung into her egg sac with all his might. The queen's abdomen did not burst, nor did it break, but the metal studs in Veriasse's gloves left a long gouge in her carapace.

A great hissing noise of displeasure rose from the dronon. All around the arena, dronon put their battle arms over their heads, crossing them in token of surrender. Yet they were not looking at Veriasse. Instead, they turned to face Everynne to do obeisance, their drumming voices crying out over the translator, "Behold the Golden! Behold our queen!"

Veriasse held his lungs, sucking air with great pain. The room seemed to spin, until he was forced to his knees.

Twenty

Maggie rushed to Veriasse. The skin of his face was red, burning away. She looked around desperately, then dabbed at his face with the hem of her robe and called to Everynne, "Help me, please!"

Everynne stood alone watching. The dronon were clattering their battle legs in token of surrender. She walked over to Veriasse, with Gallen and Orick in her wake, but Everynne said, "You have to clean him. They call me a Golden now. I cannot be seen doing work." She looked into Maggie's eyes, pleading. She could not jeopardize what she had gained thus far.

Gallen pulled a canteen from his backpack, bathed Veriasse's face. Veriasse knelt on one knee, panting.

"How badly are you hurt?" Everynne asked. She had been surprised at the ferocity of the battle. With his upgraded nervous system, Veriasse was phenomenally quick. In two minutes she had seen him take apart a dronon Lord Escort, his fists and feet blurring. Yet he had done it at great cost. His face was terribly burned, and she'd heard something crack when he'd fallen.

Veriasse pulled the microphone away from his mouth. "My ribs," he groaned. "I think some are broken."

"What can we do for you?" Gallen asked.

Panic took Everynne. She could not think. She only knew that if Veriasse failed the next battle, she would die.

"Rest. I need to lie still for awhile. My nanodocs should be able to heal the wounds in a couple of hours."

Everynne's mantle told her that he was wrong. It would take days for his nanodocs to heal the breaks. She needed to get him away from here, take him somewhere so they could speak in private.

Everynne turned to the hive queen and said, "We have won the Right of Charn. We now demand that you alter the course of your hive city. Speed us on our way to Queen Tlitkani."

The hive queen clicked her mouthfingers against her voice drum, and Everynne's earpiece translated. "She is not on this world. She has moved her hive to another world, to facilitate her use of the human's mechanical mind."

"You mean she has taken up residence on the omni-mind?" Everynne asked.

"Yes," the queen said.

"Where has she taken the omni-mind?"

"It is orbiting our sun."

Everynne said, "Then take us to the nearest spaceship."

The queen spoke to one of her Lord Technicians, then turned back to

Everynne. "Our technicians will prepare a ship for you immediately. We will send a squadron of our Lord Vanquishers as an honor guard."

The dronon queen watched Everynne for a moment. "We have received orders from our ruling dronon. She asks that we relieve you of the Terror you have been carrying."

Everynne reluctantly pulled the ball from her pocket. It had been her insurance, and part of her was loath to give it up. But it had accomplished its purpose.

She held it out for the queen, but a trio of Lord Technicians rushed forward and carried the thing away, presumably to be destroyed. The dronon queen turned her back, began dragging her bloated egg sac away.

When they were alone again, Maggie touched Everynne's arm. "We can't leave yet. Veriasse needs time to heal."

"Neither can we delay," Veriasse said, pulling on Gallen's arm as he staggered to his feet. "We have won Right of Charn, but according to dronon order, we must leave in all haste."

Everynne doubted that Veriasse could fight another battle in his condition.

Gallen stood tall, his hands on his hips. "Veriasse, you're in no shape to fight. It would be wrong to even try. You can't take a chance with Everynne's life this way. Let me fight the next battle."

Veriasse looked up, his jaw firm. "I wore the mantle of a Lord Protector for six thousand years. You have worn it for less than three days. You are a good man, Gallen, but you're not a Lord Protector yet. Even though I am injured, you couldn't beat me. How could you then take my place?"

"I watched you fight," Gallen said. "I know I could win! Veriasse, you're all done in."

"You can't just take my place, Gallen," Veriasse said. "I am Everynne's Lord Escort. By dronon rules of conduct, she can only take another Lord Escort if I die."

"I could switch clothes with you when we're alone," Gallen said. "The dronon would never know."

Gallen turned to Everynne, pleading. "You decide between us. It's your life."

"And yours," Everynne said. She looked at the two men. Gallen was probably correct. The dronon might never know if the two men switched places. Veriasse was gravely wounded, and Gallen still fresh. Yet Veriasse had proven himself in combat against a dronon.

"Will you, too, hold with my choice?" Everynne asked Veriasse.

He glared at her. His next words seemed to cost him more than the pain of drawing breath. "Gallen is right. You should have a say in this." By those words alone, Everynne knew he was severely wounded. Veriasse would never relinquish his title if he thought he could still fight.

Everynne turned her back on them, looked out over the arena. Orick ran to the center of the arena, retrieved Veriasse's goggles. A few meters away, the dronon had circled the corpse of Dinnid and were dismembering it, feeding it to the royal grubs. Everynne could not help but think that within a matter of hours, other dronon might be doing that to her.

She considered her options. Veriasse was sorely wounded, but his nanodocs would ease his discomfort. Within an hour, he should be feeling somewhat better. And Veriasse outweighed Gallen by thirty kilos. When he'd managed to break the carapace around Dinnid's air holes, she'd found it hard to imagine a human with such strength. Everynne doubted that Gallen could equal the task.

Yet, even with all of Veriasse's great accomplishments of the past, somehow at this moment, she trusted Gallen more. He was still healthy. And even though he didn't have an upgraded nervous system, Gallen was fast. Veriasse had been astonished by his strength when they first met. She considered choosing Gallen and wondered at the wisdom of such a move.

Maggie put her arm around Everynne's shoulder. "You can't let Veriasse fight anymore!" she whispered. "It would be murder."

Everynne looked into Maggie's eyes. They were no longer the eyes of that innocent child she'd met on Tihrglas a few days before. Instead, her eyes were filled with wisdom, the kind of knowledge that comes only through pain.

"You love Gallen, don't you?" Everynne said.

"Of course," Maggie answered. And in her mind, Everynne heard Maggie's accusation of a few days before: *You took him, just because you could.*

Everynne nodded. She had stolen something from Maggie once before. She determined not to do it again. Even if I die, Everynne thought, I will not steal from her again. She turned to face the two men. "I choose Veriasse as my champion."

Gallen gasped in astonishment, obviously hurt, and Veriasse breathed deeply, tears of gratitude glistening in his eyes. "I will not disappoint you, my lady. Give me a few moments' rest. I promise I will not disappoint you."

The journey to the omni-mind seemed shorter than it was. The dronon technicians took only an hour to remove a spaceship from the bowels of their city, and another hour to alter accommodations so that humans could travel in it. The alterations were limited simply to removing some seats and installing a pallet for Veriasse to lie on.

The old warrior lay on the pallet, put himself in a meditative trance to slow his breathing as they traveled. The ship was light and fast. With its antigrav drives, it moved fluidly between worlds, its rapid acceleration apparent only as one looked out the windows and watched Dronon shrink to a tiny glowing ball, lost between the stars. Forty dronon fighter ships escorted them.

After two hours, they swooped low over the omni-mind, and Everynne got her first glimpse of the great machine. It glowed with a soft silver light. Trillions of computer crystals lay upon its surface, reflecting sunlight like a sea of molten glass. Here and there across the planet, vast tachyon communication towers rose above the plains, pointing like metallic daggers to the heavens. Beyond that, there was no hint of the monolithic processors built into the planet's interior, no sign of its power supplies.

It was beautiful.

The dronon ships flew in a V to a great city, perhaps thirty kilometers across, ringed with light. Everynne watched from the portals. The city was built under large domes, and parts of it were green with grass, blue with pools of water. She could see hills and forests under the glass, and clear streams.

The dronon ships hissed low over the city, taking nearly half an hour to make their slow procession. Everynne gazed down on small estates that had once belonged to her mother's Tharrin advisors. Hundreds of thousands of people could easily live there.

The dronon went to the interior of the city, circled the largest central dome. There was a small palace beneath it situated in some woods. Nothing exotic or costly, simply a functional building where her mother had sometimes performed her duties.

The dronon fighters circled this building twice, then dove toward a gray docking portal at the dome's edge and landed so softly in the docking bay that Everynne never felt them touch down. She went to Veriasse, stroked his cheek and whispered, "Come, Father. We're here."

Unaccountably, Veriasse had fallen asleep. They had not really rested much in nearly twenty hours, and Everynne herself was exhausted. She felt a bit dizzy, unconnected from her body, but she could never have fallen asleep with the end of the journey so near. She jostled him again, and Veriasse woke, blinking. "Yes, yes. I'm coming."

She got him up, and he stretched, walked straight and tall through the ship's exit. Gallen, Maggie, and Orick followed them down a long glass corridor into one of the domed cities.

The dronon waited at the entrance to the dome. A wall of dronon vanquishers had formed under the clear canopy, and it seemed strange to Everynne to see their black carapaces shining in the pristine daylight.

Everynne breathed deep in amazement at their sheer numbers. She estimated that at least forty thousand vanquishers had gathered to meet them. Their acidic stench filled the dome, overwhelming the scent of the green grass that they trampled. In the distance, beyond the woods, she could see the palace, a building of purple-gray stone with ivy trailing up its sides.

Atop the wall of living dronon stood their leader, a Lord Escort with facial tattoos that looked like white worms strung beneath his eyes. Veriasse had talked of him often. Xim.

Xim shouted insults in dronon, and Veriasse gave his ritual hand signals, shouted insults in return and challenged the vanquisher to ritual combat, so that he and Everynne could take their rightful place as Lords of the Swarm.

Whereas earlier she had been terrified, now Everynne felt some sense of calm. She controlled her breathing. Xim called for the Rite of Examination, flew down and stalked around her. Unlike Dinnid, he was thorough. He used his whiplike sensors, grasped her dress and pulled it up to examine her skin. Xim tasted her scent thoroughly and stopped at the back of her neck, his sensor brushing against her small scar.

"What is this strange substance?" the vanquisher asked, rubbing at the body paint.

"It is a perfumed soap that our Golden uses to clean her skin," Veriasse said evenly. "Do you not like the scent? We find it quite pleasing."

Xim rubbed at the paint. "What is this mark?" Behind Everynne, she heard Maggie gasp.

"It is the mark of a Tharrin," Veriasse said reasonably. "A coloration variance similar to that found on our nipples. It is common to some of our Goldens." Everynne was not surprised that Veriasse had chosen to lie. The burn would heal in a few days, but it would be difficult to explain its presence now.

Xim hesitated, and Everynne imagined that he would kill them now for the attempt at deception.

He raised on his hind legs, crossed his battle arms and shouted, "I am Xim, Lord of the Swarm. Our larvae shall eat your corpses. Our vanquishers shall claim your domain. Your hive shall submit!"

His wings flashed, and he flew high into the air, buzzed around the ceiling. All around them, the dronon vanquishers beat their battle arms together, and their carapaces rustled as they shifted, creating a tunnel of living bodies for Everynne and the others to walk through.

They stepped into the dark cave. The dronon vanquishers had stacked themselves so that they could watch the procession, and myriads of heads swiveled to follow their progress. Sensors writhed overhead like black snakes, and many a battle arm hung overhead threateningly.

They did not have far to go. A field of grass lay a hundred yards beyond, ringed with countless dronon. The Golden Queen stood on the far side, proud and tall, whip sensors waving above the crowd. She wore the mantle of Semarritte on her head, a silver headdress with long flowing rows of medallions. Everynne looked at the mantle, the icon she had sought across light-years. To win it would mean her death. To lose it would mean her death.

Royal larvae huddled under Tlitkani's legs. Xim circled her in the air, then landed in front of her protectively, raised his battle arms high and crossed them. He shouted, "Veriasse, Lord Escort of the Golden Everynne. I have watched your battle with Dinnid. I come now to kill a worthy opponent!"

Veriasse raised his own wrists and crossed them. The two proceeded over the field. All around, dronon began their chant. A familiar thrumming filled the air, and the sound of it raised the hair on the back of Everynne's neck.

When they were ten meters apart, Xim's wings flashed and he soared into the air. The ceiling was far higher here than it had been on Dronon, and the vanquisher took full advantage of the larger area, sweeping in faster than Dinnid ever had. He flew toward the setting sun, then turned and screamed toward Veriasse, battle arms outstretched.

Veriasse stood tall and proud in his black robes of office, the dark chains of his mantle flowing down his shoulders. He raised his fists as if to strike, but Xim flashed his battle arms in a rolling blur and flew straight at Veriasse.

Veriasse was forced to dodge, roll away.

Xim repeated the tactic four times, each time veering nearer to Veriasse, and each time Veriasse had to retreat. On the fourth pass, Veriasse got up, holding his ribs painfully. He gasped for breath, and Everynne suddenly saw Xim's plan. The dronon knew of Veriasse's injury. Xim sought to aggravate it.

Xim circled the room, continued his charges. On the seventh swipe, he swerved near, slashed with a sensor, whipping Veriasse across the forehead, knocking Veriasse's goggles aside. Veriasse tried to dodge the attack, rolled to his feet and staggered. Jagget's black mantle fell from his head.

Blood flowed down his face, covering his eyes. Veriasse tried to wipe the blood away, and Xim swerved short of the roof to the glass dome, pressed the attack. He shot low over Veriasse's head, spat the contents of his stomach. The acid hit the wound, and Veriasse rolled to the ground, writhing. He tried to wipe his face with his robe.

Faster and faster Xim circled the great room with seeming effortlessness, his legs pumping rapidly as he flew.

Veriasse staggered to his feet, got up and spun in a circle, blinking frantically, his eyes a swollen mess. He tried to wipe the acid from his face. "Everynne!" he shouted.

Everynne cried, "I'm here!" She reached into her pocket, pulled out the bottle of Hope that Grandmother had given her on Cyannesse, opened it and sprinkled a drop on the ground.

Veriasse was still blinking, and though he fixed on the sound of her voice, he didn't seem to see her. Yet he suddenly breathed easier, stood tall. He closed his ravaged eyes, listened for the sound of Xim's wings.

Xim came screaming in from above, and Veriasse blurred as he leapt high into the air and blindly kicked.

Yet the dronon had anticipated his attack. Xim had come in high, and now he lashed down with the claw of his hind foot. It cut through Veriasse like a knife, and blood spattered darkly across the grass.

Around the arena, the dronon vanquishers' humming raised to a roar, and thousands of them began beating their battle arms together. The sound was deafening. Some of them rushed into the arena a couple of paces, as if they would tear Veriasse apart and begin feeding now.

Veriasse climbed to his feet, blood streaming from his leg, and he shouted. His voice came to her faintly, "Everynne? Everynne?"

"I'm here," Everynne called. Xim had swerved back into battle, letting the roar of dronon applause block out the warning sound of his clattering wings.

Everynne shouted, "Watch out!"

But it was too late. The dronon vanquisher dropped to the ground, simultaneously chopping with his battle arms. One huge serrated arm crashed down on Veriasse's head, slicing him nearly in half. The other fell at an angle, chopping him across the belly.

Xim picked up the mangled corpse, held it overhead and paraded with it a few steps, then tossed it to the ground. All across the great arena, the vanquishers fell silent as Xim turned his attention to Everynne.

Twenty-one

Everynne backed away, feeling faint. Xim leapt into the air, landed before her at ten yards, and advanced with battle arms fully extended.

Everynne recalled dully that her gloves were weapons with metal inserts in the knuckles. She raised her hands and shouted.

Suddenly Gallen jumped in front of her, arms crossed at the wrists. He fell down on his knees and shouted, "Lord Xim, I beg you to show mercy to our Golden, as Lord Veriasse showed mercy to your queen. Do not kill her, but mar her only."

Everynne did not know if the dronon understood Gallen. He did not have a translator. Everynne repeated his words, shouting so that the microphone roared her plea.

Lord Xim leapt over Gallen, advanced on her. His mouthfingers tapped over his voice drum. "I will not spare a Tharrin. You have lost your right to live."

For one second, Everynne stared up into Xim's faceted clusters of eyes. Each eye reflected a small image of her, fists raised, defiant.

Xim lifted his battle arms for the killing blow, and she suddenly realized that he thought she would make it easy, he thought she would submit to his punishment as if she were a dronon queen.

She screamed and leapt, smashed his right eye cluster with a fist. Xim twisted, caught her with his sensor whips, and smashed her to the ground. There was a great rushing in her ears, and the world twisted violently. In the distance, she could hear Orick shouting her name.

Gallen leapt up from his kneeling position, spun. He had not understood Xim's reply to his plea for mercy, so he had remained kneeling.

Now Xim had Everynne on the ground. He raised a battle arm and clubbed her. The blow struck home with a sickening thud, and Orick roared in grief, jumped on the dronon and grabbed Xim's rear leg, biting into it and pulling back.

The dronon vanquisher leapt, trying to flee the unexpected attack, and part of his carapace came away in Orick's mouth. Gallen could suddenly see Everynne's body, crimson blood washing over her golden clothing. Her hand trembled violently.

Orick roared and charged in for a second attack, but Xim backed away, raised his battle arms and chopped a slicing blow that ripped through Orick's right shoulder.

Orick yelped in pain, spun away from the battle, and Xim buzzed his wings and jumped into the air. He flew a lazy pattern while Orick madly danced in circles, blood and hair spattering across the grass. The dronon's intent was clear. Orick was already mortally wounded. He did not need to engage in battle until the bear weakened further.

Maggie shouted at Gallen, "Do something! Save them!"

Gallen watched it all, and knew that by dronon law he could do nothing. If he tried to protect Everynne, he would only be destroyed, and he had promised Veriasse that he would clone Everynne, come at some time in the future and challenge the Lords of the Swarm again.

He shook his head at Maggie, shouted, "We can't," and saw the horror in her eyes. He recalled Primary Jagget's predictions. Now that the dronon had formed gate keys, they would march through the Maze of Worlds. The Lords of the Swarm would conquer every realm. There would be no future. He had to act.

Everynne twisted on the floor, struggled for something in her pocket. Gallen stood, amazed that with such a wound she could still be alive. He watched her pull out the small vial of Hope. It rolled from her hand.

If I were the greatest warrior in the world, what would I do? Gallen wondered. And he stood, closed his eyes, and tried to clear his mind. He waited, but nothing came.

Maggie shouted at him, raised her hands over her head, crossing her wrists. "Gallen, I am Golden!"

He studied her face, wondering at the possibility. Could she challenge the dronon? And even if she won, what could she do. Maggie had suffered tremendously by wearing a Guide. The knowledge that it so ruthlessly imparted had ripped at the very fabric of her sanity, yet it was nothing compared to the wisdom of the omni-mind. To wear the mantle of Semarritte would destroy her. Even if it did not crush her as the Guide would have, it would tear away her identity.

All of Maggie's hopes, all her thoughts and dreams would be like words written on a sandy beach, waiting to be erased by the onrushing tide.

"Are you sure?" Gallen shouted. No matter what happened, he was consigning her to destruction. Yet she alone had worked under the dominion of the Lords of the Swarm. She knew the price that whole worlds would pay if she failed.

"Please!" Maggie cried.

Gallen turned. Lord Xim was flying low over the arena, circling back to finish Orick.

Gallen raised his hands, crossed his wrists. "This world is ours! All worlds are ours! A Great Queen comes among you. Prostrate yourselves in adoration, or prepare to do battle!"

The room fell silent, and ten thousand vanquishers looked to Gallen. Lord Xim flew low over Orick, dropped in front of Gallen. The dronon began clicking his mouthfingers, and Gallen went to Veriasse's corpse, pulled out the translator from his ear, plugged it into his own.

"You claim this woman is also Golden?" Lord Xim asked.

"Yes," Gallen said. "She is a Golden from the world Tihrglas. All who know her adore her. I am Gallen O'Day, Lord Protector of that world, and her Lord Escort."

He looked at Maggie, standing there with her long red hair streaming out, her clear blue eyes. He'd seen the longing in men's faces as they watched her work in the inn back home. Nothing he said was a lie.

Yet Gallen feared that his plan would not work. The dronon lived by their rigid order, their code of honor. He only hoped that his actions and words fit within that order.

Xim seemed agitated by Gallen's claim. His head swiveled from side to side, and he walked in a circle, dragging his injured leg. "You bring two Goldens and two Lord Escorts?" he asked, confused.

"Yes," Gallen said. "We humans are soft. We did not think that one pair would be enough."

Xim stopped in his tracks, raised his head questioningly, whip sensors waving. He tilted, so that his rear eye cluster faced his Golden Queen. "You must rule on this," he begged.

The Golden Queen raised her head, studied Maggie and Gallen. "She is not a Tharrin," the queen said, "and therefore cannot be a Golden among the humans."

"Do you accept challenges only from the greatest hives in your realm?" Gallen asked. "Do only the Goldens who come from your greatest families deserve the privilege of battling for the Right of Succession? Maggie and I come from a small world, a Backward world. We don't have any fancy lineage. We had never even heard of the Tharrin until a week ago, but on my world, Maggie is as Golden as they come."

The Golden Queen's whip sensors stopped waving as she considered his argument. "The omni-mind contains no useful information about your world or your culture," she said after a long moment. "I cannot corroborate your claims. Still, if you seek to battle Xim, you will find only your own death. You may battle."

Xim stalked over to Maggie, his whip-sensors waving. He pulled at her clothing, searched her scalp. Gallen didn't know if Maggie had any scars. He'd never seen her undressed. Gallen held his breath. Xim's prodding revealed a few moles on her back, nothing more. Throughout the search, Maggie simply glared at the lord, as if she wished only to bash in some more of his eyes.

When he finished, Xim raised his wings and shook them angrily. "Our offspring shall eat your carcasses! We shall rule your land! Your hive shall submit!"

Gallen could not remember what challenge Veriasse had called out next, so he was forced to innovate.

"Bullshit!" Gallen raised his fists. "I'm going to knock out your brains and use your hollow skull for a planter!"

Xim stood silently, apparently perplexed by this nonstandard verbal affront. All around the arena, dronon vanquishers began making thrumming noises.

Xim launched into the air, circled high above the arena. Gallen watched him, considered how best to handle the creature. Veriasse had opted for low dodges, a kicking attack. Gallen's mantle flashed images before his eyes, showing the dronon's weak spots.

Gallen wondered what Xim would do if Gallen opted to go over the top.

Xim swerved, dove toward Gallen, a frontal assault with his battle arms extended. Xim swept low to the ground, as if afraid Gallen would dive from his reach. Gallen rushed forward, vaulted into the air and twisted, kicking at the vanquisher's face with all his might, hoping that he could avoid its serrated arms.

Xim was traveling at tremendous speed, and Gallen's assault took him by surprise. His face smashed into the steel-toed boot with more force than Gallen could ever have mustered.

Gallen felt a sensor whip snap off at the impact, and Xim's head slammed into the ground. Gallen tumbled through the air, fell on his back. His mantle got knocked off his head, was tangled in the claws on Xim's rear leg.

Somehow in the impact, one of Xim's battle arms had grazed Gallen's leg, slicing it open. It bled profusely, but Gallen didn't have time to bandage it. Gallen scrambled to his feet as Lord Xim rushed toward him, but Xim suddenly buzzed his wings, flew high in the air, and tossed Gallen's mantle over the crowd.

Only seconds before, Gallen had felt confident, controlled. Killing a dronon in unarmed combat had seemed not only possible but easy. From moment to moment, the mantle had sent him images of the weak points on a dronon's carapace, but suddenly he felt emptiness, a yawning void.

Gallen got up, struggling to recall where he should strike on a dronon, remember the films of Lord Xim's previous fights.

His leg felt numb from the blow it had taken, and he shook it, tried to keep limber.

He recalled that Xim was supposed to be a consummate tactician. In his first fight with Veriasse, the dronon had sliced the old man open with a wing, using an appendage that could not serve as a weapon against other dronon.

Now, Xim was fighting a battle of attrition. He had removed both Gallen's and Veriasse's mantles, played against their weaknesses.

Gallen stood, sweat streaming down his face. He had plenty of weaknesses. If I were the greatest warrior in the world, he wondered, what would I do now?

He cleared his mind, let the old peace settle over him. He was breathing hard, and his tongue felt dry. The dronon vanquishers were humming loud, and Xim's wings buzzed above the crowd.

God, I love a fight, he thought. All his senses were alive, and he reveled in the energy that flowed into him.

He watched Xim buzz around the room, and he realized that Xim fought a battle of attrition because with a fully armored dronon opponent that was the only kind of battle there was. Strike at an eye cluster in this pass, rip off a wing on the next.

Xim circled the great dome, gaining speed. Gallen realized that it was a ruse. The dronon knew of Gallen's bleeding leg, and he was waiting for the loss of blood to weaken the human.

Gallen couldn't afford to fight this kind of battle. He was already losing.

Gallen closed his eyes, focused, and all of the sounds went away. He tried to ignore the numbness in his leg. Faintly, he tasted the sweet scent of flowers, and energy coursed through him. Maggie had retrieved the bottle of Hope, removed the stopper.

Gallen opened his eyes and looked up. Xim was diving toward him from the top of the dome—sweeping in with the sun behind him.

And suddenly Gallen understood why Veriasse had lost. He'd performed countless tests, trying to discover how much pressure it took to shatter a dronon's exoskeleton. But he'd performed the tests by striking the skeleton of a stationary body. He'd never calculated how much force a dronon added to a blow when its body slammed into a fist at a hundred and twenty kilometers per hour.

Gallen couldn't afford to fight a battle of attrition. He stood his ground. At the last moment, he feinted a left dodge.

Xim swerved to intercept, swung a battle arm, and Gallen veered back right, simultaneously dodging a blow and striking at the dronon's head, putting all his force into the blow. His fist connected with a loud smack, and instantly pain flared up his arm, into his shoulder. Xim's momentum threw Gallen back, and human and dronon rolled together in a tumult. Gallen's arm was loose in its socket.

He rolled to his belly, climbed up, blinded by pain. He reeled in a circle, dazed, looking for Xim. Gallen suddenly spotted the dronon lord a dozen meters off, crawling away.

He raced toward the dronon. Xim swung around to meet his attack, and Gallen leapt into the air before the dronon could raise his battle arms. Gallen's kick landed in Xim's face, and Gallen fell backward.

He looked up. Xim wobbled feebly, raised on his hind legs, extending his battle arms in the air. There was dirt and grass all over Xim's face, rubbed into his broken eye clusters. A thin grayish ooze dripped from a crack in Xim's skull.

Gallen panted, scrabbled backward to get out of Xim's reach. The dronon dropped his battle arms, rested a second.

Gallen stood up. His shoulder was dislocated, and the bones made a sickly rasping noise as they grated together. His leg was spurting blood.

Xim raised back up on his hind legs, prepared to meet Gallen's attack. Gallen staggered forward and stopped just out of Xim's striking range. He stood for a long moment, looking into the dronon's eyes. Xim waved his single remaining feeler in the air. His head leaked a gray-white fluid; an eye cluster was gone; one of his rear legs was ripped. Gallen had seen a hundred men back down from a fight, and though he didn't know what might be going on in the monster's mind, he decided to give it one last chance.

"Beg for mercy," Gallen said, "and I'll spare your life."

"Fight me!" the dronon clicked.

"If you insist." Gallen leapt in, feinting a strike. Xim swung his battle arms, and Gallen danced back. The creature's reaction time was slow, terribly slow.

Xim raised his battle arms again. They were wobbling, and Gallen fell back, panting.

Xim stood on his hind legs for a moment, and his battle arms waved feebly. He tired and dropped his arms. The white ooze was running thickly from his skull, and Gallen knew then that the creature was dying.

All around him, dronon vanquishers began thrumming, and the translator in Gallen's ear whispered, "Kill him. Finish it."

Gallen shouted at them, "You're a morbid mob." And he turned, advanced on the Golden. The small white royal larvae skittered away from beneath her legs.

She raised her battle arms, crossed them in surrender, and put her head to the ground. Behind him, Gallen heard clattering, glanced back. Xim toppled to the grass.

Gallen went to the Golden Queen. She kept her battle arms crossed in token of surrender.

"Under the rules for conquest, you may choose only to maim me," the Golden said. "If you so choose, I will not fight you."

Gallen stopped in front of her. She raised her head to look up at him. "Why should I spare you?" Gallen asked. "So you can continue to breed? So your children can challenge me?"

Her mouthfingers clicked over her voice drum. "I have already given birth to many Lord Escorts. My children will hunt you down. You cannot escape your fate."

Gallen stared at her distantly. He stepped forward and removed Semarritte's mantle from her head. She really did have a nice golden color.

He slammed a fist into her face.

He discovered that his wrists must have been stronger than Veriasse's, for instead of merely gouging her, his blow cracked her head open.

All around him, the dronon raised their battle arms and clattered them together, crying, "Behold the Golden! Behold the Lords of the Swarm!"

Gallen raised his hands for silence, looked out over the assembly. The room fell quiet. "You tell them, Maggie. You're the queen now."

Maggie glared at the dronon and shouted, "All of you: get off our worlds!"

Gallen turned away from the carnage, wiped the sweat from his forehead with the back of his left hand. Around the arena, the dronons' carapaces scraped and rattled as they evacuated the dome.

Maggie hunched over Orick. The bear was badly cut, and he breathed shallowly. Blood soaked much of his fur from groin to chin. Yet her mantle whispered to her that the nanodocs in her pack might still save him, so she forced the seven pills down his throat and waited.

Everynne was lying in a pool of blood, too, but she already had nanodocs working on her. The tiny machines were closing her wounds, had slowed the bleeding. There was nothing more that Maggie could do.

Gallen came and threw Semarritte's mantle down at Maggie's feet, then sat and petted Orick's snout. Maggie picked up the mantle, held it under her arm. All around them the room rustled as dronon fled the premises, and within five minutes, they sat alone on the grass. The sun was setting out on the horizon, and shadows lengthened. From here, she could not see the vast sea of molten glass on the omni-mind's surface, only the other domes nearby. Overhead the stars shone more fiercely than any she had ever seen.

Gallen went to Veriasse's pack, got some water, and gave drinks first to Everynne, then to Orick. He bandaged his own leg, and had Maggie pop his shoulder back into its socket. Then he sat beside Maggie and held her hand for a long time, neither of them speaking, except once when Gallen said, "Oh, my, look at that!"

She looked up just in time to see a falling star. A moment later, dronon ships began streaming away in a solid convoy.

After an hour, both Everynne and Orick were still breathing deeply. The nanodocs had closed their wounds, and Maggie's mantle whispered to her that it was a good sign. Both of them would probably survive.

Maggie sat still for a long time, then began crying. Gallen held her for awhile, and said, "I'm really tired. Do you think it gets cold here at night? Should we get some blankets for these two? Build a fire?"

"Och, you're kidding me, aren't you Gallen?" Maggie said. "You know this place has to have heaters in it. I'm sure it won't get cold."

"Heaters?" Gallen asked. "What's a heater?"

Maggie slapped him, thinking he must surely be joking, but then she looked deeper into his eyes, and she wasn't sure. Could he have learned so much in the past week and still never have heard of a heater?

He laughed at her confusion. "So, are you going to put that mantle on, or aren't you?"

"I don't know, come to think of it," Maggie said. "There's no one here making me wear it. To tell the truth, I sort of like learning slow. I could put it on and learn everything there is to know at once, but it seems to me that that would be sort of like eating all the desserts you would ever want in your life all in one day—if you take my meaning."

"Aye," Gallen said. "It does sound nasty."

"Besides," Maggie said, "it belongs to Everynne."

"That it does." Gallen sighed. "Even if she doesn't want it."

He got up, walked away in the darkness, and Maggie thought he'd gone to get his bedroll, but a moment later she heard him digging in the dirt.

Gallen had a wavy-bladed dagger, and he used it to scrape a long, shallow hole in the ground. Then he put Veriasse in, covered him with clumps of grass and a bit of dirt. Maggie went and stood beside Gallen. He gazed down at the grave for a long time and asked, "Do you think there's a heaven?"

Maggie sighed. "It's damned possible."

Gallen said, "If there's a heaven, I think Veriasse will find himself guarding the gates. You know, keeping out the rabble."

"Aye, he'd like that job," Maggie agreed.

Gallen walked over to a good spot of grass, then lay on his back, his hands folded behind his head, and stared up at the stars through the dome. The last of the dronon ships had left.

Gallen looked like some country boy back in Tihrglas.

"Gallen," Maggie said, "what are you going to do when you get home?" She didn't ask him to include her in his plans. She didn't intend to go back, and even though they'd spoken of finding a world together, she didn't know what he might be thinking now. She wanted him to come with her voluntarily.

"I've been thinking. It's been a long time since I've gone fishing, and I've got a craving for salmon. I think that first I'll go fishing in Forrest's Creek. Then I'm going to travel for a bit, see the world."

"And when you're done?"

"Well, I don't know. Tihrglas is sort of a quiet place. I could grow old there, sit in a rocker . . ." He looked up into her eyes. "But I don't think I could be happy for more than a day or two, lazing about like that. Besides, there's this woman I know, and life would be . . . dreary without her."

Maggie smiled, lay down beside him, felt the warmth of his chest against her breasts. He took her face in his hand, kissed her long and deeply.

When he finished, he whispered, "You've got no family left back in Clere, but I've got my mother to take care of. I need to go home, say good-bye, hire someone to watch after her at the very least. And I'll need to make trips home from time to time, to be sure she's okay."

"Of course, you couldn't leave her there forever alone," Maggie said. "You can just tell her that you're working, guarding ships for some merchant. Then you can stop back and see her once in awhile."

Gallen nodded, closed his eyes. Maggie lay with him for a long time, and he fell asleep. Part of her was angry with him for sleeping, but the more sensible part said, "Ah, poor boy, he needs his sleep. It's been a long week, and he's exhausted."

Yet Maggie could not rest. She checked on Orick and Everynne. Both were resting peacefully, and she washed them off a bit, then sat on the grass, looked at the silver mantle. It had thousands of tiny silver disks woven together in the chain mail. They were smaller than the disks she had seen on any other mantle, and she realized that they were made using a higher technology.

At long last, she could stand the temptation no more, and she put on the mantle, felt the cool weight of the chains running down the length of her back, over her shoulders, and between her breasts.

For an endless moment, she waited, expecting the mantle to take her, ravage her with light as the Guide had. Yet at the same time, she waited in stark terror.

She tried to clear her mind, wipe away that fear, but the knowledge never came. Nothing happened.

At last, when she was ready to throw the mantle away in disgust, a woman came to her in a vision. She had long dark hair and skin as smooth as cream. Every line of her form was perfect. Maggie did not have to beg her name.

"Your brain waves do not match mine," Semarritte said. "I can bond with you, and you will gain some use of the omni-mind, but like the dronon before you, your ability to control the device will be impaired. Still, I am loath to take you, if you fear me so. What do you want of me?"

"I want a home," Maggie said. "You know everything about ten thousand worlds. I thought, perhaps I could learn of them."

Semarritte reached out a finger, touched Maggie between the eyes. She felt a strange dizziness, and Semarritte pulled her finger away. Her demeanor changed. She looked at Maggie with a new understanding. "You would not be satisfied if I taught you all that I know about every world. You will only be happy if you go to each world and learn about it for yourself."

"That's right," Maggie said.

"So you are not searching for a world for yourself. You are searching for a world where you can be happy with your love, Gallen. I am not sure that such a world exists."

"But where should I start?"

"Tremonthin." Semarritte laughed softly. "There you can learn much, and Gallen will find his abilities sorely tested."

"Thank you," Maggie said, and she removed the mantle. Almost immediately, the vision seemed odd to her, like a dream that is forgotten upon waking, and she wondered if she had imagined it. She went to sleep beside Gallen, and he threw his arm over her protectively.

Twenty-two

For ten days, Gallen and Maggie nursed Orick and Everynne, watching them recover. In that time, many people began to arrive from distant worlds, ambassadors and powerful lords who celebrated the end of dronon rule. The first to come were Tharrin, delegates from distant parts of three galaxies who simply appeared the next morning on the road in front of the palace. They had come through their own gates. There were dozens of them—men and women with an eerie presence, a sense of light and peace that filled the air around them.

Gallen asked several of them to help clean up Everynne and Orick and move them to beds in the palace. Several Tharrin gingerly carried the two inside, and the physicians ministered to their wounds behind closed doors, then said that both would be up and about soon.

Afterward, the Tharrin came before Gallen and Maggie, requesting audience. They retired to a quiet chamber of the palace, and a powerful man named Lord Meron spoke with Maggie soberly. He was a tall man, with a barrel for a chest, long, flowing brown hair, and penetrating green eyes. He took Maggie's hand, looked into her face.

"You know," he reasoned, "it is not in the best interests of your people for you to try to claim the omni-mind."

"I know," Maggie answered. "I never wanted the thing in the first place. Gallen and I only won it by accident."

Meron patted her hand. "Still, you won it, and the dronon will hold you accountable."

"Can't I just give it away?" Maggie asked. "Give it back to Everynne?"

"The omni-mind you can give to Everynne," Meron said, "but the burden of ruling the dronon now belongs to you. They perceive you as their Great Queen, and they will seek counsel from you. If they do not receive guidance, their swarm will be overwhelmed by others."

Meron did not say it, so Maggie said it for him. "Still, they'll try to kill me, won't they?"

Meron nodded slightly in assent. "We can set barriers between them and you, protect you. We've already begun moving the omni-mind from orbit, and we'll hide it so they can't easily regain control of it. But you, you will need to hide yourself, keep moving from world to world, as Semarritte did."

"How am I supposed to hide from the dronon and lead them at the same time?" Maggie asked.

"You can appoint a regent, someone to rule in your stead."

"Everynne?" Maggie asked.

Meron nodded. "She'll do. In a way, you will be doing her a great favor.

The dronon will not perceive her as a target, and she will be free to reign without fear."

Maggie nodded thoughtfully, and Gallen saw that they had won a mixed bag of goods. Gallen patted Maggie's shoulder, whispered, "It will be all right. We can make the best of it."

"Och, sure," she said. "I wanted to visit other worlds anyway. This will just keep a fire under my toes, give me a little more incentive."

By that evening, Everynne and Orick were both able to sit up and take a bit of food, and Everynne began directing the withdrawal of dronon hives from the occupied worlds.

Over the next few days, delegates from many worlds continued to gather.

The omni-mind soon began to fill with joyous people, and it became as crowded as any inn during the Autumn Fair at Baile Sean.

And in that time, Everynne grieved for Veriasse, and put on Semarritte's mantle for the first time.

It was on the fourth evening, just after sunset. The dronon had all left, and a few hundred dignitaries had arrived on the omni-mind. But Everynne did not invite them to her investiture. She planned a public ceremony for later, but for the moment she met with Orick, Gallen, and Maggie in private. "You three battled for me across the worlds. You helped me win this moment, and I owe you my life. I want you to come with me now, to witness the death of Everynne and the rebirth of Semarritte."

They were in the throne room in the palace. The room had no ceiling, just a vast chair covered in red cloth, where one could sit and gaze out at the stars through the clear dome. Maggie, Orick, and Gallen sat around her feet in a semicircle.

"Do you have to wear this thing?" Orick asked. "The dronon left without it."

Everynne smiled at him. "The Tharrin are preparing another to take my place, but his training will take many years. In the meantime, there are ten thousand worlds that must be governed. I do not rejoice in this task, but yes, I must put the mantle on. In your time, Orick, I suspect that you too will have to accept responsibilities. You will go home and become a great and wise leader among bears."

Gallen said good-bye, kissed Everynne one last time. Everynne cried and hugged him, then hugged Maggie. Last of all, she hugged Orick for a long moment and wept in his arms.

When she was ready, Everynne sat back in the chair and placed the mantle on her head. She was shaking, and Gallen took her left hand while Orick held her right.

At first, she sat regally with the silver chains cascading down her neck, and nothing seem to happen. After a moment, she got a faraway look in her eye, then stared off into eternity.

"It's so beautiful!" she cried. Tears streamed from her eyes freely. Gallen squeezed her shaking hand, then looked up into her eyes. And in that moment, Everynne was transformed. She smiled so beatifically that she seemed to radiate light.

She breathed deeply and gave a rapid succession of sighs, crying out in wonder. At last it became too much for her, and she fainted.

Gallen watched it all and realized that part of him felt jealous. She had left him behind, traveled to a far place he could never reach.

And Gallen suddenly remembered being a child, running under the trees as his father rode away on a dark horse into the mountains. Gallen recalled how desperately he had wanted to follow. He felt the same now.

After Everynne fainted, Gallen and the others waited silently with her for nearly two hours. Orick simply held her hand, did not move from her side. But Gallen got up, walked around the dome, staring out at the stars. He wondered at them. He'd stood on worlds that orbited five of those stars. Maggie came and put her arm around his back, watched the sky with him.

A few minutes later, Orick said, "She's waking up!"

Gallen and Maggie went back to Everynne's side. Everynne stirred a bit and opened her eyes. She smiled at them, and she looked as if she had gained some contentment she had never before achieved. Her eyes were filled with a terrible light.

"Semarritte?" Gallen asked.

Everynne shook her head. "Semarritte is dead," she said. "Her consciousness was stored in the omni-mind until I put it on. But she knew I feared her, so she welcomed me, and then she died."

"How could she know that you feared her?" Orick asked.

"Maggie told her," Everynne said. She leaned forward, patted Maggie's hand, and did not explain herself. Gallen was left to stare at the two women, mystified.

That night, Everynne was invested publicly with the omni-mind before a multitude of Tharrin counselors and ambassadors from many worlds. And on that night, Maggie, the new Golden Queen, publicly named Everynne as her regent to the dronon, leaving her with that undesirable burden.

In a sense, that was almost the last that Gallen saw of Everynne.

Over the next few days, he tried to speak to Everynne again on several occasions, but found it difficult. In each conversation, she anticipated his words. She would answer questions without being asked, tell him more about himself than he wanted to know. And always there was that terrible light in her eyes, frightening in its intensity. In those days, he lost his desire to travel to Gort Ard and look upon the statue that Saint Kelly had carved. Gallen had only to gaze at Everynne to see the face of God.

On the morning of the ninth day, so many dignitaries began arriving that Everynne was constantly being pulled in several directions by those who sought her ear. Each night for the past five days, the lords of the worlds had thrown parties to celebrate, and Gallen saw the way that things would go.

These parties would be held every night for years, and though at each party the dignitaries were eager to bestow honors upon him as Lord Escort, Gallen felt somewhat embarrassed by the whole affair, and he wanted only to get away.

So he went to Everynne and said, "I'm thinking of leaving. I can't stand it here any longer."

"You know you are welcome to stay as long as you like," Everynne said. "And you are free to leave."

"It's my mother," Gallen said. "She's getting old and sickly, and I'm worried about her."

Everynne nodded, smiled at him. "And there is something you want from me. You have more than earned any reward that I could give you. Is that what you have come for?"

"Yes," he said. He expected her to ask what he wanted as payment for saving her life, for defeating the Lords of the Swarm. Among the things that she could offer there were many great treasures, but only one he desired. He feared that his price was excessive. He'd prepared all kinds of arguments for the occasion, but before he could ask, she said, "Yes, you may have a key to the Maze of Worlds, but only on one condition: you must put on your mantle often, and if I call for your aid, you must come."

"Of course," he said, grateful that she had agreed. But she touched his cheek, turned his face so that he had to look up into her eyes.

"Don't make that promise lightly," she warned. "You don't know what I have in mind."

And in her eyes he saw that terrible light, and fear struck him to the core of his soul. She reached into her pocket and pulled out a new medallion to wear in his mantle, a receiver that would let him hear her call, and she gave it to him along with the key. It appeared that she had only been waiting for him to ask for these things.

That evening, they went to a gathering in a large dome, where four thousand lords celebrated in a great throng. Gallen had seldom seen so many people in one place, and Orick stared across the crowd in wonder. All of the lords were dressed in their finery in a rainbow of colors. Hundreds of robotic servants had prepared vast sumptuous meals, and all evening long, people crowded around them, thanking and congratulating Gallen, Orick, and Maggie. Everynne was on the far side of the room, and at the end of the evening, Orick seemed worn.

Gallen escorted him out into the hall, and Orick said, "I've got to get out of here, Gallen. I'm feeling well enough to travel. I planned to stay for Everynne's sake, not wanting to leave her alone. But she's got so many of those Tharrin counselors around her now, I don't think she needs me."

"Perhaps," Gallen said. "Why don't you ask Everynne what she wants? She has many people at her ear, and all of them admire her, but you're her friend."

Orick grunted, went back into the great dome and pushed his way to Everynne. A moment later, the two of them got up and escaped to a side room together.

Late that night, Orick came to Gallen's room, and the bear seemed ecstatic. "Do you know that those pills Maggie gave me will keep me alive for at least five hundred years?"

"No, I didn't know that," Gallen lied.

"And I talked to Everynne. She's not going to stay here forever," Orick said. "In ten years, another Tharrin will come take her place as regent, and she's going to come back to Tihrglas to live for awhile. I promised to show her around."

"Good," Gallen said.

"So are you ready to go home?" Orick asked.

"Yes."

"Good," Orick said. "I'll go tell Maggie. Everynne is going to lead us to a gate in a few minutes."

Gallen bundled up his belongings—his outfit and weapons, along with the mantle and weapons that Veriasse had worn—and together the three went to meet Everynne one last time.

Everynne was dressed in her blue traveling robe, as if she might come with them. She said, "Next time you see me, I'll be wearing this." She led them down through unexplored passageways of the omni-mind, down to deep caverns that Everynne said even the dronon had never been told of. Behind a hidden door, they found an ancient gate the color of brass, covered with dust. It was marvelously decorated with images of people and creatures from many worlds, and Everynne told them, "This is the gate that leads to all worlds, all destinations. Enter, and I shall send you home."

A pale green light shone under the arch. Gallen, Orick, and Maggie each hugged Everynne, said their last good-byes.

Then together they stepped through the cold mist between worlds.

They found themselves on a forest road, beneath large pine trees in the mountains. The morning sun was just breaking over the mountains, a radiant pink ball. Kiss-me-quick birds called from the edge of the roadside, and in the distance an owl hooted. The air tasted as sweet to Gallen as Maggie's kisses, and he breathed in deeply.

They walked along the road for most of the day until they reached a small town called Gort Iseal and learned that they were in the north of County Obhiann, many miles away from home.

At the inn that night, people looked at them oddly, and Gallen found himself apologizing for his strange attire and hid his mantle in his pack.

Maggie and Gallen took a table near a roaring fire and had a large dinner. Afterward, they sat and talked softly. Some bears came to the door of the inn, begging for leftovers. Orick went outside to talk to one young female. Afterward, he came up to Gallen and Maggie all excited. "That young she-bear has invited me to the Salmon Fest. Can you believe it? We've been gone all that time, and we still didn't miss it!"

Gallen nodded, studied Orick's face. He was eager, that seemed sure. "So why don't you go? What's stopping you?"

"Well," Orick said, "I took this vow a while back. I promised God that I'd only make jolly with one she-bear in my life."

Gallen looked deep into Orick's eyes for a moment, then said, "Orick, there are as many ways to serve God as there are men who serve God. In the past few days, you helped saved every person on this planet, not to mention everyone on ten thousand other worlds. And now this she-bear wants you to serve her, and you're only feeling guilty because you'll get a little pleasure out of it in the process. Why don't you help her out? Why don't you make it two?"

"Yes," Maggie said. "I'm sure you'll be the thrill of her life."

Orick frowned. "All right, you talked me into it." Orick hung around a bit, promised to come back soon for Gallen and Maggie's wedding, then left with the she-bear.

The next morning, Gallen sold an oxygen exchanger to a sailor and used the money to buy a brace of horses. He and Maggie began to ride home in style.

But that night, they were almost in County Morgan when a bad storm tore up the sky. They took refuge at an inn, and Gallen and Maggie sat discussing their wedding plans. With Father Heany dead, no one would block their marriage. Gallen would have his cousin in An Cochan perform the ceremony. As they talked of their plans, one of the locals at another table said, "Och, what a nasty storm we have a blowing outside—and it not even yet mid-September!"

Maggie turned to Gallen and whispered, "What day was it when we left here?"

"September fifteenth," Gallen said.

Maggie turned to the stranger. "What's the date today?"

"Why, the fourteenth," the man answered.

And Gallen sat there, stunned. That trickster Everynne had sent them back in time again. He suddenly recalled that later on tonight, he would meet several robbers and a sidhe on the road to An Cochan, some twelve miles distant.

"Maggie, my love," Gallen said, "would you excuse me for a few hours, darling? There's something I have to do. I promise, I'll be back for you early in the morning."

"I suppose—if it's important," she said.

"It's not a big job," Gallen said. "But I think I need to save a man's life."

He went up to his room and dug through his clothes, put on his mantle. In one corner of his pack, he found the mask of lavender starlight he had picked up on Fale. In Veriasse's pack, he found the wavy-bladed dagger the sidhe had been carrying.

Gallen dressed himself all in black, like the Lord Protector he was, then strapped on his sword and rode out in the rain and darkness to meet his destiny.

BEYOND THE GATE

One

After his recent adventures with Gallen and Maggie, risking his hide on half a dozen planets, Orick felt that his life was somehow charmed. A few weeks ago, he couldn't have imagined sitting here, a hairsbreadth from winning the title of Primal Bear.

Along the banks of Obhiann Fiain the bears had gathered by the hundreds for the annual Salmon Fest. The icy waters of Obhiann Fiain thundered through a gorge, and many a cub was perched on the large rocks, waiting to swipe at any salmon that tried to leap past.

The older bears had gathered near the dark pines that morning. Fires burned low along the hillside, and salmon skewered on stakes were cooking slowly so that smoke crept along the ground.

But Orick the bear did not have his mind on fish. After over a week of athletic competitions and feasting, Orick felt as sated as he'd been in his life—or at least as far as his gustatory appetites were concerned.

But now came the final athletic event of the Salmon Fest—the much-anticipated pig toss. After all the contests—the tree-climbing, the wrestling matches, the log pull, and the salmon-catch—Orick lacked only five points to take the lead in the competitions. The pig toss would make or break him.

Orick's nerves were frayed. He watched dozens of younger bears toss the "pigs"—burlap bags filled with forty pounds of rock. Legend said that in the old days, bears had actually tossed live piglets, but Orick couldn't imagine his ancestors engaging in such brutish activities.

Anxiously Orick waited for the toss of old Mangan, an aging bear with an especially large snout and a blaze of white on his chest. For five years—since before Orick was even born—Mangan had held the title of Primal Bear for the twin counties, an honor which allowed him the privilege of selecting ten or twelve mates a year. Orick had matched him in nearly every competition.

The competitions proceeded. Each bear snagged a pig and then took it to the tossing ring—a small circle of stones. The bears in the crowd would cheer and jeer in their deep voices.

Orick watched the first few throws, his heart pounding. He wanted to win, could taste victory. He looked out over the crowd, scanning for the females he'd most admired during the past weeks. He particularly liked one big she-bear, one with a thick, glossy coat, long, shiny claws, and large teeth. Certainly there were some fine specimens in estrus, and their scent left Orick dizzy, reeling.

He met the eyes of one young she-bear, but the undisguised lust in her glances left him feeling empty, hollow. Am I nothing more to her than a breeder? he wondered. The boar that might sire her cubs?

And he knew it was true. She-bears did not form strong attachments. God had so fashioned them that they desired but one thing from a male, and after their sexual appetites were sated, they would become irritable, chase him away.

Even now, many females huddled around Mangan, the favorite to win the games. They tempted him with their scent, gazed imploringly with their deep brown eyes.

And Orick, watching those she-bears, suddenly felt empty, desolate.

If he won this contest, what would he win? A few nights of frolicking with she-bears who would hold him in contempt a week later? It seemed an empty prize. For months now, Orick had considered entering the priesthood, giving himself into the service of God and mankind. It seemed a noble thing to his mind, yet here he had let his gonads bring him to this Salmon Fest to engage in these bestial contests.

If he bred widely, he would perhaps gain some form of immortality through his offspring. But if I give myself into the service of God, he told himself, wouldn't I gain a more sure form of immortality?

And so Orick was at war with himself, disconsolate. Before he knew it, old Mangan marched up to the circle with a burlap "pig" in his teeth. The she-bears in the audience called out, "Hurl that pig! Make it fly, Mangan!" Many she-bears cast him demure glances. Some stood on all fours and arched their backs, raising their tails seductively.

Old Mangan turned to Orick, a calculated gleam of malice in his eyes. "Looks like you'll be taking second pick this year," he shouted.

Mangan stood on his hind legs. He was tall, over six and a half feet at the shoulders. This gave him a real advantage in the toss, for he could swing with a long arc. And he had a great deal of muscle in those shoulders.

The old bear reached down with a contemptuous swipe and snagged the pig. Then he stood majestically, a sudden gust of wind rippling through his fur. He swayed back and forth, swinging the pig in long arcs, then with a snort that was almost a roar he swung one last arc and tossed the pig high. It sailed over the playing field, far past the longest mark from the younger bears, and slammed into the gray trunk of a pine tree. The burlap bag split on impact, spilling red clay dirt down the side of the tree.

Around Orick, bears hooted and cheered, shouting Mangan's name. But Mangan looked at where his bag had landed, and his upper lip curled into a snarl. Obviously, he had not counted on hitting the tree.

The other real contenders for the title of Primal Bear hung back, waiting to see who they would have to best. But Orick was suddenly tired of the games.

He rushed forward, looked at the "pigs" in their pile. He doubted that he could toss a burlap pig as far as Mangan had. Throwing was never his strong point.

So he would have to gamble. He found a bag that was halfway torn open, giving it a little more length so that it could be swung in a wider arc and would come free without snagging into his claws. Still, the bag could also rip halfway through the toss, losing mass so that ultimately Orick might not get as long a throw as he hoped.

Orick bit the thing in a fit of frustration and carried it up to the circle in his teeth. He was dimly aware of the cheers from the females in the camp behind him, and he looked out over the field. He needed five points. He would have to beat Mangan's toss by more than five feet in order to win the title, and even then Orick would have to wait to see if the other contenders would best his own mark.

He had never tried throwing a bag underhand the way that Mangan had just done. The only advantage Orick might really have was that he was younger and stronger than Mangan. But Mangan, having a long reach, had thrown his pig in a long arc that Orick could not match. Which meant that he would need to hurl that pig with a sidewise toss.

Orick took his well-ripped bag back to its pile, found one that was still new. He carried it to the circle, closed his eyes, twisted a three-quarter turn, and roared in frustration as he threw with his might.

The pig sailed toward the same tree Mangan had hit, and for one moment Orick thought he would repeat the older bear's performance, but the bag missed the tree trunk, lofted past it a few feet and tangled in the branches, then fell to the deeper grass beyond. Orick could not tell how far the pig had gone.

A dozen cubs rushed up with the measuring rods in their teeth, and a moment later they announced that Orick had beat Mangan's mark by twelve feet. For the moment, Orick was leader in the race for Primal Bear, and roars of delight came up from all around, from males and she-bears alike, for now it marked the end of Mangan's reign. This year, there would be a new Primal Bear.

Still, at least two other bears could possibly beat Orick, and as he walked back to the crowd, he listened to the deep cheers, and for one moment, just one moment, he wished that Gallen and Maggie could be here to see what he'd accomplished. But they were off in Clere, planning their wedding.

He looked over the crowd at old Mangan, who scowled at the ground, defeated, and Orick suddenly felt no victory.

He sniffed the delicious scent of the females in estrus, looked at their lustrous fur and the shining eyes that watched, and suddenly he knew what he had to do.

Orick turned his back on them all and walked away.

Perhaps he would win the title of Primal Bear, and perhaps he wouldn't. In either case, he wasn't going to stick around the Salmon Fest to find out.

He marched past the crowd, into the woods. Perhaps the others thought he went into the woods only to relieve himself, but Orick trekked on up a trail through the sheltering pines where the salmon sat cooking on their skewers.

Ahead, at the top of the hill, the trail forked. One branch led north to Freeman, the other led southeast to An Cochan and beyond that to Clere where Orick's best friend, Gallen, would soon wed. All through this past week, Orick had imagined that after the contests he would sate his lust upon at least one female before heading home.

But suddenly he thought of Gallen's wedding, and a longing came over him that was too painful to name. If he dirtied himself by breaking his vows of chastity—for he had taken those vows in his heart, though he never had spoken them to God or man—he wouldn't return home with any sense of real victory.

So Orick went to the fire pits, stood in the blue-gray wood smoke, and began pulling salmon off their skewers, swallowing them hot from the fire. A full stomach was all he would take from these contests, he decided.

Farther up the hill, a feminine voice called to him. "Are you leaving already? Aren't you going to wait to see if you've won?"

Orick looked up. A young she-bear lay sprawled under a tree, and before her was a large, leather-bound book. Orick realized with a start that she'd been sitting here reading while all of the others watched the game. This in itself marked her as an unusual kind of bear. Furthermore, she did not ask the question with the batting of eyes and coyness he would have expected. Instead, she asked with a tone of apathy, as if she were intrigued by his answer, but it wasn't especially important to her.

"No, I'm not waiting. I've done my best, and that is all I wanted to do." Orick studied the young thing. Her eyes looked bright, alert. He guessed that she was perhaps four years old, but rather small for her age. He hadn't met her before, didn't know her name.

"What about the she-bears in heat?" she asked. "They're all drooling for you. I've seen the looks they give you. And 'a she-bear in heat is the best kind to meet,' or so I hear."

"I'm not interested," Orick said. He pulled another bit of salmon from a stick and swallowed, savoring its smoky flavor with bits of ash on it.

The she-bear pricked up her ears, sniffed the air as if testing for his scent. Orick sniffed back, wondering if she was in estrus. She wasn't. So perhaps her questions were not the byproduct of some sexually induced intrigue, but were rather guided by a sense of curiosity. The she-bear was not particularly attractive. She had a dull coat of black hair with brownish tips. Her nose was petite, her paws rather overly large. Finally, she asked, "I don't get it. You could mate with any she-bear down there. Why don't you?"

Out of curiosity, Orick sauntered over to the she-bear. She was reading from a book on how to rig sailing ships—perhaps the most useless topic a bear could study.

"I don't know," Orick answered honestly. "I guess I want more from she-bears than they're willing to offer."

She studied his eyes. "You're that bear that runs with Gallen O'Day, aren't you? So what is it you are after—fidelity?"

Orick hesitated to answer, afraid that she would laugh at him, but something about her demeanor said that she wouldn't. "Yes."

She nodded. "I've heard of some males who want things like that," she said. "It's the cub in you. You still want someone to care for you, even after your mother chases you off. You'll grow out of it."

"Perhaps I want someone to care for—as much as I want someone to take care of me," Orick said. "Perhaps I have something to offer."

"Perhaps." She nodded. "So where are you going?"

"To Clere. My human friends, Gallen and Maggie, are getting married."

"Hmmm . . ." she said. "I was heading that way myself. Do you mind if I come along?"

"Only under one condition."

"What?"

"If you tell me your name . . ."

"Grits," she answered.

Orick wrinkled his nose in distaste. "That's not much of a name," he said, perhaps too honestly.

"I'm not much of a bear," she answered. She flipped her book shut with her paw, then gingerly picked it up in her teeth and carried it to a red leather pack under the tree. She nuzzled the book into the pack, then stood and slipped the pack straps over her head. Within moments the pack was on, two leather containers dangling at her side when she walked on all fours, as if she were some pack mule carrying its burden.

Then they padded off up the worn trail. By late afternoon they reached Reilly Road, which led south along the coast to Clere. As they flitted beneath trees, the sun shone warmly on them, almost as if summer had returned. And each time the road crossed a stream, Orick was obliged to stop and slake his thirst. His mouth was made dry by more than the constant exercise, for he talked long with Grits about many things—about his interest in religion and her interest in the ways that ships were constructed. They talked of far lands, and of the strange rumors they'd heard of heavenly and hellish creatures walking alive and in the daylight down in County Morgan.

Orick didn't tell Grits about his part in such matters, how he'd just returned from a journey with Gallen O'Day and learned of the vast universe beyond their small world. Although all the rumors said that Gallen O'Day was up to his neck in affairs with creatures from another world, and though Orick was Gallen's best friend, Orick preferred to feign complete ignorance of the matter, hoping that Grits wouldn't press him with questions. The poor she-bear just wouldn't be able to comprehend such talk, and, if it frightened her, he feared that she might blather the news about willy-nilly.

So it was that they climbed down out of the tall hills and into the green rounded hills of the drumlins. By dusk they reached the village of Mack's Landing, beside a long gray lake where geese and swans gathered out on the flat waters. Jagged clouds hung on the horizon, curtains of rain falling from them. The town itself was nothing more than a grove of old oak house-trees that sprawled at the bottom of the green slope of a long hill. The house-trees' rust-colored leaves flapped in a small wind.

The wood smoke from the cooking fires left a pall over the glade, and two large flocks of black sheep had come down to huddle for shelter under the trees. Orick hurried his pace, hoping that he and Grits might be able to earn a meal before dusk. Yet as they neared the town, he got an odd, uneasy feeling at the pit of his stomach. He slowed.

There were travelers in town—four dozen sturdy mountain horses, so many men that some were forced to camp outside the only inn. The men wore brown leather body armor over green tunics, carried longswords and spears. He knew they were sheriffs from the northern towns, but he'd never seen so many gathered together. It could mean only one of two things: either they were chasing a huge company of bandits, or they had gathered for war.

Orick stopped, raised on his hind legs and sniffed the air. The scent told him little. He could smell leather saddles, horses, well-oiled weapons, the common odors of a camp.

"What do you think they're up to?" Grits asked.

And Orick suddenly had a sinking feeling. "With all the stories we've heard in the last week of angels and demons warring openly in County Morgan, I fear that we've attracted some defenders." Orick licked his lips. "Do me a favor, Grits. I'm a known companion to Gallen O'Day, but I don't want *them* to know it. Call me what name you will, as long as it isn't Orick."

"Of course, my dear Boaz," she whispered.

They plodded silently along the dirt road, Orick with his nose down, until they reached the camp under the trees. These were not grim soldiers, worn with experience. Most of them were younger men out for an adventure, strong and limber. One played a lute, and several of the fellows sat beside a campfire, singing drunkenly a rousing old tavern song,

"My lady fair, my lady fair,
was drunk as a duck and fat as a bear.
And if you saw her prancing there,
You'd lose your heart to my lady fair."

There was merriment in the sheriffs' twinkling eyes, and they laughed and boasted as they gambled at dice and drank themselves silly with beer, hardly noting the presence of two bears wandering into town. One young man with long brown hair and a thin vee of a beard spotted Orick and shouted at him, "Och, why, we have strangers in our camp. Would you like to work your jaws a bit on something to eat? We've just boiled up a pot of stray lamb stew."

"Stray lamb stew" was another way of saying "stolen lamb stew." By law, a traveler could claim a stray lamb if it wasn't with a flock and its ragged appearance made it look as if it were lost. In practice, if men traveled in a pack of more than six, they tended to butcher any lamb they came across, figuring that they could intimidate the rightful owners.

Orick sniffed at the stew from outside the circle of the campfire. It was well seasoned with rosemary and wine. Bears were notorious for begging food from travelers, and were therefore not often so welcomed to camp. "Why, I thank you, good sirs," Orick said in genuine surprise at the offer.

The lad got up from the rock where he sat, staggering from too much beer, went to the stew pot and made up two heaping bowls. He came and bent over, set the steaming bowls before Orick and Grits—then pulled them back.

"Ha!" he laughed, seeing how the bears' mouths watered at the stew. "Not just yet. You have to earn it."

"And how would I go about that?" Grits asked.

"With a tale," the lad laughed. "You've likely heard more news out of County Morgan than we have. What tale have you? What rumor of demons? And make it straight for me!"

Orick was in no mood to humor the lads. Sheriffs or not, this was a dangerous company of men, rowdy and full of themselves. "I'll give you no *rumor* of demons," Orick grumbled in his loudest, most belligerent voice, "for I've seen them, and what I have to tell isn't the kind of idle gossip you've likely heard up north!"

Suddenly, the lutist stopped and over two dozen heads turned Orick's way.

One old sheriff with a slash under his left cheek looked up and sneered, "Out with it, then. What did you see?" His tone said he was demanding an answer, not requesting it.

Orick looked at the sheriffs. They were weary from the road, and they weren't in the mood for any slow tales. Orick licked his lips, remembering. "Two weeks ago yesterday night," Orick said, "I was in the city of Clere, on my way north for the Salmon Fest, when the first of the sidhe appeared. It was a man and woman who came into town, late of the night, in the middle of a storm. I was begging scraps at the tables of John Mahoney, the innkeeper at Clere, when the sidhe opened the door and stepped out of that damnable rain.

"The woman was a princess of the Otherworld, more beautiful and powerful and fair than any woman who walks this earth. Oh, she had a face that an angel would envy." Orick recalled Everynne's face, and he let the memory of her beauty carry in his voice. Some of the men grunted in surprise at the sound, for it was obvious that Orick loved her, and the sheriffs seemed amazed that a bear would love a fairy woman, so they leaned closer. Orick decided to stretch the tale a bit, try to fill these men with the proper sense of awe. "Beside her was her guardian, an old bearded man who was stronger than any three men I've ever met, and swift as a bobcat. He guarded her jealously, with two swords that glowed magically. And though the rain was pelting the inn like a waterfall, neither of the two had a drop on them."

Orick stopped a minute, gauging his audience to see if they believed that last bit about people walking dry through the rain. Some of the rough lads had their eyes popping out at his tale, and they gaped with open mouths.

"I've heard rumors of the sidhe coming to town, but I've never heard report of these two," the old scar-faced sheriff said.

"That's because you never heard the tale proper, from someone who was there," Orick continued. "At first, no one quite believed what they saw. The princess sought dinner and a room for the night, and she asked to hire someone local to take her into the woods, to Geata na Chruinne, the Gate of the World."

The sheriffs hunched nearer, and one of the younger ones muttered, "That's where the demons were headed, too."

"Aye," Orick said. "Gallen O'Day, who legend says is the best of you good lawmen, happened to be in the room, and when the princess turned her eyes on him, he must have fallen under her spell—as we all did—for he agreed to guide her, never dreaming the consequences."

At this point, Orick licked his lips. The sheriffs listened with rapt attention. He had begun to hear rumors of late, nasty tales where Gallen was named a conspirator with the sidhe. Orick couldn't come right out and say that such tales were lies, couldn't tell men that the Lady Everynne was no more a magical creature than any one of them, that she was just some woman from another world, trying to defeat the swarms of alien dronon that were sweeping across the galaxy. What did it matter if she carried weapons that could demolish worlds? She was still only something akin to human, and even though she had no magical abilities, she was still more marvelous and powerful than these men could comprehend. And Gallen had done right in becoming her servant and protector. But Orick could never convince these men of the truth, so he bent the tale, making it seem that Gallen had been a slave who couldn't control himself, and maybe that wasn't far from the truth, for even Orick had fallen under the spell of the Lady Everynne.

"So it was that the princess sought rest and refreshment that night, for she had been running long and hard, trying to escape monsters straight out of hell."

"You saw them?" one of the young sheriffs asked, leaning nearer and spilling a wooden cup of wine in the process. His hands were shaking.

"Aye, I saw them up close, I did," Orick said. "And I'll never sleep deeply again. Some of them were giants, and the biggest of you would hardly stand above their bellies. Their skin was green, and they had large orange eyes as big as plates. They were strong creatures. When they walked into town, I saw one of them kick a wood fence just in passing, and it splintered into kindling. Others had the same green skin and walked like giant dogs, on all fours, sniffing for the scent of the princess and her bodyguard. And with them was a major devil. A creature with wings the color of ale and a skin blacker than night. It had great clusters of eyes both on the front and on the back of its head, and it had feelers like a catfish's under its jaw, and when you saw him, you knew his name: Beelzebub, the Lord of the Flies.

"The demons walked into Clere just after dawn, and Father Heany confronted their master. Now Father Heany, there was a man of God. He had no fear for himself, only for his parishioners, and he rushed to block the path of the demons. And Beelzebub raised a magic wand, and a bolt of lightning flew out of it, striking Father Heany dead right there in the street, right in front of every woman and child in Clere. And when that lightning hit him, it melted the man. The flesh stripped from his bones and melted in a black puddle as if it were pudding.

"Then the demons marched on to Mahoney's Inn and asked after the princess and her guard, but the princess must have slipped out in the night. When the demons learned that she was gone, Beelzebub flew into the air and bit John Mahoney, ripping his head off."

Orick fell silent, and the eyes and ears of every sheriff were upon him.

"What happened next?" Grits asked.

"I can't be sure," Orick answered. "At that moment, I turned and ran from Clere for my life. It was in the first dawnlight of the morning when I took off, and I didn't stop running until the moon set that night, and even then, I hid. I went to the Salmon Fest, and from there I've heard stories the same as you—about how Gallen O'Day came back that day at dusk, with the sidhe warriors at his back, and the Angel of Death himself walking at his side, and then hunted the demons until nightfall. Some say that the sidhe chased the demons back to hell. Others say that the two sides are still fighting in Coille Sidhe. All that is sure is that no one has seen any sign of the demons, or of the sidhe, but Gallen O'Day rests easy in the village of Clere and is making plans for his wedding day."

"And other folks say that it's Gallen O'Day who opened the door to the Otherworld in the first place, at Geata na Chruinne," the scar-faced sheriff said. "They say that in order to save his own life, he prayed to demons in Coille Sidhe and opened the doors to the netherworld."

Orick considered the threat implied by that story. If these men believed Gallen was consorting with demons, they'd put him to death. Orick wondered if he might be able to turn these men from their course. "I wouldn't believe such talk," Orick said, hoping to calm them.

"It's true enough," Scarface said. He nodded toward a small fat man that Orick hadn't noticed before. "Tell him."

The fat man looked uneasy, bit his lip. "A-aye," the fat man stammered. He had a bowl of stew in his hands, and he tried to set it down out of sight, as if he'd just been caught pilfering it. "It's true. Me and my friends were planning to rob Gallen O'Day's client, but he—Gallen—put four of us down before we could defend ourselves. It was only a lucky blow from one of us that felled him, and then that Gallen, he began praying long and low to the devil in a wicked voice. That's when the sidhe appeared.

"I—I know it was wrong to try to rob a man, but if we'd known a priest would die from our wickedness. . . . Now, now I just want to wash my hands of it."

Orick looked at the greasy little man and imagined sinking his teeth into the rolls of fat at the man's chinless throat. The robber was glancing about, as if daring someone to name him a liar. Orick would have shouted the man down if he dared, but he knew that now was not the time.

Scarface said, "We intend to arrest Mister O'Day and put him on trial. Bishop Mackey signed a warrant"—he nodded toward the town's inn—"and the Lord Inquisitor himself has come with us, along with two other witnesses who will swear that Gallen O'Day prayed to the Prince of Darkness. Aye, this O'Day is guilty of foul deeds, all right. And we'll not let any *southern* priests conduct the questioning—not with their soft ways. We'll wring the truth from him, if we have to skin him alive and salt his wounds."

Orick raised a brow at this, then licked his snout. A full Bishop's Inquisition would involve days of torture and scourging. They might even nail Gallen to the inverted cross. And though Gallen had a lot of heart in him, even he couldn't endure such punishment. The lad would have no recourse but to fight these men for his life.

"Are you sure there's enough of you to take Gallen O'Day?" Orick asked. "They say he's a dangerous man himself. He's killed more than a score of highwaymen and bandits. And if the Angel of Death *is* on his side, you'll need more than thirty men to take him—even if you have the Lord Inquisitor to back you."

Some of the younger men looked about to the faces of those around them. Fighting against Gallen O'Day was foolhardy enough. But no one would want to be found fighting against God.

"Hmmm . . ." Scarface muttered, squatting on the ground to think. "Things to consider. Things to consider." He got a wineskin from his pack, filled a bowl, then looked up at Orick darkly, his thick brows pulled together, and said, "You've earned yourself more than a little supper. Sit with us tonight. Drink and eat hearty, Mister . . ."

Orick did not like his probing look.

"Boaz," Grits answered quickly. "And I'm his friend, Grits."

"Keep those bowls filled," Scarface ordered his men, and he offered the wine to Orick.

Orick thanked him and began lapping at his bowl of stray lamb stew. He intended to eat his fill. He'd need the energy later tonight, when he ran to Clere to warn Gallen of the danger.

Two

"Maggie," a man's voice called. "Maggie Flynn? Are you in there?" His voice trailed to a garbled string of words Maggie couldn't make out. She knew everyone in town, and whoever was hollering for her was a stranger.

Maggie looked up from sewing ivory buttons onto the back of her wedding dress, stared up toward the door of the inn, expecting the stranger to enter at any moment. It was a bitter cold day in early fall, with a sharp wind—sharp enough so that the fishermen of Clere had dragged their boats high onto the beach. A dozen of them were lounging about the fire, drinking hot rum.

Danny Teague, a stable boy who had shaggy hair and a fair-sized goiter, opened the door and looked out. A horse cart had drawn up outside the door. Its driver was a stranger in a gray leather greatcoat, a sprawling battered leather hat pulled low over his face. He had piercing gray eyes and a neatly trimmed sandy beard going gray. Still, at first glance, Maggie knew that it was his moustache, waxed so that the ends twirled in loops, that she'd remember when he was gone.

"I'm calling after Maggie Flynn!" the stranger shouted at Danny. "You don't answer to that name, do you, man? What's the matter with you—did your father marry his sister or something?"

Danny closed the door and sort of stumbled back under the weight of this verbal insult, and Maggie shoved her wedding dress up on the table.

"It's all right, Danny," she said with obvious annoyance. "I'll have a word with Mr. Rudeness out there!"

Already, several fishermen had got up from their seats by the fire and were rather sidling toward the door. If the stranger had hoped for an audience—and folks who stood in the street and hollered usually did want an audience—well, he had one. And whatever Maggie said to him now was likely to be talked about in every house tonight—as if the town didn't have enough to gossip about after the past few weeks: with demons and angels and fairies battling in the forests outside of town, the priest and innkeeper murdered.

Maggie got up, straightened her green wool dress and a white apron so that she looked the part of a matron who kept an inn—albeit a very young matron. Her long dark red hair was tied back.

She went and opened the door, gazed into the biting wind that smelled of ocean rime. The man's wagon was old and battered, and it was drawn by a bony horse that looked as if it hoped to die before it had to plod another step. The blacksmith's hammer had quit ringing across the street, and he stood squinting from the door of his shop. Elsewhere, an unusual number of people suddenly seemed to have business on the streets.

The stranger set the brake on his wagon and greeted her. "Damn it, Maggie, you look too damned much like your mother."

She studied him. Since he spoke so familiarly, she thought she should know him, but she'd never seen his likeness before. "I'll thank you to speak more reverently of the departed, Mr. . . . ?"

"Thomas Flynn. Your uncle."

Maggie glared at him, trying to consider what to say. Her mother had been dead for three years. Her father and brothers had all drowned a year and a half before that. And in all of that time she'd not seen so much as a whisker of Thomas Flynn's beard nor got a single message expressing his sympathy.

"That's right," Thomas said, "your only kin has come to call. You can close your mouth now."

From across the street, the blacksmith cracked a huge smile that barely showed through his bushy black beard. "Will you be giving us a song, Thomas?" he called.

In answer, Thomas reached behind him and pulled out the rosewood case for his lute, stood, and shook it over his head. "I'll give you many songs in the days to come!" he shouted, and his coat opened. Beneath it, Maggie could see a beautiful plum-colored shirt tied with a gold belt, pants that were forest green. His outfit was slightly festive, slightly dignified, and slightly absurd—as befitting a minstrel. Indeed, she realized now that he had been striving to draw a crowd by shouting for her from the streets. He was a man of wide repute, a satirist with some reputation for having a quick wit and, as they say in County Morgan, "a tongue sharp enough to slice through bones."

Such folk were always good for songs and tales of faraway lands, mixed with a fair amount of political commentary so burning hot that you could use it to scald the hair off a pig.

Maggie said, "We've heard of you—even in this little backwater. Everyone knows Thomas Flynn, who goes about aping the great men of the world."

"Aping great men? Oh, heaven forbid! I'd never ape a truly *great* man." Thomas grinned, removing his hat to show a full head of close-cropped hair. "They're too strange and fine a thing. But, now, for those who call themselves 'great,' but who are in fact deceivers—those men I will not spare. For through my aping I can sometimes prove that those who call themselves 'great' are nothing more than great apes."

"So why have you favored us with your presence, Uncle Thomas?" Maggie said in a tone that flatly admitted she wanted to be rid of him quickly.

"Oh, it's worried about you that I am, darlin'. Rumors. I've been hearing disconcerting things, Maggie. Rumor says you plan to marry a man named Gallen O'Day, even after he prayed to the devil and got your village priest murdered."

"Och, and what would you know of it?" Maggie asked. There was far more to the story than she ever planned to tell her uncle—or to anyone else.

"I'm only repeating the tales that I've heard on the road," Thomas answered, "tales everyone is telling nowadays.

"Some say that Gallen called upon the devils, unleashing them on the town, and others say that the demons came of their own accord and that Gallen struggled against them until God's angels came to fight beside him. In the last two weeks, every person in twelve counties has worn out their jaws yapping about it."

"Sure, and I suppose you don't believe such stories?" Maggie challenged, unwilling to so much as venture an opinion about the recent happenings. "So you've come to write a song to mock the good folks of Clere—and my beau Gallen, too, I imagine."

"Ah," Thomas said, looking around at the folks in town. "I've seen no proof that the accounts are anything more than fables. Why, I just drove forty miles from Baille Sean, and I spotted nothing more menacing than an old red fox that was slinking from pine to pine, hunting partridges. If there be green-skinned demons about, I've had no sight of them. And as for the tales of angels or fairy folk with flaming arrows, I've seen no flames at all— except in my own campfire. If I were called to write a song right now, I'm afraid that I'd have to damn you all as liars."

"I'm not surprised that you saw nothing in the woods," Maggie said. "The militia says the roads are clear."

"And I'm not surprised that I saw nothing, neither. Little surprises me anymore. In fact, the only thing that surprises me more than the human facility for prevarication is some people's nearly equal facility for staring a known liar in the face and believing every fantastic word he utters. That's a fair *part* of why I had to come—to see if there's any truth to this gossip about demons and angels and fairy folks in the woods."

Maggie half closed her right eye, stared up at him. Out behind the inn, a sheep bleated. The same damned sheep she'd had penned out back for two weeks, waiting for slaughter. But since word of the goings-on in Clere had spread, no one had dared the roads, and the inn had remained empty, except for locals who came to drink and exchange theories on what had happened.

Maggie smiled faintly. "There's some truth in those tales, Uncle Thomas. Satan himself came marching up that road not two weeks ago, parading at the head of a band of demons. And they heartlessly murdered Father Heany and John Mahoney—but those demons were never conjured by Gallen O'-Day." She watched his face for reaction. "And angels came that snowy night and drove the demons from town, and one of them fought at Gallen's side— the angel Gabriel—that part is true.

"But now Gallen's enemies—cutthroats and thieves all—have been telling tales on him, naming him a consort of the devil, hoping to discredit him."

Thomas scratched behind his ear, and Maggie tried to imagine what he was thinking. Maggie knew that he wasn't a simple man. He'd never heard a tale that featured demons walking in broad daylight, or angels fighting with magic arrows. But everyone within fifty miles swore that it happened, and the tales were stranger than any lies these unimaginative folks could conjure.

He looked about at the crowd that had gathered. "Well," he said. "I suppose that there's more than one song in such a tale, so I'll have to stay a couple of days at the least. You wouldn't mind preparing a good room for an old man, and maybe heating up a mug of rum for me to wrap my cold fingers around."

"I'd like to see the color of your money first," Maggie said, giving him no quarter.

Thomas raised an eyebrow, fumbled under his coat and muttered, "Och, so you're a frugal lass, are you? Generous as a tax collector. Well, I like that in a woman, so long as she's my niece." Thomas pulled out a rather large purse and jingled it. Maggie could hear heavy coins—gold maybe—in that purse. Only a fool would display so much money in public, Maggie thought. So her uncle was ostentatious as well as cantankerous. And with so much of a purse, she wouldn't be able to toss him out on the streets any time soon.

Thomas grabbed his lute and climbed down from the wagon, and Danny the stable boy was forced to suffer the indignity of tending the horse of a man who'd abused him.

Thomas stumped into the common room of the inn, looked about. The inn was built inside an ancient house-pine that had a girth of some sixty feet. The rooms rose up through three stories. Like all house-pines, over the years this one had grown a bit musty, and the walls creaked as the wind blew in the pine's upper branches. The smell of pipe smoke and hard liquor filled the air. The windows were large and open, covered with new white curtains that Maggie had made the week before. The common room featured six small tables, and chairs set in a circle around a fireplace. A small bar separated the kitchen door from the common room. The bar had two barrels on tap—one of beer and one of rum. The ale, whiskey, and wine were stored in back this time of year.

"A fine place you have here, Maggie," Thomas muttered.

"Oh, it's not mine," Maggie returned. "It belonged to John Mahoney. I'm just running the place till one of his kin comes to claim it."

"Nope, nope." Thomas sighed heavily. "It's yours, now. Or it will be when you reach your majority. Mahoney sent me a copy of his will two years ago, and I stopped in Baille Sean and had the deed transferred into your name."

Maggie was rather dumbfounded by all of this. John Mahoney had never bragged much on his family. He'd once mentioned an older brother who lived "down south," and he'd posted letters once in a while, so Maggie had assumed the brother would come to take possession of the inn.

"I don't understand," Maggie said, a bit breathless. "Why would he give it to me? I mean . . . I don't understand this. I've never much liked working here, and I'm not even sure I want the damned place."

"Well, now," Thomas said, "for a frugal woman, you don't sound over-joyed with your new fortune. I'll tell you what. Why don't you and I go find a quiet corner, and let's talk about it."

Maggie led Thomas to the corner table where she'd been working on her wedding dress. He stopped at the taps and took a large tin beer mug, then filled it up with rum and set it on the grate at the edge of the fire. "A man who has been driving a cart all day in the cold needs something warm to wrap his hands around," Thomas chided her. "You should know that." Maggie looked at the full mug. It seemed her uncle planned to be drunk in an hour.

Then he came and sat across from her, folded his hands, and looked her in the eyes. She knew that he was no more than fifty-five, but he looked older. His face had grown leathery from years on the road, and his stomach was going to fat.

"Well, Maggie," Thomas said. "I've been driving for over a week to reach you, and—och—to tell the truth, I'm not sure you're going to like what I have to say. So it's begging you that I am, to not take it too hard." Thomas reached into his shirt, pulled out a yellowed envelope. "This here is a paper that your mother made out on her deathbed. She was always harping on me to take more responsibility for the family, sending me letters and whatnot. So she wrote out her will and had John Mahoney witness it, then had it sent by post. By the time the letter found me, it was months after your dear mother's death. But in this letter, she acknowledged me as your only living kin, and made me your legal guardian. So . . . the burden of seeing that you're properly cared for falls to me, don't you know?"

She sat back as suddenly as if he'd dealt her a physical blow. She gaped at him, then the words tumbled from her mouth. "Mother has been dead for years—and in all of this time, I've not had so much as a letter from you!" But now I have an inn, she thought, so you've come to make yourself my legal guardian.

Thomas held up his hands, as if to ward away the accusation in her voice. "I know, I know . . . and I'm dreadful sorry. But I've lived the life of a wandering man, don't you know, and I couldn't have cared for you properly on the road."

Maggie looked over her shoulder. Several townsfolk had slipped into the inn, and all of them had listening ears. They were gathering at nearby tables like a flock of geese to a fistful of grain.

"Anyway," Thomas said, "your mother appointed me to be your legal guardian until the age of eighteen. It's all signed by the bailiff, proper and legal." He held the paper out for her inspection.

Maggie gaped at him, astonished. "Now don't take it so hard, darlin'," Thomas offered. "It's true that I didn't split my britches running to your side after your mother's death, but you were fourteen, old enough to work, and there's nothing that will build character in a person faster than having to look after one's self. Besides, did you ever know a teenager who wanted an obnoxious old man like me hovering over her shoulder? Oh, I've worried long nights about you, worried that you might make wrong decisions or worried that you might take sick, and I exchanged letters with your old employer, John Mahoney, on the subject. But I knew you were in the hands of a good, saintly person, and you didn't need me to meddle in your affairs. But now things are different."

Maggie wondered what he meant, when he said that now things were "different." Were things different because she was wealthy, or was he planning to meddle in her affairs? Or maybe both.

Thomas leaned back, smiled a charming smile, as if considering what to say next. "By God, you're a beautiful young woman, Maggie," Thomas said, condescending, and she remembered an old saying: compliments are so cheap to give that only a fool would hold one precious. "I can tell that John Mahoney cared for you well. He said in his will that you were a special kind of person, one who doesn't let life just happen to her, but one who would likely go out and make a good life in spite of what happens. He had faith in you." More compliments, she mused.

He glanced at the wedding dress spread out on the table. "So, when are you planning to marry?"

"Our wedding is set for Saturday," Maggie said, not sure what else to answer.

Thomas frowned. "And when did this Gallen O'Day propose to you?"

"Two weeks ago."

"The day John Mahoney died?" Thomas looked skeptical.

Maggie nodded.

Thomas gazed at his hands, cleared his throat. "It seems that he decided to fall in love with you at a very convenient time—just when you were ready to come into a nice, juicy inheritance."

Maggie said nothing at first, couldn't quite think of what she should say for there was too much to be said all in one breath. Neither she nor Gallen could have known anything about the inheritance, and there were so many things that Thomas didn't know. She'd spent time on other worlds, risked her life fighting the dronon to save rascals like her uncle.

"It's not like that at all!" Maggie said. "You—and you don't care about anything but my money! In all these years, you've never so much as written me a letter—but now that I have an inheritance you come banging on my door! I should sic the sheriff on you, you nasty old lecherous thief!" She threatened him with the law, suspecting that she couldn't legally get rid of him, but willing to give it a jolly try. Still, she wanted to frighten him.

She saw a flicker in Thomas's gray eyes, a slight flaring of the nostrils as he drew breath. She knew she'd struck him right. "You plan on moving in here, don't you?" Maggie said. "You plan on coming to the inn to lord it over me until I'm old enough to toss you out on your ass."

"That's not a fair assessment," Thomas said calmly. "I'm well-known as a minstrel. Many a satirist my age takes up a winter residence in a hostel, and we enrich the landlords with our talents. I'll earn more for you than my keep."

"So you admit it: you plan to live here—for free—while you lord it over me? My mother wouldn't have made you my guardian. You must have forged that letter."

Thomas licked his lips, stared at her angrily. Obviously, he had not expected her to see through his ruse, and he hated having it discussed openly, here in front of everyone. He called himself a "satirist," but he was a professional backbiter. He was used to bullying others, pouncing from behind like a wolf. He'd tried to put her on the defensive, keep her mind occupied. Now she was turning to attack. "I'll thank you, Uncle Thomas," Maggie said, struggling to sound calm, "to take your wagon and ride out of my life forever!"

"I don't begrudge you your hard feelings," Thomas said. "If you were a filly that I'd left in the pasture for three years, I expect that I would have to use a strong hand to break you. And, alas, that is what I intend to do now.

"Maggie, darlin'," he said, "whether these magnificent stories told on your beau are true or not, your name—our family name—is mixed up in this scandal. I've heard you spoken ill of fifty miles away. You're running about, making mad resolutions that will most likely ruin your life, and I have to step in. I'm afraid I can't allow you to marry this Gallen O'Day."

Thomas pulled at the wedding dress on the table, as if he'd take it, and Maggie grabbed it from his hands.

"There will be no wedding," Thomas said, slamming his fist on the table. "How could there be? What kind of priest would perform a marriage for a girl so young?" His tone made it sound as if he were naming her a dreamer or a liar. It was true that she was young to marry.

"Gallen's cousin—Father Brian of An Cochan!" Maggie said, feeling a thrill of victory by being able to name such a priest.

"Father Brian, eh? Not without my permission, I'll wager." Thomas glared at her coldly, and Maggie realized he'd just tricked her into telling the priest's name.

He reached into his purse, and tossed a shilling to a boy of fourteen. "You're a bright-looking lad. You look as if you know where the cat's hid its kittens. I want you to carry a message for me: run to An Cochan and tell Father Brian that Maggie's wedding will have to be called off for the time being. Tell him I'll arrange a suitable donation to the church in order to . . . compensate him for his trouble."

"Don't do this," Maggie said.

Thomas stiffened at the dangerous tone in her voice, and his own voice took on a hard edge. "I didn't come all this way just to acquiesce to your wishes, child. And I'll not haggle about it. The wedding is off!"

"You can't," Maggie cried. "Gallen's a fine man. I love him!"

"This isn't about love!" Thomas shouted. "This is about *judgment*. Judgment—a damned fine quality that you're too young to have in abundance. So the wedding is off! Your mother gave me the right and the moral obligation to use my judgment in raising you, and I'll exercise that right now. And quit giving me the evil eye!"

"I'll not let you do this—" Maggie hissed. She shook with rage, and her jaw was set. She thought of the big carving knives in the kitchen. She could hardly believe that a stranger would walk into her life intent on causing so much trouble. It was like getting mugged, only Thomas was doing it legally. She wondered if she should get that letter from Thomas, try to prove that the will was a forgery; but she suspected that it was real, that in a moment of despair her mother really had sent the letter to Thomas, asking his help. And if that were the case, Maggie would be stuck in the boiling pot, certain.

The butcher Muldoon came in through the front door—apparently having heard that Thomas Flynn was in town. Both Maggie and Thomas had lapsed into silence, and Muldoon called, "Give us a song, Thomas!"

Thomas got up, went to his mug of rum that had warmed on the fire, and he took a few stiff drinks, then got his lute out of its case and began plucking strings.

Maggie sat numbly, wondering about her options. She could stay here and put up with this man, which seemed impossible. Or she could get a knife and stab him—which right now felt like a desirable thing to do, though she didn't like the thought of getting hanged afterward. Or she could try to talk Gallen into running away with her, and she wished that right now Gallen was here instead of being off in the woods.

Maggie's attention was suddenly caught as Thomas began his song. In his youth, Thomas had had a famous voice. Maggie had a handbill that she kept in a box upstairs, advertising one of Thomas's performances. On it, another bard said that Thomas's voice was like a mountain river, all watery and rippling light on the surface but with deep currents that could sweep you away, and beneath it all was a rich and abrasive gravel that could cut a listener to the bone.

And so in a moment, Thomas sang to the local fishermen an old ballad called "Green," the tale of Claire Tighearnaigh in her green days of love, raising daisies and sweet red roses on the hillsides to sell in the gray streets of Finglas. Thomas had the finest voice that Maggie had ever heard, and she tried to shut it out, but he sang the ballad with warmth and richness, so that she could almost feel the sticky flower stems in her hand and bask in the scent of bloody-colored flowers.

And when he sang of Ian Phelan, who loved a good fight as much as he loved his young fiancée, Thomas let his melody wend its way around the hearts of his listeners, sucking them down into a turbulent morass where their bodies were constantly spinning in the eddies and whirlpools, torn between the worlds of water and sky.

And when Thomas sang of how Ian Phelan was brutally stabbed at the hands of a jealous suitor, Thomas let his voice become gravel, so that his listeners could see how Ian's corpse had been left on the rocky hillsides above Finglas, his lifeblood leeching into the green flower beds of Claire's youth, the reds and greens tumbling together like lovers rolling down a hill, caught forever in a place where pain and beauty fuse into one.

When he finished, every rugged fisherman was weeping into his drink, and someone cooed, "Ah, now *that* was worth missing a day's work for." Several folks called loudly for another song, but Thomas refused, saying, "Come back tonight, and I promise you'll tire of listening to this old voice croak out its songs."

And Maggie saw that despite her personal problems with Thomas, he was already winning over the hearts of the townsfolk. Sure, and many of them would agree with Thomas, that Maggie was just too young to marry. They'd take his side.

He asked Maggie to escort him to his room. She led him upstairs to a cozy room above the fire, and opened the door for him.

"I'll expect you to behave as any other guest, Thomas Flynn," she said. "No sleeping on my clean sheets with your boots on."

Thomas went to the edge of his bed, set his lute on it, and looked up at her. "Well, Maggie," he said conspiratorially, "how do you think they liked our performance?"

"Our performance?" she asked.

"Aye. We gave them a good fight, and a grand song. I swear, the inn will be full tonight. You've never seen such drinking and carousing as you'll see tonight. I'll make you a fortune, sure."

"What?" Maggie asked, taking a deep breath. "You mean that was all an act?"

"I know about love," Thomas said, and from the way he had sung, Maggie knew it was true, and she wondered if he secretly intended to let her marry Gallen after all, but his next words dashed that hope. "But it's for your own good that I'm keeping you from your beau."

"For *your* profit, you mean," Maggie grumbled.

"That, too," Thomas said honestly. He watched her for a reaction, but she didn't give him the pleasure. "Maggie dear, if you live long enough, you're going to find that sometimes you have to play the villain in another person's life. It's just the way of things, that sometimes our goals cross. You'll have to spoil someone's plans, ruin their day—maybe even stick a dagger in someone's back. Just remember this: when that day comes, make no apologies for what you're doing. If you must play the part of the villain, play it with gusto. It's one of the sweetest sensations in life." He held his breath a moment, then said, "At least, that's how I intend to play it."

Then he lay down on the bed, put his dirty boots on the blanket. "Now there are rules in this world that tell us how to get along in polite society.

I didn't make those rules, but we have to live by them. One of those rules is that we don't go marrying children. So, you'll wait to get married, till you're the proper age. That's final."

"What if Gallen and I don't follow your rules?" Maggie said. "What if we marry, and run away?"

"Think about what you would be giving up, woman: your young beau has won himself a reputation as the finest bodyguard in seven counties. Rumor says that he's killed as many as forty highwaymen. It's a grand reputation, a romantic reputation.

"And as if his reputation as a fighter weren't enough, now folks are saying that angels—the Angel of Death himself, by God—have come down from heaven to help Gallen O'Day drive Satan from the village of Clere.

"Why, with such talk, Gallen could find himself sitting in the seat of the Lord Sheriff of Tihrglas in a year, and in five years he might be Lord Mayor of the whole land.

"But on the bad side, Gallen has also been accused of consorting with devils, and for that he could be hanged.

"Now, I doubt both stories. But, as they say in the south, 'You could spin the wool from a whole flock of sheep and never come up with such a marvelous yarn.' "

Thomas sat up, leaned closer. "In any case, the wedding must be canceled for now. If things go ill for Gallen, then your good name won't be besmirched. There's not a man or woman alive who didn't fall in love at your age, and they'll forgive you for your wrongheadedness. On the other hand, if things go well, then Gallen will need to wait to marry you, if only to enhance his political career, and in another year you can marry the man you love, and someday you'll find yourself living in one of the finest houses in the land! Oh, oh, oh, wouldn't that be grand?"

Thomas smiled and shook his head. "Och, I think you've got a future, darlin'. I can hardly wait to meet this Gallen O'Day."

Three

That afternoon in a forest glen high above Clere, Gallen O'Day practiced fighting alone with his knives. He wore some attire he'd earned while fighting off-world to save the Lady Everynne: a robe woven of thread that held small nanotech machines that could change colors to fit with any background, and others that could mask his scent; tall black boots and gloves that had a selenium matrix worked into various parts of the toe, heel, palm, and fingers so that his blows carried more punch. And most importantly, he wore his mantle, a personal intelligence made of small black metallic rings, strung with silver knowledge disks.

As Gallen practiced, the mantle fed him images that he could distinguish from reality only because the mantle fed him no audio: five swordsmen with sabers and small shields swirled around him in a fevered dance. They wore white robes that swished silently as they leapt over the forest floor, kicking up humus, grimacing and sweating with every slash and thrust.

Gallen leapt and ducked, weaving between them, seeking to block or avoid their blows as much as possible, slice them with his own daggers. When he scored a hit, his blade would mark them with blood, so that after hours of practice, the swordsmen now appeared as gory apparitions.

Yet they were extraordinary swordsmen, each man fighting in a different style, using his own tactics. One was a whirling madman whose sword blurred in continuous motion; another stood back and studied Gallen, seeking to strike only at the most opportune moment, then jab with deadly precision. Another used the cutting edge of his shield as much as he did his sword, while the other two seemed to change fighting styles to suit their needs.

Gallen was struggling for air, sweat pouring from his body. Yet his enemies showed no sign of slowing due to fatigue. Gallen had wanted to stop for nearly an hour, but he was trying to build his endurance, so he kept up the gory battle. Time and again, his foes stabbed him, and each time, the mantle sent him a searing phantom pain at the point of impact.

When Gallen's arms were impossibly heavy from fatigue, his mantle suddenly dispersed the image of the fighters, and Gallen stood panting.

"Why did you stop?" he whispered.

"You have an incoming message from the Lady Everynne," the mantle whispered. "Are you ready to receive it?"

Finally she sends word, Gallen thought, after two weeks. "Yes," he answered, and Gallen sat down in the shade on a rock encrusted with yellow lichens. He closed his eyes, stilled his breathing, waited for Everynne's image to appear.

Instead, the sky darkened, as if it were covered with a curtain, and he heard the rumbling of thunder in the distance. His heart pounded in terror, and he found himself in a strange city on a cobbled street, leaning against a stone wall in an alley.

What's this? he wondered, willing his head to turn and look about. But the view did not change. Instead, he only saw the view as if he were staring ahead, and Gallen realized that this vision of another world must be a part of Everynne's message.

He looked about, watching the narrow streets to his right, the smooth stone buildings with enormous doors and huge windows set high off the ground. He was in a business district of a large city, and all the shops were closed for the night. The black cobblestones gleamed wetly. Through the thick storm clouds, he could make out the muted light of three separate moons, and dim lights shone from a few windows down the street. But the alley behind him was dark and sheltering. He looked farther down the street to his left, hoping for more darkness, but there was a tavern there with a lantern burning from a hook outside its doors. He couldn't run that way. The light would show him up.

Not again, not again! he thought, and his lips emitted a high whimper. Yet Gallen knew it was not his own thoughts or words, but the words of someone else. The fingers that clutched the edge of the stone wall were slender, on pale feminine hands, and Gallen felt the unfamiliar weight of a woman's breasts on his body, and wondered at it.

"I am feeding you the memories of a dead woman. This is Everynne's message to you," his mantle whispered.

Off in the near hills, light flashed in the clouds, then thunder snarled and echoed, washing away all sound. He waited breathlessly, listening for sounds beneath that booming echo. Down the stone street, around a corner, he heard booted feet thudding against stone, saw three men rush into the square. Their sabers were drawn, and they silently moved into the shadows, scanning ahead.

Gallen—or the woman whose memories Gallen was reliving—moved farther back into the alley, suddenly looking about for safety. There were no windows, and the lip of the roof was ten feet above her head. Her only hope lay behind a heavy oak door.

She went to it, tested it. The door was securely locked from the inside. Its brass handle was too heavy for her to break. Lightning flashed overhead, and thunder boomed. She rattled the door as loudly as she could under the cover of that noise, not knowing even what type of business this was, hoping desperately that the shopkeeper slept at the back of the shop, that he would hear her and come to her rescue.

She thought she heard the heavy thump of a foot on wood floors behind the door.

"Is someone in there . . . ?" she whispered fiercely.

No answer.

She couldn't wait again. "Help me!" she whimpered, hoping that the person behind the door was human, that he would taste the pheromones of her Tharrin body and be forced to respond to her plea. "Please, open the door," she begged. "The Inhuman is coming!"

She rattled the door again, this time without the covering echo of thunder. Perspiration beaded on her forehead, and she wiped it away just as a thin drizzle began falling. From behind the door, a woman's voice whispered. "Go away! I have children in here to care for. Don't bring trouble down on this house!"

And with those words, the Tharrin whimpered, knew that she had just heard her death sentence. By her very nature she was forbidden to harm anyone. She could not endanger this family. She lurched back from the door as if it burned her, and a new steadiness came over her. She whispered to the woman inside, "Stay in with your children, then. There is only enslavement out here."

She wondered if there was a place to hide, but as she glanced back at the mouth of the alley, she saw a swordsman standing in the open, looking at her. The wind was growing wild as it will before a storm, and his shadowy cape twisted and fluttered behind him. He whistled softly, and with his free hand motioned to his companions. Presently, they joined him, and the three proceeded toward her abreast. A heavy, steady rain began sweeping toward her in a curtain. The alley filled with the hiss of rain slapping against stone.

The Tharrin sniffed the air, smelling rotting food and dust from a trash bin behind her, then let out a bloodcurdling cry, something that might have come from the throat of a child, Gallen decided, for it did not sound like the voice of a woman, and suddenly he understood that this was no woman's body he was in, but the voice of a girl barely into her teens.

The three men rushed toward her, one of them pulling a heavy bag out from behind his back. "Shush, child," he hissed. "We do not want to harm you! We only want you to join us!"

The young woman went rigid. She had a knife sheathed at her hip for just such an emergency, a knife tipped with deadly poison. But she was a Tharrin. She could not harm another sentient being, and the men before her were not evil, only the victims of evil, hosts to the Inhuman.

She pulled out her knife, waved it before her, hoping that the threat would hinder them. "Stay back!" she warned. Then she shouted once again, "Help me! Help!", hoping that perhaps someone at the tavern down the way might hear her.

One of the men laughed. "You won't use that," he said with certainty, and the young woman strained her ears, hoping desperately to hear the sound of running footsteps, of rescuers. But she only heard the steady rain, and realized that it must have covered the sound of her cries.

The servants of the Inhuman marched toward her warily. They were almost upon her. Lightning flashed above them, gleaming off their swords.

They think I can't use the knife, she considered, and she stood up straight and tall, knowing what she must do. She reached up quickly and slashed her own throat from ear to ear.

The searing pain was exquisite, shocking, and she felt the hairs on her head stand on end in reaction. Her heart thumped wildly, kicking in her chest, and hot blood spattered down between her breasts, a seeming river pouring out of her. She staggered back against the wall, felt the poison doing its work, numbing her jaw and neck. She tried to remain standing for a moment, but the knife slipped from her hands, and she slid down the wall.

Suddenly the three servants of the Inhuman were upon her, and one of them, a man with a dark red moustache and crazed eyes, grabbed her by the head and shouted in her face. His voice was a roaring watery echo in her ears, the voice of a waterfall or a storm rushing through trees. "You think you can escape us so easily? You think you can hide in a temporary death? When you next take a body, we will hunt you again! We will not give up so easily!"

And then he let her hair go, and she was falling, falling into pain and darkness, and the cold rain sizzling on the stones was the only sound as she silently gulped, crying as she died.

A woman's voice, Everynne's voice, rang in Gallen's ears, but he did not see her image, only a gray light in the distance. "Gallen, these are the memories taken from Ceravanne, a Tharrin who somehow managed to stay alive on Tremonthin for the past sixty years. When last I saw you, I told you that I would call upon you again for service. Her clone has been infused with all her memories but the last. I charge you to go to Tremonthin and protect her. I charge you with becoming Lord Protector of the planet for now, and as part of that charge, you must seek out and destroy the Inhuman."

Four

Thomas Flynn bolted the worn wooden latch to his room at Mahoney's Inn, then sat on the plump feather bolster, tasting the scent of a cold room that had been closed too long. It was a simple room—a chest of drawers with a small brass oil lamp on it, along with a white ceramic basin and pitcher of water should he want to wash off the dust from the road. He looked out the window with its old wavy glass, past the few small house-trees and sheds to the mountains beyond.

Everything in Clere seemed so normal, so restful. Yet he was the only guest at the inn this night—the only person brave enough to have stayed here in the past two weeks, so rumor said.

But Thomas Flynn knew a bit about people. Rumors of demons might keep folks away, but a demon itself wouldn't—not if it was safely stored in a jar of brine. Thomas had seen oddities displayed that way—a cat with two heads, a midget child. And he wondered if he might be able to preserve something as large as one of these demons in such a fashion.

Thomas could imagine how the sign out front might read: Thomas Flynn's Curious Inn. Aye, people were afraid to come around now, but in a couple weeks, he might have them pounding the doors.

Thomas had never believed in demons or angels, but something had frightened these people, and if a battle had been waged, then there would be corpses about.

It was early afternoon, but he had several good hours of daylight. He rested on the bed for a while, feeling his brain swim around in his skull from too much rum, then went downstairs to the common room. It had begun to fill up nicely. A good thirty men lounged about.

He managed to warm himself another bit of rum without falling into the fire, then drank it and clattered the empty cup against the bricks of the fireplace to get attention. "Good afternoon, gentlemen. I'm after finding myself the corpse of a demon. I imagine they should be in the woods about, and I'm offering a bounty. I'll pay twenty pounds to the first man who brings me one!"

One customer had been drinking, and he began coughing his beer up through his nostrils. Another had been leaning in his chair, and he barely saved himself from falling over backward.

"Uh," one lanky woodsman said, "talk to Gallen. He's the only one who goes about these days. He's in the woods now. Some say he's still hunting the last of the demons down!"

"Hunting demons, is he, eh?" Thomas shook his head.

Thomas looked out over the crowd. There were some stout men in the group, but none of them were eager to take him up on the offer. They stood drinking, studiously ignoring him.

"All right, fifty pounds, then!" Thomas said.

No one stirred, and frankly, he could go no higher.

"Man, you don't have to kill the buggers, mind you!" Thomas said. "If I understand right, they should already be dead." But no one budged.

"Och, there must be a trapper hereabouts, someone with the need and gumption to hike the woods?"

Several men shook their heads, and Thomas was a bit amazed at their lack of spine. "Then come outside and point the way to Geata na Chruinne for me. I'll go myself!"

A couple of men led Thomas outside, pointed down to the ridge of a nearby mountain. "At the foot of the ridge is the gate. If you wander around enough, you'll find it in a dark hollow there. It's about four miles by foot, and no man in his right mind would get caught off the road there after dark. The wights are thick in Coille Sidhe."

Several onlookers stopped to see what Thomas was up to, and Thomas said loudly, "Oh, sure I'll be back by sundown. I plan to have a word with the man that wants to marry my Maggie."

Thomas went to his wagon, got out his walking stick and half a skin of stale water. His joints felt loose, and his head was a bit foggy. And he found himself watching the gray woods, wishing that Gallen was here now. The men of town were spooked, sure enough, and he convinced himself that that was good news, for it meant that perhaps there was something for him to find out in those woods. Perhaps he'd find more than he could handle.

He headed north, walking to the edge of the forest, and a shout went up from some of the boys. Soon there were forty people walking behind him, children and women, curious folk, but most of them stopped at the edge of the wood, frightened to go in.

Thomas turned and addressed them. "If any of you older boys have a mind to come with me, I've a mind to go and collect some artifacts. I'll be looking for the skulls of demons or angels, any of their clothing or weapons. I'll pay a pound for each boy that comes with me to pack the bounty out."

Many of the boys looked around a bit as if trying to think what business they might have elsewhere, but one young lad stepped forward on shaky legs, a tough-looking boy with a broad chest and intelligent eyes. "I'll help, for five pounds."

"Five pounds then, if we find anything," Thomas said.

The boy nodded in agreement.

"Good lad," Thomas said, and he turned, leading the way. The boy rushed across the street, grabbed a hatchet from the doorstep of a house-tree where someone had been chopping kindling, then hurried up, walking right at Thomas's heel, gripping the hatchet in white fingers.

They walked under the pines for a hundred yards, until the limbs of the tall trees began to block the sun. The humus was thick and held a print, and in no time at all, they came upon a trail that held stunningly odd prints: some of the tracks came from booted feet that couldn't have been less than eighteen inches long and ten wide. Other tracks were handprints of some creature with a span of twenty inches, but the monster had only four fingers.

Thomas stopped and surveyed the prints for a long time, found his breath coming ragged, and his mouth felt dry. He took a swig of his stale water.

"Those are demon tracks, certain," the boy said. "The ones that look like handprints are from the creature that walked on all fours."

"By all that's holy!" Thomas mouthed. "To tell you true, I wasn't certain we'd find anything."

"What do you plan to do if we get a demon skull?" the boy asked.

"I'll mount the damned thing on a wall in the inn," Thomas said, perhaps being too forthright.

"Aye," the boy breathed, "that would be something! I'll tell you, the reason I came is I want some of this stuff, too. A demon head maybe, or something from an angel. When the angels came through town, I climbed the steeple of the church and looked out over the woods. That night, there was smoke and fire coming from the forest, flashes of lightning. I reckon there was a fearsome battle, and I prayed to God and the saints something fierce. But what happened out here, no one knows—only Gallen O'Day. He came out to battle with an angel at his side, and he's not breathed a word about what happened. But no angels came back, and no demons, either. I figure Gallen bested them all."

Thomas glanced up at the boy, saw that his face was pale, frightened. "What's your name, boy?"

"Chance," the boy answered.

"Well, Chance, if we find a demon skull, it's mine and I'll pay you the five pounds I promised. But if we find two, the second is yours. Beyond that, if we find the mother lode, I'll give you some of the booty."

Chance smiled at that, and they took a pee, then hurried down the trail.

Thin high clouds were coming in, making it darker and cool, promising rain. Thomas hurried, and the forest went silent. No birds sang, no squirrels leapt in the trees. It was a strange, ominous quiet. Even the trees seemed to refrain from creaking in the small wind.

Thomas had been in the woods plenty of times when the forest was just as quiet, but this silence got his heart beating. He kept stopping, looking behind him. He felt as if he were being watched.

"Sure this is an unholy silence," Chance breathed at one point, loosening his collar.

And Thomas stopped, his heart was beating too hard. He kept thinking of that nice warm inn, with its mugs of beer, and he wished he was back there.

But they followed the tracks over a long hill, up a ridge, and back down to a creek. There the trees opened up, letting in more light. Still, the deathly silence reigned in the forest.

Chance began slowing, and to hurry him, Thomas said, "Pick up your pace, you old cow—it's not as if you're pulling a plow!"

The boy picked up his pace, and ten yards farther he grabbed a stick and walloped Thomas in the back of the head.

Thomas turned so fast that he fell on his butt. The boy was so mad he was in tears. "I'll not have you talkin' down to me, like I was some cur. My name is Chance O'Dell, and you'll address me proper, or you'll find yourself in trouble with me and my clan! I'm *Mister* O'Dell to you!" The boy shook his stick in Thomas's face, and Thomas took a moment, trying to think how he'd offended the boy. His mind was still foggy from too much rum, and it took a few seconds for understanding to burn through the haze.

"I'm sorry if my rudeness wounded you, young Mister O'Dell," Thomas said. "I meant nothing by it. I say such things by force of habit. And if you think me evil for it, think on this: what is in another man a vice, is in me a virtue. As a satirist, I walk behind the proud men of the world, making rude noises. And the louder and ruder I get, the more good folks like you pay me. So, it's true that I've got no common sense when it comes to addressing decent, honorable folk like yourself."

"Well," Chance growled. "If you make more rude noises about me, I'll pay you fair, all right. I'll pay you with a stick!" He shook the stick in Thomas's face, then threw it aside.

Thomas laughed. "Well, next time I want a good spanking, I know who to come to. Come now, friend, help me up, and let's go find us something grand!"

The boy gave him a hand up, and they hurried along, and the boy seemed to calm down quickly. In minutes the whole incident was perhaps forgotten by the boy, but Thomas filed it away in his brain. A boy who was that brutal and quick to take offense likely came from a family with a strong sense of honor, and it wouldn't be wise to ever cross one of them O'Dells again, or else Thomas would end up in a blood feud. And with only two Flynns left in the world, it would be a short feud.

At the foot of a mountain, in the shadow of a glade, they came upon some booted footprints that were more proportioned to the size of a man.

"See," Chance muttered. "This is where the angels came on their track. It looks like there were four, maybe five of them, and they came stalking the demons."

"Some say that it was the sidhe who came, not angels," Thomas ventured.

"Angels, I think," Chance whispered. "You've never seen people so beautiful, so regal. And Gallen said it was the Angel of Death that walked at his side."

Thomas just grunted. He had a hard time imagining angels that wore boots—slippers maybe—but he didn't want to argue. Besides, he wondered, would an angel even need to walk? Didn't they have wings? He thought it more likely that they would just flap about like giant white crows.

They followed the trail along the creek, both of them stalking warily, looking about. Suddenly the brush exploded just before them, and Thomas's heart nearly stopped. A stag leapt off through the forest, but Thomas had to stop to let his pounding heart rest.

He looked back, and poor Chance had a face whiter than sea foam. "Come on," Thomas said. "Let's look just a bit farther."

A hundred yards on, they smelled the scent of burnt brush and left their trail to find a large circle of scorched earth. There, in the center of the burn, lay a huge pile of bones from some manlike thing that would have stood nearly nine feet tall. Its flesh had melted into the bones, and for all the world it looked as if it had been struck by lightning.

Thomas walked around the thing, afraid to touch it. The giant was sprawled out flat on his belly, arms wide. He held a long black rod in one hand. Bits of metal were fused into his bones in some spots, as if necklaces and bracelets had melted into him.

"So, this was a demon?" Thomas asked, circling the thing.

"Aye, that was one."

Thomas went to the head, kicked it off, then rolled it over to look at its face. The skull was covered with a black tarry substance from the melted flesh, and the eyes had burned out of their sockets. The eye sockets were large enough so that Thomas could easily fit his thick fists into them. But it was the massive jaws and teeth that attracted him. Those teeth were big enough for a stallion, and twice as yellow.

"They had orange eyes," Chance said, "and skin as green-gray as a frog's."

Thomas just knelt there, shaking his head in wonder. "Who'd have thought? Who'd have thought?" He sighed. "Well, here's one oddity for my inn."

He tried to lift the head, but there was still a brain inside, and the thing was as heavy as a good-sized boulder. They rolled it over to the edge of the creek, onto a worn path, and determined to leave it while they searched ahead.

They hiked along for an hour heading up Bald Mountain, finding nothing more, and Thomas began to feel doubtful, and he began to rest more easily. They'd been out for hours and seen nothing horrific. He hoped, he'd hoped for the mother lode, but all he had to show for his day's work was one misshapen skull.

They finally climbed up past the road to An Cochan, and near the mountaintop they came to an old burn where there were no trees. The air was cold up here, and chunks of ice lay in the ground. Even now, it felt as if it might snow. It was beginning to get late, and Thomas was thinking of heading back, but they climbed up onto a log, looked up over a little valley where a fire had burned off the larger trees years earlier. Many great logs lay fallen, and ferns had grown chest-high in them. Here and there were clumps of snow from the two storms that had swept over the countryside in as many weeks. Thomas looked for any blackening in the ferns, any sign of a recent fire.

They stood, heaving from effort, looking up the little valley to the mountain beyond, and a few pigeons began cooing from their roosting tree at the edge of the forest.

It was silent, peaceful. A cool wind played with Thomas's hair, and his breath came out and blew away in a fog from his mouth.

Then for no discernable reason except to ease his stress, Chance let out a long howl, as if he were a wolf. In the center of the clearing below them the ferns erupted and a jaybird flapped into the sky, chattering angrily, searching for the source of the howls.

Thomas and Chance looked at each other, both of them realizing at the same time that the jaybird had been feeding, and as one they jumped into the deep ferns below them, raced tripping and fumbling until they climbed on a wind-fallen tree and looked down. Chance hooted for joy, for there in the ferns lay a dead demon with one massive hand wrapped around the throat of the most beautiful woman Thomas had ever seen.

She had golden hair that she wore in tiny braids, and over her hair she'd worn a net of silver with teardrop-shaped disks of gold. Even now, a blue jewel glowed in the net just above her eyes. She wore a cloak that was colored the green and yellow of ferns, and beneath it was some kind of armor made of a material that Thomas imagined to be some sort of exotic spun metal, like silver maybe. Her face was regal, and her arms were strong, with sensitive hands.

For her part, she had thrust a magic sword through the heart of the demon before she died, and even now, the sword shimmered and its blade looked as if it were liquid quicksilver in motion, baffling the eye.

Behind the demon lay its severed right hand and its magic rod, just where it must have fallen when the angel lopped it off.

The bodies were well hidden from the sun. The icy ground had preserved them remarkably well. The jaybird had been having a go at the face of the demon, scoring on its huge eyes, which were glassy yellow-brown in death.

Thomas caressed the flawless skin of the woman's face, and she looked as if she were sleeping, her mouth in a tiny frown as if she had just had a disturbing dream. Her skin was stiff from cold, and the wind blew through her delicate eyelashes. Thomas saw that as he touched her, his own hand was shaking, and he sat and considered just how he felt right now.

For years he had lived on the road, plying his trade as a minstrel and satirist, and though he had seen many beautiful women in the far corners of the world, he had never before seen anything quite so exquisite and wondrous as what he beheld right now.

Thomas had always been a cautious man, unable to trust others. He'd never much believed in God. The imperfections of the world had always seemed ample evidence that there could not be a powerful and compassionate god. Yet now he quivered inside as he touched the dead angel, and he felt somehow transformed, holy.

It was as if a great light welled up within him, burning away years of doubt and cynicism that he had carried as some burden, almost unaware, and he dared not look up at Chance, lest the boy see the tears forming in his eyes. This is as close to heaven as I may ever get, Thomas thought. And he wondered if this was the true reason he'd come back to Clere. In part he'd wanted to take care of his niece Maggie and spend a profitable winter away from the cold, but deep in his heart, he'd hoped to see this wonder, to see an angel and be certain.

So, God, he thought. You've played a good joke on me, letting me go on in my doubts for all these years. And yet he wondered, he wondered what kinds of creatures these were—demons and angels as mortal as men. Perhaps their own immortal powers had somehow canceled each other out, so that they could kill one another. No doubt the priests would find some explanation. Yet here he was, caressing the cheek of a fallen angel, daring to hope that she would come back to life under his touch.

"Let's get into town," Thomas whispered to Chance roughly, his voice tight from emotion. "We'll hire some men and bring my wagon. She died to save us. I can't let her sit here through another night."

Five

Just after dusk, Maggie served in the common room at Mahoney's Inn. The place had filled up with fishermen who knew how to draw their own rum from the tap and could be trusted to leave the proper coins on the table.

They were a nervous lot, wondering aloud how soon Thomas might come in from the woods, speculating as to whether it would be wights—a very common threat in this neck of the woods—or demons who got him.

And of course there were many there who wished him well, for they'd come to hear him sing.

Thus it was that Maggie's uncle came bustling in a fluster, smelling of the road, with an odd expression—something between exultation and manic joy. Thomas just stood in the doorway for a moment, grinning.

"I found them—" he said softly to the crowd. "A dead demon and an angel with it, and they'll both be on display in the stable in an hour!"

For one moment, no one spoke, then suddenly everyone was talking.

Thomas hurried Maggie into the kitchens, and began pulling sacks of flour and sugar out onto the mixing table. He said urgently, "Old John Mahoney must have had someone who helped out during his busy season. You'll need to round up those folks—anyone who's handy at cooking and serving. Then you had better go to the butcher and buy a pig and a goose and get them roasting. We'll need dinner for a hundred tonight."

"A hundred?" Maggie said in astonishment.

"Aye," Thomas said with a wink. "At the very least. I know you resent me, but I promise you, Maggie, I'll make you a fortune at this inn. Between my singing, and heavenly hosts on display—this place will be a madhouse within a fortnight!"

And Maggie said in frustration, "The larder is empty and I don't have coin to buy so much food. The shops are closed or closing for the night—"

Thomas reached to his belt and pulled out his purse, heavy with coins. "Hurry, then, and buy what you can for tonight and tomorrow."

Then he rushed into the night, out the back door. Maggie grabbed her shawl and ran to the butcher's and the miller's. She saw Thomas and four men go rumbling off into the dark in a wagon moments later, and half wished that the wights would take them all.

In an hour the town was bustling and the inn was deluged. Whole families who had never set foot in the inn were too flustered to fix dinner for themselves, and they pounded on the tables. Maggie muscled a hundred-pound pig onto the spit, planning to carve off the meat as fast as it roasted. Ann Dilley came in of her own accord and began cooking potatoes and loaves of bread, while Ann's daughters waited tables.

Gallen came in just after dark, and he took Maggie's hand, went into the kitchen with her, and stood beside the woodbox. "What is this I hear? You've got an uncle who has called off our marriage—and brought the bodies of a Vanquisher and one of Everynne's guards into town, all in the same afternoon?"

"Aye," Maggie said angrily. "The jolly old bugger. He's paid Father Brian to call off the marriage!"

Ann Dilley rushed into the room at that moment, hurried past them. "You might as well bring the ale and wine out front and save us some trips," she said, grabbing a small keg of whiskey, then she hurried out.

"I'll have a word with your uncle," Gallen said.

"Don't stab him!" Maggie said, suddenly fearful at the note of anger in his voice.

Gallen looked at her askance. "Stab him? What do you take me for?"

Maggie realized it had been an unwarranted thought, but tried to explain. "You never know." She shook her head. "He's the damnedest man I've ever had the misfortune of meeting. *I've* thought of stabbing him today—more than once!"

"Well, don't!" Gallen laughed. Ann Dilley plodded back into the room, frowned at Maggie as she got a flagon of wine and pulled some rolls from the oven. "Look, I can tell you're busy," Gallen said. "Let's talk tonight, after you close up. It's important."

Gallen left.

Maggie was grateful when the wagon rolled into town moments later, and for a while nearly everyone cleared out while Thomas displayed the corpses in the stable. That gave time for the meat to cook. And yet, it was only the beginning of the night. Soon the tables began to fill with villagers from An Cochan, three miles away. They were coming as fast as they heard the news, walking over the mountain road by lantern light, the wights be damned, bringing whole families by wagon.

Thomas raised the price on his rooms and food and liquor and stabling, and by eleven he was selling sleeping space on the floor of the common room, and he'd rented out the lawn to campers.

The amount of work to be done piled up like snow before an avalanche, ready to topple at any moment. There was more work than twenty people could do. Maggie was forced to just grit her teeth and bear it. She cooked and served dinner, took money, cleaned the cooking pots, churned the butter, and prepared the ingredients for breakfast. By twelve-thirty the common room was more crowded than she'd ever seen it, and Gallen came to help her wash dishes, while every other person who'd ever lent a hand during the traveling season helped prepare food for the morrow.

Maggie could sense that Gallen wanted to speak to her as he worked, but with a dozen people bustling in and out of the room, he didn't dare. There was a certain tenseness in his movements, and twice she put her wet arms around him to hug him, give him comfort, wondering what was on his mind.

By two in the morning, the place was a madhouse—folks had come from twelve miles away, and Maggie wondered at how they were all making the trip so fast, on such a dark night.

They closed the common room then, with four dozen folks asleep on the floor, and every bed in the house taken. Thomas came to the kitchens. "Leave the rest of those dishes until morning, darlin'," Thomas said. "I'd like you to lock up the stable. I don't want folks mucking about there in the middle of the night."

"And what will you be doing, your lordship?" Maggie asked.

Thomas hefted a bag of coins—more money than Maggie had ever seen in one spot. "I'll be tallying receipts."

"Uncle Thomas," Maggie said angrily, "what will you be doing with all that money? It's a shame before God for a man to make so much in one day! Why, it would serve you right if someone knocked you in the head and danced off with your purse!"

Thomas laughed. "As the good Lord said, 'The poor you have with you always'—and might I add, they're always red-faced indignant when someone else falls into a bit of money. So don't go getting all self-righteous on me, Maggie Flynn. After all: you own this inn. I'm just helping you run it, until you're eighteen. I'll take a cut for showing the demon, but the vast majority of this fortune is yours!"

"And you can have it all, for all that I care!" Maggie said. "And the inn with it!" For I'm going away, and plan never to return, she wanted to say.

Thomas grinned. "Oh, you're speaking out of your anger and weariness. Get some sleep, and your head will be clearer in the morning."

Thomas looked at Gallen as if he'd just seen him. "This purse would make a *fine* start for a dowry, don't you think, Mr. O'Day?"

"Aye," Gallen nodded. "A start."

"I meant to have a talk with you, Mr. O'Day, about your intentions toward my niece—"

"Let's talk, then." Gallen pulled a worn chair away from the cutting table. The cooking fire was nearly out, and the oil lamp above the sinks was burning low so that Gallen was just a shadow moving in the dark.

"I know you're in a hurry, young man. In a hurry to talk, in a hurry to marry my niece. But it would be unpolitic to hurry the marriage, and as for the talk—I'm afraid I'm all stove in for the night," Thomas said. "Besides, it wouldn't be proper to discuss the matter in front of her . . . you know." He nodded toward Maggie.

"I'm not some heifer that you'll be bartering over," Maggie said. "I should have a say in any deals you go making. It's my money you'll be spending for the dowry!"

"I didn't say you were some heifer," Thomas growled. "But you're young.

You're just too damned young, and your mind isn't as fully developed as"—he waved vaguely toward her breasts—"the *rest* of your body. So I'd like to have a delicate talk with Gallen, man-to-man, and I don't need your meddling!"

Maggie stared hard at him, and she could feel her face burning. She wanted to scream or shove him into the big baking oven in the corner till his skin turned black, but she only glared at him.

Thomas said to Gallen, "It's time for you to go, young sir. I suspect you're an honorable man, but it wouldn't be proper for you to be skulking around here so late of the night without an escort."

Thomas turned and disappeared into the common room through the swinging doors, giving them one last moment alone. Maggie was so mad she wanted to follow Thomas out and shout to his back as he walked up the stairs to count the money, but there were too many folks camped out on the floor of the common room, and she didn't want to make a scene. So she just stood with her fists clenched until she realized that she still held a wet washrag and she had squeezed water from it onto her foot.

She spun and tossed the rag into the sink. "Well, how do you like *him*?"

Gallen chuckled at Thomas's back. "I see what you meant about wanting to stab him. 'Skulking around' he calls it. The nerve of him! Well, he's a nuisance, all right. But don't judge him too harshly. He thinks he's making you rich, and you can't fault him for that. And if your mother or father were alive, they wouldn't be talking to you much different. They'd be against you marrying so young, too."

"Oh, don't take his side. He's just a big tick trying to suck the blood from me, and he wants me to feel fine about it."

"Any sixteen-year-old woman," Gallen whispered, "who can steal a key to the Gate of the World, make her way across half a dozen planets, pilot a hovercar under a nuclear mushroom cloud, and face up to the Dronon Lords of the Swarm is surely a match for one dried-up old crooked uncle," Gallen whispered. "I'm sure you can handle him."

Maggie smiled, still angry, but subdued by weariness. "Sure, I'd gut him in a second if he wasn't my only kin," she teased. She buried her head in his chest, just resting her eyes, swaying gently. "Gallen, we've got to get out of here. I won't stay here and be his slave, working in this place for another year!"

"Of course not," Gallen said. He wrapped his strong arms around her and just held her. She could feel his heart beating strong and steady in his chest, smelled the clean scent of his cotton tunic. He didn't speak for a long time. The cooking fire crackled as a log shifted.

"Let's go lock up the stables," he whispered. "We can talk in there."

Maggie went to the cabinet where John Mahoney had kept his locks, took out the big iron lock that he used for the stables when he bothered to lock them at all. Gallen went to a peg by the back door, took down Maggie's shawl and put it over her shoulders, and they hurried out under the boughs of the house-pine.

A blustery wind was blowing, and all under the tree that formed the inn there were tents pitched, and up on the hill north of town, Maggie could hear whinnying. She looked up, and spaced along the mountain road were lanterns as people wended their way down the road.

"This is madness," Gallen whispered, watching the lanterns. "I've never seen the likes."

They picked their way carefully around the side of the inn, went to the stable. A lamp burned inside, and a couple of young boys were staring into the wagon at the corpses. Gallen shooed them out.

In the stable, the horses were backed into their stalls, staring out with tired eyes. Gallen pulled the door tight, locked it with a cross-beam.

As soon as they were alone Maggie tumbled into Gallen's arms and kissed him, a sweet, slow kiss. She'd been craving his touch all day, and now they just held each other, satisfying that urge. She shook as she held him, and Maggie found her eyes tearing, and Gallen whispered, "Oh, my sweet Maggie, what's wrong?"

"Thomas," she said. "He's mucked it all up for us."

"He can't muck it *all* up, so long as we still love each other," Gallen whispered. He pulled back, held her hand, and looked steadily into her eyes. "Maggie, we don't really have to get married here. You and I could go to any world your heart fancies, and the marriage would be just as valid."

Maggie's heart skipped. "I know," she said. Yet she felt cheated. Clere was her home. By tradition, a proper woman wouldn't marry outside her own hometown, even if the groom came from another country. It was a matter of propriety. Only a girl who had come down with a child would marry in a far county, and if Maggie were to run off now, everyone would suspect her. And even though through her travels Maggie had learned that she no longer wanted to live on this world, she was saddened by what her friends and neighbors would think.

"Yes, I've always wanted to get married here," she said. "I wanted to marry in my own hometown, dressed in white, with a priest."

"I'll talk to your uncle, tomorrow," Gallen said, "press him for an early marriage. Maybe he'll listen." She looked up into his blue eyes, and with her fingers combed a wisp of his long hair back from his face.

Gallen pulled away from her, walked over to the wagon, looked down at the corpses of a green-skinned Vanquisher and one of Everynne's personal guard, a beautiful female soldier. The night air was chill, and Gallen's breath steamed from his mouth.

Maggie could tell that he had some distressing news to tell.

"What's wrong?" she asked.

"Maggie, I got a message from Everynne. She wants me to go to a planet called Tremonthin to protect someone, a Tharrin named Ceravanne. It's important that I go soon."

"Protect her from what?" Maggie asked. "The dronon?" She shivered involuntarily as she imagined the huge insectlike alien that the townsfolk had mistaken two weeks ago for Beelzebub, Lord of the Flies.

Gallen had defeated the dronon Lords in single combat, winning the title of Lords of the Swarm for himself and Maggie, and as the new queen of the dronon Swarm, Maggie had banished the dronon from the human-occupied worlds before she returned home to Tihrglas for her wedding.

Still, she imagined that some dronon would cause trouble. They didn't think like humans at all. Certainly, when the next dronon hive queen matured, she would bring her Lord Escort to battle Gallen and Maggie, hoping to win back the title of Lords of the Swarm, believing that the title gave them the right to control ten thousand human-occupied worlds.

So Maggie's return to Tihrglas served a purpose beyond allowing her wedding, for it kept her hidden from enemy dronon.

"No, it's not the dronon," Gallen said. "There is something called 'the Inhuman' on Tremonthin. I'm not sure what it is—a secret society, perhaps. A group of people seeking control." Gallen's jaw was set, rigid. Maggie knew that look. He was ready for a fight, and God forgive anyone who stood up to him.

"The Lady Semmaritte warned me of Tremonthin before she died," Maggie said. "She wanted us to go there, and she said that your skills as a warrior would be sorely tested."

In the past two weeks, Gallen had been preparing for battle in ways that Maggie had never seen before. With this mantle of a Lord Protector that he wore during practice, this artificial intelligence that stored more information than a thousand libraries could hold, Gallen was learning secrets of combat that he'd never imagined. He said that he wanted to be more prepared when next he met the dronon, and Maggie suspected that he would be up for the test on Tremonthin. But the Lady Semmaritte hadn't seemed so sure.

Gallen seemed preoccupied as he looked at the corpses. Thomas had put the weapons from the dead Vanquisher and Everynne's warrior atop the bodies. Gallen picked up the Vanquisher's incendiary rifle. "We shouldn't leave these weapons functional," he said. "Some kid might pull the trigger and put the town to fire." He cracked the rifle at the stock, pulled out its power pack and projectiles, then laid it back down.

Maggie stood beside him, picked up the vibro-blade from the dead woman's hand, pulled out its power pack. The dead woman had a bag at her side, and Maggie pulled it open. Inside were rations, a couple of Black Fog grenades, a microwave bomb, a light globe that flashed blindingly when she squeezed it.

Gallen stuffed the items into his pockets, then pulled some weapons from the green Vanquisher's munitions belt.

Once he'd secreted anything that might prove dangerous, Gallen stood for a moment, then took Maggie's hand, let out an uneasy breath.

"I have to go to Tremonthin soon. A week or two at the longest. I'll try to finish the job quickly. But Maggie, darling, I think you should stay here."

"I won't have you leave me behind," Maggie said. "You could get hurt or killed or lose your key to the Gate of the World, and I'd never see you again." She didn't speak her greatest fear: that the dronon were hunting them, and without Gallen, Maggie would have no protection from the creatures.

"But if you come away with me, you'll be exposing yourself to more danger," Gallen said. "I'd rather have you safe, here, planning our wedding."

Maggie folded her arms, looked down at the ground, thinking. Gallen wanted her to stay. It might well be that he had her best interests at heart, but she couldn't bear the thought of remaining here in Clere. What if he lost his key to the Gate of the World and never came back? She could never be happy on a backward planet like Tihrglas, not when there were worlds with starships and immortals out there. And she couldn't be happy without Gallen near.

And suddenly she knew why Gallen was so distant. "You're not ready to leave Clere yet, are you?"

"Sure, I'm not happy to be going. I came home imagining how I'd snatch some rest, thinking about going fishing one last time. But we've been home two weeks, and I've thought of nothing but the dronon—how I'll handle them when next we meet.

"One day of rest—that's all I want," Gallen said. "I'll go fishing tomorrow, and we can pretend that nothing horrible ever happened to us. Come with me, okay? We can make a picnic."

Maggie squinted, wondering what Thomas would say about her leaving a hundred guests unfed at the inn. But it was her inn, and she could walk away from it if she wanted to.

"I'm coming with you, Gallen," Maggie said, taking both of his hands in hers, looking into his face. "I won't feel safer without you, and I certainly couldn't be happy without you. I'll go anywhere you want to go—fishing tomorrow, if you want—Tremonthin the day after. I'll be your wife. You know that I'd jump into pits of hell with you on a moment's notice."

"Oh, that's what I'm worried about," Gallen said solemnly. Now that that was settled, he looked around, talking as he thought. "I'll need to hire someone to watch my mother while I'm gone. I'll tell her I've got work on a merchant ship sailing to Greenland. With the wild rumors flying around about me, she'll think I'm just leaving till the furor dies. And we'll have to send word to Orick, discover if he wants to come with us."

Maggie found herself trembling with anticipation at the thought of getting back on the road. "He'll come."

There were a million things to take care of, Maggie knew. They'd have to leave town—escape Thomas—without drawing undue attention.

Gallen kissed her one last time for the night. Then he took her hand and they slipped out of the stable.

ight came with darkening clouds at Mack's Landing, and Orick sat with Grits and the sheriffs on the strand under the shade of the oaks, warming by the campfire.

He'd finished his third bowl of wine and sixth bowl of stew, and he felt more than a bit dizzy. When he'd first come into camp, Orick had been tense as a reed. But the warm wine had performed miracles. He felt drowsy, ready to sleep.

It was late, and the sheriffs had gone to telling unlikely stories. One boy told of the village of Droichead Bo far in the north, where a young witch named Cara Bullinger learned the banshee's song and sang it upon a hill, slaying every person, horse, cat, and cockroach within the sound of her voice. He said that after they took care of Gallen O'Day, they should go after this Bullinger woman. Another man agreed, saying that he too had heard of strange deaths up there—livestock and whatnot—and most likely it was this woman causing trouble.

While some younger sheriffs looked about the campfire with frightened, pasty faces, Orick just guffawed and said, "Why, where'd you ever hear such a concoction?"

"I have a cousin who swears it's true," the boy sheriff said. "He heard her singing the banshee's song."

"He can't have heard any such thing! If he had, he'd be dead, too!" Orick grumbled, not wanting to listen to such foolishness. He'd given them a real tale about how Gallen had gotten involved with otherworldly beings. Not some lie.

Across the fire, the scar-faced sheriff, who'd given his name as Sully, poured another bottle of wine into a bowl for Orick, and handed it to him. "Ah, don't get angry at the lad, Orick. He's just trying to keep the men entertained. No harm in that."

"But it's a flawed tale—" Orick began to say, and Sheriff Sully looked up at him with glistening, malevolent eyes, and suddenly Orick remembered that he'd been going under the name Boaz, and he hadn't wanted these lawmen to know his real name, for they planned to kill Gallen O'Day.

Sheriff Sully grabbed for his sword, growling, "I'll have a few words with you. I'd like to discover your part in this whole affair!"

Orick spun away from the campfire, but a young man had come up behind him, sword drawn. Orick was trapped between the two. Grits grumbled into his ear, "You told him your real name! Is there anything else you want to tell them?"

More sheriffs leapt up and pulled their swords, surrounding them.

Orick couldn't think straight, his head was spinning so badly. He worried about blades slicing his pelt, but remembered Lady Everynne's gift. The nanodocs flowing through his veins were marvelous at healing wounds.

Orick spun and lunged, pushing past one young sheriff. The sheriff's sword whipped through the air, slicing deeply into Orick's shoulder.

Orick roared at the pain, but continued running on three legs past a tree where the horses were tethered to a line. He roared again, spooking the horses so that their lines snapped as they reared and kicked. A couple of hounds rushed out from under a tree, yelping and snapping. Orick slashed one with his paw, knocking it into the ground, and the other yelped and leapt back, then Orick was running beside the lake under heavy cloud cover.

Orick could run faster than any human over short distances, so he sped out over the mud, turned toward the mountains and the highway beyond, and kept running until he was out of bowshot. Then he turned and stood. He was bleeding profusely, and he looked back toward the sheriffs. Their camp was in an uproar. Men were rushing for their horses, breaking camp. Grits stood beside the campfire on all fours, her back arched, growling as sheriffs ringed her about with swords.

Orick whined, then sniffed the air ahead toward a row of dark hills. He was nine miles from An Cochan, twelve miles from Clere. Normally it would be a casual day-long ride for the sheriffs, but they could make it in hours under a forced march.

He licked at his wound, and pain lanced through him. He got on all fours, then hobbled along as fast as he could. He'd have to reach Gallen soon.

Seven

Orick shouted, "Man, get your legs into your pants—or it's your life!" Orick shoved his snout into Gallen's ribs, and Gallen roused himself enough to sit up in bed.

Orick smelled of damp fur and the woods, with the metallic tang of blood. The bedroom door was open, and embers smoldered in the fire in the living room, enough so that Gallen could see dimly.

"What is it?" Gallen cried, trying to clear the cobwebs from his head. He'd been up half the night, and it was not yet dawn.

"There's an army of sheriffs and their deputies coming!" Orick panted. "Some northern bishop served a warrant. And they've brought the Lord Inquisitor. Some ruffians swear you prayed to the devil," he panted, "that killed Father Heany. They're coming, and they're not far behind me!"

Blood matted the fur of Orick's right shoulder. "Are you all right?" Gallen asked.

"I'll not die from this scratch. Run, man!"

Gallen leapt from bed, hair prickling on the back of his neck. He pulled on his tunic and britches.

A heavy pounding came at the door, and someone shouted, "Gallen O'-Day, rouse yourself—in the name of the law!"

"By God, they're here!" Orick cried. "Run!"

Gallen sighed, knowing it was too late to run. "Don't excite yourself, Orick. You never run from the law. If those sheriffs have got their bows strung, they could shoot me in the back, and they'd be in the right."

"Come out, now!" a sheriff roared. "Or we'll break the door in!"

"Coming!" Gallen called. He felt awake now, awake enough to know he was in mortal danger, sleepy enough to be unsure what to do.

If I was the fastest talker in the world, he wondered, what would I say to these sheriffs right now? He closed his eyes a moment, wondering.

Gallen's mother had gotten out of bed. She went to the fireplace in her nightcap and robe. She called in a frightened voice, "Gallen? What is it?"

"Open the door, Mother," Gallen said. "Tell them I'm dressing." He pulled on his soft leather boots.

"Coming," Gallen's mother shouted.

The front door crashed open, and a scar-faced sheriff rushed in, shoved Gallen's mother to the floor. She cried out, and the sheriff stood over her, backed by two rough-looking men with drawn swords. Behind them, in the shadows, stood a tall man with a narrow face, wearing the crimson robes with the white cross of the Lord Inquisitor. Gallen's mother put her hand up to protect her face, lest the sheriff beat her.

"Come out here!" Scarface ordered.

Gallen slowly strapped his knives over the outside of his tunic, and the sheriff simply raised one dark eyebrow and watched him, licked his lips, and studied Orick.

"You have a warrant?" Gallen asked.

"I do." Scarface answered just a bit too slowly. "You're to be taken north to Battlefield, where you'll be tried for witchcraft."

Gallen looked into the man's dark eyes, and saw that he was frightened.

"If you've got a warrant," Gallen said, "let me see it."

The sheriff hesitated. "You'll have time enough to study it on the road north."

"I'll study it now," Gallen said. "And we'll have a talk with the local sheriffs. You had better show just cause for breaking down my mother's door, and you've no right to hit an old woman in any case," Gallen said. "I'm going to make you pay dear for that!" Gallen tried to keep the deadly tone from his voice. He'd never killed a sheriff, but just at this moment, anger blossomed in him, and he was fighting the urge.

Scarface studied Gallen. "Are you threatening me?"

Gallen looked up at the Inquisitor standing behind Scarface. The churchman had glittering, calculating blue eyes. He was waiting for Gallen to give him the slightest pretext for an arrest. "I wouldn't think of threatening you," Gallen said calmly. "But I'll swear out a complaint on you for battering my mother—now, show me your warrant."

"Just come peaceful," Scarface said, "and we'll take it easy on you." He stood straighter, widened his stance, and put one hand on his own short sword.

"You know who I am," Gallen said softly. "I'm a lawman, just like you—a licensed guard with my oath-bond posted at Baille Sean. You're fifty miles out of your jurisdiction. Now, the law says you can arrest me if you've got a warrant," Gallen said softly. "But if you don't have it, I can defend myself from wrongful arrest, *if need be.*"

Scarface signaled to a man behind him, and the fellow produced a wooden scroll case, painted in thick lacquer.

"Here it is." The Inquisitor spoke from behind Scarface, taking the tube in his own hand. Gallen was surprised at the softness of his voice. He sounded like some gentle monastic brother who tended lambs, not the fearsome torturer he was reputed to be.

"There should be no need for all of this posing, for hiding behind legal technicalities," the Inquisitor told Gallen softly. "Sir, you have grievous charges leveled against you. A priest has died, and this is a matter of deep concern to the clergy. I should think that you would welcome the opportunity to clear your name. After all, if it were commonly believed that you were guilty of witchcraft, your family's reputation would be stained. . . ." He looked meaningfully to Gallen's mother. Gallen was not fooled by such soft words. This man was hinting at retribution against Gallen's whole family.

"If there are charges against me," Gallen said, "then they're leveled by false witnesses, and I'll fight those charges as best I can. I'll have a look at your warrant." Gallen stepped forward and took it from the torturer's hand, carried the paper over to the wan firelight. His mother got up and looked over his shoulder with Orick. The Inquisitor and his men shifted uneasily.

"This paper isn't legal," Gallen realized. "You can't take me north without the signature from the Lord Sheriff at Baille Sean."

Scarface said forcefully, "We were on our way to Baille Sean for the signature when we met that bear friend of yours! He came to warn you. We couldn't just let you go running off into the night!"

Gallen shrugged, handed the paper to Scarface. "I'm afraid you'll have to go to Baille Sean and talk to Lord Sheriff Carnaghan. And say hello to him for me. He's a good friend. I once saved his son from some highwaymen."

Scarface shook his head angrily, growling from the back of his throat. "Damned southerners! How am I supposed to execute a warrant against you?"

"Legally—" Gallen said, "or not at all." He rested his hands on his knives. If the man was going to attack, now would be the time.

Scarface studied Gallen, eyeing the knives that he wore. Gallen almost hoped that he'd make his move. But the Lord Inquisitor backed up a step, told the men, "Surround the house. I'll go to Baille Sean and speak with Lord Sheriff Carnaghan personally."

He backed out slowly, and Scarface closed the ruined door. Gallen let them go. Gallen's mother shoved the door tight, bolted it. "That sheriff is a blackguard, sure," she said. "The nerve, breaking into an old woman's house and knocking her off her feet!" She looked at Gallen disapprovingly, as if he should have come to her rescue.

Orick hurried to Gallen's side. "Gallen, you're not going to let them get away with this, are you?"

Gallen looked from his mother to Orick. There was little that he could do. A moment later, Thomas Flynn pushed his way through the door, followed by Gallen's cousin, Father Brian from An Cochan. The sheriffs were so thick around the house-tree that the two men could hardly get through.

Thomas Flynn seemed unperturbed by the whole affair, but Father Brian looked about with wide eyes. The young priest had obviously rushed to get out the door at his own house. He had on his black frock, but without the white collar. His face was red from the night air.

"They've got Maggie," Thomas said to Gallen. "They say they're taking her north as a witness against you. They're already filling out a subpoena."

"Those . . . rascals!" Father Brian said. "They're low, dirty rascals, that's all I can say of them! The thought of it—holding the girl hostage!"

"They only took her to keep Gallen from running," Thomas said. "And she gave one of them a bloody nose for it. I like that."

Gallen clenched his fists, looked about. There was nothing he could do to stop them from taking Maggie. They couldn't arrest Gallen without a warrant signed by the Lord Sheriff, but they could subpoena a witness, and they could hold her in prison for questioning for weeks.

"It's that damned Patrick O'Connor," Father Brian said. "He's been telling everyone false tales about you! I should have had you kill him!"

"Patrick O'Connor?" Thomas asked.

Gallen was deep in thought, so Father Brian offered, "He's the son of a sheep farmer, Seamus O'Connor, from An Cochan. Two weeks ago, Seamus hired Gallen to escort him home, and they were set upon by robbers. Gallen fought them, but the robbers had him down and would have slit his throat, when the Angel of Death came and rescued Gallen and Seamus, too. The next day, Gallen and I caught that blackguard Patrick with soot on his face and blood on his shoes. We discovered that the boy had set the robbers on his *own father*, hoping for a cut of the money! I thought to have Gallen kill the boy, but Gallen is a merciful sort, so we outlawed him from County Morgan. But now Patrick is mucking about the countryside, telling stories on Gallen, causing trouble!"

"It wasn't just Patrick who caused the trouble," Gallen said, grateful that the priest was willing to bolster Gallen's good name by claiming that it was his idea to show some mercy to the lad. In truth, neither of them had thought of killing the boy. "He's down south telling his tales. But some other robbers from up north escaped. They must have heard of Patrick's efforts to smear my name. Now Orick says that they've put a story together and plan to testify against me."

"Like as not," Orick grumbled, "some of those sheriffs out there are relatives to the robbers!"

"Granted, I'll give you that," Father Brian said. "Some of those northerners are an inbred lot, but a man can't choose his kin." He thought a moment, pacing nervously, and said, "I could raise the town in your behalf, Gallen! Most everyone is awake already, circling the house. We'll show these *northern* sheriffs!"

"If you do," Gallen said, "there will be bloodshed. We don't want that. I can't think of a man in town who I want to see dead. Besides, even if you won, you'd find yourself on trial."

Gallen's mother sat heavily on the sofa before the fireplace. She wrapped her arms around herself protectively. Gallen wondered at how small she'd become in the past few years. When he was young, she'd seemed beautiful and tall and strong. But over the past few months, since the death of Gallen's father, she'd gone into decline in a terrible way. Now she was a mere potato, a lumpy, frail woman with graying hair.

Her jaw trembled. "You'd better get out of here, son," she said, as if the words were bitter on her tongue. "You can fight your way past these sheriffs, I'll wager."

"I won't do that," Gallen said, wondering. His prowess with weapons seemed to be growing to legendary heights if even his own mother thought he could fight his way past dozens of well-armed opponents. The really frightening thing was, Gallen was tempted to give it a try. "I won't play the outlaw. I couldn't make a run for it without a fight first, and I'd have to kill some of them. And even if I won through, Maggie would still end up in their prison, and there's no telling what the Inquisitor might do."

"If the girl loves you, nothing would make her happier than to help you, whatever way she can," Gallen's mother protested.

"No," Gallen said. "I won't play their game. We have to fight them legally."

He looked up, saw that Maggie's uncle was watching him, measuring him with his eyes, and he wore a look of respect. Thomas was an odd one, in Gallen's book. He'd been around the world, probably been in his share of scrapes. He'd come to lord it over his niece, stop her from marrying in order to line his own pockets, and that showed a bit of larceny in his heart. And he had a commanding way about him. While others here were all floundering about for solutions, Thomas seemed unperturbed, as if he knew how Gallen could get out of this spot, but just wasn't saying. Gallen decided to ask him bluntly.

"You've been around, Thomas. Have you got any ideas?"

"If you let them take you north, you're a dead man, sure," Thomas grumbled. He went over to the rocking chair by the fireplace, pulled a pipe from his pocket, and began tamping it full of tobacco. "They don't like southerners much, and they're a close-knit lot. Inbred, some of them. You've killed their kin, and even if you got off with a whipping, some of them are likely to lie in wait for you and slit your throat on the road home. You need to stay here, fight them on your own ground. Take this thing to trial here. That's your legal right. And make sure your friends and cousins are all sitting in the jury."

"That's correct, a man has a right to be tried in his own town!" Father Brian said.

"Not in his own town, but in the jurisdiction where the crime was committed," Thomas corrected. "Which is one and the same, in this case. But to tell you straight, I'm worried that these sheriffs will go carting Gallen and Maggie off, in spite of the law. There's not much here to stop them."

Father Brian frowned. "Then there's only one thing to do. I'll go to Baille Sean and talk to Lord Sheriff Carnaghan. I'll raise an army of sheriffs and deputies to make sure that Gallen gets an open trial here in town. That way, these damned northerners won't be able to torment him in secret, and they won't table a jury stacked with his enemies."

Thomas nodded, and Father Brian got up, went outside into the darkness, shoving past the sheriffs and grumbling, "Out of my way! Get out—or I'll excommunicate the lot of you!" Outside the door, the sky had lightened a crack. Dawn was approaching.

Moments later, Gallen heard a horse race by on the road south, and Gallen was surprised that Father Brian would ride with such daring in so little light.

Silently, Gallen prayed that Father Brian's horse would race surefooted over the mountains.

Orick nuzzled up to Gallen, putting his face against Gallen's ribs, and Gallen stroked his nose absently. He could see no easy way out of this.

His mother got up from the couch. "It's going to be a long day, what with everyone running off to see the Lord Sheriff. At least we don't have to wait on an empty stomach."

"Aye, what a day," Thomas said. "Between the trial and my oddities, the inn will be bustling. We might as well put a tent over the whole town. Why, all we lack for a circus is a few dancing horses and a singing dog—the clowns and ringmasters are already in attendance."

In the kitchen, Gallen's mother began mixing dough and banging pots.

Orick lay at Gallen's feet. The bloody wound to his shoulder was all scabbed over, and the poor bear lay for a bit, licking himself.

When Thomas was sure that Gallen's mother was occupied, Thomas leaned forward. "Lad," he said, "I'm afraid that this trial might go bad for you. It's said that the angels have come to your aid before. Is there a chance that they'll come now?"

"I'm afraid not," Gallen said.

Thomas licked his lips. "Then they're gone now, to whatever world they hail from?"

Thomas looked into Gallen's eyes quizzically, and Gallen wondered how much he knew—or had guessed. "Yes, they're gone, and I don't think they'll be back."

Thomas leaned forward conspiratorially, and whispered, "You've talked to an angel? Wha—what did the creature say, man?"

Gallen found his heart hammering. He was torn between the desire to speak the truth, and the desire to keep his secrets. "There are many worlds beyond Geata na Chruinne," Gallen said, "and people there are not so different than they are here. Some of them are far more beautiful than anything you dream. Some of them are wise. Some of them live forever. In many ways, life is easier there than it is here, but there are also greater perils."

Thomas sat back, stunned, his face a mask of hope and confusion. "Well, I'll be . . . I wonder . . . I wish I could see . . . I wish I could have talked to an angel."

Gallen could see Thomas's secret desire written plain on his face. The man wanted to see what lay beyond Geata na Chruinne, and Gallen had promised Maggie that he'd talk to Thomas about a quick date for the wedding. He wondered if he told Thomas the truth, if Thomas could understand how important it was for Maggie to marry soon.

"Maggie and I have both been beyond the gate with the folk that you call angels," Gallen said. "And now that Maggie's been there, she won't rest easy until she washes the dust of this world from off her feet once and for all."

Orick had quit licking his wounds, and now he looked up. "Well, if you're going to say that much, you might as well tell him the whole truth, Gallen." Orick turned to Thomas. "Gallen and Maggie are people of some import out there now. They have to return. The fate of ten thousand worlds rests on their shoulders."

Thomas sat back, as if expecting Gallen to sprout horns from his head or wings from his back. It was an utterly fantastic tale that Gallen was telling, yet the dead "demon" and "angel" in Thomas's shed gave some proof of it. Thomas must have believed him, for the old minstrel began to weep. "People there can live forever?" Thomas asked. "And all you have to do is walk through Geata na Chruinne?"

"You need a key to the gate," Orick said.

"And have you got one?"

Gallen nodded.

"Can I see it?" Thomas begged, making little grasping motions with one hand.

Gallen checked to make certain that his mother wasn't watching, then he went to his room, came back with the key—a glowing crystal globe with golden wiring inside.

Thomas stared in awe, held it in both hands. "This is not of this world, that's sure," Thomas said. "But I don't know if it's a thing of God, or of the devil."

"Neither," Gallen said. "It was made by the Tharrin, a race of good people who rule the heavens."

Thomas licked his lips, handed the key back to Gallen, who scooted it into his pocket. Thomas said, "So why haven't you gone already? Is it those green-skinned devils?"

"Something like that," Gallen said. "Maggie and I have enemies who will begin hunting us soon, and this is a good place to hide. Maggie wants to get married here, before we leave. And to tell the truth, I wanted to say goodbye to my friends."

"So that's why Maggie is so hot to marry you now," Thomas said. "She doesn't care about your political future, because your future lies elsewhere."

Gallen nodded.

Thomas folded his hands, stared at them thoughtfully for a long time. "And if you don't like it out there, you can always come back here, I suppose?"

"Aye," Gallen said. "We could."

Thomas leaned back in his chair, studied Gallen a moment, his gray eyes measuring the boy. His beard and moustache were impeccably trimmed. His body was leathery, but he had a gut growing on him. He was at that stage of life where he was still tough, but somewhat worn. And in his bright purple pants and a peach-colored shirt, he looked as if he should be out juggling or singing in the streets. "I want to go with you," Thomas admitted at last.

"Are you sure?" Gallen asked. "It's a big place, stranger than I have time to tell."

"Hmmm . . ." Thomas eyed the boy thoughtfully, almost grudgingly. "I've never put much faith in God and heaven, or any rewards in the afterlife. But dammit, boy, *I want to live forever!*"

"And if I were to take you with me," Gallen mused, "what could you pay?" He said it as a joke, but Thomas didn't see it as one.

"How much do you want?" Thomas asked, licking his lips.

And Gallen realized that there was only one answer. Nothing that Thomas took with him would be of any value out there. "Everything you own," Gallen said. He watched the old man smile weakly, thinking he would balk at the price. "All of it. You'll give it all to my mother, and go into the next world as broke as a babe."

Thomas watched him calculatingly. "I'll need my lute and my mandolin and flutes."

"You can keep those," Gallen said.

"A fitting price," Thomas agreed. "I'll make out the papers this morning."

"And one more thing: I want consent to marry your niece."

"No, no," Orick said. "You can't barter for her like that, Gallen. It's not proper."

Thomas smiled greedily, and he scratched his beard, thinking.

"Maggie won't care. We'll all get what we want," Gallen said. "What does it matter what price Thomas and I agree on?"

"It's a deal," Thomas said, and he reached out his hand. The two men shook. "I'll go tell her. She's got her dress made, so you can marry as soon as the priest gets back."

Thomas got up, swaggered to the door, opened it and looked out at the sheriffs all gathered around out there. "Oh, it's going to be the damnedest long day you ever saw," Thomas bellowed, and he was out the door.

After Thomas left, Gallen's mother fixed a huge breakfast of ham and eggs with sweet rolls, and in the early morning dawn, Gallen, his mother, and Orick sat down to eat, watching the sheriffs outside through the windows, who all stared in at the banquet with envy.

All through the morning, there was nothing to do but sit, and Gallen waited with a heavy heart, considered routes of escape. But escape was out of the question. Orick tried to go outside, for the sheriffs had one of his bear friends, a female named Grits, in custody, but the sheriffs would not let him past.

And so they sat. In a couple of hours, Thomas came back and sang to the sheriffs a bit, sat with them and drank, laughing, as if they were all as thick as thieves. He came in for a minute, warned Gallen to lock all the doors and windows, and keep his weapons handy. "There's some sentiment for a lynching out there among those boys. They've come a long way to get you, and they don't want to go back empty-handed. But I think I can cool their heads," Thomas whispered, then he was back out the door.

In the early afternoon, the scar-faced sheriff came back to Gallen's door, offering him a bargain. "If you come with us now," the sheriff said, droplets of nervous perspiration on his brow, "I'm prepared to set your fiancée free. No harm will come to her."

"And if I don't come with you?" Gallen asked, wondering why the sheriff wanted a bargain, what had spooked him.

"Who knows?" the sheriff said. "We'll take her north for questioning. It's a dangerous road. Prisoners have been known to get killed while trying to escape. And the interrogations can get brutal. Even if your girl does make it through all of this, she'll have a long walk home, over lonely roads, where robbers sometimes would rather take a woman's virtue than her purse."

"You wouldn't dare," Gallen said. There was some shouting outside, townsmen arguing with sheriffs, and Gallen suddenly knew why the sheriff was getting nervous. The crowd was growing, becoming unmanageable.

"With fifty men to back me?" the sheriff said. "Oh, I'd dare."

Just then, Thomas came up to the door behind the sheriff. "Say, Gallen," Thomas chortled. "It looks as if you're getting pretty thick with Sheriff Sully here. He's the leader of this band of merry lawmakers, you know."

He pushed past the sheriff, carrying his lute in its case of rosewood, leaving the door wide open. He sat on the couch, pulled out the lute.

"Why don't you invite Sheriff Sully in, Gallen?" Thomas said. "I've been working on ballads about this meeting—the meeting of Gallen O'Day and Sheriff Sully—and I'd like you to hear them. They may be sung all over the world for many years, so I'd like your opinion."

He began fingering his lute, then apologized. "This is an early draft of the song, as you'll gather. It's a bit simple, a bit crude, but I always think a song should reflect its subject matter, don't you?"

Gallen looked to Sully, and he shrugged.

"Now, there is one point I want to be clear on," Thomas said. "You've got a nasty scar on your face, Sheriff Sully, and with a man in your line of work, one might imagine that you got it fighting some notorious outlaw. But that's not how you got the scar, is it?"

"No," Sully said.

"As I understand from your townsmen out there, it came about through a whittling mishap?"

Sully squinted and nodded.

Thomas plucked a few notes on his lute, then sang sweetly,

"Come near and listen girls and listen boys,
Whether you be virtuous or bullies
Learn good from bad while you're still young
Don't let your name be Sullied."

Sheriff Sully stiffened, reached for the haft of his sword, a sneer spreading across his face.

"Och, now!" Thomas stopped, looked up. "Do you know the penalty for drawing a blade against a minstrel?" Thomas said. "We carry a license for this work from the Lord Mayor, you know."

"You can't sing songs about me, unless a judge approves them!" Sully cried.

"I can't sing songs *in public*," Thomas said. "But I can compose them in private. I'm sure I can clear the song through the review process before going public. It contains nothing slanderous, only the facts. Here's how it goes . . ." His hands strummed, and he continued in a sweet voice,

"Now, when Sheriff Sully was a lad of ten,
he slept in his own piddle.
He drowned young rats in his grandma's well
And sliced his face up when he whittled."

When Thomas sang the word "whittled," he hit a sour note on his lute, smiled up at the two of them. "That's the first verse. Sheriff Sully was a bed wetter, Gallen. Did you know that?" Sully's face had turned a bright red, and he stood there mortified. Several other sheriffs were standing outside the door, and Thomas had sung loud enough for them to hear. Their guffaws reverberated through the room, and they pressed closer. "Anyway," Thomas said, "here's my idea for the chorus!" His voice took on a gravelly note as he pounded the strings of his lute and snarled,

"But who knew,
that when his body grew,
his mind would stay so damned little?
Yes, he wounds himself when he whittles!
And you never know where he'll piddle!"

Thomas got up and strolled the room as he sang through the next two verses. And Sully's eyes became more and more wild, more desperate and full of rage.

"Sully matured into a fearsome lad,
He turned his knife on others.
And as sheriffs go, he wasn't bad,
at poking the wife of his own brother!

But who knew,
that when his body grew,
his soul would stay so damned little?
Yes, he wounds himself when he whittles!
And you never know where he'll piddle!
And with his sister-in-law he diddles!

Now Sheriff Sully knew he was brave,
And he vowed to stamp out sin!
So he hunted that worthy Gallen O'Day
backed by only a hundred well-armed men!

But who knew
that when his body grew
his heart would stay so damned little?
Yes, he wounds himself when he whittles!
And you never know where he'll piddle!
And with his sister-in-law he diddles!
And what he calls 'valor' is a riddle!"

"Enough!" Sheriff Sully screamed, reaching for his sword. But one of his men, who had been inching in through the open door, grabbed his arm and wrestled it behind his back.

"Oh, I don't think it's nearly enough." Thomas grinned. "I've got several more verses."

"I challenge you to a duel . . . you," Sully roared. "You knave!"

"Oh, a duel, is it?" Thomas said. "Well, if you're going to abuse me with language like that, then I accept."

Gallen looked back and forth between the men for a moment. Sully was younger, bigger, and stronger than Thomas, and in any match, the minstrel was sure to lose.

"I accept your challenge," Thomas said, "and since you've offered the duel, I shall choose the weapons!"

He walked over to the sheriff, who suddenly was glancing about worriedly, wondering what trick the minstrel was playing. Thomas glanced meaningfully at Gallen's knives, looked over the swords of a couple of Sully's men. "It shall be a duel . . . of tongues," Thomas said. "You and I shall stand and hurl insults at each other for an evening, and we'll find out who wilts first under the weight of a good tongue-lashing."

"You . . . you bombastic, overdressed . . ." The sheriff could not think what next to say.

"Ah, how right you are!" Thomas said, looking down at his own peach-colored shirt and purple trousers. "You wound me with your foulmouthed invectives, sir—mortally!"

Thomas plucked at his lute, a tune that was now becoming familiar, and Sully let out a scream of frustration. He shouted at his own men, herding them outside, and rushed from the house, slamming the door behind him. Gallen could hear Sully's own men guffawing as he passed.

"You shouldn't have done that," Gallen said. "You've only infuriated him."

"No," Thomas said, putting the lute away. "I've done right. Every man who abuses power as he does will come under scrutiny in time. He wants to be your judge and executioner, but his deeds here will be judged by others for years to come. My song only reminds him of this fact."

"He might kill you for what you just did," Gallen said.

"Very likely," Thomas agreed. "And if I died tonight, every minstrel in the land would come to sing of it, and Sully's fate would be far worse than he fears. Mere mortals cannot withstand the muse."

Gallen stared at the door a moment. "I find it odd that this Mister Sully should hate me so much. As far as I know, I've never harmed him or his kin."

"You're a great lawman, Gallen," Thomas said. "And he's not much of anything. You wound his pride just by being alive. You'll find that he's much like small men everywhere."

Gallen studied Thomas, and found that he felt a new respect for the man. He'd just sliced Sheriff Sully to the core as easily as Gallen would gut a highwayman. There was no remorse, no fear of recourse, and now Gallen saw why Thomas carried himself with a lordly demeanor.

"I don't mean to sound critical," Gallen said. "But that wasn't much of a song you sang. I mean, it was a nice ditty, a catchy tune, but I think it needs some work."

Thomas looked up at Gallen with disinterested eyes. "You're a critic, eh? Don't fear. That bit of bawdy wasn't meant to immortalize Sully, only intimidate him. In the business we call it a 'driver,' for it is meant only to drive a man away from his hometown. The real ballad will have to be much longer, with entire stanzas devoted to Sully's bed-wetting, and whole movements devoted to exposing his acts of incest. I feel sorry for the man. Few men's lives can bear such close scrutiny." Thomas sighed. "And now that my day's work is done, I think I'll take a nap."

He yawned, made his way back outside. The sheriffs hooted and cheered as he passed.

In the early evening, Father Brian rode back on a winded horse with a writ from Lord Sheriff Carnaghan deputizing every man in Clere to make sure that Gallen wasn't taken from the city, and he forbade the prosecution from securing testimony by torture, and ordered Maggie Flynn to be freed. Because of the fear that open warfare might break out between the northern sheriffs and the locals, the city of Baille Sean was sending a judge in great haste.

Gallen had hardly heard this news from one of the local fishermen, when Father Brian came banging on the door, calling, "Out with you, man. Get on your finest duds, and out of the house with you!"

"What's happening?" Gallen asked, opening the door enough to see the sheriffs all crowded about, with Father Brian standing there, looking a bit worn.

"Today is to be your wedding day," Father Brian said. "It seems that Thomas Flynn has taken a sudden fondness to you, and he says that if you so desire, he wants you to marry his niece before nightfall!"

Eight

Gallen and Maggie's wedding was perhaps the strangest that ever took place in the village of Clere. By dusk, nearly everyone from as far as fifteen miles away was in the village, so that tents and wagons filled every field within half a mile of town. And over two hundred men came north from Baille Sean, driving hard, hoping to see what all of the hoopla was about.

Between having a minstrel in town, along with a display of a demon from hell and an angel from heaven, and an occupying army of northern sheriffs who'd come down to hang the local hero, an impending trial on witchcraft, and the marriage of Gallen O'Day—it was all too much for anyone to miss. The poor old church couldn't have held a tenth of the number of people who wanted to view the wedding; and, as Orick grumbled, there was a grand lot of speculation as to the cause of the sudden marriage.

The most evil-minded folks figured that Maggie had come down with a child, and this was all an effort to make it right.

But many a bedazzled maid believed that Maggie loved Gallen, and so she wanted to make him her husband all in one grand gesture before he got hung.

But some old deacon remembered an obscure verse in the Tome of Law, where it pointed out that it was illegal to hang a man within a month of his wedding day, for to do so would not only deny him his life, it would deny him the chance of having posterity.

This last bit of news thoroughly enraged some of the northern sheriffs, who saw this all as some grand scheme to keep Gallen alive for another month, even if they could convict him, ensuring him greater chances of escape.

But the northern sheriffs didn't cause much of an uproar, for to tell the truth, the majority of them began to join in the festive attitude. While the rest of the sheriffs, seeing how with every wagon that pulled into town they were more and more outnumbered, decided to remain quiet. So the sheriffs paid their shillings to go see Thomas's angel and demon, and one sheriff, after seeing the demon, said, "Well, if Gallen O'Day fought those monsters, he's a better man than I am." And he rode off toward home to much applause.

And so the wedding was held in an open field, just before sundown, Maggie in a white dress that made her look radiant, and Gallen dressed in his finest blue tunic with gray hose.

Gallen's cousin, Father Brian of An Cochan, wedded the two, administering the oaths.

Orick the bear played the part of Gallen's "best man," and that caused many a stare. Thomas sang, with the church choir joining him, and never had so sweet a music been heard over the city.

Folks from all over Counties Morgan, Obhiann, and Daugherty tried to outdo one another on wedding gifts—trying to show those northern sheriffs how much they admired Gallen. Seamus O'Connor gave Gallen a nice carriage, while a friend of Gallen's father gave the couple a brace of white stallions. Silver teapots took all of one table, while blankets and coats and saddles and all other manner of finery filled up others.

Someone brought out a whiskey keg, and those folks who had nothing else to give began filling it with money, and more than one gold coin was seen therein. Over the past years, Gallen had saved more than a dozen locals from highwaymen, and the roads around Clere were notoriously safe—all because of Gallen O'Day. So folks let their money flow freely in gratitude.

It was just an hour before dusk, and the dancing was in full swing, when the Lord Inquisitor rode into town in a hired coach, his face clenched and frustrated.

Obviously, the terms of the trial were not to his liking. "We'll begin jury selection tonight!" he announced to his men, and they rounded up Gallen and his young wife and herded him back to Gallen's home.

Gallen selected Deacon Green to be his defender in the case, and within the hour the townspeople drew lots for jury duty. All of the northern sheriffs put their lots in, and to Gallen's great dismay, four of them won seats on the jury, along with two men and a woman from nearby. Even in his own village, the jury was stacked against him.

Gallen was given copies of the affidavits sworn against him, and he and Maggie and Orick and Deacon Green studied them for a bit. Three men out of County Obhiann told how they had planned the robbery two weeks ago, how they had taken Seamus O'Connor down, then Gallen, and were beating the men, planning to rob them (they omitted the fact that they were planning to cut Gallen's throat), when they swore that Gallen uttered his prayer and hell itself disgorged one of its minions, a magical man with wicked swords and a face that glowed like starlight. Later, as they ran away, they claimed that they looked back over the hills and saw a strange light, as if the very bowels of hell had opened.

Technically, their case had some weaknesses. In many places their sworn testimony had been copied verbatim from one document to the next, so it would be easy enough to prove that they had been in collusion. Second, they were all felons—robbers who nevertheless swore that murder had never entered their minds that night.

And there were some holes in their testimony. None of them had actually witnessed the bowels of hell open, and they did not claim to have seen any other sign of the demons that troubled the area the next morning.

Yet as Deacon Green, a tall, balding man with round spectacles, studied the testimony, he muttered under his breath. "Och, Gallen. You're in a tight spot, sure, lad. I don't see a way out of this. You'll do prison time, at the very least."

"How can that be?" Maggie said, sitting on the sofa, holding Gallen's hand. "Why would anyone believe those robbers, instead of Gallen?"

"The Bible says that out of the mouths of two or three witnesses, every word shall be established," Deacon Green said. "And so according to law, if three witnesses testify against a man in a capital case, then that man will . . . well, he'll hang—unless we can shake the accusers."

"What about Seamus O'Connor's testimony?" Maggie asked, biting her lower lip. "We can put him on the stand."

"But what can the man swear to? He was so drunk he had to hire Gallen to keep him from falling off his horse, and then he got a knock in the head halfway through the battle and didn't wake up for four days. He says that he's willing to swear that the men who tried to rob him were murderous bastards, and he hopes they all go to hell. But I'm afraid people can only laugh at any testimony he has to give."

"But we can prove that the witnesses here have something against me," Gallen contended. "Mason and Argent Flaherty both had a brother and a cousin killed in the attack that night. They have a blood debt against me."

"But both of them swear that they came forward to the law out of remorse," the good deacon said. "Both of them are to be whipped with forty lashes for their crime, once they testify against you. If they only wanted revenge, they could have lain in wait for you of a dark night and cut your throat. Now, I know that you feel they have something against you, but the fact is that their remorse seems genuine, and this could sway the jury."

Gallen shook his head, wondering, "Could they have worked out a deal with that Bishop Mackey? Perhaps they'll get a commuted sentence for testifying against me."

"All three men claim that they sought such a bargain, but that Bishop Mackey never spoke a promise in return."

"And what of the reward?" Maggie asked. "Isn't there money for proving witchcraft against a man? These men are robbers, so why wouldn't they be willing to lie for some money?"

"Fifty pounds." Deacon Green sighed. "Not enough to risk your life for."

Gallen wondered. There is always someone who holds life cheap. All three of these men were desperate. To some degree, they had all risked their lives in trying to rob Seamus O'Connor of fifty pounds, but then it had been nine men against two—and the robbers had never expected Gallen O'Day to be among those two. They'd hoped to get five pounds per man then.

Would they go to so much trouble for a share of fifty pounds split three ways? Not likely, not when you considered that they could be whipped within an inch of their lives, in the bargain.

No, there had to be some other reason for them to bring false charges against Gallen.

So Gallen sat with his head bent low, wondering why these strangers would come like this and try to bring so much trouble down on him.

He wondered if it simply might be a matter of conceit. If they got away with this, these three robbers would be revered among outlaws all across the land as the men who had killed Gallen O'Day. And the very irony that they had taken a lawman and had him executed by the law would be a great jest.

Deacon Green made studious notes, probing for weaknesses in the transcripts, hunting for avenues to pursue. Gallen studied with him for a bit, but his eyes ached from lack of sleep, so he and Maggie went to his room to rest. Maggie just sat on the edge of the bed, holding him for a while, as Gallen considered.

If I were the greatest counselor in the world, Gallen asked himself, what would I do? He rested in Maggie's arms for a long moment, waiting for some insight to fill him, to send knowledge coursing through his body until it seemed that understanding flowed from his fingertips. So often in the past, this technique had served Gallen well. But Gallen waited long, yet no insight came.

Finally, Gallen realized that the deacon's expertise in such matters was far beyond his, so he closed the door to his bedroom, leaving Deacon Green to study and Orick to sit out on the couch talking with Gallen's mother about the injustices committed by the northern sheriffs who were holding Orick's good friend, a she-bear named Grits.

The house began to feel stuffy—with that wet, earthy smell that fills a house-tree in the evening—so he opened his window a crack, looked out. Twenty sheriffs surrounded the house, and Gallen's opening of the window was the most exciting move he had made in hours. Four of them drew in closer, backlit by their campfires.

Gallen sat on his bed, and Sheriff Sully stuck his dark face through the windows. "Needing a bit of fresh air, are you?" he leered. "A bit winded, are you, from doing your business with that juicy little wife of yours? Well, I've got a bit of fresh news for you: guess what? I got on your jury. Isn't that worthy of a laugh?"

"Every juror has to swear that he has nothing against me," Gallen said, surprised at the undisguised malice in the sheriff's voice.

"Oh, and I'll swear it," the sheriff said. "I've got nothing personal against you. It's not your fault that you're so good at what you do. Why, whenever a highwayman strikes, there's always a bit of a bustle, folks wagging their tongues. 'Why can't *our* sheriffs protect us?' they ask. 'Why do we pay these louts three pounds a month, when for just a bit more, we could get Gallen O'Day up here to do the job proper?'

"And when one of us lads goes to a dance and asks an ugly young woman onto the floor, like as not she'll say, 'And who do you think you are that I should dance with you—Gallen O'Day?' So you understand, Gallen, that it's nothing personal, but after the trial, I for one shall be glad to be rid of you!"

Behind Sully, several other sheriffs laughed, as if this were all just part of some great meaningless hoax. They'd come for entertainment, and they didn't care if they were cheering Sully on, or Thomas, or Gallen. It was all just fun.

But there is a look that a man gives you just before he seriously tries to kill you. It is a fixed stare with constricted pupils and a face that is set and determined. It's a look that is both relaxed and calculating, and Gallen saw that look now in the eyes of Sheriff Sully. The man was jealous of him, so jealous that he thought it a small thing to kill Gallen.

The sheriffs turned away, walked back to their campfire. Gallen stood at the window, watching them.

Gallen could smell the scent of fires. "That croaking old frog," Maggie whispered. "I'd like to gouge out his eyes and use them for earrings."

"That isn't a ladylike thing to say," Gallen whispered. A cold pain shot up the back of his spine and through his heart. Never had he felt so weak, so unable to defend himself.

So this is the way it ends for me, he wondered. He had done his job as a bodyguard, perhaps done it too well. Now, highwaymen with blood debts against him would stand as witnesses in his trial, and jealous lawmen would cast their jury ballots against him. And there was no way that he could win.

All of this time, Gallen had believed that others respected him, believed that by fighting so hard against the evils of the world he had won their favor. But now he saw that some of them only feared and hated him for what he'd done.

He laughed under his breath. He'd come home to Tihrglas after his adventures on far worlds, come home with the hope of going salmon fishing in the river, of resting and tasting the scent of the clean air under the pines. He had done it so often in his youth, casting his yellow wet-water flies out into the flood and jigging through the rippled stream until a salmon struck, bending his old hickory pole to the snapping point.

But he hadn't been fishing now in years. Sometime a couple of years ago, he'd put the rod away, and now it looked as if he'd never have the chance to take it up again. Sometime, while trying to win honor and right the wrongs of the world, he'd given up the things he'd enjoyed most.

Gallen glanced into the living room. Deacon Green sat on the sofa, still studying the testimonies of the felons. The creases in his brow and the singular concentration with which he studied showed just how worried he'd become.

It was getting late, and Gallen looked out the window. People were still pouring into town to see the demon and angel in Thomas Flynn's stable.

The trial of Gallen O'Day would be an added sideshow that few would want to miss. Even now, the sheriffs had a fire beside the road, not twenty feet from the door, and they sat together with their three witnesses. Perhaps two hundred observers had gathered around the house to listen while the false witnesses drunkenly railed against Gallen O'Day, telling how he'd summoned demons from hell, and how he'd laughed about it after.

Gallen studied the faces of the men. The two Flaherty brothers were difficult to miss. Mason was a tall man, hard and strong, and Gallen couldn't even recall having seen him in the battle on the night that Seamus was attacked. The younger Flaherty, Argent, was one that Gallen recalled well. He had put a knife to the boy's throat, tried to hold him hostage so that the robbers would back off, let Gallen and Seamus go free. Now, Gallen wished that he had killed the boy in cold blood when he'd had the chance. He doubted that he would be able to get either of the Flahertys to change their testimony.

The third man, though—he interested Gallen. His name was Christian Bean. He was a small man, fat and soft, with a rounded face accentuated by a thin beard. He kept more to himself, seemed almost afraid to talk. Gallen remembered him from the battle, too, but only dimly. The man was a coward who had hung back during the robbery.

Gallen looked up at the stars, thought for a moment of the planet Tremonthin and the young Tharrin woman whose whole world was in jeopardy. Gallen licked his lips, enjoying the way his pulse quickened. Gallen always felt most alive in battle, when the threat of death was imminent. Gallen smiled, for at the moment he felt the thrill.

The spectators at the front of the house began plying Christian Bean with liquor, and he railed against Gallen. Gallen could see the man's face only by firelight—little piggy eyes that glanced worriedly, hunting the shadows around the house as he described the demon he'd seen, its face glowing like a blue star, the swords in its hand.

"It's a shame you don't have another witness in your behalf," Maggie muttered absently from the bed.

With a start, Gallen realized that there *had* been another witness to the attack: the very demon that these men accused Gallen of summoning. Little did anyone realize that the demon was Gallen O'Day himself, in disguise. Everynne had sent him back in time after his journey, so that he would return from his long foray to other worlds before he'd even left his home.

And with a second shock, Gallen realized that Christian Bean didn't fear Gallen or fear that his testimony would be controverted and shown to be a lie. He feared the fairy folk of Coille Sidhe who might yet come to Gallen's aid. With that recognition, Gallen laughed aloud and rushed to Maggie's side and kissed her. He knew what he had to do.

The wind came in blustery just after midnight, and the limbs of the house-tree swayed and cracked. Gallen wore his silver mantle, and his robe of changing colors had taken on a deep black to match the night. He wore his black boots and black fighting gloves, carried a single sword, and in his pockets he had the mask of Fale, a mask of palest silver-blue that shone like starlight.

"Are you sure you should be going out there?" Maggie whispered, as she tied the hood of his robe over his mantle.

"It's the only way I know to shake the witnesses," Gallen said. "If I can scare them into admitting the truth, there will never be a trial."

Maggie gave him a kiss for luck, then sent him on his way.

Under cover of darkness, and with the sound of the wind and the chattering of voices and the singing accompanied by lutes in the distance, Gallen climbed to the attic of the house-tree and slid open the service door. Slowly, and ever so quietly, he crept out on a limb, then reached back and closed the door behind.

There were people everywhere below him. There could not be less than a hundred just under the bough he was on. Some were sheriffs, but many were just curious onlookers.

Gallen closed his eyes and let the sensors on his mantle show him the scene in infrared. He climbed from limb to limb, until he was nearly over the little knot of sheriffs who sat beside the fire.

Taking a small dronon translator from his pocket, he clipped it to his lapel, then flipped off the translator so that its microphone would simply amplify his voice.

All night long, travelers had been forcing rum and beer onto the sheriffs and the witnesses, and Gallen sat listening to them talk, until at last Christian Bean began raging in a loud whiny voice. "Aye, that Gallen O'Day is half a devil himself. He's more than a murderer. Mark my words: if he can pray to the devil once and raise hell itself, surely he can do it again—so none of you are safe!"

With those remarks, Gallen grabbed the mask of Fale from his pocket and quickly pushed the rubbery thing over his face. The nanotech devices within the mask immediately flowed into position, conforming to his face, and pulled energy from his body heat, releasing it as photons.

Gallen leapt from limb to ground, so that suddenly he stood in the midst of the crowd. With a roar, he drew his shimmering vibro-blade and pointed it at Christian Bean.

"Behold, a liar and murderer who shall himself soon be a denizen of hell!" Gallen shouted.

There were screams, and all about him, the people fled. The sheriffs were a swirl of motion as they stood, drawing arms. One of them clutched at his sword and stumbled backward, falling into the fire.

Christian Bean just sat, his face lit by the twisting flames of the campfire, his mouth opened wide, clutching a bottle of wine in one hand, a goblet in the other. He was shaking, and Gallen watched in dismay as he soiled his pants.

There was a great uproar, and people from all over town began rushing toward Gallen.

"I warned you," Gallen said loudly, pointing his sword toward all three of the robbers, "that those who commit murder in Coille Sidhe would have to answer to me." His voice carried over the town and reverberated off the walls of the stable. No one on this small world had ever heard such a shout. "Yet now you have returned, and you seek to bring death to a man through your false witness!"

The sheriffs faded back a few steps, leaving the robbers alone beside the fire. All around Gallen, the curious onlookers were quietly retreating, leaving a larger and larger circle.

Gallen moved toward the robbers, and the young Argent Flaherty stood, tried to back away. Gallen commanded him to stop with a roar, and the boy froze, knees shaking.

Gallen moved to within a dozen feet of the men, and suddenly the Lord Inquisitor rushed forward with Sully at his side, and the two put themselves between Gallen and the witnesses. The Lord Inquisitor looked up at Gallen with his piercing blue eyes, and of all the people in town, he did not seem frightened.

"What are you?" the Lord Inquisitor asked, raising a hand as if to stop Gallen.

And at that moment, Gallen realized that he felt odd. Wearing his mantle and the clothing of a Lord Protector, he somehow felt as if he had been endowed with power. Surely, the artificial intelligence within the mantle did give him knowledge beyond the understanding of men, and Gallen felt that he was no longer a common man.

"I am more than a man, less than God," Gallen said.

"And I am Brother Shayne," the Lord Inquisitor said softly. He seemed to be wary, and he looked about, trying to see in the distance behind Gallen. Gallen wondered if the Lord Inquisitor wasn't signaling with his eyes for one of the sheriffs to rush him from behind, but the sensors on his mantle assured Gallen that none were so foolhardy. "You are an angel, then?"

Gallen did not consider. "I am the Lord Protector of this land. I come to protect the righteous, and to bring evil men to judgment."

Gallen did not want to answer more questions, so he thrust his hand into a fold of his robes and pulled out the light globe he had taken from the corpses in Thomas Flynn's stable the night before. He raised the globe aloft and squeezed so that a piercingly brilliant light burst over the town, and he stood as if in sunlight while all around him the townsfolk gasped and groaned, shielding their eyes.

"Behold the light of truth," Gallen shouted. "No mere mortal can look upon it and lie, for he who lies shall be consumed in holy fire!

"You—" Gallen waved his sword toward Christian Bean. "You seek to kill a man by bearing false witness. You have admitted to church authorities that you are a robber. What boon were you granted for bearing false testimony?"

Christian Bean half stood, and the poor man began gasping in fear. Though it was a cool night, he was sweating profusely, and he stammered, "M-m-money. B-Bishop Mackey said he prayed, and God told him that Gallen was responsible for Father Heany's death. He offered us each a hundred pounds to testify!"

Young Argent Flaherty was nodding his head hugely in agreement, and

Gallen stepped closer. "Yet you are under the penalty of a whipping. How do you hope to live through such a beating?"

Christian Bean's eyes opened wide, and he began wheezing heavily. He dropped his brown bottle of wine and his goblet, and he stumbled backward, moaning incoherently. Gallen advanced on young Argent Flaherty and pointed his sword. "Answer me, Argent Flaherty!"

"H-he promised to commute our sentences after the trial!"

"Yet you have sworn in your affidavits that you asked this boon, and that Bishop Mackey denied it?"

"We said that he 'never spoke a promise to us'—and he never did! He wrote the promise in a note, then told us to word our testimony this way so that we wouldn't be lying."

"Keep silent!" Mason Flaherty shouted at his younger brother, grabbing the boy's arm. "If you answer no questions, you'll speak no lies!"

"Och, you child of a serpent!" Gallen sneered at Mason. "Hardly shall you escape the wrath of hell! What does it matter if you worded a portion of your testimony with half-truths, when the brunt of your tale is a lie? I was never summoned by the prayers of Gallen O'Day or any other man, nor have I opened the gates of hell. What of this tale you tell?"

Gallen pointed his sword at Christian Bean, who was writhing on the ground. He was so terrified that Gallen was sure he could get the man to speak, to admit to perjury, but Christian Bean looked up through slitted eyes, gulped at the air loudly, and suddenly grabbed his chest. He began shaking uncontrollably, muscles spasming in his legs, his eyes rolling back in his head. A deep rattling noise came from his throat, and Gallen suddenly realized that the man had just died of fright.

Young Argent Flaherty stared at Christian and gasped, lurched away, rushed toward the crowd. He tried to beat his way through, but several townspeople caught him. The boy pulled his knife and took a swing, and some worthy drew his own blade and plunged it in the lad's ribs. He gave out a startled cry and sank to the ground.

Gallen went to Mason Flaherty, looked down at him steadily. The man was shaking, but stood his ground and met Gallen's eyes. Gallen had never seen such controlled hatred in a man's eyes.

"And you," Gallen said. "You alone are left to bear witness. Tell us now: was your testimony false?"

Mason gritted his teeth, spat his words. "I'll-Not-Speak-Of-It! You cannot force me to talk! Gallen O'Day killed my brother and my cousin, and I've got nothing to say to you!"

Gallen looked at this man and wished that Mason would give him some other choice. He couldn't leave the man alive. The man had tried to kill him on the road, and he'd tried to do it in court. To let such a stubborn and evil man live would only bring trouble later on.

Gallen looked up at Sully. The sheriff stood beside the Lord Inquisitor, shaking. "Do with him what you will," Gallen told the sheriff, and he turned and walked away.

As Gallen passed the front door of his home, he clenched his fist over the glow globe so that there was a bright flash, then he quit squeezing his glow globe so that the light suddenly failed, and he ripped off his mask and headed into the woods.

At his back, he heard Mason Flaherty's sudden scream and the sickening sound of a sword slashing through flesh, snicking through bone. Once, twice, and the head was off. Sully had done a poor job of it.

Gallen reached the edge of the woods, and there he stood panting. Hot, bitter tears were streaming down his face, and he found himself breathing heavily, gasping. He hadn't cried in ages, not since that first time he'd been forced to kill a highwayman three years before. Then, he'd cried because he'd felt that somehow he'd been robbed of his innocence, but with every killing since then, he'd felt justified.

Now, more than ever, he could feel that his innocence had been stripped away. He'd just killed three men, and though they were highwaymen and would have used their testimony to nail him to the inverted cross, still they had not held any weapons, and because of their ignorance, they had been powerless against him.

Gallen rushed up the hillside, under the shelter of an old apple grove. There he fell to his knees and began praying sincerely for the first time in years, begging God for forgiveness.

And as he prayed with his eyes closed, the amplified words hissing from his microphone, he suddenly saw a weak light before him.

He opened his eyes. A pale-blue glowing figure stood before him, leaning against the tree. A wight.

Two weeks ago, the sight would have frozen his heart. But now he knew that it was only a creature formed from luminescent nanotech devices, like the glowing mask he wore from Fale. Yet this creature had the thoughts and memories of a long-dead human inhabiting it. It was a heavyset man with lambchop sideburns.

"I don't know who you are," the wight said, in a deep voice, "but this is an interdicted planet. By charter, you cannot be carrying the kinds of weapons you have on you."

"Then why don't you take them from me?" Gallen said. He didn't need a sword. His mantle whispered that it could incapacitate the creature with a burst of radio waves at any time.

"Och, there's not much that *I* can do against the likes of you," the wight answered. "But I can raise the hue and cry against you. I'll call you a demon. At my word, every townsman in a thousand miles would come marching to war against you. Sooner or later, we'd get you."

"You would let that many people die—just to rid this world of one man?" Gallen whispered.

The wight didn't answer. "We've chosen how we will live here on Tihrglas."

"Eighteen thousand years ago you chose how you will live. But you're dead, and this isn't your world anymore," Gallen said.

"It is filled with our children. If they wish to change the planetary charter, they may do so."

"Yet you don't even let them know that there are worlds beyond this. How can they choose?"

The wight sat down a few feet from Gallen, folded his hands into a steeple and stared at them thoughtfully. "You know of the worlds beyond this, of the wars and horrors found in the universe. Of what value is such knowledge? Our people lead simple lives, free of care. It is a commodity that cannot be purchased."

Things had changed much in the past eighteen thousand years. New sub-races of humanity had been engineered. The Tharrin had been created and given leadership of most planets, ending the petty conflicts and wars that the galaxy had endured under the corporate governors so long before. Gallen did not know much about how the galaxy had been run millennia ago, and he wondered how much the wights understood about how it functioned now.

"I fear," Gallen said, "that much has changed in eighteen thousand years. When you built this world, if I remember my history right, corporate wars raged between planets, but mankind has come far toward making peace with itself."

The wight smiled wryly. "From your words, I guess that mankind has not managed to bring about perfect peace?"

"As long as men are free to do evil, and have the power to do so, there will be evil," Gallen answered. "But the evils of today are perpetrated on a smaller scale than in the past."

"In other words, you've cut the balls off the bigger predators. You've taken away their power."

Gallen considered a moment. He'd seen how heavily modified the Tharrin were, and in a sense they were no longer even human. Yes, mankind had stripped their leaders of the capacity to do evil. "We've modified mankind to some extent. Most people do not have the same level of desire to do evil that your people had in your time."

"Aye, we knew it would be done. It was such a seductive solution to the problem, that we knew others would not resist the temptation. You can place evil men in jail, or you can make the flesh a prison in itself where evil cannot enter. There's not much difference. But you're still restricting people's freedom."

So you created bars of ignorance, Gallen thought, and imprisoned them anyway. "The point is," Gallen said, "that the universe is not so dangerous now as it was in your day. Perhaps it is time for your children to join it."

"Mark my words—" the wight said, suddenly angry, "if our feral children go into the universe, in two generations they'll pose such a threat that none of your peaceful planets would want them!"

Gallen studied the wight, and realized that he had a point. Gallen had just seen the face of evil on his own world, and if highwaymen like the Flahertys were given power, they would take their criminal ways out into the larger galaxy. He envisioned pirating fleets and judges who had been purchased.

In the greater universe, others had chosen to reengineer their children, rid them of the desire to dominate and oppress others. On some worlds, he knew, huge police forces had been created to handle the problem. No matter how you looked at it, bars had been created, and Gallen's ancestors had chosen to control their children by giving them an inheritance of ignorance. Perhaps they had been right to retreat from the future.

Yet Gallen and Maggie had both seen the larger universe, and they had grown from it. Gallen had come home only to find that there was nothing left for him here. He had few friends. And something inside him had changed. He'd outgrown this place, and he felt free to leave now.

He thought of the Tharrin woman, Ceravanne, whom Everynne had shown him on Tremonthin, and he was suddenly eager to be off.

Gallen sighed, looked at the wight. He was an older man who had graying hairs among his sideburns, someone who looked as if the heavy burdens of life had bent him low. "If the only other worlds out there were inhabited only by humans," Gallen said, "then perhaps I would be content to admit that this world should stay as it is. But there is a race of beings called the dronon, and they will come here. Perhaps, someday, they will come to war against this world. If they do, your people will need to grow up, or they will be destroyed."

The wight gave Gallen a calculating look. "We saw one of your dronon not two weeks ago, and wondered how it came to be. I'll take this bit of news to Conclave. Perhaps we must reconsider how this world is run." He stood up.

"And I," Gallen said, rising, "will leave this world with all possible haste, without alerting anyone else here of the universe beyond."

"Not just like that," the wight said, shaking his head. "I'll not let you go at your own pace. We'll escort you, if you please. Just tell us where your ship is."

Suddenly, there was an uproar in town. Gallen looked back down over the small seaport. Hundreds of glowing wights were striding through the edge of town, past the fires and tent cities. The townsfolk were terrified. The wights only came to town if a priest tied someone to a tree for breaking the laws found in the Tome. And a person taken for such an offense never returned.

"My mother lives down there," Gallen sighed, realizing that the wight must have had a built-in transmitter. It must have called its companions. "I'll go down to say good-bye."

"I wish you wouldn't," the wight said with just a hint of force.

"You can't stop me," Gallen replied.

"You wear the mantle of a Lord Protector," the wight said. "If you would protect those people below, then you will leave now. It is against the law to wear such mantles on this world. You know that. And things have already gotten out of hand—what with off-worlders coming through the gates. But things aren't too bad. For now, we will clean up the evidence of off-world intruders, and in a generation these shenanigans will all be forgotten, the stuff of legend. But if you go back to town and pollute those folks down there with more knowledge, we will be forced to eradicate them."

Gallen studied the wight's face. The old creature was not bluffing. Gallen pulled out the glowing mask of Fale, considered putting it back on his face, but decided against it, and then walked unmasked down through the apple grove in long easy strides.

As he passed the china shop, he looked into its windows and thought, I shall never see this place again. And as he passed the quay with its little boats pulled up onto the pebbled beach, he inhaled the sea air. He moved like a wraith through the streets, and all ahead of him, people stepped aside, and the wights drifted in behind him.

He stopped at his own home, and his mother stood outside the door of the little pine house-tree, looking more haggard and world-weary than he'd ever seen her. He hugged her briefly. "I don't know if I'll ever be back," he whispered into her ear as he stooped to hug her, and she reached up and managed to hug him around the ribs.

"Where will you go?" she demanded in a tone of disbelief.

"To another world, to dance with the fairy folk and fight demons."

She squeezed him tight. "Be good," was all she managed to say between sobs. Gallen reached into his pocket and pulled out his coin purse, gave it to her. "The money, wedding gifts, the inn—they're all yours," he said.

Then he went into the house, retrieved his sword, daggers, and the incendiary rifle he'd brought home from his previous trip. Maggie had already gone to fetch her own things.

When Gallen got out of the house, Sheriff Sully came out of the crowd, and growled in a bitter voice. "You—you made me kill a man," he said, rubbing his hands on his shirt as if they'd been soiled.

"Not I," Gallen said. "I told you only to do with Mason Flaherty 'what you will.' You came here with murder on your mind, and murder is what you've accomplished."

Gallen pushed him away, and some of Sully's own men grabbed him, placed him under arrest.

Orick rushed to Gallen's side. "I'm with you, Gallen!" the bear called in his deep voice, and a young female bear padded along beside him. Gallen was glad to finally meet Grits.

Maggie Flynn was calling, "Out of my way! Get out of my way!" and Gallen could see her trying to break through the crowd over by the inn. Within moments she came huffing through the crowd with nothing but a small valise in her hand.

Her uncle Thomas nearly skipped at her side, and he came bustling up with his own bag in one hand, his lute over his shoulder, smiling. " 'Tis good that I didn't even have time to unpack!" he told Gallen.

Then he bowed to Gallen's mother and handed her his purse. "Everything that I own is now yours, good woman. Spend the money in good health."

Some wights had moved in behind the crowd. They'd gotten into the stables across the street from the inn, and they pulled out the bodies of the dead Vanquisher and Everynne's defender, then carried them toward the sea.

Father Brian pushed his way through the crowd, a look of profound fear on his face as he studied the wights who'd gathered behind Gallen. He looked as if he would speak, but he managed to say only, "God be with you, Gallen. I don't know what's happening here."

"Perhaps it's best if you never know. Look in on my mother from time to time, will you?"

Together, the little band began moving through town, and the townspeople parted to let them pass. Some of them shouted out, "God be with you, Gallen, Maggie," and "Go with God!" Their voices were high and troubled, like the voices of small birds that call querulously in the night.

It was obvious that the townspeople did not understand what was happening, but they were afraid. Only witches and sorcerors and those who knew too much were ever taken by wights, and they never returned.

Gallen looked about the town with a profound sense of loss, feeling as if someone had died. He wondered at his own numbness, at his sense of mourning, and knew that it was because everyone he had ever known, everyone he had loved and trusted and played with and hated, all of these people with their odd quirks and petty vices would be dead to him now.

And thus it was that he walked stiffly out of town, an army of wights dogging his step, a few loyal friends beside him. None of the townsfolk followed, for most of them feared that Gallen and his friends were going to their deaths, and none wished to share their fate. Gallen took out his glow globe and squeezed it, let it light his footsteps as they made their way into the forest.

Thomas stopped at the edge of the wood and whispered, "I want to give them one last song, Gallen."

He sang thunderously, yet sweetly,

"Many roads I've traveled down,
And many more I'll follow,
Past lonely woods, and shadowed fens,
And fields too long a-fallow.

But when night breathes on the land,
When fear makes my walk unstately,
I'll remember you, my friends,
And good times we've shared lately."

When he finished, Thomas waved good-bye, and the whole town shouted farewell.

"That was kind of you, Thomas," Maggie said as they walked, "to send them away with a song. It eased their hearts."

"Ah, well," Thomas said, "being as it costs me nothing, a song always makes a fine parting gift."

After an hour they reached a secluded glen at the foot of a mountain. Lichens hung thick on the trees, and the leaf mold was heavy.

There, sheltered under the dark pines, lay Geata na Chruinne, an ancient arch of dark stone with dancing animals and glyphs carved into its side. The forest was alive with the blue and green lights of wights, circling the small group.

The air around the arch was cold, and Gallen fumbled through his pack until he found the gate key. He picked it up, realized that he didn't even know how to use it. He handed it to Maggie, asking, "Show me how to work this thing."

She thought a minute, punched in a sequence of numbers on the key, and suddenly the arch shimmered. A pale lavender light shone beneath it. Maggie handed the key back to Gallen and took her uncle Thomas's hand. "Come on. This way," she said.

They walked through together first, followed by Orick.

The small female bear stood and watched Orick go, apparently too afraid to follow. She had not voiced a word since they'd left town. Gallen bent and whispered into her ear. "There are marvelous worlds beyond the gate, but if you come, it is doubtful that you will ever return to this place." He could see the confusion in her eyes.

"Tell Orick good-bye for me," she said, then she licked Gallen's face.

He sighed deeply, patted her head, then walked to the gate. She gave a short growl, lunged toward him just as he stepped into the cold light, and he realized that she had come too late, for she couldn't enter behind the key-bearer. Then he felt the familiar sensation of winds blowing, as if he were a leaf borne by turbulent storms between worlds.

Nine

Orick stepped through the opal wind between the worlds and found himself in a clearing surrounded by a lush forest, thick with undergrowth. A cool dawn breeze whispered through the trees. Overhead in a sky full of lavender, twin suns rose above the forest, weaving shadows in the woods, while white birds swirled among the trees calling out in creaking voices.

Thomas was staring up with mouth open, and Orick remembered his own sense of awe upon first visiting Fale. "'Tis a sight to behold," Maggie whispered. And Thomas nodded, too dumbfounded to speak.

Orick looked behind him and suddenly a glowing white form appeared, like a mist streaming through the jungle, then Gallen strode into view, his face rigid and worn. The gate could not be seen from this side.

Orick waited, hoping that his bear friend Grits would come through, but the female had stayed behind. Orick gave a little bawl, and weaved his head back and forth as he tried to catch a scent of her.

"I'm sorry, Orick," Maggie said softly, coming to his side. She knelt by him, touched his brow. "She seemed so nice. And you've been looking for love so long. I had hoped she would come."

"That's all right," Orick grumbled. Maggie seemed so distraught that he wanted to calm her. "I couldn't hope for any better from a she-bear. I left her alone with those sheriffs. How could I have hoped she would be more true to me?"

"She wanted to come, Orick," Gallen said. "But she was afraid. Don't blame yourself."

Maggie scratched behind his ears, and Orick licked her hand in gratitude.

Thomas stared about at the skyline. His lute case was strung over his shoulders, and he held to the strap with both hands, a gesture that showed his insecurity. Tall creepers climbed some of the trees, and a few orange birds began chattering loudly as they fed on berries.

Gallen knelt on a clump of grass, pulled out his map of worlds—a thin piece of film that showed a three-dimensional representation of Fale with tiny red gates displayed at various points. "We're not far from a gate to Tremonthin," he said, a tone of relief in his voice. "It's about two thousand kilometers. We'll need to go into town, hire a vehicle."

"What is a kilometer?" Thomas asked.

"Just a stupid way to measure things," Orick grumbled.

"It's a little less than half a mile," Gallen said.

"Do you think it's safe to go into town?" Maggie asked. She had put down her pack—for they'd just walked with them for an hour—and she was looking to Gallen.

Gallen shrugged. "I'll not lie. It has been only a week in this time-line since you and I defeated the Lords of the Swarm. The dronon should have abandoned their military installations here on Fale, but that doesn't mean that we're safe."

"Well, now, you're the optimist today," Orick said.

Gallen hung his head, downcast. Maggie knelt next to him, touched his knee. Orick looked into Gallen's pale blue eyes, and for a moment he felt as if he were looking into the eyes of a stranger, there was so much pain behind them.

"See here, lad—" Orick told Gallen, "just because you've got kicked off your own home world, you don't have to wilt. Things can't be worse than last time we were here."

Gallen smiled up at him. "Aye, you're right, Orick. But we must take care. We have enemies here—men who were evil before the dronon ever set hand to corrupt them. Lord Karthenor and men of his ilk may hold power, for all we know."

"Och, well, if he does," Orick said, "I'll bite his butt so hard he'll never want to sit on a toilet again!"

Yet Orick's playful threats could not brighten the mood. Karthenor had been a powerful servant to the dronon rulers, perhaps powerful enough to wrest control even after the dronon retreated.

"So, Gallen, you've taken my money and led me astray, have you?" Thomas said. "I thought you said this was a decent sort of place, where folks live forever?"

"I also said there were great dangers here," Gallen reminded him. "Some folks here do live a mighty long time, but you still have to take care. . . ."

"Ah, don't listen to him," Orick said. "It's good enough for the likes of us. You'll never taste better food, and they pass it out free to strangers as a courtesy. Why, it's so easy to grow here, that they esteem food as nothing. That's why they give it away."

"Really?" Thomas asked, his face showing that he doubted Orick's every word. Now, some bears have a reputation for stretching the truth, but Orick had never been that kind of bear, so Thomas's raised brows got Orick riled.

"It is indeed the truth!" Orick said. "And I'll tell you something else: there's wonders here that a pudding-head like you couldn't imagine—"

"Tell me about them as we walk, then." Thomas laughed, and with that laugh, Orick looked up. It seemed to him that Thomas was somehow a younger man, less weathered and worn than he had been just hours before, and Orick began to tell Thomas of the things he'd seen on his last trip here.

Maggie donned her own mantle and the cinnamon-colored robes of a technician. In moments they were off, striding through the forest. Gray lizards skittered from their feet, and as they marched, Orick used his keen nose to follow the trail they'd blazed on their journey here two weeks earlier.

Orick told Thomas of the wonders he would behold here on Fale—of starships and men who wore wings, of teaching machines and ancient merchants who lived for ten thousand years, of machines that let one speak with the dead or breathe underwater, and of horrifying weapons that could burn worlds to ashes. He described the armies of insectlike dronon that had infested the place and boasted of the heroic efforts of common people who sought to end their tyranny. He told how Gallen had defeated the dronon Lords of the Swarm in single combat, when even the brilliant Lord Protector Veriasse had failed the challenge, and Orick minimized his own part in all these affairs. For a long while he described the Tharrin woman Everynne, who now reigned as Maggie's regent, as far as the dronon were concerned, over the ten thousand worlds.

From time to time, Orick would pause along the path to eat a slug or a large wood snail. In two hours he had just begun to fill in the details of what Thomas should know when the group reached a small cliff that looked out over Toohkansay, a sprawling purplish-green city grown from a coral-like plant. It stretched like beach foam across the hills, spanning a wide river.

They climbed down the cliff and walked to the city along a ruby road, past rich farms. Hovercars and magcars sped past them, much to the wonder and dismay of Thomas.

And when they reached the outskirts of the city, little had changed. They could still smell the sweet fragrance of foods from a roadside cantina, music swelled from the city walls, and within the shadows under the city gates they could discern human-looking inhabitants from various stock (the impish Wodari with their large eyes, tall bald men out of Bonab who wore nothing but tattoos), along with gold serving droids that still reminded Orick of men in armor.

Several Lords of Fale sat together at one table in the shade of the cupola outside the inn. They wore the multicolored robes of merchants, with masks of palest lavender.

Thomas stopped and surveyed the scene, his mouth gaping in wonder, as if he'd just reached the gates of heaven and feared that Saint Peter would come out and wrestle him for the right to enter.

And as the group approached the archway that led into the cantina, one woman looked up from her table and gasped, "Gallen? Maggie? Orick?"

Orick had never seen the woman before, of that he was certain, but immediately the diners at all the tables turned to stare. Here and there among the crowd, people shouted, "It's them!" "They've returned!" "Welcome!"

And suddenly a human tide surged from the inn, people shouting, hugging them, giving thanks. A Lord of Ethics, wearing her purple robes of office, rushed to Maggie and fell at her knees, kissing them and then kissing Orick's paw, thanking them all for their part in ending the long siege by the dronon.

As the cry went up, a clamor issued from the city, and soon there were hundreds upon hundreds of people shouting the good news, their voices swelling and blending together in a roar.

When Gallen had first defeated the dronon's Golden Queen and her escort, he'd received accolades from the ambassadors of ten dozen worlds, but Orick had never witnessed anything like this, not this overwhelming, spontaneous outpouring of gratitude.

Someone picked Gallen up on his shoulders, and for one moment Orick saw his golden hair limned in the morning light. Orick suddenly envied the man—a hero on ten thousand worlds—while Orick didn't even know if he'd won the title of Primal Bear of Obhiann and Morgan counties. Only two days before, Orick had been reading the parable of the talents in the Bible, and he wondered if he himself was progressing as God would have him. So often, Orick was content to be—well, just Orick. And somehow that didn't seem enough. He silently vowed to do better.

But just as suddenly, Orick too was lifted by strong hands, and he and Gallen and Maggie and Thomas were carried upon human shoulders into the city.

Orick bawled out for the people to let him go, for it was rather precarious for a fat bear to be carried by humans, but to his delight, they ignored his pleas.

Orick looked forward, and Gallen smiled, pleased but embarrassed by this show of affection, and Orick felt glad for him. Gallen had been cast off from his own world, but it appeared now that he'd won back more than he'd lost.

Maggie, for her part, looked resplendent, a huge grin on her face that you couldn't clean off with lye soap. And Thomas shouted to Orick in glee, "Some welcome, eh, Orick?"

They entered the city of Toohkansay with great fanfare and were treated to feasts. And that night, painters decorated the sky with incandescent clouds of plasma in Gallen's and Maggie's honor. A band of twelve people from various worlds played beautiful instruments that could sing as sweetly as birds or cut a man to the heart, and Thomas took up his lute and played and sang with them, astonishing the people of Toohkansay with his prowess. Upon hearing a ballad that Thomas had composed, a Master Musician honored Thomas by giving him his own mantle, as "just recompense" for the performance. As soon as Thomas had placed the silver mantle upon his head, his eyes began to water as he learned the music of the universe.

Shortly afterward, Thomas was forced to ask Gallen to take him to his rooms for the night, for he needed seclusion.

"I think it's time for all of us to make a night of it," Gallen said.

The mayor of Toohkansay himself offered to escort them to an inn that had the finest rooms in the city, and when they reached the door, he asked Gallen if there was anything he needed for the night.

Gallen said, "I need access to an ansible. I must talk with Lady Everynne."

"Even with an ansible, it takes several hours to send messages so far," the mayor said. He was a tall, bald man whose skin shone as if it were oiled. "Is there a question you have, so that we can ask a response?"

"She set me a task. Tell her that I would like more direction. I'll want to review her response in private."

"As you wish," the mayor said, then he departed.

Gallen and Maggie took one room as man and wife, and they went in.

Orick and Thomas were each given separate rooms across a wide hallway, and they stood for a moment. Thomas closed his eyes and whispered, "Ah, Orick, have you heard the fine music here?" And Orick knew that Thomas was listening through his mantle.

"I've heard some," Orick said.

Thomas shook his head, as if words could not convey what he wanted to say. "I can hear the music of ten thousand worlds, composed over the past thirty-eight thousand years. . . . All of my life has been so . . . cramped, so stilted." Hot tears were flowing from his eyes, and Thomas was weeping bitterly. "How could I have been so blind? There is so much to explore!"

"How do you mean?"

"We're babes, Orick! On Tihrglas, I thought I was at the end of my life. But I'll need an eternity to perfect my skills as a musician, and another to compose my songs!"

Orick looked up at Thomas, at the gray streaks in his hair, and he could see that the aging man was at the beginning of his own incredible adventure. At this very moment, Thomas had his foot stuck in the door of heaven, and he was set to put his shoulder to that door and force it open.

"Well, then," Orick said, for lack of anything better to say, "it's good night to you."

Orick went into his own room, and he sat and thought. Thomas, right now, Orick was sure, was in his room getting his head crammed full of knowledge, probably weeping his eyes out for joy. Gallen was hailed as the hero of ten thousand worlds and was most likely frolicking with the woman he loved most in life.

And Orick, well, Orick tried to sleep on a soft bed, but found it to be too odd. It was large enough, but it hadn't been made to hold a bear, and he sank so low into it that he kept having a spooky feeling that he might drown. So instead he lay on the floor beneath an open window, watching the galaxies pinwheeling overhead, and skyships streaking through the night like meteors. He wondered if he would ever find happiness.

When Orick had been a cub, his mother once told him a tale. She'd said that the hummingbird was the sweetest-tasting of all fowl, for it alone of all birds fed upon the nectar of flowers. She'd said that the sweetest honey tasted bland in comparison.

And so Orick had taken to hiding in a thicket of summer lilies, leaping up after hummingbirds whenever he heard the trill of their wings. But no matter how well he hid, or how quickly he leapt, the hummingbirds would always lift themselves just out of his reach.

Orick drifted asleep, dreaming of jumping, jumping, leaping impossibly high to catch honey-scented hummingbirds, which he held gingerly in his teeth, savoring them.

He heard a chiming noise as Gallen's door opened across the hall, and Orick got up groggily, stepped out into the dark arching corridors of the inn, where gems in the ceiling lit the dim way.

Gallen was standing in the corridor, fully dressed in the black of a Lord Protector.

"What are you about?" Orick asked.

"Shhh . . ." Gallen signaled for Orick to follow him, and they crept down the familiar streets. It was soon obvious to Orick where Gallen was heading: to the quarters where Lord Karthenor dwelt with his aberlains.

But when they reached those offices where Lord Karthenor had enslaved Maggie and dozens of other workers, the buildings were stripped bare. The Dronon guards were gone, the machinery removed.

Gallen walked through a dozen dark rooms, until he reached the last, then stood, staring into nothingness.

"Couldn't sleep, thinking about him?" Orick asked.

"I wondered if he was still here. He would have heard that Maggie and I were back."

"From the scent, I'd say he's been gone a while," Orick said. "The aberlains probably left the day the dronon pulled out."

"Maggie says that the women on this world will conceive children built in the image of the dronon hive," Gallen said distantly. "Some women will have swollen bellies, and they will be breeders, giving birth to six or eight children at a time, as if they were hound bitches.

"Other women will be born to labor, never able to give themselves to a man in love, barren except for an irresistible craving to work from dawn to dusk.

"Some men will be thinkers and planners.

"And some men will be born to war, bred to fight and hate and bully others into worshiping the dronon Golden Queen. And all of this happened because people like Lord Karthenor were willing to sell mankind's secrets to the dronon.

"In all probability, we will suffer for a thousand generations for what Karthenor and his aberlains have done."

Orick didn't understand much about how Karthenor and his aberlains manipulated unborn children into becoming something so strange, but he knew that Karthenor had done unmentionable evil. He'd known it from the moment when Karthenor had placed his Guide upon Maggie's head, enslaving her so that she could be his worker. "Aye, no beating would be great enough to suffice for that man," Orick grumbled.

Behind them, someone cleared his throat, and Orick turned. A man stood in the shadows in a corner, a man wearing the robes and mantle of a Lord

Protector. His robes had so blended into the night, that Orick had not seen him. And Orick could still not smell his scent. "Perhaps he is already paying a penalty," he said.

Gallen turned and studied the stranger.

"I'm Laranac," the man said, "a Lord Protector for this world."

"Do you know where Karthenor is?" Gallen asked.

"He left in great haste, I believe, when the dronon evacuated, taking many of his creations—and his slaves—with him."

Gallen frowned. "How can that be? I've been in a dronon hive city; the stench of their stomach acids fills the air. And the acids dry into a fine powder that blankets everything. A closed ship would be—impossible to bear."

Laranac nodded. "Their kind and ours were not meant to live together. Karthenor knew that. Yet he will suffer for his choice, constantly burning from the acids on the dronon hive ships. The nanodocs in his blood will keep him alive, but at what price? I suspect his exile is a great torment to him."

"A fit ending for the man, as far as I'm concerned," Orick said. "Death would have been too nice."

"No, this is not his end," Gallen whispered, "only a reprieve in torment. Such a painful exile will only madden him, make him want to return that much more quickly."

"And so I keep watch on this place," Laranac said, "hoping for his return. I found a cache of weapons and credit chips hidden in a secret room behind that wall. If Karthenor returns, he will come searching for it, but all he will find is me. I will give him death, when next I see him."

"What of the law?" Gallen asked. "Will you give the man no trial?"

"His memories were on file, along with his gene samples, so that the dronon could rebuild him if he died. Those memories were all the evidence we needed. Karthenor has already been convicted and sentenced to death. I wait now only to mete out his punishment."

Orick considered this bit of news on how evil men were tried here on Tremonthin, and he thought it much better than what had happened with Gallen, back home.

Gallen smiled up at Laranac. "You'll not mete out his punishment, if I get to him first."

"That is unlikely," Laranac said.

Gallen mused, "I am Lord of the Swarm. If I asked the dronon to turn him over, they would do it on a moment's notice."

Orick did not like the idea of having to deal with the dronon. He never wanted to see one of their black carapaces again.

Laranac smiled back at Gallen. "Then do it. Karthenor is a dangerous man, and the fact that he is on a dronon starship hardly hinders his work. He must be stopped."

"Soon," Gallen said. "I'll make arrangements. But I've urgent business elsewhere for the moment. If it takes a week for him to be delivered, I'm afraid I can't be here to meet Karthenor at the spaceport."

"I can," Laranac said. "Send for him."

"I will, first thing tomorrow. Until then, keep watching this place," Gallen said. "And I shall sleep better tonight."

Gallen turned to leave, but Laranac caught his arm. "Be careful," Laranac whispered fervently. "A new government is forming on this world, one that recognizes the Lady Everynne as Semmaritte's heir and as a rightful judge. They are eager to join once again in the Consortium of Worlds. But there are other voices crying to be heard on the councils. There are other Karthenors on the loose—brutal people who lost profit and prestige when the dronon evacuated. Such people would not bear you into the city upon their shoulders. They would rather trample you under their feet."

"You think I am in danger?" Gallen asked.

"The mayor of Toohkansay is protecting you now, the best he knows how. But if you left soon, you would be doing him a favor—and perhaps you would save your own lives."

Gallen nodded almost imperceptibly. Gallen and Orick returned to their chambers, and when Orick was alone, he offered up more than his usual nightly prayers.

The next day dawned bright and clear. Gallen sent a message to Everynne to be relayed to the dronon Vanquishers, asking that Karthenor and any other such humans carried away in Dronon ships be returned to their home worlds for judging and sentencing.

For a bit in the morning, Orick was edgy, watchful, but the mood soon vanished like the morning mists burning off the wide river. The celebrations continued all throughout the day, and Orick found it difficult under such circumstances to believe that anyone would wish Maggie and Gallen harm.

On the contrary, at every turn people sought Maggie and Gallen out to offer favors. The finest clothiers arrayed Gallen, Maggie, and Maggie's honored uncle Thomas in their best wares, and perfumers brought their most exotic scents. Musicians and actors played before them, while chefs plied them with fine food and technologists brought tokens of knowledge for Gallen and Maggie to place in their mantles.

Those who were poor came and told tales of woe, describing the horrible tyranny they had suffered under the dronon. Those who were weak, or deformed, or belligerent, or brave had been annihilated under dronon rule. Their bodies were processed for fertilizer by unfeeling dronon overlords.

And so the poor people of Fale told unending tales of woe, then thanked Gallen and Maggie. From all across the planet, the grateful people of Fale came to give honor.

The whole affair was dizzying and extravagant beyond anything that Orick had ever dreamed, and all through the day he watched Gallen, gauging the look upon his face. He seemed worn, worried, and not until that evening when the brewers of Fale convinced him to try their dearest vintages of wine did those lines of worry begin to ease.

That night, as they returned to their rooms, the mayor of Toohkansay walked with them once again, and he was laughing, smiling. Thomas had his lute out, and he sang softly as he walked.

Outside the door to Maggie's apartment, a large, intricately carved crystal vase held a perfect white rose with petals so lustrous they shone like pearl. A note beneath the flower said, "A Token of Our Esteem."

"Ah," the mayor said, "it looks as if the hotel has left you a special gift."

Thomas cooed in appreciation, and reached down for the vase, but the mayor said, "Let me get that for you!"

As he touched the vase, the rose petals suddenly whirred and spun like a pinwheel, blurring into the air, striking him in the face. Blood and flesh spattered across the hallway, and there was cracking as the rose cut through his skull, then rose petals exploded outward.

The mayor's head seemed to implode, the broken skull sagging in on itself, and he fell face first to the floor.

Maggie screamed and backed away, and Orick looked up. Thomas stood in shock, holding his wrist. A delicate-looking petal of rose had lodged in his wrist, like a knife blade.

Gallen spun, looking down the hallway, as if expecting attackers to come, and in seconds, four men rushed down from both ends of the corridor, all of them with weapons drawn. They looked at the mayor, watched down both sides of the corridor.

One of them was shouting into a tiny microphone at his lapel, "Security breach, code one! Man down!"

The men took defensive postures on either side of the corridor, placing themselves between Maggie and any would-be attackers.

In another minute, a dozen more soldiers arrived, including several of the green giants like the "demon" that Thomas had displayed at the inn. The sight of those creatures dismayed Thomas more than anything, so the soldiers were forced to rush Thomas and the others into their own room, where they waited for a medic, who used clamps and nanoware to begin healing the cut ligaments in Thomas's wrist.

Thomas just sat on his bed during the whole procedure, cursing the folks who had done this.

"It was nanoware," Maggie said to herself once in the room. "They were after me and Gallen."

"Aye," Thomas said, "it looks as if you've made some enemies here, while collecting worshipers."

"But I don't understand," Maggie whispered. "They could have found so many easier ways to kill me—a bomb, a poisoned scent in the flower. Even if they'd wanted to use nanoware, there were so many things they could have done. They could have stripped every atom of copper from my body . . . torn away my ability to remember—any one of a thousand things. So why the rose?"

"They weren't just trying to kill you," Thomas suggested. "Perhaps the saboteur wanted to do more than kill you. He wanted to send a message."

"Of course," Gallen said. "Whoever put the flower there believed that killing Maggie would be pointless. Her memories could just be downloaded into a clone. So the flower was a message from her enemies."

"But what does it mean?" Orick asked.

The medic who was attending Thomas's wound looked up. "Beware of beautiful appearances," he said, with almost too much certainty. "Things are not as they seem."

"Are they warning us away from the Tharrin?" Gallen asked. "Lady Everynne?"

"That may be. Not all people trust the Tharrin. Though they are beautiful, they are not truly human. On the other hand, perhaps the rose was not meant as a message to you," the medic said. "Perhaps it was a message to the rest of the world. This weapon was intended to kill Maggie, and she too is beautiful. Perhaps the killers were trying to warn the people of Fale away from her."

"You're talking gibberish, man," Orick said, certain the medic was on the wrong track. Maggie was not a leader on Fale. No, the rose had to signify the Tharrin, but Orick knew the Lady Everynne well. The Tharrin were good folks, and only a person with a warped mind would fear otherwise.

The medic shrugged. "I'm only making wild guesses. The only person who really knows what the message meant is out there somewhere." He waved toward the city.

He applied some nanodocs to the wound, then bandaged it, and left.

When they were alone, Gallen took an object from his robe—a white metal triangle with a lens set at each corner.

"You've a message?" Maggie said, taking the contraption from his hand.

"The mayor gave it to me earlier. It's from Everynne."

Maggie set the thing on the floor, and asked the room to lower the lights.

"Everynne," she called softly, and suddenly the image of Everynne appeared in the room, her dark hair gleaming, resplendent in a pale blue gown. Thomas gasped at her beauty, and Orick studied the fine bones of her jaw, the keen intellect behind her eyes. In the brief weeks since Orick had last seen her, he found that time had blurred her image, so he tried to burn the Tharrin woman into his memory.

"I had suspected that you would call me, Gallen," the holoimage said, "and I will give you what little help I can. I need you to go to Tremonthin, a world like yours where mankind has rejected most technologies, with one exception: in the City of Life the Lords of Tremonthin have dedicated themselves to developing life-extending technologies. There they download memories into clones of those worthy for immortality. There, they fight disease and suffering. And for twenty millennia the world has had but one export—children who are engineered to live on worlds that other humans cannot inhabit, or who are engineered to fulfill roles that other humans cannot. Many of these altered people live on Tremonthin still, for the Lords of that world do not force their creations into exile but give them their choice of staying or leaving.

"My ancestors, the Tharrin, were created on Tremonthin eighteen thousand years ago to be judges and rulers of mankind, and for this reason Tremonthin was one of the first worlds that the dronon sought to conquer. It appears that they murdered all of the Tharrin there, but one survived with the help of technicians from the City of Life. And she has been hunted by a thing called the Inhuman.

"I have no information on the Inhuman. It seems to be a secret society, formed by the descendants of genetically upgraded people. We lost ansible contact with Tremonthin years ago, but rebels working on a ship that visited the City of Life in the past three months were able to smuggle out the small recording that I sent you, along with a request that the rebellion send a Lord Protector. They must have known that Veriasse and I were traveling between the world gates, for the message says that someone will meet you at the gate.

"Gallen, this will be no easy task. Those who are genetically upgraded and who choose to remain on Tremonthin are often banished from human lands, and in those lands the fiercest variations of mankind thrive.

"I would come with you if I could, Gallen," Everynne said, and her voice caught a little as she said it. "Since I don't know the dimensions of this problem, I fear the worst. Certainly, the rebels on Tremonthin were desperate, for they sent their plea knowing that the dronon would almost certainly discover the recording. Still, they hoped that one Lord Protector, alone, could handle their problems—as I also hope.

"Be strong, but be wise," Everynne said. "Come back to us alive."

The message ended, and Gallen stood looking at the holograph thoughtfully.

"Well, we'd better get going," Orick offered after a moment of silence, hoping to prod the others into immediate action. It would feel good to be back in Everynne's service, to be doing something important.

"The mayor spoke with me earlier," Gallen said. "He'd readied a flier. We can leave in the morning."

"But folks are waiting for us!" Orick said.

"They've been waiting for months," Gallen countered. "We'll need our rest. They can wait one night longer."

Thomas had been sitting quietly, watching the holograph, and he cleared his throat. He was waxing the tips of his moustache, twirling them thoughtfully. "Gallen, Orick, Maggie—you may do as you please. But I'll be staying."

"No you won't," Gallen said. "There are only four people on this planet who know where Maggie and I are going—and all of them are in this room. And sometime in the next few weeks, at least one dronon hive queen will come hunting for Maggie, and I'll have to be at her side to protect her. I'd rather they didn't find us, so I can't leave any witnesses behind. So, you see, sir, that I can't let you stay!"

Gallen's jaw was set, his eyes stony. Orick knew that look. It was the same look that hill robbers always saw just before Gallen pulled his knives and gutted them.

"I'll not have you talking down to me in that tone," Thomas said. "I've got my own dreams in life, my own path to take, and I don't fancy that running off with you will get me where I want to go. It appears to me that you three are just targets for trouble: you bring it down on yourselves wherever you go, and I'm not a fighting man. If I stay long in your presence, I'm sure to get killed."

Thomas quit twirling his moustache and tentatively held his bandaged wrist, clenching and unclenching his fingers experimentally.

"You'll be under my protection," Gallen said forcefully. "I've never lost someone who was under my protection."

"Well, it's mighty convenient that you weren't hired by that fellow who is lying dead out in the hall, isn't it?" Thomas grumbled. "We wouldn't want to ruin your reputation."

Gallen frowned at the haughty tone in Thomas's voice.

Orick realized that this argument was beginning to escalate. As a bear studying for the priesthood, he felt it his duty to calm these folks.

He rose up on his hind feet, catching their attention. "I'm sure that Thomas is no coward, Gallen. After all, he's smarted off to every mayor and usurer in Tihrglas for forty years. So, if he doesn't want to come, he must have his reasons."

"I know what he's after—" Gallen said, "he's after a comfortable retirement!"

"I'm sure you misjudge the man. . . ." Orick soothed, but Thomas began laughing, deep and hearty.

"Oh, Orick, Gallen has judged the man right! I've *earned* my rest. The food here is good, the people gracious . . ."—he flexed his fingers experimentally—"for the most part. And, frankly, I'm a paying customer. I paid to come here—not to go to someplace worse off than Tihrglas!"

"Nevertheless, that's where we're going," Gallen said, as if the discussion were final.

"Look," Thomas said. "I'm an old man. You can't be ordering me about!"

"You were quick to order *me* about when it suited your fancy!" Maggie countered.

Gallen was staring icily at Thomas, and he took the older man by the collar. "You're coming with us," Gallen said. "I'll leave no witnesses behind—at least not live ones. This isn't a game I'm playing, Thomas. If you stay here, you put us at risk, and I'll not be looking over my shoulder because of you! Once this is all over, I'll bring you back here, if you want, or send you to any other planet!"

Thomas fixed him with a gaze, and Thomas's own face took on a closed look. Orick suddenly found that he didn't trust the man. "So, the ferryman has taken my money, and now he plans to row the boat where he will! Well, it sounds to me as if you're cheating me out of my life savings, Gallen. I commend you for that. I admire a man who is willing to take what he wants." He sighed, and his gaze turned inward. "All right then, Gallen, I'll come with you to your damned world—but it *is* a comfortable retirement I'm after. I'll find me a nice inn and settle down for a bit, work on my music. When you're done with your task, you can come back and bring me here, if I so desire. Agreed?"

Gallen nodded, and the two men shook hands.

Thomas stood taller, stretched and yawned. "Very well, then. I suspect that tomorrow will be a long day. Wake me in the morning."

Orick sighed in relief, now that the matter was settled. Gallen, Maggie, and Thomas went to their rooms.

Sometime well before dawn, Maggie rushed back into Orick's quarters, waking him. Orick had never seen her so mad; she had tears in her eyes.

"Orick, get up! We've got problems. We just got another message from Everynne. We've got to leave Tremonthin now! The dronon are here, and I just went to that lousy Thomas's room. He left us a good-bye note, and ran sneaking off sometime in the night!"

"Oh, damn him!" Orick grumbled, realizing that Thomas had only made a pretense of being reasonable. She held a note in her hand, and Orick read it quickly.

Dear Maggie:

Now, don't be cross at me, darling, but by the time you read this, I'll be off on my own adventures. I'm afraid I'm getting old and plump, and if you don't mind, I'd rather spend some time on a nice, safe world like this. You go ahead and tramp down the dark roads, if that's what your heart is after, but for me, I want nothing more than a warm mug of whiskey by the fire, some soft music, and a woman who loves me just for warming her bed.

I know that Gallen is worrying that I'll tell someone about you folks going you-know-where, but I promise not to whisper a peep about it, even in my dreams. So don't you fret. And don't waste your time trying to hunt me down. I've eluded my share of assassins in my time, and I know how to disappear when I want to.

Now, I must say that I've been pleased to be making your acquaintance, Maggie. You're a fine-looking woman, and I'm glad you're a

Flynn. But you do have your mother's way about you. I sometimes think my brother drowned himself just to escape your mother's vile temper. And if I know you, you're probably so mad right now, I could fry an egg on your forehead. But someday, maybe you'll thank me for leaving.

With no apologies,
Thomas

Maggie placed a holoprojector cube on the floor, then went to Orick's pack, began throwing it together.

The holoprojector flared to life, and an image appeared—a dronon Vanquisher with a dusty black carapace and glistening amber wings. The insect-like creature squatted on four hind legs, and its forward battle arms were crossed on the ground. The dronon's head was to the ground, so that his forward eyes looked at the dust while his backward eye cluster pointed upward. It was the dronon stance of obeisance.

"Oh, great Golden, admired by all," a translator said in English while the dronon's mouthfingers clicked over the voice drums beneath its jaws. "I bear messages of congratulations from the Tincin and Tlinini, Lords of the Fourth Swarm; and from Kininic and Nickit, Lords of the Fifth Swarm; and from In and Tlik, Lords of the Third Swarm; and from Cintkin and Kintiniklintit, Lords of the Seventh Swarm. All of these speak their adoration, and announce their intent to challenge you and the great Gallen O'Day to combat for the right to rule the Sixth Swarm of Dronon."

The image faded, and Everynne stood in the creature's place. "Maggie, I wanted to give you and Gallen time to prepare, to rest. But that time has been cut short. I received this message, and immediately afterward registered a power fluctuation to the Gate of the World. The Lords of the Seventh Swarm are coming, and they know you are on Fale. They may be there already. Flee."

Orick's heart began beating hard. He had imagined that in time, Golden Queens from within the swarm that Gallen and Maggie nominally controlled would grow and demand to battle for the right to govern, but he had not considered that lords from the other swarms of Dronon would seek them out.

"They're all coming for you," Orick muttered, in shock. "The dronon attack only those that they believe are weak. They must think that you and Gallen are the weakest lords of all."

"We are," Maggie said. And she handed him his pack.

Ten

After notifying Orick of the danger, Maggie rushed to her room, then took off her nightgown and dressed in the burnt-orange-colored robes of a Lord of Technicians and donned a pale green mask to hide her face. Gallen threw her nightgown in her bags.

After she dressed, Maggie stood for a moment, trying to wake, thinking furiously. She wondered where Thomas might have gone. Her uncle seemed willing to cause her any amount of trouble. She doubted that he would willingly betray her—his notions of the duties to kin would extend too far for that—but Maggie knew too well that what he was willing to tell and what he would be forced to tell were two different things.

"Quickly," Gallen said as he took Maggie's hand and they rushed out the door. "My mantle is picking up dronon radio signals. The Lords of the Swarm are heading for the city."

Orick was in the hall. Gallen did not slow for him, but as they hurried down the corridors, Gallen kept watching down side passages, as if hoping to find Thomas wandering the halls. "That old fool will cost us dear," Gallen murmured. "The dronon will have the city in an hour."

In two minutes they were on the roof of the city, where half a dozen fliers were parked. Gallen rushed to them, spoke his name and commanded the fliers to open.

Only one of the fliers obeyed his command—a four-man flier. Maggie jumped in the pilot's seat, while Orick scrambled to fit into a space entirely too small for a bear of his bulk.

"Hurry! They've reached the city," Gallen shouted. As if to emphasize his point, emergency sirens began whining all across the city. Orick squeezed in, filling two seats.

"Head north at normal air speed. We don't want to attract attention," Maggie commanded the flier's on-board intelligence while Gallen took out his map and looked for the coordinates to the gate to Tremonthin. The flier lurched into the air, and Maggie looked down.

An army of dronon Vanquishers was marching in the night, carrying lights before them. They churned and seethed, like giant ants seen from a distance. They had nearly reached the city. Fortunately, the entrance to the Gate of the World was too small to allow them to bring in their own heavy fliers, and Maggie sighed in relief.

They surged upward for ten minutes, then slowed. In that brief time, the flier had traveled a thousand miles, and in moments they were on the ground beside an ancient metal arch in a northern desert. The rocks stood out in sharp relief all around them, and in the distance, Maggie could hear wild dogs barking. The night was warm, yet she shivered.

Maggie commanded the on-board intelligence of the flier to erase its memories of this trip, then sent it back to the city, arching up toward a high cloud whose edges were silvered in the moonlight.

Maggie stood breathing the air of Fale for a moment as if she were readying to plunge into cold water, then pulled out the key to the Gate of the World and began entering codes. The air under the gate shivered a brilliant magenta.

"Remember," Gallen said. "We are traveling in disguise. Do not mention our names."

Maggie took her bags, handed Gallen the key, then walked into the magenta light. She felt the familiar sense of being lifted impossibly high into the air, and in a moment she was standing in a field yellow with ripe wheat, white with the bitter-smelling flowers of wild carrots. Tall daisies with beer-colored hearts swayed in the wind. They were in the folds of a valley, and on the hill behind her, golden oaks swayed.

Maggie could hear the distant sound of a marketplace, the cries of street vendors, the bawling of goats. She glanced over her shoulder. A light building rose above the oaks not two hundred yards away—a curious temple the color of the wheat, with five spires rising high above the hill. Banners flew from each spire, red with images of twin orange suns. Along the parapets of the temple walked a man, a broad-shouldered man in a red tunic, with thick braids of golden hair. Maggie studied him a moment, vaguely distressed by his appearance, until she realized that the man could be no less than nine feet tall.

White ghosts blurred into existence at Maggie's side, as if emerging up from the grass, and suddenly Orick and Gallen stood beside her.

They stood for a moment, looking about, and Orick growled, pointed to Maggie's left. On the next hill, a dronon's walking hive city squatted on six giant legs, like some great black tick. The incendiary gun turrets that bristled on its back were unmanned, and had in fact been stripped off, but the red lights at the hatches glowed like squinting eyes.

Maggie found herself suddenly wary. The hive city was uninhabited as far as she could see. Yet it served as an unsavory reminder that this world had been under dronon control only days before.

"Where do we go now?" Orick asked, looking about.

"To find the Lady Ceravanne," Gallen said uncertainly. There was a depression in the hill, a hollow where someone had perhaps mined rocks. Gallen went to it, hunching down beneath the shelter of an odd, twisted green stump to get out of sight of the temple walls. The others followed. Gallen reached into his bags and brought out his map of Tremonthin. It showed two large continents near each other, and from the map Maggie could see that they were on the eastern coast of the northern continent, but the map did not show cities, for it was far older than cities, so it showed only images of the approximate terrain and the nearest gates.

Maggie studied the map. "Ceravanne could be anywhere, thousands of miles from here."

"The dronon can't have left more than a week ago," Gallen pointed out. "A Tharrin will be precious rare on this world. If Ceravanne is near, perhaps others will know of her."

But Maggie was not so certain. This world was nearly as backward as her home on Tihrglas. She looked up the hill and noticed that the stump above them had a faded rope tied to it, with a small leather purse attached. She wondered if it had been left there on purpose. Perhaps there was a letter inside, bearing instructions. She began climbing toward it.

Gallen sighed heavily. "I want to travel secretly," he said, hunching lower into the grass, "stay on back roads and sleep in the woods."

"And if I had your face, I'd keep it hidden, too," Orick jested, trying to lighten Gallen's mood. "Any sack would do fine."

"The young man has a fine face," a strange whispering voice said. The voice was almost a groan, or the yawn of a waking man. And most startling of all was that it came from the stump!

Maggie looked higher, and saw that the tree stump was staring down at her. The creature that watched them was the most amazing thing she had ever seen: it had deep brown eyes set high up on the uppermost ridge of its long, narrow head, and leaves crowned its top. Its long arms and legs each had many knobby growths, so that no two joints were at the same height. And it had been holding its hands up toward the sun as if it were praying, or warming itself. Each long hand had many fingers. Its mouth was a leathery crack at the bottom of its head, and two holes in its face might have been a nose. But Maggie could see no ears on the creature, and it wore no clothes. She could see no sign of sex organs or an anus.

"Soooh, you have come at last," the creature said slowly. "But I am patient, as *she* is patient."

"She?" Gallen said. "You mean Ceravanne?"

The green man did not answer, but instead looked down in concentration. It twisted its right leg, pulling many toes from deep in the rocky yellow soil. Then, with equally great effort, it pulled its left leg free from the earth.

Its skin looked like forest-green leather, and the three-pronged leaves on its head rustled as if blown in the wind.

"What are you doing?" Orick demanded, as if he were questioning a young rascal.

"Drinking rainwater, tasting sun," the green man answered.

"And who are you?" Orick asked.

"I have no name, but you may call me Bock, for I am of the race of Bock, and we are all one."

The green man swiveled, and began walking slowly down the gully on long legs that covered a great distance. In two steps it was staring at them in the hollow.

"So, you have taken shelter?" the Bock addressed them. "Sitting with backs to the wall, facing out." It seemed to consider this for a moment. "That is a human trait." Maggie had never noticed it before, but it was indeed a human trait to take such a stance, one that humans shared with bears.

"Aye," Gallen said, climbing out of the hollow, eyeing the Bock.

"You speak strangely," the Bock said. "Were you born speaking this way, or did you learn to speak by listening to your parents?"

Maggie had never heard of anyone who had not been born knowing how to talk. "I was born speaking thus," Gallen muttered. He rested his free hand on his dagger.

"Good," the Bock said, his strange eyes widening at Gallen's threatening action. "Then you are not from feral human stock, but have had some genetic upgrading. I see that you also wear heavy clothes, which speaks of a strong *enclosure* quotient."

"A what?" Gallen asked.

"Humans of most subspecies seek enclosure," the Bock said in slow, even words. "They house themselves in cavelike enclosures at all opportunities, and drape their bodies in bits of hide or vegetation. The amount of covering they desire is a guide to their enclosure quotient, and this can help me make a judgment as to how *human* the specimen is."

"You mean that different people want to wear different amounts of clothes?" Gallen asked.

"It varies by subspecies of human," the Bock said.

"That's mad," Gallen said. "We wear clothes to protect ourselves from the weather."

"You are a Lord Protector," the Bock said, half a question. "The weather is warm. Why don't you take off your clothes? You don't need them here."

"I would rather keep them on," Gallen said. "I need the hood, to hide my identity."

"No one will recognize you," the Bock assured, putting his long green hand on Gallen's shoulder, pulling back his robe to expose flesh, and Maggie counted nine fingers on that hand. "Here on Tremonthin, you are unknown. You may show your face freely. You may show your whole body freely."

The Bock's actions were strange and frightening, but Maggie could also sense that it meant no harm. Its touch was not rough or lecherous. It seemed instead to be—*perplexed* by Gallen. Curious about him, and totally alien.

Gallen stared up at the creature, shrugged his shoulder away from it. "Why are you so intent on taking off my clothes?"

"Why are you so intent to keep them on? Does the thought of your nakedness frighten you?" Gallen didn't answer, and the Bock whispered, "What kind of fear must you possess to be a Lord Protector, to feel so threatened that you must kill all the time?"

"Gallen's not afraid of anyone, you green galoot," Orick said.

"It's all right," Gallen said, studying the Bock.

"Soooh, if you are unafraid," the Bock said slowly, "take off some of your clothes. You wear your weapons as casually as another man wears his belt. Take them off, and your robes also."

Gallen smiled up at the creature's challenging tone. He unbuckled his knife belt and dropped his weapons, watching the Bock carefully. He then pulled off his robe and mantle, stripped off his tunic so that he wore only his hose and tight black boots. The Bock made a gasping noise as if in approval. "Some subspecies on this planet could not divest themselves of clothes or weapons so easily," he said. "Their enclosure quotient is too high. But if you are truly courageous, you will come with me now into the marketplace, unarmed."

He turned and began walking uphill. Gallen didn't move, and the Bock reached back and took his hand, leading Gallen. "No one will harm you. You will be in the company of a Bock."

He led Gallen forward, and Orick growled. "What about us?"

"Stay here," the Bock said. "We will return shortly. Gallen should come naked into this world."

"Wait one minute!" Maggie said. "I don't know if I like the idea of you taking off with that—thing! Leaving us alone!"

Gallen looked up at the Bock quizzically, then glanced back at Maggie. "I . . . don't think he means us any harm," Gallen said.

"No," the Bock said. "We wish no harm, to you or anyone else."

"But is it safe for us to be alone here?" Maggie asked.

"No one disturbs the temple grounds by daylight," the Bock said. "I have been here for weeks, and only the priests come into this field. But people like you would best seek shelter at night." The Bock took Gallen's hand and led him off up the hill and into the trees.

Maggie and Orick waited in the little hollow until one hour passed, then two. Heavy clouds rolled in. Still, Gallen did not return with the Bock.

Near sunset it began to rain, a light warm drizzle. Minute by minute, Maggie began to worry that perhaps the Bock was not as harmless as he seemed, that perhaps he had set some kind of a trap. He'd said he would be back before dark.

As darkness drew on, a huge gonging rang out, and the cries of street vendors in the village over the hill went silent just as the rain stopped. The thick gray clouds created a false darkness. It seemed somehow spooky the way the vendors all stopped crying out so suddenly.

Whenever Maggie mentioned the time, Orick had encouraging words to say. "Gallen will be back shortly. He won't get lost. Nothing bad has happened." But at last, Orick admitted, "I don't know what Gallen's thinking, but he should be back by now!"

"Shall we search the city?" Maggie asked. "You can probably track Gallen by scent."

Orick nodded uncertainly, began sniffing. Maggie bundled up Gallen's packs, wrapping them all in his robe. They climbed over the hill, to the back of the temple, walked around it, and looked out over a large bay filled with sailing ships. Tall, elegant stone buildings surrounded the bay, and the nearer hills were filled with homes made of fine wood. Twin suns had just set golden in the distance. The air carried the smoke of evening fires and the tempting odor of food cooking, heavy with the scent of ginger and curry. Night was coming quickly.

Overhead, the clouds were whipping away, and ragged patches of evening sky came into view, showing a small scattering of stars.

"Don't worry," Orick said softly. "I'm sure I'll find Gallen soon."

Maggie shook her head violently. "Don't give me that. Something's wrong. Gallen wouldn't just leave."

"Perhaps that Bock creature has him jumping through hoops somewhere," Orick said.

"I don't understand Gallen sometimes," Maggie said as if to herself, "running off unarmed with some strange . . . *thing*, on a world he's never set foot on."

"Och, he's a young man," Orick said. "You have to let them act the part of fools—you couldn't stop them anyway."

A wind was blowing in off the sea, carrying an evening chill. Orick stood just beside Maggie, close enough so that she could feel his body heat. She trembled slightly, stroked his back.

Down the street several blocks, a man turned a corner, walking toward them, but when he noticed them, he immediately turned back, ducking behind a house.

Orick licked his lips, raised his nose in the air to taste the scent. Maggie started forward, but Orick stopped her. "Wait a minute, darling," he whispered. "You had better strap on one of Gallen's swords and a dagger. I've got a cold feeling that an unarmed person wouldn't last long on these streets at night."

Maggie reached into the bag, pulled out Gallen's vibro-blade, felt it begin to activate as it registered her body heat on the handle. She strapped on a knife belt for good measure.

"What should we do?" Maggie asked.

"I'd feel more comfortable in a nice crowded building," Orick said. "This is a port. Surely there's a hostel down at seaside."

"I've decided to stay out of off-world inns," Maggie whispered. "Every time I go in one, I get into a hell of a lot of trouble."

"Well, a young girl traveling with a vicious bear to protect her, what kind of trouble could she get into?" Orick reasoned, and he led the way, heading through the broad streets toward the sea..

• • •

After a half mile, they entered the business district, where four-story buildings lined the street, each with its own elaborate columned portico. The doors were all locked. By the docks they found an inn where they could see inside broad windows. A cheery fire was set in a large hearth, and the inn was so crowded that many of the patrons stood around drinking and laughing, unable to sit down at a table to eat. Maggie took the door handle and began shaking it, trying to get in, but the door was locked. She rapped it with the butt of her dagger, and a man with a thin face came to the window beside the door, shaking his head, shouting, "Too dark! Go away!"

"Let us in!" Orick called, but the innkeep turned away. Maggie could tell when a man acted out of fear and when he could not be pushed. She didn't bother rapping at the door again.

Maggie wandered out into the middle of the street, looking both ways. It seemed safer out there, where no one could creep up on them unawares. It was getting quite dark now, and moths banged softly against some of the more well-lighted windows. A mosquito buzzed at Maggie's neck, and she slapped it.

"Which way do we go?" Maggie asked. "North or south?"

Orick stood sniffing. "Back over the hill," Orick said. "I can't taste Gallen's scent at all. Maybe they'll come back for us."

But if Gallen were here on the streets, Maggie figured that she'd spot him half a mile away, and it seemed likely that he'd be coming down the street to find her. Maggie turned up the north road, and Orick followed. A bat swooped in front of them, dipping twice for mosquitoes. Maggie welcomed its presence, figuring that for every mosquito it ate, there was one less mosquito to dine upon her.

Just as the bat swooped in front of them a third time, something enormous fluttered over Maggie's head—something large enough so that its wingspan could have been no less than fifteen feet. Orick bowled Maggie forward, and as she fell she saw the creature grab the little bat out of the sky with a quick snatching motion of one wing.

Then the dark creature flapped up the road where Maggie and Orick had been heading and landed atop the portico of a building.

Maggie blinked. The creature had the wings of a bat, and a bat's catlike ears. It looked for all the world like a bat itself, except for its milky golden eyes. It sat on the portico, staring at Maggie and Orick, and gingerly began feeding on the bat it had caught.

Maggie got up off the muddy road, dusted off her hands, then slowly advanced. The creature sniffed the air as she approached. "Niccce night," it whispered as they neared. "The sstarsss glimmer like firesss in the bowl of heaven." It glanced up. "And the moonsss cassst their golden light on the earth."

Something about the way the creature spoke bothered Maggie. There was a threat behind its words, and she felt as if she should answer. The creature tore a wing from the bat, stuffed it in its mouth and began crunching the tiny bones.

Maggie looked up at the sky. There were no moons shining, and she guessed at the coded message the bat-thing had given her. It had said the word "golden," and immediately it brought to mind the golden color of the dronon's hive queen that Gallen had killed a couple of weeks before. She stammered, "Yet their light is not so great as that cast by our Golden Queen."

The creature on the portico looked at her long, stopped tearing apart its prey. Instead, it took the remainder of the body, stuffed it in its mouth, and swallowed the bat in one gulp.

"My brother and sissster, how goesss your hunt tonight?" the creature asked.

"The streets are empty, as you see. We've found no one," Maggie said, praying that she answered correctly. Maggie felt tense to the breaking point. If this creature chose to attack them, there would be no way to escape it. Not with all the doors in town locked against them. She'd have to fight, and she was no great hand with a sword.

"In the harbor liesss a ssship, the third to the north. I sssaw a hatch open, and men inssside were making merry. They think themsselvesss ssecure."

Maggie forced a smile. The creature's intentions were clear. It expected Orick and Maggie to prey upon those men, in the same way that it preyed upon the bat.

"Thank you," Orick said, touching Maggie's hip with his snout, turning toward the harbor. She could hear the tautness in his voice. "Come," he whispered to Maggie. She could tell that he was frightened, that like her, Orick only wanted to get out of there.

We're in this deeper than I'd imagined, Maggie realized. They'd come to this world seeking the Inhuman, and if she guessed right, the Inhuman had found *them*—in a matter of hours.

Maggie forced herself to turn, follow Orick on legs that felt as unresponsive as wood.

The bat began whistling, an odd, meandering tune that sounded more like some code than music. Maggie silently prayed that no one was listening, for she felt sure that if other creatures like this one were near, they would attack. She slipped Gallen's dagger from its sheath. Sometimes, when things had been slow in the inn back home, she had sat in the kitchen with John Mahoney, throwing knives into a target on the wall, above the bread table. John had always insisted that it was a skill that could come in handy someday. Maggie was fairly accurate at a distance of thirty or forty feet, but this creature was more like sixty feet away. Still, it was her only chance.

She hefted the knife half a moment, testing its balance, then whirled and threw high, fearing that the knife was heavier than she was used to.

The knife sailed through the air, and the batlike creature jumped. The heavy knife glanced off the creature's face, and it squealed and fell from the portico, flapping its wings as it tried to fly.

In half a moment Orick was there, leaping atop the creature with all of his weight. She heard the sickening snick of bones cracking when Orick landed, and Orick took the creature's head in his jaws before it could cry out. Orick swung his mighty head back and forth, decapitating the creature. He slapped the dead body and lunged away in disgust, then changed his mind and pounced on it again.

"Enough, enough! It's dead!" Maggie cried.

Orick looked at her and roared, choking out strangled sounds, shivering violently.

"Come—come away from here," Maggie said, and she turned.

They hurried north, up the broad avenue, away from the bloody mess behind them, running from the horror of it rather than searching for Gallen.

Somewhere in the air high above and behind them, Maggie heard a shrill whistle, as if from a seaman's pipe—but the sound moved toward them. She glanced back, and in the light of three small, swiftly rising moons saw a huge bat-shape flapping toward them.

In a moment it was overhead, and it landed on a tall building before them, out of throwing distance. It held something shiny in its mouth, and the shrill whistle came again.

Maggie froze, turned to head back down the street, but three men were rushing up the street behind them—if men you could call them. Two were large men in dark robes—too large to be human, but a third hairy man with a misshapen head was hunched low on the ground, running on its knuckles.

Maggie glanced forward, saw another huge brute rush into the street ahead of her.

"This way!" Orick growled, gingerly nipping Maggie's arm in his teeth to guide her. They ran to the nearest shop, and Orick charged the door full force. The door splintered and broke into pieces, but Orick had hit his head against a metal crossbeam that held. The poor bear was knocked unconscious, and he lay there like a sack of flour.

Maggie glanced both ways up the street, saw the four men closing the distance rapidly. She climbed past Orick. Orick lay on the ground in a tumble of splintered wood. He was groaning, and looked up at her weakly, squinting, then his head sagged to the ground.

Maggie turned and brandished her sword, weaving the weapon forward. She'd seen how much damage it could do. It could rip through a human body as easily as slicing melons. From inside the shop, the streets seemed washed in moonlight.

The great hulk reached the building first, stood gazing in the doorway, looking down at Orick, who was still unconscious.

In seconds, the others stood outside the building, panting. One of the men smiled, said easily, "What do you think you're doing? Running? What do you fear?"

"Not you," Maggie said, brandishing the sword.

One hulk held a club. He went to a huge window of the shop where bowls and urns were displayed, and began shattering the glass, widening his access to Maggie.

"Was that your handiwork down the street?" the first man said, a worried expression on his brow. "That poor scout. Not much left of him now."

Maggie glanced at the broken panes in the window. One piece thrust upward like a tooth. Absently, the hulk outside kicked it, breaking it off.

"Stay back!" Maggie warned. "Move along." Her hands were sweaty, and she gripped the hilt of the sword more tightly. The sword seemed to hum, reacting to her fear.

The man in the doorway laughed uneasily. "Come with us. A pretty young thing like you, you belong with us."

"Ah, I'll bet she's human," the hulk said. "She wants nothing to do with us."

"Is that it?" the smiling man asked. "Are you too good for us? Are you sure? I can show you something beautiful. I have a Word for you. You might like it." He reached into the pocket of his tunic, and she knew she did not want to see what he brought out.

Orick moaned at her feet, shifting the shattered door as he tried to get up, then he fell down, and Maggie realized that he would not get up, would not be able to come to her aid. And Maggie recalled something Gallen had once told her: when opponents know that the odds are vastly in their favor, they never expect you to leap into battle.

With a shout, Maggie bounded over the windowsill, swinging the sword with all her fury. The blade caught the hulk at the midriff, slicing through his belly. She whirled and let the blade arc into the smiler, slicing him in two before he could get his hand out of his pocket. Suddenly, Maggie was on the sidewalk, dancing past two dead men.

The hairy man on his knuckles shrieked and tried to leap backward, throwing his hands up to protect his face, and Maggie whacked off his hands while slicing open his face, turned to her last foe who shouted, "Ah, damn you!" and leapt backward.

He drew his own sword ringing from its sheath, and from the cornice of the building above them, the batlike creature blasted its shrill whistle three times.

The swordsman didn't give her a second to think, merely advanced on her, his sword blurring in the moonlight. Maggie was far outmatched in swordsmanship. She stepped back, and in her haste stumbled over the corpse of one of her victims.

The swordsman pressed the attack, swiping maliciously. She managed to parry with her own blade. His sword snapped under the impact, and hers flew from her hand, landed three yards away.

Her attacker jumped at her, landing a foot on her chest, knocking the air from her. For a moment, Maggie's vision went black from the pain, and she raised her head feebly. Her attacker held his broken sword, its jagged edge lodged in her Adam's apple.

"Here now, sweet lady," he panted. "You see, all of your resistance has come to naught. I never wanted to hurt you." Maggie looked up into his face, and a shock went through her. Though the man was tall, his narrow face was a pale yellow, and he was unnaturally handsome, lustrous, almost as if his face were cast in ceramics. And there was a kindness to his voice. He believed what he said. He didn't want to hurt her.

He struggled with his free hand to untie a pouch wrapped to his belt, opened the pouch and pulled out something small and silver that glittered in the moonlight. It moved like an insect, a large praying mantis perhaps, but its body was sleeker, longer, and more angular.

"Here is the Word. Let it set you free!"

He put it on her chest, and the creature poised for a moment with one huge claw ready to stab into her chest. Then, carefully checking each direction, it began stalking toward her face.

Eleven

The Bock led Gallen over the hill and into a city market, on a wide street where canvas tarpaulins fixed to poles provided some shelter. Under the tarps, small, tan-colored men and women haggled with customers over the prices of exotic fruits and trays of fishes. The locals wore short colorful tunics that left their legs exposed. On their shoulders they wore hooded half-capes made of soft, oiled leather.

The vendors' stalls smelled strongly of curry, anise, saffron, vanilla, and pepper—salt and spices beyond number. The pair moved past brass potmakers, past coils of hemp, bags of wheat, down toward some docks where they had to pass human guards.

Forty ships had put into port, and the docks were awash with all types of cargo—bales of wool and cotton, silks and hemp. Crates filled with beans and furniture, ingots of brass and steel. The Bock explained that most of the people in the crowd were nonhumans, come to trade from far-off lands.

A batch of red-furred sailors in heavy leather armor were unloading a scow, singing a high nasal song. Gallen looked at them in wonder, feeling that something more was wrong with them than their fur, when he realized that they had no ears.

Among bales of cotton, a dark woman dressed in yellow silks sat upon a palanquin that was at the moment unattended. On a long metal chain she held a pitiable creature, an emaciated girl with greenish skin and sad eyes who squatted naked atop a coil of hemp. There were no other men about to bear the palanquin, and as Gallen looked at the woman, she squatted on her hands, and smiled at him. She moved in an odd manner, scratching her arm with her teeth in a way that was distinctly unlike anything he had seen before, and as she stared at him with glimmering eyes, the look of undisguised lust in her eyes frightened him, for Gallen understood immediately that she did not lust for his flesh, except to eat it.

"What is that?" Gallen asked in disgust, leaping back from the woman.

"That is a Herap," the Bock answered. "Among her people, ten men are born for every female. Once she•mates with a man, she dines on him, if she can."

Gallen was truly dismayed by all of this, and soon the oddities he noticed among the locals—grotesquely enlarged chests, huge grasping toes, violet skin—all began to meld together in his mind, a seething collage of monstrosities.

A warm shower started, but despite the downpour, the people milled about freely, oblivious to such weather. If it had truly been the Bock's determination to simply parade Gallen through the streets, it could have taken

Gallen back to Maggie then. But instead the Bock led him resolutely past the marketplace, down toward a district where the buildings began to close in, stone houses flanking the narrow streets, each house with its pillars and portico protruding out so far that they had to walk around them.

"Where are we going?" Gallen asked at last, wiping the rain from his face.

"Consider for a moment," the Bock answered, "but do not speak your guess." And Gallen knew that they were going to see Ceravanne.

The Bock led Gallen down around the bay, and over a hill, farther up the coast. The city extended on for miles, stretching among the hills, and Gallen realized that they had been only at the very southern tip of it. The sky began to darken, and the streets emptied far too quickly, until few people walked the streets, and those who did glanced about furtively and would duck into alleyways when they saw Gallen and the Bock approaching.

"This part of the city isn't safe," Gallen said.

"If you wore weapons or more clothing, this would be a dangerous neighborhood," the Bock answered. "But obviously you are carrying no money. A half-naked man and a Bock—no one would bother with us. Besides, are you not a killer?"

"A Lord Protector," Gallen answered uncomfortably.

"A killer," the Bock argued, a hint of distaste in his voice.

"And you disapprove?" Gallen asked.

"I am a Bock. We respect all life."

"You must eat."

"I have a mouth so that I may speak," the Bock answered. "Beyond that, I take nourishment from the rain and the soil. I cannot comprehend killing. Life is precious—in all its forms. Unfortunately, not everyone agrees with me. Some peoples are esteemed as less than others. For example, in the wilderness of Babel, there are creatures called the Roamers. Their ancestors were humans, but the desire for enclosure was bred out of them, and they were given hair and great strength and stamina, so that they might thrive in the wilds without shelter. They wear no clothes, and many in Babel think of them as somehow less than human, animals. The Roamers do not have human rights—access to human technology and the human system of justice."

"That doesn't seem fair to me," Gallen said. "Why, back home, every man can have his day in court."

"But for many subspecies of human," the Bock countered, "the human system of justice itself is unfair. It requires them to think and act like humans—something they cannot do. And so we cannot hold them to human laws."

"But what if a nonhuman kills someone else?" Gallen said. "Certainly you can't just allow that."

"All beings are held accountable equally," the Bock answered. "In such cases, our courts hire a champion to hunt down the offender, and slay it."

And suddenly Gallen knew why he was here. "The Inhuman . . ."

The Bock glanced at him sideways, the wide portion of his head swiveling.

"Yes. Champions have been sent to Babel to hunt the Inhuman, but they never returned, and still its power spreads. That is why our leaders requested a Lord Protector from off-world, someone licensed to use weapons that we keep restricted here."

"So you want me to hunt down and slay this Inhuman?" Gallen asked.

"*I* want nothing of the sort. Whether the lion or the jackal wins this conflict does not matter to me. It does not matter to the rocks and sky and water. I see little difference between the goals of the Inhuman and your goals, nor do I see any difference in your methods for gaining control. Ceravanne says that your people fight for freedom, but freedom is an illusion, so long as the light within you is encased in a body made of dust. You are all slaves to your animal desires—"

"And you're not?" Gallen asked.

"I am not an animal," the Bock said. "That is why the Tharrin . . . worship me." Gallen caught his breath at this last bit of news, for he imagined the Tharrin to be the highest life-forms in the galaxy. It had never occurred to him that the Tharrin would look up to other beings, much less that they would so admire another species that they would worship it. For the past hour, Gallen had felt that the Bock had been trying to show him something, had been trying to get across a message that somehow wasn't connecting. Now Gallen focused more attentively.

"Gallen, I desire that both sides find a path to peace, nothing more." The Bock stopped in a narrow alley. A chill wind swept through the alley, and overhead several pigeons flapped about, trying to find the best roosting spot on the crumbling stone lip of a roof. Gallen could see over the edge of town, and the suns setting out over the ocean were shining on some near hills. He could see the front of the temple near where the Gate of the World opened, and near the temple's huge doors, an enormous brass disk reflected the dying suns. Two giants in yellow robes began to beat the disk with great clubs, so that the gong flashed golden like the wings of a fiery bird, and the sound of it echoed over the town. There was silence for the moment. "Those giants are called Acradas. In many ways they are wise, but each night they try to call the suns back, fearing that unless their sun disk tolls, the suns will never return." The Bock hesitated, and Gallen pitied such ignorant creatures. "You and I look at the Acradas, and we think them strange. As you are to Acradas, I am to you. My thoughts are incomprehensible to you, and you and the Inhuman are equally alien to me. But we—each of us—are held prisoner by our own bodies. We sense the world in our own way, and we act toward it in ways that our mind allows. No man can truly be comprehended by another. Here on our world, in the City of Life, our people design new forms of humanity to inhabit other worlds. They have created over five thousand subspecies of human. Many of them have far-reaching enhancements that cannot be detected by eye alone, and with others, apparently major enhancements are merely cosmetic. For some subspecies, their paths of thought so differ from those of mankind that they cannot be held accountable to the laws that govern life here in the human lands. Still, their lives are precious to them. They cannot help what they are, and they cannot change it. They are not capable of being human, but you, Gallen O'Day, I hope will look upon them with empathy and understanding."

"You want me to *judge* the Inhuman?" Gallen asked.

The Bock whispered, "Many people have been absorbed by the mind of the Inhuman. Few of the people who have become Inhuman did so of their own free will. For each Inhuman that you meet, you will have to decide whether to slay it or let it live." The Bock sighed, and its mouth opened and its eyes half closed.

For a moment, it gave an expression of such profound sadness that Gallen feared it would break into tears. "And yet, Gallen, I suspect that you will have no chance to reason with or prevail against this . . . thing. The Inhuman is powerful, and if the rumors we hear are true, it controls hundreds of thousands of beings. . . ." The Bock glanced up, then whispered, "See, there is one of its scouts now! They come to the city every night!"

Gallen looked skyward, and from the clouds above a dark form swooped, a wriggling tatter of night that suddenly resolved into a creature flapping on batlike wings. As Gallen watched, he almost imagined it to be an enormous bat. And suddenly he knew why the streets here cleared at dusk. The servants of the Inhuman owned the night.

"Quickly now," the Bock said. "We must get indoors."

Gallen had a sudden cold fear, and he wondered if Maggie and Orick were all right. He would need to get back to them soon.

Gallen stopped, unwilling to go any farther with this strange creature. The Bock turned and looked at him expectantly, waiting for Gallen to follow.

"Wait a minute," Gallen said. "What of Maggie and Orick? Shouldn't we go back for them?"

"Soon, soon," the Bock promised. "All in time."

And Gallen wondered. He was a stranger to this world, still unsure of its dangers. The Bock knew more than he did. Perhaps the fact that the Inhuman was sending scouts to the city at night did not mean that Maggie was in danger—but Gallen had seen the fear in the eyes of the locals as they hurried off the streets.

"I'll go no farther with you," Gallen said.

"Please, hurry," the Bock said. "It is not much farther—a moment more."

Gallen hesitated, greatly torn. But Maggie had Orick to guard her, and Gallen suspected that another moment would make little difference. Reluctantly, he followed the Bock.

The Bock led Gallen to the side entrance of a building, and they stepped under the portico and hurried down a maze of dark hallways until Gallen was completely turned around. Then the Bock stopped and whispered a name at a door that looked like all the others. "Ceravanne."

Gallen heard a bolt sliding, then the door opened, and behind it stood a young woman wrapped in a dark cloak that hid most of her face. Yet Gallen could see the precisely sculpted cheekbones and brow that marked her kind. He found himself wishing that she would speak, so that he might hear her voice. Her dark eyes were haunted, and she looked at Gallen hopefully for a second, then turned and led the way into a dusty store room filled with barrels and crates, moving with a delicate grace that could only belong to a Tharrin.

Gallen entered the room behind the Bock, feeling extremely ill at ease. As he stepped through the doorway, the door closed a little and a large man moved in behind Gallen, placing a sword at the side of his neck. "Far enough," the man said, putting just enough weight on the blade to force Gallen to step sideways and back. "Face the wall."

Gallen stood against the wall, bridling at the thought. He'd come here unarmed, without so much as a knife or his mantle. His legs were shaking, and Gallen forced himself to breathe deeply, hold down his anger. The guard kept the sword to the back of his neck, then ran one hand through Gallen's long hair, checking carefully around the base of his neck. "He's clean, milady," the guard said. "No weapons, and no scars near the neck."

"The Lord Protector, Gallen O'Day, did not come alone," the Bock told Ceravanne. "He brought a woman and a bear. I left them behind with the weapons, as ordered."

The guard stepped back, and Gallen glanced at the Bock, realizing that this seemingly innocuous creature had a duplicitous streak to it. "You tricked me," Gallen said.

"Ceravanne asked me to bring you to her alone, stripped of weapons," the Bock answered. "But I asked you to come so for my own reasons."

So the Bock and Lady Ceravanne worked at cross-purposes, and Gallen realized that he might be working at cross-purposes to them both. The Bock wanted the Inhuman left alone. Ceravanne perhaps sought only to stop its encroachments. And without knowing anything about the Inhuman, Gallen had halfway decided to kill it.

Ceravanne was about to speak, but she stopped, as if a sudden thought had occurred to her. "Bock, isn't it getting dark out?"

"It is late," the Bock agreed.

"But—Gallen's friends, where did you leave them?"

"In the field, at the opening to the gate."

Ceravanne frowned, plainly worried. "Bock, we can't leave them for the night—the Inhumans . . . !"

"I will go get them," the Bock said.

Ceravanne said, "Can you retrieve them before full nightfall?"

"If I hurry across the fields, over the hill!"

"Rougaire, you go with him," Ceravanne said.

The guard, a giant with a bulbous red nose and weathered features, put one hand on his sword and said, "Yes, milady."

"Should I go, too?" Gallen asked.

Ceravanne frowned. "No," she said after a moment. "I think not. I still need a guard. And if your friends stayed put, the Bock and Rougaire should reach them soon enough. Four people traveling together in the early evening are not in great danger—especially not when Rougaire is among them."

The giant Rougaire took a heavy robe from atop a nearby crate and put it on, then strapped his swords to his back. Gallen studied the man's movements. He was all strength and no grace. When he was ready, the giant handed Gallen one of his swords, a weapon that seemed just a bit too long and heavy for convenient use.

"For you, sir," Rougaire said, bowing deeply.

"I'd rather have one of your daggers," Gallen said. The giant frowned a bit at Gallen's choice, then took one of his daggers from its sheath at his knee and handed it to Gallen. It was large enough for Gallen to use as a short sword. Gallen just held it, for he'd left his belt with Maggie and had nowhere to put the weapon.

"Thank you, Rougaire," the Lady Ceravanne said to the guard. "Go quickly!"

The guard bowed to her, then hurried out in company with the Bock. Gallen bolted the door behind them.

Ceravanne studied Gallen, and the haunted look did not leave her eyes. She appeared to be a child of thirteen or fourteen, but she held herself with a dignity, a wisdom, far beyond her years. Her platinum hair cascaded in waves down over her shoulders, and she watched him from green eyes, paler than any eyes he'd ever seen or imagined. She wore a delicate white dress with white birds embroidered upon it, and she looked like something not quite human, like a fragile fairy bride in a dark glen. But there was the pain in her eyes, and Gallen wondered idly how many cloned bodies she had worn out.

"I'm sorry for asking the Bock to bring you stripped *and alone*," she said. "I asked him to bring you alone because curious children sometimes follow the Bock, and I didn't want them tagging along. The Bock . . . is very wise in his way, but he does not think on our level. He often takes the things we say too literally, and he does not comprehend the import of our struggle. He meant no harm, and I hope that no harm will come of it."

"My friend Orick is handy in a fight," Gallen said, trying to put her at ease, still uneasy himself. "I suspect they'll be all right."

"I am not worried that they will be injured or killed," Ceravanne said. "I'm worried that they will be infected by the Inhuman."

"Infected?"

"The Inhuman sends agents—small creatures—to burrow into their victims from the back of the neck, and then the creature infects its host with the Inhuman's propaganda, downloading information into the victim's brain. Those who have recently been infected will bear a scar at the base of the neck."

Ceravanne went to a large barrel, used a match to light a single candle, then set it on the barrel. She sat down cross-legged at the base of it, and motes of dust rose up, floated in the light.

"I asked the rebellion to send someone I could trust. Can I trust you?" she asked.

Gallen stared into the child's eyes, and his heart felt as if it would melt. He had forgotten how powerful the scent of a Tharrin woman could be, had forgotten how the pheromones she exuded could tug at his sanity. One look at her frail, perfect figure, and he wanted only to fall to his knees, pledge his fealty. And because she was Tharrin, because she was bred to rule in kindness, he could see no reason not to do so. Yet Gallen remembered the deadly rose in its glass last night, someone warning him against trusting the beautiful Tharrin? He stood aloof from her. "Of course you can trust me."

"You are new to our world," Ceravanne said. "I forget my manners. Is there anything you need? Food, drink?"

"No," Gallen said.

"I suppose you have questions?"

"Your friend, the Bock—he said that you Tharrin worship him. Is this true?"

"Worship?" The question seemed to make her nervous. She shook her head and looked away a bit guiltily. "I'm afraid he does not understand all of the nuances of our language. I revere him, certainly. I respect him, seek to emulate him. He is my teacher, and I love him as a friend. . . . Perhaps 'worship' is close to the right word." She looked at him squarely. "I do not worship him any more than you worship the Tharrin, I suspect. Do you worship the Tharrin?"

Gallen puzzled at the question. In many ways, he almost did. He found that when he was in their presence, he could not help but serve them faithfully. He admired them. He had loved the Lady Everynne. Still . . . "No," Gallen said. "I do not trust them completely. I have learned that despite all appearances, we are not the same species."

Ceravanne smiled wryly at that. "In some ways, I trust the Bock completely. He is a man of peace, who can do no harm. But it seems that I cannot trust him to fetch a Lord Protector to me, without botching the job."

Gallen changed the subject. "Why does the Inhuman want you?"

"I'm Tharrin," Ceravanne answered. "And therefore am born to lead. The Inhuman may want me as a leader."

"I am surprised," Gallen admitted. "With the dronon gone from this world, I would have thought you would be a Lord Judge, wearing a mantle."

"No," Ceravanne said. "The human lords in the City of Life act as judges on this world, not me. I act as a counselor to them only—should they seek my counsel. I have not held much power for the past several centuries. Still, I am the last of the Tharrin here, and so the Inhuman seeks to control me.

"Beyond that, what I can tell you about the Inhuman is mostly guesses.

We began to hear rumors of it three years ago. At first it was only one or two odd reports, borne from the interior of Babel by nonhumans who came with wild tales. The lands there are very rugged and backward, and we imagined that it was only some new religion. But when our leaders sought to send scouts to the area, the dronon opposed us. Among the Rebellion, there was some talk of sending our own scouts in secret, but we erred—we ignored the rumors for the moment, and concentrated instead on fighting the dronon.

"So the Inhuman seemed to grow slowly, until last year. Among the peoples of Babel, there is a race called the Tekkar, a brilliant people, engineered to live on a brutal world so hot that men can only safely move about at night. They have purple eyes that see in the dark, and they are themselves stealthy and dark. Within weeks, all the tribes of Tekkar were converted, and then they began to attack their neighbors by night, converting those they could, slaying those who opposed them."

Gallen said slowly, "The Bock showed me some of the peoples who live here, and he warned that some were more powerful, more vicious than humans. Yet I wonder: the Tharrin are peaceful people—why would you create such beings?"

"Once again, you overestimate my influence," Ceravanne said. "The human lords in the City of Life choose which races to create, which attributes are needed for those who will inhabit other worlds. Some of the beings they've created were designed before the Tharrin were born. Others I see as abominations that should never have been formed. Still, I have long sought to maintain peace between our various races."

"You were telling me about the Inhuman?" Gallen said.

"Yes. It was about a year ago that the Inhuman sent its first scouts to the City of Life, where I had been in hiding from the dronon for many years. The agents of the Inhuman tried to abduct me, but I resisted to the death, and my faithful followers downloaded my memories into a new clone.

"Then sailing ships began arriving from Babel, ships filled with refugees, and they warned us of the darkness growing in the land of Moree. Only then did we begin to recognize the true size of the danger, but we could not mount an attack against the Inhuman. The dronon still ruled here, and they refused our pleas. At first, we thought they were only refusing to take sides in a local squabble, so we sent out scouts then, in secret. Even I went with that first scouting party, but most of our people were killed, and those who survived returned as Inhuman converts who betrayed the Rebellion by pointing out our operatives. Some small bands of our people went to war secretly then, but they were no match for the Inhuman.

"Then three months ago it became apparent that the dronon were openly siding with the Inhuman. They put a marching hive city in each of our ports so that we could not mount an offensive. We could not defeat the dronon's aircraft and walking fortresses with spears and swords.

"And so we began to lose hope. We thought we would all be consumed—until a few days ago, when the dronon left our worlds. And suddenly our hope is reborn!"

"And what is the Inhuman's cause?" Gallen asked.

"It was created for the purpose of convincing mankind that our species can coexist peacefully—as subjects within the dronon Empire."

"So the dronon created the Inhuman?"

Ceravanne frowned. "Not exactly. It is beyond their technology—in some ways, it is beyond ours. Here on Tremonthin, we have adopted a simple way of life. Nearly all technology is proscribed, except that which is used in the service of extending life. In the City of Life we download memories into clones, perform our great work of adapting mankind to fit within alien ecosystems. Because it is our sole technological export, our life-enhancing technologies are among the best in the galaxy. The dronon incorporated our technologies into the Inhuman. Some of our scientists aided them. We found the perpetrators, and those who aided them willingly have already been dealt with. The rest are working to undo the damage."

"You say that the dronon helped create the Inhuman," Gallen said. "What is the Inhuman?"

"The dronon saw that with the thousands of subspecies of mankind living on this world, it was the perfect place to experiment, learn which breeds might most easily integrate into their society.

"So they made an artificial intelligence that stores the memories of dronon technicians, along with those of nonhumans from our southern continent.

"And this artificial intelligence is struggling to infect our people with a new world view—a complex web of memories and beliefs and lies that lead those infected to convert to the doctrines of the Inhuman," Ceravanne sighed. "We couldn't fight such sophisticated weaponry."

"Then why don't you get better weapons?" Gallen blurted out. "Bring in forces from off-world."

Ceravanne looked pointedly at Gallen. "Our world is distant from others. Even with the fastest ships—and such ships are on their way—it will take months for help to arrive. Even then, it will be hard to mount an attack on Babel. It was created as a refuge for nonhumans, and many of the species there fear us. If we attacked in force, they would see it as an invasion and would seek to turn us away. So even those we count as allies could turn against us. But more importantly, many of the nonhumans in Babel are genetically upgraded. They are stronger and faster than us, tougher, and often more cunning. We could not defeat them on their own ground. We can hardly hope to repel an invasion."

"So you want me to sneak into the southlands and destroy this Inhuman, this machine?" Gallen asked.

Ceravanne studied him a moment, then looked down at her feet. Her jaw trembled, and an expression of utter hopelessness crossed her face. "Oh, Gallen, I wish that were all I was asking of you. . . ."

Gallen went to her, knelt and put his hand on her shoulder, trying to comfort her. She looked up, reached up with one hand and stroked his cheek, then kissed him softly.

For one long moment, he allowed it—reveling in the sweet, intense taste of her lips—then pulled back sharply, as if he'd been struck. He wiped her kiss from his mouth with the back of his arm, yet the scent of her pheromones lingered, and he had to remind himself that as a Tharrin she was made so that he would love her. "I, I—" He fumbled for an explanation. "I'm married."

"I need you!" Ceravanne said fiercely. "I need you to give yourself to me completely. Gallen—I don't know everything about the Inhuman, but I believe that it is more dangerous than you or I can imagine. It isn't just a machine, it is a technology that has fused the minds of millions of beings—and they will oppose you. It is not just the machine, it is the talents and wisdom and hopes of all those people. I can't tell you what I think I must ask you to do for me! But I need you to trust me. If my guess is correct, it will be harder than anything you can imagine. I need you!"

Gallen studied her face. It was obvious that she planned to face this challenge with him, that she did not want to reveal her part in this fight. It annoyed him that she would hold her plans so secret, but looking into her eyes, he suddenly realized that he trusted her. "It seems that I do trust the Tharrin completely," Gallen said. "Or at least I trust you. I'll do whatever you ask—but don't ask me to give you my heart."

"I need *that* most of all!" Ceravanne whispered fiercely. "I need a Lord Protector to serve me wholly. Listen: in Moree there is a leader, a very powerful person that the servants of the Inhuman call 'the Harvester.'"

That name struck a chord in Gallen, and he found his heart pounding. He was sure he'd never heard of this Harvester—yet he suddenly remembered something, a bit of information that only his mantle could have planted in his memory.

"Are you sure it's human?" Gallen asked. "A thousand years ago, on a planet from the Chenowi system, a few hundred machines were built, machines called the Harvesters. They are nanotech devices which carry downloaded human memories. They can assume dozens of forms, change colors. They were designed to be the ultimate assassins. Over the centuries, most of them have been destroyed. But on a low-tech world like this, a Harvester would be almost invulnerable. It's possible that one survives here."

This bit of news seemed to disconcert Ceravanne. "I—never considered such a possibility," she said.

"I'll have to kill it," Gallen said, almost certain that this Harvester was more than a mere person.

Ceravanne looked up at him, startled, and there was resignation in her eyes. Though she was a Tharrin, and could never bring herself to harm another, she understood the need for killing at times. Still, she seemed tormented. "I hope it does not come to that," Ceravanne whispered, and Gallen wondered at her naïveté. "But if it does, it won't be easy. At the very least, I suspect that you will bear scars from this—scars on your soul, scars that you will abhor. I . . . am loath to ask this of you."

"I've killed before," Gallen said calmly, wondering what Ceravanne knew of this Harvester, and even as he said it, he remembered the three men back home, the empty-headed oafs who had forced his hand by testifying against him. He still felt marred by those killings, stained.

Twelve

Orick woke at the doorway to the store, his vision blurred. He could smell the cobbled roads thick with dust and tiny flakes of dried manure from sheep and some other animal, and Orick wished that he could stand up and walk on his hind feet, put a little distance between himself and that unclean scent.

A whistle blew, and its sound was a cold wind that froze Orick to the heart.

The Inhuman, Orick remembered. The hair on the back of his neck bristled, and Orick opened his eyes, spotted Maggie in a patch of moonlight, lying on her back in the street, corpses stacked around her. A tall fellow hunched over her, holding what looked to be a broad dagger at her throat.

Orick lay for just a moment, and suddenly there was a shout from down the street, the way they had come. Two forms moved in the shadows—one was the familiar shape of the Bock, the other was a giant, and they were running, but they were too far away to help Maggie before the villain could cut her throat.

Orick jumped up and charged, digging his claws into the floor planks for all the purchase he could get, bounding forward so that parts of a broad wooden door were flung away from him.

Orick roared, and the fellow glanced up from Maggie, then fled down the road, between two buildings. Orick lunged after him, and the fellow grunted and zigzagged into the shadows.

A giant bat swooped in front of Orick, trying to distract him, and Orick stood up, swatted at the creature, catching a corner of its wing. The bat veered away clumsily.

Orick was so angry he felt as if he were invulnerable, as if he could run forever, and he continued to chase Maggie's attacker, rushing till he could nearly take the man's neck in his teeth.

The fellow glanced over his back, shouted "No!" and, in a burst of redoubled speed, made it around a corner and jumped over a high wall.

Orick came up short against the wall, knowing he couldn't make it, and decided that it was best to go care for Maggie.

He rushed through the streets to Maggie, found her on her back, holding some strange insect in her hand, keeping it at a distance. Her face was pale, frightened. The giant and the Bock stood over her, gasping for breath.

"What is that thing?" Orick asked. The insect was mantislike in appearance, but its front legs were oversized. Maggie had them pinched firmly.

"I'm not sure," Maggie said. "It looks like a machine, but I'm not sure what it does."

"That is an Inhuman's Word," the giant said in a deep voice, taking the thing from Maggie's fingers and smashing it. "It turns a man into an Inhuman. You had better watch out. There might be more."

The giant immediately began dusting off Maggie's back while watching for the bugs on the street.

When he was sure she was clean, Maggie retrieved Gallen's sword. One of the insects was there beneath it. It began to scurry over the cobblestones, so she swatted it with the flat of the sword. After more searching, she decided there had only been two Words. Up the street from them, that damned bat-like creature had made it to the top of a building, and it blew its whistle in three sharp bursts.

Maggie looked up at the giant bat. "Shut off the whistling already, damn you!" she shouted. "If any more of your black-hearted friends come around, we'll give them just what we gave the others!"

The scout looked down at them in the moonlight, his eyes glowing golden. He growled, "You'll pay for dessstroying the Wordsss." He let his whistle dangle from a chain about his neck, glared at Maggie for a moment, rubbed his face with the little black hands at the joint of his wings, then hurled himself from the building, swooping just over their heads.

Orick wished that Maggie had been carrying a stick or something. One good knock on the head would have busted the creature's skull open like an acorn.

"I am sorry that I got back so late," the Bock told them, waving its arms emphatically. "When we reached the meadow, you had already left. We've been looking everywhere for you!"

Maggie shook her head. "No harm done," she said, hefting her packs. "Let's go." They began hurrying north, but the Bock was striding along slowly. The giant walked ahead, leading the way, his huge sword in hand. He stopped at each side street, checking both ways.

"Can you hurry?" Maggie said, trying to help the Bock along by pulling at its arm.

"I'm sorry," the Bock said. "I have no energy after dark. There were huge clouds at sunset, and it slowed us. I should have found you long ago!"

Orick looked at the creature—half man, half plant. They could not leave it behind, and they could hardly wait for the thing to move at its own pace.

Maggie was sweating heartily from her fight, from her fear. She looked at Orick a moment. "Orick, could you have a go at giving him a ride?"

Orick considered. His ears were ringing, and he felt woozy from the bump on his head, but he could probably carry the man. Still, just because he had four legs, it didn't mean he'd let people treat him like a pack mule. "All right," he grumbled, "but it's undignified."

Maggie helped the creature on. Orick ran with Maggie at his tail, and they managed to make good time with the giant leading the way.

They were running into the wind, and once Orick smelled the fresh scent of strangers ahead. Orick called to the giant, then turned aside, lurching off around several blocks, certain that he'd avoided an ambush. As if to prove his point, moments later he heard excited whistling behind him as the batlike scout realized what had happened. Just then, the giant had Orick duck into a little side alley that led to a warehouse, and within moments they were inside.

Maggie closed the door tight behind her, threw the bolt home, and sagged against it in the dark. There were no lanterns, no lights in the building at all, and the dark was utterly impenetrable. Orick half turned. He could smell her warm sweat, and she was breathing hard, as much from fright as from the exertion. He couldn't smell any other people in the hall, though Gallen had passed here shortly. There would be no ambush waiting ahead of them.

"Orick?" Maggie said. "Where are you?"

"Here," he grumbled.

"Come here, where I can touch you."

Orick ambled to her, and Maggie petted his snout affectionately. It was one of the most intimate pettings she had ever given him, and he closed his eyes, relishing the way she scratched him. He groaned with pleasure, and Maggie bent down and kissed him full on the snout. "Thank you," she said. "You're welcome at my table anytime. You really saved me."

And at those kind words, Orick's heart warmed. He led Maggie, the giant, and the Bock down the maze of twisted halls in something of a blur, until he got to a door. He could see candlelight winking through the cracks, and the Bock called out softly for Gallen.

Gallen slid the bolt, pulled the door open, and at sight of the blood on Orick's face he cried, "What happened to you?"

Maggie told them then of their skirmish with the servants of the Inhuman, and Ceravanne frowned and paced the room, then had Gallen and Rougaire check Orick and Maggie for neck wounds.

When she was satisfied, Ceravanne shook her head, plainly worried. "I had hoped to wait here for a few days so that we could provision our trip at our ease, receive counsel from the Lords in the City of Life. But we will have to leave first thing in the morning."

"Why?" Orick asked.

"Their scout has your scent," Ceravanne said. "It will call its fellows, and by dawn there may be a dozen or more of them hunting for you and Maggie. The Inhuman will not hold harmless those who have slain its members. We must flee at dawn."

Thirteen

Zell'a Cree heard the shrill warning of the scout's whistle from over a mile away, and rushed through the darkened streets until his infrared vision could make out the fiery forms of his men. He came upon the corpses of his men, pack brothers lying in pools of their own blood. Their bodies glowed like faint embers, and the blood still hot in their veins was like twisted rivers of light under their skin.

Besides the scout Ssaz, who sat nursing an injured wing from the stone gutters of a building, three other hunters from Zell'a Cree's pack had gathered—two were unnamed Tekkars, swathed in black robes cut at the thighs, wearing tall leather boots tied above the knees. The Tekkars' purple eyes gleamed darkly from their shadowed hoods. The third was a small man named Ewod who might have been human, except that he wore fur-lined winter robes on a balmy evening and his skin was pale yellow. He stared at the ruined corpses and shook, and Zell'a Cree watched him closely. He had seldom seen so much fear upon the face of a man.

Zell'a Cree felt calm himself. Fear had been bred out of his people thousands of years ago. He had never wakened with his heart thumping from a bad dream, had never felt an uneasy tingling at the sound of running feet in a dark alley. And now, looking at his brothers, he felt only sadness, a profound loss at such a waste.

He went to the corpses, closed the staring eyes. "The wheel turns, and we must now travel the road without you. Come to us when you can," he whispered to the dead, bidding them to seek rebirth soon, then reached into his travel pouch and brought out wafers of bread and placed one in the mouth of each of his dead comrades to feed them on their spirit journeys.

Zell'a Cree was disturbed by the sounds of the little man, Ewod, crying, and Zell'a Cree also wanted to weep at the waste of life. But as leader of this hunting pack, he could not afford the luxury.

"Don't dawdle," the scout Ssaz hissed at them from its perch, its canines gleaming as gold as its eyes in the moonlight. Zell'a Cree could smell the sweet copper scent of its blood, but couldn't immediately see the wound. "The humansss may return, hunting usss thisss time!"

"What happened?" Zell'a Cree spoke only in a hushed whisper. All of the men here had hearing far keener than any human.

Ewod said, "Me and my brothers chanced upon a bear and a young woman, and we thought they would make easy converts. The bear wounded himself trying to escape, but the girl came at us with a sword and slew my brothers before they could react."

"Fools!" one of the Tekkar spat, his voice the sound of loose gravel shifting under one's feet. Because the Tekkar did not name themselves, Zell'a Cree was forced to bestow names upon them in order to keep them straight. He called this one Red Hand, for the man had his right hand dyed red. "They should have taken more care. They deserved to die!"

"No one deserves death," Zell'a Cree said.

"The humans who did this deserve to die!" Red Hand countered. "We must make an example of them, teach the humans to fear us."

Zell'a Cree knew that the humans no longer walked abroad at night because they were afraid of his hunting pack, and it was only that fear that made it possible for his people to penetrate so deeply into the human lands. If the humans banded together and went abroad in the dark, his hunters would be no match for them. But the humans did not know this, and so fear protected Zell'a Cree's men. He could not gainsay Red Hand's argument, no matter how repulsive he might find it.

"What do the rest of you think?" Zell'a Cree asked, hoping that the imaginative Ewod might be able to find a reason to extend mercy.

The second Tekkar, whom Zell'a Cree called Garrote because the man always kept a garrote wrapped at his waist to use as a belt, said, "If an Inhuman kills a human, the humans send their assassins to take vengeance. We should do no less."

"And if we kill these humans, will we not be lowering ourselves to their standards?" Zell'a Cree said. "The way of the Inhuman is a way to peace."

"Yes," Ewod said nervously. "I tried to tell the humans that. But they feared the Word."

Zell'a Cree glanced at his men. "The Inhuman does not seek vengeance, it seeks converts above all. Yet justice must also be done. We shall hunt this woman and offer her a choice: she may accept the Word, or lose her life."

Zell'a Cree held his breath a moment, and his men grunted their assent. The Tekkar immediately raised their heads, trying to catch the woman's scent, but whereas their night vision was stronger than Zell'a Cree's, his sense of smell far outmatched theirs. He could smell the woman now, the subtle aroma of strange perfumes about her, like nothing he'd ever come across before. And he could smell the bear, its heavy fur.

He rushed down the street, under the cover of darkness, his men flitting behind him like shadows. For nearly an hour he tracked them through the streets. It was a difficult task, even for Zell'a Cree, for it was not long past dusk, and the odors of thousands of travelers were still fresh on the night air.

Their scout flew ahead, and once he spotted the humans and they tried to set a hasty ambush, but the humans turned aside from their course.

Still, it was not hard to pick up their trail again. Zell'a Cree held to the exotic scent of the woman, a scent utterly alien, until at last he came to a warehouse that covered most of a block. It was an old stone building that had once been a great covered market, but now the huge arched doorways had been filled with new brick, leaving but one small opening under a portico.

Bending near the door, Zell'a Cree tasted the scent—and discovered the earthy vegetable odor of Bock. He inhaled deeply, closing his eyes, so that he would remember those smells, recognize their owners as if they were old friends.

Zell'a Cree pulled on the door, but it was barred inside, as he'd expected. He backed up, looked at the building from outside. The old warehouse had two high windows that were barred. Ssaz was already at the bars, tugging on them. But the batlike creature didn't have the strength in his hands to pull the bars loose.

"We could pry open the door," one of the Tekkar suggested, breathing down Zell'a Cree's neck. The Tekkar's voice was annoyingly loud to Zell'a Cree's sensitive ears.

"We don't know if they're in there," Zell'a Cree said. "They may have left another way. Besides, if they remained within, they may have accomplices. I can smell several people who have entered here recently."

He nodded toward the Tekkar. "Each of you circle the building, checking for other doors. If you catch the woman's scent there, call us. Do not try to fight this woman alone. I will go up on the roof and listen for them, see if I can hear them inside."

He only hoped that the Tekkar would follow his orders. The Tekkar had been bred for life on a violent world, and were prone to viciousness. Both of the men were likely to kill their prey without notice. And given their skill in battle, their blinding speed, the woman would not stand a chance against them.

Zell'a Cree's ancestors were designed for life on a world where the air hung so heavy it would choke humans, and the gravity would make the blood pool in a human's legs till the vessels burst. It was a dark world, swathed in eternal mists, and so Zell'a Cree's ancestors had been gifted by the Immortals with compensations—eyes that could see in the dark, a sense of smell as keen as a wolf's, hearing as sharp as an owl's.

Zell'a Cree looked more human than any of his companions, but even now, the sensitive hairs in his ears twitched, and he listened for the sounds of voices.

"Ssaz, fly up and make certain that our prey does not leave the building," Zell'a Cree whispered. "Ewod, you hide in the shadows and watch this door. I'll try to find them inside."

The scout unfurled his wings and leapt into the air, swooping down and then flapping madly. Zell'a Cree grasped the rough stone walls of the building with his fingertips, finding chinks in the stone with his fingers and toes, then climbed up quickly two stories to the roof, crawling over the moss-covered slate tiles, listening, trying to catch a scent.

In moments his knees were wet and bore cuts from the slate roof, but he hardly noticed, he was so intent. Several times he heard the sounds of rats in the rooms below him, their shrieking voices and feet padding over the wooden floors, but Zell'a Cree passed them by, straining to hear above the softly gusting wind, until at last he heard voices echoing in a room beneath him, and he stopped.

The night was nearly silent, and the humans below him, with their dull senses, were utterly unaware. ". . . . The Inhuman will not hold harmless those who have slain its members." A girl was speaking, or a young woman, more likely. He imagined that it was the swordswoman speaking. She had a commanding voice, which was at the same time soft and mellifluous. "We must flee at dawn."

"Are you sure you want to come with us?" a young man asked. "It will be a long trip, and if I'm to protect you, it seems to me that the best way to do that is to leave you here."

"I need to come," the young woman replied. "Many servants of the Inhuman respect the Tharrin. You will need their help in finding the Harvester. You'll get that easier with me around. Besides, we requested a Lord Protector simply because I can no longer trust anyone here. The number of those who have been converted by the Inhuman is growing. I would not count myself safer here than in your presence."

"What of the giant, Rougaire? He seems trustworthy."

The woman lowered her voice, and by this Zell'a Cree guessed that the giant must still be in the building, and the woman did not want him to hear her words. "Trustworthy, yes, but he is not your match as a warrior. In battle he is both as graceful and as dangerous as a dancing elephant. Still, he has a great heart. But if we are to win through to Moree, we will require stealth, and Rougaire lacks that capacity."

"And will the Bock be coming?"

"No," the Tharrin said. "He's ill-suited to travel and is incapable of defending himself in an attack." She hesitated. "And what of you? You say the High Judge sent you here. How did you earn her trust?"

"Maggie and I killed the Lords of the Swarm, and Maggie banished the dronon from the human worlds."

There was a pause, and Zell'a Cree sat openmouthed at his good fortune. To find a Tharrin and the new human Lords of the Swarm both at once—it was incredible. "You did that?" the Tharrin asked.

"Aye," the young man said, and his voice was weary. As if to change the subject, he said, "You said the servants of the Inhuman will be hunting us. Will they attack tonight?"

"That is doubtful," the Tharrin said. "Maggie killed several of them, so they will respect her for that. And now she has reinforcements, while the hosts of the Inhuman are scattered in their hunting packs. No, I think it more likely that they will band in larger numbers—then try to hunt her down. That should give us time to escape."

"How can we manage to escape them undetected?"

"Our best hope is to travel quickly, over water," the Tharrin said. "The scouts have keen noses, but they are blind in the daytime. We can flee at dawn, but we cannot leave our scent on any road leaving town. With luck, they will search the buildings here in town for a couple of days before they realize that we are gone. I think we should leave in the morning, on the first ship that sails with the tide."

Another feminine voice broke in, a young woman, "Gallen, the beds are made up. . . ."

Zell'a Cree inched away from the room, taking immeasurable care not to make a sound. The rainwater trapped in the moss had wet his tunic so that he shivered with the cold, but when he was well away from his prey, he merely turned on his back and looked up at the stars and three small golden moons that whirled dreamily through the sky like juggler's balls. He breathed the sharp air, and considered. A Tharrin, a Lord Protector with his woman—the newly proclaimed Lords of the Swarm—all heading toward Moree to do battle with the Inhuman.

What better converts could he desire?

Zell'a Cree thought furiously, considering his resources. Here on the frontier he had nearly run out of his copies of the Word. And Zell'a Cree wondered if even the vicious Tekkar would be a match for a Lord Protector. Here, Zell'a Cree lacked the necessary resources for a confrontation, both in technology and in manpower. But if the humans were heading toward Moree . . .

"When you reach the Harvester's throne," Zell'a Cree whispered, "you will bow before it."

Fourteen

Once they reached the shadowed recesses of the warehouse, the Bock was dismayed at the sight of blood on Orick's brow, so while Ceravanne and Gallen talked in the other room and Maggie and the giant made up beds nearby, the Bock lit an oil lamp and set it on some crates. Then it brought forth a pouch of blue dust from its belt, and began slowly rubbing it into Orick's wounds, his sticklike finger probing tenderly.

"I see blood," the Bock exclaimed, "but your hair is so dense, I cannot find a wound."

Orick wasn't sure if he should tell the creature that he healed quickly—ever since Maggie had fed him some capsules of nanodocs that would extend his life for a millennium or more.

"What is that?" Maggie asked of the powder, looking up from one of the bedrolls.

"Healing Earth," the Bock said. "It will ease the swelling, mend the cuts. It is a small wound. He should be well in a few hours."

Maggie came and pinched some of the dirt in her fingers. "Where does it come from?"

"Legend says that ages ago, the Immortal Lords brought it from the City of Life and put it in the land. Now it is there for the benefit of all people, to be used in curing all wounds."

"Nanodocs," Maggie whispered, looking at the powder. "Does it extend one's life? Regenerate nerve tissue?"

"No," the Bock said, leaning away from Orick. "Only the Immortals in the City of Life have that power. But it cures wounds, mends bones. If you travel, you will find the Healing Earth in many places, beside the springs where the ground is wet."

Maggie nodded thoughtfully, then said, "I'm going to let Gallen know that the beds are ready." She went back behind the crates, into the main room.

The Bock stood perfectly motionless, slightly hunched, and there was a vacant look in its eyes.

"Are you all right?" Orick asked.

"Pardon me," the Bock said. "I fell asleep. I'm exhausted. I must rest soon." The Bock stepped back into a corner, raised his arms up toward a dim window, and stood with eyes squinted, unfocused.

The Bock began asking questions, in his slow way, about Orick's habits, his interests in theology and the possibility of becoming a priest. And with each question, the Bock grew steadily more incredulous, more awake and more interested.

The Bock asked, "So you have been working with Gallen for three years, yet never has he paid you? If you receive no compensation, why do you stay with him?"

"Oh, Gallen does buy me an odd meal now and then, but there's more in this world than money," Orick said. "After all, the Bible says that it's easier for a camel to get through the eye of a needle than for a rich man to enter the Kingdom of Heaven. I'd have to be a wretched creature, indeed, to base my relationship with someone on money."

"So why do you work with him?" the Bock said, his brown eyes gazing steadily at Orick.

"He's my friend."

"So you remain with him for companionship?" the Bock said, as if it were an alien concept, vaguely understood.

"Of course."

"But what of your own kind? Why do you not seek out other bears for companionship?"

"Oh, I don't know," Orick grumbled, not wanting to admit the painful truth. But he was an honest bear, so he continued. "On my world, bears don't run together. Mostly the males eat too much, and they wouldn't want to share food with me. The females love to have us during mating season, but they commence snarling soon afterward, and then, well, they just won't have you around, and they let you know it."

"Have you sought company with many females?" the Bock asked.

"Some," Orick admitted. "There was one I met just before I came here. I had hopes for her."

"You wanted to bond with her?"

Orick hesitated to admit to such a crazy notion. "Marriage is an honorable and holy state . . . or at least that's what the Bible says."

The Bock stopped, and in the dim lamplight he opened his mouth wide in surprise, as if he had just had a fantastic idea. "You are human, Orick!" the Bock said excitedly.

"I'm a bear!" Orick argued.

"Few of us are what we seem," the Bock said. "Our flesh is our disguise, hiding our desires and notions. Many who seem human are mere shells, so why should it be improbable that a creature such as yourself, who inhabits the form of a bear, would be a human at heart? Your thoughts, your beliefs and needs, are all those that a human would understand and agree with. And if you are human at heart, then by our law I have the right to extend the invitation: you may live within our society and enjoy the blessings of human company."

"Great," Orick murmured. He'd had human companionship for his whole life. It didn't seem a great privilege. "So what does that get me?"

"A great deal," the Bock answered. "Few nonhumans may ever enter the City of Life and obtain the blessings granted there. You will find many non-humans here in the port, but they cannot travel the roads beyond. Instead, they must leave with their ships, returning to exile in Babel."

The Bock seemed so distressed by the plight of the nonhumans that Orick found himself sympathizing with them. He imagined how things must be in Babel, a seething madhouse of incompatible species, preying upon the weak and upon one another, a vast continent laid waste by perpetual warfare. Orick's heart went out to such creatures, for he understood what it was to be outcast, to never belong.

"So," Orick grumbled. "Gallen will be surprised when I tell him that I'm as human as he is."

"Are you sure that he *is* human?" the Bock said.

"Why, what else would he be?" Orick asked.

"He could be many things," the Bock said. "I have not yet determined whether he is human, and so I cannot grant him the privileges that come with humanity."

"Why, that's the most absurd thing I've ever heard!" Orick said.

"One's flesh is often a disguise," the Bock countered. "On your home world, did you not often meet others whose thoughts and actions seemed strange to you—so strange as to be incomprehensible?"

Orick considered the blackguards who had tried to frame Gallen. Orick couldn't quite understand how someone would go to so much work to destroy another. It just wasn't in his nature, and on that count, Orick had to agree. Outwardly, men looked the same, but on the insides they could be strangers.

Maggie, Gallen, Ceravanne, and the giant Rougaire came back at that moment, and Orick said in glee, "Did you hear that, Gallen? The Bock says I'm human!"

"Well"—Gallen shrugged—"I've always known you were a better man than me, Orick, but I wish you would do something about that excess body hair."

Orick chuckled, but Ceravanne said quite seriously, as if she were offended, "Do not take the Bock's word lightly, Orick. For five hundred years, this one has been a Lord Judge in the City of Life. A million times he has judged the subspecies of peoples who came before him. In many ways, this Bock knows you better than you know yourselves. If he has proclaimed you human, then he is granting you legal rights and protections. This is a great boon, though you may not know it."

"Well, thank you, then," Orick said to the Bock.

Ceravanne turned to the Bock and said softly, "You know a human when you meet it. So, what do you think of Gallen O'Day?"

The Bock blinked and looked at her from the corners of his eyes.

"I approved the bear, Orick, as human. Not Gallen. As for Maggie, I cannot make a determination, since I have spoken with her so little," the Bock admitted.

"And why do you not think that Gallen is human?" Ceravanne pushed him.

"I sense within him . . . a struggle. He desires to become more than what he is."

"So perhaps he is only a human with high aspirations?" Ceravanne countered.

"Perhaps," the Bock agreed. "I suspect that his are a strong-willed people, with only minor genetic upgrades, very close to feral humans in temperament. I could name him human," the Bock said, "but I am loath to place him so low on the scale of sentient life."

Ceravanne laughed daintily and half lowered her eyes, as if at a private joke. "I suspect you are right," she said to the Bock. "To be a Lord Protector, one would have to be more than human." She lowered the flame on the lamp, then with the giant in tow made her way to the other room.

Orick lay tasting the scent of cobwebs and thinking of the spiders spinning their webs above his head. He was unable to sleep for a long time.

The next morning, Orick woke to the cries of gulls and the smell of sea fog, a salty tang that seeped through every crack in the floor boards and clung to every fold of the blankets. Rougaire the giant had roused the others, and they grabbed their belongings then made a quick breakfast of bread and cheese from Ceravanne's pack.

Gallen and Maggie sat alone and talked for a moment by the door with the giant, while Ceravanne had gone to the back room with the Bock.

Orick went to tell them that breakfast was ready, and what he saw surprised him: Ceravanne and the Bock stood in the dim light shining through a small window, and Ceravanne was holding the Bock's long fingers, looking down at them, like a shy lover.

Orick stopped in the shadows of a crate, and the Bock said, "Are you sure you want to go with them? They killed so easily last night."

"I too am horrified by their violence, but what can I do?" Ceravanne asked.

The Bock thought a moment. "For three hundred years you have studied with the Bock, learning the ways of peace. You are more one of us than you are of them."

"Three hundred years . . ." Ceravanne echoed. "It is time I return to my people, and teach them the ways of peace. If I can." Orick wondered at the words "my people." Was she saying that the nonhumans of Babel were her people?

"We are our bodies," the Bock said. "I fear that you cannot teach peace to these creatures. And I fear that the violence you must endure in their presence will maim you. Should that happen, do not hesitate to seek us out. In the woods, in the high mountain glens, you can find peace with the Bock."

Ceravanne had been holding the Bock's hand, and suddenly she bent forward and kissed it. "Three hundred years among the Bock—passed all too quickly. . . . I often wish to see the world as you do. I often wish that I could be you."

Suddenly the Bock's face twisted into a mask of profound regret, and he reached out his long fingers to stroke her hair, cradle her head in his hand. "We are our bodies, with all their hopes and dreams, all their limitations. But you, Ceravanne, even among the Tharrin—you are special. . . ." The Bock wailed in its own tongue, "Assuah n sentavah, avhala mehall—" and Ceravanne stepped back as if astonished at this.

"I love you, too," Ceravanne said. "As much as I have ever loved."

The Bock reached up to its head and fumbled among the green leaves at its crown, then plucked something loose and held it out for Ceravanne. It looked like a small greenish-tan nut, something that Orick hadn't noticed before among its foliage.

"You are going away, and I may never see you again. Should you need a Bock, plant this seed, and in time I will be with you once again."

Ceravanne took the seed gratefully, held it close to her chest as if it were precious. The Bock reached out his long fingers, cradled them around her hair so that she looked as if she were caught in the bushes, and then the Bock leaned forward. His face overshadowed hers, and he kissed her softly on the lips.

Ceravanne wept.

Orick sneaked back to Gallen and Maggie, unwilling to tear the Bock and the Tharrin away from each other. In moments, Ceravanne came out of the back room and placed the seed in her pack, then ate a brief breakfast.

When she finished, she hugged the giant Rougaire and said, "You can see us off at the dock, but afterward I need you to go to the City of Life. Tell the Immortals there that the Lord Protector has come, and that we have gone to confront the Inhuman. If our task is not accomplished by mid-winter, they will have to prepare for war in the spring."

The giant nodded, and they made one last quick search of the room.

Ceravanne wrapped her hair back with a red rag, then pulled her hood forward low over her eyes. She got some soot from a corner, dusted it on her cheeks and under her eyes, making her look worn and wasted. Obviously, she was assuming a disguise.

"Won't people recognize you as a Tharrin?" Gallen said.

"Most people alive today on this world have never seen a Tharrin," Ceravanne said. "And so I tell them that I am a Domorian dancing girl. They look much like the Tharrin. But few people ever even question me about my race. I wear a young body, and children are often ignored, invisible."

She pulled her hood up, affected a slumped posture, a slightly altered body language that somehow completed her disguise. Orick was amazed at the transformation.

Then they hurried out of the warehouse into the streets, and crept to the docks in a dawn fog so thick that they could not see a dozen paces ahead.

It felt good to be on the road again with Gallen and Maggie and a Tharrin, and Orick was somehow eager for action, so he was disappointed when they reached the docks without incident and were able to quickly purchase berths on the second ship they found heading toward Babel.

Because of the thick fog, they had to take the purser's word as to the seaworthiness of the ship; he described it as a lofty five-masted clipper—a worthy ship whose wood held no worm, a ship that could outrun pirates.

So with trepidation they left the docks as several crewmen rowed them to the ship in the fog. The Bock and Rougaire stood on the docks and waved goodbye, seeming to recede into the mist.

Once aboard the ship, the purser escorted them to their berths in three of the six small cabins near the captain's quarters, then excused himself to handle other business.

A brief inspection showed that the ship was all they had been promised—comfortable, immaculate. The ship was already heavily laden with goods, so Orick and Maggie went up to the weather deck in the fog and watched one last time for sign of the Inhuman. Dozens of sailors came aboard in small boats, many of them obviously drunk.

"Watch for a man with bright yellow skin," Maggie breathed into Orick's ear, and Orick sat, listening to the creaking timbers of the ship, the water slapping against the hull. Certainly, most of the crew was made up of an eccentric lot. Dozens of small, bald men with red skin came aboard wearing little more than breechcloths and knife belts. They were filled with nervous energy and were soon everywhere, manning the lines, checking the ties. A dozen grim-faced giants in leather tunics, all armed with oversized bastard swords, seemed relegated to the more strenuous tasks of hoisting sails.

Other crewmen were more eccentric—tall men with tremendously large pale yellow eyes. Black men with horny growths sticking up under their long white hair. Two men with black hooded cloaks came in the last boat, so tightly bundled that they looked as if they wanted their faces hidden, and Orick strained to see the color of their skin. When they climbed up the ladder to the main deck, they moved with incredible swiftness. He glimpsed bare arms the color of slate. One had tattooed his right hand red.

The men passed Orick and Maggie on their way below deck, and Orick caught a glint of their eyes—a deep purple. The second of the pair bore a tattoo of a white spider between his eyes.

And though neither man had the markings that Orick sought, he found that the hair on his neck raised just a bit, and he fought the urge to turn and see if the men were staring at him. When at last he did turn, they had gone off into the fog, yet he wondered what those men might be able to see with such eyes.

When the last sailors boarded the ship, Maggie breathed a sigh of relief. "Thank heaven," she whispered. "Not a yellow man nor one of those bat people among the lot."

The crew weighed anchors and hoisted a single sail, and the ship slid out of port slowly, still under cover of the thick fog.

And Orick soon forgot the chill he'd felt at the sight of the dark-cloaked men. Now that they were away, he found that his heart was light. He heard children laughing out over the water, and spotted some tots—little girls and boys swimming among the many jellyfish alongside the ship. He was amazed at the children's speed, till he noticed that they wore no clothes, and they had tails like fishes.

"Hello!" Orick called to them, and the children laughed and waved at him and Maggie, shouting, "Hello, funny man! Hello, funny lady!" Then one of them threw a jellyfish and they all dove deep, as if they were afraid that he and Maggie would hurl rocks at them.

"Oh, do you think they'll come back?" Maggie cried in delight, and they watched the white-tipped waves for a time, but saw no more of the water children.

Maggie and Orick ambled over the decks for the next half hour till they reached the open sea, where the air swirled and the oppressive fog was left behind.

Orick's spirits soared as they came out under blue skies. The giants began hoisting all sails, and when they filled with air, the ship suddenly surged over the water.

Orick glanced up to the white sails, full of wind, his heart thrilling, just as three giant bat shapes swooped out of the fog to land in the rigging.

He cringed and Maggie cried out, and they moved a bit to see where the creatures went. All three of them scurried to a roofed crow's nest, where they began to cover their eyes with their wings, hiding from the sun.

One of them shouted, "All clear! Night watch out!" then blew a seaman's whistle.

Orick had heard that voice dozens of times in the fog, but never realized that it came from one of the loathsome batlike scouts.

"Hah, they're just part of the crew," Maggie laughed in mock relief. "Who better to sit watch in the crow's nest?"

"A crow would be better," Orick growled, recalling how the scouts had blown their little seaman's whistles in town. "I don't like the looks of them!"

"You can't damn them for their looks," Maggie said, studying the creatures as they huddled in their dark nest.

Her red hair was flying in the wind, and she brushed it out of her face. "Just because they're scouts, it doesn't mean they're Inhuman."

"But it does mean that they're ugly, and I'd just as soon not have their kind near me!" Orick grumbled. "I've seen no good from them."

Maggie whispered, "Speak softer. There's no telling how well they hear." She bent closer, and Orick listened tight. "Orick, those things may not be Inhuman, but it's just as possible that they are. We're on a ship full of people from Babel, and it's likely that at least one of them, and probably more, are Inhuman."

Orick grumbled, turned away, and padded over the deck, his claws scratching the well-scrubbed planks. Maggie's voice had sounded calm enough when she talked of the creatures, but Orick noticed how quick Maggie was to follow at his heels.

That evening, Orick and the others dined at the captain's table. The dinner was a fine feast, with a unique wine that both stimulated the mind and elevated the mood, and along with it they had plates of candied meats, five types of melon, sweet rolls, and breads with cheese baked in them. Orick was delighted, for he seldom found a table larger than his appetite.

In the captain's cabin, the brass lamps kept the room well lit, and the captain had only two other guests at the table—a fat merchant and a shy albino girl.

Captain Aherly sat at the far end of the table from Orick, with a steward boy in a gray smock at one shoulder and his nervous bodyguard at the other.

They made polite conversation for a while at dinner, and Orick was plainly curious about the other guests at the table, so he was almost relieved when the captain said to Gallen, "I've never heard someone who spoke quite the way you and your friends do."

"They're from the village of Soorary, in the north," Ceravanne put in, covering for them.

"Ah, a far country," the captain said, plainly trying to disguise the fact that he wasn't satisfied. "So, do you travel to Babel on business, or pleasure?"

"Adventure," Gallen said. "My friends and I are out to see the world, and I understand that a lot of it is south of here."

"Hah." The captain laughed. "Well, if you're going south, there are some sights that will have your eyes popping out."

"What of our other guests?" Gallen asked. "Why are you aboard?"

The albino girl, a shy girl who had not spoken all evening, looked to the merchant as if asking him to speak, but when he remained silent for too long, she leaned forward and said softly, "I went to the City of Life, for Downing."

Ceravanne supplied the proper response. "You seek resurrection? I hope you were judged worthy!"

The girl looked away demurely. "I was not. They read my memories, but felt that my contribution to society does not merit—" She choked off the words.

Orick felt a small shock go around the table, and wondered what it would be like to be judged unworthy of future life. It would be as bad as getting a death sentence, he decided.

"You are young yet," Ceravanne said. "Redouble your efforts. All is not lost. I am but a lowly Domorian dancer, yet I got the Rebirth."

The young woman looked at Ceravanne, gratitude in her pink eyes. "As one whose skin is young, but whose eyes are old, I appreciate your reassurance. But—I am considered to be a great teacher among my people. I have worked so hard. I don't know what more I can do. . . ."

She abruptly drew her head back, a graceful gesture, like the movement of a deer in a forest, and Orick realized that she was not shy or reticent as a personality quirk, but that her timidness went much deeper. Her life might well be defined by it.

"Be kind and generous, as is your nature," Ceravanne offered. "It is said that the Immortals value such more than other accomplishments."

The albino woman lowered her eyes, blinking them as a sign of acceptance.

"Perhaps, instead more life, seek meaningful death," the captain's body-guard said, pacing across the room. The guard, a woman named Tallea, was like a panther, stalking to and fro, and she spoke in quick, sharp tones, as if unable to slow her speech down. She was well muscled and wore a short sword on her right hip and a dueling trident on her left. Her decorative tunic of gray with blue animal figures was covered by a thin leather vest. All in all, her clothes seemed to be merely functional rather than protective. Despite her pacing and her bunched muscles, she seemed serene.

"A meaningful death?" Gallen asked.

Tallea paced across the room, flexing her hands. She wore many rings of topaz and emerald. "Among Roamers, death is accepted. It comes to all, even those who run long, as Immortals do. They say, is duty of young to live, to care for herd. But when you old, is duty to die, to free others from caring for you. Death, like life, should have purpose. So, seek meaningful death."

"And how would you do that?" Gallen asked.

"Life has meaning only if serve something greater than selves. Give life in service."

"You mean, in battle?" Gallen asked.

The woman half nodded, half shook her head. "Maybe. Or in work."

Captain Aherly laughed. "You must forgive Tallea. She is a pure-bred Caldurian, but she is also a devotee of the Roamers, with their odd ways."

"Why do you want to be reborn as a Roamer?" Ceravanne asked.

The woman turned, her dark hair flying. "Peace. Caldurians never at peace." She turned away, began pacing.

"And what great thing do you serve?" Ceravanne asked.

The Caldurian woman shot a glance over her shoulder, a bright-eyed, mocking look. "I raised in wilderness of Moree, but I left. I serve truth."

There was an uncomfortable silence at the mention of Moree. By saying she'd left to serve truth, the woman seemed to be openly siding against the Inhuman, and none of the others at the table would dare be so bold. The burly merchant who was sitting beside Orick spoke evenly. "My name is Zell'a Cree. I'm a trader myself. For fifteen years now, I've been traveling."

"And what do you sell?" Gallen asked.

"Oh, this and that," Zell'a Cree said. "It used to be that trade was good between continents, but now, most folks don't want to go to Babel. I keep thinking it's time to get out of there, come home and settle down."

"So you are human?" Orick asked, somehow unnerved by the man. All evening, Orick had found that Zell'a Cree sat a bit too close. And now, his tone of voice was off—too mellifluous. The women had just been talking about death and hope, their deepest fears. Yet this man's tone hinted that such things did not bother him. It struck Orick that the man lacked social graces, or some quality that Orick couldn't quite name. At the very least, he didn't know when to keep his mouth shut.

"Yes," Zell'a Cree said, affirming his humanity.

"Liar," Gallen countered, unaccountably furious at the man.

The fellow raised an eyebrow, but did not recoil at the accusation. Gallen raised a hand, as if to strike him.

Zell'a Cree just looked at him calmly. His pupils did not constrict. He did not tremble or sweat.

"You're not human," Gallen said. "You don't even know how to fake it. You have no fear at all, do you?"

"Here, now," the captain said. "We all have our secrets. I make it a policy never to dig too deeply into the private lives of my passengers. A man's sub-species is his own business. Why, I even have a pair of Tekkar aboard—the black-hearted devils."

Gallen put his fist down, but carefully watched the burly Zell'a Cree.

"Tekkar?" Ceravanne asked, and Orick could tell by the tone of her voice that these Tekkar had a nasty reputation.

The captain's face took on a closed look. "Aye, two of them. I invited them to dinner, but they declined, so they're holed up in their cabin. They said that they too went to the City of Life, seeking the Downing."

"But you think they have other schemes in mind?" Gallen asked.

"A Tekkar?" Captain Aherly laughed. "You think they would get the re-birth? Weasels will sooner get reborn as doves."

"Is this what things have come to?" Ceravanne asked. "You knowingly transport agents of the Inhuman?"

"It's not something I can prove or disprove," Captain Aherly said. "I may suspect that a man is a scoundrel, but even the guards at the City of Life will turn no man back who desires the Downing. As long as we keep the gates of the city open to all, I can't prove that the Tekkar have no business in Northland."

"I suspect," Ceravanne said, "that the Immortals would have closed those gates to the Tekkar—if not for the presence of the dronon. Now that the dronon have fled, the Tekkar will not be allowed into the northlands."

"A shame, a shame," Captain Aherly said, "that things had to come to this. Ah, it's not like the old days, when the Tharrin judged men honestly, and there was goodwill among peoples."

"You believe there ever was such a time?" Zell'a Cree said. "Some say that it is a myth."

"The harbor at Tylee has old dry-docking facilities for a hundred vessels," Aherly said. "But I've never seen more than ten ships put up at any one time. There must have been more people coming and going, not too long ago."

"It's true. There was never such fear or animosity between peoples when I was young," Ceravanne said. "The gates to the City of Life were unguarded, as were the ports. People traded freely, and it seemed we were rich."

"If ever there was such a time, it is long past," Zell'a Cree said.

"You were born after the dronon came," Ceravanne said. "Ask the old ones you meet, they will tell you. Our world was at peace."

"Yes," Captain Aherly said. "It's true that we had some peace, an unequal peace. There was always peace in Northland. But even without the dronon, it was harder to come by in the south. You can't let people like the Tekkar mix with folks like . . . the Champlianne here"—he waved to the albino woman—"and hope to have any peace. You might as well raise wolves in the rabbit pen."

"Yet even the Champlianne had the faithful Caldurians to protect them," Ceravanne said, looking up to the warrior woman who paced the floor. "And as long as the Caldurians are strong, there can be peace again. Especially now that the dronon have fled."

"Ah, the dronon have fled but the Inhuman remains," Aherly said. "And I fear that those who desire peace will be swept away before it. Those who have just come from the City of Life say they have seen preparations for war. Armies gathering in Northland."

Maggie gasped, unable to hide her astonishment.

"It makes sense," Zell'a Cree said. "With the dronon gone, someone will have to take charge."

"I have heard this rumor, too," Ceravanne admitted reluctantly, eyeing Gallen for his reaction. "But mark my words, the Immortals will not let their human soldiers cross the oceans. They will not carry their war to the Inhuman, whatever the provocation."

"Pity, Inhuman does not feel same," the Caldurian guard said. "No one has counted people of Babel, but they outnumber humans. They will strike first, and they will strike hard. Humans can't stand against them."

"You seem certain," Ceravanne said, setting down her fork, watching the Caldurian for a confirmation.

The Caldurian shrugged. "I hear things."

"What kinds of things?" Ceravanne asked.

"Rumors." Aherly laughed, too nervously. "Rumors are all you've heard."

The Caldurian studied his face, and seemed to take a warning from it, as if perhaps it was unsafe to speak further. "Rumors," she agreed.

That night in Gallen and Maggie's room, when the waves rode high and the boat tossed on the sea, Orick lay sprawled on the floor while Ceravanne reclined on his stomach, as if it were a pillow. Gallen and Maggie gathered round and held a council, speaking softly.

"What is this about a war?" Gallen demanded from Ceravanne, his voice almost a hiss. "You said nothing about it last night!"

"It's a rumor started by the Immortals," Ceravanne said. "So long as the hosts of the Inhuman believe that we have troops massed and prepared, we hope that they will not march against us. Meanwhile, we are trying to gather armies. A muster has gone out. Our lords fear that now that the dronon have left, the Inhuman will try to seize power. As to whether the Inhuman has gathered armies, we do not know. So far, we have heard only rumors, no more substantial than those we have spread ourselves."

"What if those rumors are true?" Gallen asked, incredulous. "You want us to march into an armed country?"

"We have no choice," Ceravanne said. "But think of this: if armies are now gathering, a muster could work to our advantage by drawing soldiers away from Moree. It could aid our quest.

"Gallen, you must understand something," Ceravanne said. "We don't know how many foes we are up against. As the Caldurian told you, the people of Babel have never been numbered, and we can't even guess how many have joined the Inhuman. But there is one thing we do know: we know the quality of their troops. The Tekkar are swift and brutal in ways you cannot comprehend. They live in dark warrens carved into the stones, and no one can guess their numbers. They alone would sorely test our defenses. Their swift-winged scouts can fly long and far, coordinating armies in ways that we cannot match. And there are thousands of lesser races in Babel, each with its own unique strengths.

"Gallen, the message we sent to the rebels was recorded six months ago. It took a long time to contact you. I've been waiting for you now for months, and you may have come too late to do much good. It may be that we cannot avert a war.

"I fear that the hosts of the Inhuman will sweep across Northland, and the human hosts of Tremonthin may be decimated.

"But no matter what our quest may accomplish, we must at least try."

"If I'd known this last night," Gallen said, "we could have hurried!"

"Hurried where?" Ceravanne said. "It would have been foolish to try to leave port in the dark, even if we'd had a trustworthy captain handy who was willing. We left as soon as we could, and we cannot make the wind blow us any faster. We've hired a lofty ship—but until we reach port in Babel, you and I have no power to even begin the race to Moree.

"Gallen, there may be more dangers ahead than I have told you, depending on our route. There are peoples in Babel who do not think as we do, and we may be unsafe among them. Some, like the Derrits, are uncivilized and eat other peoples for food. Some, like the Tekkar, are civilized and more brutal. And we are just as likely to find unexpected friends. It has been five hundred years since I left Babel, and I do not know what people occupy the lands now. Mostly, I fear the Inhuman and its Tekkar. But I do not want to burden you with possible dangers."

"Tell me this, then, at least," Gallen said. "Why are you here? Why did you insist on coming? Why do you insist on facing the Inhuman yourself?"

"I came for many reasons," Ceravanne said. "I came because you need a guide, and few in the human lands could do this. I came because I fear that you may not have the heart to do what is required, and I hoped to give you strength, and to help rally the people of Babel to our need, if possible." She leaned closer and said softly, "Gallen, it is not enough to destroy the Inhuman—I have come to undo the damage it has wrought."

"Ooh! How can you do that?" Gallen asked.

"I'm not sure," Ceravanne said. "I can only try." She plainly did not want to say any more.

"Right, then," Gallen mumbled. He turned away from her in frustration, bit his upper lip. There were volumes that needed to be spoken between them, but they would not be spoken now. "We must take stock of our situation.

"What did you think of our dinner guests tonight?" Gallen asked, looking between Ceravanne, Orick, and Maggie. "It seems to me that other folks had secrets to keep. Not just us. I don't trust Zell'a Cree."

"Why not?" Ceravanne asked.

"He claimed to be a merchant, but when I asked what he sold, he didn't tell. Every merchant I've ever met is quick to grab your collar, and if he's any good, he'll try to unload half his wares before you get away. That man is no merchant, and he's no human."

"He is a Tosken," Ceravanne said. "Outwardly, he can pass as human. Inwardly, he is something else entirely. Still, they are a peaceful people."

"You don't think he is dangerous?" Gallen asked.

"He has no fear—of death, of pain, of strangers. And because he has no fear, he is not likely to harm us."

"And what of the captain?" Maggie said, bending down close to Gallen, taking his hand in hers. "He practically admits that he transports those who are in league with the Inhuman."

"If he were secretly in league with the Inhuman, would he admit to transporting them?" Ceravanne asked. "No, I think he is like any merchant. He would rather make money than ask dangerous questions."

"And if he is loyal only to money," Orick said, "then he's loyal only to those who pay the most—or last. As long as our purse has a bottom, I won't trust him."

"Tallea said she was loyal to the truth," Maggie whispered.

"Yes," Orick said, excited. "A curious sentiment. Which truth, do you think? And why did she leave Moree? To escape the Inhuman?"

"She's not loyal to the Inhuman," Ceravanne said.

"How can you know?" Maggie asked.

"She wore no belt."

"What do you mean?" Gallen asked.

"Tallea is a Caldurian," Ceravanne said. "Her people are often called 'the

Allies.' They were created long ago—long before the Tharrin were formed—by corporate warlords who sought total devotion from their workers. When they are young, Caldurians may bond to a certain patron, and they remain faithful throughout life. And when they bond, they wear a belt as a sign of their bondage. She is not bonded to Captain Aherly, or to anyone else."

Orick looked at Ceravanne appreciatively. She seemed to have a keen eye, and he saw now that her presence on this journey would be invaluable.

"Which means that she might hire her services out to us," Ceravanne considered. "She would make an excellent escort."

"Wouldn't you rather have a man?" Maggie asked. "Someone who is stronger?"

"A Caldurian woman is stronger than a man of most other races," Ceravanne said. "You saw the rings on her fingers? Six master rings of emerald for her swordsmanship. Four rings of topaz for staff. When a Caldurian proves equal in training to a master, he or she gets a ring. To win more rings, they must cut them from the fingers of their dead foes.

"She is an accomplished warrior, and it is rumored that the Caldurians cannot be turned by the Inhuman."

"Why not?" Gallen asked.

"Some think that it is because they are so highly disciplined," Ceravanne said. "Others think that their minds are just too different from ours, so the Word cannot function properly with them. It is whispered that the Inhuman does not even bother to try to convert them now. Instead, they are killed outright."

"I don't know about the rest of you," Orick said, "but I'm getting nervous with all of this talk. I think there's trouble on this ship. I saw those Tekkar. Even without your warnings, I knew they were dangerous."

"Yes," Ceravanne agreed. "The Inhuman is with us, but does it know of our plans? Will it seek to thwart us?"

"I don't think any of them followed us from the city," Maggie said. "Orick and I watched the boats, and we saw no familiar faces."

"That's a good sign," Gallen agreed.

"But the Inhuman is often subtle," Ceravanne warned. "Just because you do not see it, that does not mean it isn't here. We should take care. We should stay to our cabins as much as possible for the duration of the trip, and never speak openly about our quest again. I know that it is much to ask for you to agree to such seclusion, but it should only be six or seven days till we reach Babel."

Well?" Captain Aherly asked.

Zell'a Cree pulled his head away from the cabin wall where he'd been listening. "They don't suspect either of us strongly," he whispered. "But they are wary of the Tekkar."

"You should have left the Tekkar in Northland," Aherly said. "They'll be nothing but trouble. They've already asked my permission to kill some of our guests. I denied them, but they're thirsty for blood."

"Yet we may need their services before this is over," Zell'a Cree whispered. He considered. He had only three copies of the Word left in his pouch. He couldn't harvest all of the souls in the neighboring cabin. But perhaps he didn't need to. The bear was expendable. Still, most unwilling converts would fight the Word, and there was no way to be certain that three copies would be enough.

"The Tharrin woman, Ceravanne, is beautiful," Aherly said. "I have often longed to see a Tharrin. And yet I find that if I had seen this one on the street, disguised as she was, I would have passed her, never knowing what she was, knowing only that she was lovely." His tone became hard, commanding. "Whatever happens, I don't want you or your men to kill her."

"She's more than just beautiful, she's useful. I'll order the Tekkar to stay in their room," Zell'a Cree agreed.

Aherly shook his head in bewilderment. "Are you sure these people are what you say they are? Gallen and Maggie look like . . . well, just nice kids. Not Lords of the Swarm. And Ceravanne looks like their younger sister. They're practically children!"

"Were we not children before the Inhuman claimed us?" Zell'a Cree said.

"Well, yeah," Aherly fumbled.

Zell'a Cree sighed, obviously fatigued. "We'll find more copies of the Word when we reach port. It seems that time is against our friends. From now on, at night we will put the sails at quarter mast."

"You bastard!" Captain Aherly said. "I've got cargo to carry. You'll cost me days!"

Zell'a Cree scowled at the man. Aherly might be Inhuman, but he was still greedy, a vice that Zell'a Cree could not claim for himself.

"If you have complaints about how I treat you," Zell'a Cree whispered dangerously, "perhaps you should take them to the Tekkar." Zell'a Cree was a broad man, incredibly stocky, so that even in spite of the fact that he was not much taller than Aherly, Zell'a Cree seemed to dwarf the captain.

Aherly's jaw quivered, and Zell'a Cree studied the movement . . . wondering if he could learn to simulate fear.

Fifteen

That night, Gallen wore his mantle to bed. The heavy metal ringlets were uncomfortable, and the many tiny knowledge crystals dangling from it tinkled when he moved his head. But he cared little for sleep this night. He needed knowledge, and so he lay thinking for a long time, wondering how best to speed their trip to Moree.

With his mantle's many sensors, he could see around the room clearly, and he let the mantle heighten his hearing, until the creaking of timbers and water lapping the hull were well amplified. Maggie slept beside him in the narrow bunk, facing the wall, and Gallen enjoyed the sweet scent of her off-world perfumes.

He lay curled against her, smelling her hair, just holding her.

Outside, there was the occasional sound of a scout calling his reports, and the scurry of feet over the weather deck.

Gallen tried to call up files about the Tekkar, but he was using Veriasse's old mantle, and Veriasse had never battled that race. His mantle carried information about the planet Tekkar—a fiendishly hot world where near-sentient dragons hunted by night. Gallen could guess at the specifications one might set in creating a subspecies to dwell on that world, but the reasons for colonizing the place at all were baffling.

And so after a bit of study, Gallen let his mantle seek files on other sub-species he would find on Tremonthin—size, coloration, distinctive features; visual, auditory, and olfactory sensitivity; speeds and strengths; various traits. The information he received was very discomfiting. He found that many races had been boosted for sensitivity, for dexterity, for intelligence, for fierceness.

The Lords of Tremonthin were designing subspecies to colonize thousands of worlds in this galaxy and beyond, yet Gallen saw that the attributes given to some made for incredibly dangerous combinations. He shook his head in wonder, wishing vainly that Ceravanne and the other Tharrin would have had more control over such decisions.

Late in the night, Gallen suddenly became aware of soft footsteps outside his door, and he realized that for several minutes he had heard stealthy sounds—the creaking of timbers at long, infrequent intervals.

For a moment, he watched his door. He'd thrown the bolt home before retiring, but he watched the door handle. His mantle let him see it clearly in the dark, and Gallen silently willed the mantle to let him view the scene in infrared.

He spotted two people standing on the other side of the door—their form revealed by the warmth of their body heat striking the planks.

For a long time they stood, then one of them gently pulled the wooden door handle, testing to see if the door was locked.

Gallen silently sat up, pulled his knife from his sheath, and began stalking toward the door, thinking to pull it open, surprise the men.

He slid his feet across the floor, careful to make no sound, and his mantle detected none.

But suddenly the man at the door froze and distinctly hissed to his companion, "The Lord Protector!" They turned and fled above deck.

Gallen rushed to his door, threw it open, and raced above deck. The deck was cluttered with the lines and mast, dozens of nooks where someone might hide. There was a swift, cold breeze outside, and a dozen sailors were on deck, but Gallen couldn't be certain which of them had been at his door. He looked at them in infrared, and their bodies seemed to shine while flames flickered across their skins as if they were demons from hell.

He addressed one giant who stood at the wheel above him, back turned. "Did you see anyone come up here just now?"

The giant looked over his shoulder. "No. But I heard a noise. Could have been someone."

Gallen nodded. There was no one else close enough to have been keeping watch. He looked up, noticed that the sails were at quarter mast.

"Why are the sails lowered?"

The giant shrugged. "Cold wind from up north, I guess. Might bring a squall. Captain said to lower them. It's his ship."

Gallen pulled his tunic up tight around his throat. It was a cold wind. Very cold.

He looked to the deck to see if there were any prints. The blackguards' body heat should have left its mark. But the men had run too quickly, and he could see no trail. At least the sensors in his mantle weren't strong enough to pick it up.

He asked the mantle to give him an olfactory boost, but this was a feature of his mantle that Gallen had not used before, and the heavy odors that came to him meant nothing.

He grunted, went below deck, and bolted his door. Maggie had slept through the whole thing.

Gallen lay back rehearsing what had just happened, and he could not recall making a sound that would have alerted the intruders. He had his mantle play back the recorded sounds of the incident, and there was nothing that could have alerted the intruders.

Which meant there was but one alternative: they had to have seen him. His foes could see infrared.

But far worse, Gallen realized, was that even though he had kept his mantle and weapons concealed, his foes knew that he was a Lord Protector.

•   •   •

The next morning, Gallen asked Orick to check the corridor, see if he could track the intruders by scent. But the cabin boy had already come through the hall that morning, swabbing the decks with lye.

So Gallen went to the captain's quarters to speak with Aherly, and Orick followed. Gallen had hoped to meet the captain in private, but his body-guard, Tallea, was there. The captain sat in a stuffed chair at his desk, writing in his log, and Tallea stood at his shoulder, her eyes alert, muscles bunched.

Still, Gallen felt he needed to speak now. "Two men tested the doors to my room last night, trying to break in," he informed the captain.

Aherly looked at him askance, his balding head gleaming in the light from the portal. "That's a substantial accusation. Was anything taken, anyone harmed?"

"No," Gallen said. "But they did try my door."

"Did you see them? Could you point them out to me again?"

"I didn't see their faces, but they were of normal height."

"Of normal height?" Aherly pursed his lips. "That's not much of a description."

"And I know that they can see in infrared," Gallen added, hoping to narrow the field.

"It's a common trait in Babel—or even in Northland, for that matter." Aherly shrugged. "Half of my crew has it—all of the night watch. I insist on it, for safety's sake. I would love to resolve this situation, but—is there anything more I could go on?"

"Nothing," Gallen said. "Except—could it have been the Tekkar? Were they out last night?"

"I'm sure they were, but it would prove nothing. The Tekkar prefer darkness, and they sleep during the day."

Gallen stood thinking, and Captain Aherly said, "Look, sir, I don't know what I can do about this matter. But it does concern me. So, I have but one question for you: do you feel unsafe on my ship? Do you feel threatened in any way?"

Whoever had tried his door last night knew Gallen was a Lord Protector. And if he knew that, he would almost certainly know Ceravanne's identity, and Maggie's. Gallen could not ignore that threat, and it was so horrific that he wished he could hide it from his companions. At this moment, he wanted nothing more than to get off this ship. "I do," Gallen admitted. "I feel threatened clear down to my boots."

The captain frowned. "Then there is only one thing to do. I deal with many kinds of people, some who feel threatened by things that are real, others who feel threatened by things that are imaginary. . . ."

"Och, here now," Orick grumbled, "Gallen's not one to go about imagining devils and banshees—"

"Oh, I didn't mean to imply . . ." the captain said, studying Gallen's eyes, "I just mean that—it is . . . it is my policy to make all of my customers feel safe aboard my ship. Welcome and secure. Which is why I hire the Caldurian.

"Would you feel safer if I assigned Tallea to watch your rooms at night?"

Gallen studied the warrior. She had short dark hair with streaks of gray, and deep brown eyes that were very intense. She moved with a grace and power that he only someday hoped to match, and Ceravanne had said that the woman could not be Inhuman.

"Yes," Gallen said. "I would feel safer."

"Good," Aherly smiled. "She will be outside your doors from dusk to dawn." He began to fumble with a drawer of his desk, as if he would open it. "Uh, look," he grumbled. "I assure you that I want to catch these intruders as much as you do. I try to run a clean ship. I pay my crew well, but it may be that one or two of my men—or even some of the other passengers—were intent on pilfering. If that's the case, it's bad for my reputation, you see?"

Gallen nodded, for he could ask no more of the man, but as he turned away, he muttered under his breath, "That's not the case."

He went back to his cabin, and called a meeting. When Ceravanne heard his tale, she was terrified.

"Are you sure that the intruder called you 'Lord Protector'?" Maggie asked Gallen.

"Certain," Gallen answered. "I was wearing my mantle. I've played back the recording a dozen times."

"Then the Inhuman's agents are on the ship, and they know who we are," she said.

Maggie and the bear looked at the porthole, then at the door, as if the In-humans would come piling in at any moment. "What can we do?"

Gallen had been sitting cross-legged, but he pulled his legs up, wrapped his arms around his knees. "I see only one thing that we can do. I have to find the servants of the Inhuman, and eliminate the threat."

Ceravanne said, "Perhaps you're wrong in imagining that it is the Inhu-man. Perhaps these intruders know only that you are a Lord Protector. We were gone from our room for a time last night. Perhaps someone entered the room and went through your pack, found your mantle and incendiary rifle."

"Perhaps," Gallen admitted. "But I think you are only hoping for the best. If they were thieves, why didn't they just take my things, then?"

Ceravanne could come up with no answer.

"There are lifeboats aboard," Maggie said. "We could sneak off the ship some night, try to make it to shore."

"The night crew can all see in the dark," Gallen countered. "To them, you glow like a firefly. You'll not get off this ship unnoticed."

"Then we'll have to be patient, and courageous, and wait," Ceravanne said.

"For what?" Orick demanded.

"For them to come to us," Gallen said.

Sixteen

They sailed that week without further incident, and after a couple of days, the group began to rest easier. During the days they walked the decks of the ship, but in the evenings none of them journeyed abroad.

Orick in particular soon began to wonder. After five more days without a sign of trouble, he began to wonder if Gallen had not dreamed of the danger.

So Orick took to scrambling across the decks longer and longer during the days, watching over the railing as porpoises leapt in the waves and salmon swam in lazy circles, tantalizingly close to the surface of the water.

Each day, the sun came up clear and bright, and the wind filled the sails. Orick spoke to some of the sailors—the red-skinned men of Penasurra were boisterous and always had a joke handy, while the strong Annatkim giants seemed more wistful, always dreaming and talking of their homes in the White Isles far to the south and east.

But it was the warrior Tallea who sat night after night guarding their rooms who most captured Orick's interest, and so one night, he went to speak to her.

He opened the door to his room, found her in her accustomed position outside, standing in the light of a small oil lamp. Orick just stood for a moment, looking at the woman, embarrassed.

She watched Orick's face. "You want from me?" Tallea said.

"I'm curious," Orick said freely. "You're a Caldurian, but you devote your life to following the teachings of Roamers—so that means that when you die, you hope to be born again in a Roamer's body?"

"If I worthy of honor, yes, my memories put into body of Roamer."

"I knew that some folks could be reborn into young bodies made from the old," Orick said, licking his lips, "but I never imagined that they could give you a *different* body. Could I be reborn—as a human?"

"Perhaps . . ." Tallea said doubtfully. "Body is shell. What lives inside, is important, judges say. But rebirth not granted to many. Immortals in City of Life, they judge. Sometimes strangely."

"What do you mean? How do they judge strangely?"

"They read memories, thoughts. Sometimes, person not given rebirth, even when all other peoples think person should be. Judges make hard for person who is not human to get rebirth."

"Maybe it's not just the actions they base their judgment on—but also thoughts and desires," Orick said, "so that everyone who knows the person thinks well of him, but the judges at the city don't. That's how I'd handle it, at least." And that's how God does it, Orick thought.

"Sometimes," Tallea admitted, shaking her head as if to say he was wrong, "I think humans judge human ways, not peoples' ways."

"What do you mean?" Orick asked, licking his nose. He could smell something annoying in the air—lye soap.

"I abhor violence, but excel at it," Tallea said. "Among Caldurians, those who fight best are honored. They would be reborn. But among humans, those who *serve* best reborn. We do not value same."

"Then you feel cheated by the humans?"

"They gave life," Tallea said. "How I feel cheated?"

"Because your people die young?"

"You forget, I am devotee of Roamers. They own nothing. No land, no clothing, no honor. Not even lives. This is wise, to know you cannot own life. It passes."

He left then, but Orick could not help but wonder at the Caldurian.

After a week, Ceravanne began to worry. "We've been at sea too long, with such strong winds," she said. "It's but a five-day journey to Babel under such winds. We must be off course."

Yet when she spoke her fears to the captain in his office, he only scratched his bald head and muttered, "Aye, we're not making good time. We're heavily laden, and that slows us. And we've faced some strong head winds two nights in a row. Give it a day. We'll find land tomorrow."

But it was two days before they sighted land, just after dawn, a line of blue hills barely discernible where the water met the sky. But the scouts knew those hills. The ship was still two days from port.

It rained that afternoon, and everyone was forced to remain inside for most of the day, so it wasn't until evening that the weather cleared. Gallen seemed tense, his muscles tight, and he stared into the darkness.

Maggie knew he was thinking about Moree, wishing that the ship was already there. To ease his tension Maggie convinced Gallen to walk with her under the moonlight.

So it was that they left their room in the evening, well after dinner. The Caldurian, Tallea, stood outside their door, a solid presence.

And as they went topside, Tallea touched Maggie's hand and whispered, "Take care. Tekkar are out."

Gallen was wearing his black-hooded robe, with his mantle concealed beneath. He had his knives and his fighting boots, though he wore no gloves. Maggie felt safe in his presence, so she merely nodded at the Caldurian.

They walked under the moonlight, talking softly, and Maggie held Gallen's hand. As always, his touch was electric. They hadn't made love yet that day, and under the cold stars, she welcomed his touch. They went to the bow of the ship, and stood looking off to sea. To the south she could see the lights of a city sprinkled over a distant hill.

The boat rocked gently, and for a while they stood and kissed, long and passionately. So many times during the day, while Gallen worked out with his swords in their room until the air was filled with the humid scent of him, Maggie found that her lips hungered for his. But now she hesitated to give herself to him too completely, to satisfy her cravings, for she felt the weight of other eyes upon her. Yet she trembled under his touch, and for a while, it was good.

She leaned into him, and her breasts crushed against the strong muscles of his chest. She drew back his hood so that the links of his mantle gleamed in the moonlight, and the memory crystals in it shone with the reflected light of stars. He wore the metal netting over his blond hair, and she considered taking it off so that she could run her fingers through his hair, but decided against it and only bit his ear. "I'd give you more of a honeymoon tonight," she whispered, "right here, if no one were watching." She whispered the words only to tease him, for she knew Gallen to be a gentleman with more self-control than she sometimes wanted him to have.

But she felt him tense, look around, as if to find some handy corner where they could be alone. Suddenly he drew back from her and asked, "Why are the sails at quarter mast?"

Maggie looked up. The evening breeze was cool and steady, without a sign of clouds in the sky. There was no threat of storm, no reason for the sails to be lowered.

"Look at this," Gallen said, gazing over the bow. "We're nearly dead in the water!"

Suddenly a feeling of dread came over Maggie. They'd been aching to reach port for days, and the trip had taken them at least three days longer than expected, though the winds had seemed good the whole time. And even though the captain had complained of head winds at night, she'd never been aware of them.

Gallen looked up over the deck to the helmsman and asked, "Why aren't we at full sail?"

"The captain orders them lowered after dark," the fellow answered, a giant of a man.

"And why would that be?" Gallen asked.

The giant shrugged.

"Has he always lowered his sails at night?"

"Just this trip," the giant answered.

"Gallen," Maggie whispered. "Something smells. Do you think the captain has cost us time on purpose?" But she couldn't imagine how that could be. They'd never spoken of their need to make haste in public. Could the man read minds?

"Aye, the captain," Gallen whispered. "I think I'll have a talk with him."

He took Maggie's hand and began leading her along the weather deck. Aft of the forecastle were two stairs on each side of the ship, leading down to the main deck. The moons were low on the horizon, and shadows from the sails kept the main deck as black as it could get. On a ship back home, the sailors would have rigged a lantern for light, but there was none here. Maggie dreaded having to feel her way down the steps in the darkness, but Gallen stopped, squeezed her hand.

Barely, she saw something black moving in the shadows—a cloaked form.

"Get out of our way," Gallen said evenly.

The shadowed figure barely moved, and Maggie saw light glint from a steel blade. "Get out of *our* way, Lord Protector," a mocking voice replied. It had a hissing grate to it, and Maggie was sure that nothing human spoke with a voice like that. The ship listed as it wallowed in a trough, so that for a brief moment she saw figures in the moonlight—two black-robed Tekkar, sitting on the opposite stairs.

Gallen pushed Maggie back with one hand, drew his sword and a dagger.

"Oh, a wicked man, a wicked *human*," one of the Tekkar laughed.

"With a *big* sword!" the other mocked.

Maggie glanced behind her. There were four crewmen walking along the weather deck toward them, clubs in hand. She stiffened.

"I know—they're coming," Gallen whispered.

"Let, let us through!" Maggie cried.

"We're not stopping you," one of the Tekkar said. "We have no business with you—for now. Go and talk with the captain, if you wish. . . ."

Gallen crept forward cautiously, and Maggie followed so close behind she could feel the warmth of his body.

Just as they reached the doorway to the cabins, Zell'a Cree opened the doors, stood for a moment backlit from a lamp in the hallway. He yawned, then seemed to realize that something was amiss.

"What's going on?" Zell'a Cree asked, looking to the Tekkar. "I thought you two were confined to quarters?"

Maggie realized that Zell'a Cree had known something she did not. She hadn't known that the Tekkar were confined to quarters. Maggie thought it odd that the captain hadn't told the others this comforting bit of information.

One of the Tekkar leaned a bit closer so that light from the hallway fell upon him—a menacing figure all draped in black. Maggie could see just a bit of the man's face, eyes gleaming like wet stones, a white spider tattooed into his forehead. "Even weasels must come out to hunt," the Tekkar said. And then Maggie knew that these men had heard them talking through the walls. The Tekkar pointed. "This *human*—thinks we are a problem, so he wants the captain to tell us to go away. But we know the captain does not like to be disturbed after dark. We thought we'd stop him from squawking."

"You like the hunt, don't you?" Gallen said to the Tekkar. "It's not enough to just kill. You like to bully your prey first. Like cats, batting around dazed mice. Och," Gallen laughed low and dangerous, "I've known plenty like you. Well, come and get me." Gallen thrust his sword forward, letting the tip move in slow circles. The Tekkar was ten feet away.

"Meow." The Tekkar smiled. Then he lurched forward and spun back so fast it baffled the eyes. One second he seemed to be attacking, the next he was over behind the rigging.

"Watch out," Gallen breathed to Zell'a Cree. "We're coming past."

Gallen began to inch past the heavy man, and Zell'a Cree turned his back to the Tekkar and reached up and put his hands on Gallen's and Maggie's shoulders. "Here, here," he said, "let's all be reasonable. Surely there's no cause to draw weapons!"

Gallen slipped past him, drew Maggie into the corridor. Zell'a Cree seemed taken aback by his quick retreat, and he leapt into the hallway with them as if afraid to be on the main deck in company with the Tekkar.

Gallen slammed the outer door, throwing home the bolt. Zell'a Cree stood beside the door dumbly, as if pondering what to do next. The guard Tallea stood at the far end of the hall, a small oil lamp at her feet casting a comforting glow.

Gallen went to the captain's cabin and knocked at the door until it opened.

"What's the matter?" the captain asked groggily through a cracked door.

"Have your lads hoist sails," Gallen said. "I want no more delays from you."

"What do you mean?" Aherly cried.

"I mean, you've ordered the ship to sail at quarter mast every night. I want the sails hoisted."

"What?" Aherly cried, indignant. "I gave no such orders! Wait a moment. Let me get my clothes."

Maggie wondered if this were all a mistake, if some crewman had sabotaged the journey by giving false orders in Aherly's name. He closed his door and bolted it tight. For two minutes Gallen and Maggie waited, until Gallen rapped on the door again with his knife handle. There was no answer from the captain. And Maggie was left to wonder if he was merely frightened of Gallen, or if he was indeed in league with the Inhuman.

The door was made with thick planks, and it hinged on the inside. Maggie doubted that they could break it easily.

"Go," Gallen growled to Maggie. "Warn the others. We're getting off this ship now!"

"Careful," Tallea said at Gallen's back, and she drew her own sword, stepped between Maggie and Zell'a Cree. "He's of them! I in captain's office when he came aboard. He said you would seek passage on ship."

"How did he know we'd choose this ship?" Gallen asked, eyeing the heavy man.

"He knew you traveling, so he bought every berth on every ship. He set trap for you!"

Zell'a Cree stood down the hall, his hands behind his back. Before Maggie knew what was happening, he opened the door to his own room and leapt inside, slammed his door shut, and held it tight as Gallen threw himself against it, trying to knock it open before Zell'a Cree could lock it.

Zell'a Cree threw the bolt home, and Gallen cursed and kicked the door.

Tallea stepped forward and watched the doors, said to Gallen, "Go to cabin and pack. I guard."

Gallen pulled up his hood, glared at the door that Zell'a Cree had fled behind. He stood for just a moment, frustrated, then cried out as if in pain. He threw back his hood, rubbed the back of his neck.

His hand came away bloody, and he looked at Maggie, stricken. For one moment he wobbled, and cried "What's happening?" then Gallen crumpled to his knees.

Maggie rushed to his side. He was looking around, dazed, and Maggie pulled his long hair away, studied the back of his neck. There was a sickly purplish welt under his skin, with blood dribbling from it, as if some pus-filled boil had popped. She couldn't imagine that thing having been on his neck without him noticing it, and then suddenly the whole welt heaved, as something moved under his flesh.

Maggie's stomach turned at the sight, and she gasped.

"Maggie?" Gallen asked. "What is it? I can feel something moving! Something's burrowing into my head!"

There was a crackling noise of bones chipping away from his skull, just beneath the flesh.

"Ah, Christ," Maggie muttered, and her first impulse was to take a knife and cut into his flesh, pull out whatever was burrowing into him.

Tallea rushed over to Gallen, looked at him, aghast. Then she reached into the hood at the back of Maggie's cloak. "Careful," she said.

She brought out a creature that could have been a mantis, with a wide body and a single spade-shaped arm. She held the back of its body gingerly between two fingers.

"The Word is inside him," Tallea said. "The Inhuman is inside him."

"Ah, God," Gallen gasped, and he dropped to the floor, reached behind his neck, tried to pull the thing away.

Tallea dropped to her knees in front of him, peered into his face, curious. "You fight it!" she whispered fiercely. "You must fight!"

"Help me! Help me!" Gallen cried, and his plea terrified Maggie. "I feel it moving in my head." She had never seen him plea for help, had never seen him despair. His eyes grew large, and beads of sweat dotted his forehead.

Maggie fell to her knees, held him close, so that he rocked back and forth, his face buried against her breasts. "It's all right. You're all right," she whispered, yet she could not keep the tone of panic, the pure desperation, from her voice.

"How do you know?" Gallen cried.

"Some resist Inhuman's Word," Tallea insisted. "They not die. They not injured. You must say no to Word!" She took the insectlike machine in her hand and crushed it with emphasis.

Gallen looked up at the Word crushed between her fingers, and his eyes became vacant, as if his mind were far, far away.

Then his attention snapped back, and he looked up at the women, as if embarrassed. "My mantle? The Inhuman is trying to communicate to me through its Word, but my mantle has blocked the transmissions."

There was infinite relief in his voice, yet the precariousness of his situation was not lost on him. Maggie could see by the manic gleam in his eye that he was horrified. Maggie had never seen Gallen like this—so terrified, so utterly alone, and she clung to him as he climbed to his feet.

"It was Zell'a Cree," he whispered fiercely. "The bastard slipped those things into our hoods when we were outside!"

Maggie knew that it must be true, but there was little they could do about it. Gallen ran and leapt, kicking Zell'a Cree's door, but the door held. He kicked at it again and again, then looked over his back at Maggie. "Damn, they build solid doors here!"

"Get packed, and get the others," he said, and there was a fury in his voice. She dared not argue.

Maggie ran into her room, threw her things together, and helped Ceravanne pack.

By then Orick was in the hallway, drawn by the noise, and Maggie came and stood at the back of Tallea, vibro-sword in hand.

"Do you think we can make it out?" Gallen asked Tallea.

"Inhuman seeks converts, not corpses," Tallea said. "They might let us go. But if choose to kill—" She shrugged, as if to say that neither Gallen nor anyone else could stop them.

Maggie pounded on the door of one last passenger—the albino girl who was too frightened to leave her room during most of the trip, but the girl would not open her door now.

Gallen rushed up to the end of the hall, peeked through the door's small window out over the deck, then backed up slowly. "They've got half the crew out there."

Tallea nodded. "We should wait. I can't see well in dark."

"I can lighten things up for you," Gallen said. He grabbed his pack from Maggie, pulled out his incendiary rifle, and connected the barrel to the stock.

He opened the door and fired once. Burning white plasma streamed out, bright as the sun, and sprayed over the crowd, dousing the mainmast. Gallen shouted for the others to follow, and he leapt out onto the main deck.

Silently, Tallea raced out after him, followed by Orick and Maggie. On the quarterdeck, one Tekkar was a seething inferno. For a moment his skeleton remained standing, blazing like a torch, the bones fusing together, and then the skeleton crumbled. Several of the small red-skinned sailors had taken minor hits as plasma splattered from the rifle, and they screamed and spun about, madly dancing as they tried to escape. But with plasma heating to ten thousand degrees on their arms or torsos, even a minor wound was cooking them alive.

The bottom of the mainmast incinerated in a moment, and the sail began to topple forward, held only by the rigging. Maggie shouted for Ceravanne to follow her.

Ahead of her, Gallen and Tallea were in a deadly duel, pitted against a dozen hosts of the Inhuman. Maggie saw Tallea lop the hand off one red-skinned foe, stab a giant in the eyes with her dueling fork. Gallen cut a giant down at the knees, and engaged two black sailors with bony ridges on their foreheads and long white hair.

The remaining Tekkar, a man with his hand tattooed red, rushed forward, his body a blur, and stabbed one of his own men in the back to move him out of his way as he sought to engage Gallen.

In seconds, the two were spinning madly, exchanging parries and thrusts. Maggie had imagined that with his mantle—which helped speed Gallen ten-fold and which had the fighting experience of six thousand years stored in its memory crystals—no one should have been able to challenge him in single combat. But for fifty seconds the two traded punches and kicks, slashing and blocking with their swords, and it soon appeared that the match was even.

Each blow was jarring, so that when Gallen parried the deck rang with the sound, and Maggie was surprised that the swords didn't splinter under the impact. And Maggie knew that Gallen was strong. He'd been training as a guard from his childhood, and his wrists and arms were far thicker than a normal man's. Yet each blow by the Tekkar would knock Gallen back.

One sailor swung a pole at Gallen's feet, trying to divert his attention, and the Tekkar dove in low, throwing his whole body forward in a deadly lunge, sword thrust outward. Gallen parried the sword away with his knife, and blood went splashing over the deck—though Maggie could not see whose—then the Tekkar's body slammed into Gallen, knocking him back onto the deck.

For a moment they struggled together, the Tekkar on top trying to wrestle Gallen's knife away, and it was growling.

Orick rushed to Gallen's aid, but a sailor moved in to intercept him.

Maggie tossed the vibro-sword at the sailor, so that it flew end over end. It caught the man in the neck, slicing him open, and Orick barreled past, jumped on the Tekkar, and bit his shoulder.

In that second, Gallen wrested the knife away and brought it up into the Tekkar's kidney with a violent jerk, so that the blade shot upward, spraying blood.

Then Gallen shoved so hard that the Tekkar flew back three yards and lay clawing the deck. Gallen surged up into the fray. He gutted the sailor who'd swung at his feet, leapt and kicked another in the head so hard that his neck snapped. Four sailors rushed away from him, and Maggie turned to see how Tallea was doing.

The woman knelt on the deck, holding her guts in with one hand, astonishment on her face. Three bloody-handed sailors advanced on her, aiming for a killing blow.

Maggie had no weapons, but without thought she shrieked and leapt forward, tossing her pack. It hit one man, driving his own sword back so that it split his nose.

Then Maggie was in front of them, shouting furiously, "Get out of my way, or I'll cut your nuts off and send them home to your wives!"

All three sailors stared at her, seeing that her hands were empty, yet somehow not trusting their own eyes.

And Maggie had a sudden thought. There were thousands of subspecies in the southlands, more than any one person could know, and you couldn't always tell the dangerous ones by looking at them.

"Believe me, friends," she threatened. "You don't wrestle a Tihrglassian, and walk away alive."

The three servants of the Inhuman stood watching her, uncertain. Maggie raised her hands and bared her fingers threateningly, as if she had talons on them, and two of the men actually backed away.

One of them leapt forward with a roar, jabbing his sword swiftly for a killing blow. Maggie heard a gasp behind her, and suddenly the Caldurian's own sword darted out, caught the tip of their foe's sword and knocked it away with a flourish. With a deadly lunge Tallea let her own sword slide up the attacker's arm, till it bit deep into the sailor's ribs. The last two foes turned and fled, knowing themselves to be no match for Maggie and the wounded Caldurian.

The sails had become sheets of flame, and suddenly the mainmast fell forward, crushing the forecastle, sending up a shower of sparks.

And then Maggie was running, pulling on Tallea's arm. The warrior woman slumped to the deck, crying weakly, "Leave me!"

And Maggie pulled her up, shouting to be heard above the flames. "Not for a fortune. I want to hire your services, if you live through this!"

"Agreed," the Caldurian said.

Someone pushed Maggie from behind, and she looked back. Orick had her pack in his teeth, and Ceravanne was stooping to grab Gallen's incendiary rifle. Gallen was leaping toward them all through the flames.

Maggie saw with relief that the timid albino girl had come out, that she was running to the far side of the ship.

In a moment, Gallen was beside Maggie, half carrying Tallea. They rushed to the aft of the ship, found sailors lowering a lifeboat. It had just hit water, and already some of them were scurrying down the rope ladders to get in.

Gallen aimed his incendiary rifle, shouted to them, "Go on, all of you. Get away from the boat!" And the sailors stopped. One man leapt off the ladder, began swimming for shore, while another raced back up to the deck.

The sailors at the ropes all rushed to the far side of the ship, hoping to get to the other lifeboat before the ship burned.

Gallen stood on the weather deck, keeping the sailors at bay, while Maggie and the others climbed the rope ladders down to the boat. Maggie held the Caldurian in her lap, for the woman had saved her life, and with her own hands she pushed the woman's intestines back in place. The Caldurian's brown face was a mask of pain, and she looked up toward the stars, her dark eyes fixed, unfocused.

Then everyone was in the boat, and Ceravanne was pulling at the oars, splashing them all with water in her hurry to leave. Gallen stood in the prow, balancing on a seat, incendiary rifle in hand.

Fire-lit smoke streamed across the water, and the ship was a roaring inferno. Maggie looked up. The batlike scouts were circling the burning ship, and Orick said to Gallen sadly, "You can't let them get away, lad. It's a man's work you have to do."

Gallen nodded, took his incendiary rifle, sighted for a second, and fired into the sky. Plasma streamed high, lighting the darkness, and hit one of the scouts, splashing enough so that a second also fell.

A third wheeled out over the water, and Gallen fired. But the scout was far away by then, and it dodged the incoming plasma.

Gallen fired twice into the ship for good measure, and Maggie watched several men throw themselves overboard. A dozen men rowed into view from the far side of the ship, and Gallen fired into their boat at a hundred yards. The plasma rushed toward them, a bolt of lightning, and for ten seconds after the hit, the sailors sat burning in the inferno, flesh melting from bones, so that they were skeletons that crumbled in the furnace.

And then the horror of what had just happened—of the murders Gallen had just been forced to commit—fell upon Maggie like a solid weight, like an invisible stone falling from heaven. She saw him standing with head downcast, shoulders limp, limned in the light of the fires.

"Oh, god forgive us," Ceravanne whispered, and then it was over.

They were rocking in the lifeboat, and the sea was fairly calm. Gallen made a little whining noise, a cry of shock and disgust and fear, and he let his rifle clatter to the hull of the boat.

Men were out in the water, swimming for their lives, and the flaming ship was sailing to oblivion, making a sound like the rushing of wind, while spars and timbers cracked. And Maggie knew that some of those men were her enemies, servants of the Inhuman, and it was dangerous to show them any mercy. She knew that they should row out there and cut the men down.

But none of them had the heart for it. Gallen shook his head, muttering, "I know what I'm fighting for, but what in the hell am I fighting against?"

No one answered. Instead, Ceravanne brought out her bag of Healing Earth and began to administer to Tallea. Maggie watched out the back of the boat, to a cloud on the horizon, and at that moment, she saw that the Inhuman was but a shadow, a vapor. Every time they tried to strike against the Inhuman's agents, they faded back and disappeared. She wondered how they would be able to strike against enemies who would not face her.

As Gallen took the oars and rowed toward the distant shore, where the city lights dusted the hillside like flour, Orick began reciting the last rites for those who had died.

Zell'a Cree dove deep beneath the burning ship, and looked up. It seemed for a second that the sky was aflame—or as if the water had turned to amber that scattered the sunlight. Then he climbed for the surface, broke through.

The burning ship roared like a waterfall, and Zell'a Cree floated a moment, floundering, then a wave lifted him and he saw a dark ball floating in the water. He swam to it. It was Captain Aherly, his bald head lolling as if it had been crushed.

Zell'a Cree clung to the floating corpse, and gritted his teeth, looked up at the scouts who were wildly flapping about the ship. All of its masts were aflame, and there was nowhere for them to land, yet the scouts seemed to be circling in the hope of helping survivors.

One of them spotted Zell'a Cree and dove toward him, just as a finger of light arced up from the sea. The scout turned into a flaming skeleton that dropped like a meteor, splashing not far away.

Poor Ssaz, Zell'a Cree thought. Some of the sailors were getting away in a boat, and another finger of light touched them, sent them screaming into torment.

And then Zell'a Cree was nearly alone in the water. Dead, nearly all his men were dead, and of those in the water, he couldn't guess how many might make it to shore. One lone scout had escaped.

Zell'a Cree fumbled for the bag tied to his belt, feeling the contents. His last Word was there, whole and safe, more precious to him than diamonds. Zell'a Cree let his eyes adjust, until he could see Gallen's little lifeboat tossing in the waves, and beyond it the lights along the distant shore, and then he struck out.

It would be a far swim, but Zell'a Cree was Tosken. He ripped the bag from his belt, put it between his teeth, and his mood grew foul as he followed the boat.

Seventeen

The wind and current carried the lifeboat east for many miles, so that as Gallen began rowing, they drew farther and farther from the city.

Ceravanne lay in the boat, stunned by what had happened. She carried the memories of her own suicides, suicides that she had been forced to endure in order to evade the Inhuman, but she had seldom seen such butchery. She'd seldom actually seen men seek to annihilate one another, and she was shocked to the core of her soul.

There was nothing to do but tend to the wounded. She administered the last of her Healing Earth to the Caldurian. The woman had a slash across her belly. It was long, but ran little deeper than the flesh at its deepest point. No vital organs seemed to be hit. Still, Ceravanne did not know if the woman could heal.

Maggie was talking to Tallea, trying to keep the Caldurian calm, her mind occupied. "Are you well? Are you comfortable?" Maggie asked. "Here, let me move, so you can lean your head back."

Tallea leaned her head back at an odd angle, and after a minute seemed to register the question. "Comfortable. I'm comfortable."

Maggie held her hand over Tallea's wound, and blood seeped through it. It was a large wound, too big for the Healing Earth to help much.

"Is there anything more that you can do?" Maggie asked Ceravanne.

"No," Tallea answered, apparently believing that Maggie had asked a question of her.

Ceravanne considered. The nanodocs in her own blood were far more potent than the Healing Earth, but she was proscribed by law from giving her blood to a nonhuman. The nanodocs could establish a colony in her, which would extend her life by decades. Ceravanne pulled a knife from Tallea's sheath and cut her own wrist in violation of the law. Then she let the blood flow into Tallea's wound. In a moment, Ceravanne's own bleeding stopped as the nanodocs closed her cut.

"That is all I can do for her," Ceravanne said. "It may be enough, if no vital organs have been punctured."

So Maggie held the woman as Gallen rowed the boat, long into the night. Soon, Tallea faded to sleep.

In two hours, while the moons were riding high, they landed upon a rocky beach where a large creek spilled into the ocean.

Gallen, Ceravanne, and Maggie carried Tallea from the boat, then dragged the boat ashore into deep brush, and set it down.

Ceravanne helped Maggie form a bed of leaves under the shelter of a large tree, and they placed Tallea in it. Orick was gathering wood, while Gallen made a small fire with matches from his pack.

When he got it going, everyone sat beside it for a while, and Ceravanne looked over to Tallea. She was surprised to see the woman conscious again, watching her from the corner of her eyes.

Ceravanne went to her side, to see if the Caldurian needed anything.

Tallea clutched at Ceravanne's robe and whispered, "Life brings joy, only if serve something greater than selves." Her voice was weak.

"Yes, you said that to us several nights ago," Ceravanne said. Ceravanne looked at the woman helplessly. "Is there anything you need? Water, food?"

Tallea shook her head fiercely and whispered, "A year ago, you came to Babel. I served you then. Not well."

Ceravanne caught her breath, studied the woman's face. "Yes, one of my clones came here, before I was renewed," Ceravanne whispered low enough so that the others would not hear. "It was lost, and never returned. What happened to it?"

Tallea wet her lips, looked away, and closed her eyes. "Dead, I think. That one dead. I wanted to tell when I saw you, but I not want Inhuman to hear." She coughed, then winced at the pain in her side.

Ceravanne bent low, brushed her lips over the woman's forehead, and held her for a long time.

"I need rope, to use as belt," Tallea whispered.

"You don't have to bind yourself to me," Ceravanne whispered. "I don't want slaves."

"I not slave," Tallea wheezed. "I ally. I serve freely."

"But the clone you served is dead. I am not that woman."

"No, I not be bound to you—to Maggie."

Ceravanne looked at Tallea, taken aback.

"She saved me," Tallea said. "I promise live for her."

"You promised wisely," Ceravanne said. "Sleep now, and keep your promise. When you wake, I will have the belt for you."

Ceravanne gently laid Tallea's head back down, then went back to the fire. The others were still all wide awake. "I wish we had more blankets for her," she said, nodding toward Tallea. Maggie had put a thick robe on the woman, but it was hardly enough, and the blankets had gotten wet in the bottom of the boat. They'd have to sleep without for the night.

"When my fur is dry, I'll lie next to her," Orick offered.

Ceravanne laughed. "And may I sleep on the other side of you?"

"If you do, you'll do so at your own risk," Orick said. "I tend to toss and turn in my sleep. I'd hate to squash you."

"I'll take the risk," Ceravanne said.

No one spoke for a minute, and they all sat gazing into the fire. At last, Gallen said, "I'll hike into town in the morning and buy a wagon, if we've got any money. We'll need it to carry supplies—and to get *her* to a doctor."

Ceravanne said, "Her fever is low. If she makes it through the night, she should do well. There's nothing more that a doctor could do. Still, she will need a wagon. She won't be walking much for a few days."

The others spoke on for a while, but Ceravanne began to tire. She went and lay beside Tallea, and sometime later she woke. Orick was beside her, his fur all warm from the fire. The bear put one big paw over Tallea's chest, and Ceravanne hugged him from the other side, lay for a moment, watching his chest rise and fall. He began to sing in his deep voice, a song she guessed that bear mothers would sing to their cubs on his home world:

"Little bear running,
little bear running,
with burrs in your hair,
and dirt on your paws.

May your spirit linger,
long may you wander
in woodlands hallow
with dirt on your paws."

When he finished, Ceravanne realized that it was a song to comfort dying cubs, and her heart ached to think that anyone should have to compose such a verse. Yet she was glad to have Orick here, comforting the woman in his own way.

When Orick and Ceravanne went off to sleep, Gallen and Maggie rested together beside a small fire that flickered and twisted among a few sticks.

Gallen sat in the darkness far under the tree, and Maggie lay in the crook of his arm, holding the crushed Word, its white metal body limp in her fingers as she scrutinized it. Aside from Tallea, only Maggie knew that Gallen had been infected by the Inhuman, and she seemed greatly distressed, unable to sleep.

Gallen tuned his mantle, listening as far as its range would extend, calling upon its sensors to amplify the light until it seemed that he sat in daylight, beneath cloudy skies. Yet there was a surreal quality to his sight. He could see mice hunting for food among the leaves in the distance too clearly, their body heat glowing like soft flames. And small deer in the near hills shone brightly. The songs of ten thousand crickets and katydids filled the woods, and he could hear the rustling of mice under dead leaves. No people lurked nearby.

Yet despite his sensors, Gallen was worried. Even with ample warning, Gallen feared the servants of the Inhuman. The fear gnawed at him, kept him awake.

When battling on ship, he'd found the giants and the red-skinned sailors to be no great challenge, but he had come close to dying in the grasp of the Tekkar. The little man had been incredibly fast, incredibly strong, and he had the focus of one who does not fear death but only wishes to kill. While struggling with the creature on the deck of the ship, Gallen had watched the white spider tattooed on the Tekkar's forehead. As the man grimaced and struggled, the legs of the spider had seemed to move as his skin stretched and tightened. And Gallen realized that the man had done it purposely, seeking to frighten him. The Tekkar had worked its hand slowly, inexorably toward Gallen's esophagus, despite Gallen's best efforts to fight the creature off. It had been playing with him, Gallen was sure, lengthening the seconds until it took Gallen's esophagus in hand and crushed it.

Gallen did not want to frighten the others, but he worried, for it had only been their combined strength that let them defeat one Tekkar.

"How are you feeling?" Maggie said, still looking at the machine in her hand. She wore her own mantle. "Your head—is it all right?"

"I can't feel anything moving in it anymore," Gallen said, and even to himself his voice sounded stretched, hollow.

"What are you going to do?" Maggie whispered. "You can't just ignore it. The Word isn't going to go away."

"What are our options?" Gallen asked. "What have you learned from the Word that Tallea found?"

"It's a fairly simple device," Maggie said. Maggie had on her own mantle, and she was studying the creature as a technologist would. "Its body has a few sensors—smell and sight only, as far as I can tell, and the main shell is built with invasion in mind. Its streamlined build helps it get under the flesh quickly. Beyond that . . ." She pried off its largest arm, with its spade-shaped blade, then pulled off the head. Something like a green-blue gel oozed out. "On the inside, it's all nanoware interface. The Word is designed to burrow into your skull and create an electronic sensory interface."

"So the Inhuman can send its messages?"

"Yes," Maggie said.

"Can it control me?"

"It's more primitive than a Guide," Maggie said, referring to personal intelligences that were designed to enslave their wearers. "It's not large enough to carry the machinery needed to take total control of your central nervous system. I believe it simply carries a message to you. The Word."

"What if I resist it?"

Maggie considered. "It may punish you. The nanoware sends circuitry, strings of neural web, into your brain. It might activate pain and pleasure centers—cause fear, send hallucinations. But if Tallea is right, people *can* resist it. If you resist it enough, I suspect that the circuitry may just fry certain nerve sites, activating them over and over until they burn out. Once that happens—there's probably nothing more that it can do."

She tried to make it sound easy, as if freedom were only a thought away, but Gallen knew that it would be much tougher than that. He could resist it, but if neurons were getting fried, then he'd have some brain damage as an aftereffect. But it was better to die for his friends than to live for the Inhuman.

"I have to see if I can fight it," Gallen said. "I have to test it. I've had my mantle knocked off in battle before. I can't let myself get in a position where I'm fighting on two fronts at once."

"I know," Maggie said, and she threw the dead Word into the brush, turned to look up in his face. She kissed him slowly, and the reflected firelight flickered on her face. He breathed deeply, relishing the clean scent of her hair, the faintest hint of perfume.

"I'll ask my mantle to shut down its signal block for two minutes," Gallen said, silently willing the mantle to stop. His ears went numb, as if all the sound in the world—the song of the katydids, the rush of the wind, the bark of a distant fox in the darkness—all disappeared. Then his legs buckled from under him, and Gallen tumbled to the ground, looking out, struggling to hear the sound of his own heartbeat, and he could not move, could not speak. He was vaguely aware of Maggie grabbing him, trying to lift him up, hold him in her arms.

And then the visions started, and Gallen remembered. . . .

He was in a beautiful village in Babel growing up in a home that was a work of art, a mansion formed of stone and wood. As a child he would watch the cornices of his bedroom, which were sculpted by hand, and he would imagine that the animals and people carved there would speak to him of their lives in wood. And he remembered his ancient grandmother, draped in robes of purple silk with black lace, the black feathers woven into the white mass of her hair. She was greatly venerated for the cloth she wove and dyed, but he loved her for her sweet voice as she sang him to sleep, and he loved her even more for the attentiveness with which she listened to the tales he would tell from the lives of the wooden creatures carved on the cornices of his room. Once, his grandmother had told his father, "He will be great among the Makers, for with him, the art is not something that he sees, it is something that he lives."

He remembered the green fields of his childhood, where the yellow cows on his father's farm drank from elaborately decorated brass containers shaped like moons and suns and stars and boats all set out on the green pastures.

He learned in time that his people were called "the Makers," and in his village, creating things of beauty was the goal of every person. They did not seek to own beauty or horde it—only to create it. And not only were the things of their hands beautiful, but the thoughts of their hearts, the lives that they lived, also were shaped and molded into beautiful forms.

And so Gallen remembered that from the youngest age he desired to do nothing but shape stone, to release the people and animals and gods hidden under stone—whether he was carving walnut-shaped tubs from marble or forming statues of giant whales that seemed to be leaping out of lawns. As a child, he would seek the hills where cliff faces were exposed, and there he would chisel and smooth the granite, creating wondrous scenes of gods from his private pantheon, battling their demons.

By the age of twelve, he was given his name and his rank—Koti, a master craftsman. He was one of the youngest ever to become a master, and small, brown-skinned Makers from all across Babel came to study at his feet, learn his techniques.

By the time he was forty, sixteen thousand students he had, and great was their work—greater than that of any Makers who had ever lived.

At the Tower of Serat his pupils worked for seventeen years to carve scenes from the tales of the life of the hairy prophet Janek, and tell of his ascent into heaven on the back of a flaming swan from that very pinnacle. Though the tower was six hundred feet tall, the Makers worked every inch of the stone, until it became one of the great wonders of Babel, so that millions of people undertook pilgrimages to gaze upon Janek at the top of the tower, his long beard whipping in the tempest as he straddled the back of the giant flaming swan.

When he finished, Koti took his pupils to the edge of Andou, where the river Marn flowed in from the Whitefish Mountains. There a great sea of rounded boulders had lain for millions of years, deposited by glaciers.

Koti's students worked diligently among the boulders for twenty years, carving each of them into great images from their tradition, showing the War of the Gods that would someday come, when Goddess Peace would finally put down the Dark Spirit of Strife, when Fertility with her many orifices overcame the sexless Barrenness, when all the ten thousand gods of virtue ascended to their rightful domain.

The place was renamed Valley of the Gods, and one could walk through it for weeks staring at marvel after marvel.

And Koti did not only create great works in stone, he married a wise woman who had a talent for shaping lives. They loved one another passionately, and well Gallen remembered the countless times they wrestled as one while making love in their garden bed, under the evening stars at their summer home. His sweet wife Aya gave birth to eleven talented children, so that together Koti and Aya became a great patriarch and matriarch, admired by all.

After sixty-two years, Koti's body grew frail even though he was still young, for he had worn it out in the service of his art and of his family and of his people.

By then, Koti's fame had grown so great that his own people built him a throne and begged him to slough off his mortal body so that he could reveal himself as a god, for the works that he had designed for his apprentices were not only apparently without number, they were also without equal.

But Koti convinced the crowds to stifle their acclaim, and he prepared for death.

And so it was that the Makers gathered fifty thousand men and women, and they bore Koti's ravaged body upon a pallet carved of sandalwood, and they sailed with a thousand ships across the sea, as he lay dying.

Together they marched to the City of Life, where the great columns of crystal memory rose high and haughty and gray against the white mountains on the skyline.

His people came arrayed in their finest garments of scarlet, and they swung golden censers of incense before his pallet, filling the sky with sweet-smelling smoke of green. The drummers and flutists played before him, and women danced with bells on their feet and tambourines in their hands, their voices rising in haunting music.

At the City of Life, he had his memories recorded and gave the humans samples of his skin, and fifty thousand people wept upon the stairways to the Hall of Life and petitioned the human lords to prepare a new body for the greatest of Makers.

And there the memories of Koti ended, but the memories of his disciples were recorded thus:

And so the humans studied Koti's works, studied his memories, and they judged him: "We know that Koti's work is magnificent in form, but it is flawed in content. His work is filled with boundless passion, but we fear the images of the gods he has formed. We fear that his work will fuel a danger-ous resurgence of idolatry. He has impeded the cause of mankind, and therefore will not be reborn."

And so his disciples took Koti home and tried to nurse him back to health, but on the cruise home, Koti was so humiliated by his treatment at the hands of the humans that he swore to eat no more. Because of his poor health, he died within the week.

So all Makers swore a vow that none of them would ever go back to the human lands seeking rebirth, and none would sell their wares to humans. Since the greatest of them had been judged unworthy, the Makers knew that mankind esteemed them as dust.

Gallen felt the weight of Koti's life in a great surge. He lived through the passion, the genius, the years of toil, the intense love he'd felt for his family, all in moments, gained the insights that Koti had had, then witnessed the fi-nal humiliation and death.

And Gallen knew, he knew surely, that mankind had judged Koti wrongly, that they had been blind to his greatness.

And suddenly, the colors swirled in his head, and Gallen began to recall the life of Doovenach, a humble woman of the Roamers, the hairy people of the plains.

She had been born under a weathered oak tree in a warm rain, and had lived her life on the open plains beneath the sky. As a child, she had learned the call of the thrush, the scent of the rabbit. And during the summer storms, when forks of lightning beat the earth, the tribe would huddle under wide trees, and Doovenach would huddle under her mother's sagging breasts and watch the dark clouds, listen to them growling.

For countless days she had wandered the golden plains, under Tremon-thin's suns, harvesting handfuls of wild oats, rose apples, and black peas. She grew to hate the biting black flies that followed her herd, never realizing that they were so tormented only because her people had a law against bathing—for when one bathed in the infrequent pools of the grasslands, he dirtied water that others might drink.

But mostly, Doovenach remembered a sense of peace that flowed as wide as the prairie, and she remembered the good times hunting for mice to eat with her sisters, or the time that the tribe wandered east all summer until they reached the end of the world, where it dropped over cliffs to salty water, and together the whole tribe jumped off into the ocean and swam about every day until the weather turned cold, then they climbed out and headed west for another three years until they bumped into the mountains.

At times it would rain or snow, and Doovenach would huddle beneath a tree, her furry hide wet and cold, and she would curse her life on such miserable days.

Like others of her tribe, she had been born into a society that knew no possessions. Her people ate the wild grasses from the plain, hunted with sticks and rocks. When they brought down a deer or an antelope, they squatted and cut the fresh meat with knives, divided it equally among all.

Other races sometimes hated them, for the Roamers could not understand the concept of ownership. If they found a cow in the wild, they would eat it. If trees were filled with fruit, they fed. And afterward some person of another tribe would come and claim that they owned this cow or this tree.

And so Doovenach remembered times when other peoples would chase the Roamers and beat them. They once found a field of peas, and men with clubs came to chase them away, and when one of the men hit Doovenach's mother, his long club also struck Doovenach's baby brother, crushing his skull.

And she remembered a time when her people wandered into a town, hoping to drink from the troughs where horses drank, and people in hats and tunics and dresses laughed at her nakedness, and their children threw rocks at her. Doovenach found a beautiful dress as blue as her eyes drying on a bush, and she tried to put it on, but some people came out of a house, shouting, and their dogs bit her legs and drove her away.

And when she was eighteen and beautiful so that the males of other clans wanted to mate with her too much, Doovenach ran away and crossed through a great town, and while she was hungry, she went into an inn and began to feed from a table.

The people of that town gathered around and laughed at her nakedness, and a man claimed that she was eating his food. She tried to run then, for she feared he would beat her, but he only laughed and said that he would trade her for the food, give her something good, then he took her into an alley and beat her and savagely mated with her.

When he finished, he threw coins on her, and other men from the inn also came and mated with her, too, ignoring her cries but leaving more coins, until at last when the men had all finished, a wench from the inn came and explained to Doovenach how to use the coins.

Doovenach had never owned anything. It seemed to her that her very bones whispered that the root of all evil came from lusting after the possessions of another. And her very bones told her that the earth and all of its riches belonged to all. And because Doovenach had never possessed something to call her own, she had never learned the great secrets of exchange.

But once she learned this great secret, Doovenach returned to her people with money and sought to teach them. She told them that their lives would not be so harsh in the winter if they took money into town and bought food, and she explained that they could mate for money, but her people could never seem to comprehend her words. Or perhaps they never believed them.

So Doovenach returned to the city and rented a corner in a stable where she could sleep in warm straw, close to the sweet smell of horses. She made money by breeding with any man who would have her, and she learned to both take and give great joy in the act. Many were the men who would suck at her hairy breasts and cry out in ecstasy as they made love. And though she never bore children, she helped care for children of the streets who had no homes. For many years she studied other races and learned their ways.

Often in the winter, younger Roamers would come in off the plains and Doovenach would share her food with them, let them sit under her shelter, but the others never learned her ways. They respected her and knew she was wise, but she was wise in ways that they could not comprehend.

And so, when Doovenach began to grow old and ugly and could no longer earn much money, she journeyed to Northland with a friend and sought rebirth, hoping to be young again, hoping to become a teacher for her people.

The human judges in the City of Life recorded her memories and took her skin sample, and Doovenach's memories ended there. But she gave money to her friend, and her friend's memories were also recorded. After many days the humans passed judgment on Doovenach, saying, "Although you claim to be a devotee of human ways, you have never understood anything but the most surface concepts of capitalism. You have rented the barest shelter in a stable, and sometimes bought food, but beyond that, you have never gained any possessions, never sought to obtain the virtues that would assure rebirth."

"But I have advanced the cause of mankind," Doovenach protested. "I gave joy to many men."

The human judges said: "You sold them pleasure. You were only a whore, catering to their most basic instincts." And they sent her away.

Doovenach shrugged, and she was not angry. She had lived her life, and she reasoned that if the humans had given her another, then perhaps on some cosmic scale the universe would have been thrown out of balance, and someone else would have had to go without being born.

But after that, the Roamers did not go to the human lands seeking rebirth, for even the wisest and most human among them had been found unworthy.

And the colors swirled, and Gallen began to recall the life of Entreak d'-Suluuth of the bird tribe. And just as suddenly, he was in the night again.

There was a searing moment of pain, and Gallen found himself lying on the ground. He could smell grass and mud. There was a familiar weight of his mantle on his head and shoulders.

The night felt so strange, so cold. Gallen struggled up, until he could see Maggie squatting over him, her dark red hair limned by moonlight. She was holding his hands.

"Oh, Gallen, are you all right?" she asked. Gallen's mantle heightened his vision, and he could easily see the lines of worry in her face. In the darkness the pupils of her eyes dilated to a seemingly unnatural width.

Gallen struggled to his feet. It was well past midnight, and silver-lined clouds rolled across the night sky. Two minutes. He had been under for two minutes, and in those moments, he somehow felt the weight and pain of two lifetimes. He'd tasted the flavor of those lives, of people's feelings, in a way that he'd never imagined. "We are our bodies," the Bock had said. And Gallen wondered if that creature really understood the depth of those words—understood the sense of peace the Roamers felt in traveling the wide earth, or the passion the Makers felt while kneading mud for the potter's wheel.

Gallen recalled dozens of experiences, all whirling like butterflies in his head—Doovenach tasting wild anise for the first time; an old man of her tribe dying of hunger. Koti as a young man, painting a tin glaze over a pot before it went into a kiln.

Gallen felt as if he were tumbling, tumbling; his emotions were still jangled. He felt exultation that was somehow displaced, without a reference to any experience he could imagine. Right now, he thought he should be feeling relief at getting free of the Inhuman, or disgust at his own humanity . . . or something. But the Inhuman's probe seemed to be stimulating his emotions directly.

"I . . . can't think. I can't think!" Gallen said.

"Why not? What are they doing to you?"

"Memories—" Gallen said. "I'm remembering lives."

"The dronon made the Inhuman, and they don't want you to think!" Maggie said, squeezing his hands. "Whatever the dronon show you, they don't want you to think. Gallen, I know how memories are recorded. They can be edited. They can be misremembered. It's easy to fake them. But even if these are genuine, the dronon don't want you to think: you might disagree with them, and the dronon don't tolerate that."

Gallen looked up at her, knew that she was speaking what she believed was the truth, yet dangerous thoughts kept flooding through his mind, welcome snatches of memory. He felt far more experienced in life, far wiser than ever before. He reveled in his new memories, as if they were a new great cloak that weighed heavily on his shoulders, but was yet new and comforting. The memories that the Inhuman offered were sweet and exotic and tinged with pain, and he hungered for more.

Maggie was human, and she accepted the human agenda without question. But neither she nor Gallen had ever looked beyond the human agenda. Neither of them had really considered whether the benevolent Tharrin were running the universe in the best possible way. Gallen remembered the deadly rose, left as a warning on Fale. And now, Gallen recalled the lives of the people of Babel, saw how their lives were thrown away, how their needs were ignored. They suffered. They suffered. Ignorance, poverty, lawlessness, death. The humans of Tremonthin could protect the people of Babel, sweep all of these ills away, but they did not.

"Maggie," he whispered. "I need to go under again. I need to know more!"

"Not right now," Maggie said, squeezing his hand. Her eyes were frightened, and he knew that she didn't want him to ever go under again. "Give your head some time to clear. Rest."

"Soon, then," Gallen said. "I want to go under soon."

Maggie's eyes were large and frightened, but Gallen suddenly knew that there was nothing to fear. The Inhuman had never sought to kill them, had never sought to harm them. Gallen felt dazed, as if he were whirling, and he knew he was too tired to stay awake much longer.

"Promise me," Maggie said, her voice tight, "that you won't go under again without telling me. Promise me that!" She took him by the collar, held him, her lips just inches away from his.

Gallen gazed into Maggie's wide eyes, and wondered how he would tell her of the things he'd seen, the things he was beginning to guess—about the Inhuman's beautiful plans. . . .

Eighteen

When Maggie woke at dawn, Gallen was gone. She hoped that he had not tried to wrestle with the Inhuman once again. Whatever he'd felt the night before, she had seen in his face that the Inhuman was more dangerous than she'd imagined. It had seduced him in only a moment, and she feared that he had wakened hungering for its touch.

She stalked around the camp all morning, wondering if she should tell the others, wondering if Gallen would come back at all. She retrieved the broken Word from the bushes where she'd thrown it the night before, then went outside of camp, put her mantle on, and Maggie silently asked her mantle to feed her information on the creature—its probable functionality.

Immediately, the mantle showed her a schematic for the creature, detailing the known hinges in its joints, its sensory apparatus, its own brain and system of energy storage. The body of the Word was just a simple machine designed for invasion. It was too small to be self-aware, and therefore would try to complete its only task rather doggedly, and stupidly, at times.

But the information she needed most was not available. Once the creature invaded its host, the nanoware inside was extruded into the host's brain, and that nanoware could not be studied without microscopic sensors that Maggie's mantle did not have.

So Maggie asked it to make a guess about the most logical functionality of the thing based on current technology. The mantle suggested that the system required several components: an antenna system to receive signals; an amplifier to boost the signal; a power system to power the amplifier; and a neural interface that would let the Inhuman's message be sent directly to the brain.

Beyond those four systems, Maggie didn't know what else the Word might have incorporated into it. But Maggie considered each of these systems, wondering how to sabotage them.

The antenna was first on her list. Her mantle said that since the human body already worked as an antenna, receiving radio signals due to the electromagnetic field created by ionized salts within the body, the Word would need to do very little to actually receive the signals. The body already could receive signals, it just wouldn't recognize them. But solar interference during the day might distort signals, weakening them to the point that they would be worthless. And beings living underground might not receive the signals at all. And the dronon may have taken these factors into account.

Her mantle whispered that the human body could be greatly enhanced as an antenna by temporarily introducing small amounts of metallic salts, and Maggie suspected that such metallic salts would disperse evenly throughout the body.

But the main thing that the Word needed was not a better antenna, but a good amplifier, and that amplifier would be powered by converting body heat into electrical energy.

Maggie noted that the servants of the Inhuman had kept the Word close to their bodies, kept them warm, and she suspected that the biogenerator was concealed in the body of the creature, probably with the amplifier. If she could get that biogenerator to cool, the Word would die.

But the Word had burrowed to the base of Gallen's skull and had actually inserted itself inside the skull, making it almost impossible to remove.

Gallen had said that he felt it "moving in his skull," and Maggie had the very disturbing notion that he might have been right. Once the creature made its entrance at the base of the skull, it might well have moved higher into the brain to protect itself.

Once there, it had little difficulty sending a chain of nanoware devices into the brain and spinal column, forming new neural pathways so that it could send its message to its host.

Once there, the Word had only to receive its signals from the Inhuman, then convey the information to Gallen. He recalled two lifetimes in only two minutes, which suggested to Maggie that an incredible amount of information was being downloaded rapidly.

But those possessed by the Inhuman were not being controlled individually, of that she was sure. If they were all connected through a transmission network, they would have been able to send and receive information instantly, coordinating their attacks without even voicing commands.

But back in town, the hunting packs of the Inhuman had relied upon their scouts to convey verbal communications.

Which meant that the Inhuman, once it fed its propaganda to a host, released the host, expecting it to act at its own discretion.

The Word. . . . Maggie recalled how her attacker in Northland had talked about it almost reverently, as something to enjoy. And Gallen had been seduced by its touch, and now craved to hear more. When she'd first looked at his face, he had been filled with joy and peace and loss. His eyes had been shining with an emotion she hesitated to name—ecstacy.

And Maggie realized that the entire process, rather than being dark and frightening, had been designed to be something far more palatable for its victim—perhaps even something desirable. Perhaps that was why the Tekkar were converted so quickly; instead of running from the Inhuman, they embraced it joyously.

Maggie considered the Word, as she walked up a steep incline, wondered how to combat it.

If she were a surgeon and had the proper equipment, perhaps she could have destroyed the neural network. But she wasn't prepared to perform brain surgery out here in the woods. Likewise, she couldn't risk trying to open Gallen's brain to get to the Word's amplifier or biogenerators.

She wondered if it might be possible to damage the Word, corrode the nanoware with chemicals—but her mantle whispered that such an attempt would be dangerous. The nanoware would be more resistant to most chemical attacks than Gallen's own body would. Doubtlessly, with the many human subspecies on Tremonthin, the dronon would have created the Word to be suitable to a broad spectrum of creatures.

"The nanodocs in Ceravanne's body form an artificial immune system, designed in part to rid the body of excess metals," her mantle whispered, and Maggie considered. It was possible that the nanodocs could—over several days—corrode the Word, but her mantle also whispered that it would take the nanodocs from a liter of Ceravanne's blood three days to have much effect. It was hardly a workable solution.

Which meant that Maggie had to figure out how to disable the antenna. Her mantle had suggested that metallic salts would stay in the body for only a few days. And she realized with a start that this was all the Inhuman would need: it was probably designed to download its information in a matter of hours, then never be used again. In fact, Maggie realized that it probably *couldn't* be used at long distances after a few days, not if the antenna system were only temporary.

Her mouth became dry, and she grew more excited.

Is there a way to get rid of these metallic salts? she wondered.

"You cannot attempt to deprive him of them," the mantle whispered, "for he needs some to live. But if you feed him small amounts of potassium chloride and large amounts of water, his body should flush out any of these metallic salts quickly, within a few days."

Beyond that, Maggie could guess what to do. In the daytime, the natural solar activity would help Gallen's mantle block the radio waves. In fact, Maggie suddenly realized why the Inhuman attacked after dark—so that their victims would be converted immediately, instead of having to wait for the night.

And after dark, it would help if Gallen could get underground, where the Inhuman could not communicate.

So Maggie realized that she would have to begin flushing the excess salts from Gallen's system. Until that was completed—a task that her mantle suggested would take a week—Maggie would have to do what she could to lower Gallen's susceptibility. They could probably travel during the day, but at night they would have to seek shelter underground.

And still, given all of that, the Inhuman's Word would still be lying dormant within him. Once Gallen got close to the Inhuman, or close to one of its transmitters, the Word would no longer require a strong signal, and it would be able to overwhelm him.

"One battle at a time," Maggie told herself. "I must fight one battle at a time."

At noon, Gallen returned to camp with food—a plump goose, a burlap bag filled with apples, plums, pears, squash, new potatoes, and a pouch of cherry wine.

Gallen passed the food out, then told the others, "There is a road just south of here, with a farmhouse. The master of the house was good enough to sell us some stores, but no wagon. We're twenty kilometers east of a fair-sized town. I'll buy a wagon there, and drive back to you tonight. Keep your heads low. We've no way of knowing these folks around here, whether their intentions toward us would be foul or fair."

Maggie watched his eyes as he spoke, and she could detect no change in his features, no change in how he acted toward them. If he'd been seduced by the Inhuman's Word, she could not tell. She could sense no struggle.

Maggie told Gallen that she would come with him to town. Orick said he also wished he could be off with them, but he looked around camp and decided that his greater duty lay here, to guard Ceravanne and Tallea in case an armed mob came searching for them.

Maggie was getting ready to leave, eating a brief lunch of plums and raw corn, and Ceravanne was caring for Tallea. Orick began plucking the goose with his teeth—a thankless job that he complained would leave down stuck between his teeth for days.

When Maggie finished eating, she and Gallen climbed the hillsides through the thick woods until they reached a dirt road wending through forests at the foot of the mountains.

Gallen seemed somber, distracted.

"Tell me more about what happened last night?" Maggie asked, hoping that he would at least acknowledge that something had changed.

He said, "It doesn't matter. They were just someone else's memories, someone else's thoughts. I'm over it now."

He hurried his pace, as if he were angry, and looked about. She could tell that he was still deep in thought, deeply troubled, trying to work things out.

She told him then of her own studies, and the things that the mantle had revealed, how they would need to travel during the day and go underground at night, how he could reduce his own reception of the Inhuman's signal by drinking heavily to rid his body of any metallic salts that the Word introduced.

Gallen smiled mirthlessly at that news, and when they passed a small stream, he knelt on all fours and drank to his fill. Afterward, Maggie took his hand as she walked with him, and the sun was shining, and the road was clear, and she felt somehow relieved, hopeful that all would be well.

Maggie had not known what to expect in Babel. She'd imagined armed encampments, each city a fortress. But as they walked along the dirt road, past stands of alder, maple, and oak, the hills seemed little different from her home in Tihrglas. The autumn colors were on the trees, and the soil smelled rich.

And in each little valley that they came to, a few quaint cottages huddled.

Most of them were of gray stone with round clay shingles. The hay houses and sheepfolds and dovecotes were made of mud and wattle, with thatched roofs made of reeds.

Instead of armies, Maggie saw children working beside their parents at cutting wood for the winter or bringing in the corn.

In the afternoon they came to one green valley, where the emerald grass had been cropped short by the sheep, and Maggie stopped and looked out. The maples and alders lit the hillsides with flame. Three houses clustered together on the side of a hill at the foot of the valley, and a small smokehouse was letting its blue smoke rise lazily up. The scent of cooking sausages was strong. And beside the road, where a bridge spanned a clear river, a dozen naked children were swinging from a rope into a wide pool. Some of the little boys had thick red hair, almost fur, that covered most of their bodies, and one little girl had a face that was strangely deformed—with eyes that were unnaturally large, and a heavy brow that jutted over them. The children were screaming and laughing, splashing water at each other, and for a moment, Maggie grasped Gallen's hand, forcing him to stop.

"Look," she said. And Gallen suddenly became wary, scanning the hillside.

"No, you muffin, look at those children—this place!"

"Aye, it's a pretty valley," Gallen admitted.

"I . . . I think I could be happy here," Maggie whispered.

Gallen looked at her askance. "Here? But I thought you loved fiddling with gadgets—technology. There's nothing here for you, nothing like that. You'd be splitting logs and butchering pigs just like back home. You—your neighbors wouldn't even be human, damn it, Maggie!"

"I know," Maggie said quietly. Her sudden change of heart surprised even her, and she remembered the mischievous grin she'd seen upon the Lady Semarritte's face when she'd told Maggie of Tremonthin. Somehow, Semarritte had known that Maggie would like this place.

"I don't understand," Gallen said. "If you want to live on a backward planet, there are valleys just as pretty as this back home. I know a place near An Cochan. And if it's a stone house you want to live in rather than a housetree, well, one could be built."

"No," Maggie said. "It wouldn't be the same. On Tihrglas, you can't go to the City of Life to be reborn. On Tihrglas, you're told what you must be. But here—"She suddenly got a glimmer of what it was she really was after, and she waved toward the motley assortment of children. "Here you'd never want for interesting neighbors. They'd be nothing like you, and they'd never try to tell you how you must act or what to wear."

"You're not making sense, Maggie," Gallen said, shaking his head. But he stared out across the valley, thinking, considering what it would be like, and his voice had held no conviction. "What about the Tekkar, and the other warrior races? You would be scared to step out of your door at night."

"Och, and who would be so bold as to come threatening the household of

Gallen O'Day?" Maggie asked. "I know you, Gallen. You wouldn't mind it a bit, finding some village in the wilds and becoming a sheriff, keeping the peace for those who want it. . . ."

Gallen said no more. But as they walked on, he eyed the homesteads and hamlets and the fertile valleys keenly, looking beyond the exterior, as if considering the possibilities.

In the late afternoon, the road became cobblestone and wound down out of the hills to the sea, leading to an oddly shaped granite bluff, where the road led into a vast cave.

There were a few buildings perched next to the bluff—a sizable stable, some shops, but no houses—and people were going into the cave with wagons filled with wood and produce. Maggie realized with a start that the inhabitants of this city all lived within that monolithic rock.

She studied the place a bit—some rounded pillars had been carved into the rock, and they thrust up high, carrying a bit of smoke. In other places, holes had been gouged into the roof, giving light and air. In some holes, she could see through to whitened walls.

As with the temple she'd first noticed back in Northland, this place was built by someone who had no concept of symmetry. Each of the chimneys was a different height, and the windows were each shaped in their own ways. And yet there was a gracefulness, a peaceful organic feel to the structure, that was both comforting and inviting.

Cormorants and gulls wheeled out over the gray ocean, and the skies were getting dark, promising rain. Maggie and Gallen went down to the city.

Under the arching entrance, they could see the city before them—a vast cavern filled with people and noise and the smells of smoke and sweat and fish. The rock had been carved away so that long stone staircases led away under great arches. The walls were not only painted white, but crystals had been set in them, casting light back like stars.

Between the skylights and the guttering lamps on wrought-iron posts placed strategically beside the roads, the caverns sparkled with light.

Maggie looked up, and along the roads going up the hill were side corridors, where people of a dozen races lived. Children screamed and played in the corridors, and clothing was left along stone walls to dry.

There was the smell of seawater in the air, and off to the right, a path led to the ocean. There, on broad stones at the sea's edge, sea people swam through an underwater channel, bringing up fresh fish and crabs. Maggie saw a gaggle of hooded merchants who were bartering loudly for the fish, offering brass bracelets and sacks made of fine cloth.

Directly ahead, just above sea level, a central pillar, like an enormous stalagmite, filled the middle of the complex, and carved at the column's center were several shops and a large pub where a dozen burly giants guzzled mugs of beer at wooden tables. The delicious scent of fish and sausages filled the air.

As Maggie and Gallen headed toward the pub, a grizzled giant approached.

He wore a green tunic over black leather pants, and had a rope tied around his waist. His dark brown hair was tied back, and he wore beads of aqua and cardinal woven into it. His enormous beard spilled down his chest, thinning into a ragged wisp at his belly. It wasn't until he was nearly on them that Maggie realized how truly large he was—eight feet tall, with broad shoulders. He wore a short sword on his hip, but he handled himself like a man who wouldn't need weapons.

"My name's Fenorah," he grumbled, studying Gallen's sword. "Welcome to Battic, where land kisses the sea."

"Thank you," Gallen said, lifting his chin high to stare the man in the eye.

"We're a peaceful town," Fenorah said, scratching his nose. "I'll be straight with you. You carry a sword, and from the way you wear it, I'd say you know how to do more than split kindling with it. And there's blood on your boots—and I'd rather not know how it got there. But these are my folks, my town. There's peace here."

He looked deep into Gallen's eyes, as if trying to gauge what lay beneath their cool blue surface.

"I appreciate an honest man," Gallen said. "And I admire one who seeks peace. As long as I'm given it, I shall give it in return."

The giant laughed, slapped him on the back. "You look hungry from the road. I saw how you eyed the pub. May I buy you dinner? We've the finest flounder you'll taste on the coast." Gallen hesitated, but Maggie could sense something in this giant, a lack of guile, that she found refreshing.

"We would be honored," Maggie said, and the giant took her arm, led them into the pub, where they dined on sea bass roasted in rosemary and a fruity wine. Other giants like Fenorah lumbered around.

Fenorah talked long and boisterously, asking Gallen's business. When Gallen said that he wanted to purchase a wagon and draft animals, Fenorah called a serving boy and ordered them, as if he'd been ordering dinner, and the boy rushed to fetch them.

Then, Fenorah took them down to the "docks," the stones where the sea people rose from the dark waters, their tails flashing silver, and there Fenorah talked to Gallen of the city's trade agreements.

He showed Maggie and Gallen a great cavern where the annual fairs were held, where images of the city's founders were carved in three giant stalactites, so that their beards were hanging shards of stone. Fenorah then took them to the upper chambers above the city, where small swarthy men and women of the Ntak race still carved, singing in high voices as their picks and hammers rang, with each blow extending the city back deeper and deeper into the bones of the earth.

The giant seemed to Maggie to be enormously proud of his city. He was obviously a man of wealth, a man of worries. And at last when they were in the far upper recesses of a cave, looking back down over a vast stairway of a thousand feet, and the ringing of hammers and picks below them rose like some strange music, Fenorah motioned for Gallen and Maggie to sit on a rock. Then, with a grunt, he knelt down beside them, and stared down into the distance.

"Gallen, my friend," the giant whispered, his voice a mere grumble, hard to be heard over the ringing hammers, the piping music. "There was a ship that burned last night, a ship not far off the beach. Its sails lit up like a bonfire, and we could see it sailing as if it would fall off the edge of the world."

"Aye?" Gallen asked, curiously.

"Aye," the giant grunted. "The sea folk went to investigate, and they brought back some survivors." The giant sighed, measured his words. "They told . . . stories, about a swordsman with two beautiful women. They hinted that he was a great warrior, and that they would pay well for his capture. Too well."

"And what did you tell them?" Gallen said.

"I sent them away, though I've thought better of it since. They had broken none of our laws, and yet . . ."

"And yet what?"

"And yet I found it hard to spare them their lives." Fenorah dug his hand into the stone at his feet, broke off a small boulder. Maggie had not seen any sign of a chink in the stone, and even Gallen caught his breath at witnessing the giant's tremendous strength. "The thing is, Battic is small for a sea town, and distant from other cities. We don't even have a port. And we've been careful to watch one another, protect each other. Perhaps for this reason, we have escaped the Inhuman's scrutiny. We have been . . . beneath notice. But I fear that now the Inhuman will turn its face our way, if it is searching for you. It's a small fear, perhaps unfounded."

Maggie took all of this in. If the agents of Inhuman had been turned loose from town, then perhaps they would be out in the countryside, hunting even now. She suddenly feared for Ceravanne, who had only Orick to protect her. More importantly, she understood that Fenorah, despite his great strength, was asking them to make a hasty retreat.

"I suspect," Gallen said, "that such fears *are* unfounded. Did you see which way they went?"

"Four of the Inhuman's servants went to the south, toward the wilderness of Moree," the giant whispered. "Five to the woods to the east."

Maggie caught her breath. Despite their best efforts, the Inhuman's agents were still searching for them in greater force than she'd imagined. It would be easy for a few servants of the Inhuman to find others like themselves, raise the countryside against them.

Fenorah studied them from the corner of his eyes. "I . . . have to admit that I am not above spying on a stranger. When the nine were alone in the medic's chamber, I listened to them from the hole above. They spoke of a Lord Protector who should not be allowed to reach Moree."

Gallen did not answer for a moment. "Even if it is true that you have escaped the Inhuman's scrutiny so far," he said, "it will not remain so forever. Unless the Inhuman is destroyed, you and your people will be found."

"And what can one man do against it?" Fenorah grumbled. "I fear that the Inhuman is more powerful than you know."

Gallen said, "There is more than one warrior here, unless I miss my guess. Perhaps you and some of your kind would join me."

Maggie held her breath, for she wished that this strong man would come with them. An army of them would be formidable.

"I am of the Im people," Fenorah said. "I could not travel inland with you, away from the sea. Me and my brothers cannot drink your fresh water. We would die after a few days' march."

Maggie's heart fell, and she wondered what Gallen would do without the giants' help. Somehow, though she had not admitted it to herself, to go into that wilderness alone seemed . . . unthinkable.

"Then let me have a wagon," Gallen asked, "and tell no one that I came this way."

"Done." The giant nodded. He looked at Gallen from the corner of his eye once again. "And more. I'll come with you, and bring my brothers, so long as your road leads by the sea. The Inhuman will have to show some restraint, with us at hand."

"I accept your offer, gratefully," Gallen said.

"Good." The giant slapped his knee and he got up, took Maggie's hand and helped her to her feet.

"One thing more," Maggie said. "Among the survivors, did you find a pale woman?"

"The Champlianne?" the giant said. "Aye, she's safe."

"She's not Inhuman, I don't think," Maggie said.

"Neither do I. She's well, resting in my own house," Fenorah assured her. "My wife is caring for her."

Maggie found herself suddenly teary-eyed with relief. As far as the others on the ship went, she had trusted none of them, but she hated the thought that this innocent woman might have died in the skirmish. Gallen put his arm over Maggie's shoulders, hugged her for a moment.

Then Fenorah led them back down the long stairs, to the mouth of the city, where the serving boy had readied a fine wagon carved of cherrywood, with ornate scrollwork and bas-reliefs of trees and dancing rabbits on every panel. Gallen slapped the wagon, commenting on its fine Maker build, and Maggie wondered at his knowledge of it.

To pull the wagon, Fenorah had provided a beast that Maggie had never seen before, nor ever imagined. It stood tall as a horse, but was built more like a cow. It had a great hump at its shoulders, and while most of it was a creamy golden brown in color, shaggy black hair covered its head. Its small horns curved like those of a ram, and it glared about with small red eyes. It was both a fearsome creature, and powerfully built.

"What is this thing called?" Maggie asked.

"A travelbeast," Fenorah answered, obviously surprised that she did not know. "His kind are greatly prized. He has greater endurance than a bull, and greater speed than a horse. He sees in the dark, and is smart enough to understand a few small words." He hissed a little lower. "And he will trample anyone who gets in his way."

Maggie climbed up into the seat of the wagon, saw that it was lightly loaded with baskets of fruit, a barrel of salted fish, and plenty of blankets.

On impulse she grabbed the giant, hugged him tight. "Thank you," she whispered fiercely, and found herself fighting back tears once again.

"It is my pleasure," Fenorah said, and he went to find some men. In half an hour, six of the giants had gathered. Three ran out ahead of the wagon, while three others followed close behind.

Then Gallen nodded and slapped the travelbeast with the reins, and they lurched off, out the door of the tunnel. The twin suns were already down outside, and the moons had not yet risen. Clouds scudded across the sky, obscuring the stars. In the darkness, she could barely see the broad backs of the giants, rushing ahead into the shadows.

Gallen hunched at the reins, his face an unreadable mask in the darkness, and she felt distant from him. She could sense a change in him, a new uncertainty that he dared not voice.

As the wagon rattled over the cobblestones up toward the woods, Maggie had a sense of foreboding. It was dark under the trees, so dark that she could hardly see her hand in front of her face, and somehow she sensed that she was crossing into a darker realm than she could have ever imagined.

Nineteen

As night fell, Zell'a Cree ambled along the rutted roads east of Battic. His men had been following the road since just after dawn, sniffing for the scent of Gallen O'Day and his party. They'd crossed forty kilometers of mountain, hugging the coast, and never caught a whiff of him.

Forty kilometers seemed too far. Zell'a Cree knew that the currents and the wind had carried the little lifeboat east along the coast, and for a good time, he'd kept them in sight as he swam.

Still, they should have landed somewhere closer to Battic. But Zell'a Cree's nose didn't lie: they hadn't set foot on the road.

They're learning, Zell'a Cree realized. They must have known that if they walked on the road, I would catch their scent. And the coastline here was so rocky in places, that Zell'a Cree could not easily hunt them by following the beach.

He wondered idly how it would be to be a human—living in a world where the senses were so limited, where sight and smell and hearing were so dull. Humans must feel terribly vulnerable, terribly open to attack, and they would have to be wary at all times. No wonder they had developed fear as a basic component of their emotional makeup.

Yet Zell'a Cree could hear a twig snap a mile away, and at night, even in a deep fog, the heat of living things blazed like torches. Zell'a Cree did not need to suffer from mankind's irrational fears. He was better than that.

At dusk, he stopped, weary to the bone, and said to the three other men, "It may be that we have passed the Tharrin's trail. I for one believe that we should go back."

"Bransoon told us to head east. He's first mate," a sailor grumbled, a small red-skinned man with yellow eyes.

"But we've been walking all day, and still have no sign of them," Zell'a Cree said. "Don't you think it likely that we passed them already?"

"Maybe," the sailor said, scratching his ear with a long knife. "But what if you're wrong? What if they're a kilometer down the road, or five kilometers? The wind and current are strong. Maybe they decided to follow the coast by boat. If they're ahead of us, and we turn back now, we could lose them. But if they're behind us, most likely they'll just come down the road right into our arms."

Zell'a Cree studied the men. It seemed just as likely to him that Gallen and the others would run off into the woods and never be found again. There were hundreds of small hamlets scattered throughout these mountains, with roads going everywhere. It would be easy to lose them on back roads.

The three sailors seemed nervous, and they kept looking east, as if in a hurry to be off. "I'm not sure that you men want to find Gallen," Zell'a Cree said. "I think you're afraid of him."

One sailor licked his lips. "It's not healthy to tangle with him, that's for sure. What can four of us do against him?"

And Zell'a Cree had to admit that tangling with the Lord Protector had proven to be an unhealthy pastime.

"Aye," the others agreed. "We're heading east, and when we find the next town, we'll notify someone in authority that Gallen may be coming. Then I for one will sit and have a long beer, and thank my ancestors to be quit of this mess."

Zell'a Cree saw his mistake. He couldn't trust these men to hunt Gallen properly. In all likelihood, the first mate and his men would just as soon never meet Gallen again, either. But there was a reason why Zell'a Cree had been given his own hunting pack to lead. He had to trust his own wits, his own instinct. "I'm going back," Zell'a Cree said, "to check the road again."

And he turned back, heading west. It was cool under the trees at night. Even for a Tosken it had been a long day. He felt worn through, but he picked up his pace and began jogging along the road.

At a farmhouse, he suddenly caught the scent. Gallen, Maggie, Orick, and some others had come out of the road here, just minutes ago. And the smell of Im giants was heavy all around. In the dark, he could see warm glowing footprints where someone had stood by the road for a bit—a giant—waiting for the others to come.

But at the roadside, the scent suddenly became very weak. Gallen and the others were not walking, they were riding.

And Zell'a Cree detected the heavy, malodorous fur of a travelbeast. Since the creature had not passed him, it must have gone west toward Battic.

Zell'a Cree redoubled his efforts, running over the hills, pumping his legs with a fury. If Gallen had fallen in with Im giants, and if he had a travel-beast, then any creature afoot would be hard-pressed to catch them.

So he ran as if to outrace the wind; Zell'a Cree stretched his legs, letting them pump in steady rhythm, the sweat pouring down his face. "I am Tosken, I am Tosken," he repeated over and over as he pounded the dirt roads, racing under trees past farmhouses where dogs rushed out barking and snapping and then finally fell back in defeat when they tired. Zell'a Cree's mind retreated from thought until there was only the race.

He heaved great, gasping breaths. He'd been made for great strength and great endurance, but he had not been formed to breathe such thin air as this planet offered. Most times, it did not bother him, but running, the constant pumping of legs, wore him down.

In an hour, he reached Battic, and dared not take the tunnel into the city—not if Gallen was with the Im giants. At Battic one road branched south, and the first mate and his men were to have followed that road. A second road went west.

Zell'a Cree scrambled over the hills, until he found the exit heading south, and there he did not find Gallen's scent. Which meant that Gallen had anticipated an ambush, and he was circling around it.

Zell'a Cree raced through the woods till he reached a hillside above the west road. There the woods had burned away in ages past, and only low brush survived on the stark, windswept hillsides. He could see parts of the road for six kilometers, and there, at the edge of his vision, burned the forms of the racing giants as they sprinted down the road, protecting their wagon.

Suddenly, the wagon stopped. The giants waited for a moment, glancing about anxiously.

A man climbed up in the back of the wagon and stood looking toward Zell'a Cree. He wore a dark robe, and wore a sword at his back. Gallen O'Day.

To most peoples, even the Im giants, Zell'a Cree would be invisible at this time of night, at such a distance. But Zell'a Cree had been running, and he imagined that the heat of his own body must be radiating like a torch. Yet of all those below, only Gallen O'Day could see him.

The tricky little man could see in infrared. Zell'a Cree had had no idea that the Lord Protector possessed such talents.

They stood for a moment, gazing at one another across the distance, and Gallen raised an arm, as if to wave, then suddenly clenched his fist, drawing it downward—one of the secret hand gestures of the Inhuman—a beckoning call. Then the wagon lurched forward, the travelbeast rushing over a hill, and was gone.

For one moment, hope flickered in Zell'a Cree. If Gallen knew the hand signal, then he had been infected by the Inhuman. The Word had indeed entered him.

Yet something was wrong. If Gallen was Inhuman now, then why did he run? Why did he not bring the others so that they too could be converted? The only answer seemed to be that Gallen had been strong enough to resist the Word. Had Gallen beckoned him in mockery?

Zell'a Cree licked his lips, angry. Sweat poured down his face, and he gulped for air. He'd been two days without sleep, and he'd just run twenty kilometers. He could go no farther tonight. He let himself collapse into a sitting position.

So Gallen O'Day was not as blind and helpless as other men. He had more resources to draw upon . . . and he had resisted the Word.

Zell'a Cree considered his own resources. He imagined the roads south, drew a map in his mind. The Inhuman had given him a great gift—the memories of a hundred lives lived and wasted. Over six thousand years of memories. Twelve of those lives had been spent in cities and villages between Battic and Moree. He recalled childhoods spent playing on obscure tracks, the life of a tinker working between towns, the days of a Thoranian guard who traveled with a tax collector. Zell'a Cree concentrated, recalling each road, each main track.

Gallen might go far west to avoid detection, but he was in a hurry. If he went too far, he'd have to cross the Telgood Mountains, and that would cost him many days. At the most, Gallen could go four hundred kilometers out of his way, but then he'd have to go south, closer to the hosts of the Inhuman.

Sooner or later he'd turn up on the road to Moree. Zell'a Cree had no choice but to race south now, checking for Gallen's trail, hoping to enlist other servants of the Inhuman in his quest.

Perhaps I've been too naïve, Zell'a Cree considered. I'd hoped to take Gallen alive, but he really isn't as essential as Maggie and the Tharrin. The practical thing would be to kill him.

Once the decision was made, Zell'a Cree felt an enormous calm.

Twenty

As the wagon stopped, Orick looked up at Gallen, saw him study the distance behind them, then make the strange pulling gesture at the sky as if trying to wrap clouds in his hand and draw them to earth. Gallen's expression was distant, and Orick could see that some heavy burden was upon him.

"Gallen, what's wrong?" Orick asked.

"Nothing . . ." Gallen said, obviously disturbed himself. "It's just—I saw Zell'a Cree behind us."

"How far?" one of the giants asked, drawing his sword as if to do battle.

"He's back several kilometers—at Battic."

The giant grumbled, sheathed his sword, and took a moment to swab the wagon's axles with grease from a bucket.

Gallen turned and sat back down in the driver's seat, urged the travelbeast forward, and the giants began running. The travelbeast was terribly strong, much faster than a horse. Although the huge wagon carried four people, a bear, and supplies, it fairly sang over the roads. The craftsmen who had built it had invested a great deal of time in carving every panel, and they'd spent equal care in designing the suspension. Orick had never ridden in a wagon that was its equal, and he was grateful for the smooth ride, not for his own sake, but for Tallea's. The warrior's wounds had healed at the surface, but the giants had carried her from the camp to the road, and every jarring step was a pain for her.

So as they raced through the night, Orick lay beside her, keeping her warm, singing to her.

Everyone was silent. Since Maggie and Gallen had been hiking all across the countryside, when they tired the giant Fenorah took the reins and Ceravanne sat hunched beside him with her cloak draped tightly about, to keep out the cold. Gallen and Maggie lay in the back of the wagon.

Gallen stretched out beside Orick under a blanket, with Maggie beside him, and Orick could feel a certain tenseness in Gallen's muscles.

Orick took a moment to consider, trying to remember how far a kilometer was. He was still not accustomed to measuring things as the starfarers did. When he was satisfied that Zell'a Cree was far away, he breathed deeply, quietly, trying to get back to sleep, but it wasn't much use. They traveled under the clouds for a while, and then the stars came out—a vast panoply far brighter than the dim stars back on Tihrglas.

Maggie was looking up at the sky, too, and she whispered, "Ah, Gallen, look at all of the stars."

"We must be close to the galactic center here, closer than we are back on Tihrglas—"

"Not much closer," Maggie said. "We're on the far side from Tihrglas, closer to the Dronon worlds. They're out on the rim, but we're halfway to the galactic center here, a little above the spiral. See that bright band—how wide it is?"

And Orick saw. Indeed the Milky Way was but a dim river of stars back on Tihrglas, but here it took up the whole night sky. The starlight alone was enough to see by, fairly well.

"Gallen," Maggie whispered, changing the subject, worry in her voice, "what was that hand signal you gave Zell'a Cree?" Orick could barely hear the question over the sounds of running feet, the creak of wagon wheels, the jostling of springs.

"I don't know," Gallen whispered.

"What do you mean, you don't know? Is it something you learned from the Inhuman?"

"I really don't know," Gallen said. "I was just standing there, and it came to me. It seemed the right thing to do."

Maggie seemed to take this in, and Orick realized that they were discussing something private, something dangerous. What would Gallen have learned from the Inhuman? Orick wondered. They were whispering, and with the way the backboard for the driver's seat leaned, it would baffle the sound for Ceravanne and Fenorah.

Maggie sat up and readjusted her pack, using it for a pillow. "I wish we were underground this night, Gallen," she said. She looked at Orick.

"Orick, are you still awake?" Maggie asked.

"Huh, ah, yes." Orick yawned.

"Oh, good night, then," she said; she rolled over.

Orick saw his mistake. If he'd feigned sleep, then Maggie and Gallen would have kept talking. Instead, Maggie drifted into a light sleep. But Gallen lay for a long time, his muscles rigid, until the rumble of the wagon lulled even him to sleep. Orick roused enough to look over the backboard, and a hundred yards back, the giants were running three abreast behind the wagon, a strong, comforting presence.

Orick lay watching the sky, and the marvelous wagon moved so gently over the road, he felt that he was floating under the stars. They passed through several small towns, and each time, dogs would bark and geese would honk, and then they'd be left behind. But then the trees closed over them, and for a long time there were no houses to pass. They were moving deeper and deeper into the wilderness.

A few hours before dawn, they came to the sea and clattered over a long bridge, then at some woods along an empty beach the giants stopped for the night. Two of them stayed up as sentries, watching the road, and the others built a small fire and napped. Ceravanne and Fenorah camped under a tree, while Orick slept in the wagon with the others. At dawn Orick got up, while the giants fixed breakfast—salty corn cakes covered with peaches, dried apricots, and cream.

Orick walked along the road, and quickly realized that they were on a small island between two branches of a river. And on the island two enormous cliff faces, each over two hundred feet tall, were carved with the images of eagles. One eagle, with its wings raised, faced the north sea. The other, with its wings folded, looked upriver, its beak wide as if it were screeching.

And the bridge they had crossed was a marvel—nearly a mile of vast granite pylons held stonework that was intricately carved along the side with a massive frieze that displayed images of grotesque gargoyles, squatting and grunting as they shoved handcarts over the bridge. The images were somehow both comic and beautiful. And the bridge was enormously wide, enough so that four or five carts could have gone abreast.

On the far side of the island was a shorter bridge, just as intricately decorated, and Orick suddenly saw why the giants chose to camp here: the island could be easily defended.

Orick climbed a steep, pine-covered ridge until he reached the top of the eagle that gazed out to sea. There, on the head between the eagle's wings, he found Gallen sitting, dangling his feet as if unaware that he was perched above a deadly drop. Gallen wore the black gloves and boots of a Lord Protector, along with his robe that would stay black unless he willed it to change some other color or let it blend into whatever background he happened to be standing in.

Orick climbed beside him, sat gazing out to sea, resting his muzzle on his paws. The double suns had just risen, and the sea was flat, smooth, a deep, pristine blue. Orick could see salmon finning in lazy circles out in the water, and cormorants were flying out to sea, shooting just above the waves.

Orick said, "Did you see the bridges?"

"Indeed." Gallen sighed. "This place is called Profundis, and those unbreakable bridges were carved long ago by a race called the Thworn. If you look west, on that bluff over there, you will see the walls to an ancient city, Tywee." Orick looked over to a dome-shaped bluff beside the sea and noticed for the first time some crumbling walls among the trees. "Eight hundred years ago, a young man named Omad fell in love with a beautiful princess, and she agreed to marry him if he took her armies and unified this region. He did so—by making pacts and trade agreements, so that never a drop of blood was spilled. And after their wedding he wisely built the bridges—not only to facilitate travel in his own lands, but to keep enemy ships from sailing upriver into the heart of his realm.

"You see, this river accepts drainage from all the land within a thousand kilometers in any direction, and so it is the major artery leading south into the heartland."

"Did the king build these statues, too?" Orick asked.

"Yes. A bloody, barbaric race called the Dwinideen were great seamen, and they had often raided deep into the fertile inland. As the bridge was being built, the Dwinideen harried the craftsmen, slaughtering many people, much to the dismay of Omad. But the Dwinideen were superstitious, and they feared Capúl, the sky god who appears in the shape of a fish eagle. They believed that if one dies, and the fish eagle gets at the body, the eagle will carry off the dead person's spirit to be eaten so that the dead can never be reborn. So the King of Tywee carved this statue, and when next the Dwinideen attacked, Omad took thirty of the Dwinideen captive. With his own hand he hurled them from the eagle's head to the rocks below, crying, 'Thus shall my enemies die!' There were many fish eagles living here then, as there are now, and they fed on the carcasses. Afterward, the Dwinideen feared this place and never returned. For the rest of his days, Omad regretted that he was forced to shed blood to protect his kingdom."

Gallen fell silent. His voice seemed grim. Almost, Orick thought, as if he were grieving for the long-dead king, and there was pain in his eyes, a quiet wisdom that seemed out of place on Gallen's features.

"Hmmm . . ." Orick said, wondering how Gallen had learned so much. Gallen must have spoken of this place with the giants.

In the distance, toward the ancient city of Tywee, Orick saw the white flashing of wings as a fish eagle swooped to grab a fish from the water.

"If this bridge is so important, why isn't there a city here now?" Orick asked.

"The kingdom fell into ruin. It was attacked from the south, by men who came out of the desert. The villagers who live here now are weaker men, too divided to stand against their overlords. They pay a small tribute and live in relative peace."

"And who might these southern warriors be?" Orick asked, knowing that they would have to go south soon, and might have to pass through their lands.

"Can you not guess?" Gallen said. "They're the Tekkar."

Orick licked his lips. "I don't like the Tekkar." He'd known that they served the Inhuman, but somehow he imagined that they would be far away—not a present danger. "Will we meet more of them soon?"

Gallen said, "We made good time last night. A hundred kilometers since sunset. And it's a beautiful, clear day. We'll go a hundred more kilometers before the day is done. But we are almost a thousand kilometers from the desert, and the Tekkar do not like climates as cool and wet as this. It will be a few days before we find them."

Orick grunted in relief, and Gallen sat brooding, looking out to sea. Orick headed down between the dark pines to see if breakfast was ready. Squirrels were out in the morning sun, searching for nuts, chattering. At the foot of the trail, Orick found Maggie.

"Have you seen Gallen?" she asked.

"He's up top."

"Is he all right?"

"Quiet," Orick said. "He just seemed to want some time alone, to think."

Maggie bit her lower lip and frowned. She glanced up the trail, then headed up in a hurry.

Orick watched her leave, and something in her face bothered him. She'd been panicked, as if she didn't trust Gallen to sit and think for five minutes.

Orick almost headed to camp, but curiosity got the better of him. Maggie was nearly running up the steep trail, darting between trees.

Orick turned and rushed after her, but halfway up the trail, Gallen met Maggie coming down, and Gallen had obviously seen Orick. The two of them walked down together, arm in arm, and Orick tagged along, certain that once again he had missed out on a chance to hear their secret conversations.

When they got back to camp, the Im giants all sat around a small cooking fire, circled by dark trees. Their tunics were stained by sweat, and they smelled none too sweet to Orick, but the humans next to them didn't mind. Breakfast was ready, and they passed out the corn cakes, tasty enough fare for the road. Even Tallea was up to sitting a bit while she ate. It felt good to Orick to be in the daylight, with the sun shining on his fur.

Ceravanne addressed them all as they ate. "Today we must make some decisions. The roads to Moree are many, and each is fraught with its own dangers. We've come west out of expediency, but how far west shall we go? And when do we head south? I walked abroad in this land many years ago. The hills and mountains look little changed, but rivers have turned, old roads are forgotten and new ones are unknown to me. So I think it best to ask our friends, the Im giants, for their advice, and to ask Tallea the Caldurian for her help."

"I not been to this land," Tallea said.

"I know the roads along the sea," Fenorah said, "and I know the roads inland by reputation. You could head south this morning at Marbee Road. It's a wide road built upon a bed of stone, and it follows the river where it passes through many small hamlets, and borders many a field. The folk along the way are friendly enough, and accustomed to strangers. But I fear it is a dangerous road for you: the hosts of the Inhuman have already gone south on Battic Road, and Marbee Road will meet it in one hundred and twenty kilometers. They may be waiting for you there or beyond. Still, if you hurry, the chances are good that you could keep ahead of them."

"What other choices do we have?" Ceravanne asked.

"Beyond Marbee, fifty kilometers, lies the Old King's Road," Fenorah said. "It is a winding road among the hills, built to connect old fortresses, many of which no longer exist. But there is many a farmstead along it, and a few villages."

"And some places along the road often flood," Ceravanne said.

"In the spring, this is true, but the roads should be clear this time of year," one of Fenorah's men protested. "But once again, it meets Marbee Road in two hundred and forty kilometers, at High Home. Beyond that, the next best trail would be the ancient highway at the foot of the Telgood Mountains. Only a few wild people live in those mountains—Derrits and the like. The road is mostly unused and has gone to grass. Some would claim that it is no longer safe, but I have hunted along its trails, and a sturdy wagon should make it through."

"I know that way well," Ceravanne said. "In younger days it was called the Emerald Way. The caravanserais would come out of Indallian, and at night when you camped in the valleys you would see the lights of their fires burning like winding rivers of stars along the hills."

"That could not have happened within the past three hundred years," Fenorah mused, a faraway look in his eyes, "though my grandfather recalled those days—the glory and the wars."

"Indeed, it was the richness of this land that destroyed it," Ceravanne said.

"If Derrits along road, road not good," Tallea said. "Troublesome people."

"What are Derrits?" Orick asked.

"They . . . are solitary giants," Ceravanne said, "built for life on a sterile world. They are very strong, and very cunning."

"They're cowards and killers," Fenorah said, glaring, grasping the hilt of his sword as if he wanted to cut one down.

"Eat other people," Tallea said. "Build traps."

"They can eat just about anything—from carrion to raw soil," Ceravanne said, "and they will eat you, if you're alone and fall into one of their pits."

"We can't use that road," Maggie said, "not with a quick-running animal."

"I agree that it is a dangerous choice," Ceravanne said thoughtfully. "But beyond that old highway, there are no roads south until you cross the Telgoods. They're a high mountain range, and we couldn't cross easily."

"Six hundred kilometers," Fenorah said, "just to cross the mountains, and that land is so distant, I do not know the roads there."

"I have been there," one of Fenorah's men said. "The roads south are good, better than any we have here, for the Lords of Telgood keep them. But the mountains also veer west, and if you go to Moree, then you will be spending much time in the high passes. The wingmen live there, and it is not safe to travel in parties as small as yours—especially without bows."

"More importantly," Ceravanne said, "we would be traveling hundreds of kilometers out of our way. And we need to hurry."

"So," Gallen said, "it sounds to me that perhaps our best choice is the Old King's Road. It gives us a chance to race against the Inhuman, and it sounds safer than the far roads, more civilized."

"But therein lies another danger," Ceravanne said. "If we pass through hamlets and villages, undoubtedly we will meet more servants of the Inhuman. Do you suppose that they pose no threat?"

"All roads may lead astray," Orick said, "and the longer we sit here, the more dangerous they become. I think Gallen is right in his choice."

Ceravanne looked to Fenorah, as if the giant held the final word. "The choice is yours, dear lady," he said. "No one should make it for you."

"Then I will follow Gallen," Ceravanne whispered. "Still," she said more loudly, "there is another matter we must consider. And that is the question, Who of us shall go? We know that the servants of the Inhuman are rushing ahead of us, we know that they will be prepared. If any choose to come, they will be risking great danger. So, I have spoken with Fenorah, and he has agreed to let any who desire return to Battic." Her eyes rested on Maggie.

"None of us will return to Battic, I wager," Maggie said. "None of us are cowards."

"Yet there is good reason to consider the offer," Gallen said loudly, and he stood, resting his hand on the hilt of his sword. "For one among us has already been infected by the Inhuman's Word, and all who travel are imperiled by it!"

Orick looked around the camp. One of the Im giants leapt to his feet as if ready to attack the traitor, and Ceravanne looked from Gallen to Maggie, her face a mask of fear.

"Who?" Orick cried.

"*I* am infected, my friend," Gallen said, and there was a sadness in his eyes. "Forgive me. The Word burrowed into my skull while we were aboard ship, and the Inhuman has been sending messages to me for the past two nights."

"And what kind of messages does it send?" Fenorah asked, scratching his thick beard.

"It sends memories of lives spent and wasted. It tells me that the world is unfair, and that the peoples of Babel have been treated shabbily. The Inhuman cries out for justice, and reparation, and equality. But the humans of Northland will hear none of it." Gallen paused and closed his eyes, looking inward. "The Inhuman teaches me to be ashamed of my own species, and to mistrust them and the Tharrin who lead them." There was a long moment of silence.

Tallea, who had been leaning weakly against a tree, pulled herself forward, fixed her eyes on Gallen with desperation. Until now, she had always spoken crisply, breaking off her words and her sentences. But now, as if to emphasize their import, she spoke as others on Tremonthin did, in her harsh voice. "You can fight those voices, Gallen," she said. "I know those who fought and won. At first, when you hear those voices, see their memories, it is like falling into a great darkness, and your own small voice is a tiny light—"

"No," Gallen growled. "It is like falling into a vast and yawning light, and *my* voice is the small darkness!"

"Why did you keep this infection hidden from me?" Ceravanne demanded.

"Because I hoped that my mantle could defeat it. Because I believed that it could jam the frequencies that the Inhuman sent its signal on."

"And your mantle fails you?" Ceravanne asked.

Gallen looked away to the north. "The Inhuman is switching frequencies, sending messages in short bursts. I have . . . memories flowing into me, like water gushing through a swollen dike. In the past few hours, I have recalled five lifetimes."

"No, Gallen!" Maggie cried. "It can't have!"

"But it has," Gallen said.

"I don't understand," Maggie said. "The Word shouldn't be sophisticated enough to do what you're saying."

Gallen shook his head, and there were tears glistening in his eyes. "Apparently we have underestimated the Inhuman once again. The Word *is* sending signals in coded bursts. My mantle tries to block them, but when it does, the Inhuman then begins sending on a different frequency. My mantle doesn't have enough power to block both signals."

Maggie frowned in concentration. "This is worse than anything I feared." She took his hand and looked up into his face steadily, searching his features. "We can stop this! We can stop it! We could—take you underground."

"Aw, and what use would it be, my love?" Gallen shook his head. "You can't just hide me away from it. I'm fighting. My mantle is fighting, but it cannot stave off the attack. I must warn you: you go to battle the Inhuman, but by the time we get to Moree I may be Inhuman."

"The Inhuman's Word can be defeated, as Tallea said—" Ceravanne intoned hopefully, "by those who are strong of purpose, by those who are wise. I can help you defeat it."

Gallen glanced at her, and there was a gleam of anger in his eye, and Orick's heart froze at the sight—anger at the peaceful Tharrin, a folk who'd never done Gallen any harm.

"Thank you," Gallen said coldly. "But I do not want your help."

"Why?" Ceravanne asked, unable to hide how his tone had hurt her.

Gallen's face took on a closed look. "I'm not sure I trust you—or any Tharrin."

Two of the Im giants got up, throwing the remains of their corn cake to the ground, confused and hurt by Gallen's words. They brought their hands to their short swords, as if ready to do battle over such talk. And Gallen half pulled his own sword.

"Wait!" Orick said. "Gallen here has always been a trusty lad. I've never seen him back away from any bandit or outlaw! So if you're going to draw swords on him, you'd best be sure of your cause. And you'd better be ready to die."

"Orick is right," Ceravanne said. "Put your weapons away. We are all friends here. I'll not force Gallen or anyone else to serve me."

Ceravanne stared deep into Gallen's face, and the giants rested, seeing no immediate danger. But Gallen held his own sword halfway drawn, as if ready to sweep the blade free. The sunlight shone on Ceravanne's platinum hair, and her pale green eyes reflected the light like cut gems. The sunlight caught her blue-white dress, and it gleamed like a bolt of lightning here under the dark pines. In spite of her strength and wisdom, she looked like little more than a frail child who could be easily swept away, and Gallen's sword was nearly out. If Gallen had wanted to cut her down, he could have put a swift end to her.

"If you are willing to go to Moree to risk your life, then I will walk beside you," Ceravanne said. "I know that the Inhuman teaches that I am its enemy, that the people of this world are but pawns in our hand. But you can trust me, Gallen. I desire harm for no one. I've come to bring peace to this land, not war. I have long been a friend to the people of Babel."

The Im giants stirred restlessly at these words, studying her, and Fenorah said hopefully, "Unless I miss my guess, you are an Immortal? But I am not sure that I have heard of a Tharrin who was a friend to Babel."

"For three hundred years I have been studying with the Bock," Ceravanne whispered. "And for over two hundred years before that, I exiled myself. But I lived here before your grandfather was young—for two thousand years. In Chingat they called me the White Lady. On the island of Bin I was Frost Before the Sun, and in Indallian they called me the Swallow—she who returns. If you have memories from the Inhuman, Gallen, then you have heard these names, and you know why I have come here!"

"By the gods!" Fenorah swore. "The Swallow has returned from the dead! The Immortal is with us!" And the giants of Im all fell to their knees. Some lowered their eyes in respect, while others stared at her in amazement. One man drew his sword, as if pledging it to her service, while the others set their weapons on the ground before them, as if swearing to put them away forever. It was obvious that all of them knew her name and her reputation, but none of the giants was certain how to react.

For one moment, as the giants sat with their heads lowered, it looked as if Ceravanne stood among a field of huge boulders.

And to Orick's utter amazement, Gallen himself, who seemed but a moment before ready to draw his sword on her, suddenly opened his mouth in surprise and fell to one knee at Ceravanne's feet, as if she had slapped him for some insult and he were begging her forgiveness. He watched her steadily. "I know of the Swallow, and how her gentle people fell in ancient days at the hands of the Rodim," he said, "but I have not heard that she was a Tharrin. Truly, you are a friend of the people." Gallen's voice became husky. "I would be more than honored, if you would accompany me to Moree."

"My Lady," Fenorah said, "will you again build the Accord?"

"For long I've tried to bring peace between all peoples," Ceravanne said. "And the Accord was my best effort. When the Rodim slew whole villages,

I could hardly bear it. In anger I turned my back on them, and let my disciples ruin them. The slaughter was horrible, and I could not live with what I'd done. I had sought peace by giving in to war. For centuries I have been in the North, studying the ways of peace at the hands of the Bock, purifying myself. But now I must return to my people. The Tekkar and the Inhuman are forming a deadly alliance, one that could shake the stars."

"I would fight them with you," Fenorah said, and all of his men shouted, "Aye."

"Then draw your weapons upon no man, except in self-defense," Ceravanne said.

"But—how can we fight the servants of the Inhuman without drawing upon them?" one giant asked.

"Your people are tied to the sea, and I forbid you to shed blood. But that does not mean that you cannot fight. There are ships in the harbors of Babel preparing for war," Ceravanne said. "Set them afire. See that the Inhuman does not cross the ocean. And in every ear, with everyone you meet, tell them that the Swallow has returned to build the Accord, and that she begs human and Inhuman alike to lay aside their weapons."

"But the Tekkar will not listen to you," Fenorah said. "They are as deadly and vile a race as ever the Rodim were. We cannot let them live."

"How do we know that we cannot reason with them, if we have not tried?" Ceravanne said. "They are violent and cunning and bloodthirsty. But their men love their women as passionately as you love your own wives. And their mothers love their children."

The Im giants shook their huge heads in disbelief, doubting that the horrid Tekkar could share any brotherhood with them.

But Fenorah looked to his men. "Anabim, Dodeo, the Swallow has spoken her wishes. I charge you to return to Battic and raise some men. Go east along the coast, and set fire to any ships that are preparing for war. And tell people what you have learned here today—that the Swallow has returned to rebuild the Accord. It will set fire to their hearts."

The two giants turned and ran from the grove, heading toward the bridge east.

"You know, Great Lady," Fenorah said, "that news of your presence will put you in greater peril. It now becomes imperative for the Inhuman's agents to kill you, lest some among their numbers give you aid. Legends of the golden days of the Accord abound, and long have we hoped for your return. Still, some people may be slow to believe that you have returned. In past years, there have been rumors. . . ."

"What kinds of rumors?" Ceravanne asked.

"It was said that you had died and that the Lords of the City of Life would not let you be reborn. It was said that they feared a new Accord. It has even been said that the Inhuman has sought to rebuild you, so that you will come and lead it to victory."

"Those were lies spread by the dronon and their Inhuman," Ceravanne said. "The dronon tried to kill me when they learned that they could not turn me to their violent ways, when I would not champion the cause of the Inhuman. Four times the Rebellion brought me the rebirth, and each time I tried to return south to my people, but the Inhuman stopped me."

"Of course," Fenorah said. "Some had guessed as much, and all will be glad of your return." He lowered his head in thought. "Look, when I heard the Servants of the Inhuman talking yesterday, making plans in their cave, I knew only that they sought to turn you because you are a Tharrin, and because you brought a Lord Protector to fight them. I am sure that they did not know your real name, or the full scale of your mission."

"I have been careful not to reveal that until now," Ceravanne said.

"Well," Fenorah said, "what I mean to say is—we had planned to take you inland for a hundred kilometers. But maybe we could go farther."

"Yes," one of the giants echoed.

"And what will you drink?" Gallen said. "Without seawater, you will die of thirst in a matter of days."

"We could buy sea salt in the villages along the way, and add it to fresh water," Fenorah said. "I have gone far inland in such a manner. Indeed, I brought a small pouch of salt just for such an emergency."

"Bless you," Ceravanne said, and tears suddenly shone in her eyes. "But I fear that it would put you in danger. Four giants, all searching for sea salt in those small villages? No, I would be asking too much."

"One giant, then," Fenorah said. "I am Lord Sheriff for this region, and I will accept the risk. I will run two thousand kilometers at your side, all the way to Moree."

"There are vast deserts between here and Moree." Ceravanne shook her head. "You will not find the salt you need to purchase, and even water may be scarce. No, my faithful friend, I cannot accept your life as a sacrifice."

"It is mine to give," Fenorah said.

"Then give it in service. Two hundred and eighty kilometers you may come, to High Home, where the Old King's Road meets the Marbee Road. If we are in peril from the Inhuman's servants, that is where we will most likely find them, and I would welcome your protection."

"Agreed," Fenorah said. "And now, we must be on our journey, for every second matters."

With that, the giants leapt to their feet, and in a moment the travelbeast was harnessed. They did not clean their cooking pans, only pushed them under a bush for later retrieval, then Orick and the others climbed into the wagon.

The giants were no longer content merely to run loosely behind the wagon. Instead, two of them got behind and pushed, and in moments they were off, the wheels singing down the road, the travelbeast lowering its head and huffing as its hooves thundered over the bridge.

Orick looked out over the broad river, saw the folding wings of a fish eagle as it dove, and he gazed along the cliffs at the gray statues of the birds that rose above the trees, gazing out to sea, in to land, their wings and heads splotched green and white and yellow with lichens. Gallen sat beside Orick, an old friend and confidant, yet now Orick knew that Gallen was a stranger. Indeed, the man he'd befriended and trusted most was gone, if Orick understood correctly, becoming submerged under layer after layer of other beings.

Orick recalled how Jesus once met a man near the region of the Gadarenes who was afflicted with demons, and he spoke to the man, asking his name, and the man said, "Legion, for we are many."

And Jesus commanded the demons to depart, and they begged to enter a herd of swine. So Jesus allowed it, and two thousand pigs immediately ran downhill into the raging sea and were drowned.

Ah, Gallen, Orick wondered. Will you let your demons pull you into the sea? And Orick wished that he were a priest, with the authority to cast out demons. Indeed, Gallen needed an exorcist now, as deeply as any man ever did.

But I've always been too weak to accept the priesthood, Orick realized. Too much tempted by the things of the world.

Orick looked at Gallen, all draped in black. And he wondered if he might yet have to fight Gallen at some lonely spot down this road.

Orick could not examine such possibilities for long, and somehow he found himself mourning for lost Profundis and the people who had lived in hard-won peace under these sun-drenched skies. For he knew that, like them, he would never see this place again.

Twenty-one

For two hours that morning the giants ran west along the coast as Gallen drove the wagon. When the road abruptly turned south, heading between two low hills, the giants stopped to rest. All four of them went down to a calm sea, as blue and sparkling as sapphires, and waded into waves up to their chests. For ten minutes they stooped and slowly drank their fill. Afterward, each of them bathed, then clambered back up the long sandy beach, looking refreshed, but as bedraggled as if they'd washed up in a flood.

Then the group headed south through the wooded hills. Tallea was healing nicely, and she and Orick took advantage of the opportunity to rest, while Ceravanne only sat gazing out the back of the wagon.

Maggie had time to wonder. According to Gallen, during the previous night his mantle had begun picking up memories in short bursts, so she put on her own mantle of technology and questioned Gallen about the problem.

"Gallen," she whispered as the travelbeast charged down the dirt road, rounding a corner, "you said that the Inhuman is switching frequencies, trying to communicate with you. Did it do that only last night, or has it continued today?"

"It kept up until just past dawn," Gallen said, "then it stopped."

That was good news, at least. As she'd imagined earlier, the Inhuman's ability to transmit seemed hampered in daylight, so it would be safer to travel by day. But she didn't like the fact that the frequencies were changing at all. "Dammit, Gallen, the Word is more complex than I thought: at the very least, it is equipped with a transmitter so that it can communicate with the Inhuman."

"But how much can it communicate?" Gallen said. "Is it just telling the Inhuman 'I'm here,' or does it send more information?"

Maggie considered. She'd thrown away the broken Word she'd had in camp yesterday. If she had it in hand, she might have been able to find its memory. Most likely, it would have been a small crystal, and by knowing its size, she would have been able to calculate exactly how much information was stored in the Word. But she knew that it couldn't have stored much. *If* the Word's memory was large at all, she'd have noticed its crystal earlier. Which meant that it wasn't equipped with much memory—probably just enough to walk and move and recognize potential targets. It was probably not much smarter than an insect, and it might have had a transmitter in it just so that it could let the Inhuman know when to begin sending messages and whether they had been properly received.

But what bothered Maggie was that the Word didn't *need* much memory to do some rather devastating things. With its transmitter, it *might* be able to download Gallen's memories, his thoughts and ideas, and inform the Inhuman. It *might* be able to send direct transmissions to let the Inhuman know what he saw, what he smelled, what he heard.

In other words, without his knowledge or approbation, Gallen could very well lead them all into a trap, all the while believing himself to be fighting the Inhuman's sway.

"Gallen, I don't know how much the Word in your skull might be able to communicate with the Inhuman," Maggie said hopefully. "But from what I've seen, the agents of the Inhuman don't work in concert. Information doesn't seem to be transferred directly between people. So that transmitter can't be sending much."

"But . . ." Gallen said, "I can tell that something worries you."

Maggie leaned close to Gallen and a wave of dizziness passed over her. What she was about to say was so horrific, so undesirable, that she could hardly express her fears. "If the Word has a transmitter built into it, I've got to believe that it was put there for a good reason. I don't know how much memory the Inhuman has. It couldn't possibly hope to control a million or fifty million people all at once, so it downloads thoughts to you and lets you all act as if you were autonomous. But what if you're not? What if the Inhuman *could* read your mind? What if it could take control of your body the way that Karthenor's Guide took control of me? It wouldn't take a lot of memory for the Inhuman to control a couple dozen people."

"That can't happen to me," Gallen said. "My mantle is blocking its transmissions—at least during the daytime."

Maggie looked meaningfully at Gallen and considered the problem. She didn't want to speak so openly of such possibilities in front of Gallen and the others. She wanted to believe—she needed to believe—that the Inhuman had weaknesses, controllable limitations.

She whispered to her mantle, You have transmission capabilities. Can you help Gallen block the Inhuman's signals?

Done, her mantle whispered. Static will be transmitted in a steady burst. Maggie understood that as long as she stayed within three meters of Gallen, the mantle would add an extra layer of protection.

Maggie silently asked her mantle to provide a schematic for the Word's transmitter, and the mantle provided her with an image. The transmitter, it indicated, would most likely still be inside the metal body of the Word that had burrowed into Gallen's skull. Because it was powered by a biogenic cell, the transmitter would have to be very weak, and would best communicate at ultralow frequencies, lower than those normally used by mantles. Maggie's mantle was unable to read any such frequencies emanating from Gallen's Word. And Maggie wondered if the Word was conserving energy. Perhaps it recognized the futility of trying to communicate during the day.

So Maggie sat next to Gallen, her mantle leaning up against his shoulder, and she rested as he drove.

During the late morning they began to pass others on the road—farmers with handcarts traveling to markets, old men with barrows carrying bundles of firewood, children herding pigs along the road.

Each time they passed such folk, the travelbeast was obliged to slow for safety's sake. And on the occasions when they passed some small hamlet in which buildings made of stone seemed almost to stoop out into the streets, the beast was brought to a walk.

But once they passed such villages, the race would begin anew, and the giants ran. They startled herds of wild pigs sleeping under the oaks by the roadside, and often deer would bound away at their approach, crashing through the brush.

Thus in the early afternoon they topped a long grassy hill, and rested under the shade of an oak. The wooded valleys spread out wide below, thick with oak and alder. As far as they could see, the land looked barren of habitation.

With heavy hearts, three of the giants stopped, begging Ceravanne's pardon for leaving. "You will have to go in the care of Fenorah from now on," one young giant apologized, "though he's not much good for anything but eating your stores."

The giants were covered with sweat, but Ceravanne stood in the back of the wagon and leaned out, kissing each on the forehead. "Go with my blessing," she said, "and know that I am grateful for your service."

The travelbeast was winded, and it lowered its shaggy head and began tearing great clumps of grass from the ground. One of the giants took a bag of rotting pears from the back of the wagon and fed them to the beast, explaining that if it was to run all day, it would need something better than grass to eat.

Then the giants turned as if to walk back toward the sea, but they were slow to leave. And for her part, Maggie was sad to see them go. With them at her side, she'd felt safe, like a child in its father's arms. One of them told a joke that Maggie could not hear, and the three laughed.

Gallen stood in the wagon and shouted in a strange tongue, "Doordra hinim s Duur!"

The three giants turned as one, raising their fists to the sky, and cried, "Doordra hinim!" Then they smiled, as if with renewed energy, and raced away.

Fenorah chuckled. "Stand tall in Duur! Indeed. Where did you learn that old battle cry? The Im giants abandoned the ancient tongue centuries ago."

Gallen took a seat, but his eyes flashed, and he looked up into Fenorah's face. "I learned it a few hours ago," he said softly. "From a man who has been dead for five hundred years. He served beside the Im giants, and with them he hunted Derrits in the mountains of Duur until he swore fealty to the Swallow, and for her slew the Rodim."

Gallen fell silent and his eyes lost their focus as he gazed inward. It was a magical thing for Maggie to see him as a boy one day, then suddenly turning into an old man the next, with too much pain and too much wisdom in his eyes.

Gallen began to sing, and though Maggie had heard him sing a few tavern songs, in the past she'd never thought him to have a fair voice. But now he sang in a voice that was both beautiful and startling, like the scent of a fresh rose filling a room in late autumn, and Maggie realized that it was a talent he'd learned from the Inhuman.

"In Indallian, the peaceful land,
among dark pines glowering,
the hills were hollowed by Inhuman hands
in the days of the Swallow's flowering."

"Hold," said Ceravanne from the back of the wagon, and she reached out and touched Gallen's hand, silencing him. "Please, Gallen, do not sing that song. It is long forgotten by those who dwell here, and . . . it hurts too much. Perhaps if it came from the voice of another bard—but not you. You remind me too much of Belorian."

"He has been dead for many centuries," Gallen said. "I would have thought that time had brought you peace."

"Not today," Ceravanne whispered. "The memories of him seem fresh today, and the pain still hot. If you must tell your friends of Indallian in its days of glory, I beg that you do not sing of it around me."

"What's Indallian?" Orick asked.

Gallen waved toward the wild hills before them, golden with fields of grass, green with forests. "All of this is the land of Indallian—from the rough coast to the ruined halls of Ophat beside the city of Nigangi, and beyond, even to the deserts south of Moree where the Tekkar dwell. Long ago Ceravanne ruled the empire from the great city of Indallian with her consort the good King Belorian, until the Accord fell. Even today if I judge right by Fenorah's account, their love is remembered as the stuff of legend."

"It is spoken of," Fenorah said beside the wagon, "though I must confess that I have not heard that song. And the Land of Indallian is no more, while its capital is spoken of with dread."

"Belorian was more than a consort," Ceravanne said as if to correct Gallen. "He was my lover, my husband in all but name—for by the laws of his people, we could not marry. Yet our love was fierce, before he died."

"I do not understand," Orick said to Ceravanne. "Your people can bring the dead back to life. Why is he not beside you now?"

"Because," Ceravanne said, "a man is more than his flesh. He is also his memories, his experiences, his dreams and ambitions. And shortly after Belorian died in battle, the crystals that stored his memories were destroyed, and that is a far truer and more permanent death than the sloughing off of the flesh. We could rebuild his body, but we cannot remake the man." She looked sharply at Gallen, as if to censure him for bringing up such a painful subject, then turned away.

In the uncomfortable silence that followed, Gallen urged the travelbeast forward with some strange words foreign to the human tongue. The beast responded as if Gallen had spoken in its own language, and it rushed through the hills.

And as Maggie rode that day, she watched the land roll by. Often she would see ancient lichen-crusted stones tumbled in the grass as they passed some ruin, and twice they passed ancient fortresses that sprawled upon the hills, covered with moss, with oaks growing in the courtyard, their branches reaching over the stone walls like great hands.

As the day drew to its close, a brief squall blew over, and Fenorah, unwilling to risk that his travelbeast should injure itself by slipping in the mud, decided to set camp in an old fortress, in a great hall without doors or windows. So they brought the travelbeast inside.

The walls were made of huge stones, a meter thick, carved so that various grooves fit together. Maggie suspected that the stone might not deter the Inhuman's signal as well as a dozen feet of solid dirt, but she hoped it would serve nearly as well. She found the most secluded corner and directed Gallen to sit there and rest.

Dried horse dung left by the mounts of previous travelers served as ample fuel to set a small fire, and Fenorah brought out stores for dinner. They had not had a formal meal since early morning, and everyone was tired, and the poor giant was most weary of all. He curled into a corner while Maggie cooked dinner, and he fell asleep before it was done.

After a brief dinner Ceravanne withdrew from the group, going out a back hall that led to a tower. Outside, the rain was falling steadily, hissing as it struck the leaves of trees, and the heavy scent of moisture pervaded the room. It was chill and dreary.

"That song you began to sing today," Orick said. "Will you sing it to us now?" And Maggie hoped that he would, for the sound of music would do her heart good.

Gallen sang in a low voice the same tune he had begun earlier in the day, and Maggie was amazed at his voice, at the easy grace and power in it, as if he'd been born to sing.

He sang of Indallian, the riches and glory that made it the envy of all the world. He sang of the peaceful peoples drawn by the Swallow to form the great Accord, where each species had equal voices in the open counsels.

But then the Rodim came, a greedy race lured by tales of the rich deposits of emeralds and gold found in Indallian, and they ravaged whole villages, looted and burned the caravanserais.

The Swallow's love, Belorian, was a strong man, and he sought to protect his people by arming them. But the Swallow urged him to counsel with the Rodim peacefully, to reconcile with them, bring them into the Accord.

Yet when Belorian met with the savage chieftains of the Rodim in their mountain camps, they slew him and put his body upon a pole, then danced through the night, proclaiming victory over the land of Indallian, and they sent their armies to Belorian's throne at the city of Indallian, where they heaped contempt upon the dead by destroying the crystal that held Belorian's memories.

Ceravanne was there, in her tower, and she witnessed the abuses committed upon her people, and upon her lord. Then the Rodim's head chieftain ravished Ceravanne in Belorian's bedchamber.

Because of the atrocities, the peaceful people of Indallian gathered together and slaughtered the armies of the Rodim without mercy, then fell upon the villages of their women without restraint and murdered their children, removing the Rodim from the face of the land.

Many went to the Swallow, asking her to have mercy before the final slaughter of the Rodim, hoping to spare some remnant of the race.

But Ceravanne turned away so that not one child remained.

And when the Rodim were all dead, the Swallow put a single red rose upon the grave of Belorian, and another upon the grave of the chieftain of the Rodim, to signify that she forgave him and his people, though she had not spared them. Then she proclaimed a year of mourning for the Rodim who lay dead, and for those who were forced to kill them.

None who beheld her could miss the horror on her face, nor deny her torment. And hours later the Swallow disappeared, and her crystal scepter was found in the mud of her courtyard. Many thought she had chosen to die rather than live without Belorian; while others imagined that she was so horrified by the genocide that was done in her behalf that she turned her back on mankind forever; but her friends swore that she would return when her grief had run its course, and so the legends said that someday she would come back to lead the Accord.

"Four hundred and eighty years ago the Swallow left rich Indallian," Gallen intoned. "And still her heart knows no peace. Yet in songs and legends, people here remember the days of the Accord."

Maggie looked toward the door that led to the tower, understanding why Ceravanne sought refuge in silence. Ceravanne had said earlier that her love, Belorian, was fresh on her mind, and Maggie felt the pain of knowing that she was surely losing Gallen to the Inhuman, just as Ceravanne had lost Belorian to the Rodim.

Gallen lay beside Maggie and stared into the fire, unable to sleep for a long time. Sometimes, he thought he could hear snatches of whispers, and he saw brief visions, tatters of memories that belonged to other people. But the song of the Inhuman was weak tonight, possibly because of the storm. Even as this thought struck Gallen, he heard the distant rumble of thunder, confirming his suppositions.

He got up quietly so as not to rouse Maggie, and he put some twigs on the fire.

"How many lives you recall?" Tallea whispered, letting the sound of her voice fill the night.

"Just the seven," Gallen answered. Then to fill up the silence that followed, he said, "I wonder how many more the Inhuman has in store for me."

"A hundred lives to be remembered," Tallea said. "You fortunate, remember them slowly, over days. Should be easy."

"Yes." Gallen smiled wanly. "I'm fortunate." A cold shiver of fright wriggled down his backbone. He went to his pack, dug around for a moment, then pulled out a thin film of translucent material and applied it to his face.

His face suddenly shone like blue starlight as he put on the mask of Fale, and he stood for a moment, his black robes draped over him, weapons bristling on his back and thighs. He recalled how the witnesses at his trial back home had imagined he was a sidhe when thus garbed, a magical being with malevolent intent, and now Gallen could indeed feel it. With his face gleaming in the dark like a ghost, there was little human left in him. He looked like a thing.

Gallen stood at the door, as if he would walk out into the night rain, and for a moment he wanted to do that, just walk away into the dark and the cleansing rain that was sweeping down in misty sheets.

Instead he went to a back corridor of the great hall. The floors were thick with dust and moss, old leaves, and the husks of pine nuts carried in by squirrels.

He stood for a moment, testing the air to see whether the Inhuman would try to send him more memories. But there was nothing. It seemed that for the time being, he was free.

Using his mantle's night, vision, Gallen negotiated the passageways until he found some stairs curving up the wall of a tower. Muddy footprints showed that Ceravanne had been here recently, and though Gallen mistrusted her, he felt drawn to her.

He climbed the winding stairs for twenty meters, till he found a room that opened at the top. There, several arching windows were still intact; weathered stones surrounded casements that had long ago rotted into dust. Ceravanne stood beside one such window. Ivy grew in dust on the floor, so that she stood as if in a meadow, surrounded by foliage, staring out into the rain. Her back was to him, and she shivered.

Gallen went to her, stood for a moment. He could feel the heat of her body near his, and he inhaled her clean scent. He knew that it was only pheromones that drew him so vigorously, yet he found himself wishing to hold her, to comfort her.

"I hoped you would come," she said, and she turned. With the light amplification provided by his mantle, he could see that she'd been crying, and she stared into his face, at the mask, and he wondered what she saw. A blue glowing phantom, with dark holes for eyes.

She took his hands, held them lightly, and studied his face. She was breathing heavily, and she said, "That song—I have to ask—from whom did you learn it?"

"From a minstrel named Tam, who lived here ages ago," Gallen answered.

"But this man, did he remember me? He didn't know the Swallow in person?"

"You were but newly gone when he composed the song," Gallen said.

"And Belorian? Did he know Belorian?" Her voice was nearly hysterical, as if she hoped for some word of her long-dead lover.

"No," Gallen whispered. "He never knew Belorian."

Ceravanne gasped and began weeping, fell against Gallen's chest. "Ah, I thought he had. I thought you remembered his face." Then she sobbed from the core of her soul, and Gallen clumsily put his arms around her, tried to ease her pain.

"So many tears, for one long dead," Gallen whispered.

Ceravanne looked up, stroked his chin. "You look much like him," she said. "When we first met, I kissed you inappropriately. I guess I wanted you to love me. Being near you has been hard. Forgive me if I've offended you with my affection."

Gallen licked his lips, stepped back. He'd been aware of Ceravanne, of her graceful movements, of the longing glances she sometimes gave him. He'd imagined that it was all a ploy, a sly attempt to manipulate him. And the Inhuman, with its clever tongue, whispered that this was true—another cruel attempt by the Tharrin to ensnare him. Gallen had never dreamed that Ceravanne could really have felt anything for him, and now he saw that he was but a shadow to her.

"I'm sorry." He found himself unaccountably apologizing. "I didn't know."

She looked at him oddly, as if wondering if he told the truth. "Of course you couldn't have known." She turned away. "What of Maggie? Have your feelings for her changed?"

"Today, I learned of the most marvelous people, far to the south. The Yakrists, they are called, and they care for others more than they care for themselves. They love one another perfectly, and as I lived the life of a Yakrist, I came to understand how weak and imperfect my love for Maggie has been."

"So your feelings for her *are* changed?"

"I will try to be more . . . understanding of her needs," Gallen said. "Perhaps if I were Inhuman, I would love her more perfectly."

Ceravanne nodded, obviously distraught, and Gallen realized that she had hoped he would answer differently, that he would say he was abandoning Maggie.

"And you believe that by enslaving others, the Inhuman is showing that kind of great love?"

"Ceravanne," Gallen whispered. "I think there is something you should know. The Inhuman is not completely wrong, here. It only wants us to understand one another, to help one another."

There was a cruel laughing, something that Gallen could almost not imagine hearing from Ceravanne's throat. "Don't tell me that," she whispered fiercely. "I've seen what the dronon are up to. They care nothing for us, nothing for each other. They love only their Golden Queen, and they serve her ruthlessly."

"And yet they want peace," Gallen said. "They want us to unite with them, and they're offering . . . so much in return."

"What are they offering?"

"Life. Rebirth," Gallen said. "They're going to open restrictions on giving rebirth to nonhumans. And anyone can be reborn into the body of their choice, experience life as they desire.

"And peace!" Gallen continued. "In the past, the people of Babel have been slaughtered in ruthless wars, with everyone trying to conquer their neighbors. But among the hosts of the Inhuman, everyone will live fuller lives. I know what it is to be a Yakrist, and now that I know them, I could never harm one of them. That is what the Inhuman offers, a knowledge of our own brotherhood. And the Dronon will take care of the people of Babel."

"Gallen," Ceravanne said, looking at him as if he were mad, and a knife of fear stabbed him, for Gallen wondered if he was mad. "The dronon don't care for us," she said reasonably. "You can't imagine that they do. When their own infants are sick or crippled, they grind them up to fertilize their fields. You're trying to make sense, but the dronon are using your own compassion against you. And it's damned unfair of them to ask you to be compassionate, when they lack that capacity themselves. They don't want to free us from our wars and infighting, they want to create nations of slaves with them as our masters. All of the technologies they offer to benefit mankind are technologies we've already developed. If they succeed in taking over, just watch them. They'll give rebirth only to those who serve them best. And they want you to feel good about it."

Gallen listened to her words carefully, tried to hold on to them, but somehow their meaning evaded him. I used to think like she does, Gallen realized. But when? It seemed to him that his fears of the dronon had stemmed from a dream—a long time ago. Something about Maggie, wearing a Guide, while trapped in a dronon fortress. But just at the moment, he couldn't recall. Instead, a more pressing argument came to mind. "You are no more human than a dronon is," Gallen said, brightening. "Why should you rule us?"

"Because humans created me for that purpose," Ceravanne countered. "And I crave to serve them. But unlike the dronon, I never force my rule on anyone. If humans desire to elect a human leader, that is their option. But the dronon will not let you serve as equals. They will never accept human leaders."

There was a long pause, and Gallen listened to her words but could not understand how any sane person could arrive at her conclusion. He finally managed, "The Dronon will accept *us*. Maggie and I, we are the leaders of the Sixth Swarm. We could take our rightful place, show them how to live together with us in harmony!"

"But humans don't want to live with *them*!" Ceravanne said.

"Agreed, most of them don't," Gallen whispered, and there was an unusual intensity in his voice. He felt almost as if his mouth moved of its own accord, and he merely listened to the words it said. "But what of the people of Babel? They are not humans. Can't you see how your policies afflict them? They have no sense of purpose, so few social bonds across tribes. They have no law, no access to technology. You created them, then abandoned them. They need what humans and the dronon have!"

"Gallen, I was not formed to be a judge of the peoples of Babel. I *can't* take care of them, any more than the dronon could. I don't understand all of their needs, all of their hopes. I don't even force my judgments on humans.

"But let me ask you this, Gallen. Is it our obligation to govern other peoples, or to find a purpose in life for them, or to be their friends?" Ceravanne asked, and her voice was desperate. "You are human, from a world not unlike Tremonthin: who ever tried to give you a purpose in life? Who ever protected you? Can't you see—all of these things that you say the humans owe the people of Babel, in your own country, you don't even force them on your own children. It would be wicked to do so. If these people in Babel want law, then they have to figure out how to create and enforce their own laws. They weren't designed to live by human standards, and I can't take the right to govern themselves away from them."

"But you deny them life. . . ." Gallen objected, angry that she would not or could not see his point.

"And we deny most of our own people more than one life," Ceravanne said. "Even the best of us often only get our lives extended by a few decades."

"But the humans of Tremonthin created these people," Gallen objected. "You owe them!"

"Since we created them, doesn't it stand to reason that they owe us for the blessing of life?" Ceravanne countered. "Think of it. Do we owe them more than we owe our own children? Even for our own children, we make no guarantees. We make no promises of love or acceptance or wealth. No society can promise all of these things to its individuals. Happiness comes as a reward for a life well lived. It cannot be an entitlement."

"But . . ."

"There are no buts," Ceravanne said. "Gallen, all of your thoughts, all of those confused feelings, those are just the Inhuman talking. Those notions don't make any sense when you look at them closely. But the dronon want you to believe them. The dronon want you to believe that their Golden Queen will take care of us. But you've seen what the dronon offer on other worlds. They want to feed off us, as parasites. Gallen, the dronon showed you the lives of a few folks. They told you a story, providing the sights, the smells, the emotions. They told you a lie.

"But more importantly, I want you to realize that you are spouting danger-ous dogma that doesn't necessarily follow from the information you've been given. Think about it, and you'll know I'm right. The dronon are teaching you on a subconscious level, altering your thought patterns. The memories they feed you only serve to cover the deeper alterations, and to make you think that you changed your mind on your own."

Gallen was stunned. She had all the answers, all waiting in her hand like needles to prod him with. It seemed obvious that she had argued against the Inhuman before. He felt confused, and a buzzing sounded in his ears, sounded so loudly that he had a hard time thinking. He wanted to speak against her, but he could not think what to say next. The room seemed to be spinning, and Gallen found himself wanting to take Ceravanne by the throat, shake some sense into her. For the moment he seemed certain of only one thing: she was his enemy.

He grabbed her neck and pushed her against the wall. "Liar! Deceitful lit-tle vixen!" he said, and the room spun mightily so that he wondered if he could even stand. In his mind, her presence registered only as some hateful creature, a woman with long skeletal hands, groping for him.

Ceravanne hit the stone wall and slid down, her mouth open as if she would cry out, her eyes wide with fear, and Gallen knew that if she spoke again, he would have to silence her. Lightning struck outside—once, twice, a third time.

But the Tharrin only sat heavily in the ivy leaves. For a long moment, she only breathed, and Gallen's anger began to pass. The room quit spinning, and Gallen's mantle whispered, Seek shelter below, next to Maggie, quickly! And suddenly Gallen knew that the Inhuman had been communicating with him, trying to download its arguments directly into his mind.

Gallen stood gazing down at Ceravanne. "Don't hurt me," she pleaded, and she folded her arms, sat gazing up at him, a helpless child.

Gallen found that his sword had unaccountably appeared in his hand. Some time in the past minute, he had drawn it. And he'd been prepared to kill her, without thinking.

He shoved it back into his scabbard, and he wanted to run then, wanted to rush down the stairs and hide in the woods for what he'd almost done. He felt terribly embarrassed.

"Forgive me," he whispered, white shock registering in his brain only as numbness. "The Inhuman can be . . . subtle."

"You're forgiven," Ceravanne said with a tiny nod. She reached up her thin hand, so that he could help her up.

He took it, pulled her to a standing position. His heart was hammering with fear, and something else. . . . The air in the room was moist and closed, and Ceravanne's scent was thick. She was trembling, frightened, and he wanted to ease her mind. So he kissed her hand, looking into her eyes. She was small and pale, like a porcelain figure. Her hand, when he kissed it, tasted sweet. He'd almost forgotten how sweet the taste of a Tharrin could be.

Ceravanne reached up, and she was shaking, leaning against him. Her whole body trembled. She gazed deeply into his eyes. "You see," she whispered desperately, "that I was right when I told you that I needed your heart. If you do not give it to me, the Inhuman will take it. Gallen, give me your heart!"

She kissed his chin experimentally, then brushed her lips against his. A burning passion rose in him, and Gallen kissed her full on the lips, pulling her close. She drew tight against him, her flesh folding into his like a lover's, her arms embracing him. All thought retreated, and for one moment, there was only that passionate kiss blossoming like a field of wild poppies in his mind. Every nerve in his body tingled, her touch was lightning, and she groaned, tried to pull him to the floor there among the ivy.

Desperately, he pushed her away. "No!" Gallen cried. "I am married to Maggie!"

And he fled across the room from her, stood by the doorway. Ceravanne was on her knees now, breathing heavily, gazing at him, stunned. "No man has ever rejected me," she said, hurt in her voice.

He turned for the door, and she said, "If it is Maggie you want, then be faithful to her, Gallen—remain as faithful to her in Moree as you have been tonight."

Gallen hurried down the stairway, almost running. When he reached the bottom he found the fire still going. Tallea was hunched over it, putting in some more dry dung. Everyone else had gone to sleep, but Gallen stayed awake for the rest of the night while the others rested. He stared off into the rain, letting the full powers of his mantle keep watch while he remained on guard duty.

And through the night, ghosts came, the memories of people long dead, and they took him on journeys he could not sleep through and could not hope to escape. He felt like a child on a sandy beach, with water rushing in upon him with tremendous force, and with each crashing wave, the sand beneath him would shift, so that he felt as if something essential were being dragged away.

It did not matter where he stood in that little room. It did not matter that his mantle tried to block the signals. The Inhuman was overpowering him moment by moment, so that sometimes while the others slept, Gallen sobbed or cried out softly.

Long before morning, Gallen woke the others, and they headed south.

Twenty-two

By dawn the companions were on the road again, and Tallea felt . . . decent for the first time in three days. She was able to sit with little pain, and in fact could feel herself mending, and to her it seemed miraculous. As a Caldurian, she tended to heal fast anyway, but the Immortal's blood had worked wonders on her wounds.

More importantly, the support that these people had given her was working wonders on her spirit. A year earlier, when Ceravanne's other self had come to Babel, Tallea had hired on with her band, had led them into the wilderness of Moree, and there she lost them to the Tekkar. At the time Ceravanne had not announced herself as the Swallow. Indeed, Tallea had only thought her to be a beautiful woman, traveling as a companion to the valiant swordsmen who sought to destroy the Inhuman.

But one night, when they had neared Moree, the Tekkar ambushed their small band. Many good men died before their swords cleared their scabbards. Tallea herself had been sorely wounded and left among the dead. And Ceravanne, beautiful Ceravanne had been carried away into Moree where the Tekkar would do unspeakable things to her.

For a year Tallea had been serving on ships, waiting for a new band to make its way into Moree. And this time, she vowed, they would slay the Inhuman. For a year she had suffered alone on the ships, refusing to bind herself to anyone. It was an untenable situation for a Caldurian, and only her training, her devotion to the ways of the Roamers, had helped her survive.

Yet now, as they rode in the oversized wagon through a gray dawn, she could not help but feel concerned. It seemed that some cosmic balance was being maintained. Minute by minute, her pains decreased, and she blossomed to greater health.

Minute by minute, Gallen was crumbling, falling in on himself like an old house toppling under its own weight.

He hadn't slept all night, and during the morning he just sat, huddled in the driver's seat of the wagon, his mouth slack as he stared into nothingness. The travelbeast was guiding the wagon more than Gallen was.

Orick whispered to Maggie about it. "There is a horror on Gallen's face that I've never seen before. Gallen has always been a feisty lad—nothing like this."

And so the travelbeast ran on, its head rising and falling as it drew the wagon along the bank of a winding muddy river. Ceravanne took control of the wagon for a while, and Maggie took Gallen and cradled his head against her breast tenderly, and he stared out the back of the wagon, at the trees falling behind.

Gallen muttered, "Eighteen . . . eighteen. My defenses are crumbling."

Maggie said that her own mantle whispered insistently that it was doing all it could to block the Inhuman's transmissions. And when Maggie asked Gallen to tell her about this latest life he had lived, he said nothing for many minutes.

"God, I wish I were home," Maggie whispered in his ear. "I wish we both were home, that we'd never come. This trip is changing us, destroying you."

"So the journey changes us," Gallen said wearily, surprising Tallea by responding at all. "You can't walk from your house without your hairs growing whiter. You can't walk down to the gate without taking a risk. And from the death of the old, the new is born."

"This isn't a walk to the gate," Maggie said. "Ever since you went to the teaching machines on Fale, you've lost some of yourself, some of your accent. Now, you hardly sound as if you're from Tihrglas at all."

Gallen said no more for a long time, and Ceravanne, who was sitting up front, exchanged worried glances with Maggie.

One of the rear wheels began squeaking a bit, and Tallea climbed up, ignoring the stabbing pains in her side, got the swabbing rod out of the grease, and daubed each wheel.

No one spoke for a long time. They passed through several small villages in the space of a few hours, and Fenorah stopped at the largest to grain the travelbeast and to purchase salt, food, leather for shoes, and a number of small items that they had not had a chance to carry.

All during that stop, Gallen went and stood leaning against a hitching post, and the townsfolk took great pains to avoid him. Even a pair of yellow dogs that were running together crossed to the far side of the street.

As Fenorah began loading the wagon in preparation to leave, he glanced at Gallen and mumbled, "Only twenty demons in him, and he's ready to crumble. If an apple spoiled in our food barrel, would we not throw it out?"

"What you saying?" Tallea asked.

Fenorah nodded toward Gallen. "I'm worried. He's a danger to us now—perhaps more dangerous than he knows. If we left him, I do not think he'd notice."

And Tallea realized that Fenorah truly was entertaining thoughts of leaving Gallen behind. Sometimes, it seemed that people who were not of the Caldur were so unaware of how the tenuous threads of friendship could bind people together, lend them support. To her, those feelings were almost a visible thing, they were so strongly felt.

"Now he needs us most," she said, struggling into a more comfortable position. "Servants of Inhuman want you reject him, so he turn to them for companionship."

Orick pricked his ears forward and stood still for a moment. "You're right!" Orick shouted in a voice that echoed from the buildings, and he got up from the bed of the wagon and stood clumsily with his two front feet on the backboard. "This is no time to turn our backs on him."

He jumped from the wagon, ran to Gallen's side, and stood, wrapping his paws around Gallen's shoulders. By applying his weight, he pushed Gallen to the ground. "I've had enough from you!" Orick said, putting one great paw on Gallen's chest. "You spirits, I adjure you to come out of this man, in the name of the Father, the Son, and the Holy Ghost. Amen!"

Gallen grunted, gave half a laugh, and his eyes suddenly cleared, as if he'd wakened. "Orick, I wish it were that simple!"

"Och, well, it was worth a try," Orick growled, looking from side to side as if for another answer. "Look, Gallen, my friend, you remember your Bible: and if Satan can appear as an angel, then it's no great feat for the dronon to disguise themselves as our friends. But I tell you, Gallen, even if you had a head made of straw and a belly full of whiskey, I'd expect you to know better! When the dronon came to Clere, they didn't pass out bags of gold and welcome us to paradise. They chewed off John Mahoney's head, and shot Father Heany, turning our priest into a puddle. And on Fale, they didn't come ask Maggie if she'd like to be their slave. They put a Guide on her and dragged her off—me fighting them tooth and claw. You know better than to trust a word they say!"

"Get off me," Gallen choked, "I can't breathe!"

"I'll not get off you until you start making sense!" Orick growled, and he put both front paws on Gallen and bounced his weight on him experimentally, as if to prove the point. "I don't care whose memories are rolling around in your head, Gallen. Your own memories are in there, too. You've got to take control of yourself!"

Gallen stared up at Orick, and there was a bleakness to his countenance, a look of utter desolation, and then a smile crossed his face, and he began laughing. It was not a happy laugh, though it held a tone of relief. "Well said, my dearest friend. I hereby take control of myself."

"Good," Orick grumbled, " 'cause I'd hate to have to crush you." He backed off Gallen's chest, sniffed the air. Then reached down and nipped at Gallen's mask, pulling it halfway off. "And take off that ugly mask."

Gallen crumpled the blue mask, put it in a pocket of his robes. Then he rolled over, began climbing to his knees. Orick bit the collar of his robe and began dragging him forward playfully, growling, "Come on, into the wagon with you." By now, a dozen locals began gathering to watch the spectacle, creeping out of shops, openly asking one another what was going on, and for their benefit Orick said loudly, "We'll have no more public displays of drunkenness, young man!"

Orick climbed up to the wagon, and in moments they were off.

Gallen looked to be himself, smiling around at his friends, and he put his arms around Orick gratefully, and for the moment, Tallea knew that they had him back.

When they passed out of town, beneath the shade of chestnut trees that lined the road, Gallen looked up at Ceravanne. "You told me once that you could help me fight this. I need your help."

Ceravanne, who had been sitting up front to drive, turned back around, pulled the reins and brought the travelbeast to a halt, then set the brake. "Lean your head into Maggie's lap, and stare into her face."

Gallen lay back, so that his long golden hair spread about Maggie's lap, and he gazed up into Maggie's face. Ceravanne climbed down beside them, and the back of the wagon bed was suddenly crowded, but Tallea herself did not mind the close bodies. It reminded her of her childhood in the crèche at Wind Mountain, sleeping with her sisters among the pile of blankets in their dormitory.

"Maggie is the woman you love," Ceravanne said softly, and only the gentle hiss of the wind through the trees competed with her voice. "You have loved her since you were children, and you gave your heart to her long ago. Look into her eyes and concentrate, try to recall every detail of her face, and re-member that she is the one you have chosen to give yourself to. . . ." She hesi-tated, and Gallen stared into Maggie's face, his mouth working as he silently spoke to himself. Cool clouds were scudding overhead, and the wind played delicately in Maggie's hair. Ceravanne's voice was fragile, dreamy. "Maggie is the one you've loved forever. Tell this to yourself, over and over. A hundred times is not enough. A thousand times is just the beginning. A hundred thou-sand times, you must repeat this, though it take the next year of your life."

Gallen stared up at Maggie for a long time, and she held his face. The sun shone through the clouds on him, and Tallea could see on his nose the pale remnants of freckles that might have been more pronounced in childhood. He had a strong jaw, and clear blue eyes, and for a few moments, all the pain and worry seemed to leach away. Maggie was holding Gallen's chin, stroking it, and he was gazing up into Maggie's eyes. So Gallen did not notice when Ceravanne reached down and brushed his lips with the back of her forefinger.

Tallea had heard much about how the touch of a Tharrin could calm a person. Indeed, Gallen licked the back of Ceravanne's finger, sensually, kissed it, thinking it was Maggie's caress.

Then Ceravanne pulled her finger away gently, took Maggie's hand and moved her forefinger into the same position, and he kissed it. Suddenly his eyes became clear, focused, and he stared at Maggie, unblinking, for several moments, then fell asleep.

He rested for a long time in Maggie's lap, and Maggie said, "What did you do to him? Put him to sleep?"

Ceravanne shook her head. "No. He has hardly slept in three days. I think that we just eased his mind enough so that fatigue finally took him."

"But what did you do?"

Ceravanne said softly to Maggie, "Every woman's touch can have a power over man, but a Tharrin's touch is very strong. There are . . . agents, pheromones in my skin that he craves, that can cause him to bond to me. I exude them at all times, but I do so more when I am afraid. It's a defense mechanism that your ancestors gave me. He tasted those pheromones, but it was your face he was watching. He will be more strongly bonded to you now."

"I envy you that power," Maggie whispered.

Ceravanne shrugged. "Don't envy me. I think that it is a power that causes as much harm as good. It has saved me at times, but it ill serves the men who throw their lives away in my defense. I envy you his love, for it *is* you that he loves above all others." She watched Gallen sleep for a bit, and whispered, "He will hunger for your presence as never before, and you must stay close to him. Still, the draw of the Inhuman is strong. He may need more treatments before this is over."

She climbed out of the wagon bed, got back up front into the driver's seat again, and eased the wagon out slowly.

"I'm glad he's resting," Orick said, watching Gallen. "I know that if Gallen were thinking straight, he'd never doubt us." Orick was lying on his stomach, resting his nose under his paws, watching Gallen thoughtfully with his sad brown eyes, like some great dog studying its injured master. The sight of it warmed Tallea's heart, for she valued faithfulness above all traits, and instinctively she knew that Orick would never betray Gallen or be unsteady. Orick looked right at Tallea and said softly, "Thank you for reminding me how to be his friend."

The way that they were sitting, his rump was near her hand, and she patted his rear paw. In response, he began licking her ankle with his broad tongue, and she found this show of affection . . . curiously sensual.

For a moment she looked around at these strange companions—to strong Fenorah up ahead of the wagon, running in his rolling, lumbering gait; Ceravanne at the wagon's reins; Maggie and Gallen, resting together with eyes closed; while faithful Orick lay at Tallea's feet.

It seemed remarkable to her how these people had a way of weaving themselves into her heart, with a song, a sigh, a touch.

Tallea's Caldurian instincts were having their way with her. Perhaps it was only because she had denied bonding with someone for so long. Perhaps she would have chosen to serve these people anyway. But she felt a sharp need to protect them.

The wagon left the wide valley and began heading up a long road again, into some lonely hills where the trees grew thick and wild. It was a likely place to find Derrits or Sprees, or some other wild animal.

Tallea pulled her sword from its scabbard, a blade heavy near the guard for parrying, and deceptively long and thin, for thrusting. The sunlight gleamed on its edges, and the blade was in fair condition, but over the past few days Tallea hadn't felt well enough to take proper care of it. It had been nicked and blunted in the battle at sea, and she'd managed only a cursory cleaning the day before.

So as the wagon rolled ever closer to Moree, she took her stone from its pouch tied at her back, and began grinding out the nicks, honing the blade to razor sharpness, buffing off the rust, and she considered. If they were going to Moree, she'd need a bow and some arrows.

The travelbeast was running steadily through the brisk air, over the rolling hills. At the rate they were moving, they'd reach High Home by nightfall. She hoped to buy some weapons there.

Twenty-three

In the early afternoon Zell'a Cree had reached the mountains a few kilometers north of High Home when he limped to the junction to the Old King's Road.

He'd killed two stolen horses to get here, and he'd run without much sleep for most of the past two nights. His right boot was held together with a strip of cloth torn from his tunic.

But his work was paying off. South of Battic he had met up with five servants of the Inhuman who had given him a Word. And more importantly, last night he'd spotted a scout, flying high beneath the clouds. With a gesture he had pulled it to earth and asked it to carry a message south, warning the Inhuman that a Lord Protector was coming.

With that done, Zell'a Cree had felt a great sense of relief. The scout flew south, and it would deliver its warning long before Gallen's wagon got to Moree. Still Zell'a Cree could not rest. He wanted to capture this band himself.

Marbee Road met the Old King's Road at the mouth of a small valley where an old wooden bridge crossed the river, its boards whitened by the summer sun. Zell'a Cree stood for some time, tasting the scent of the air. There was no stench of travelbeast, no perfume of the Tharrin or taste of the others, but it was hard to tell for certain. An orchard had been planted here many years ago—Zell'a Cree recalled it from the memories of Anote Brell, a soldier who'd died six decades past—and still there were many apple trees growing on both sides of the road. The smell of the pungent, fallen apples filled the air, so much so that Zell'a Cree could smell little else.

Still, after a bit, he felt sure that the wagon had not passed. More good news. If the Tharrin's company had not passed, he had managed to stay ahead of them.

He hurried along the road south to High Home, and soon began climbing the long hills. He was well up into the mountains by now, and the air was growing thinner, too thin for a Tosken to breathe comfortably.

Yet Zell'a Cree managed the climb until he reached the crown of the mountain and stood in the small hamlet. Iron ore was mined from ridges above town, so that on the upper slopes there were red holes gouged in the earth, and the miners had tunneled deep into the hills. Down below town, sheep farmers grazed their herds on the green slopes.

The homes here in town were not your standard northern fare. They were built of heavy stone, mudded over on the outside with a white plaster the color of bones, topped with tile roofs that were an ash-gray. The houses kept cool in the hot summers when the wind blew out of the desert, but in the winters when the snow flew, the folks hereabout would have to fasten tapestries to their walls and stuff straw behind them to provide insulation against the cold.

In the summer, frequent cool winds blew down from the mountain slopes so that High Home had a reputation among desert folk as something of a mountain resort with "healthy air," a place where the rich could escape the blistering summer months.

But now it was fall, cool but not unpleasantly so, though the three fine inns in town were fairly deserted, as were the streets. In the summer, the streets would have been filled with merchants out to sell their wares, but now there were only a few shops open, their doors thrown wide in invitation to potential customers.

Zell'a Cree asked around until he found a bootmaker who was willing to throw together something cheap and durable.

In the bootmaker's shop, Zell'a Cree put his foot on the thick leather for the soles and let the old man scratch his cutting marks, then they chose something more supple for the uppers. In moments the old man had cut the leather and begun sewing, when Zell'a Cree heard the rumble of hooves and the clattering of wheels.

He glanced out the window of the shop toward the wide avenue, and his heart skipped a beat.

Sure enough, Gallen's wagon rolled into town, the huge travelbeast frothing at the mouth from its exertions, one lone giant in the lead, the chest and armpits of his tunic stained with sweat.

The suns were setting, and the Tharrin's company cast long shadows over the cobblestone streets. The white stone buildings gleamed intensely in the sunlight, and Zell'a Cree ducked behind the doorpost and listened.

"The travelbeast needs grain and rest," the giant told the others, walking up to set the wagon's brakes. "He's nearly done in for the night, and won't be able to carry you much farther along these mountain roads. We might as well eat here—the inns are highly renowned."

"Thank you," the Tharrin said, as the giant took her gently by the waist and set her down from the wagon. "I don't know how we can repay your generosity."

"Your safety is repayment enough," the giant said, and Zell'a Cree nearly laughed. The others were climbing down from the wagon now, and Gallen O'Day stretched sinuously, reaching for the sky.

Zell'a Cree put his back to the doorpost, so that none in the company would have even the slimmest chance of spotting his silhouette in the doorway.

Darkness, a lonely town, and Gallen unaware. And in my pouch, two copies of the Word. Zell'a Cree could not quite believe his good fortune.

And yet, and yet he was worried. He felt alone with his troubles. New converts often rejoiced at the sense of fullness that communion with the Inhuman gave them, the sense of boundless knowledge, the feeling of buoyancy, as if they were children who had been lifted up and were looking at the world from the height of tall shoulders. But in time, that sensation wore thin. After years of not hearing from the Inhuman, one sometimes felt lost, cast adrift. It was said that some great leaders were in constant communion—the Harvester, certainly, and the commanders of the armies and navies to a lesser extent. But not Zell'a Cree. Not once over the long years since his conversion had he heard the sweet voice of the Inhuman. And at this moment, he wished that he could be certain of the correct course—to let these people proceed to Moree, where the Inhuman could arrange a more appropriate reception, or to kill Gallen now and seek to convert the others.

He stood for several long minutes, pondering his choices, then peeked out again. The company had gone inside, with the exception of the giant, who was busy unharnessing the travelbeast.

Zell'a Cree crept back to the bootmaker's bench. "Just sew up the right boot for now," he said softly. "I'm in a hurry."

The bootmaker glanced up at him in surprise and grunted, "Don't think I can have it done by dark, and I close soon."

"In the morning, then," Zell'a Cree said. He checked out the door. The giant was leading the travelbeast away to the stables down behind the inn. The suns were falling rapidly, and in the cool evening air, some crickets had begun chirping. A few people scurried along the streets, heading home. Even here, the Inhuman's agents were known to hunt at night.

Zell'a Cree pulled up the hood of his cloak, covering his face, and hurried across the shadowed avenue to the wall of the inn. From its shade, he could see the wooden stables in back, down a small hill. The giant had reached the stables, and he opened the broad doors, took the beast inside.

Zell'a Cree knew that he had to get Gallen alone, had to strip Ceravanne of her protectors. The giant himself was a formidable adversary. The Toskens were smaller in stature than the Im giants, and were not so strong, though they could endure greater hardships. And as a Tosken, Zell'a Cree knew no fear.

He ran down to the stable, slipped into the door. His eyes did not need to adjust to the dark. He saw the giant plainly enough, stooping over a feed bin, dumping in a bag of grain. The travelbeast was already stabled, nuzzling the feed.

The Im heard Zell'a Cree's approach, turned his head partway. "May I help you with your beast, sir?" Zell'a Cree asked, taking the role of stablehand, hoping that the giant would not recognize him. "Does it need water, or a comb?"

"Aye, it will take a couple of water buckets," the giant said, not bothering to look back, dumping the whole sack of grain into the bin.

"Good enough, sir," Zell'a Cree said, only a step behind.

Zell'a Cree grasped the haft of his sword, pulled it free, and plunged the blade deep into the giant's back, just beneath his rib cage. He'd hoped to hit a kidney, send the giant into deadly shock, but the Im shouted and spun, hitting Zell'a Cree in the head with the bucket.

There was a moment of pain, and horses began neighing in fright, kicking at the doors to their stalls, and Zell'a Cree found himself struggling up from the stable floor to his knees. The giant had taken a step to the middle of the room, and he pulled the sword from his back, stood gazing stupidly at the blade.

Zell'a Cree jumped up, rushed at him, but the giant bellowed loudly and took a step back. Zell'a Cree tried to pull the sword from the giant's hand, and for one brief moment they struggled together, both of them fighting for the blade.

The short sword twisted from Zell'a Cree's grip, and the giant made a weak stab. Zell'a Cree leapt backward as the sword slashed at his midriff.

The giant stood, panting as if from long exertion, holding the sword. He sagged to his knees after a minute, dropped the blade, then fell facedown into the straw.

The horses were all neighing frantically now at the smell of blood, and Zell'a Cree knew that the noise would draw attention. He had hoped to commit a nice quiet murder.

Instead, he grabbed the short sword, stabbed the giant in the back of the neck to sever his spinal cord, then rushed to the rear door of the stables and stood panting, trying to get some air.

He wondered whether anyone had heard the giant's bellowing. He did not know if he should run now or set a trap for Gallen and the others.

Gallen had settled into his seat at the inn and ordered dinner. The place had few patrons, and they were all sitting up in front of a little puppeteer's theater, where marvelously decorated puppets were used to play a tale about a greedy king who was being robbed by some highwaymen. Gallen could not hear all of the dialogue, but two of the highwaymen were speaking aside to one another, and it sounded as if they were the king's own wife and daughter, robbing the man in the hopes of curing him of his greed.

Gallen had just asked his mantle to amplify the sounds of the room, hoping to hear the puppeteers, when he heard Fenorah cry out.

He jumped from his seat, seeing the surprised faces of Maggie and the others. He had been trying so hard for the past few days to seem normal that he did not want to cause them alarm. "Trouble!" Gallen said, then he went tearing out a back door, where two cooks stood looking toward the stable.

"I'm sure I heard yelling, back here!" one said, though neither seemed inclined to go see who had screamed.

Drawing his sword free from its scabbard, Gallen raced down to the stable, pulled the door open, and let his mantle magnify the light, show him the scene.

Fenorah lay in the straw, facedown. Gallen rushed to him, found blood flowing all down the back of his neck, soaking into his tunic. Gallen could see no sign that he was breathing, and for a brief moment, stinging tears came to Gallen's eyes. The giant had never harmed anyone, had sought to do only good. He'd shared his food, given of his time and wealth.

"Goodbye, my friend. The wheel turns without you for a while," Gallen whispered into his ears, and realized that he had subconsciously chosen to voice a death farewell common to the people of Babel.

He bit his lip, tried to calm himself. He was afraid, for he could feel the weight of years on him. He felt that he was struggling to control the voices inside him—strong Amvik of the Immatar, a scholar and physician, wanted Gallen to check Fenorah more thoroughly for signs of life. "Turn him over. Try to revive him," the doctor warned, but Gallen knew it was no use. Even if he managed to revive the giant for a few moments, he had lost far too much blood.

Gallen noticed that someone had stepped over the body, making bloody footprints in the straw, and had rushed out a back door, leaving it open.

The horses and the travelbeast were standing quietly in their stalls, looking out. Gallen glanced upward to the haylofts and empty stalls where tack and fodder were stored. He listened closely for any sound of the murderer, then took one last look at Fenorah.

The Inhuman has done this, a voice whispered at the back of Gallen's mind.

Gallen went to look out the rear door with a heavy heart. Suddenly he heard movement to his side, and his mantle warned him to duck. Gallen spun in time to see Zell'a Cree exploding out of a stall where hay had been piled high. The stocky man had been hiding under the hay, and he threw some at Gallen's face.

Gallen almost did not see the blade of Zell'a Cree's sword, arcing through the flying straw, but fortunately he had his own blade up high enough to parry the blow.

Zell'a Cree's sword hit Gallen's with such force that Gallen barely held on. The blow knocked Gallen back a pace, and Gallen spun away from Zell'a Cree's charge, feigning a loss of balance as if he'd fallen, then he whirled as he fell and thrust his own blade up into Zell'a Cree's chest, a brief, biting kiss that left the tip of Gallen's sword bloodied.

Gallen rolled to his feet and sat, hunched low, his sword weaving slowly before Zell'a Cree's eyes.

Zell'a Cree spotted the well-bloodied sword, and seemed to react more to it than he had to the touch of the steel. His free hand rose up to his chest, and his eyes grew wide in surprise at the severity of the wound.

"Damn your hide for that! I'll split your belly and strangle you with your own guts!" he cried, and he kicked a bucket at Gallen.

Gallen dodged it easily, and waited en garde. "Come, then," Gallen hissed, "and find out why I'm a Lord Protector!"

Zell'a Cree almost rushed him, but instead halted, watched him warily. And in half a second he turned and fled out the back door, slamming it behind.

Gallen ran to give chase, but when he threw himself against the door, it wouldn't budge. Zell'a Cree had bolted it from outside.

Gallen rushed back to the front, then circled the stable and stood gazing over the valley. Along a trail downhill were dozens of stone houses and buildings with white stucco exteriors, many with low courtyards where someone could easily leap a wall to hide. Bright stars pierced the indigo sky, and Tremonthin's three small moons were rising all in a close knot, shining like molten brass over the countryside. Gallen could see far to the south, across a great valley where dark hills rose as forested islands from a moonlit sea of fog.

There was no one on or near the road, no sign of Zell'a Cree. But in infrared Gallen's mantle detected hot points of light on the ground, splashes of blood.

He stooped low and ran, following the trail. A dog began barking far ahead, perhaps a kilometer off, and Gallen wondered if his quarry were getting away.

He raced low a couple hundred meters, responding to the voice of Fermoth, a great hunter who whispered that he should be quiet, refrain from alerting his quarry, and Gallen found a bright pool of blood on the ground on the far side of a stone well. Zell'a Cree had rested here momentarily, dripping blood over everything.

More bright flecks beckoned farther on, and Gallen began stalking through dark alleys, over a wall. His prey moved like a fox—backtracking and zigzagging, and Fermoth whispered to Gallen, Yes, yes, this is how I would do it. This is the direction I would go, till Gallen wondered if the shared experiences of the Inhuman might not be a disadvantage to his quarry.

Gallen reached the far end of town and began circling back along a hill, at which point even Fermoth wondered what the quarry was up to, and Gallen began to wonder if Zell'a Cree was Inhuman after all.

Yet it was obvious that Gallen's quarry was failing. Perhaps he was no longer thinking clearly. The droplets of blood were getting brighter, warmer. The man was slowing, weakening, until Gallen felt sure he was near, and that he would be weak, and dying, when Gallen found him.

Gallen felt confused. He was beginning to understand the servants of the Inhuman. Indeed, he thought that they might be friends, or that at least they thought themselves good. None of the voices inside Gallen were evil. They had just been people who were concerned with living their own lives, people who wanted to continue living. And though Zell'a Cree had killed Fenorah and was an Inhuman, he was also someone like Gallen who had become infected against his will. Gallen recalled the Bock's warning, in which he told Gallen that at times he would have to choose whether to kill an Inhuman or spare it. And as he hunted, Gallen's resolve to kill Zell'a Cree weakened.

Yet Fenorah had also been innocent, had not deserved to die, Gallen reminded himself. And Gallen could not understand how it was that basically good people could do this to each other.

After nearly twenty minutes, he reached an alley behind a store.

Blood was smeared on a white stucco wall in the moonlight, and Gallen could see droplets on the dusty road. He heard the sound of coughing ahead.

He rounded a corner, and a beefy man was there in the moonlight, lying on his side in the alley, his pale eyes looking almost white. Zell'a Cree. He held his wound and lay gasping, bubbles of blood dribbling down his chin.

Gallen held his sword point forward, carefully stalked up to the man, to the *Inhuman*, he reminded himself, and he stared into the man's face. We share so many memories, Gallen thought, looking into Zell'a Cree's eyes. The Inhuman struggled to run, moved his legs about feebly, and stared forward into the dust, his eyes blind. He breathed furiously, and small puffs of dust rose up near his chin. His face contorted in a grimace, and beads of sweat stood out on his forehead.

"Boots. Boots are inside building," Zell'a Cree whispered to Gallen, as if it were terribly urgent, and Gallen could smell the tanned leather scraps outside the back door of the bootmaker's shop. Indeed, Zell'a Cree's right boot was tied together with a scrap of cloth. And Gallen suddenly realized that this man had circled back to town to get some new boots.

Now that Gallen had caught him, he considered stabbing him again, but didn't have the heart. Gallen shared the memories of twenty lives with this man, and all of those people had lived extraordinary lives. They were not small-minded killers.

"Damn you," Gallen said. "Why did you have to stab Fenorah?"

Zell'a Cree didn't answer. Gallen suspected that Zell'a Cree had taken a mortal wound. Yet Gallen could not afford mercy. His friends' lives might still be at stake. Gallen stuck his sword at Zell'a Cree's throat, demanded, "How many of you are stalking us? Where are your men camped?"

Zell'a Cree did not answer, merely turned his head up at the sound of Gallen's voice.

Gallen put the sword to his chin, and asked again, "How many more are you?" Zell'a Cree said nothing, and Gallen wondered if he were past talking.

"Join us," Zell'a Cree breathed, "and we will stalk you no more."

So Zell'a Cree still felt himself at war and would give up no information. Gallen respected that. He studied the creature. Zell'a Cree looked human, simply a beefy man with pale eyes that were much like Ceravanne's. He could have been a baker or an innkeeper in any town that Gallen had ever visited, and Gallen felt ashamed at wanting him dead.

"What did you do, before the Inhuman converted you?" Gallen asked.

"I . . . farmed," the big man panted. "Apples. I make, uh, cider."

"I think you're going to die," Gallen admitted softly. "There's little that you or I or anyone else can do to stop it now. I can let you die slowly, in your own time, or I can take you quickly." He let the tone of his voice ask the question.

"Slowly," Zell'a Cree asked. "Life is sweet. Savor it."

Gallen was dismayed by the answer. How could life be so sweet that you looked forward to coughing up your own blood for five minutes? But the voices of the dead within him bubbled up, all of them clamoring, "Yes, yes, life is sweet." They craved it, even a miserable few moments of pain.

Gallen looked back toward where he imagined the inn might be. He was tempted to leave Zell'a Cree on the road, head back to check on the others, but he was acutely aware that Zell'a Cree had lost his life at least twice: once when the Inhuman had converted him against his will, and once when Gallen had plunged a sword into his lung.

So Gallen sat down in the dust, prepared to wait with Zell'a Cree, stay with him to the end.

"Forgive me," Zell'a Cree asked, grunting, his words raising small puffs of dust. "I never wanted to hurt you . . . anyone."

Gallen wasn't sure what to answer, but settled for "I know."

The voices of the Inhuman rose within Gallen, crying out across the centuries. "Join with us."

Gallen felt torn. For several minutes Zell'a Cree only lay breathing, gasping at an ever more frenzied pace, droplets of sweat rolling down his face into the dust. At first, Gallen feared the man, but Zell'a Cree made no move against him, seemed less and less capable of moving at all. He wheezed for a bit, and coughed until fresh blood began foaming from his mouth.

Zell'a Cree closed his eyes and began weeping, concentrated on breathing.

"Let me take you now, friend," Gallen said. "There's nothing left to savor."

"Please . . ." Zell'a Cree mumbled after a long moment, "water. A drink first. Then kill me."

Gallen looked about. His own water skin was back in the wagon, but there was a rain barrel under the eaves of the shoemaker's roof. Gallen went to the barrel, found that it was nearly full. He sheathed his sword, cupped some water in his hands, and went back to the dying Zell'a Cree, put his hands down under Zell'a Cree's lips.

The dying man didn't take the water. Just lay there breathing heavily, lapsing into sleep.

"Wake up," Gallen said. "I brought your water."

"Unh," Zell'a Cree grunted, twisted his head to try to get his lips to the water. Gallen held his hands down lower, and to his surprise, Zell'a Cree tried to sit up to drink, put a hand on Gallen's shoulder as he steadied himself.

Gallen held his hands to the man's mouth, let him drink it for a moment, and Zell'a Cree leaned back against the wall, his eyes focusing on Gallen. He seemed only a bluish shadow in the moonlight, all colors washed from his face, as if he were already fading into dust.

The cicadas and crickets began singing in the still night, and a little breeze whipped through the streets, raising the hair on Gallen's back.

Zell'a Cree smiled weakly, stared up at the sky, and Gallen thought he would die now. "Thank you," Zell'a Cree whispered as if addressing the universe, and then he looked into Gallen's eyes. "It has been so long . . . so long since I have heard the voice of the Inhuman . . . but now, I know what it wants me to do."

Gallen leaned closer, curious, and looked into Zell'a Cree's eyes. "What does it want from you?"

Zell'a Cree reached up quickly, and there was the jingle of metal rings as he pulled at Gallen's mantle. Gallen grabbed at the Tosken's wrist, but like the Tekkar he was immensely strong—so their struggle lasted only a brief second, then the knowledge tokens flashed in the moonlight as Zell'a Cree ripped Gallen's mantle free.

It went sailing through the air and clanked against the wall of the bootmaker's shop, and Gallen gasped and drove his sword into Zell'a Cree's neck.

For one moment, Gallen still could not feel the Inhuman's presence. He was not lost in strangers' memories, and for a brief few seconds he dared hope that the Inhuman would spare him, and he lurched toward his mantle in the moonlight.

And then there was a surging in Gallen's ears, dozens of voices clamoring, as if a tide were swelling from a distant shore. His arms and legs fell out beneath him, and Gallen could almost imagine that someone had reached into his body and pulled his spirit free. He felt disconnected—the sounds of crickets and cicadas suddenly ceased. Gallen crumpled to the ground, barely conscious of the fact that his head bounced off the dirt street.

And he felt them come leaping and tumbling after him, the hosts of the Inhuman, the ghosts with their iron will. Until now, they had taken him gently, slowly, but now he could feel something akin to desperation emanating from the machine, the desire to crush him before he could resist.

Far away he heard a desperate shriek, a harrowing wail that shook him and demanded aid, but Gallen hardly recognized that it was his own voice.

It had been thirty minutes since Gallen jumped up and rushed from the inn. Maggie and the others had gone down to the stables where they found poor Fenorah lying in a pool of blood.

Ceravanne was still beside his body, weeping, while Maggie tried to comfort her. Orick had headed south along the outskirts of town with Tallea, sniffing Gallen's trail.

At last Maggie went and stood outside the barn, hoping to see Gallen's shadow against the white stucco walls in the moonlight.

A maid from the kitchens was up at the inn, beckoning to her, urging Maggie to "Come back indoors, where it's safe!"

Then Maggie heard Gallen's bloodcurdling scream.

Gallen's voice rang out over the small town, echoing from the hilltops and from the buildings so that she couldn't be sure where it came from. Almost, it seemed to rise from the earth itself, but she thought it might have come from a ridge to the west.

Maggie's heart began pounding, and she looked about frantically. She wondered if it really had been Gallen's voice—it had been blurred and distant, after all—but she knew that it was. It sounded like a death cry, as if he'd taken a mortal wound in the back, as Fenorah had done. She raced toward the sound for a moment, looked about hysterically, realized that anyone who could have killed Gallen could also kill her.

And yet it didn't matter. If Gallen was dead, she didn't really care to live anymore.

So she ran uphill, west toward the ridge, and began searching. For an hour she wandered through town, investigating every street, until she met Orick and Tallea coming up from the south of town.

"Maggie, girl, what are you doing out here?" Orick demanded.

"I heard Gallen scream," she said.

Orick and Tallea looked at each other. "We heard a shout some time back," Orick said, "but I couldn't say it was Gallen's. It sounded to us as if it came from the north."

"No sign of Gallen?" Maggie asked.

"Whoever he was chasing," Orick said, "knew how to cover his scent. He ran me in circles, and his scent didn't stick to the dust. And Gallen's wearing that damned cloak of his, which hides all smell. So we've lost their trail."

Maggie filed that information away. She hadn't known that a Lord Protector's cloak masked his scent.

"Maybe Gallen went back to inn," Tallea said, and Maggie realized that she *had* been gone for over an hour. If Gallen were hurt, he'd have gone back to the inn, if he could.

And it seemed her last hope. So they went back to the inn, down to the stables. A maid from the inn had brought a lantern down, and Fenorah had been washed and turned on his back. A clean quilt was stretched out over him, but it was too short for the giant, so that it covered his feet, but not his face.

Shivering from a chill wind that was beginning to blow down the high mountain passes, the companions sat in the stable, waiting for Gallen's return for several more minutes, until at last Ceravanne said in her clear voice, "All things pass away. It is time, my friends, to consider the possibility that Gallen is gone, and what that means to the quest." She stood above Fenorah, and the lantern's sharp light reflected from her angular face. She seemed somehow washed out, unreal under such light.

"Are you saying we should leave without him?" Orick grumbled, rising to his hind feet. He sniffed the air once again, as was his habit when he felt nervous.

"I hesitate to say it," the Tharrin answered. "Gallen has not returned, and almost two hours have passed. I doubt he would stay away so long, if he were able to return to us."

"And if he's dead, killer waiting for us," Tallea muttered, resting her unsheathed sword by letting its tip settle into the floorboards under the straw.

"And that means we have little choice but to press on as quickly as possible," Ceravanne whispered. "But there is something else we must consider. If Gallen is dead, then his killer may have taken Gallen's mantle. We will have someone with the powers of a Lord Protector hunting us, and he will have access to all of Gallen's memories. He will know where we plan to go, what we plan to do."

"So you want us to stay and see if we can find Gallen's body," Maggie asked, "just to make sure we get his mantle?" And she knew Ceravanne was right. Knowledge is power, and the Lord Protector's mantle would be a powerful weapon if it fell into the hands of the Inhuman.

"I think," Orick said, "you're all worried for nothing. If Gallen is dead and his enemies took his weapons, why haven't they come after us? He had his mantle, that fancy sword, and his incendiary rifle."

Maggie clung to his words, knowing they made some sense, hoping he was right. "Gallen may still be hunting," she said at last. "He's thorough when it comes to blackguards. He wouldn't let one give him the slip."

"Aye, that's possible," Orick grumbled. "Down in County Toorary, Gallen tracked a cutthroat for three weeks, chased him two hundred miles."

Ceravanne licked her lips, looked out the open door southward. "Perhaps we should wait," she said. "But there is something just as portentous that could have happened. Gallen has been very . . . deep in thought these past two days. We all know that his loyalties are wavering, hanging in the balance. He may have joined the Inhuman, or he may have gone in search of solitude while he considers his future course."

Maggie wanted to deny this, wanted to slap Ceravanne for even bringing up the possibility, but this too seemed very likely.

"I don't think he'd leave me," Maggie said, her voice small in the close darkness of the stable.

"I would hope not," Ceravanne offered, and she took Maggie's hand in hers to offer comfort. "But he is under great pressure. You must remember that he is living with many other voices inside him, rich recollections of other loves. Those who become infected by the Word, they sometimes become lost in the . . . history that the Inhuman offers. Their small voices are drowned out by the bitterness and despair of the Inhuman. And I fear that Gallen may be susceptible to this. Those who are most susceptible are those who are weak of purpose, or weak of mind, and those who are simply inexperienced—the young. Gallen is neither weak of purpose nor stupid, but he is young."

"You forget," Gallen said loudly from the far end of the room, "the others who are equally susceptible to the Inhuman's domination."

Maggie turned, and Gallen stood in the front doorway to the stable, all draped in the black robes of a Lord Protector. Yet there was something terribly wrong. The way he stood—with a certain swaggering confidence as he leaned casually against the doorpost—was nothing like Gallen. Indeed, a terrible light seemed to blaze from his pale blue eyes, and he wore the mask of Fale. Yet strangest of all was his voice. It sounded deeper, and it resonated more, and all of his accent was gone. Where a few weeks ago he'd been a charming boy from County Morgan, now an older and wearier man stood. It seemed to Maggie suddenly that a stranger was wearing Gallen's body, and that Gallen stood smiling, mocking their fears for him.

"What others are susceptible to the Inhuman?" Ceravanne asked.

Gallen waved his hand at her. "The trusting," he spat, then waved to Orick. "The naïve. And those who are actively evil."

Gallen reached into the pocket of his robe, pulled out his mantle, and its black rings and silver stones glimmered in the moonlight. He draped it over his head.

"So, you are Inhuman now," Ceravanne whispered, and Maggie found her heart pounding within her. "But you have never been any of those—naïve, trusting, or evil."

Gallen straightened, and he seemed taller and more menacing to Maggie as he crossed the stable, gazed out to the south, over the wide valley below with its shroud of fog that glowed like gauze in the moonlight.

"Yes," Gallen said, staring to the south. "The Inhuman has tried to claim me as its own." For a brief moment it looked as if he would collapse, and he held to the door frame as he struggled for control. Maggie could see the old Gallen. "And, my friends, it is good for us all that the Inhuman has finished its task—else I would not have suspected its plans, and we would have walked into a trap.

"Maggie, come here."

Maggie went to his side and followed his eye. He took off his mantle, placed it on her head. "Listen to the radio frequencies on the higher end of the spectrum," he said, "and look south to Bern's Pass, beneath that far mountain, four hundred kilometers from here."

Four hundred kilometers? she wondered. She couldn't imagine seeing that far. But Maggie concentrated, and the mantle brought a faint sound to her ears, bursts of radio signals squealing undiscernible messages. It was a code.

She looked to their source, beneath the far mountains that suddenly appeared in her mind as she gazed, and Gallen's mantle magnified the distant image. Something vast and black was crawling down a mountainside.

"Dronon hive cities," Maggie realized, "crawling toward us."

"Yes," Gallen said. "They are far away, but they're coming. Part of the memories the Inhuman gave me came from a dronon technician. All those who join the Inhuman know how to use dronon technologies, and now that the dronon have been forced to abandon this world, leaving the hive cities behind, the Inhuman hosts have taken them up. With these they will march against Northland, for the hive cities can also swim across the oceans, and here in Babel their guns are not dismantled.

"So the dronon who abandoned this world betrayed it, leaving behind weapons for the Inhuman to use." Gallen breathed deeply. "Ceravanne, your people are in far graver danger from the invaders than even you had imagined!"

Maggie was watching the distant image of the dronon hive city, crawling down the mountainside like a huge spider, when a second crested the ridge. And then she saw something else, a knot of large birds in the darkness, their body heat registering white, hurtling across the distant valleys. She wondered how far away they were, and her mantle flashed an image before her eyes. Two hundred and twenty kilometers.

"Gallen, there are scouts flying this way, hundreds of them."

"I know," Gallen said. "The Inhuman is coming for you. It knows where we are, and because of the interference my mantle offered, it has guessed at our purpose."

"It could only have learned our location from the transmitter in your head," Maggie said, and she looked at Gallen sharply.

"I know," Gallen admitted. "The Inhuman sent a message to Zell'a Cree in his last moments, telling him to pull off my mantle so that the downloading could be finished. The Inhuman could only have sent that message if it were tracking us and knew that Zell'a Cree and I were together."

"Of course," Ceravanne whispered.

"Then if it knows where you are," Maggie said, "the Inhuman only has to follow you to find us."

Gallen looked about helplessly, threw up his hands. "Unless Maggie can remove the transmitter, or we can somehow block it, then you will have to leave me."

Gallen took Maggie's hand, looked steadily into her eyes, and touched it to the back of his head. "Here is where the Word burrowed into my skull. I can feel a small bump there. It only makes sense that the transmitter is still outside the skull; the Inhuman would not try to beam messages through bone. Perhaps the tail end of the Word is the transmitter."

Maggie had suspected this possibility before, but dared not admit it. The implications horrified and sickened her. She didn't want to have to pry this thing out of Gallen's head. "I know what you're going to ask, Gallen, and I can't do it. The Word has inserted itself into your brain. I can't just pull it out!"

An image flashed through Maggie's mind, a vision of neural wires slicing through the gray matter of Gallen's brain as she pulled.

"We have to try something," Gallen said. "I want you to try now to cut away anything outside the skull. And if that doesn't work, you must pry the Word out. I know it's dangerous, but it is the only way for me to remain with you. Unless you do this, I might as well be dead."

Maggie looked nervously to the south. "What of the scouts?"

"They will not make it here for several hours," Gallen said. "And we can hide from them tomorrow." When next he spoke, Gallen spoke not as himself, but as the Inhuman, and it was reflected in his demeanor. "For six thousand years, I've lived in this land. I can guide you to Moree like no others, except those infected by the Inhuman. But I cannot help you, unless you do this for me. And perhaps it will avail nothing."

Maggie looked to Ceravanne. "I don't think I can do this."

"I can, maybe," Ceravanne said. "I've mended festering wounds, and I'm handy with a knife. But I'm not sure what you'll require of me."

"Do you have any more Healing Earth?" Maggie asked.

"A pinch, perhaps, no more," Ceravanne said. "He can have a few drops of my blood."

Maggie wondered where to perform the surgery. It seemed ghastly to do it here in the stable, in the dim lamplight surrounding Fenorah's pale corpse, but it sheltered them from the chilly night air and from prying eyes. Maggie looked for some clean straw. Some of the horses nickered querulously as she pulled the hay from a crib and sprinkled it on the floor. Ceravanne brought the lantern near, and Tallea brought her sharpest dagger from its sheath.

Ceravanne bit her lower lip, and her hands shook as she did the cutting, opening the back of Gallen's neck down to the blue-white bone. She pulled Gallen's hair gently, opening the flaps of severed skin so that she could see more clearly, and Maggie had to use a bandage from her pack to daub the blood away.

There was a small, perfectly circular hole in his skull, and two small wires dangled from what had once been the Word's hind feet. Maggie couldn't be sure what the wires were for, so she ran up to the wagon at the front of the inn and got her mantle of technology, then came back and looked closely at the wires. The sensors in her mantle magnified the image. From the Word's hind legs, tiny microfilaments, like veins, had grown out in a gray web, wrapping themselves around Gallen's skull. It was not a particularly powerful antenna for either receiving or transmitting information, but Gallen's skull acted as something of a dish.

"This is it," Maggie said. "This is the antenna. This is a more complex design than I'd imagined, but it's also easy to defeat—at least I think we can keep them from tracking us."

"Do it," Gallen said.

And to her own surprise, Maggie found that she was able to take the knife from Ceravanne. "It's too intricate to do this without a mantle," she explained. She severed the web in a circle, then dug out as much of the wiring as possible. She tried to clear her thoughts, concentrate only on doing the job. She watched for several seconds, to see if the web would grow back, but apparently this component of the nanotech weapon was too unsophisticated to regenerate. After thirty seconds, the wound so filled with blood that she could no longer see well.

Maggie blotted it away again with the bandage. "I'm done," she whispered.

"Try to pry the Word out," Gallen said.

"There's no need," Maggie argued, imagining how the webs of metallic neurons would slice through his brain if she pulled. "I've already cut off the antenna."

"I don't want it in me," Gallen shouted, his voice muffled as he yelled into the straw. "Cut it out! Pull it out partway, if you can, and then cut it in half."

Maggie found herself breathing hard, imagining the possibilities for infection in the wound, the possibilities of brain damage.

She touched the tail end of the Word with her knife, wondering if it *could* be pried out.

Suddenly, as if it had been burned, the Word lunged forward into Gallen's brain, and blood began gushing out from Gallen's brain cavity.

"Ah, God," Orick cried out in fear.

"What?" Gallen asked, moving a bit.

"Nothing," Maggie said, suddenly terrified, her knees going weak. "I'll close now."

Ceravanne held out her finger, and Maggie cut it, dropped a bit of Ceravanne's Immortal blood into the wound, and in moments the cut began to heal. Gallen lay quietly while Maggie washed the blood from the back of his neck. And when Gallen sat up, he replaced his mantle on his head and asked Maggie, "Did you get it out?"

"I couldn't get the Word out," Maggie said. "It dug itself in deeper. But I cut all of the connections to the antenna, and I dug out part of the wiring. I think the Word will be permanently disabled."

Gallen considered, got up, and gazed off to the south. "I fear that my presence could be a danger to you even still. I will not guide you south, unless you all desire me to. But I warn you in any case that we may not be able to elude the Inhuman—a great race is afoot. I suspect that those marching hive cities have come searching for us, as have the scouts. Our enemies hunt us by land and air."

He looked back, into the faces of Orick, Tallea, and Ceravanne. "Will you have me?"

And Maggie looked into the face of Gallen, the Inhuman, and one by one, the others said yes, until at last Tallea said, "For now."

Twenty-four

Late that night after a brief and belated dinner at the inn at High Home, Ceravanne made arrangements with the innkeeper for Fenorah's body to be conveyed back to Battic, then Gallen loaded the group into the wagon and led the travelbeast downhill, under the blanketing fog.

Though it had good night vision, the beast could not see in such total darkness, so Gallen led it by hand. At dawn, he left the main road heading west by way of what appeared to be an old hay trail through some fields, but the deserted track held, and for many hours the wagon rolled through the lonely woods, passing only a few shacks that belonged to woodsmen.

And all through the morning, Maggie watched Gallen in horror, studying him for signs of change. They were everywhere—in the stealthy way that he walked, almost unnaturally quiet; in the way he sometimes tilted his head to catch a sound; the new way that he spoke. Twice, when they passed small clear pools, Gallen stopped to wash his hands, and he would sit and inspect them long afterward. He'd always been tidy, but never like this.

Maggie complained about it once under her breath, whispering, "What is he doing?"

And Ceravanne whispered in her ear, "The Faylan people have olfactory nerves on their hands. They wash themselves so. I think it is a habit from another life. He will forget about it, in time."

Because Gallen and Tallea feared Derrits in these woods, they made poor time, going little faster than a horse could pull, but the travelbeast was able to work all day at this pace. Twice they bogged down in lonely places and had to get off the wagon and push, and once they had to float the wagon across a broad river, but in the early afternoon they began climbing out of the wetlands to an ancient fortress on a small hill.

When they reached the hilltop, Gallen had them turn the wagon on its bottom and he removed a wheel so that it looked as if the wagon had been abandoned. "The scouts will be searching for us tonight," he said. "We don't want them to see anything suspicious." And Maggie saw by this ruse that this new Gallen was craftier than the old.

The fortress was small—a simple watchtower that looked out over the moors and woods, several crumbling outbuildings beside the walls.

Gallen let the travelbeast graze for a bit, then took it to an underground root cellar away from the main tower and penned it in for the night.

Maggie climbed the tower at dusk, and stood for a moment watching out, wishing that Gallen would come to be with her, come to put his arms around her. Doves had flown up to the tower's tiled roof, and were fluttering about the broken window. Maggie could not see the distant mountains, where High Home sat on the slopes, and she found it difficult to believe that any scouts would come so far in a single night to search for them. But Gallen seemed certain.

When Maggie went downstairs, Gallen and the others were milling about the courtyard. Tallea had found the dungeon, and she brought up a huge turd as long as her arm, poked on a stick, and held it out for Gallen to see. "Much Derrit poop," she said, "in dungeon."

Goose bumps rose on the back of Maggie's arms at the mention of Derrits, for even the Im giants had feared them, but Gallen seemed little concerned. "Fine, fine," he said. "We'll wet it down so that it looks and smells fresh, and put it in the tower and upper halls. The scouts will not be eager to search this place if they find it marked with Derrit spoor."

So Gallen set himself the task of carrying the loathsome stuff upstairs while the others went below and ate a cold dinner. Maggie could find no place where the odious, garlicky scent of the Derrits did not permeate. It was terribly dark in the dungeon, the only light coming from the open door leading upstairs, and so before they closed the doors, she rushed outside and picked a great armload of straw to use as bedding.

When Gallen finished his task of moving the Derrit poop, he came below, and sealed them in for the night, barring the door from the inside with a rusty iron pole.

They sat for a long time. The only light in the room came from Gallen's mask, a shimmering piece of starlight. Maggie did not find it comforting, for Gallen sat away from her, as if they were strangers.

Maggie found herself getting nervous, till Gallen began singing softly, song after song from their home on Tihrglas, until her heart nearly broke at the sweet memory. Everything here was getting out of control. Everything here was not as she'd imagined. And so she dreamed of the clean mountain rivers rushing under the lowering pines, the sky so blue that she could not quite hold it in her memory.

When the others had fallen asleep, Maggie crept to Gallen's side, held his hand, and looked up into his face.

"Gallen," she whispered. "I want to tell you I'm sorry."

"For what?" he said, not turning to look at her.

"I've, I've been thinking hard on it—and I'm pretty sure that I could have stopped the Inhuman from downloading its memories to you."

"How?" Gallen asked.

"If I'd cut the antenna sooner, yesterday morning perhaps, the Inhuman would not have known how to contact you. It never would have received a signal from the Word."

"Why didn't you do that, then?" Gallen said, his voice hard. He didn't turn to look at her.

"I—wasn't certain that I could get to the transmitter. I was hoping our mantles would block the Inhuman's transmissions. I didn't want to have to lay into you with that knife!"

"You wanted to spare me pain?" Gallen asked.

"Yes!" Maggie said, and she squeezed his hand.

Gallen smiled at her, barely turned in her direction. "Then you are apologizing for having a good heart?"

"I'm apologizing for being wrong," Maggie said. "For being weak."

"Apology accepted." Gallen turned to her then, and Maggie hoped that he would take her in his arms, but instead he held himself aloof, as if he were a stranger. "And your mistake may yet cause the downfall of the Inhuman," Gallen said. "Because I know its thoughts, its ways, we have a greater hope of defeating it. Now, go to sleep, and I will keep watch."

He reached out and patted her hand, as if she were a child. Maggie curled up on the straw and tried to sleep, disturbed by a steady drip, drip, drip of water falling into a corner from the sweaty walls.

Until at long last, she fell asleep for a while, then woke to a scratching noise. At first she thought it only a rodent gnawing on some old wood upstairs. But it came steadily, and she looked around. She could see little enough by the light of Gallen's mask, but soon she realized that while rolling around in her sleep, she had misjudged where the door was. What she had taken to be a far corner of the building was in fact the bolted door directly above them.

Maggie got up warily, wondered what to do. The insistent scratching was from something large. She went to Gallen, and pushed him gently in his sleep, praying that he would not waken with a shout.

To her relief, Gallen merely opened his eyes, took one look at Maggie, and sat listening for a moment.

Suddenly Gallen snarled, letting a low rumble escape his throat. It was a sound distinctly nonhuman, like some savage animal, and the noise frightened her. Then in a harsh voice he shouted, "Ghisna, ghisna—siisum," and leapt up the stairs and began fumbling with the bolt.

Something shrieked behind the door. There was the sound of scurrying feet and flapping wings . . . followed by silence.

Ceravanne woke up, as did Orick and Tallea. "What's wrong?" Ceravanne asked.

"A scout was here," Gallen whispered, "and it thinks it was almost eaten by a tribe of Derrits. It will not be back tonight. Quiet, now. Go back to sleep."

Maggie lay down again, but Gallen did not follow his own advice. The last thing Maggie saw before she fell into a deep slumber was Gallen's mask glowing in the dark as Gallen watched the stairs, accompanied by the drip, drip, drip from the seeping wall.

• • •

Just before dawn, Gallen roused the group and began preparing to break camp. He went out and righted the wagon with Orick's help, then harnessed the travelbeast.

They headed west again, and by midday they climbed up out of the valley floor to an ancient stone highway, swept by the wind. This road headed south once more, and it led through a bleak grassy landscape where there was little shelter from prying eyes. On it, their travelbeast raced like the wind, and Gallen dared not slow down, though Tallea warned him repeatedly to beware of Derrit traps.

During the day, Maggie asked Gallen how he'd been so familiar with the old stone fortress, and he explained, "I played there as a child. My mother went there daily, to take provisions to my father, who was kept prisoner in the dungeon."

Maggie did not ask him more about who those memories had belonged to, and Gallen offered no more explanation.

Shortly before dusk, Gallen pulled the wagon off the road, then he flipped it and removed the wheel again, and led the group up a narrow defile to a small cleft that went back twenty meters into the rock. Scrub oak covered the opening so fully that when they got inside, they could not see out. Nevertheless, Gallen insisted on fortifying the entrance by stacking stones around it.

As he stacked the rocks, Gallen said, "If I know of this place, then the servants of the Inhuman may recall it, too. I think it will be safe, but we must still keep watch!"

"To me, it seems more dangerous to stay here than to find somewhere else," Ceravanne warned him softly.

"Perhaps," Gallen said, "but last night I learned a lesson. I went to a place familiar to me, and the Inhuman searched that place. I hope not to repeat that experience. I've never actually visited this cavern in one of my former lives. Indeed, I was told of it only once, and sought it, but never found it. It wasn't until weeks later that I guessed where it might be. So my memories of this place are tenuous. I hope that the Inhuman's servants will not even consider searching for this old haunt."

They ate another cold dinner, and afterward Orick slept on guard near the entrance of the cave, while Gallen curled up next to him and finally took some rest.

Maggie wondered at this, for it had been two nights now since Gallen had held her, and she felt that her new husband was a stranger.

She tended the fire and sat with her arms wrapped around her knees for a long time, watching Gallen's sleeping form and thinking.

Ceravanne and Tallea had been talking softly together, and Tallea must have seen how Maggie watched Gallen. "Not worry," Tallea said. "He remembers love for you."

"Are you sure?" Maggie wondered aloud. She did not fear that Gallen would hear her. He was so tired, he was dead to the world.

"If not," Tallea said, "he would not try save us."

"She's right," Ceravanne offered. "It takes a great deal of willpower for someone to fight off the Inhuman's conditioning. The fact that he is working so hard is a sign of his commitment to you."

Maggie bit her lip, feeling that something was still terribly wrong. "Aye, he's fighting the Inhuman, but there's something amiss. He doesn't touch me. He doesn't kiss me. It's keeping his distance that he is."

Ceravanne frowned, and Maggie could see that this news dismayed her. "Maggie, I think he loves you more than you give him credit for."

Something in the way that she said it, something in the way that her voice quavered, made Maggie curious. "Why do you say that?"

Ceravanne took a deep breath. "I have something I must confess: twice now, I've asked Gallen to give me his heart. I wanted him to give himself to me completely, just in case this happened. I wanted him to bond with me more strongly than he might with the Inhuman."

Maggie looked at the Tharrin and knew that Ceravanne was talking about more than just some mental bonding. The Tharrin was admitting that she had sought Gallen's complete love and devotion. She'd tried to seduce him. "But," Ceravanne continued, "Gallen has already given his heart to you. You're the reason he fights the Inhuman now. But if he isn't seeking you out, if he isn't touching you, you need to go to him. In his mind, he's been separated from you for a hundred lifetimes. The dronon have tried to put an incredible amount of emotional distance between you. He needs to fall in love with you all over again. You need to remind him why he loved you in the first place."

Maggie bit her lip, looked around the cave desperately. Tears came to her eyes, and Tallea went to her side, put her hand on Maggie's shoulder.

"Why cry?" Tallea asked.

Maggie shook her head. "That's not Gallen anymore. That's not the man I married. He doesn't talk like Gallen, or move like him. He's six thousand years old." Maggie did not dare say what she was thinking. Ceravanne had more to offer Gallen than she did. Ceravanne was more beautiful than Maggie, and the lure of her pheromones could undermine a man's resolve. Ceravanne, like Gallen, had apparently lived for thousands of years. On the face of it, she was a better match for him, and something in Maggie made her wonder if Ceravanne hadn't tried to seduce him based upon such cold reasoning.

"Why did you do it?" Maggie said bitterly. "Why did you try to make Gallen love you if you knew that he already loved me?"

Ceravanne sat across the fire and licked her lips as she considered her response. "The first time it happened was when the Bock brought him to me. I didn't know then that he loved you."

"And the second time?"

She took a deep breath. "Was three nights ago."

Maggie considered the depth of the betrayal. She had a strong desire to pull a knife and gut the Tharrin right at the moment, but by telling Maggie of her betrayal, Ceravanne was also promising never to do it again. Still, a month earlier, the Lady Everynne had lured Gallen into her bed, and now Ceravanne was trying to do the same. Maggie wondered if all Tharrin were inherently untrustworthy that way. "Why did you do it?" Maggie asked. "Why do you Tharrin do this?"

Ceravanne was breathing hard, and she looked away, but she knew that she owed Maggie an answer. "I could tell you that it is because of Belorian, because Gallen looks like Belorian, and I love him still. It was dark, and I was frightened and lonely, as frightened and lonely as I have felt in five hundred years, and out of the goodness of his heart, Gallen was trying to comfort me. That was temptation enough for what I did.

"But . . ." Ceravanne gasped as if the truth were being physically wrung out of her. "If we Tharrin have a weakness, it is one that our human makers designed into us. Maggie, you know that we exude pheromones that attract you humans to us. You know that we are constantly aware of how we look, of a thousand tiny ways that our expressions and actions can manipulate you. But there is something else about us that you must know: as much as humans desire to serve us, we also desire to be served. I . . . crave devotion, as you crave air. I sometimes wish that I could be different, that I could be free of this, that I could be dead."

And suddenly, for Maggie it all made sense. The Tharrin had been formed to be leaders. They'd been given wisdom, beauty, an innate ability to sway others. But all of that would have been worthless if they didn't also, to some degree, crave power.

"We are our bodies," Ceravanne whispered. "We are all imprisoned in a cage of flesh, doomed to sometimes think and act in ways we would prefer not to. You, I, Gallen, the Inhuman. Maggie, I hate myself for what I tried to do, and I am grateful to Gallen for resisting me. I won't let this happen again."

Maggie took her fists and rubbed her eyes with them. It was so late, and she was confused. She wanted to be angry, and it might have been that she was tired, or it might have had more to do with Ceravanne's ability to manipulate her, or it might have been that it was just the right thing to do. In any case, Maggie just shook her head. "All right, then," she said, and she went over to Gallen and lay beside her husband.

My husband, she thought. Mine. And I won't let any damned Tharrin or any damned Inhuman take him away from me.

She slept soundly that night, with no disturbing visitors. And such was Gallen's woodsmanship that for the next day, they saw no sign of pursuit. The only evidence that someone might live in this region came when they passed a small stream, and enormous footprints could be seen in the mud. Tallea was driving the team, and Orick sat beside her, but when Orick asked what made the tracks, she only urged the horses faster and said, "You don't want to know."

Maggie was sitting in the back of the wagon, and she'd been holding Gallen's hand, and she squeezed it as they passed the muddy tracks, and

Gallen squeezed her hand back. He sat watching her for a bit as the wagon rolled away, and at last he bent forward and kissed her, experimentally, as if it were the first time.

On the evening of the third day out from High Home, Gallen left the ancient highway, taking the wagon up a narrow pass, beside ruins so ancient that no single building still stood.

For the first time, Ceravanne seemed uncertain of his direction. "Where are we going?" she asked. "Are you heading to Ophat? The Nigangi Pass is down below to the east."

"And it may be closed to us," Gallen said. "So we're heading to Ophat. I need to get some height, and from this peak, I should be able to see all of the way from here to Moree."

Thus he led them up an ever steeper trail, past ancient ruins above the tree line. Long the travelbeast climbed, until it was exhausted, foam dripping from its mouth. Often the road was ruined, and portions had dropped from the sides of the treacherous cliff to the chasms beneath.

Still, the road wound on, up through cold ruins where bitter winds blew among the rocks until at last they reached one sheltered niche between two arms of the mountain. There, some ancient hallways still stood, carved back under recesses of stone, a hundred meters in from the treacherous road. There was a great pillared hall, and beside each of its massive doors was a carved image of a somber giant in breastplates, carrying heavy spears in one hand, a gem in the other. Ancient cobblestones littered a broad courtyard, empty of all but the sparest dead grasses.

The stonework here was cracked and old, far older, Maggie guessed, than anything that she had seen before.

"The travelbeast can safely climb no higher," Gallen said, "and forage is scarce enough here as it is. You can camp inside the hallway, and may even build a small fire. No scouts will trouble you here tonight."

"Why is that?" Orick asked.

"We have been climbing for the past four days, and now we are at nearly three thousand meters on this peak. The scouts' wings give them little purchase in such thin air. Though they could walk up the road as we do, they are not likely to bother. Besides, we are on the far side of the mountain from where they will be searching."

So Gallen had them unload the wagon and let the travelbeast graze in the courtyard. Huge cisterns in the courtyard were full of water, though a green moss had built up all along the basins. Still it seemed drinkable.

Maggie went inside the ancient palace and found that some passages led to caves that delved deep under the mountain. Some Derrit dung littered the great hall, but it was old, dry dung that could have been there for years. Still, Gallen insisted on securing a defensible room, and he left Tallea in charge.

"I have much scouting to do on my own tonight," Gallen said rather formally, "and I will be climbing the road higher. You should be all right."

"I'm coming with you," Maggie said.

"That isn't necessary," Gallen said, and he looked into her eyes with some relief, as if he'd wanted to beg her to come, but was somehow afraid that she wouldn't. "It will be bitter cold up on the mountaintop, and I'm not even sure if there's a shelter."

"I'm not going because it's necessary. I'm going because it's desirable," Maggie said. She took his arm in hers. "And I'll just have to trust you to keep me warm."

Before they left, Maggie kissed Orick on the snout, and Gallen patted his head, and then they were gone, heading out the doorway to the tower atop the mountain.

Something about the formality of their departure bothered Orick. It was as if they were newlyweds, scurrying off for their honeymoon. In a way, they were formally bidding the rest of the world good-bye. Orick felt a ponderous emptiness in his chest, for Gallen had been his closest friend, and now Orick felt somehow deserted. He went and curled up on the floor feeling empty and barren.

Ceravanne must have sensed his mood, for she came to him after a while, put her thin arms around him.

"Why do you think he did that, went off without me?" Orick asked.

"It may have been my influence," Ceravanne whispered. "I strengthened Maggie's bond to him when I let him touch my skin. The Inhuman tried to break that bond in him, but I think Maggie has reawakened it. It is a terrible thing to be alone when you become so deeply bonded. Gallen needs her now, as he needs water or air. And I suspect that she has needed him as badly all along. We should rejoice that they have each other."

Orick listened to the words, but found little comfort in them.

"And maybe it is also the fear of battle," Ceravanne said at last. "We are about to cross the Telgood Mountains, into the desert of Moree. None of us can be sure what our future holds. So he seeks to show his love for her, in case he dies."

Orick just grunted, and Ceravanne went back beside the fire. A burning cold was seeping through the stone walls, though Orick hardly minded. But a minute later, Tallea came and knelt beside him.

"When I young, I live in crèche," Tallea whispered into his ear. "My sister slept with me, fought beside me, for many years. When grow, she go to marriage, I go to war. It hurt, when she slept with another."

Orick didn't answer, but Tallea went on. "Someday, you find bear woman to sleep with?" She said it half in comfort, half as question.

"No," Orick whispered. "Bear women don't love the way that human women do."

"Oh, very sad," Tallea said, and to Orick's surprise, she lay down beside him, curled up against his thick fur. And she just held him, like a friend, until he fell asleep.

For his part, Gallen took Maggie up an ancient stair, and on his back he carried firewood and some blankets. There, at the peak of the mountain, the memories newly downloaded in his head told him an ancient race with powerful vision had once built a tower to keep watch over the valleys below.

Indeed, he found the tower as legend said, though it was but a small, cylindrical shack carved from stone, stuck between a crevice in the rocks. Still, it contained two large beds carved into stone, and a dome-shaped fire chamber with a tiny chimney. Gallen built a good fire, and soon the room was surprisingly warm.

And there by the fire, wrapped in blankets, he made love to his wife and lay with her, holding her tenderly long after she fell asleep.

Once, just before she closed her eyes, she asked, "When the Inhuman finished downloading, and you came back to the stable at the inn, how long did it take you to decide to stay with us?"

"I decided when I saw how you feared me," he whispered honestly. "Until then I was unsure who I would keep allegiance with. But I could not stand to see you fear me."

"Oh," Maggie whispered, and she fell asleep, never guessing what a truly difficult decision that had been for him to make. At times, the sea of voices, the memories, still threatened to overwhelm him. But always there seemed to be one bright corner in his mind where he could retreat, and in that place his memories were clear, and he could recall what the dronon had done on his home world and on other worlds, and in this way he could bear witness against it.

And somehow, that helped. One by one, the voices in his head were going silent, like candle flames snuffed out under his finger. Over the past few days, his thoughts had begun to clear.

And yet he was afraid that somehow he would slip back into that dark place in his mind. He feared it, and he needed Maggie to help him remain strong.

So Gallen lay and thought for a long time, recalling the dronon's atrocities, planning for the days ahead. He still had the Harvester to contend with, and if he guessed right, it was an ancient killing machine. So he let his mantle read out the files on its weaponry and defense systems.

Afterward, in the cold night, he wrapped his black robes around him, and took his mantle, and went out under the stars. It was bitter cold, and he softly spoke to his robe, asking it to reflect all heat back to his body.

He climbed to the top of the small tower, and there he sat upon a simple stone dais. And if anyone had seen him there, wrapped in dark robes, gazing out over the land, they would have thought him only to be an image carved in stone, so little did he move, for he closed his eyes and let his mantle gaze for him.

The sky was clear of clouds below him, and for a long while he sat, letting his sensors pick up sights and feed the magnified images to his mind. Letting the mantle scan radio frequencies, so that he could listen to the Inhuman's distant communications.

What he saw and heard disturbed him. Down in the Nigangi Pass, only forty kilometers to the west, three hive cities scoured the land, calling to one another, searching for him, and all along the valley floor he could see the scouts, flapping on swift wings as they fluttered from ruins, to cave, to crowded inn.

To the south, in the deserts of Moree, he spotted seventeen more of the hive cities, crawling like great spiders across the land, heading north to war through the desert. He could see the glowing lights of their plasma engines, red in the night, and could see tiny figures of men running about the upper war decks.

He'd never imagined that the dronon had left such fearsome arsenals.

Yet far more disturbing than either of these were the armies. The whole south of Babel must have been coming northward, for warriors swarmed across the desert. He could see great armed encampments of giants in blood-red robes, sleeping in the open beside huge bonfires. And beyond that were tent cities of the blue-skinned Adare warriors, numbering in the hundreds of thousands. Vast armies of Tekkar marched through the night, running northward in their fluid gait, all swathed in black robes. And all of them were heading to the north and east, out to ports where they could cross the seas.

And their movements were stirring things up in the wilds. Twelve kilometers below, at the foot of the mountain, tribes of wild giant Derrits had gathered, apparently to defend themselves from the sudden encroachments of others. The giant Derrits were said to be solitary creatures, seldom traveling in more than small family groups. But Gallen spotted at least a hundred of the creatures in one great war band.

And down a curve of the mountain trail, a glowing figure walked. Gallen watched it, a scout with wings folded, scurrying up the road in small lunges, stopping every few meters to sniff. Indeed, as it studied the fresh wagon tracks, it seemed both hopeful and apprehensive. Gallen wondered why the creature had not spotted him—it was only six kilometers down the road—until he recalled that he'd asked his robe to reflect all of his body heat inward. Obviously, it cut down his infrared signature to the point that the scout could not detect him.

But most disturbing of all to Gallen was the great city of Moree, eight hundred kilometers distant. At such a great span, his mantle could make out little. Water vapors in the air, oxygen itself, formed a barrier.

Yet the images his mantle accumulated showed him one thing—five huge silver domes spread out equidistantly around the city. Gallen had seen such domes before, when he was on Fale, and so he recognized them.

The Inhuman was building starships.

Gallen sighed, and slipped from the tower, heading down to kill the scout.

Twenty-five

I don't like it," Ceravanne said the next morning, in the great hall. "The Tower Road is our best chance," Gallen urged, standing over the corpse of a dead scout. "The servants of the Inhuman have little knowledge of it. I remember it as a dark and dangerous track, a place of terror—one I would not willingly brave again. I was lost in the tunnels under the city of Indallian once, for many days—and so I think that the servants of the Inhuman will avoid the place. But you, Ceravanne, must have used the road. You were the queen of this land."

"That was five hundred years ago," Ceravanne said. "Even then, the road through the Hollow Hills was a maze. Few dared the tunnels without guides. And now, who knows what might live there? Derrits at the least would lurk in those caves, but many another folk are accustomed to the dark. What if the Tekkar have established an outpost? And even when the road lies aboveground, one must beware of wingmen. They've a strong taste for blood."

"Yet the valleys of Moree are awash with the armies of the Inhuman," Gallen said. "The word has gone out that a Lord Protector seeks Moree. Scouts by the hundreds are scouring the land for us, and by our poor chance, great armies are moving through the night. We cannot go over the open roads. Already, one scout has found our wagon tracks. We must get through to Moree."

"And you think that it is better to face a hidden danger than a known one?"

"When the known danger is overwhelming, yes," Gallen said.

"I don't understand," Orick said. "What are you two arguing about?" Gallen had done a bit of scouting last night, and had decided to use an old trail, the Tower Road, to get closer to Moree. The rest of the group was willing to follow him blindly, but Ceravanne had blown up at the news.

She said, "The Tower Road is an old road that united Ophat with the underground city of Indallian, which lies west of here, under the Hollow Hills. From there, the road leads farther west, through the Telgood Mountains to the very edge of Moree itself."

"I don't understand," Orick said. "I thought we were already in Indallian. Is Indallian a city, or a country?"

"Both," Ceravanne said. "Long ago, there were many city-states in this part of the world, so the name of the Capitol was often the same as that of a country. We are already within the ancient borders of the land of Indallian, now Gallen wants to go through the city, under the Hollow Hills. But as Fenorah warned, the city is a perilous place, and has been for centuries. None go there nowadays."

Ceravanne looked about the room to the others. "We could take the

Tower Road." She sighed. "But much of it lies underground—through forty kilometers of stone. You, Caldurian, what do you say?"

"Indallian is legend to me," Tallea said. "I not know if holds danger." Yet she feared it. Many races lived underground, and they could see in the dark. As aboveground, the most peaceful peoples tended to die out, while the fierce races thrived. And if Tallea had to fight underground, she knew she would be at a disadvantage. Indeed, her wounds were not all healed yet, though she found she could swing her sword.

"It is not a legend to me," Ceravanne said. "For eight thousand years, the city called to various peoples, and the Hollow Hills were carved with measureless tunnels. For long, it was but a peaceful city where folk of the underworld lived in harmony. Then the emeralds were discovered, and peoples flocked to the city in ever greater numbers. Even in its glory, when the city of Indallian was under my full sway, it was said that 'no man knows Indallian,' for no one could explore all of the many caverns in one lifetime. Indeed, there were rumors of strange and malevolent peoples inhabiting the far bounds of the realm even then.

"And I will be honest with you all," Ceravanne concluded, visibly shaking. "I fear that place."

"Still, three hundred years ago, I heard rumors," Gallen said, "that one could travel the Tower Road for over five hundred kilometers—from Ophat to White Reed. And that is a crucial stretch in our journey. And you must consider this—the Telgood Mountains form a formidable obstacle. No army could cross it on foot, not even an army of Tekkar, so the mountains themselves will form a wall to protect us."

"So that is why you brought us to this entrance," Ceravanne said, gazing away toward the back halls. "I suspected as much. Yet the road is dangerous. In many places aboveground, it will have crumbled away. And belowground, many of the caverns have fallen in, floors have collapsed into chambers beneath. There is good reason that no one has taken that track in ages. And when we do reach the city of Indallian, what will we do for light?"

Gallen reached into the pocket of his robe, pulled out a small crystal globe, and squeezed it. A brilliant white light shone from his gloved fingers.

"I see," Ceravanne breathed. "Technologies from other worlds. And you are determined to leave the travelbeast behind?"

"I am," Gallen said. "The closer we get to Moree, the more impossible it becomes to travel openly, and the beast only marks us. Do you think you can guide us?"

"Perhaps." Ceravanne breathed deeply. "The road is easy enough to follow aboveground, and I know some paths below, though I am not certain they will be open."

And with that, they were off. Gallen went out to the travelbeast and whispered in its ear, pointing back north, and in a moment it nodded its shaggy head and raced down the mountain road.

Then they packed, and headed to a hallway where a statue of a giant stood guard beside a great stone door. Gallen pulled mightily on the handle, and cold air hit them, smelling of dampness and minerals. Ceravanne held up Gallen's glowing globe, and gazed down a stair that curved into the dark, and they began to descend, and to Tallea, the Tharrin looked as if she were a goddess, carrying a star in her hand.

"Wait," Gallen said, and his voice echoed through the corridors. He went back to the room, hoisted the dead scout on his back. "We'll leave it down below, where other scouts will not find it."

Then they began their descent. The stair went on and on, and Ceravanne led through the dark at almost a run. Their footsteps echoed off the stone. Tallea was acutely conscious of the noise they made, and she strained her ears for sound of pursuit.

Twice, during the long race down, they passed side tunnels of poor make that had been dug in more recent years, and from one of them they smelled the acrid stench of Derrit dung and cold ashes.

Beside that door, Gallen cast down the dead scout, leaving it as a meal for the beasts, and once again, as she had over the past several days, Tallea saw the craftiness in what he did. The Derrits would certainly prefer the carrion of a recent kill to hunting a party of armed men with bright lights and sharp swords.

The tunnel seemed endlessly long, and the cold of the rock seeped into her bones. Even as she ran, Tallea could not seem to warm enough to fight this cold.

In two hours they came out of the cavern under the mountain's shadow and found themselves on a broad road in the sunlight. Over the ages, stones had rolled down the hillside, so that in many places it would have been impassable by horse, but they were able to run and climb on foot.

Tallea's side ached from her recent wound, and though the sun warmed her a bit, she found that it didn't warm the wound. Instead, it burned like ice all along its length.

Still, they ran for hours, passing through more tunnels. Gallen took the lead, and twice he warned the others of Derrit traps—deep pits overlaid with a framework of twigs, then covered with hides and dust.

Tallea was glad for Gallen's sharp eyes, for she herself spent her time watching the skies for sign of wingmen, and secretly she felt relieved each time they were forced to make their way through a tunnel.

Thus, they spent the day running, and camped in a tunnel by dark. Tallea's wound throbbed through the night, and it heated up, as if it had become infected. She slept poorly, but was forced to run again at dawn.

That day, the road took a long, steady climb, higher into the bleak, gray mountains, so that the air was frigid, and they ran along a ridge that was incredibly steep and long. The mountain rose on their left like a wall, and dropped for five hundred meters below them. In places along the road, they found the splayed prints of mountain sheep, but no other sign of use.

That day they passed two ancient outposts, high stone citadels along Tower Road, and on one crenellated tower, twigs and leaves stuck out like a great nest, three meters across. Only a wingman could have carried such large sticks so far from the valley below.

Gallen called a halt, then crept up the crumbling stone stairs to the tower himself, with Tallea and Orick behind. The nest was old, the twigs whitened by age and rotted so that they could hold no weight, proving that the nest had been abandoned for years. But among the yellowed bones of sheep and deer was a human arm and skull, with tatters from a bloody wool tunic.

They climbed back down, hurried on their way, watching the skies. Gallen rounded one long arm of the mountain ridge, then dropped to the ground, warning the others with a wave of his hand to stay back.

Tallea dropped and crawled forward, and together they looked over the bluff. A wild white river churned through a gorge far below, and pines climbed halfway up the mountains in a green haze.

Sweeping over the canyon in wide, lazy circles, a lone wingman hunted on leather wings. Tallea watched the creature. Its underbelly was pale blue in color, so that it was hard to spot from below, but its back was a mottled gray and green. If it had been sitting high in a tree, with its wings folded, it would have been hard to spot from the ground. But from above, while in flight, it was easily discernable.

"It's watching the valley," Gallen said, "hunting for deer or wolves. We're lucky that it's below us."

"Not much eat up here," Tallea agreed. The wingman would not bother hunting this high road through the barren, gray mountains. She watched the creature, and wondered. According to common wisdom, all of the races on Tremonthin had been adapted from human stock to live on other worlds. But of all the peoples in Babel, she found the wingmen to be the strangest. They did not look humanoid at all. The creature was large, perhaps ten meters from wing tip to wing tip—much larger than scouts. It had a broad tail that it used as a rudder as it flew, and fierce, razor-sharp hooks of a bloody red were attached to its wings. Its long flat head was filled with great teeth that Tallea could see even from this far distance, and its scaly hide was nearly proof against a blade. And it was said that the wingmen saw other peoples not as kin, but only as food. One could sometimes reason with a Derrit, but never with a wingman.

They watched the creature circling the valley. It did not move farther west or east, nor did it seem inclined to climb higher. "I think," Gallen whispered, "that it must have seen some prey down there in the trees. It's probably waiting for it to come back into the open. It could keep circling like this all day."

"Agreed," Tallea said.

"We'll keep low, crawl on our bellies if we must. We're only eight kilometers from the gate down into the city of Indallian."

Tallea looked ahead, feeling exultant. They had traveled far and fast in the past two days. The road snaked along the ridge, vertical cliffs above and below, following a U-shaped bend in the mountain. But Gallen was right—in the distance the road met with a great iron door in the rock, a door that stood closed.

"This foolish," Tallea said. "We don't even have bow."

"There is only one wingman," Gallen said, "not a flock. And I have my incendiary rifle."

Tallea had seen how much damage that weapon had caused on the ship, and she didn't doubt that it would send a wingman tumbling in flames.

"How many fire arrows have?" Tallea asked.

"Six," Gallen whispered. "And I may need to save two of those—one to slay the Harvester, one for the Inhuman."

Tallea nodded grimly. Only one wingman—as far as she could see. But there might be dozens more around the next ridge, out of sight, or others roosting in trees below. It was autumn, when the wingmen often flocked together to head south.

"What of door?" Tallea asked, nodding toward the iron door in the distance. "What if is locked?"

Gallen bit his lip and did not answer.

Tallea's wound was icy as it rubbed against the cold stone, and she felt deeply troubled. She recalled how the cold blade of the giant had pierced her aboard ship, and it almost felt to her as if the wound were alive, calling out for her demise.

She looked up the road ahead. The thin afternoon sun shone all along its length. There were few shadows thrown from rocks to hide in.

Gallen's robe had turned slate-gray, the color of the stones, and Tallea wished that all of them wore such robes to hide them.

"All right," she agreed. "We go on bellies."

Gallen signaled the others to come forward and drop low, and he crawled to the far edge of the road, inching along the stone wall.

The others followed. Tallea took up the rear guard, and the arduous journey began. The stones here had a peculiar, powdery scent, and they were cold and sharp, cutting into Tallea's hands and knees, and the coldness of the stone was peculiar. Tallea calculated by the angle of the suns that light had been shining on the road for hours, yet it had not warmed. Apparently, the cold in the rocks went too deep for that.

Orick took the journey easily enough, inching forward, his big rump in the air.

After two kilometers, Tallea began to notice blood on the trail. Maggie had cut her hand on sharp rocks. It was rumored that the wingmen could smell blood at great distances, but it was only a small amount. Still, Tallea felt uneasy.

Another kilometer down the road, Derrit spoor was on the ledge, the first Tallea had seen in nearly two days, and it was fresh.

Normally the sight would not have left her feeling so uncomfortable, but at the moment, Tallea was struggling to hug the rock wall as closely as possible, afraid that the wingman might spot them. She couldn't bear the thought of fighting a Derrit.

She could do nothing but crawl ahead. A croaking sound echoed up from the valley below, one wingman calling to another. Gallen waved his hand, called a stop. He inched forward to the edge of the cliff, and alarm became evident on his face.

He inched back, held up three fingers. Three wingmen now. Tallea looked up at Maggie's hand. Fresh blood was dripping from the deep wound in her palm. Tallea gestured at her, pointed to her nose and mouthed the words, "Smell your blood. They smell blood."

Maggie's face paled, and she clenched her other hand over the wound. Ceravanne brought out a small piece of white cloth from her pack, gave it to Maggie to use as a bandage.

In a moment, they were on their knees again, scurrying ever faster along the road. They made it past the bend in the road, almost five kilometers, when Gallen suddenly stopped. A lone wingman rose, riding the thermal updrafts from the valley below.

Tallea and the others froze, crouched against the stone wall, and the wingman rose on up. Like many animals, the wingman looked mostly for signs of movement, and at the moment, the creature was in full sunlight, while they were in shadows.

Tallea's heart pounded, and she tried to still her breathing, tried to stop the pounding, as the wingman flew along the ridge, then swept up over the mountain, sniffing loudly for the scent of blood.

Then Gallen was on his feet, motioning to them. "Run!"

Orick raced ahead of Gallen, running toward the door faster than any human could, while Maggie and Ceravanne hurried forward.

Tallea jumped up so quickly that one of her mending muscles must have ripped, for she felt a searing pain in her side. Still, she managed to run forward for nearly two minutes.

Suddenly Gallen shouted, turned toward Tallea and fired near her head. A searing ball of flame shot three meters over her, hotter than any oven, and a croaking scream sounded. She turned to see a wingman, mouth open, swooping toward her, the white flames from Gallen's rifle billowing in its mouth. The wingman crashed into the road not five meters behind her, bounced, and flopped over the cliff.

They were nearly to the door. Tallea lurched forward, and saw more wingmen rising up from the valley floor, searching for the cause of the commotion. Five of them.

Gallen leapt over a smattering of fallen rocks, but Ceravanne tripped on one, fell onto others. Maggie grabbed her arm and nearly carried her, and Ceravanne was weeping from the pain.

Orick reached the iron door and stood looking at it.

Tallea felt a shadow, ducked and pulled her sword, swinging. A wingman was diving straight down from the precipice above, swooping over her, and it had extended the long red claw on its wing tip, hoping to snag her and sweep her off the road, over the bluff.

She twisted her sword inward, hoping to strike through flesh and bone instead of just claw. Her sword tip struck the scaly leather of its wing, and she was surprised at the fierce jolt, for it cut the beast but also tore the sword from her hand.

The wingman screamed in pain and swept past her, careening onto the road. Her sword clattered over the cliff, and Tallea drew her dagger, leapt past the wingman as it tried to get up.

She looked back, and the wingman screamed in anger, a roar that seemed to shake the very stone, and then it was after her, loping on clumsy feet, dragging its shattered wing.

Ahead of her, Gallen and Orick were at the iron door. They both pulled at its enormous handles to no avail. And then Maggie was with them, and Ceravanne, and they all stood in a tight knot.

A wingman swooped up from the valley in front of Tallea, trying to cut her off from the rest of the group, but she ducked under it, and suddenly all of them stood together outside the iron door.

Gallen held his incendiary rifle, looked back down the road. The wounded wingman was eight meters away, and when Gallen confronted it with his weapon, the wingman hissed and stopped.

"You don't want to die," Gallen shouted at the creature, aiming his weapon at it.

The wingman shrieked, raising its long neck into the air, teeth flashing. It watched Gallen with intelligent eyes, bright red, gleaming like rubies.

"Leave now, or die!" Gallen shouted.

The wingman watched him a second, its eyes filled with rage, then leapt over the side of the road, flapping clumsily toward the valley below.

"Who says you can't reason with a wingman?" Gallen asked, smiling toward Ceravanne. Then a huge stone fell and shattered at his feet.

Tallea looked up. A wingman was in the air, two hundred meters above them, and another swept over the ridge and dropped a large stone.

"Get under cover!" Gallen cried. And Tallea went to the door, pulled at it.

"It's locked!" Ceravanne said. "We need the key."

"But who would have locked it?" Maggie asked.

Tallea looked at the door. The lock was a mess of rust. Above the door was fancy scrollwork all along the lintel, images of twin suns rising above fields of wheat. At one time, gems might have adorned the centerpiece of each sun, but the gems had long ago been pried free.

Gallen studied the door for half a second. "Everyone grab the handles and pull," he said. "This lock can't hold us."

But despite their efforts, the door would not open.

"Watch out!" Ceravanne called, and she pushed Tallea backward. Tallea looked up, saw a wingman swooping toward them, a rock tumbling in the air, and she marveled to see such a deadly rain fall from such beautiful blue skies.

She dodged, and the stone hit the lintel of the door with a clang, then split and bounced to the ground. Rust drifted off the door in a thin sheet.

"Hey," Orick grumbled. "I'm not handy at pulling doors open, but I'm pretty good at knocking them down!"

The bear ran back to the ledge, then charged the door, slamming all of his weight against it.

The door creaked, and there was a snapping, and when Orick dizzily backed away from it, the door had cracked open a finger's width.

Three wingmen slid overhead, dropping stones in rapid succession, and Gallen stared up at them, raised his weapon as if trying to decide whether to use the last of his ammunition. Orick backed up and roared as he charged the door again.

The lock snapped, and one half of the door buckled under his weight. The bear climbed up onto all fours groggily and shook himself.

And then a wingman swept over the clifftop and shrieked, a long wail of alarm. Tallea was not certain, but she could almost distinguish words in that scream. Out above the valley, all of the remaining wingmen veered toward them and flapped their wings, gaining speed. They knew that this would be their last chance.

"Inside!" Gallen shouted, and several people ran for the door. But Gallen went to the edge of the road, his rifle in hand.

Tallea rushed up beside him. "Take my sword," he yelled, and she drew the weapon from his sheath. She felt it quivering in her hand, as if it were alive, and it emitted a soft and eager humming.

Tallea glanced back. Ceravanne and Maggie were already inside the iron door, but Orick was trying to squeeze his own bulk through the narrow passage, shoving mightily with his back feet, leaving claw marks in the stone.

Gallen fired at the four wingmen who flew forward in a loose formation, and it seemed that the sun blazed from his weapon. A fierce wall of heat struck Tallea's face, and the light burst out over the canyon sky, catching the foremost of the wingmen so that he tumbled downward in flames.

Two of them veered off, to avoid colliding with their dying kin, but the third came on.

Gallen fired once more, and the wingman tried to drop beneath his shot. The flames surged past the creature, but they had come too close. Even in passing, the heat was so great that it left a huge black smoking blemish on the creature's back.

The wingman screamed out in pain, diving toward the ribbon of blue river that shone in the forest far below.

Tallea looked back to the door. Orick was still trying to push through. Gallen shouted, "Get in!"

He raced to the door and charged into Orick, hitting him at full speed. Gallen bounced back, but Orick slid through the opening. Two more wingmen were sweeping from the ridge above, and Tallea ran to Gallen's side, leapt through the opening.

A huge stone hit the door and shattered, then Gallen leapt through.

The group sat inside the door for a moment, panting, looking at one another. Maggie's hand was bleeding, and Orick had lost a tuft of hair. Ceravanne may have suffered a sprained ankle, but Immortals healed so quickly that it would cause her no grief. A rock chip had struck Gallen in the chin, and he was bleeding.

Outside, the wingmen screamed in frustration, hurling rocks against the doors, but none dared land for the hunt.

Gallen sat panting for a moment, and Ceravanne held aloft the light globe. "Welcome to the city of Indallian," she said, and her voice was tight with emotion. "It has been long since I've given such a greeting."

Tallea looked up. The room flashed and reflected Ceravanne's light. They were in an incredibly large chamber, where gracefully carved stone rose high. In the distant past, the room had been painted cream or ivory, and stonework floral patterns had been painted in their own bright hues. High up, three magnificent silver chandeliers graced the ceiling, each with hundreds of sconces. Bright crystals at their base reflected back the light, throwing prismatic colors sparkling across the walls.

Beneath each chandelier was a high, arching passage that led deeper into the mountain.

The place smelled of dust and earth, and for once Tallea almost rejoiced at the cold, in spite of the tearing pain in her side, for at least they had escaped the wingmen. Yet there was more here than barren passages. Unlike the tunnels they had wandered before, this place still carried the faint scent of people, of ancient sweat and food, of tapestries moldering in distant halls.

"Hey," Orick said. "Are you certain that no one lives here?"

"Great is the lure of the city of Indallian," Ceravanne whispered. "I suppose that many people may live here yet. Miners may have ventured here in hopes of finding riches. . . . Other beings."

"That lock was rusted," Orick said, "but the door hasn't been closed for hundreds of years. Thirty or fifty maybe."

"Then whoever closed the city is surely dead and gone," Maggie said hopefully.

"Do not be so certain," Ceravanne said. "Many peoples are fashioned to live long. Even a Derrit, with its thick hide, is likely to live three or four centuries."

"But would a Derrit be smart enough to lock a door?" Maggie asked.

"Don't be deceived," Ceravanne whispered. "Derrits are not dumb animals.

They are foul, and live in their own filth, and they may eat you. But they are also clever and cunning. They were made to be workers on a brutal world, where conditions are harsh."

"But why would you make them that way?" Orick asked.

"I cannot speak for their makers, for the Derrits were formed long before I was born," Ceravanne said. "But I believe that it was not the creator's intent to form such foul beings. Often, peoples who have been created fail as a species. Their love for one another is too fragile. Their passions too untameable. Such peoples usually die out. But while the Derrits are a failure as a species, either unwilling or unable to lift their own kind by sharing their culture, they are successful as individuals."

"More than successful, I would say," Gallen put in. "For thousands of years, other peoples here in Babel have hunted them, trying to get rid of their kind. But it has proven damned near impossible to rid this world of them."

"So they're forced to live here in these lonely mountains?" Maggie asked.

"In the winter, when the snow comes on, they often move to lower valleys," Gallen said. "Where they sneak into barns and throttle sheep, or steal children from their beds."

"Let us speak no more about them," Ceravanne whispered.

"Yes," Gallen whispered. "They are unpleasant to think about."

Ceravanne raised the light toward the middle hallway, and began limping toward it. "Are you all right?" Gallen asked, taking her arm tenderly.

"Bloody, but unbowed," Ceravanne said, smiling. And Tallea followed them down into the darkness, holding her own aching gut. The pain was bad, but tolerable for a Caldurian.

Long they journeyed into the heart of the ancient city of Indallian, until Tallea felt certain that darkness must have fallen outside, but Ceravanne led them on. Several times they found corridors that were blocked by falling rubble, and once the floor had caved in beneath them to a deep shaft where great caverns had been excavated.

Ceravanne kept having to turn aside into new hallways, and once she stopped and threw her hands up, crying, "This isn't the way." They had been traveling down a well-made corridor, but suddenly it turned into a crude cave, chiseled by rough hands. Ceravanne walked back a hundred meters, found a side passage that none of them had noticed, for it was purposely concealed behind a large stone slab. It took them in a new direction, and Ceravanne seemed less and less certain of this new path with each footstep.

Finally, she called a halt.

Tallea put down her pack, and the group sat wearily. They began eating a small dinner of apples and jerky. Their provisions were failing. In two or three more days, Tallea figured they would be down to scraps.

Ceravanne looked around the corridor worriedly, and Gallen whispered into her ear, "Perhaps we should scout ahead, while the others rest."

Ceravanne bit her lower lip, looked ahead down the passage. "Perhaps we should."

Maggie took two candles from her pack, lit them, and in moments Gallen and Ceravanne departed. Orick grumbled about the small dinner, and lay in a corner. Tallea went to him. "You can have my apple core," she offered.

"Ah, I've plenty of winter fat to eat," he muttered, but when she put the apple core under his nose, he gingerly took it in his teeth, gulped it down.

Tallea lay down beside him. She was falling asleep when Orick began muttering his nightly prayers. Cold from the stone seemed to be seeping into her wound, and Tallea lay wondering why the hosts of the Inhuman would remember this as a place of terror.

Tallea's muscles had been strengthening daily, and she stretched her arms in spite of her fresh wound, hoping that she would soon be ready to begin exercise. She considered sparring with Gallen, wished that her ribs would stand for it, but she was still too weak. Perhaps in a couple of days she would be ready.

She listened long, and realized that in the distance she could hear a sound like wind rushing through trees. But it could only have been water cascading through some underground chasm. For a while she thought of searching for the source of the sound, so that she could refill the water bags. But instead she lay still, thinking to do it in the morning, and fell asleep to the gurgling of water.

Hours later, when she wakened, Gallen and Ceravanne were just getting back. Ceravanne seemed greatly relieved, and when Tallea put her head up, Gallen explained. "We've been lost in a side corridor, but Ceravanne found the main road once again."

Tallea lay back down, and Gallen went to sleep beside Maggie while Ceravanne lay beside Tallea.

Tallea closed her eyes, and lay for a long while, but something felt wrong. She looked around, counted those sleeping nearby. Everyone was there, the candles were still flickering.

She sniffed, but could feel no strange air currents. And she held her breath. Aside from the soft snoring of Orick, there was no sound.

And then it hit her: no sound. She could not hear the rushing waters. Which meant that either the underground brook had subsided in a matter of hours, or else . . . someone had closed off a door, masking the sound.

Tallea loosened her knife in its sheath, and lay for the rest of the long night with her eyes open, perfectly still. Once, she thought she heard a distant thud, as if someone had stubbed a foot on the floor, but there was nothing else.

Still, when Gallen woke hours later, she whispered in his ear: "Take care. We may have visitors."

And as they quietly slipped away from their resting place, Tallea listened down each side corridor for the sound of running water.

• • •

For the next few hours they hurried along down passageways that were unimpeded, past storage rooms and old quarters where thousands of people had been housed. They were entering a section of Indallian that had been far more than the mere service tunnels or mining camps found at the east entrance. This was the full-fledged city, in its ancient glory, and often they passed through huge chambers where sunlight shone down through shafts in the ceiling upon vast reflecting pools, or where wooden bedposts still sat in the musty ground, petrified.

In these areas, where ancient shafts and fire holes littered the ceiling, they had little need for Gallen's light, and Ceravanne nearly ran through the halls, filled with a new intensity. "This district was called Westfall," she said as they passed through one great chamber where an underground river rushed through a stone causeway, spilling out into the light. "Children used to bathe here, laughing under the icy water."

And in the next chamber, vast brick ovens sat next to each other. "Here the bakers worked night and day, cooking loaves for the household."

And in the next great chamber, the tallest and grandest of all, sunlight shone down through five holes in the roof, two at one end of the hall, and three at the far end. There were long reflecting pools under each light, and all along the great chamber were statues of ancient warriors lining the central hall—short, fat pikemen of the Poduni race; Tacian giants with great hammers; the tall Boonta men with long spears and their narrow shields, an army of warriors representing many nations.

And at the end of the hallway were two thrones. "And here," Ceravanne said nervously, "is where I ruled, beside my brave Belorian."

She stopped, and looked away shyly. Above each throne was a vast statue of marble that had once been overlaid with gold, but the images had been defaced by thieves, all of the gold chiseled away.

Maggie gasped, and rushed forward to the statues, as did each of them. The statue on the right bore the image of Ceravanne, as one would imagine she would look in a few years. But the image on the left . . .

"Gallen?" Maggie called, and she looked back at Gallen, horror and confusion on her face.

Ceravanne strode forward, clenching Gallen's glow globe so that the light shone from it fiercely, and she held it up to the statue.

The image was chipped and scarred. The hair had been cut shorter than Gallen's and the bearded face belonged to an older man. But there could be no mistake: the eyes, the chin, the nose, were all Gallen's.

"Belorian?" Maggie asked, still confused.

"When the Rodim slew him," Ceravanne said softly, "they destroyed his memories, so that he could never be reborn with those memories intact. But they did not obliterate his body. His genome was stored, so that his seed could be propagated, undefiled."

Tallea heard Gallen gasp. "You mean I'm—But how?"

"When the Dronon came, it was a dark time. Across the galaxy, the cry came out. 'We need more Lord Protectors.' And of all the Lord Protectors on our world, Belorian was judged the most worthy of cloning.

"And so, the Lady Semarritte sent technicians to our world, and they took what they needed. Seeds for the future, as they also harvested seeds from other worlds."

Ceravanne looked up at Gallen, and there were tears in her eyes. "I do not know your circumstances, but I can guess: you were born on a backward world, much like ours. Your mother and father had no other children, and it was voiced abroad that they were desperate."

"I never heard that," Gallen whispered.

"I did," Maggie countered. "My mother told me of it, when I was small."

"And so when you were born, no one worried that you did not look too much like your mother or father, for you were a gift from heaven. And you were a smart child, bright and resourceful, strong and fiercely independent," Ceravanne said. "That is the way it happens.

"In a time of peace, you would have become a trader, perhaps—fiercely competitive. But you were born during uneasy times.

"Gallen, it is no accident that you are a Lord Protector. Maggie told me how Veriasse found you only a few weeks ago, that he 'chanced' upon you in an inn. But though it is our good fortune that he found you, I suspect that little chance was involved. I suspect that he knew a seed had been planted in the town of Clere, so he sought for you in the town of your birth.

"And I am grateful that the Lady Everynne—when she learned the truth—sent you back to us, in the hour of our greatest need."

"I am a clone?" Gallen asked, and there was still disbelief in his blue eyes.

"Ah," Orick grunted, studying Gallen. "Now I see. The Bock never would tell us that Gallen was human!"

"He's not—quite," Ceravanne said. "Belorian was from a race of people called the Denars."

"The Denars?" Gallen asked.

"A race designed to be Lord Protectors," Ceravanne said. "The first race designed to be so. It is not by chance that your hands are quick or your mind is nimble. You were born with great gifts, and a desire to use them in the service of your fellow man."

Gallen folded his arms and looked up at the statue for a long minute. Then he spoke to Ceravanne, and his voice was husky with resentment and accusation. "You know these corridors. You brought me here on purpose, when you could have bypassed this chamber."

"All these past few days," Ceravanne said softly, "the memories the Inhuman gave you have been telling you what it wants you to become. I thought it best that you find out what you are."

"I think, rather, you are showing me what you want me to become."

Gallen grunted as if it did not matter to him at all, and nodded. "Let's go, then."

And Ceravanne led them from the great hall, down some long corridors. They were near the borders of the city, and now they rushed for the east gate, but a few kilometers away.

Gallen looked back once, and his eyes were full of tears, and Tallea pitied him for being a pawn in such a large game. He seemed to be running blindly, so she ran ahead of him, taking the lead in case there was danger.

They were jogging down a corridor, and entered a broad room when she smelled it—the garlicky scent of Derrits, thick as smoke.

She halted and turned, and there in the shadows, the great beasts were lying: three of them rose up on their knuckles and growled, each of them more than twice the height of a man.

"Run!" Gallen shouted, and he drew his sword. Tallea would have stood to fight beside him, but her sword was gone, and she had only a knife and her dueling trident—no weapons to pierce Derrit hide.

She rushed down the nearest passage, leading the way, with Ceravanne behind her. The Derrits lunged, their shadows dancing against the far wall. They had huge yellow eyes, and bones tied in their stringy gray hair clattered when they moved. The largest was an enormous male with dirty yellow skin and testicles as large as a stallion's. He wore a mail shirt, woven from bits of chain mail taken from a dozen human warriors, and he grabbed a massive door to use as a shield. In his other hand, he took an ancient halberd. He roared and charged, and Orick stood beside Gallen and rose on his hind legs. The two of them looked like children, hoping to withstand the monster.

And Tallea stopped and rushed to Gallen's side. Her Caldurian blood called her, and she could not leave friends in need.

Ceravanne and Maggie needed no urging to run, yet they did not go far— merely crossed the room, then stopped and turned. Ceravanne crushed the glow globe in her hand, squeezing it tighter and tighter, so that its light shone fiercely. Tallea admired the woman's bravery, for the Tharrin had no protection, and she held the light up only to aid the warriors.

The Derrits howled in pain, and raised their hands to shield their eyes, their pointed yellow teeth flashing. The huge male raised his shield, protecting his eyes. They were a shifting mass, acting as if they would charge, and Tallea dared not turn her back on them. She pulled her dagger and dueling trident, held one in each hand. They were small weapons, hardly big enough to do much damage, but she'd honed them as sharp as steel can be.

The male Derrit roared and surged forward, using his shield to slap Orick aside. The bear went flying like a doll, yelping in pain, and tumbled past Tallea. The male raised his halberd to strike, as if it were a hatchet, and Gallen danced in, struck the giant under the rib cage, and rolled away, his sword dripping blood.

The Derrit swung wide, slamming the halberd into the stone floor so hard that the weapon shattered. The Derrit raised his head and howled at the roof, never taking his amber eyes from Gallen, and swung his shield at Tallea. She ducked under its blow, felt the huge door whistle over her head, and knew that if she'd been hit, the blow would have shattered every bone in her body.

The Derrit howled again, and he must have spoken some command to the others, for the two smaller females rushed out from under his shadow. One of them lunged toward Orick, while the other tried to circle around Gallen, heading toward Ceravanne.

At the same time, the big male roared and leapt for Gallen, swinging the broken haft of the halberd like a club.

And in that moment, time seemed to stop. Tallea could see Orick on the floor, dazed, seconds from death at the teeth of a Derrit. Gallen was swinging madly, slashing open the snout of the big male as it lunged in to bite. The female on the far side of the room, rushing forward on her knuckles, headed toward Ceravanne and Maggie.

And in that moment, Tallea had to decide who she might save. Her little knife and trident were feeble weapons, but they were all she had. Ceravanne was on the far side of the room, and Tallea had served her poorly once before. Her heart was torn—Ceravanne or Orick? She could not make that choice. So she only prayed that she could fight swiftly enough to save them both.

The Derrit grabbed Orick in her claws and pulled him forward with both arms, ready to sink her teeth into him. With a war cry, Tallea leapt onto her broad snout, sinking her trident into the giant's forehead to use as an anchor, then stabbed the big female in the eye—once, twice.

Blood gushed from the creature's torn eyelids, and the Derrit shoved Tallea away, knocking her across the room, and Tallea lost her trident, leaving it stuck in the monster's head.

There was a fierce tearing pain from the old wound in Tallea's side when she hit the floor, and she rolled to her knees.

Ceravanne began shouting, waving the light, and Tallea looked up, saw the other female Derrit hesitate not three meters from Ceravanne, pawing the air with one hand, shielding her eyes with the other. Ceravanne, though she lacked all skill in weaponry, also found it impossible to leave a friend in need.

Gallen had slashed the big male across the belly and one arm. The Derrit was a bloody mess, but still had some good fight in him. He was swinging his shield with both hands now. The Derrit's solitary lifestyle showed itself in the creature's poor fighting form.

The little female that Tallea had wounded began to shriek, and Tallea looked over in surprise to see Orick wrapped around her left leg. He was biting her, ripping her leg into shreds while she tried to pry him off and escape.

"Run!" Gallen said, looking right at Tallea. "Take Maggie to safety!"

Tallea got up, felt as if some ribs had snapped. She ran toward Ceravanne and Maggie, screaming a battle cry, and the female Derrit who'd cornered the women took an experimental grab at Ceravanne, her long yellow hands darting forward.

Tallea rushed up to the Derrit, grabbed a handful of hair near the Derrit's short tail, and drove her knife deeply into the Derrit's thigh, just below her left leg, trying to hit the femoral artery.

Tallea pulled her knife out, and though her blade had not made a deep cut, it was a painful one. The Derrit shrieked and lurched away.

The Derrit struggled to turn, hoping to throw Tallea off, but Tallea thrust the knife in again and again. The Derrit screamed in fear, released some acrid-smelling urine, then turned and fled, rushing toward Gallen's back.

Tallea could not hold the female Derrit from attack, but she clung to her, slowing her down for a moment. Tallea shouted for Gallen, then drove her blade deep into the back of the Derrit's knee, hoping to cripple her, and then Tallea lost her grasp on the monster and fell.

Tallea looked, and Gallen was swinging at the big male. With a mighty blow he leapt forward and slashed it across the forehead, seemingly unaware of the female rushing in behind, then suddenly he danced to the side, and swung a terrible blow at her leg.

The female crashed into the big male, knocking them both backward, and in that second Gallen rushed to Orick's aid, shouting to Tallea, "Flee!"

With a heavy heart Tallea ran, knowing it was the best thing to do. She lacked adequate weapons, and only Gallen was equipped to fight in that room. But few men survived an attack by a single Derrit, while Gallen and Orick had three to contend with.

Tallea found tears in her eyes, and recalled the teachings of her crèche masters: "A warrior cannot afford to weep in battle. It gives your foe the advantage." And so her masters had beat her, until she could hold back the tears. Yet the tears came now, for her friend Orick was battling without her, and Tallea knew that when this was over, she would have to weave a new rope belt for Orick, for her greatest bond now—beyond all her imaginings— was with the bear.

She passed by a room where wind blew in fiercely from a hole, a deathly chill, and Ceravanne was just behind Tallea, at the back of the group, holding aloft the light to ward off any more Derrits.

Their shadows danced madly upon the floor and the walls of the corridor, and then they ran into an open hallway, where suddenly the floor fell out from beneath Tallea.

There was a flash of darkness, and she found herself hurtling down—a rough hide and dirt falling all around her—then she landed with a jolt, and a searing pain shot through her back and arm.

For one brief moment she lay looking up, and Maggie shouted, "My God!" and was staring down into the pit. It had to be a good five meters to the top, Tallea thought. Ceravanne called, "Are you all right?"

Tallea felt very confused. She could see the light above her, and her ears were ringing. She was breathing hard, panting, and a sweat had broken out on her forehead. She felt as if she'd landed on a rock, and it was digging into her back, but it hurt when she tried to move off it, and something held her in place. She tried to answer, but no words would come out.

"Are you all right?" Ceravanne repeated, and she held the light above her head so that she could see down into the pit.

"Derrit . . . Derrit trap," Tallea managed to say, and she felt lucky to say that much. She wanted to count her good fortune at being alive, but when Ceravanne's light shone on her, Tallea looked down at her own legs. A pointed stake as wide as her hand was poking up through her belly, and another pierced through the meat of her right arm. A third came through her leg just below the hip, but she could not feel it.

She could feel nothing below the waist. Her back was broken. She closed her eyes, listened. There was the roaring of Derrits in the far room, and it was getting closer. Gallen shouted something, and Orick roared in return, and Tallea's heart sang with joy at the sound. At least Orick will live, she realized, and she looked back up at the concerned faces of the women.

"Leave me," Tallea said, and her voice came out as a croak, barely audible above the yelling.

"Not yet," Ceravanne said, and she stood fast beside the pit.

There was more shrieking, more cries, and one final wailing roar. A few moments later Gallen and Orick came and looked down into the pit. Both of them were covered with blood, but little of it was their own.

"Three Derrits?" Tallea asked when she saw Gallen. "Perhaps a record."

Gallen's face was sad. Tallea felt light-headed, as if she were floating, and she almost thought she could float up to them, tell them that it was all right.

"What can we do for you?" Gallen asked, and Tallea tried to think of an answer.

"There must be something we can do for you," Maggie said, but even kind Ceravanne shook her head no.

"We're losing her," Maggie whispered.

"Save me!" Tallea found herself asking.

"There is nothing we can do," Orick said solemnly, and the bear had tears in his eyes. Tallea coughed, tried to speak.

"They say, in City of Life, Immortals with mantles can save people. Save me!"

And then Maggie's eyes opened, and Tallea realized that with all of his lore, even Gallen had not realized what she was asking.

"Not all mantles have this power," Ceravanne said.

"Of course," Maggie said. "We can download her memories into Gallen's mantle!"

"Yes, the rebirthing," Tallea pleaded.

Gallen held up the cloth woven of black rings, its glittering diadems shining in the light. "Can you catch it?"

Tallea nodded, and Gallen dropped the mantle onto her chest. Feebly, with her left hand, Tallea grasped the mantle and placed it on her forehead. Maggie called, "Command it to save you."

"Save me," Tallea begged. "Save me."

The silver rings sat cold upon her forehead, and she felt no different. She fell asleep for a moment, and she saw bright images: flashes of her childhood when she picnicked at a pond in carefree days. The time she first learned to hone a sword blade. A great meteor that she once observed streaking across the night sky for several minutes.

And then Gallen was beside her, stroking her head. He'd climbed down into the pit, though she had no idea how. He picked up the mantle, showed her a gem in the center where the mantle sat on his forehead, a gem that gleamed palest green with its own light.

"See this," Gallen said, pointing at the gem. "These are all of the memories that make you. All of your hopes and dreams. And I shall take a hair from your head, to remake you."

Tallea tried to thank him, but no words came from her mouth.

"Quiet now," he said, and he kissed her softly on the forehead. "The great wheel turns without you now for a while. Until you wake again."

She closed her eyes, and for a long time it was a struggle to breathe. She thought of one last thing she wanted to ask of the others, a gift she dearly wanted to give to Orick. But Gallen must have left her, for when she next opened her eyes, it was dark, and the stone floor beneath her was cold, so cold that it felt as if it were sucking all the heat from her.

Twenty-six

Though the remaining journey through the passageways of the city of Indallian took only a few hours, to Maggie it seemed to last forever. Gallen took the lead, watching for traps while Ceravanne told him which passages to take, and once more they heard the roaring of Derrits in distant recesses, but the company eluded them by slipping through passageways too small and narrow for the Derrits to negotiate.

Once, when they stopped to rest in an ancient hallway where dried and faded tapestries still hung on some walls, Gallen said, "I'd hoped we wouldn't find so many Derrits here. I saw a tribe of them in the Nigangi Pass. I think that the movements of armies has driven them here."

"With nothing but dirt to chew on for these past few weeks," Ceravanne said, "they'll be mad with hunger. How many did you see in Nigangi Pass?"

"Perhaps a hundred of them."

Ceravanne squinted her eyes, and her mouth opened in a little O of shock. "So many? Derrits only band like that in fear."

Yet Maggie had to wonder how many might be hereabout. They'd fought off three Derrits and been chased by more. Perhaps Ceravanne was thinking along the same lines.

"We'll have to take care," Ceravanne whispered. "We may be the only food these Derrits see this winter—though they are known to feed on their own young, if necessary."

"What are you saying?" Orick asked.

"They'll hesitate to follow us into the sunlight," Ceravanne said, "but surely they will be hunting us tonight, and perhaps they will dog our trail for weeks to come. We can only hope that their band is smaller than the one Gallen saw in Nigangi."

"Right then, let's move out quietly," Gallen said, and Ceravanne held the glow globe aloft while Gallen led the way.

Thus it was that the group came out of the city of Indallian at sunset and found themselves on a long gray road. But they were still too close to the lairs of the Derrits, and Gallen kept them moving at a run over the long road for many hours, until the pack on Maggie's back felt as if it would burrow into her flesh, and her legs felt as massive and unyielding as stone.

At last, well past midnight, they could run no more. They came to an ancient guard tower dug into the mountain alongside the road, and prepared to make camp there. It was a good spot, out on a spur of a mountain ridge where they could see the road gouged into the cliff for four or five kilometers in each direction. The Derrits would not be able to come upon them unawares, so long as someone kept watch.

Maggie shrugged off her pack as soon as she got in the door of the guard room, then merely threw herself on the ground in exhaustion, glad to sleep on the rocks. She was almost blind with fatigue, still numbed with grief at Tallea's death.

But Gallen took her elbow and lifted her up. "Come," he whispered, "just a bit farther."

"No," Maggie whispered, but she was too tired to argue, so she let him guide her and the others to the back of the guard room, into a tiny shelter that had once been used as an armory. There, he got out the packs and began laying out blankets.

Maggie stood watching him stupidly for a moment, wondering why he bothered, and then said at last, "Wait, let me help."

"I can get it," Gallen said, spreading out the last blanket. He began setting out the food and wine, and Maggie watched him and realized that for the past couple of days, whenever it was time to eat, Tallea had been quietly preparing the food. She'd taken that as her job, and now she was gone. It didn't seem fair that Tallea should be dead, while all of them walked around.

"Sit down and get some food in you," Gallen said. "You'll need your energy tomorrow."

"What if the Derrits come tonight?" Maggie said.

"I'll stand watch," Gallen whispered, looking up at her.

But she knew that he could not run all day and then stand watch all night. Indeed, he had dark circles under his eyes already, and Orick had been keeping more than his fair share of watches. And though Ceravanne was bright and intelligent, she was so small that Maggie feared the woman would be useless in battle.

Which meant that Maggie would need to take over some of Tallea's duties. Maggie felt the loss of Tallea as a sharp pain that sucked the air from her, and she realized that Tallea's death had given her an added responsibility. Tallea had saved them more than once. Maggie had felt secure with her solid presence on the ship as she guarded their door each night. And certainly Gallen would have been overwhelmed in battle with the Derrits and the wingmen had Tallea not come to his aid. Always, Maggie had imagined that Gallen and Orick could hold their own in any skirmish, but Gallen had never had to fight anything as big as a Derrit, or as swift as a Tekkar.

Maggie closed her eyes momentarily, and felt a slight disorientation, as if she were falling. And suddenly she found herself back in the hive city on Dronon, and ten thousand dronon warriors surrounded her in the dark arena at the city's belly, their mouthfingers clicking as they chanted in unison. The air was heavy with the biting scent of their stomach acids, and only a dim red light of their glow globes in the high ceiling lit the room.

Gallen was battling a dronon Lord Vanquisher who had spat his stomach acids into Gallen's face, so that Gallen stood with his flesh blistering, blinded as Veriasse had stood blinded in his final battle, while the dronon Lord swooped overhead, slashing with his battle arms.

And in the dream, Gallen listened intently as the dronon Lord made his approach, and he leapt incredibly high and kicked at the Lord Vanquisher one final time. Their bodies blurred together as they collided, and there was a spray of blood—both red and green—and Gallen tumbled back to the ground, the flesh ripped off half his face, to reveal a pale blue mask underneath. He was no longer breathing.

The Lord Vanquisher tumbled to the ground beyond him, wounded, the exoskeleton of his skull badly crushed, so that white ooze dripped from it. His left front cluster of eyes was shattered, and one of the sensor whips beneath his mouth had been snapped off. The Lord Vanquisher was almost dead, and he flapped his pee-colored wings experimentally, but was unable to lift his weight off the ground.

All around the room, the dronon's voices were raised in a gentle roar of clacking, as if rocks were falling onto the metal floor, and the Lord Vanquisher turned toward Maggie and raised his serrated battle arms high for a killing blow, then began stalking toward her.

And Maggie looked up at him helplessly, feebly, knowing that she would die, just as surely as Gallen had executed the dronon's weak and bloated Golden Queen after defeating her Lord Vanquisher.

And as the Lord Vanquisher came to destroy her, Maggie heard a voice whisper in the back of her mind, "This is what becomes of the Lords of the Swarm. Prepare."

Maggie's heart began hammering wildly, and she looked about, suddenly realized that she'd fallen asleep on her feet, and dreamed a dream that she knew she'd had on many nights before but that had been so terrible, she'd put it from her mind.

Perhaps her own feelings of inadequacy now brought it to the surface. Without Tallea to guard her, Maggie realized that the time had come for her to learn to fight for herself.

They ate a brief dinner, and Gallen urged Maggie to bed.

"You sleep," Maggie whispered. "I'll take the first watch."

"Are you certain?" Gallen said, eyeing her carefully.

"I feel better with some food in me. I'll thank you for the loan of your weapons though, and your mantle," Maggie said.

Gallen gave her his sword and incendiary rifle, then Maggie put on his mantle. "Are you sure?" he asked.

Maggie nodded. "I have to start sometime," she said and went into the large guard chamber where slits cut into the stone let her watch out into the darkness. The moons were out, but the road was deep in shadows, and Maggie wished that she could see better. Suddenly the whole scene lightened as Gallen's mantle complied with her wishes, and Maggie watched the snaking road. There was nothing alive out there except an owl that swooped silently down the length of the road, hunting for mice.

In moments, Maggie heard Gallen and Ceravanne settle down to rest, but Orick whined and barked, as bears will when they cry.

Maggie went back to check on him, and he was sitting up beside the door, shaking with the hurt. With the mantle on, she could see the tears in his eyes, and Maggie realized that Orick's feelings for Tallea had been stronger than she'd known, and no one had thought to try to comfort him.

"Are you thinking of Tallea?" Maggie whispered, and Orick nodded. Maggie patted his head, then petted him behind the ears. "She was a good one. We will all miss her."

"I know," Orick grumbled.

There was a rustling in the far corner as Ceravanne came awake, and sat up and looked over toward them, as did Gallen. "Do not be too hasty to grieve for Tallea," Ceravanne said from across the room. "Death is but a temporary state for many. She lived her life to the benefit of others, and she died to save us. The Immortals will be loath to let her perish."

"But she feels dead to me," Orick grumbled.

"Think of her as a friend who sleeps, but who will waken again."

"Aye, but when she wakes again, she wants to be a Roamer. She'll be different."

"I should think you wouldn't mind the differences," Ceravanne said. "She'll have fur, and she'll look more like you. You were becoming close friends. I should think that when she is a Roamer, you will be closer still."

"Och, she may resemble me," Orick said, "but I have to wonder what thoughts will lodge in her head. Certainly not human thoughts. And what will her heart feel? No, Tallea is gone forever."

Maggie patted his head. "By her own will she is gone," she whispered. "She died well, as she wanted. We should be happy for her in that. But I think she lived a sad life. She wanted others to depend on her, to own them and be owned—too much. It was a burden for her."

"So it's love you're accusing her of?" Orick said. "And I should be happy that she'll feel it no more?"

No one spoke for a long moment, and at last Gallen said softly, "I lived as a Roamer once. You are right to mourn for her, Orick. Roamers feel a certain closeness, but it is not love, and so Tallea now loses some of her humanity. Still, they can be happy. They revel in their own freedom, and their days pass quickly because they are unencumbered. She will learn to hunt for grass seeds on the plain, and squat beneath wide trees in a fireless camp, where she will have no care while she sings at the stars.

"And so, while you mourn her, take care not to mourn too long. This is the reward she has chosen, and if you had ever suffered under the emotional encumbrances of a Caldurian, perhaps you would feel that she has chosen wisely."

Orick thought for a long time, and his spirits seemed to lift a little. Maggie quickly kissed him on the snout, and when Orick said, "You know, I'm at least as hungry as those Derrits," she knew that he was feeling better, but he was also reminding her of her duty.

She went back and watched the road, letting the others sleep through the long night. And as she waited, she clasped her hands and twisted, exercising her wrists as she often saw Gallen do, and she whispered of her need to Gallen's mantle, saying, "Teach me!"

And so during that night, she moved in the darkness, exercising her body in new ways, swinging Gallen's sword as best she could while the mantle sent her visions of foes.

Only once that night did she spot a Derrit—a great brute of a male walking down a ridge on the far side of the canyon, carrying a greatsword in one hand, with a war hammer in the other.

Twenty-seven

wo hours before dawn, Gallen woke Orick with a kick. And Orick lay on the floor while Ceravanne packed, listening to the others talk in the main room of the guard shack. Maggie had chanced a small fire in the guard house and made a quick breakfast of cooked oats with cinnamon. It was their first hot meal in days, and to tell the truth, they would not have risked the smoke from a fire except that they had eaten all else. The cheeses were gone, as were the wine and corn, the plums and peaches. They were down to apples and oats, and they couldn't tell when they'd eat a cooked meal again. So it was the oats.

Orick had been living off his store of winter fat for days now, and he was beginning to feel a gnawing hunger that the others would soon share. Yet bears are tough, and Orick knew that the hunger that was a mere annoyance for him would quickly become dangerous for the others.

He was lying on the floor, thinking of these things, when Gallen came back and kicked him again. "Wake up, sleepy," Gallen said, laughing.

Orick felt as if he'd hardly slept at all, and he grumbled to Gallen, "Why must you rouse me so early? I'm dead tired."

"Better dead tired than merely dead," Gallen said, squatting beside Orick's ear. "We ran a good bit last night, but the next few kilometers of road are well exposed. Once dawn comes it won't be safe to travel that road for the wingmen, and we must make good time today. I fear the Derrits will be hunting us tonight."

"Och, I thought we left them all behind?" Orick grumbled.

"The Derrits and the wingmen own these mountains. The wingmen flocks are everywhere, and as for the Derrits, you saw how big they are. You saw their stride," Gallen warned. "They can run a hundred kilometers in a night without breaking a sweat, and they can track by scent as well as any wolf. We ran for six hours last night, but if a Derrit hunting pack gathers, they'll reach this spot in less than two."

"Do you think they'll come after us?"

"I think they'd have come for us last night, except that you and I made a good accounting against some of their number. But they won't be satisfied to eat the dead we left behind." Gallen leaned closer and whispered so that Maggie and Ceravanne wouldn't hear. "I told you once that this road is a place of terror for the Inhuman. They would not likely brave it this time of year. In the fall, Derrits do their hunting for the winter. They kill men and animals, and bury them in a cache to eat later. In one of my former lives, I was a soldier who hunted Derrits here. Thirty-two men were in my command, and a dozen Derrits fell upon us in an ambush, slaughtering them.

They buried my men in a huge pit, piling the dirt upon them all. I was sorely wounded, and I was buried with them. I dug myself out of the grave after four days, and for the next week I dragged myself across this rocky road, trying to escape, until the Derrits came for me again. It was only by chance that they lost my scent, passed me as I hid in the night. The next day I was able to make it down into the river, float for hours in the icy water until the Derrits had no opportunity to catch my scent again. A fear of this place must burn in the memory of every Inhuman."

"So you think the Derrits will come for us? We only heard one other Derrit back there."

Gallen leaned close, watching through the open door as Ceravanne and Maggie hunched over the cooking fire. "I did not want to tell you, but twice I had Ceravanne turn aside into smaller hallways because my mantle smelled Derrits ahead. We heard one, but I smelled dozens. Believe me, we'll not get away from them this easily."

"Are you going to tell the women?" Orick asked.

"I think Ceravanne already knows the risk, but I do not want to frighten Maggie. What will come, will come, and perhaps our best efforts will avail us nothing. So now, my friend, if you will pick your shaggy carcass up off the floor, I think we should eat quickly, and then be running."

Orick obliged him, and in moments they were off, jogging on nearly empty stomachs through a maze of gray canyons, over the barren road. Their only light came from stars and moon, and just as the sky began to lighten, the road dipped precipitously, leading them deep into the gorge.

Before they could take the road down, Gallen stopped, and they stood panting while Gallen gazed far behind along the mountain slopes. A light snow dusted the tops of the peaks silver in the moonlight, and down near the bottoms were dark clots of pine forest running the slopes. But Gallen watched the gray middle slopes, almost featureless in the night, where the ancient road was bordered on one side by a precipice, on the other by walls of dark stone. The mountain chain here formed a huge S, so that though they had run perhaps forty kilometers since sunset, they were only fifteen kilometers as the wingman flies from the gates of the city, and with his mantle Gallen was able to see much of that road from this last bluff.

He stood for a long minute, then his breath caught in his chest, and his face became hard, impassive. Orick knew that look.

"What is it?" Ceravanne said, panting. "What do you see?"

Gallen looked up at the sky. It was growing light, a dimming of stars on the horizon. "They're after us," he said.

"How many in the hunting pack?" Ceravanne said, looking back up the trail.

"Twenty . . . or more." Gallen pulled out his incendiary rifle, checked it. He had only two shots left, as they all well knew.

"So many?" Ceravanne asked in dismay. "We'd hardly make a meal for a dozen of them."

"They're hungry," Gallen said, slipping his rifle back into its holster. "Let's go. They'll have to hole up for the day in that guard shack. But they'll be after us again tonight."

He turned and sprinted down the road, into the depths of the gorge where the dark trunks of massive pine trees rose above them, and the road was overshadowed by vine maple and ironwood. On the slopes above, the world had seemed dead, sterile, but Orick was surprised that down here there was plenty of game—rabbits, squirrels, jays—things too small for the Derrits to bother with, all of them rustling through the detritus as they searched for their morning meals.

For that day they ran, scurrying from thicket to thicket like mice as Gallen watched for signs of wingmen.

So it was that near dusk, Gallen led them into the woods along the river. From high above, Orick had seen the river as nothing more than a silver ribbon in the canyon below, but down here he could see that it was more. Now, in the early fall, a cool flow rushed over boulders, flowed rippling across gravel bars. But all along the riverbank were great logs, cast up on the shores by the raging floods that tore down this canyon in winters past. Often, the river had gouged passageways through narrow chasms or left huge piles of flotsam. For nearly two hours after dark, the group made its way downstream through this mess. Then well after dark, under the light of the triple moons, Gallen led them all into the water, and they waded back upstream for several kilometers, often sloshing through pools that were chest-deep, until they passed the point where they'd first set foot off the road.

The water did not seem very cold to Orick, but all of his human friends complained of it, and Ceravanne often slipped on the mossy rocks.

When the women could wade no more, Orick let them sit astride his back, and carried them surefooted up to a tiny tributary creek that had become only a small flow of water. In the spring the creek must have been much larger, for it had eroded a deep and narrow gorge into the hillside.

"This will have to do for the night," Gallen whispered when they stopped at last, sheltered in a tiny nook. He pulled out the blankets from the packs, and they made a dismal camp behind a small tree.

Orick looked up and down through the gorge. He estimated that the walls were perhaps a hundred feet high here, and twelve feet wide. "I'm not very cozy with your strategy, Gallen," Orick whispered. "Sure, the Derrits could easily swagger through here two abreast."

"Aye," Gallen said, "that they could. But I'm hoping that they'll think we've headed downstream through the woods. The road takes us downstream, to the southeast, and I'm hoping they'll believe we've still gone that way. If they waste enough time hunting downstream, then we'll win through the night and they'll have to continue the hunt tomorrow. But even if we don't fool them, at the very least they'll have to split up and check the banks both upstream and down. That leaves us maybe five or ten to contend with at a time—not twenty."

"I thought the three we fought gave us more than ample exercise," Orick grumbled. "I really would prefer to leave these ones alone."

"Well, go to sleep," Gallen said, "and maybe you'll get your wish."

Orick tried to stay up the night, but in time he settled onto his paws. His heart was hammering heavy in his chest, and he was cold and hungry and miserable, but he thought of Tallea lying dead in the city of Indallian, naught but Derrit food, and though he missed his friend, he was glad to be alive.

"Gallen," Orick whispered, for both Maggie and Ceravanne had fallen asleep and were already snoring lightly.

"Aye?" Gallen asked.

"You've got Tallea's memories stored in your mantle, right?"

"Aye," Gallen said.

"Well," Orick wondered aloud, "how many people's memories can be stored in that thing?"

"Just one."

"And what would you do, I mean, if tonight a Derrit caught you? You couldn't save yourself the way you saved Tallea, could you?"

"Not without erasing her memories," Gallen said. "The memory crystal holds a lot, but I'm part of the Inhuman now, and I've probably got more memories than this one crystal can handle."

"So would you do it? Would you erase her memories to save yourself?"

Gallen thought for a moment. "The Inhuman in me would. Most of those people desperately want more life. They crave it. But the Gallen O'Day in me wouldn't do it."

Orick grunted. "I think that if you have to do it, you should. You should live for Maggie. Tallea would understand that, and she would forgive you."

"I'm not sure that I would forgive myself," Gallen whispered. "It's an un-pleasant thing to have to consider. Go to sleep, now."

"No, you go to sleep," Orick said. "I'll take watch for a bit."

Orick lay watching quietly for a minute. Maggie had kept watch last night, so Orick was hoping to split it tonight with Gallen. Orick figured that the lad was worn to the nap, and he needed some time off, so tomorrow he considered taking watch with Maggie.

For a long time, he stared down the slope, and only the croaking of a lone tree frog kept him company.

Orick closed his eyes to rest them for a moment, and when next he woke, there was a fierce wind blowing down through the canyons. It did not buffet the small group much, sheltered as they were, but it was singing through the rocks and the trees.

He looked over at Gallen, who sat up awake and alert. "Any sign of them?" Orick asked, and Gallen looked over at him.

"I heard five or six of them walking upriver about an hour ago," Gallen said, "but the wind must have blown our scent away. Go back to sleep. It's nearly dawn."

Orick could not go back to sleep, since he felt so guilty about falling asleep during his watch, so he asked Gallen to catch some more shut-eye, then in an hour he woke them all. They ate a cold breakfast of the last of the apples.

"That was a good trick you gave them," Orick said after finishing his two apples. He eyed the cores that the others were eating as he talked. Without any more food to keep them going, he wanted to accentuate the positive. "You knew the wind would blow the scent away?"

"I hoped it would," Gallen admitted. "I've been through these canyons many times, and often at night the cold mountain air funnels down these slopes. It was a chance we had to take."

"Well," Orick said, "you've pulled us out for the day, but what about tonight?" He only hoped that Gallen had some kind of plan.

"That is a tough one," Gallen admitted.

"Farra Kuur?" Ceravanne asked, tossing Orick an apple core.

"Yes," Gallen said, "that is what I was hoping."

"It's a long stretch of road before us," Ceravanne considered. "We'll be hard-pressed to make it."

"Farra what?" Maggie asked.

"Farra Kuur," Gallen said. "A few kilometers south of here, the canyons narrow again, and down the road fifty or sixty kilometers, there was a fortress called Farra Kuur, virtually impenetrable. If we can make it there, and if the bridge is down after all these years, we should be able to hold the Derrits off for another night."

"If the bridge is down?" Orick said.

"Drawbridges," Gallen said. "Farra Kuur is burrowed into the spur of a mountain between two very steep chasms. Drawbridges were carved from great sheets of stone to span the gap, and the Makers created giant gears to raise and lower them."

"Certainly the bridges aren't in working order," Ceravanne said.

"They were three hundred years ago," Gallen said hopefully. "And the gears and chains were all well oiled back then. The Makers build for permanence. But even if the bridges aren't working now, so long as the bridges are down, we should make it into Farra Kuur. And once we're there . . . well, we'll see what I can do."

Orick didn't want to talk about the battle that would inevitably come tonight even if they made it to Farra Kuur, so he said, "Making it to this fortress of yours sounds like a fine idea, but it won't do us much good if we starve. You wouldn't happen to know where we might find some food around here?"

"Keep watch for mushrooms, berries, nuts," Gallen told him, "pick anything you find. We'll be running through the forest all day, and if we're lucky, maybe a young deer will impale itself on my sword," he joked.

"Are you sure that's wise, eating these strange berries?" Orick asked. He'd seen some small red berries the day before, but he'd been afraid to harvest any, not knowing if they were poisonous. And he didn't even want to chance the mushrooms he'd seen, for none were of varieties familiar to him.

"All mushrooms, berries, and fruits that you will find here on Tremonthin are edible—" Ceravanne said, "but one. The deathfruit grows on a bush low to the ground, and is dark purple, darker than a plum. It is to be eaten only by those who are sick or horribly injured, those who seek death."

Orick considered this good news, and they took off, climbing up the narrow gorge till they hit the road once again, and for most of the day, Orick foraged as he ran, eating a snail here, swallowing a few acorns there, nibbling a mushroom.

That day they ran among rounded hills beside where the river flowed, and once they stopped by the riverbank where the soil had a blue tinge so that Ceravanne could harvest some of the Healing Earth. They took off again, but shortly after that they lost the road altogether, for lush grasses and woods now covered the ancient road as if it had never been.

Still, Gallen kept a straight course, and on some high hills they would find themselves climbing over the remnants of a stone road that was worn and cracked, until well before noon they came to an ancient fortress that lay nearly all in ruins. One of its walls stood intact, rose to an incredible height of perhaps two hundred feet.

"Druin's Tower," Gallen called it, and he stood on the hill and studied the landmark wistfully, as did Ceravanne.

"Who was Druin?" Maggie asked.

Ceravanne answered. "Druin was a kindly scholar who united many people. He built this tower to study the stars, and he delved in forbidden technologies, hoping to carry the peoples of this land away with him to other worlds. But then he became old, and bitter, and turned away from peace, manufacturing weapons of war."

"I did not manufacture weapons," Gallen growled, gazing hard at Ceravanne, and it was as if another person spoke from his mouth. The memories the Inhuman had given Gallen were so strong, that for one moment, Druin spoke. "The Fengari workers turned against me, making cannons without my knowledge."

Ceravanne studied Gallen a moment. "The Immortals studied your memories most carefully, Druin. You were not guiltless in this affair."

"I was guiltless!" Gallen spat, and then he seemed to struggle for control and said heavily, in his own voice, "But that was long ago."

"The memories of the dead can be easily edited," Ceravanne said softly. "Druin's memories are in the archives at the City of Life. Someday you may see for yourself and learn the truth of it. Druin was a great man, a man of peace for most of his days, but his goodness died before he did."

"And if you read those memories and find that you have wronged him?" Gallen asked.

"We can review the records, and if he deserves a new life, then he will be granted one. But you must understand, Gallen, that he violated our strictest laws. Certain technologies are forbidden on this world, yet Druin sought them out. He may have been a well-meaning criminal, but he was a criminal nonetheless."

Gallen turned away from her, as if to lay the matter aside. The icy-gray river they'd been following flowed down below them through a green valley, where it joined an even broader muddy flow that came in from the north. For a moment, they sat and rested. There were no roads, no signs of homes or settlements. All of that was long gone. Gallen spotted some distant wing-men circling closer toward them, so they headed out for the shelter of the trees.

Orick could smell the garlicky scent of Derrits throughout most of the morning along the road, so he knew that they had gone ahead during the night. But an hour before noon they were climbing back up a long hill when the group passed an old mining tunnel carved into the stone cliff face along-side the road. There the odor of Derrits became so strong that even Maggie and Ceravanne could smell it.

The suns were shining bright and full, hidden only by the thinnest gauze of high clouds. Everyone crept quietly past the mine, and when they were well past, Gallen stopped and looked back toward it longingly.

"Give me the glow globe," Gallen said to Ceravanne.

"You aren't going in there?" Maggie hissed, grabbing Gallen's arm.

Gallen's face was pale, wooden. "They've got too much of a lead on us," he said. "I don't want them so close."

"What kind of plan do you have rolling around in that head of yours?" Maggie asked.

"I was thinking," Gallen answered, "that it would be interesting to see if they've posted a guard. Derrits normally don't, and I'm thinking I could kill two or three before any of them wake."

"No!" Maggie said. "It's not worth the risk!"

Gallen licked his lips. "The Derrits are not above eating their own kind. If I kill a couple, it leaves that much more food for the others to eat."

Ceravanne had fished the glow globe out of her pack, and she handed it to Gallen. "He's right," she said. "A well-fed Derrit is not as ferocious as a hungry one."

"Go ahead on up the road," Gallen said to Orick. "Derrits don't like the sun, but if they're angered, they might come out after us, and there's no sense being within arm's length if you don't have to."

"I'll come with you," Orick whispered.

"No, thank you." Gallen sighed. "With my cloak covering my scent, they won't smell me coming, and with my mantle, I can fight in the dark, so I won't alert them that way. I'd prefer to keep those advantages."

Orick's heart was sore to follow Gallen, but he knew it would not be wise, so he took the lesser course of action, and he hurried Maggie and Ceravanne up the road a couple of kilometers, where it turned around a wide bend, then had them hide in some bushes.

Gallen waited till they were set, then crept back to the huge entrance of the mine. It seemed he had hardly stepped in when they heard the bloodcurdling roar of Derrits.

Gallen staggered back out the door as if he'd been knocked backward, and he had his sword up in one hand, the glow globe blaring in the other. A huge yellow Derrit lunged through the narrow doorway after him, a stream of red blood at its throat, raking the air with its claws.

Gallen ducked beneath its grasp, slashed at its belly, then turned and ran. The Derrit careened around drunkenly for a second, then fell to the ground, and Gallen did not stop to watch it, for four other Derrits were lunging through the doors.

One of them stopped in the sunlight, raised his long snout skyward and roared his contempt, while three of the smaller Derrits gave chase to Gallen.

They were so swift, he could not hope to outrun them. Gallen sprinted for a hundred yards, pocketed his glow globe, then reached back and drew his incendiary rifle, whirled and fired.

A meteor of white plasma struck the first Derrit full in the face, and bits of plasma splashed backward, where they dropped and burned into the stone road and into the Derrits behind. The fire of it was bright as the sun, and even the Derrits inside the tunnel shrieked and grabbed their eyes, wailing like the damned.

The single shot managed to fry two of the Derrits and burn the leg of a third. Those monsters who were still alive stayed back in the mine.

Moments later, Gallen hurried up to Orick and the others, sweat dripping from his face, fresh blood spattered all across his robes. Behind him, the plasma fires from his rifle were still burning.

"They had a guard," Gallen said, shaking his head, stopping to catch his breath. He glanced back. "They sure don't like the incendiary rifle. Too bad we have only one shot left."

"Maybe this little display will have them thinking better about following our trail," Orick said hopefully.

Ceravanne shook her head. "Derrits are not easily dismayed, and they are a cunning people. They will try to outwit us."

Gallen merely grunted. "They will have to catch us first," he said and set off at a run.

That afternoon their trail took them through a land of broken hills, a wild land, with little game in it. They did see some rabbits from time to time, and once they saw three dark wolves fading away into the shadows under some trees.

Gallen and the women were wilting from lack of food and from the fast pace, so Orick made it his job to find something edible. Often that day, he imagined himself in Gallen's shoes, playing the hero. But he wasn't Gallen, he realized, and food is what they were lacking now.

While Gallen watched for wingmen and Derrits, Orick watched for mushrooms and pine cones, wild onions and berries. So it was that he managed to scrounge some snacks on the run, and near sunset, as he crossed a large stone bridge over the river, he smelled wild blackberries, and led the others upriver a hundred yards to a patch of berries that hung thick from the vines.

They picked what they could, stuffing as many berries as possible into their mouths, and when they set off again a few minutes later, it was with renewed vigor.

At dusk the road left the riverbanks and began to meander up through some dark hills, thick with scrub and the stone ruins of old buildings.

Gallen kept them running till well after dark. Clouds were blowing in, and it looked as if it would rain.

An hour after sundown, they topped a rise and found themselves once again on a high canyon wall. Gallen called the others together for a council.

"If I guess right," he said, "the Derrits cannot be far behind us. We can either leave the road now and try to hide, or we can hope that the bridge is down at Farra Kuur, and try to fend them off there. Either plan may fail, so I ask you, which do you prefer?"

Orick looked down the cliff toward the river, then looked up at the sky. Their trail was still fresh, and the rains had not come yet, and might not come for hours. To run in hopes that the Derrits would lose their scent seemed foolhardy. Yet the path ahead was unknown. What if the bridge wasn't down, or what if it had been destroyed over the centuries? What if Derrits also lived in this fortress? There seemed to be no easy solution.

"The river here is not as wide as it was last night in the woods, and there are fewer places to hide," Ceravanne said. "You still have one shot for your rifle, and the Derrits will be loath to charge us so long as you wield that weapon. I think we should go ahead."

"I'm not sure," Orick grumbled. "How long could the bridges last at Farra Kuur before they weather away? At least if we leave the road now, we know what kind of a mess we've gotten ourselves into!"

Gallen looked at Maggie, who just shrugged.

"Farra Kuur, I vote, then," Gallen said. "Even if we get backed into a corner, the road behind us offers little room for the Derrits to maneuver. I think that up there, I might be able to hold them off until morning."

He nodded ahead, and Orick worried. Gallen had slept only lightly the night before. He was in no shape for battle. Still, Gallen had six thousand years of experience on this world, and Orick had but a few weeks. Orick had to bow to Gallen's wisdom.

They ran then. Blackberry vines crossed the road under their feet, attesting to the fact that even the game did not use this road as a trail, and as they ran, a burrow owl glided ahead before them, watching for any mice that they might disturb.

The moons were up enough so that they shed some wan light, and the four of them ran with their hearts, until at last they rounded a bend and saw a huge cliff face jutting out from the arm of the mountains, with broken towers crumbling along its rim, and all of the towers were riddled with dark holes that once had been windows. It was difficult at first to see much else, for the moonlight shone only on the upper towers, while the valley before them was in shadow, but the towers looked almost like living things, like giants tall and ready for battle, and Orick realized that indeed the whole face of the cliff was sculpted with their images. Four giants, their eyes hollowed out by age, their great beards hanging down to their belts, stood ready with huge axes in their hands, ever vigilant, ever ready for battle. Orick's eyes focused on those images.

As they ran, Gallen shouted in triumph, "The bridge is down! Hurry across!"

Behind them Orick heard the roar of Derrits.

Gallen spun about and shouted at Maggie, "Take the light. I'll hold them off!" He passed her the globe from his pocket.

Maggie squeezed the glow globe, and its bright white light flooded over the ridge. Then Ceravanne and Maggie rushed headlong, running faster than before, their stained cloaks flapping in the breeze, carrying a piece of the sun in their hand as they raced toward the dark tower.

Orick stayed beside Gallen. It was dark, with a thin blanket of clouds above, but not too dark for a bear to see by.

The Derrits were rushing uphill toward them in a disorganized pack, growling and hissing. They moved at a loping pace, sometimes lurching forward on their knuckles more than their feet, yet they moved at an incredible speed, so that a span of road that had taken Orick twenty minutes to cross took the giants only two. In the darkness, the Derrits' crude gait reminded Orick of nothing so much as that of an otter, with its head bobbing down and up as it ran. He counted seventeen of the brutes.

Yet when they were a hundred yards away, Gallen shouted at them. "Siisum, gasht! Gasht!"

The Derrits stopped, and stood gazing at Gallen and Orick. The ones in front would not move forward, but those in the back came inching up, shoving the others aside to get a look at the prey.

"Siisum s gasht! Ooongu s gasht!" Gallen shouted, and his voice was a snarling roar that mimicked that of the Derrits.

One of the Derrits called out to Gallen quizzically, a sound of grunts and snarls, yet Orick was sure that he heard words mingled in that growling.

"I told them to stop or die," Gallen said. "But their leader says that we are warriors of great power, and they want to eat us, to gain our power, so that even in our deaths our power will live on in them. He says that he will not be hungry for me, however, if I only give him you and a woman to eat."

Orick snarled and stood up on his hind feet. "Siisum a gasht!" he growled.

The Derrits lurched forward a step, as if angered, and Gallen fired his last shot into the pack. The plasma arced up into the night, then dropped in a spray. The whole side of the cliff lit up like noonday, and some of the Derrits screamed and toppled off the road in their haste to escape while others roared and lurched, trying to brush the flaming magma from them. In the light, their yellow hides were suddenly revealed, the white flashing of their fangs.

"Gasht!" Gallen roared, and he held his rifle up menacingly.

Those Derrits who could rushed backward down the hill at full speed, but four of the tribe were either killed outright by the blast, or were burning slowly, or had already toppled over the cliff.

Orick and Gallen turned and headed back toward Farra Kuur, and by the wavering light of the plasma fires, Orick could now see the great stone bridge spanning the chasm ahead, with its ancient guard posts still intact.

Orick started to hurry up the road, but Gallen whispered savagely, "Don't run! Don't let the Derrits see you run, or they'll know we're afraid, and they'll try to hunt us again."

And so they walked slowly up the road, and Orick felt as if a great weight had been lifted. With so many of the Derrits in flames, Gallen seemed confident that the others would not dare to attack again.

They could see the light up ahead, shining from within the walls of Farra Kuur on the far side of the bridge. Maggie and Ceravanne had gone deeper into the fortress, and the light shone from an archway far back along the northern wall.

As Orick approached the bridge, he could hear the sound of water rushing over rocks in the gorge below, could smell the faint vapors of water—and he caught a strange scent, something smoky and oily, a scent he recognized just barely. He was about to shout a warning, when suddenly a dark shadow detached from a corner and stood on the far side of the bridge, a man dressed in the dark, hooded robes of the Tekkar, which went down almost to his knees. And he wore tall black boots.

He held out a strange metallic device pointed at Gallen, and Gallen drew a startled breath at the sight of it. Orick could only guess that it was some type of gun, but it had an odd stock, one that required its user to hold the weapon forward with one hand on a trigger, the other on the stock.

"Well done, Lord Protector." The Tekkar's voice was soft, almost a hiss.

In the dim light, Orick could see that the man's face was all a tattoo—of a pale yellow skull. "We've been waiting. You've saved us from an inconvenience with the Derrits, and for that, we owe you. Now, throw down your weapons, or we'll execute the women."

Orick's heart pounded in his chest, and he considered what to do. He wanted desperately to rush forward and tear off this man's limbs.

But the Tekkar nodded, and from the archway where the lights shone, seven more Tekkar came out in a tight knot, holding Ceravanne and Maggie. One of the Tekkar held a gun to Maggie's head.

Twenty-eight

Orick growled and paced back and forth, as if at any moment he would lunge ahead, and Maggie stood with the gun to her temple, her head cocked painfully to one side under the Tekkar's rough grip, unable to move. She remembered some of the basic kicks and punches that Gallen's mantle had taught her two nights before, but three of the Tekkar had her. She knew nothing that could help her now.

"Don't," Gallen warned Orick, to keep the bear from charging, and Maggie's heart went out to poor Orick. "Those are dronon pulp pistols, made to pierce a dronon's exoskeleton. You don't want to see what kind of damage they do."

Orick stood up on his hind legs and bawled, his claws raking the air, obviously confused. Maggie could see how much he wanted to save her, and she feared he would charge now to his own death.

"Please, Orick, stay back!" she called, and the bear roared loudly, got back down on all fours.

"Quite sensible," the Lord of the Tekkar hissed. "Now, Lord Protector, take off your mantle and throw it at my feet. Then drop your rifle belt, sword, and knives."

Gallen looked up once to the towering images of giants overhead, and he stood with eyes closed, as if meditating for a long moment, considering his chances if he should choose to fight, but at last he did not resist, simply threw his mantle down.

Maggie realized that the Tekkar couldn't know that Gallen's rifle was empty. If she fled now, the Tekkar might not chase her, since they wouldn't want to turn their backs on Gallen. She wondered if she could twist away, run through the dark tunnels of Farra Kuur to escape, but she knew that the Tekkar were terribly fast and Gallen had said that they could see in the dark, that to their eyes the heat from her own body glowed. She could not hope to escape them.

Gallen unbuckled his sword belt and knife sheaths, put them down on the ground, then kicked them forward with his foot and backed away. For one final second, Maggie almost hoped he would pull his sword and fight, but she knew that resistance would be futile. He was outgunned.

Gallen raised his hand out to the Tekkar's Lord, made a pulling gesture, as if summoning him, and Maggie recognized it as the same gesture he'd made days ago to Zell'a Cree. But the Tekkar ignored the Inhuman hand signal, kept their weapons trained on Gallen.

Only when Gallen had backed well away did the Tekkar Lord stride forward, watching Gallen as he carefully picked up the mantle.

Once he had it in hand, his men came to his side, and one held a dronon pulp gun and kept Gallen and Orick covered while their Lord placed Gallen's mantle into the pocket of his robe.

The Tekkar Lord ordered Gallen to turn around, and two of his men went forward, pulled back Gallen's hands and began to bind him.

"What is this, my brothers?" Gallen said, addressing the Tekkar. "This isn't necessary. I was bringing the Tharrin to Moree—a goal that both she and the Harvester shared, though with different ends. I planned to deliver her into the Inhuman's hands."

And in the farthest recesses of her mind, Maggie worried that Gallen might be telling the Tekkar the truth. Perhaps in all of this journey he had been the unwitting accomplice of the Inhuman. At the very least, Maggie had felt his distance during the past week. The Inhuman had formed a barrier between them.

"And for bringing them here, I thank you," the Tekkar Lord answered Gallen.

When Gallen's bands were tight, one of the Tekkar reached up, pulled the hair back from Gallen's neck, and said, "My brothers, he does bear the mark of the Word!"

Ceravanne had the presence of mind to gasp and to look around in astonishment. "No!" she cried, as if horrified at the news. And because Ceravanne had been studying how to manipulate humans for nearly four thousand years, her performance carried a sense of conviction that few others could match.

All faces turned toward her, though the Tekkar Lord just glanced at her with a flicker of his eyes, but it gave time for Maggie and Orick to manage similar exclamations of horror and surprise.

The Tekkar Lord studied them, then addressed Gallen. "If you were delivering them to Moree, then why the subterfuge? You could have taken a more direct route."

Gallen looked up at him steadily. "I wanted to bring them in alone. It was to be my first and noblest act of service to the Inhuman. We all serve it in our own way, and I prefer to use deceit rather than force."

The Tekkar Lord reached into a pocket, pulled out a small ball. Maggie recognized it as a dronon message pod. Like the dronon weapons the Tekkar bore, it was an odd piece of work, an artifact that the dronon must have left behind. The Tekkar hissed, "We have the Lord Protector and his company in custody at Farra Kuur. We are bringing four of them in. Request air transport for twelve to Moree."

He threw the ball in the air, and it flew with a hissing noise high up, heading southwest toward Moree. Maggie had seen the dronon message pods before, even had some broken ones of her own, but she'd never seen a working model at such close range, and she longed to tear it apart to see how its miniature antigrav unit functioned.

"Perhaps you are indeed Inhuman," the Tekkar Lord said to Gallen, "and if so, we welcome you. But if you are Inhuman, then you will not fight your fetters, and you will rejoice with us as we introduce your friends to the mysteries of the Word."

He reached into his pocket, pulled out a small silver insect that struggled in his gloved hand. The Tekkar held it up, walked over to Ceravanne, and looked her in the eyes. Maggie could see from the way that his lips were gently parted, from the anxious breaths he took, that he enjoyed torturing others, but Ceravanne did not flinch away from him, did not let him see her fear, and thus denied him his pleasure.

"Hold!" Orick called out, still standing on the bridge. "You can't be doing that to her. This is the Swallow, come back to rebuild the Accord!" Obviously the bear hoped that his words would have some kind of influence on the Tekkar. Perhaps he even hoped that they would fall to their knees as the worthy Im giants had done.

But the Lord of the Tekkar only laughed at Orick. "Have you not heard? The Swallow is already in Moree, and she has gathered her armies. She is set to harvest this world, and the stars beyond."

He spread his hands, waving toward the stars shining above the fortress, above the dark canyon walls, then turned to Maggie.

"This one is for you, child," he whispered, and he dropped the Word into the hood of her cloak.

Maggie cried out, tried to struggle free of the Tekkar's grip, but two of them viciously twisted her arms up behind her back and held her wrists, forcing her to bow down on her knees into the dirt.

Gallen was still at the far side of the bridge, his hands tied behind his back, unable to do anything but watch. Orick could not come to her rescue with the Tekkar holding him at gunpoint.

Gallen stood watching, his face a carefully controlled mask, unable to do anything for the moment. There was no movement, only the sound of the tumbling waters in the chasm far below the stone bridge, breaking the silence.

Maggie grunted, breathing hard, and waited in cold terror for the Word to attack. In a moment, she felt a sharp stabbing pain at the base of her neck, then a rapid push as the Word burrowed under the skin at the base of her skull.

She cried out, and watched Gallen through tear-filled eyes. He was standing thirty meters away from her in the edge of the darkness, and she looked across at him as if across some great gulf, and she realized that she had been looking at him this way for days. Ever since the Word had infected his skull, he'd inhabited a place she could not quite reach.

And now I'm going there, Maggie realized, and it filled her with a new thrill of hope, mingled with fear. I will share the lives he has lived, feel what he has felt. And in the end, we will no more be strangers.

But only if I renounce the Word. And so Maggie conjured an image of the dronon on Fale, and how they had tormented her, until the white hate boiling in the pit of her stomach burned away all fear, all pain.

She heard the sound of bones grinding in her skull, and she shrieked, "Gallen!" And suddenly, the world was turning, and Maggie felt herself dropping forward into the dust.

When Maggie woke, she lay for a long moment, her eyes opened to slits, and her first thought was to wonder if she were dead.

The room was dark but for a small fire, and Maggie recalled lives past, in bodies where she could see more keenly, smell through the palms of her hands, hear the rustling footsteps of mice through stone walls. In comparison, this body seemed sluggish, its senses dulled. She remembered her sense of power living as a Djudjanit under the ocean and swimming as fast as any fish, and re-called as Entreak d'Suluuth flying on hot summer thermals for days, never needing rest, and so she felt weak now in comparison. And this was the Inhu-man's first message to her, that because of her humanity, she was inferior.

She thought for a moment of times spent gazing placidly at campfires, of passionate loves lost and won over the course of a hundred lifetimes, of bat-tles and defeat, and she saw how whole lives were often colored by emo-tional themes, recurring cycles of anger or despair or hopeful delusions. People were too often cramped by their own inadequacies, or made pawns in the larger affairs of men. Maggie thought back on her lives and saw them as a painter's palette of colors, each with its own distinctive hue and texture.

And the experience made her feel rich, and buoyant and wise and old be-yond the counting of years. And this was the Inhuman's second message to her. Be grateful for what I have given you.

The lives and customs and thoughts and ideals of a hundred different people roiled around in her brain, and Maggie had learned much from the Inhuman. It was as if before there had been only a night sky, and now a vast and yawning galaxy of stars suddenly burned before her.

Almost without exception, the lives the dronon had shown her were lived by people of passion, people who loved life and wanted to continue indefi-nitely, and now Maggie saw how truly precious a gift it was, and she wanted to live over and over again, each time experiencing a new form. And in her mind, the Inhuman whispered, Follow me, and I will give you endless life.

And she recalled the hundred lives lived and wasted, and felt how each of those people had seen their own deaths as unfair. And the Inhuman whis-pered, The Tharrin-led humans are your enemies.

But as she cast back into her new memories, she also recalled thousands of nonhuman people who had been granted the rebirth. So she reconsidered the lives she had led, and recalled from each person something of the unbri-dled passions that might have kept them from being reborn. For Entreak d'Suluuth it may have been his contempt for the "wingless," for another it had been complacency, for another greed.

So Maggie felt unsure as to whether the human lords had misjudged these people. Perhaps the human lords had been right to let them pass away, forgotten. And the Inhuman within her cringed at such thoughts, tried to get her to consider other arguments.

Then Maggie recalled her own captivity under the hands of the dronon, and her rage began to burn in her. A wave of confusion washed over her as the Inhuman sought to take control of her, but Maggie focused on her own memories. And she saw without a doubt that the information she'd been given was tainted, an emotional argument designed for the naïve and inexperienced. Her own experiences with the dronon precluded any possibility of being drawn into their cause, and her resolve to destroy the Inhuman had not weakened. Indeed, the Inhuman's Word had not been able to have the slightest effect in changing her view of the world, and she marveled at how Gallen had been so strongly influenced by the Word.

It seemed almost a defect in his character to have become so misguided, but she recalled Ceravanne's warning that some people found it easier to fight the Inhuman's Word. Indeed, the Bock had not even feared that Orick could be infected. So Maggie wondered if it were some biological difference in her that let her defeat the programming so easily.

She opened her eyes to slits and looked around. She was lying on the floor in a large room—the same room that the Tekkar had hustled Maggie and Ceravanne into when they first entered Farra Kuur. The room may have once been an inn. It was large enough for one—twenty meters on one side, thirty long, with a huge hearth on the far wall and a couple of entryways that might have led to kitchens or sleeping chambers. Maggie's head was pillowed by the packs that Gallen, Maggie, and Ceravanne had carried.

In the far corner of the room, two Tekkar had built a fire in an ancient stone oven, and they were cooking some fry bread and beans seasoned with desert spices. The scent made Maggie hungry.

Her legs and arms were not bound, which suggested that the Tekkar believed that she would be converted when she woke—or perhaps they thought only that she would pose no threat.

Maggie looked around for the others. Two Tekkar had Gallen sitting in one corner, guns trained on him. The other Tekkar did not speak much, and then only in whispers, but they moved about the room as if in a dance, each performing his own task—cooking, packing, guarding—and Maggie noticed something odd about them: the Tekkar had set themselves up around the room so that none were really close to the others. They did not congregate. Instead, they moved about the room evenly, almost gracefully, but always chose their path so that they maximized one another's body space. It was a distinctly nonhuman behavior.

In another corner, Ceravanne sat, hands bound in front of her. Orick was at her side, both of them under heavy guard. Maggie was surprised that they had not yet been infected by the Word.

The Tekkar Lord had Gallen's mantle in his hands, and he turned it over and over, studying it. Finally, after a minute, he put it on his own head, and smiled at his men. He stood for a moment, breathing deeply, and said, "Ah, now *I* am a Lord Protector."

Maggie knew that she had to get the mantle back. It was too powerful a tool to leave in the hands of a servant of the Inhuman. She got up, stretched, and smiled warmly at the Tekkar. Their leader saw her and hurried over, the memory crystals of Gallen's mantle glinting under his hood.

Maggie waved toward Ceravanne, her voice expressing confusion. "Have we no Word for our sister, or for the bear?"

The Tekkar Lord gazed into her eyes, and his own purple eyes looked like black holes in his dark skin. "None," he hissed, his voice whispery, as is often the case with those who have keen ears. "An aircar will be here soon. Perhaps more will be provided."

Maggie looked about the room, still wondering what to do. "I . . . want to serve the Inhuman," she said. "But I don't know how."

The Tekkar nodded graciously. "The lives you have lived—they train you in the use of technology and weapons, strategy and history. All that remains is for you to be assigned to a unit."

Maggie considered. She had the lives of forty-one men and women who'd gone to war—swordsmen and bowmen, tacticians, scouts, squires, kings, and supplymen. Merchants who understood the economics of war, a dronon technician and worker from the City of Life.

She hadn't considered before, but she was prepared for just about any situation that the future could throw at her, and she also realized that much of what she'd learned was designed to help accommodate other nonhuman species. The passionless Wydeem would learn about lust and the desire to build. The gentle and shy Foglarens would learn how to be confident in open spaces and understand the thrill of battle. The Roamers would learn of trade and economics.

"Yes," Maggie whispered for the first time. "I see what you mean. May I be in your command for now?"

"Of course," the Tekkar hissed. "It is always an honor to work with a kitten whose eyes have just opened."

Maggie gave him her hand, let the Tekkar help her rise. She nodded toward the food. "May I? We haven't eaten well in days."

"Of course," the Lord said. "But you will need to hurry. The transport will be here soon."

Maggie made up a plate, and the Tekkar Lord knelt beside her, watching her every move. Maggie nodded toward Ceravanne. "I almost envy them."

"Why?" the Tekkar asked.

"Because soon they will hear the voice of the Inhuman, and they will feel what I felt upon awakening. That first moment of being alive."

"Yesss," the Lord hissed, obviously pleased.

Maggie sat eating, wondering what she might be able to do to help the others break free. Probably nothing. She noticed the furtive glances the Tekkar gave her. They were watching her closely now, and had not yet offered her a weapon. She knew that they wouldn't offer her one until she had been safely delivered to Moree.

She had just finished her plate, when the building began to rumble and vibrate as the gravity waves of a dronon flier bounced against it.

"The transport is here," the Tekkar Lord said, and his men began picking up their packs. They had great mounds of food and blankets, and most of the men had to fill their arms.

The Tekkar Lord himself was about to grab his pack, but instead ordered one of his men to do it and took both of the dronon pulp guns, waved Gallen and Orick forward, and they went out into the night.

On the stone bridge outside Farra Kuur, a lone flier had set down. It was a large military job, an oblong blue disk with rows of windows. One of its doors swung upward automatically on landing. It was large enough to carry twenty men, and its forward weapon array held twin plasma cannons and several smart missile mounts. No one had come with the flier, so obviously it was piloted by an AI. Maggie was not wearing her mantle, but she knew upon looking at the flier that this was a completely new machine, not more than a week old and designed for use by men, not some artifact left by the dronon.

So the Inhuman was building its own arsenal.

The Tekkar carried their bundles and went ahead, stopped to look down the road. The Derrits had come back to retrieve their dead. The whole pack of them were gathered out in the darkness far down the road, growling low and snarling.

But they seemed disinclined to charge up the road to the military transport and attack a squad of Tekkar.

Gallen, Orick, Maggie, and Ceravanne were herded behind by the Tekkar Lord, waving his gun. He'd put the spare in his belt.

Just as Maggie got to the main gate of Farra Kuur and stood under its black stone arch, Gallen stopped and looked back at the Tekkar Lord.

"Veriasse, kill them now!" he whispered.

The Tekkar Lord's eyes suddenly rolled back in his head, and he leapt sideways and fired the dronon pulp pistol in a frenzy. It made burping noises as it fired, and Maggie looked to see a Tekkar take a hit to the head, opening a hole. The whole side of his face exploded outward, the shattered bones of his skull stretching the skin incredibly taut, and then his skull seemed to shrink in on itself, and he crumpled to the road.

Another Tekkar took a body hit, and the left side of his chest ripped away as the shell of the pulp gun exploded, spattering blood and bits of bone and lung all across the transport.

One of the Tekkar managed to pull a knife and fling it at his Lord, but it was a hasty throw, and the Tekkar Lord simply dodged aside, then finished shooting down his own men.

And then he pulled the spare gun from his belt and dropped both weapons, and merely stood. Maggie watched him in confusion, wondering if the Lord were changing sides. Down the mountain, the Derrits began to roar quizzically, as if trying to decide whether to charge.

"Quickly!" Gallen shouted. "Cut us free! There is no telling how long the mantle will be able to control him!"

Maggie grabbed the fallen knife from the road, went to Gallen and cut his bonds, then did the same for Ceravanne. Before Maggie could finish with Ceravanne, Gallen went to the Tekkar Lord, pulled the man's knife, and plunged it into his heart.

The Tekkar dropped with a sigh, and Gallen grabbed the pulp pistols and his mantle. In moments he had hurried to the flier, and they began throwing in the packs that the Tekkar had carried, then leapt in and closed the doors just as the Derrits charged up the road.

"Vehicle, rise eighty yards and hold position!" Maggie commanded the flier's AI.

The flier rose up in the air and hovered.

"I don't understand." Orick grumbled. "What happened?"

Gallen had already put his mantle back on, and he whispered, "Not any man can wield the power of a Lord Protector's mantle. The mantle is a living machine, and it partakes of the desires and intents of its makers, and of those who use it. And like a Guide, it has some measure of control over its wearer. Most of the time, it gives me free rein to do as I please, but I have felt it tugging at my limbs, using me in battle as much as I use it. So when the Tekkar asked me to surrender it, I asked my mantle if it could protect me. It said that it could not serve an evil man. It warned me that it might be able to battle the Tekkar, once one of them put it on. I knew that the Tekkar would covet the thing, and eventually one would try to claim it, so I had only to wait my chance."

Maggie looked out the window at the dead Tekkar strewn across the road. She recalled how the Tekkar Lord had innocuously obtained both the guns. She realized that Gallen's mantle had been prodding him even then.

Maggie had understood that her mantle was designed for a special purpose, and that its abilities and memory were all aimed at fulfilling its own desires and objectives. She had felt her own mantle tugging at her mind, filling her with curiosity when she'd studied dronon technology, but she hadn't quite grasped how symbiotic the relationship between man and mantle might be— until now. And Maggie realized that she would need to begin studying mantles more explicitly, learning more of their creation, abilities, and desires.

Down on the road, the Derrits fell upon the bodies of the dead Tekkar, grabbing them and scurrying away. Food for their babies, Maggie thought.

"Where to now?" Maggie said.

Gallen looked at her quizzically, the green running lights of the flier soft on his face, and she smiled. "I'm not Inhuman, if that's what you're wondering, Gallen O'Day!"

"I didn't imagine you would be," Gallen said. "But one can never tell."

After a moment of thought, he said, "We've got air transport, and we've got food. We might as well fly to Moree."

"Surely we can't just fly into the city," Ceravanne said. "They'll be waiting for us."

"We can land nearby," Gallen said. "Close, but not too close."

Ceravanne closed her eyes, thinking. "I'm not sure, but I believe I know just the place."

here should we go?" Maggie asked again, staring hard at Ceravanne, but Ceravanne was still thinking, unsure if hers was the right course.

"If I judge right," Ceravanne said, "we cannot just go straight into Moree in this vehicle. We will have to set down outside the city. Is that right?"

Gallen nodded curtly.

"And I have seen the dronon aircars streak across the sky like meteors," Ceravanne said, "so that a journey of a thousand kilometers takes but an hour."

"More like six minutes in this car," Maggie said.

"We need rest and food before we go into Moree, and a place of safety," Ceravanne continued. "Could we go back to Northland for one day, to the Vale of the Bock on Starbourne Mountain?"

Maggie and Orick both dropped their jaws. They had been struggling so hard to reach Moree that both of them thought only in terms of that small goal, and so they had imagined landing as close as possible to that place.

"It might not be a bad idea," Maggie said. "When this aircar doesn't return on schedule, the Tekkar at Moree are going to become suspicious. They'll close the gates tight, and start looking for us. It wouldn't be a bad idea to stay away for a while."

Gallen stared out the window, considering. "But every moment we waste only allows the Inhuman's agents to get stronger. They've already got the Dronon hive cities, and now they are building armed and armored air transports. I think we should go in immediately."

"It is hours till dawn," Ceravanne said. "The Tekkar are awake, but most of them will be sleeping by morning. We should wait to infiltrate the city by daylight."

Gallen nodded in acquiescence, and Maggie told the aircar to take them to Northland, to Starbourne Mountain. The aircar did not know the coordinates, so Ceravanne gave it an approximation, and the transport rose in the air and swept away. Ceravanne looked out her window and saw the small campfires and lights of villages down in the cities below, and she watched the clouds, like floating sheets of ice on a swollen winter river, sliding away beneath her. She had never been in an aircar before. Though the thing sounded noisy from the outside, there was absolute quiet within the vehicle, and this seemed somehow wondrous to her.

Gallen sighed, then said, "With all of their military buildup, I don't understand why the hosts of the Inhuman haven't attacked Northland yet."

"Perhaps they are afraid that Northland is stronger than they know," Ceravanne said. "In the City of Life, we have long allowed our guards to carry weapons that are restricted elsewhere on the planet, and our resistance fighters became expert at using those weapons on the dronon, and at sabotaging the dronon walking hive cities."

"Even with that," Gallen said, raising a brow, "I suspect that the Inhuman has amassed enough weaponry to wipe out your people. Something else is holding it back."

There was a long moment of silence, and at last Ceravanne said, "Could it be compassion?"

Gallen studied her a moment, wondering. "Why would you say that?"

Ceravanne shrugged a little. "It was something the Tekkar said when Orick told him that I was the Swallow. He said that the Swallow had already returned to Moree, and had gathered her armies."

Gallen whispered, "And she was set to harvest the stars?"

Ceravanne nodded. Gallen had been so convinced that the Harvester was a machine that for a moment he did not understand what she implied.

"Could it be that the dronon have set up an imposter?" Maggie asked Ceravanne. "Someone who could take advantage of your reputation."

Gallen blurted out, "Why would they bother, when they could have the real thing? They would only need to clone Ceravanne and fill her with the Inhuman's memories—and they'd have their Harvester." He spoke the thought as quickly as it came to him. And finally, she saw that Gallen understood.

Orick gasped, and Maggie looked crestfallen as together they saw the simplicity of it. Ceravanne turned away, for she could not face them.

Gallen looked into Ceravanne's eyes and said more gently, perhaps only realizing the truth now, "And that is why you insisted on coming with us, isn't it? You knew that the Harvester is not a machine. You came to face your darker self?"

Ceravanne hesitated to speak, and Maggie shook her head in denial. "Certainly the dronon couldn't turn a Tharrin—even with the Inhuman's conditioning. It wasn't able to turn me!"

Ceravanne wondered, as she had wondered on countless nights, just how susceptible she herself might be to the Inhuman's persuasion. The Inhuman had come after her again and again with such persistence, and always she'd managed to kill herself to avoid being taken. But she had not been able to defend her dead body. The dronon had had countless opportunities to recover her genome, create a clone, and fill it with whatever thoughts or memories they desired.

Ceravanne looked into Maggie's dark eyes. The young woman had been losing weight due to the rigors of their journey, and for the first time Ceravanne really noticed how this was wearing at her. "I have never wanted to talk to you about these things until now," Ceravanne said. "I didn't want to betray how much I knew of the Inhuman, nor did I want to betray my plans on how to deal with it once we reach Moree. You see, there was always the possibility that one of you could be turned. But now Orick and I are the only ones who have not received the Inhuman's Word, and Maggie, you and Gallen will need to continue my battle without me, should I die."

Ceravanne looked deep into Maggie's eyes, took a deep breath, and said, "Maggie, you are wrong if you think we Tharrin can withstand the Inhuman's Word. The sad truth is that the Inhuman's Word, as a weapon, has proven to be more effective against my people than any others. It was designed to persuade us to join the dronon's cause. It is almost by accident that the Word has also worked so well against the Tekkar and other races."

"Oh, Ceravanne," Maggie said, and she crossed the hull of the ship, took Ceravanne in her arms, and for one sweet moment, Ceravanne wept and let Maggie embrace her.

"We are our bodies," Ceravanne whispered close to Maggie's ear. "You see, the Tharrin were made to serve mankind, and men, by their very nature, are predispositioned to serve us in return. The dronon knew that if they could control us, we Tharrin might hold the key to controlling mankind. None of us can escape what we are. And in some cases, we cannot escape what we feel, what we must do."

Ceravanne wiped her eyes, leaned back, and looked at Maggie. "The Inhuman argues for greater compassion, and to the Tharrin its arguments seem persuasive, for the Tharrin have always sought to rule with compassion above all else. And so the dronon use our most basic needs to undermine us. But the Inhuman's Word does more to us than that—it seeks to manipulate its victims subconsciously. It convinces them that only by surrendering their individual freedom can they hope to serve mankind with total compassion—"

Gallen and Maggie both said at once, "By best serving the state, we best serve mankind." They looked into each other's eyes, recognizing that the idea they'd spoken had not been their own, but had been planted in them by the Inhuman.

"Exactly," Ceravanne said. "But of course when the state becomes supreme, it inevitably becomes corrupt, catering to some undefinable mass rather than to the individual. By trying to serve everyone, ultimately it serves no one well. You've seen how ruthless the Tekkar are, yet even they believe that their ruthlessness toward others is in fact a compassionate service to the state.

"The dronon do not care about this flaw in their system, for they are hopelessly enthralled by their Golden Queen, and they have no ideals beyond serving her. But we Tharrin agonize over the problem. We are trained to consistently review our actions so that we leave humans as much individual ability to make choices as they desire—"

"But you can never leave us totally free," Maggie said. "You always have the desire to manipulate us. I've seen it in the way that you treat Gallen."

"I was wrong to try to control him," Ceravanne said. "If I had not felt that my own world was at stake, I would not have done it. I . . . was so afraid, that I was not thinking well. What I did was contemptible. Please forgive me."

Maggie watched her, and though her expression showed only compassion, there was a hardness in her eyes. She might forgive Ceravanne, but she no longer trusted her completely, and she would not forget what Ceravanne had done.

"Sometimes I wonder," Maggie said. "How do I know you are not trying to manipulate me now?"

Ceravanne studied Maggie and considered how she might best address this question. She could have said something to placate the woman, but she did not want to frost the hard facts with sweet-tasting half-truths. "I am trying to manipulate you, of course," Ceravanne said. "I have shown you my world's need, and I have asked you to enlist with me and risk your lives in my cause. But I have not tried to deceive you about the dangers involved. I ask you to come willingly.

"But of course," Ceravanne continued, "on the larger scale we must also consider your biological needs, your inborn desire to serve your fellow man. That is what motivates you now. And in fact, Maggie, I suspect that whether I am a Tharrin or not makes little difference at the moment. If I were a Derrit leading you on this quest, you would still follow me, despite my odor and ungainly appearance.

"But as to the larger question as to whether you are free, of course we cannot lead men who are totally free, because none of us is free of the basic human desires that define what we are. So, ultimately, none of us are free, and all must share responsibility for our group acts.

"Perhaps only if you were a Tharrin could you understand completely how dependent we are upon one another—and how much responsibility a leader has for the group: if I call a man into battle, and we win, I must always wonder if I've done the right thing, if my enemies deserved death. But if we lose the fight, and the man I've called into battle dies, then I have to wonder if I'm responsible." Ceravanne took Maggie's hand and squeezed it. Maggie sat down beside her on the soft, green bench. "I can ask myself, Did the man die because our enemies were too strong? Did the man die because he was too weak or too unprepared? Or did the man die because I failed to resolve the conflict peacefully long before that?

"It may be that in any given defeat, I am totally at fault. It may be that the man died because of all my failures. And so when we resort to battle, we Tharrin always count ourselves as having lost the conflict, for we are ill-prepared to tolerate such guilt.

"For this reason, we prefer never to resolve conflicts through violence. Often we accept the responsibilities of leadership only so long as they do not lead into battle.

"This resolve is so strong that when my people here on Tremonthin saw what the Inhuman could do, most of my brothers and sisters removed the records of their genome and their memories from the City of Life, then destroyed themselves outright in order to avoid capture. We had to avoid becoming pawns in the dronon's game."

Orick had been sitting quietly on the floor, resting, but he perked his head up, raised his nose questioningly in the air. "But you said earlier that the dronon had *killed* your people?"

"I've never said 'killed.' They *destroyed* my people," Ceravanne corrected. "Those that they did convert became . . . monsters, creatures that we Tharrin find reprehensible. And so they were no longer Tharrin. And by forcing upon us this conflict, others of my people were forced to seek oblivion. I did not lie when I said they destroyed us."

"How many Tharrin are under the Inhuman's domination?" Gallen said.

"The Resistance killed the others. As for the Harvester—I am still not even certain that she is Tharrin," Ceravanne said, "though I have greatly suspected that my sister is there. . . . But if they do have my clone, it is just one."

Gallen's focus turned inward for a moment, and he rocked in his seat. The flier was equipped with benches with thick green cushions that were very comfortable, and he leaned back casually and said, "When we first met, you suspected that you wanted me to kill your dark sister?"

Ceravanne nodded. She knew that to their eyes, she still looked very much like a child of fourteen. She'd thought that by keeping a younger body, it might afford her some protection, provide something of a disguise. Adults in power tended to discount youth. And yet she had also felt the need to try to attract Gallen sexually. "I knew when we met that you might have to fight off the influence of the Inhuman, and that you might be forced to kill my dark twin. I wanted your commitment for those things only."

She did not admit that she wanted him because she'd known immediately that he was the clone of her beloved Belorian, and that she was in love with the image of the man she remembered, and that she hoped that Gallen might become that man still. Perhaps both he and Maggie might recall her reasons, but Ceravanne spared reminding them of this sad fact. She spared reminding them most of all because as she looked at Gallen, saw how faithful he'd remained to Maggie, he reminded her more than ever of Belorian. Indeed, he had been reborn both in body and spirit, but had given himself to another, and Ceravanne could not seek his affection in good conscience, though the pain of being so close to him tore at her heart. And so she was resolved that she would leave them gracefully, with a lie.

"So," Gallen said, "Maggie and I have tasted the persuasions of the Inhuman, but you, Ceravanne, still seem to know our enemy better than either of us can. What is the Harvester's next step?"

"I'm not certain. I cannot guess what memories my clone might have, and those memories could turn her on paths that I might not anticipate," Ceravanne said. "But I fear that she may have all of my memories, along with those of the Inhuman. But even if she doesn't, as the Bock were fond of reminding me, we are our bodies. I know what she feels. I may know how she thinks. And so I imagine myself in her place. . . . If I were the Harvester, I would try to minimize the amount of force needed for the operation. I would seek converts, not corpses."

"And how would you do that?" Gallen asked.

"I would seek to indoctrinate every man and woman on the planet by supplying them with the Word. If a person remains neutral after indoctrination, I would accept this. But if they actively tried to fight after their indoctrination, I would do nothing . . . just let the Tekkar handle it, as—to my shame— I let my people handle the Rodim ages ago. And all of the evidence leads me to believe that this is precisely the path that the Harvester is taking."

"So you don't believe the Harvester will go to war?" Gallen asked.

"I can only guess," Ceravanne said. "And I imagine not. Yet we in Northland can't not prepare for that eventuality."

The deep voice of the ship's AI sounded—"Approaching destination"— and Ceravanne herself was forced to go to the front and describe how to reach the Vale of the Bock.

The aircar settled down then in a valley at the foot of the mountains, and Ceravanne looked out the windows. Snow was on the ground on the mountain peaks, silver in the moonlight. And in the Vale of the Bock, a single teardrop-shaped pool also glowed silver, its water unrippled. It gave off only a thin mist, which was odd, for at this time of year the hot springs here often fogged the cold air. Which suggested that it was an unusually warm evening, almost summer weather.

All around the pool, the Bock stood with arms raised, looking for all the world like twisted stumps. On a gentle hill above the vale, a temple made of white stone glowed yellow in the night because of the fires burning at the twin beacons beside each temple door. The gentle Riallna devotees who tended the Bock were already locked in for the night. Yet Ceravanne was concerned that the air transport landing so near the temple would frighten the Riallna, so she decided to let them know that it was she who had come.

She ran out into the evening air, using Gallen's glow globe for light, and hurried up to the temple, knocked at the door. In a moment, to Ceravanne's surprise, a Riallna devotee actually opened her door just a crack and peeked out, terrified. The devotee was a plump woman of middle age for her species, a woman named Alna, and Ceravanne had known her for a hundred years.

"Do not be afraid," Ceravanne whispered. "I've been to Moree, and we captured an aircar. I've come back tonight to speak to the Bock. We will sleep in our car, and leave in the morning."

The dear Alna gazed out at her in surprise, unconcerned about the possibility that Ceravanne might be Inhuman. "You'll do no such thing. You'll have a good dinner and some music by the fire, and sleep with us tonight," and then she opened the door wide and gave Ceravanne a hug.

"Oh, thank you," Ceravanne said.

"But first," Alna said, reconsidering, "I think that you and your friends should bathe, while we fix your dinner." The tone of her voice clearly let Ceravanne know that a bath was not optional, it was required.

Ceravanne went back into the main cabin of the transport and found Gallen and Maggie searching through the food stores.

Ceravanne said, "I've been informed by the priestess of the temple that if we would like a nice dinner and a warm bed tonight, we need only to take a bath and wash out our clothes. The night is warm, and the pools here are heated by hot springs, which is why the Bock winter in this valley. Would anyone care to join me?"

It had been so long since they'd had a chance to bathe in anything but an icy river, that Ceravanne was not surprised when the others eagerly came out and enjoyed the luxury together, swimming naked in the moonlight. Orick the bear began slapping water at Ceravanne, and she splashed him back, and soon they were chasing one another around the pool and having a great time.

Afterward, they returned to the transport to get their packs, and in the darkness, Gallen said, "Ceravanne, when we first met, you asked me not to question you about your plans. You asked me to simply trust you, and till now I have. But we'll be going into Moree tomorrow. I came with the idea of destroying the Inhuman, dismantling the artificial intelligence that drives it. But you obviously hope to reclaim the Harvester. Is that your plan?"

"If I can reason with her," Ceravanne said, "yes, I think I can reclaim her. But there is much more that I hope to do."

Ceravanne went to her pack. It was a small pack made of brown leather, and she'd carried it a long way without anyone becoming suspicious of its contents. It held but one change of dirty clothes and a comb, and in all these past weeks, she had never given the others a clue as to what else might be inside it.

She pulled out a small but heavy parcel wrapped in fine leather and laid it out on the floor, then began to unfold it. The thin golden chains that formed it tinkled as she worked, and the memory crystals woven into it glittered like diamonds. When it was all laid out on the floor, the huge mantle looked like the treasure of some ancient king. "This is what the Inhuman looks like," Ceravanne said. "This is an exact replica. Over the past two years, we gleaned information from all of the technicians who worked on it. In the City of Life, our technicians are not well versed in making such things, and so it was a great task. But we were able to learn whose lives are stored within the Inhuman, and so we went to our archives and retrieved those lives, whole and unedited, and placed them in this mantle. We could not get them all, for the dronon were careless, and so some of those people's memories were lost forever. And in those cases, we replaced the lost crystals with new ones, showing the lives of those who *were* successful in obtaining rebirth.

"And our technicians created a program that will nullify the subliminal teachings that the Inhuman tries to plant in its victims."

"You mean you are going to fight the Inhuman's indoctrination?" Maggie asked, for like Gallen, she had assumed that the destruction of the Inhuman was their ultimate goal.

"We will do what we can," Ceravanne said. "If we can only destroy the Inhuman, burn it forever, then much will have been accomplished. But I fear that if that were to happen, our world would continue in civil war. You've seen the weapons that the dronon left: if it comes to war, this world will yet be destroyed. But even that is better than letting the Inhuman's influence spread to the stars.

"Better still, the Council of Immortals in the City of Life hopes to diminish its influence. We hope to combat it on its own terms, counter its lies by telling the truth."

"But," Orick growled, "you'll be little better than they are. You'll have your own Word burrowing into Maggie's skull!"

Ceravanne shook her head violently. "I do not understand a great deal about how this technology works," she said. "But I know this: everyone who has ever been affected by the Word already has a built-in receiver, and this mantle can send to the Inhuman's frequencies. But our mantle isn't fully operational. If it were, we could send our message out now and be done with it."

"What more do you need?" Maggie asked. "Maybe my mantle can help you make it?"

"We need the *key* to the Inhuman," Ceravanne said. "When a Word burrows into its victim, it sends a coded message telling the Inhuman to begin sending information. The memories are then sent, but they are only readable by the Word that requested them."

"So this 'key' contains an encryption program?" Maggie asked. She sounded so much like one of the technicians in the City of Life that her question startled Ceravanne.

"Yes, that is what the technicians called it."

"And they couldn't just break the encryption program?"

Ceravanne shook her head. "The key was made by the dronon, using their own technologies. Our people cannot duplicate it. But I do know that if you take the key off the mantle, the Inhuman will cease to function, for the key also bears the power source for the memory crystals on the mantle."

"And so in the most favorable scenario," Gallen said, "you would capture this key intact. Is that what you imagine?"

Ceravanne nodded. "If I can speak to the Harvester, I hope she will give it to me. If not, you may have to kill her and take the Inhuman's key."

Gallen rubbed his chin thoughtfully. Perhaps he had imagined rushing into a room, killing everyone and everything there, considering that the job would be finished. But Ceravanne had come to see that it could not be done so easily. She had imagined that the journey into Moree itself would be an easy walk, with only minor elements of intrigue—not a constant mad dash for her life. And now she saw that stealing the key to the Inhuman would be no small feat. Obviously, by the way that Maggie and Gallen furrowed their brows, they were thinking along the same lines.

Gallen got up, paced in the darkness, gazed off south toward Moree. The windows in the aircar showed only the mountains. He rubbed his hands together as if to warm them with the friction. "Moree is a hive worse than the city of Indallian, and its keepers are more fearsome than any tribe of Derrits. Do we even have an idea where to find the Harvester in that maze?"

Ceravanne went to her pack again. "Traders have been to Moree often enough, and some of them have been to the old king's throne room. It is well defended, and we believe that the Harvester is there. I have some intelligence on the place." She brought out a large map on thick gray paper. It showed three routes into the city, and from each route it displayed the number of doorways and chambers to the Harvester's throne room.

Gallen studied it for a moment, and his brow furrowed in dismay. Much of the map consisted of blank spaces, unknowable regions of the city that could easily house warriors. But what the map *did* show was that with each route, there were several guarded entrances, fortified gates. The Tekkar were a fierce race, created for a harsh world where survival seemed improbable, and their inborn need for a strong defense showed in the design of their city. It made for an impossible journey through the warrens of the Tekkar.

That evening, Gallen was relieved to find that instead of another sleepless night sitting among cold stones, he was able to enjoy the company of the Riallna in their temple at the Vale of the Bock.

The Riallna devotees were all women, with cream-colored complexions and hair that was long and as soft and golden brown as corn silk, and though he knew that they were each hundreds of years old, they looked as if they were only handsome women of middle years. Their lives were simple and peaceful, and in their own way they were as devoted to making the world a place of beauty as any of the Makers.

On the outside, the temple seemed to be only a large blockish building of ivory-colored stone with a row of four fluted-stone columns that rose in front to form a large porch. It was a variation on a theme common in this rainy region, and it was a simple design, and graceful.

But inside, the temple was a masterpiece of functionality and comfort. The walls were covered over in some gold cloth and decorated with large wooden panels of ash, carved with delicate scenes of the suns rising over mountain fields.

On the main floor, low beds were laid out on rich carpets around a central fireplace that was shaped into a tall cone, with perhaps a dozen small holes near the bottom so that heat and light could escape the fire, while the smoke would be drawn up the chimney.

Various oil lamps burned around the room, keeping the place bright inside, but the soft wine-colored sofas and the forest-green carpets muted the brightness, creating a lighting that reminded Gallen of a forest glen at dusk, rampant with earth tones.

Evidence that the Riallna had a strong sense of smell was also abundant. Gallen noted a cleanness, a freshness to the room that had seldom been duplicated among other cultures. The scents of lightly seasoned foods were evident, but no harsh perfumes, and perhaps it was the scent more than anything else that gave the room a sense of wide spaces, an openness that size alone did not account for.

In moments, the Riallna began serving them silently, bringing in warm water to wash with first, followed by plates heaping with food. Some of the priestesses played flutes and cymbals at the far side of the great hall, so that the music of woodwinds floated dreamily through the air, and Ceravanne's friend Alna sat quietly with them, anticipating their needs, willing to let them steer the conversation in any direction they desired.

After a while, it became evident that the priestesses were seeking to serve their every whim, to give themselves completely in a manner that Gallen had seldom seen, even among the many lives the Inhuman had shown him, and he was pleased by the effect. He knew that this night, he was free to do whatever he pleased—whether it be to eat, sleep, listen to others, or talk quietly, and he realized suddenly how shallow the Inhuman's training had been.

Among the lives that he'd been shown, none of the peoples he'd met had been as generous as the Riallna. Instead, they'd often been grasping and outright selfish. Perhaps not overtly so, but it ran like a strong current beneath all of their actions. Even the best of the people he recalled had been . . . unconcerned about anyone beyond their own kin.

And as Gallen considered where he most would like to be this night—home in Tihrglas listening to some old hand playing the violin, or among the Suluuth listening to the piping song of the winged people, or on the plains singing at the stars with the Roamers, he realized that he was most content to be here.

Almost effortlessly, he fell asleep beside Maggie upon one of the couches, unaware of when the music ended.

Shortly after dawn, Gallen woke to the sounds of women cooking. Orick was asleep on one couch, lying on his back, his paws in the air. Maggie slept beside Gallen, and he gently disentangled himself from her arms. Ceravanne was no place to be seen, and Gallen imagined that she might be out bathing in the pool again.

He got up, wanting to plan for the day's coming battle, so headed out to the transport.

The suns were just rising in a soft violet haze over the mountains, and down the slope below the temple, the Bock had gathered near the pool, where they were dipping their feet into the pool's edge.

Ceravanne was sitting down with them, dressed in a clean green tunic that one of the priestesses must have given her. She was talking energetically to the same Bock that Gallen had met before, though something odd was happening. When they'd first met a few weeks before, the Bock had been a dark green in color, but now the color of its skin was tinted with a grayish-brown, like the stalk of a plant that is dying. Gallen walked toward them.

The Bock spoke back to Ceravanne, slowly, in dreamy tones, telling her, "Too late, too late for me to come now. Winter is upon us . . . task falls to you!"

Gallen stopped beside them for a moment, looked up at the green man, with his knobby joints, his long fingers splayed up toward the sun.

"Is everything all right?" Gallen asked Ceravanne.

She looked up at him. "The Bock are not awake yet. They have trouble this time of year. When the sun rises a bit more, and the blood warms in his veins, he will understand me more."

"Can't . . . can't go," the Bock said dreamily, the voice of an old man, long senile.

"I'll leave you two, then," Gallen said. He went to the transport, got Ceravanne's map out for further study, laid it out on the floor, trying to imagine alternate routes into the Tekkar warren that might exist somewhere in the gray unknown spaces the map did not show.

In a few minutes, Maggie came to join him. "The Riallna are making breakfast for us," she whispered, kneeling behind him. "I told them we'd be there in a while." She too was wearing her mantle and a new green tunic, and she knelt over the map just behind him to his right. Gallen inhaled her clean scent, tasted her exotic perfumes from Fale, and was very conscious of the way her left breast pressed against his arm. He felt somehow old. I should be rutting with her, celebrating with her, instead of making plans for war, he considered, but he put the stray thought from his mind.

Maggie stroked him quickly up the spine with the back of her hand—an act that made the nerves tingle all along his body. It was an odd caress, one that the Worren women used to good effect in their lovemaking. They were a lusty people and Gallen smiled at some of his memories.

"I love it when you smile at private little dirty jokes like that," Maggie said. She put both hands on his shoulders, knelt behind him, and nibbled his ear. "You know, darlin'," she said in her rich brogue, "I know more tricks than any madam in Baille Sean. In fact, I'll bet the Inhuman taught me more than the whole lot of them know together."

Gallen licked his lips, considered what it would mean to have someone with the memories of an Inhuman as a lover. "Then I'd say our time here has been well spent for that, if for nothing else."

Maggie giggled and twisted him down to the floor, then straddled him, commanded the car's AI to close and lock the security door to the transport, then she smiled at Gallen and wiggled enticingly. "It would be a shame if we disturbed the others with all of our moaning and yelling, now wouldn't it?"

Gallen nodded, and Maggie bent over and kissed him, and her breasts brushed against his chest. She just knelt there for a moment staring into his eyes, and then she began to untie his tunic slowly, sometimes reaching up to stroke his face or to snatch a kiss in gestures that he recalled from dozens of lovers over a hundred lifetimes. And yet being with her was better than being with any of the others, for Gallen saw that she knew all of the women he had ever loved, and with her gestures, she showed that she was willing to become all of them, to give what each had given before.

Gallen reached up and began to untie the strings on the front of her tunic, but Maggie shook her head, did it herself, and pulled off her clothes.

For the next half hour, Maggie led him on a tour of wonderland, and what they shared was as pure and beautiful as any moment he ever remembered. Somewhere in the lovemaking, he recalled some of the things he'd learned about women over the past six thousand years, and he began to give as good as he'd gotten, so that at the height of her excitement Maggie actually let out a jubilant shout of "Thank God and Gallen O'Day!" though when he teased her about it later, she denied recalling that she'd ever said it.

When they finished, Gallen held her for a long time, just lying on the cushions of the benches, and realized that for the first time in weeks he'd been able to completely forget about the Inhuman, about the world, and just enjoy the one woman he loved.

For a long time, he said nothing, till the suns began to shine higher through their window, and then Maggie said, "I was meaning to ask, what did you come in here for, anyway?"

"I was studying the map of Moree," Gallen said, "trying to figure out how to get in, but I don't see any easy path."

Maggie smiled at him. "That's because you're looking at the wrong map." She looked up toward the ceiling, to the crystalweb in the cryotank above the doorway. "Car, can you see the map Gallen has here spread out on the floor?"

"Yes," the car's AI said.

"Show us a holo of the aerial view of Moree, as it was last night, and superimpose your image over the map."

A holoimage appeared on the floor, an image of hills and trees in perfect miniature. Gallen sat up, and his feet sank into the landscape just below the knees, and he felt like a giant towering over the earth. The land around Moree was a yellow desert, with but one thin river flowing through it. Gallen could see individual Russian olive and juniper trees clumped among the rocks, and along the river was a veritable sea of cattails. By looking close, he could see the smoke holes from chimneys carved in rocks, along with the rare entrances where the Tekkar let in light to their world. Much of the land above the warrens was dedicated to farms that were carefully tended at night.

The starport facilities spread out on three sides of Moree, with five separate ships, like silver globes, set equidistantly around the city.

Crouching to the north, south, and west of Moree were three dronon walking fortresses, like huge black crabs guarding the carrion from which they would make a meal.

South of Moree were parked seven aircars, lozenge-shaped vehicles like the one they were in. "Wait a minute," Gallen said, pondering the image. "Car, is this the total number of air vehicles that have been created?"

"Yes," the car said.

Gallen looked closely at the holograph. The airfield at Moree was only lightly guarded by a handful of men—and they were best positioned for a ground assault.

"Do you see what I see?" Gallen asked Maggie. She looked at him craftily, and Gallen suspected that she did. "The Tekkar are ready to fend off a ground assault, but they're not prepared to fight off an air attack."

"Of course not," Maggie said. "These are the first aircars they've ever owned, and they know that Northland has no air power. So they haven't even considered how to best defend them. The servants of the Inhuman are relying on techniques and tactics they've learned over the past six thousand years—not the tactics your mantle knows."

Gallen considered, questioned his mantle about the best way to assault the city from this transport. The other military fliers at Moree were parked too close to one another—a single rocket could blow them all into vapor. And the walking fortresses would not be able to defend the airfield from a smart missile fired a hundred kilometers away.

He considered shooting at the fortresses, too, but shook his head. His memories from Tkintit, a Dronon technician, warned him that those walking fortresses were so heavily armored that he couldn't make much of a dent in them, and they had enough firepower to devastate his little transport. But Maggie pointed out that the whole reason the starships were spaced so far out from the city was to avoid damage to metropolitan areas in case the combustible liquids stored in the exterior radiation shields leaked out and caught fire. In space the liquids cooled to below their freezing point, and there was no danger of the shields exploding on impact with a meteor. But so long as they were down here in the atmosphere, those starships were just fancy bombs, and one of Gallen's rockets could light a fuse that would blow the nearest hive fortress off its feet, and Gallen suddenly saw some interesting ways to wreak havoc on the Tekkar. Four missiles was all he had—one for the airfield, one for each of three starships.

"You know," Gallen said, "if we convinced the Tekkar that our purpose in attacking was to destroy their technological buildup, it could form a decent diversion, allowing us to land near the Harvester's throne room."

By studying the map he realized that in all likelihood, a single rocky hillside hid the chambers where the Harvester lived. The hill was nestled deep in the heart of the city, and from the air it looked rather innocuous. But if the maps were right, then somewhere on the hill's northern slope, a huge chamber had been hollowed out. Gallen imagined that if they could blow a hole in that room, they could drop themselves right into the middle of the city. But after a few moments, he shook his head in dismay. "I'm not sure. This vehicle has enough firepower to knock out the airfield and probably even take out a couple of spaceships, but I might not have enough rockets to blow a hole into those chambers."

Maggie shook her head, and her mantle jangled. "You're still thinking like some backward hick. What is it that makes our aircar fly?"

"The fusion reactor?" he said.

"No," Maggie answered, "that's the power source. The car flies on waves of directed antigravity."

Gallen looked at her, and his mantle began to hint to him what she planned, but he did not have a technician's mantle, with its own arcane wisdom, so he let her explain it. "Most of the time the antigrav generator gives off weak pulses, but I can vary those—creating phased wavelengths if I want to. And I guarantee that none of these subterranean hives here on Tremonthin were built to withstand the stresses I could put on them! If I fly over this subterranean city, spiking out harmonic frequencies—well, these Tekkar will be surprised at how quickly their stone walls can get pounded into sand."

Gallen looked up into Maggie's eyes. "Do you know how many people you're talking about killing? There may be a half million or more Tekkar in that city."

Maggie leaned back, and her hair fell behind her shoulders, accentuating the impassive lines of her face. "Gallen, when we talked to Ceravanne, you must have noticed that she has no idea how to run a war. She wants to go to Moree and 'talk to' the Harvester, for God's sake! Well, that's not how *we're* going to do it. The dronon brought technology here to use as a weapon, and the Inhuman is tearing these people apart. I think we should cram these weapons down their throats and let them know just how monstrous a war can be."

"We're talking about killing innocent women and children," Gallen said. And he surprised himself by saying "we're," for he knew that he had to consider it.

Maggie shrugged. "So hit them where they least expect it. Play on the Harvester's weaknesses, and on the Inhuman's inexperience. We can't afford to be nice. We can't afford to fight cleanly. I keep . . . I keep thinking about something my uncle Thomas told me just before we left Tihrglas. When he came into the inn, he planned to move in and use me badly. He lay on one of the beds in my inn, wearing his dirty boots, and he said something like, 'If you ever have to play the villain in someone's life, play your part well. Savor it. It's one of the greatest joys in living.' He hinted that you should stab the fellow in the back, and twist the knife with glee.

"Well, the Inhuman tried its best to make our last two weeks on this planet a living hell, and I for one don't think we should pull our punches. When you see the Harvester, Gallen O'Day, I'll not have you making any nice kissy faces at her just because she's Ceravanne's clone. If you don't blow her head off, I will!"

Gallen stared at her in wonder. "Jesus, you Flynns are a bad-tempered lot! It's a wonder the priests don't catch on and drown the lot of you when you're born!" Gallen leaned back, and his mantle was already considering the approach it would use when they attacked. He could trace the battle lines in his imagination.

He considered the carnage they would wreak on Moree, wondered about alternatives. Maggie was right. Her diabolical ideas did have the virtue of offering them the best chance at success, but Gallen couldn't bring himself to seriously consider such a plan. In some ways, he realized, Maggie was tougher than he was. She'd been the one who first put her life on the line when battling the dronon, and now she was willing to wage a full-fledged war with the Tekkar.

He looked back down at the holographic image hovering over the floor, his legs rising like giant tree trunks from the land. But the image of the land transposed over Ceravanne's map gave him an idea.

Thirty-one

That morning, after Gallen and Maggie announced their battle plans, Ceravanne took Gallen aside and argued against his method long and vigorously. Neither she nor the Bock could countenance the kind of attack he proposed. They were standing in the Vale of the Bock, beside the hot pools, which shone emerald in the morning light. It was a bright day, and fair here, and it seemed to Maggie somehow odd to be talking of such things in the bright sunlight. Around Maggie, Gallen, Ceravanne, and Orick, dozens of the Bock had gathered, and they stood nearly motionless in the morning sun, their hands upraised as if they were some strange priests gathered in convocation, offering up their prayers to Tremonthin's double suns. But Ceravanne's favorite Bock stood beside Gallen and Ceravanne, as if to referee the dispute.

"Remember, Gallen," Ceravanne warned him, her voice shaking from emotion, "I want no violence, if we can avoid it. Not all of those infected by the Inhuman are evil. Like you, they are people, just people who were infected—by something they did not understand and something they lacked the ability to fight!"

Ceravanne's eyes blazed, and Maggie was surprised, for she'd never seen a Tharrin show anger.

"But if we fail here today, this world may not get another chance at freedom."

"And I would rather lose my freedom than destroy one innocent life!" Ceravanne argued. She looked like only a young girl, with her pale green eyes blazing and her platinum-blond hair. For the first time since they met, Maggie sensed that Ceravanne was losing control, speaking openly of her deepest feelings.

"But you cannot make that choice for others," Gallen shouted. "I won't let you! I've already modified my plans so that I spare as many of the Tekkar as I feel safe in doing. If that does not gratify you, then I will leave you displeased! Perhaps I should take your mantle and fight this battle without you!"

"No, please!" Ceravanne said, and her voice faltered, as if she'd never considered the possibility that Gallen would go into battle without her. She begged, "I must come. Don't deny me that. I've already seen all of my own people destroyed in this conflict. And far too many people of other races have been maimed or slaughtered. If I can save only one life, then it will be worth it. I've convinced the Bock to come with us. He too may offer some help."

Gallen's voice became softer. "Your Tharrin compassion does you merit, but it also is your greatest weakness. I wish you would stay out of this."

"This world is my home," Ceravanne said, and she knelt forward a little, almost as if bowing to Gallen, pleading. "I must serve it as I can. There are children in the Tekkar's warrens. Innocents. Be gentle with them. Please, let me speak to the Harvester. Perhaps between us we can resolve this."

Maggie watched Gallen, and though both she and Gallen had known that Ceravanne would argue for this, and both of them had agreed that they should leave her behind, such was the quality of Ceravanne's voice, her ability to persuade, that Maggie suddenly found herself unable to argue against the woman. Indeed, to have done so would have been cruel.

Maggie knew that it was only a combination of pheromones, body language, and the use of voice that made them give in. And perhaps it was their own desires that Ceravanne was working on. But as Ceravanne leaned forward, looking like little more than a child herself, the sunlight falling on her golden hair, her words seemed to weave a powerful spell, so powerful that Gallen's voice was stopped almost in mid-sentence. And suddenly Maggie saw why Ceravanne had been admired for millennia on this world. She'd helped bring peace to warring races for thousands of years, and such was the power of her presence that Maggie felt almost compelled to throw down the Dronon pulp gun she'd stowed in her waistband.

Ceravanne took Gallen's hand. "Do you not think that the Harvester argues for peace against the Tekkar, even as I sue for peace with you now? Why else do you think they have not attacked Northland yet? We see now that they could easily take it," Ceravanne said. And Maggie knew that it must be true. Ceravanne's other self was suing for peace two thousand kilometers away. "Once we reach her throne room, there will be no need for weapons or battle. The Harvester will not let her people hurt you, if she sees me and the Bock in your retinue. That much, I feel confident, I can promise you."

"Ceravanne is right," the Bock urged in his slow voice, the brown-tinged leaves at his crown rustling in the morning wind. "She has experience with many races, even the Tekkar. I do not hesitate to put my own life in her hands."

Gallen studied the Bock, his face still set and implacable. "All right, then," he said. "I will give you a moment with the Harvester—no more. If you do not succeed in persuading her, I will kill her."

Ceravanne closed her eyes gratefully, and sighed. She took Gallen's hand and kissed it. "I—thank you," she said, too overcome with gratitude to speak more, and Maggie wondered then if perhaps they had not given in too easily.

After they had discussed their plans once again, they saw the Riallna come down from the hill, bearing a breakfast of cheeses and fresh rolls filled with fruit.

They spread the food out into a circle and ate, watching one another in the morning light, and Maggie's heart was full.

And Orick the bear ate his rolls with fruit, licking the jam from his upper lips so that his tongue almost wrapped around his snout.

Gallen and Maggie silently held hands as they ate, sharing secret glances. The Bock gathered down at the banks of the pool and stood with their toes stretching out into the water, while the Riallna washed their feet with a paste of nutrients.

And so it was that as they finished eating, a few meadowlarks began to sing, and Orick began to speak slowly. Maggie had always known that Orick wanted to be a priest, and she had imagined him as an ascetic, perhaps some monastic brother living in the woods. She'd never thought him to be one with any missionary tendencies, but he spoke softly to Ceravanne then of the things that were in his heart.

"You know," he told her, "it hasn't escaped my notice that you don't have any proper churches here."

"The Riallna have their temples, the Bock have their woods," Ceravanne said. "And others build places to worship."

"But what of Catholic churches?" Orick asked. "What of Christianity?"

"What is that?" Ceravanne asked. And Maggie suspected that because she respected the bear and saw him as a friend, she asked kindly, as if she were truly interested.

"I've had a mind to tell you about it," Orick said, and then he told her of a young man named Jesus who, like her, sued for peace among mankind thousands of years ago, then gave his life for others. Orick told her how Jesus had died, betrayed by a friend, and how on the night before his death, he had broken bread and blessed wine, asking his disciples to always do this act in remembrance of his sacrifice.

Then, to Maggie's surprise, the bear said, "Normally, I don't have proper authority from the Church to do these things, but I think that they must be done. Today we go into Moree." And with that apology he began singing the words to the Sacrament, and he took some rolls and passed them around, and Gallen fetched a skin of wine, and each of them took it.

Orick then gave a brief prayer, asking God to bless them on their journey and deliver them from harm, and Maggie felt the solemnity of the occasion.

After the sacrament they each made final preparations for the battle. Gallen checked his weapons, while the Bock stood gazing at the sky. Ceravanne laid her pack on the grass. She reached into it, put on a gray silk cloak with a deep hood. Then she unwrapped her mantle and put it on her head, its golden ringlets falling down her shoulders. Last of all, she pulled up the hood to her robe, to conceal her mantle.

Maggie saw that Orick was shaken, pacing nervously, but Ceravanne rumpled the coarse black hair on the back of his neck, and whispered, "Now, let us go, but not in haste, and not in fear. If we go to our deaths, remember that it is but a brief sleep."

Those words held no comfort for Gallen, Orick, or Maggie. Though Maggie had a mantle herself, it could not save her, and Gallen already had

Tallea's memories stored in his own mantle. And Orick looked resigned. Though he had his faith to sustain him, Maggie knew he hungered for love and a life of peace, yet the road to any greater reward led down this dark path.

And suddenly Ceravanne caught her breath as she realized that what she had meant as a comforting word was only a cruel reminder to the others, since none had their memories recorded, none of them could be reborn, as Ceravanne could.

Orick growled lightly, and bounded forward to the aircar, followed by Ceravanne, the Bock, Gallen, and Maggie.

Maggie went to the cockpit, did a manual system's check, and as she did so, Gallen came in behind her, and she slid back up out of the pilot's seat, into his arms. They held each other for a long time. Gallen kissed her, brushing her forehead with his lips, and she leaned into him. "Promise me," he whispered fervently, "that once you drop me off, you'll get the transport away quickly. I don't want you sitting there, a target for the dronon's walking fortresses."

"I may be brave, but I'm not stupid." Maggie smiled up at him sweetly. "And you promise me—come back alive?"

"I guarantee, I plan to grow old with you," Gallen whispered. Then they kissed so long and tenderly that Maggie was sure that the others must be getting impatient. Gallen was slow to leave, to close the bulkhead door behind him.

Maggie strapped herself into the pilot's seat and had her mantle silently radio the ship's AI, link intelligence with it so that the ship would know her commands before she could articulate them.

Their flight time would be short, a swift hop at low altitudes over the ocean, with the ship's antidetection equipment operating at full capacity. Once they reached the Telgood Mountains, the ship's intelligent missiles would fire, taking out their primary targets, if those were still available, or taking the secondary or tertiary targets that Maggie had already chosen.

And so they slipped quietly over the ocean for the next few minutes as Maggie's mantle displayed the view ahead. The sky was clear until they reached the coasts of Babel, and there a thin line of dark clouds showed on the horizon, an approaching thunderstorm.

"Buckle in back there and prepare for rapid descent," Maggie called to the others.

The aircar dropped low and screamed over the hills and valleys just above the treetops at mach 9. The clouds and rain obscured her vision out the windows, so Maggie relied completely on the head-up holo that her mantle displayed. The holo showed the Telgoods looming ahead, a line of bony white teeth, and Maggie fired her smart missiles, then opened her eyes and looked out the front windows to verify that they left. The missiles streaked ahead of her on antigrav, leaving a flash as the air around them became superheated.

The aircar whirled, dove through some narrow canyons, and the AI fired a burst on the incendiary cannons, blasting a lone wingman from its path.

And suddenly the aircar seemed to leap in the air as it cleared a mountain, then lurched as it plummeted toward Moree.

"Four targets hit, three destroyed—" the AI flashed a message on her screen as soon as the ship had visuals. The head-up holo displayed the scene—three of the five dome-shaped spaceships going up in mushroom clouds. A fourth had been hit, but had not exploded. Maggie looked out the windows through a heavy rain, saw the trunk of fiery mushroom cloud begin billowing up as she passed, an incredible inferno. They were diving right through the periphery of its flames.

Two dronon walking fortresses had taken fire from the explosions. One was flying apart, huge metallic chunks spewing out in odd angles as its munitions blew. The other had flames boiling out its cargo hold and was trying to retreat from the white inferno that had once been a starship. The dronon walking fortress left a trail of flames and burning debris as it crawled away, looking for all the world like some great black spider in its death throes.

A smart missile was coming in from directly ahead, launched from one of the intact walking fortresses ten kilometers to the south, and Maggie almost subconsciously fired both plasma cannons, detonating the missile in midair so that a brilliant flash blinded her for a moment.

Their aircar was still dropping toward ground—toward the perpendicular rocky cliff face where the Harvester's chambers should be—when the AI flashed a message in red letters through the head-up holodisplay: "Permission to abort mission?"

Maggie looked about desperately at the scene below, wondering why the AI would ask that, wondering why one of her missiles hadn't taken out the Tekkar's airfield instead of a starship, its secondary target. She looked toward the dun-colored fields below and saw the reason: none of the Tekkar's military transports were on the field. They'd all been moved.

"No!" Maggie shouted in frustration, but her AI took that as a rejection of permission to abort, and in half a second they slammed to the ground, and her aircar began sending pulsed bursts of antigravity through the substrata.

Maggie looked out the windows, shouted, "Gallen, the airfield was clear! The Tekkar must have their transports out searching for us!"

But Gallen was already clearing the hold, with Orick, Ceravanne, and the Bock all following. Maggie silently willed her mantle to radio the message from mantle to mantle, and she looked around.

"Message received," Gallen said through his mantle. "But we can't stop now. Do what you can, then get out of here!"

Maggie wondered what to do. She couldn't leave Gallen stranded here in Moree, but certainly the Tekkar airships, with a capability for mach 10 speeds, would be here in seconds. Even if they were out a hundred kilometers away, they could be here in thirty seconds.

Maggie bit her lip, studied her surroundings. For the moment, her ship was partly hidden under the rock cliff face to her south. To the north and east, the mushroom clouds from the exploding starships were growing redder and redder as their caps of smoke and flame rose higher into the thunderheads. Static discharges caused by the explosion were suddenly setting off a series of lightning blasts that spanned the sky. The door to the shuttle hummed shut, and almost unconsciously Maggie realized that a huge hole had opened in the cliff face to her south. From inside the aircar, with the exterior sounds shielded, she heard and felt nothing as tons of rock slid down the face of the cliff, leaving a gaping hole.

Gallen, Ceravanne, and the others were running over the ground, and now that the hole was opened, the transport's AI began emitting a cloud of Black Fog, a harmless aerial dye that blocked nearly all light.

At this moment, Maggie was supposed to move the hovercar, begin circling on a path around the Harvester's suberannean throne room, collapsing the tunnels leading to the room so that the Harvester and the Inhuman would be sealed off from aid, and from any avenues of escape.

Maggie swung the hovercar forward in a long arc, covered a kilometer in a matter of seconds, and watched as her aircar's antigravity collapsed the tunnels ahead, leaving furrowed ruins.

Tunnels fell in and chambers opened in a regular pattern. Maggie had made nearly half the circle when an alarm sounded. Her AI flashed an image of two approaching aircraft, smart missiles blurring toward her.

Maggie had no missiles left to fire back, and it was too late to escape.

Orick was running up the hill behind Ceravanne and the Bock, with Gallen in the lead. A gritty rain hammered his snout, and red pillars of fire blazed across the countryside. All around them the ground had collapsed in pockets as tunnels and chambers caved in. In those places, Orick could see slabs of broken stone protruding from the ground. In many places across these fields, there were fires coming up out of the horrific rents, and dust rising from the earth. Armageddon. It looked like some vision of Armageddon.

Orick had seen that much of the damage was already done before their transport even landed—apparently the explosive power of the starships had been more than the architects of this city could have planned for.

Orick was running full tilt when suddenly the ground at his feet began to give way, and he lunged forward just as a tunnel collapsed beneath. In front of him a hundred yards there was a sound of splitting rock, and almost all of the face of the cliff just before the group began sliding down, as if it had been a sand castle dashed apart by a child's foot.

The sounds of the splitting rock, the roaring infernos of the distant mushroom clouds, the blasts of lightning, the cries of people, the shaking of the earth—all rose together in an incredible tumult, and for one breathless moment Orick stopped to watch in the distance as one of the starships—a gigantic globe nearly half a mile across—lifted from the ground without any visible means of propulsion, heading upward for the safety of the stars.

Gallen stopped for a moment, and Orick could feel the ground weaving and bucking beneath his feet. The movement bothered the humans and the Bock more than it did Orick, and they stood balancing precariously.

Where the rock wall had collapsed, they could see at least six levels of rooms that had been in that part of the Tekkar's city. At the highest level was a tall chamber, with forty-foot ceilings. The Harvester's throne room. But to reach it they would have to climb the wall of broken rubble that lay before them, scaling the stones.

"That way!" Gallen shouted, pointing out a path over the rocks.

The whole world smelled of fire and smoke and broken stone.

Orick was vaguely aware of Tekkar running through those apartments, of wounded people crying out, but suddenly a wall of Black Fog swept over them as Maggie released their camouflage. And then they were swallowed by utter darkness.

Ceravanne pulled the glow globe from her pocket, and even its brilliant white light would not let them see more than five yards ahead.

The aircar made a deep thrumming, grinding noise as it swung around to the southeast.

Gallen called to the others, telling them to form a group as they climbed. He was merely waiting for the ground to stop shaking, for rocks to quit sliding from the cliff wall above, and Orick hoped that as Maggie moved the aircar, it would become safer for them to begin running again.

And suddenly Orick heard the whine of rockets accelerating toward them, off toward the aircar. The rockets slammed into the car with a pinging noise, and a huge explosion lifted them all from their feet.

Orick looked toward the aircar for any sign of a flash or burning. But in the inky darkness, Orick could see nothing but a brief lightening of the darkness, and then bits of metal and rock and ash began to rain down upon them.

"Maggie!" Orick cried, and Gallen stood watching the empty space, a look of utter desolation on his face. "Maggie!" Orick called again, and he began to run toward the car.

"Stop!" Gallen shouted at Orick's back, and when Orick turned to look at his face, Gallen turned away. "She's gone," he said. "She's gone, and there's nothing we can do."

For one brief moment, it looked as if Gallen would crumple under his own weight. It looked as if some invisible support had been kicked out from beneath him, and he dropped partway to one knee. But then he lifted himself and began scrambling up the rocks. Orick heard Gallen sniff, saw him wipe at his eyes with his sleeve. Then Gallen pulled his dronon pulp gun, and his robes suddenly used their chameleon abilities to turn jet-black, to match the darkness.

Somehow, Orick found that he was unprepared for this. He'd imagined that if anyone would die in this battle, it would have been frail Ceravanne or the Bock or that maybe even Gallen would take on more than he could handle—but not Maggie.

"Gallen?" Orick cried at his back.

"She's gone," Gallen shouted, and he leapt forward to a boulder, then another, running up over the broken field of rubble without thought of stones still tumbling and crashing from the face of the cliff. Ceravanne ran behind him, calling for him to slow down, holding the light aloft, but she soon lost him in the dark.

And so she stopped and waited for the Bock and Orick to catch up. With his mantle, Gallen could see in the full darkness better than any man, and within seconds there was no sound of him.

Orick stopped beside Ceravanne, and the Bock made his way slowly over the rocks. Ceravanne nodded up toward where Gallen had run, and she muttered, "He's in a foul mood. Can you track him for us?"

Orick grumbled, "Not with those damned robes on. They mask his scent. I can't smell him."

Ceravanne sighed in disgust. "Then we'll track him by the corpses he leaves behind."

They began scrambling up over the fallen rocks from the cliff, and it seemed to take minutes upon minutes to get anywhere. As they passed beneath the cliff, they could still hear boulders and scree falling through the darkness around them, but they did not see the dropping stones. By now, between the thunderheads, the Black Fog, and the deep shadows of the Tekkar's city, the air around them was darker than any night.

And as they rushed through the rooms, Orick smelled blood ahead. The rooms were like nothing he had imagined: they had a peculiar fluid form to them, and the walls were covered with some white plaster. Orick could almost sense the sleek lines of some living creature, and he realized that the walls reminded him of nothing more than bones, as if they were in some vast hollowed-out bones.

There were torches lying about here and there, bodies crushed under falling rocks, tapestries sitting in heaps on the floor, wide silver washing or drinking vessels. And along the walls were thousands of small clay pots with long stems. Many had fallen over, and lay broken, with bits of ash and bone spilling out.

"What's this?" Orick called as they ran.

Ceravanne said, "The dead. It is said that the kings of Moree were protected by the spirits of their dead." And Orick saw that it was still true, more so than ever, for the Inhuman also relied upon those who had died for protection.

The group passed a Tekkar servant woman whose head was horribly crushed, part of her cheek ripped away, and she cried out from a swollen mouth, grasped the fur on Orick's leg, begging aid. Orick looked into her deep purple eyes as he passed, saw how they were not focused, and knew that she would die whether he helped her or not.

They reached some smoothly undulating stairs with golden handholds fastened to the wall, each shaped like the head of a dog.

They rushed up several flights, climbing over debris, and Orick saw Gallen's tracks in the dirt.

A moment later, they reached a landing and found the body of a Tekkar guard, his chest blown apart. And from up ahead there came shouting, followed by the burp of gunfire and the explosion of shells.

"This way," Ceravanne cried, leaping over the corpse, and she redoubled her speed as she chased the sound of battle.

And Orick suddenly realized that Gallen was doing it all without him, that Gallen had rushed ahead and was avenging Maggie by killing the Harvester and the Inhuman. Always in the past, he had been left behind. He'd let Gallen fight the great battles and get the glory, and never had he minded.

But over the past days, he'd lost three friends. Grits had been left behind, and Tallea was now food for the Derrits, and Maggie had just been blown apart, and Orick decided that he'd rather be damned in hell than let Gallen take all the vengeance this time.

They reached a huge set of double doors, twenty feet tall and ten feet wide, made of thick wooden planks with great brass rings to pull on. The doors were already opened just wide enough for a thin man to squeeze through.

Lying at the foot of the doors were eleven or twelve Tekkar, sprawled in a bloody heap. Orick leapt up and grabbed a brass ring in his teeth, then pulled back the door, swung it wider.

Ceravanne held up the glow globe, and peered inside. There was a great chamber, sixty feet long, with ceilings forty feet high. The dim red lights scavenged from a dronon hive city glowed at the far end, and beneath the lights on a broad-backed throne of gold sat a small woman, her shoulders hunched, a golden mantle cascading over her shoulders.

Gallen himself was kneeling before the throne, his mantle spread before him on the floor, his dronon pulp pistol discarded at his side. Orick's heart skipped a beat. Gallen had come all this way to protect them, to fight for them, and now Orick saw him kneeling, helpless before the Harvester. The heavy scent of the Harvester's pheromones filled the room, sweet and cloying.

For her part, the Harvester seemed to be staring into Gallen's face, and she looked up as Ceravanne and Orick entered, her sad green eyes gazing at them, so much like Ceravanne's eyes.

All along the walls were doorways, and at each doorway stood a Tekkar guard, draped in black robes that were longer than the norm, holding a sword pointed down toward the floor. Four guards lay sprawled upon the carpet just inside the door, where Gallen had killed them.

The Harvester reached out toward them, made a pulling gesture, as the

Inhuman's agents often did when greeting one another, and said softly, "I've been waiting for you."

The room's lights shone over her platinum hair, sparkled in her pale green eyes. Ceravanne looked at herself, the Harvester.

The Harvester glanced about at Gallen and the others in confusion. "It took only four of you to cause so much destruction?"

Ceravanne nodded, and her heart pounded in her chest. She looked to both sides. The air in here was still heavy with the scent of the explosive charges from the dronon pulp gun, but there was a mustier smell of things long dead. As Ceravanne scanned the room, she recognized the source. What she had first thought to be Tekkar guards lining the walls were in fact the dead, mummified remains of Tekkar, their bodies dried, their faces painted over with some preservative lacquer. Gallen had already killed the living guards, yet he knelt before the Harvester's throne, unmoving, and Ceravanne's heart pounded within her.

"What are you doing?" Orick growled at Gallen. But Gallen did not move, did not answer.

"You have damaged him," the Harvester said, and she reached down and removed Gallen's mantle. "Someone tried to remove his Word, but enough of it is still intact. He is Inhuman still, and here in Moree, he cannot harm me."

Ceravanne looked at Gallen in horror, saw that he was breathing heavily. He grunted, a faint cry, and Ceravanne realized that he was only holding still with a great struggle. The Inhuman held him.

"Who is he?" the Harvester asked, looking at Gallen's face.

"Don't you know?" Ceravanne asked. "He is Belorian."

"No," the Harvester said angrily. "Belorian is dead. His memories are lost."

"Yet his genome lives," Ceravanne said. "You know that much. And this one was reborn on a world like ours. He is Belorian in all but name."

The Harvester looked at him thoughtfully. "I shall keep him, then, as my own."

There was an electricity between the two women, almost sizzling. For long years, Ceravanne had wondered if even she could be subverted by the Inhuman, and now she saw the proof of it. If this woman remembered Belorian, then she could not be some empty-headed clone created by the dronon. This had to be Ceravanne's older self, the woman who'd been lost a year ago. Ceravanne, with all her memories intact. Here was a Tharrin who proposed to rule a world of slaves, who claimed that she would keep Gallen as her personal pet, and yet Ceravanne wondered. Ceravanne and the Harvester were of the same flesh. How could they take such divergent paths? Though Ceravanne often felt the tug, the desire to manipulate others to her own ends, she had rejected that path a million times. It seemed to Ceravanne that at the very core of their being, there must be some commonality, some shred of decency that they still shared.

"We share much," Ceravanne said, "but we do not share a belief that we can own others. I have come to reclaim you, my sister-self. I suspected that you could not be lost among the Tekkar. Even taken as a slave, you would soon make yourself queen."

"There is nothing here to reclaim," the Harvester whispered vehemently. "I am Inhuman now."

"A lover of war?" Ceravanne whispered. "Then why have not the Tekkar already been unleashed on Northland? Instead you send spies, carrying copies of the Word. It is a frail weapon indeed, for one who professes not to value life. No, you lead a peaceful war, a beneficent war, and you tame the dogs that serve you.

"Even now, I suspect that you have guards ready to do your bidding. Have them cut us down, if you can. But I know that you can't. No matter what the Inhuman has taught you, no matter how it has sought to turn you, we still share something." Ceravanne pointed to her heart.

Silently, two Tekkar swordsmen walked out from behind the throne, confirming Ceravanne's suspicions that there were more guards in the room.

"You sneer when you speak of my converts," the Harvester said. "I can hear your ill-conceived judgments in your voice."

"It is unnatural for a Tharrin to take slaves," Ceravanne said.

"The humans created us to be their slaves," the Harvester spat. "Loving masters, wise stewards, beloved lords—or so they call us. But we were made to serve. We are their drudges."

Is that what the Inhuman had taught her, Ceravanne wondered, contempt for mankind? "They love us, and we love them in return," Ceravanne said. "Is that slavery, or something greater? We—you and I—have always *given* ourselves to them freely."

"And what have they given you in return?" the Harvester spat.

"Their love, their companionship." Ceravanne gestured toward Gallen and the others. "I came in the name of the Sparrow, and three people gave their lives that I might make this journey in safety. What greater love could I ask of them? What less could I give in return?"

"Judgment!" the Harvester said. "Control! For ages you have sought to bring peace to this land. For generations you sought to bring the peoples of Babel together in harmony! And you failed! You failed with the Rodim, and for centuries have felt the worms of guilt eating at your soul. You have sought to bring about peace and happiness among mankind, but how can there be peace when there is no self-control? The Immortal Lords in the City of Life created the Rodim. They created the Tekkar. They created the Derrits and the Andwe and the Fyyrdoken—all without wisdom, always knowing the misery that such creatures would cause. For millennia they have set evils loose upon the world, ignoring your counsel *if* they ever deigned to seek it. You know that they are but ignorant children when compared to you. You would not give a child a surgeon's knife to play with, but you have given mankind their liberty, knowing that with their liberty they would create the instruments of their own destruction. But in one year, I've accomplished more for the cause of peace than you ever did."

"But at what price?" Ceravanne said weakly. "You enslave millions to control a few. You hobble mankind so that a few evil people cannot run free. Is it worth it?"

"Yes!" the Harvester shouted. "Worth it and more! There will be generations born in peace, people who never know discontent or suffering!"

Ceravanne listened to those words, and they cut her to the soul. Oh, how she had yearned to bring about such a change. For centuries the temptation had gnawed at her, to grasp control and put an end to as much human misery as possible. It did little good for the humans to create Tharrin leaders, and then continue their barbaric ways, killing one another and squabbling over soil as if nothing had changed. But the Tharrin hoped to lead men into some golden era of peace, not sit in judgment on them as if they were children.

And yet, and yet, Ceravanne knew that to seize control, even in the attempt to bring greater peace to mankind, would be to destroy the very people she most loved.

She gestured toward Gallen and the Bock. "You feign hardness and anger, but I know you. I have brought you the two men you have loved most in your life—Belorian and the Bock. Men whom you love, but men who love freedom more than they value their own lives. They've come to stop you. If you still love them, if you seek to strip from them their humanity, then be merciful to them. Give them the death they would prefer, rather than the slavery you offer! I say once again—cut us down and be done with it!"

The Harvester began shaking, and her gaze turned deeply inward, as if she were fighting some mighty battle. Her mouth opened, as if against her will, and she made a fist, pointed her finger at the Bock as if to speak the command for her guards to slay him, and lowered her eyes.

"It's her mantle!" Orick shouted. "It's controlling her! Take it!"

Gallen raised his head, and he was shaking mightily, his muscles spasming.

Ceravanne imagined the net of tiny wires in the woman's head, like those she had seen in Gallen. The Inhuman might be broadcasting the Harvester's every thought, every action, until she was no more than a puppet, moved at its whim. But if that were true, then all of them would be dead by now. And so she realized that the Inhuman was unable to control its subjects fully. It struggled to hold both Gallen and the Harvester at once.

Orick bounded forward.

"No!" the Harvester shouted, and a Tekkar guard obediently leapt to intercept the bear.

Gallen snatched his pulp gun, shot the Tekkar as he rushed past, and the bullet popped under his right eye. His skull cracked and expanded outward for a moment like a burgeoning wine bag, and shards of bone ruptured the skin. His eyes flew out, and smoke issued from the holes. His upper teeth broke off unevenly, spitting out to the floor. White shards of skull cut through skin, and blood spattered Ceravanne's face.

The Tekkar guard crumpled in ruin, and Ceravanne screamed in horror at the sight. Time seemed to slow.

Gallen cried out, and the gun fell from his hand as the Inhuman regained control. Suddenly Gallen dropped back to one knee.

Orick stopped halfway to the Harvester's throne as the second guard rushed forward, swinging his sword in complex arcs.

The Harvester merely stood, watching them all, and Ceravanne studied her every tiny gesture, every seemingly unconscious movement of the eyes. The Harvester had not cried out at the horrible sight of her guard, crumpling in ruin. The image of it had struck Ceravanne to the very core, but the Harvester was merely watching. And suddenly Ceravanne felt very uneasy. She had come here imagining that she and the Harvester were one, single organisms that had branched out on different paths. But now she wondered just how far they might have diverged. The Harvester stood rigid, trembling, but the murder of a man before her eyes had not seemed to cause her undue discomfort.

Ceravanne knew that the Inhuman planted memories from the lives of warriors in its victims, but now she wondered what that would be like, wondered how the horror of committing such atrocities would leave their mark on the Harvester.

In ages past, Ceravanne had turned her back on the Rodim, let their kind be slaughtered, removed from the face of the earth. It had not been a sin of commission. She had killed no one herself, had never even seen a Rodim die. But she forced herself to remain silent as the slaughter began. It had taken all of her will, sapped her strength, left her unable to sleep for thousands of nights afterward. She could not imagine ever committing a crime more horrible than what she had done.

But the Harvester stood before her, and she bore memories of war, of her own hands bathed in another's blood. Somehow, Ceravanne had imagined that the Harvester would be able to disassociate herself from such memories, to recognize that she had never committed such atrocities.

But Ceravanne knew better than that. The peoples of Babel had been created because of the Tharrin's inaction, their unwillingness to control mankind. If the Tharrin asserted more control, they could end this madness. Human misery was the gauge of Tharrin inadequacy.

And so Ceravanne felt the stain of blood upon her, the stain of blood for every man who had ever died under the sword, the guilt of every good man who was forced to kill in order to defend himself. The stain was always there. Ceravanne could feel her conscience whispering to her, though she tried to block it from her mind.

But how much more horrible would it be to have the Inhuman show her true waste and destruction, to live through the horrors of becoming a killer, to suffer the atrocities committed by others? How could Ceravanne bear it, if the Inhuman were to show her the misery her people suffered? How could the Harvester even bear to stand, to breathe, to speak while under the weight of such guilt. It was not the lies that the Inhuman told that so much bothered Ceravanne, it was the threat of all the damning truths. How could anyone bear it?

Indeed, the Harvester only stood gazing at the room, and the muscles at her mouth twitched. She drew weak, rapid breaths, and her eyes gazed around in bewilderment.

The Harvester was struggling for control, struggling against the Inhuman.

Gallen climbed to his feet, turned and looked at Ceravanne. His eyes had rolled back in his head, and slowly, as if fighting a great battle with himself, he whispered, "Leave us!"

"Gallen?" Orick said, gazing deep into his eyes. "Are you in there?"

Gallen said nothing intelligible, but his voice gurgled. And Ceravanne looked at Gallen's mantle on the floor, realized that his mantle was still fighting, trying to block the Inhuman's signals, just as Gallen was still struggling against it.

Ceravanne stepped forward. The Tekkar guard swung his sword menacingly, still blocking the path, and though the guard would not let Orick pass, Ceravanne suspected that she herself might have a better chance of reaching the Harvester.

Ceravanne crossed the room, pulled back her hood, and the Tekkar stood looking at her in her splendor. She hesitated for a moment, waiting for her scent to fill the air around her, so that her powerful pheromones would have time to work on the Tekkar. By nature, Ceravanne was aware of subtle forms of manipulation. Tone of voice, gestures, scent—all worked together to create a mood.

The Tekkar stopped swinging his sword, considering, and Ceravanne watched his purple eyes. There was a hint of widening, as if the Tekkar were surprised by her lack of fear, but his eyes did not stare beyond her, losing their focus, as so often happens when one is planning to kill. Ceravanne held her hands together and hunched her shoulders, making herself seem smaller. It was a pose that spoke at once of unconscious authority and vulnerability. Her beauty and scent confused the Tekkar with a sensual aura. Ceravanne had called mortal enemies together and got them forging alliances within minutes, yet even after thousands of years of experience, she could not be sure that her persuasive powers would work on the Tekkar.

"Let me pass," Ceravanne said softly, as if reminding him that she had the perfect right to command. "I will not harm you, and I do not believe you wish to harm me. There has been too much violence already."

The Tekkar's lips parted and he looked back to the Harvester in confusion, and in that moment of hesitation, Ceravanne crossed the room, stood at Gallen's side, rested her hand on his shoulder, and looked up into the face of the Harvester. There was sweat running down the woman's forehead, and she held her jaw clenched, trembling.

"Fight it," Ceravanne whispered vehemently to both Gallen and the Harvester. "Fight with your whole souls."

Ceravanne stepped toward her, and the Harvester reached for the knife on her hip.

"Please, not one more life!" the Bock said, holding its arms high. "I beg of the Ceravanne who once was, do not let this Inhuman force you into taking one more life!"

The Harvester stood, and beads of sweat began dotting her forehead. "I can't . . . stop it. I can't hold . . . it!"

Ceravanne pulled back her hood, exposing her own mantle. "Yes you can, for a moment, at great cost. And in that moment, you are free. I've spoken with those technicians who designed the Inhuman," she whispered. "The memories it shows you are flawed, and all of its conclusions are lies. You are not responsible for the sum of human misery. I've come to bring you truth. Put on this mantle, and let it teach you peace. It will free you."

She began walking slowly toward the Harvester, who looked toward the exits. Ceravanne feared that she would jump and flee down one of those corridors. The Tekkar guard moved uneasily, as if to intercept Ceravanne, and the Bock hurried toward the throne.

The Harvester raised her hands, as if to ward Ceravanne away. "No," she whispered. "Leave now! I do not want to hurt you!"

"And I do not want to hurt you," Ceravanne said softly, all feigned vocal tones aside. The Harvester would know if she lied.

The Tekkar guard moved to intercept the Bock, and the Harvester cried, "Stop him!" The Bock stopped beside Orick, unable to advance farther.

The Harvester pulled her dagger from her hip sheath, and its shining curved blade gleamed wickedly. Ceravanne recalled how deeply it had bit into her in the past, the cold poison at its tip. "I have killed myself before," the Harvester whispered.

"Yes, to avoid being infected by the Inhuman," Ceravanne answered sadly, realizing that her sister-self was planning suicide. "The Swallow has returned to her ancient land of Indallian. She came to bring peace and unite her people. But you're infected by that which we both fear. If this is all you can do to save us, then do what you must. I forgive you."

And Ceravanne saw the pain on the Harvester's face as her muscles worked against her. She marveled at the Harvester's struggle for control, for few could hope to fight the domination of a machine designed to manipulate the human will, and Ceravanne knew that the Harvester must have been fighting the Inhuman's control for months.

"Forgive me and die," the Harvester said, and she leapt at Ceravanne. In that brief instant, Ceravanne saw her mistake.

The Tharrin compunction against taking a human life was nearly unbreakable, but it did not extend to self, and the Harvester viewed Ceravanne as self. And in that instant, Ceravanne saw that the Harvester was relinquishing control. She could not have moved so swiftly otherwise. Indeed, for that brief moment, she was the Inhuman.

And a sudden shocking urge welled up inside Ceravanne. For one moment, she wished the Harvester dead. She wanted to hide the ugliness of what she had become from the world. Expunge it. Make it as if it had never been. While humans feared most the death of the body, Ceravanne feared more for the death of her soul, and she wanted now to unmake the thing she had become.

"No!" the Bock shouted, rushing toward them.

Ceravanne grasped the Harvester's hand as her knife plunged downward. And for a moment they struggled, fighting for control of the knife. The Harvester's face was a mask of determination and rage, the face of a stranger. Ceravanne turned and kicked at the older woman's legs, trying to unbalance her, and very nearly succeeded in driving the knife into the Harvester's neck.

The Harvester cried out for aid, and her guard spun and rushed toward her. Ceravanne saw Orick leap in behind the guard, catch the Tekkar's rear leg in his teeth, and shake the man vigorously. With a mighty heave of his neck, Orick threw the Tekkar against the near wall, and bones snapped.

The Bock lunged forward past Orick, trying to throw himself between the women. With his long fingers, he grabbed for the knife as it arced toward Ceravanne a second time, reaching up. The knife pierced his hand, driving deeply along the outside of his palm. Bright blood spattered over his arm, and he backed away from the Harvester.

"She's . . . innocent! You're both innocent!" the Bock cried.

The Harvester stared at the Bock, eyes wide, and staggered backward, running from her deed.

Ceravanne stood, watching the doomed Bock collapse at her feet. "Ah," he muttered courageously, making a show as if the wound were a scratch, backing away. "I . . ." Confusion crossed his face, and he sat down heavily, his many knees buckling. "What?"

"I've killed you," the Harvester cried, as if the words were torn from her throat.

Ceravanne felt her heart pounding fiercely in her chest, but she couldn't breathe. She fell to her knees beside the Bock, hoping to comfort him.

Her eyes filled with tears, and the Bock looked up at her incredulous. "How? No, it's a small wound!"

"With the juice of deathfruit in it," the Harvester whispered.

The Bock fell back, gasping, and looked up.

And in that second, the Harvester dropped her knife to the floor. Ceravanne stood there stunned, holding the Bock, as the Harvester cried out from the core of her soul, and the cry seemed to echo from some recess in Ceravanne's mind. It was a scream that was unlike anything she had ever heard—almost bestial.

The Bock looked up, and his brown eyes did not focus. He stared blindly at the ceiling. "Wha . . . gulls crying?" Ceravanne knelt, her heart pounding, blinded by tears. The Bock looked up and said, "Ah, the cry of a child as it dies into an adult."

Then his voice rattled, and he went still.

The ground twisted beneath her, and Ceravanne fell forward, still weeping.

Ceravanne had come hoping to find common ground with the Harvester. She'd known that somewhere, despite the Inhuman's manipulations, its distortions and outright lies, there had to be some core, some essential, unchanging element, that would remain the same in them.

And as the Bock died, the one man both Ceravanne and the Harvester had loved most in this life, the Harvester was touched deep in her soul, in a place where the Inhuman could not enter.

The Harvester crawled on her knees toward the Bock. Then Ceravanne grabbed the mantle of the Inhuman, pulled off the gold clip that her technicians had told her would be its key, and laid the Inhuman over the Bock's face like a burial shroud.

Suddenly freed from the Inhuman's influence, Gallen leapt up, came to Ceravanne's side and held her a moment. Ceravanne was trying to snap the key onto a corner of her own mantle, but her hands were shaking too badly. So Gallen took the key from her hands.

From one of the side doors, Ceravanne could hear shouting as several of the Tekkar tried to clear rubble, gain entrance to the great hall.

"Quickly, put the key on my mantle," Ceravanne whispered, "if you love truth, if you seek rest."

Gallen took Ceravanne's mantle from her, placed its golden net over his own head. Then he sat down, arms wrapped around his knees, snapped the key onto the mantle's golden rings, and lived another hundred lifetimes.

For nearly two hours, Ceravanne sat with Orick.

The Bock's body cooled, and Ceravanne cleaned it up, weeping softly. She could not keep from touching him, and for a long hour after the body was cleaned, Orick nuzzled her, pressing his nose under her arm.

Orick could not believe how badly the day had gone. Gallen had not been able to fight the Inhuman, and Maggie was dead. Both Ceravanne and the Harvester had lost the man they loved, and the city of Moree was in ruins. Orick had hoped for much better, and it left a great gaping hole in his heart, to see all the pain that others would have to endure.

He kept looking over at Gallen, who sat with his arms wrapped about his knees, his forehead bowed to one knee, with the great golden mantle draped over his head and shoulders, wearing a look as if he were some philosopher, exhausted from profound thought. And in a way, Orick feared that. The teaching machines on Fale had changed him some. The Inhuman had sought to rip away his free will. And now, he would waken and be something new.

Everyone Orick loved most was being taken from him.

He had begun to fear that terrible light that was growing in Gallen's pale eyes. Now he felt it keenest. A few short weeks ago, Gallen had been little more than a boy who had to cope with his incredible talent for battle and his desire to set the world right. Now, he was growing into something new, something unpredictable.

So Orick sat and thought, trying to comfort Ceravanne. Orick remembered that when the Lady Everynne had connected with the omni-mind, she'd wakened after the initial shock, and she'd become something powerful—a goddess, with nearly unlimited knowledge. In his own smaller way, Orick knew, Gallen was doing the same, step by step. The light was steadily growing in his eyes, and Orick could see what he was becoming, could see how he was leaving ordinary men behind, leaving Orick behind.

When Ceravanne's tears had eased some, Orick asked gently, "When Gallen wakes, how will he be changed? What will he become?"

"The demons inside him should never bother him again," Ceravanne whispered. "We didn't alter the memories much, just restored the true versions, so that Gallen may see upon reflection our judges were not harsh. When Gallen wakes, everyone will know that I've returned to make peace among the peoples. Some may resent me for it. Some may still hold allegiance to the Inhuman, but we've removed the hidden thought structures that the Inhuman inserted into its hosts. People will be free to make up their own minds."

Ceravanne sat, her arms wrapped around her Bock.

"And what of those who do resent you?" Orick asked. "What if some of the Tekkar try to kill you?"

"I suspect that they will," Ceravanne said. "I've been killed before, but always I've been reborn. Still, such actions anger the faithful. The Rodim were destroyed as a people for such acts. The Tekkar know what will happen to them if they are too harsh."

Orick licked Ceravanne's hand, and together they waited for the awakening.

In the recesses of his mind, Gallen lived through the days of Druin after the fall of Indallian. He rode his huge war-horse through the forests in his youth, and suffered the pangs of lost loves, he fought many battles and learned to crave blood as much as he craved the wider world. He united many people, before he was crippled by a spear in the back.

As an old man, he became frustrated in his designs. Many admired him as a man of learning, for he could do little more than lie in his bed and study. He became devoted to the welfare of his people, yet he dreamed of walking again, of visiting the stars.

He learned to hate the walls of his bedchamber, and so he sent messengers to the City of Life and hired travelers from other worlds to come and be his tutors. He began acquiring metals to build his starships, and studied the designs.

When word reached him that the Immortals planned to stop him, he built cannons to guard his city, and great were the battles waged against him, until in ruin he was forced to put aside his weapons.

In old age, his men took him to the City of Life, and there sought the rebirth. And the judges found him unworthy. Still, they took pity on him, and gave him back his legs, sending him away. He took his gift, but turned and cursed his judges.

Thus Druin wandered far, and never visited his realm again.

So it went, life after life, Gallen saw the portion of meanness in character that the Dronon had chosen to hide.

And then Ceravanne's mantle showed Gallen other lives, the lives lived by some of those who had won the rebirth—Tottenan the Wise, from the race of the Atonkin, who felt no desire to dominate other peoples. He spent his days buying old swords and melting the steel to be used in building nails.

And Gallen recalled the life of Zemette, a shipbuilder of weak mind but great heart, a man who somehow understood by nature how to be happy, who used all of his money to buy slaves from the southlands, so that he could set them free.

And Gallen lived the life of Thrennen Ka, a Derrit who sought to teach farming to her own people.

Over and over, the lives came to him, and he was shown an equal portion of the divine and the damned. And while the dronon whispered to him that all men were equal, and therefore should serve their new dronon overlords, Gallen saw that all men were given time to make of themselves what they would, and that while some became vile, and others merely consumed, always there were a few who earnestly strove to make the world better for all, and such people were rewarded in the City of Life.

And thus Ceravanne's mantle sought to make Gallen a wiser man, full of hope and experience, and then it left him.

When Gallen finally woke, raising his head so that Ceravanne's mantle jingled, Orick came to his side. There was a noise reverberating through the darkened hive, and the shadows jangled to the querulous notes of people waking to a new world in wonder.

And when the Harvester woke, Ceravanne hungered for a private conference with her sister. So they sat close together and held one another and cried. Gallen sat listening to the women talk.

"I've killed with my own hands," the Harvester whispered, almost a wail. "I need cleansing. Can you feel it?"

"Five hundred years will not suffice," Ceravanne agreed, not concealing the worry in her voice. "I would come with you, aid you if I could. But one of us must stay here. The Swallow must return as promised, and bring peace with her."

"I know that you still hurt for the Rodim," the Harvester said. "Your healing is not complete. How can we bring peace, when we feel none ourselves?"

Ceravanne opened her mouth, but spoke no answer for a moment. "We are our bodies," she whispered at last. "Neither of us can escape our guilt. And both of us must seek to establish peace in our turns. You go to Northland, to the Vale of the Bock." Ceravanne went to her pack, fumbled out a small seed. She held the unborn Bock up with evident care, as if it were a great treasure. "Plant this in the Vale. And there you can find peace for both of us."

The Harvester took the seed, held it up in wonder, then grabbed Ceravanne, hugged her fiercely, and whispered, "Thank you. Thank you. Look for me again in summer, in some distant year, when both our hearts are lighter. A Bock will come with me."

They held each other, crying softly for a moment, and Gallen petted Orick's head, stroking it softly. There were cries in the land again, the sound of Tekkar awakening, and Gallen was looking off into the distance, into the shadows of the corner of the room. He did not mention Maggie's name, though his heart was heavy for her.

Then the main door to the throne room squeaked on its hinges, and Gallen glanced over, expecting to see some Tekkar.

Maggie poked her head into the room.

"Maggie!" Orick shouted, bounding toward her. "I thought you got killed."

Orick reached her, sat on all fours and licked her hands, wanting to jump up and hug her, but knowing she would fall over if he did. She bent forward and kissed his forehead. "Very nearly, but the AI ejected me before the car blew."

She stood looking at Gallen across the room, and neither one of them spoke or moved for several long seconds.

"I was afraid for you," Gallen said at last.

"I love you, too," Maggie said, her lower lip trembling, and they rushed into each other's arms.

He was surprised how, even now, her touch could be electric. He kissed her, looked deep into her face, and was surprised at what he saw. There was a peace in her eyes that had never been a part of Maggie Flynn before, a new clarity and softness.

The hallways leading to the Harvester's chamber had begun to fill with people, and Gallen could hear them talking reverently, saying, "The Swallow, yes, she's in here." They stood outside the doors, afraid to come in, until Ceravanne rose to greet them.

They slept that night under the bright stars of Tremonthin, with the Tekkar camped around them. The people knew the Swallow from ancient memories downloaded into their skulls, and they showed her great reverence. The Tekkar vied for the honor to become her protectors, and chefs brought her their finest meals.

Maggie looked about, and it was hard to miss the adulation shining in the eyes of the people. But all of it was for Ceravanne. Gallen, Maggie, and Orick were all but strangers in the city, people who were obvious friends to the Swallow, nothing more.

The Harvester had dressed in black robes and a hood to hide her face, and she went out into the darkness beside the river, and for long she stood alone in the moonlight.

And so at last when Maggie and Gallen staggered off to sleep in a thicket, Maggie listened to the sounds of the night, and for the first time on this world, she slept unafraid.

In the morning, they had a short funeral where they buried the Bock beside a small river. And because the Swallow herself came to the funeral, everyone from the city of Moree turned out.

Ceravanne spoke his eulogies, praising the Bock so that everyone within listening range felt as if they'd lost something important without ever knowing exactly what it was.

An engraver carved a large stone from the river's bank for the Bock, showing a treelike figure with his hands raised toward the suns, and they left it over the gravesite, beside the road, where folks would reckon it a significant landmark in the city for a thousand years.

Ceravanne offered to send Gallen and Maggie back to Northland in a flyer, but after a brief conference, they all decided that they were in no hurry. The dronon would be hunting for Gallen and Maggie across the worlds, and Tremonthin seemed as good a place to hide as any.

Orick voiced the suspicion that both Maggie and Gallen were loath to leave because they shared so many memories of this land, and Maggie thought back through the lives she'd lived here, and did not deny it.

And so Ceravanne gave them a fine cart and a pair of horses, and Gallen, Maggie, and Orick prepared to head to Northland with the Harvester.

They were in no hurry, but Maggie found that there was a great weight upon her. She needed to go north, to the City of Life, to petition the Immortals in Tallea's behalf, seeking her rebirth.

Ceravanne came to give her final farewell to them before they departed. She thanked them profusely for their help, and wished them good fortune. She gave them many gifts from the hands of the people of the city—warm blankets for their journey, good food and clothes, a bag of coins.

She wept as she hugged them goodbye, and then she was hustled off into the city by her Tekkar guardians, all dressed in their black robes, their faces hooded from sunlight.

They walked away in a tight knot, almost as if Ceravanne were a prisoner rather than a dignitary, and something about it gave Maggie the chills.

And in the afternoon sunlight, Maggie watched them heading back to the dark catacombs of Moree, leaving Maggie, Gallen, Orick, and the Harvester to make their own way back across the seas to Northland, and whatever destinations might lie beyond.

In the bright sunlight, Maggie watched Ceravanne waving goodbye from up a slope, a streak of lightning in her blue dress, with her platinum hair, all against the dark lines of the hills of Moree, and Maggie felt a profound sense of distress. Though Ceravanne's mantle had perhaps tamed the hosts of the Inhuman, Ceravanne herself was staying among the Tekkar, men who by their very nature were little more than monsters.

Maggie looked up at Gallen in frustration. "Why is she staying with them?" she asked in dismay. "That's no proper reward for her labor."

"She is staying with them because she must dismantle the armaments in Moree, tear down the starports," the Harvester said softly. "She is going back with them, because governing them will be her greatest challenge. And if she is to rule this land in peace, she must first get them under her sway."

"But . . . but Maggie's right," Orick grumbled. "She's lost! A lifetime of work is all she has before her. What kind of reward is that?"

"Perhaps by your human perspective she has lost," the Harvester whispered from beneath her dark hood, so that her soft words seemed to hang in the cool air about her face. "But Ceravanne is not human. She desires to serve, and now she has won that opportunity."

And you have lost yours, Maggie realized, studying the hooded woman.

Now Maggie saw what was really troubling her. Ceravanne had won only a new kind of captivity, just as Maggie and Gallen had. By defeating the Lords of the Swarm, she and Gallen had sought to win freedom, but all they had won was a responsibility that was too great to bear. She looked into Gallen's face, and by his troubled look, she knew he was thinking the same.

Even now, the Lords of the dronon Swarms were hunting for Gallen and Maggie, and perhaps might soon be searching this planet. But Tremonthin was a big planet, easy to hide in.

So they headed home at a leisurely pace, while the fall grew steadily colder. A week later, when they crossed the Telgoods in their travels north, there was snow on the peaks, and a bitter nip in the air.

All during their journey home, they found peace in the land, and a new sense of brotherhood among the people of Babel. Where before they had received distrustful stares when they drove through a town, now they found merchants smiling and alehouses full of people who laughed and were quick to joke or sing or tell some outlandish story.

Indeed, Maggie found herself falling more and more deeply in love with the land, and one night, when she and Gallen had snuggled in a cozy bed at an inn, and a fire was burning in their hearth, she asked him as she had once before, "Gallen, if we ever escape the dronon completely, would you want to live here?"

"We've already lived in Babel for more than seven thousand years," he whispered, and she saw that strange new peace in his eyes. "It's my home. Yes, I could live here ten thousand more."

And Maggie curled tighter against him, and felt that one thing at least had been settled. Now, if only she could figure a way to escape those damned dronon. But she feared that she would never be rid of the threat, not until they'd killed her.

And on their journey, though Maggie and Gallen continued to fall more and more deeply in love, and Maggie found greater contentment, she worried for Orick. In all of their travels, they had not found a single bear who could speak. Oh, on the trip home they once saw a bear walking along a lightly forested ridge in the wilderness, but when Orick called out to it, the creature growled stupidly and ran away, for it was only a simple animal, without Orick's genetic upgrades.

A month later, when they reached the city of Queekusaw on the ocean shores, the whole land was blanketed in white, and snow was pounding the land. They left Babel on a slow freighter in the afternoon, on dark and wild seas, and Maggie watched the gray city fade behind a blanket of soft white.

They had a rough sea voyage, and Maggie took sick, vomiting every day. Five days later she was glad to be in Northland, where muddy roads were the greatest inconvenience a traveler had to contend with.

When they landed, they bought a new wagon, and that night, as they headed north, Orick, who had been very quiet for several days, came to Gallen and Maggie.

"Once we get to the City of Life and petition the judges there to give Tallea the rebirth, what is your heart set to do?"

"I don't know," Gallen said honestly. "Everynne has warned us that the Lords of the Swarms are searching for us, so no place is safe. And some of the servants of the Inhuman escaped in that starship during the battle at Moree. They might tell the dronon where we are—if Thomas doesn't. For a while, anyway, we'll have to keep moving, search for safer worlds. Why do you ask?"

"Well," Orick growled, plainly very troubled, "you've been a good friend to me, Gallen. But I'm starting to wonder. I'm thinking maybe I should go home, to my own kind."

"But Orick," Maggie whispered, "I'm not sure there are more bears like you."

Orick sniffed, and Maggie petted his snout, rubbed the thick black fur behind his ears. It was a cruel thing to have to say to him, but Maggie knew that Orick was terribly lonely, and she knew that the she-bears in Tihrglas would never give him the companionship he deserved.

"Still," Orick grumbled, "I need to go back home."

"Then I will take you there, my best and dearest friend," Gallen said, and Gallen took the huge bear by the ears and kissed his forehead.

It was a long and lonely drive northward. The seasickness didn't seem to leave Maggie for several days after they landed, yet soon things got back to normal and they arrived in the City of Life near mid-winter. It was a vast city, with great bubbles rising up at the spaceport on its edge. Tall white buildings with lofty spires gleamed against the mountains. A wide and deep river poured through the city, and white snow geese swam, mirrored in its black waters.

There, the group checked into an inn more like something they would find on Fale, a stately building with fountains at its feet, with vast clean rooms and a beautifully constructed hearth where the fire was already laid.

Maggie said goodbye to the Harvester, who had kept her distance and never really become a close friend all during this trip. "Perhaps I will see you sometime," the Harvester said, surprising Maggie with the sentiment.

"Where will you go now?" Maggie asked.

The Harvester pointed east to the mountains. "I have friends in the Vale of the Bock. Ceravanne gave me a seed from my friend, so that at least he will bear offspring, though he will never be reborn. I will raise his child as if it too were my son."

"Then may you find peace," Maggie said, and she gave the woman a hug, then the Harvester drove off alone in the wagon toward the snow-covered mountains.

Straightaway, Maggie, Gallen, and Orick took Tallea's hair sample along with the gem of memories from Gallen's mantle and sought out the Hall of Rebirth—a vast building made of crystal that held more than three hundred thousand workers. There, they presented the items to the judges, along with their petition for Tallea's rebirth.

Because of the unseasonable weather, there were few travelers in the city, and three judges, an ageless man and two women, each dressed in white and wearing the platinum mantles of their profession, said they would be able to consider the petition that very evening.

"You can come back in the morning, and hear our decision," one of the judges said.

"Fine," Orick grumbled. "But I'll be waiting out on the steps to hear your word tonight, if you don't mind. I'll come in just when I see that you're closing your doors."

The judges glanced at one another, as if considering the propriety of this inconvenience, and Maggie went back to the inn with Gallen for a bit.

At sunset they returned to the Hall of Rebirth and found Orick waiting. A light snow had begun to fall again, powdering the streets, and the weather seemed only cool. Orick, with his thick pelt, didn't fret about the weather, but after a bit, Maggie found herself stamping her feet, trying to keep them warm.

After an hour, one of the judges came running from the building in his thin white gown, came and took Maggie by the hand, then bent low and put one hand on Orick's shoulder. "Why did you not tell us who you were?" the judge said.

"Would it have made a difference in our petition?" Gallen asked.

"No," the judge said, "but at the very least, I would not have had you standing out here in the snow. Twice these past two weeks, the Vanquishers from the Seventh Swarm came to search the city for you. Apparently, the Dronon are scouring the worlds for news of you. Right now, they've headed farther south, to a warmer clime. Still, I expect that they will return. You are in grave danger!"

"We know that they're hunting us," Orick grumbled, "and we're getting damned tired of it! Now, what about Tallea?"

"We have reviewed her memories, and I am happy to report that she will be reborn."

"How soon?" Gallen asked. "We don't want to leave the city without saying good-bye."

"Just as I am equally sure that she will want you to wait for her," the judge said. "Still, she poses a problem for us. She seeks a new body, one that will have to be modified to meet her desires, and then we will have to force-grow it in the vats for a week."

"Yes," Maggie said, "she wanted to be a Roamer."

"How soon?" Orick urged the man.

The judge breathed heavily. "Eight days, maybe ten. I will have the technicians begin within the hour, but it cannot be hurried any faster."

Maggie knew from her mantle that, indeed, the judge was offering to perform a near-miracle. "Thank you," she whispered, hugging him briefly. "Now, you had better get back inside before you freeze."

"Tell me where you are staying," the judge whispered. "I have friends who were in the resistance. They will know best how to help you stay hidden."

Gallen told him where to find them, and then they headed back toward the inn. They had not gone two blocks before two burly gentlemen in dark cloaks stepped out of a doorway, their warm breath making a cloud of fog around their faces. One of them whispered, "We're friends."

He walked up ahead, taking point, and looked at each cross street, then waved them along. Maggie had felt secure for weeks, but her guardians' behavior unnerved her. For the next four kilometers, they found themselves under such guard, and when they reached the hotel, no less than a dozen such men could be seen loafing at the street corners, watching from roofs.

When they got to their room, Gallen took off his cold winter cloak and hung it in the closet. "It sounds as if we're hotter on this world than we'd anticipated," Gallen said, trying to sound nonchalant.

He went and looked out the window, to the lights burning in the buildings, the snow falling, and Orick went and stood looking out with him.

"Eight days. Eight days from today is Christmas day here on this world, you know," Orick said. "I figured it up on their calendar."

"No one here will be celebrating it," Gallen said. "There are no Catholics here."

"I will be celebrating it," Orick muttered.

"We all will," Maggie said. "That is the day that Tallea is reborn . . . if we're lucky."

"Ah, that would be grand," Gallen said. "But don't get your hopes up."

And so, that following week they spent some time searching for gifts for one another in the shops of the City of Life. The shops carried no fantastic goods, like the near-magical items one might find on Fale. Instead, there were only good woolen coats dyed with bright colors, shoes that would last. Fine cheeses from all corners of the world.

On Christmas eve, in the kitchens at the inn, Maggie cooked a ham and made rolls and Christmas pies all filled with red cherries and topped with white sugared cream. It was a huge feast, fit for a bear, and by the end of it, Orick's snout was plastered with jam and cream.

Early on Christmas day, they exchanged gifts. Gallen got fine new scabbards for his knives from Orick, and Maggie and Gallen had scrounged together to find Orick a handsome new leather-covered copy of the Bible, for Orick had been obliged, in his haste to escape Tihrglas, to leave his Bible at home.

"Where did you get this?" Orick exclaimed, and Gallen said, "I told you that there were no Catholics on this world. I didn't say that it completely lacked Christians."

"But Ceravanne had never heard of them," Orick said. "How is it she never heard of them?"

"We found the Bible at the spaceport," Maggie finally said, unwilling to keep the bear in suspense. "Travelers from many far worlds come through there. One of them had sold it to a man who trades in . . . curiosities."

Orick and Gallen then gave Maggie their gifts—a light perfume of exotic flavor, and a green silk nightgown. Both of them were fine, indeed.

When they were done, Orick asked, "All right, Maggie, don't keep us hanging at your elbow. What did you get for Gallen?"

"Oh, nothing much," she said honestly. "It's a small gift."

She presented him with a little package wrapped in bright red paper with a white bow.

He opened it. Inside was a pair of booties and a receiving blanket. Orick looked up, his eyes wide with surprise.

"I got sick on the ocean, all right," Maggie said, "but I never did really stop feeling queasy. I checked with the doctors here. It will be a boy."

Gallen grinned, and looked away wistfully. "No blood kin left," he whispered, "so you'll make your own."

"I will," Maggie said, "with your help. And I'll have a dozen of them if I want."

Gallen grabbed her and kissed her roughly, and Orick smiled and left them alone.

It was a pleasant day, with cold suns rising up through the clouds, and a sky filled with streams of light. Later that day, Orick sat Gallen and Maggie down and read to them from his new Bible about the birth of Jesus in ancient Jerusalem, with King Herod seeking the lives of infants, and angels announcing the birth of the King of Heaven.

That afternoon, there came an insistent pounding at the door. Maggie answered it, and one of the guards stood outside. "You'll want to be leaving the city tonight," he said softly. "The dronon are back."

"We can't leave yet," Maggie begged. "We're waiting for a friend to get out of the rebirthing vats."

"I checked on it," the guard said. "They're taking her out early. Her body will be a little younger than she wanted, but they're downloading her memories now."

"We can be there right away," Maggie said. She didn't need to tell Gallen and Orick the news. Both of them were already racing around the spacious room, grabbing clothes to pack.

This will have to be a hasty farewell, Maggie realized, and she fretted for Tallea, a young girl who would be traveling alone through the winter, heading south.

In a matter of minutes, they were hurrying through the dark streets. A chill wind had picked up, and it blew frozen snow through the air. Clouds were moving in from the south, a horrendous dark storm.

They reached the great halls, which were closed for the night, just as the snow began to fall. One of the judges had come out to meet them. He was appropriately dressed in a long gray cloak and a sagging peaked hat with a broad brim.

"There you are!" he called as he saw them running up the broad stone steps from the street. "Your friend is reborn, and she awaits you!"

He waved up toward a darkened doorway, and Maggie saw movement behind the thick glass. The door opened a crack, and something hairy moved in the darkness.

Maggie had expected to see a young woman covered with the soft reddish-brown fur of the Roamers, as she remembered them from previous lives. But this creature was more heavily furred than she'd imagined, and its pelt was far darker.

Tallea lowered to all fours, and Maggie heard Orick gulp in astonishment.

"She's a bear!" Gallen said.

"Yes," the judge said. "When we read her memories, we found that at the last moments of her life, she had a change of heart. So we made her the body she desired."

The young black bear was small, and appeared to be only about a year old. She walked down the steps carefully, as if unsure of herself.

But when she was within twenty meters, she suddenly hunkered down and ran toward them at great speed, hit Orick full tilt and knocked the bigger bear over on his side. He grunted, and she jumped up on him playfully, and bit his ear. "Orick! Orick!" she shouted. "Being a bear is great! Why, you're strong as an ox and all dressed in leather!"

"Well, I've never minded it," Orick grunted, not quite sure what to think.

Tallea hugged his neck, wrapping her paws around him, and licked his face. He licked her back shyly, and Tallea growled in his ear, her voice husky with desire. "Ah, Orick, you and I will have a grand time. That is, if you'll have me?"

The little she-bear looked up at him with big brown eyes, and Orick glanced at Maggie and Gallen imploringly, as if they would tell him what to say.

"Do it," Maggie said.

"She's not like the she-bears on your world," the judge told Orick. "She loves you as fiercely as any Caldurian can, and she will stay by your side always."

Orick got up on all fours, then very gently, very passionately, licked the young she-bear's muzzle with his long tongue, softly at first, then more fiercely, and Maggie found herself vaguely disturbed at how sensual a bear's tongue could be.

And after the bears exchanged long, sweet kisses, the guard came through the dark and stood at the foot of the steps. "The dronon are coming," he urged. "We must hurry away."

"Where are we going?" Tallea asked.

"I don't know," Orick said, though Maggie was sure that Gallen had told him the name of the world. But for the moment, that information seemed to be driven from his mind. Orick just stared at the young she-bear.

"To new worlds, and safety, I hope," Gallen said, and he took Maggie's hand. They hurried down the broad steps and into the streets.

The new falling snow swirled around them in the darkness, and covered their tracks. Within moments, no one would ever have guessed that they had passed along that road.

About the Author

David Farland's career was launched with a string of highly praised paperback science fiction novels, written under the name of Dave Wolverton, that made him a writer to watch. His quartet of fantasy novels, *The Runelords*, *Brotherhood of the Wolf*, *Wizardborn*, and *The Lair of Bones*, brought him new readers and critical acclaim. With *The Golden Queen* and *Beyond the Gate*, he achieved a new level of excellence in space adventure storytelling just before his bestselling fantasy series began. He lives in Saint George, Utah.